MW01256403

YOUTH AND OTHER STORIES

MORI ŌGAI

Youth

and

Other

Stories

Edited by

J. Thomas Rimer

SHAPS Library of Translations

University of Hawaii Press / Honolulu

A publication of the

SCHOOL OF HAWAIIAN

ASIAN & PACIFIC STUDIES

University of Hawaii

© 1994 School of Hawaiian, Asian & Pacific Studies
All rights reserved
Printed in the United States of America

94 95 96 97 98 99   5 4 3 2 1

Library of Congress Cataloging-in-Publication Data
Mori, Ōgai, 1862–1922.
Youth and other stories / Mori Ōgai ; edited by J. Thomas Rimer.
p.   cm. — (SHAPS library of translations)
Translation of "Seinen" and other selected works of M. Ōgai.
ISBN 0–8248–1600–5
1. Mori, Ōgai, 1862–1922—Translations into English.   I. Rimer,
J. Thomas.   II. Title.   III. Series.
PL811.O7A2   1994
895.6'342—dc20   93–38737
CIP

Frontis: Illustration for *Fumizukai* (The Courier) drawn by
Ōgai's friend Harada Naojirō for the publication of
the story in the January 1891 issue of the magazine *Shincho
Hyakushu* (A Myriad of New Works).

University of Hawaii Press books are printed on acid-free paper and
meet the guidelines for permanence and durability of the
Council on Library Resources

Designed by Paula Newcomb

CONTENTS

FOREWORD

MORI ŌGAI (1867–1922) IS CONSIDERED one of the giants in modern Japanese literature and intellectual history. Indeed Ōgai and his younger contemporary, the novelist Natsume Sōseki (1867–1916), have long been viewed by Japanese readers as the two colossi bestriding the whole complex period in which Japan began to integrate Western culture and values into a long and very different tradition. Neither began their respective careers as writers; both were to do so by the shock of the formative experiences they received abroad at a time when Japan, after centuries of seclusion, was opening itself again to Western influences.

The writing of Sōseki, whose visit to England at the turn of the century helped shape his own aesthetic attitudes, has come to be widely appreciated by English-speaking readers, and most of his major works now exist in translation. Ōgai's reputation abroad, however, has been slower to develop. His shock of inspiration came from his years in Germany, almost twenty years before Sōseki's journey to London. Some of Ōgai's literary models, therefore, are relatively unfamiliar to English-speaking readers who remain, on the whole, far less exposed to German than to the American, French, and English literary traditions. Nevertheless, the outlines of Ōgai's life, work, and cultural significance are far more widely known than they were twenty years ago. There are two English-language biographies, a number of excellent scholarly studies, and a book-length collection of translations of his late historical works now available. For that reason, certain larger issues involving Ōgai's role in the literary, political, and intellectual world of his time have not been discussed in any detail here. The brief introductions to each story are intended merely to guide the reader in approaching the text. Larger contextual questions are well treated in the studies now available in English.

Even during the course of Ōgai's lifetime, however, when there was very little indeed in the way of either classical or modern Japanese literature available in any Western language, his work began to attract enthusiastic translators. Each, in his or her own way, attempted to render the author's spare and elegant prose, so much appreciated by later Japanese writers ranging from Nagai Kafū to Mishima Yukio, into the foreign medium of English. The first Ōgai translation published in the United States appeared in 1918, and they have been appearing in one form or another ever since.

Readers often make an implicit assumption that works composed at a later stage in a writer's career will be more highly polished, and more artistically significant, than those created earlier. Perhaps, for Americans, the overwhelming example of a writer such as Henry James, or, in the case of modern German literature, Thomas Mann, have helped reinforce such assumptions. Whatever the difficulties in understanding or appreciation such later texts present, the canon of received opinion puts, say, *The Wings of the Dove* on a higher level than James's early *The Europeans,* or Mann's *Dr. Faustus* at a higher level than *Buddenbrooks.* Ōgai may serve as a trenchant example of a writer whose writings remain of interest in all phases of his artistic career. There is no denying, certainly as far as his Japanese admirers are concerned, the laconic majesty of his later historical writings, but this fact should in no way detract from the very different appeal of his early romantic stories or the personal, ironic, and often touching narratives composed in his middle years. This anthology offers translations of a number of texts that, for Japanese readers, remain central to the work of this writer.

In order to trace these phases of Ōgai's career, the anthology is divided into five parts. The first, entitled "First Experiments: 1890–1891," provides translations of the three romantic stories that gave Ōgai his early reputation. "Self-Portraits of the Artist: 1909–1915" conveys in the course of the ten translations a sense of the range of Ōgai's determination to understand himself. "The Demands of the Day: 1910–1912" presents three texts that deal more directly with intellectual and social problems which the author held to be of paramount importance. Ōgai's own restless desire to experiment in terms of literary form are chronicled in the six texts making up the section "Later Experiments: 1909–1912." Finally, and perhaps most important, this anthology makes available for the first time in English a full translation of Ōgai's novel *Seinen* (Youth), by confirmed reputation an important document in the development of modern Japanese literary and intellectual history. The work of Sanford Goldstein and his several Japanese collaborators has long been known and appreciated because of their translations of Ōgai's other two completed novels from his middle years: *Gan* (Wild Geese) and *Vita Sexualis.* It seemed only appropriate to ask Goldstein and his colleague Shoichi Ono to complete the trilogy, and they did so with energy and grace. With the full translation of Ōgai's fascinating fragment *Kaijin* (The Ashes of Destruction), included here as well, the English reader has for the first time access to all of Ōgai's longer works of fiction in translation.

Those who examine all the stories in the anthology will appreciate the range of styles into which Ōgai's work can be rendered into English. In that sense, this book is an anthology of the history of Ōgai in translation as well. The first translation, mentioned above, was published in 1918. The last were finished in 1991. The shifts in English style from one to the other may permit, through the process of juxtaposition, something of Ōgai's own style to come through.

Insofar as possible, with one or two minor modifications, I have attempted to let the individual voice of each translator to be heard. Previously published translations were altered to follow the order of names used in Japan: family name first, personal name second. Useful information (more often than not pertaining to matters of traditional Japanese dress, objects, and the like) has been placed in a glossary at the end of the book. Occasionally, Ōgai used foreign words in his texts (usually words in French or, more often, German). On occasion, these were employed for an elegant effect in conversation between his characters, somewhat in the way in which, for example, the well-traveled characters in certain novels of Henry James lard their phrases with fashionable French. On the whole, these usages have been retained. On other occasions, however, Ōgai used foreign words in his text when there appeared no useful equivalent in the shifting and rapidly modernizing Japanese available to him. Most of these words and phrases have been simply translated into English to avoid impeding the flow of the narrative. Following the translation of *Youth,* the final selection in this anthology, is a selective glossary of references cited in that novel.

The editor owes many thanks to a variety of people who have contributed to making this anthology a reality. First of all, thanks go to the translators themselves, who so generously made new contributions or permitted their previously published work to be made available in this new format. A very special thanks, too, goes to Michael Cooper of *Monumenta Nipponica,* who kindly granted permission to use a number of translations which first appeared in that journal. Ivan Morris' translation, *Under Reconstruction (Fushinchū),* was first published by Charles E. Tuttle Company in 1962, to whom we are grateful for permission to publish the story here. Fumi Norica at the Library of Congress supplied a number of thoughtful suggestions and materials for the illustrations, and Eiko Miura looked over and improved my own translation. Most of all, I would like to thank Stuart Kiang, formerly of the School of Hawaiian, Asian & Pacific Studies, who took an early and enthusiastic interest in this project and helped in so many ways to bring it to fruition. Finally, thanks go to Stephanie Chun, who typed the final manuscript from such disparate sources, and Don Yoder, the manuscript editor, who aided in the production of such a beautiful book.

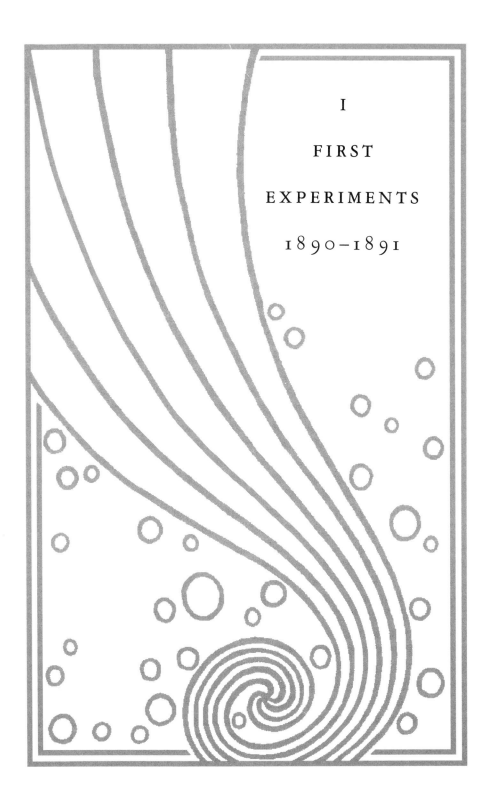

I

FIRST

EXPERIMENTS

1890–1891

IN 1881, THE YOUNG MORI ŌGAI finished his medical studies in Tokyo and was given a post in the Japanese army Medical Corps with the rank of second lieutenant. His studies with European teachers, who at that time served as professors of medicine at the university, required a command of German. Ōgai, naturally gifted, soon became adept at the language and thus seemed a natural choice to be sent to Germany by his superiors. The young officer was sent to Berlin in 1884 to make a study of methods in European military hygiene. He was to remain in Europe until 1898.

Once in Germany, the results of Ōgai's thorough linguistic preparations in Japan took a turn perhaps unanticipated even by the young medical officer himself. Ōgai's thorough knowledge of German quickly led him to discover the riches of European literature, in particular the work of the great romantic German writers of the nineteenth century; indeed, Ōgai's lifetime admiration for Goethe was to begin during these early years. Ōgai commenced his study of the classics of European literature in the same disciplined fashion with which he approached his medical studies. Along with his absorption of romantic German literature and philosophy, he extended his reading to the great works of the European tradition available in German translation, ranging in his enthusiasms from Sophocles and Shakespeare to the French naturalists. This encounter with high European culture proved perhaps more significant to his development as an intellectual and a writer than the fact of his physical presence in Germany.

That presence, however, kept him seriously occupied as well. Ōgai traveled to Munich, Dresden, and Leipzig, where he met a number of distinguished military and civilian figures; he went to the theater and attended concerts and art exhibitions, throwing himself into the highest reaches of a culture that fascinated him. His own growing self-consciousness as a Japanese led him in turn to engage in a polemical exchange of newspaper articles with Edmund Naumann, a German geologist who had worked in Japan for a decade and found the country backward and unlikely to improve. It appears as well that he fell in love with a German girl who eventually followed him to Tokyo only to be rebuffed and sent back to Europe by Ōgai's family.

These were tumultuous events for a young Japanese brought up in the narrow world of a rural Tokugawa domain. Yet even in these early years, Ōgai found he possessed one basic characteristic that permitted him both to observe and to create: his ability to put himself in the position of what he was to call at one later point the bystander. No matter how involved he became in the events around him, Ōgai preserved the ability to study them, and himself, with a certain detachment. As for the virtues of such a sense of detachment, he was to come to feel a certain poignant ambiguity, as some of his later pieces such as *Daydreams* (1911) and *Ghost Stories* (1912) reveal. Some of this ability to remove himself from emotional engagement in the affairs around him may have come from his early upbringing in the tradition of Confucian self-cultivation. Or perhaps these attitudes of mind were reinforced by the mental precision demanded of him through his medical training, a quality that can be observed in the work of another literary doctor, Anton Chekhov. More likely, however, these predilections, however they came to be developed through his studies and travel, sprang from the deepest levels of his personality.

Back in Japan in 1888 and bearing the rank of captain, Ōgai, now advancing in his army medical career, appeared, on the surface, to be moving into the kind of life pattern that his superiors might well have expected of him. But the understandings and enthusiasms welling up in him from his European experience took on an urgency of their own. Two years later, in 1890, he was divorced, began writing stories using materials drawn from the emotional wellspring of his European experiences, and engaged in a series of literary debates with his contemporaries that were to last much of the decade. He was not yet thirty when this process began.

This period of first flowering produced three short novellas: *The Dancing Girl, A Sad Tale,* and *The Courier,* all published in the brief period from January 1890 to January 1891. As works of fiction, they ultimately must stand on their own terms for the reader; still, an understanding of the context in which they were written may sharpen one's appreciation of what Ōgai was attempting to achieve in these early experiments.

In the first place, there were at this period virtually no literary works in Japan devoted to serious examination of contemporary psychology or to the spiritual significance of the experience of a Japanese living in the midst of the complexities of Meiji life. The work of fiction usually regarded—and with justice—as the first work of modern Japanese literature was the novel *Ukigumo* (Floating Clouds), which the young Futabatei Shimei (1864–1909) began to publish in installments while Ōgai was in Germany. Futabatei's literary model was Turgenev.

Nor was there a suitable written language in which to compose such works. The bookish Japanese used for literary composition earlier in the nineteenth century, with its long classical heritage, bore little resemblance to the resonances of genuine contemporary speech; it soon proved useless as a means to capture the quickly shifting realities of life after the Meiji restoration of 1868. Futabatei has often been credited with creating a flexible written language, modeled on the actual speech patterns of the time, that allowed for an adequate articulation of the modern Japanese sensibility.

Ōgai would eventually make his own contributions to these efforts to bring language and psychological reality closer together. At the time of the composition of these three stories, however, Ōgai's language still showed certain formal qualities that, for a reader of the original in our times, reveals an intriguing distance between the formal, classical linguistic structures employed and a surprisingly fresh emotional content. In that regard, these three stories are perhaps more modern in feeling when read in translation than in the original. In the Japan of Ōgai's early years, the language, like all else, seemed in a sometimes perilous state of flux.

Then, too, these three stories can be read as personal experiments—Ōgai's attempts to search out through the use of literary models the implications and imperatives of his own encounter with European culture. Ōgai was to try to deal creatively in many ways with his new and restless understandings. These efforts all seemed, in one way or another, to involve an attempt to encompass what he found in Germany that had touched him and so stimulated his own creativity. He began his work as a translator, first of romantic German poetry, then of European fiction; he took a profound interest in the development of modern Western-style painting in Japan; he read, translated, and argued the real nature of the significance of European aesthetic theory with his contemporaries. These three stories, written at the beginning of ten years of artistic apprenticeship, might best be seen as one manifestation of Ōgai's urge to understand and articulate what for him had become a virutal quest for cultural and personal self-understanding as a modern Japanese. These experiments were to come to full fruition fifteen years later, when Ōgai would again turn to fiction as a means of self-expression, this time as a mature, and chastened, man in his late forties.

Maihime

THE DANCING GIRL

THE DANCING GIRL, PUBLISHED IN 1890, was Ōgai's first work to reach the Japanese reading public, and it remains one of his best-known and most highly appreciated shorter works of fiction. Fiction, perhaps; yet what drives this romantic tale of love, madness, and death are the authentic feelings articulated by the narrator, whose adventures in Germany, and his emotional response to those adventures, closely resemble those of the author.

The story thus possesses a considerable resonance. The dilemmas caused by the pain of a gradual self-awakening experienced by the protagonist, developed during his years in Europe, were to represent for Ōgai during the whole span of his artistic career a central tension in Japanese contemporary civilization that he believed his countrymen must learn to acknowledge. Once awakened to the demands of the individual self, the author inquires, how can one find the courage, and a necessary sense of resignation, to say nothing of the appropriate means, to reintegrate oneself into a society that seeks an ideal of communal compliance, particularly when there were, from a national point of view, a number of compelling reasons to do so. In many ways, these concerns, first expressed in *The Dancing Girl,* form a thread that binds together many of Ōgai's later important works, such as *Gan* (Wild Geese) and a number of his historical tales.

Much has been written about the relation between the particulars of Ōgai's own life in Germany and the characters and events portrayed in the story. Fascinating as these matters may be to biographers or literary historians, such debates shed little light on the considerable success of the story itself as a romantic narrative. In the character of the young heroine Elise, the tale may suggest certain of Ōgai's literary debts, notably to Goethe and other romantic writers, even to Shakespeare's Ophelia, but she remains a touching and authentic creation in her own right. Nevertheless, the scene in which the narrator falls ill in the rain, suffering a virtual nervous breakdown because of the conflicting pressures brought to bear upon him, is strikingly contemporary in its psychology, even by modern standards. Here Ōgai, perhaps first among Japanese writers since the beginning of the Meiji period, pushed his narrative strongly, even relentlessly, into the psychic interior of his character. In every sense of the word it was a daring and difficult thing to do.

Nor, it must be said, have such clashes between duty and self-fulfillment dwindled to insignificance in the psychological life of the Japanese, even today. The 1989 film of *The Dancing Girl,* directed by the eminent director Shinoda Masahiro, an elaborate Japanese-German coproduction, bears witness to the fact that Ōgai's understanding of the force of these tensions over the role of the individual in Japanese society remains very much appreciated and understood.

THEY HAVE FINISHED LOADING THE COAL, and the tables here in the second-class saloon stand in silence. Even the bright glare from the electric lights seems wasted, for tonight the group of card players who usually gather here of an evening are staying in a hotel and I am left alone on board.

It is now five years since the hopes I cherished for so long were fulfilled and I received orders to go to Europe. When I arrived here in the port of Saigon, I was struck by the strangeness of everything I saw and heard. I wonder how many thousands of words I wrote every day as I jotted down random thoughts in my travel diary. It was published in a newspaper at the time and was highly praised, but now I shudder to think how any sensitive person must have reacted to my childish ideas and my presumptuous rhetoric. I even recorded details of the common flora and fauna, the geology, and the local customs as if they were rarities. Now, on my way home, the notebooks that I bought intending to use for a diary remain untouched. Could it be that while studying in Germany I developed a kind of *nil admirari* attitude? No, there is another reason.

Returning to Japan, I feel a very different person from when I set out. Not only do I still feel dissatisfied with my studies, but I have also learned how sad this transient life can be. I am now aware of the fallibility of human emotions, but in particular I realize what a fickle heart I have myself. To whom could I possibly show a record of fleeting impressions that might well be right one day and wrong the next? Perhaps this is why my diary was never written. No, there is another reason.

Twenty days or more have passed since we left Brindisi. Usually it is the custom at sea to while away the cares of travel even in the company of utter strangers, but I have shut myself up in my cabin under the pretext of feeling somewhat indisposed. I seldom speak to my fellow travelers, for I am tormented by a hidden remorse.

At first this pain was a mere wisp of cloud that brushed against my heart, hiding the mountain scenery of Switzerland and dulling my interest in Italy's ancient ruins. Then gradually I grew weary of life and weary of myself, and suffered the most heartrending anguish. Now, remorse has settled in the depths of my heart, the merest shadow. And yet, with everything I read and see it causes me renewed pain, evoking feelings of extreme nostalgia, like a form reflected in a mirror or the echo of a voice.

TRANSLATED BY RICHARD BOWRING

How can I ever rid myself of such remorse? If it were of a different nature I could perhaps soothe my feelings by expressing them in poetry. But it is so deeply engraved upon my heart that I fear this is impossible. And yet, as there is no one here this evening, and it will be some while before the cabin boy comes to turn off the light, I think I will try to record the outline of my story here.

Thanks to a very strict education at home since childhood, my studies lacked nothing, despite the fact that I lost my father at an early age. When I studied at the school in my former fief, and in the preparatory course for the university in Tokyo, and later in the Faculty of Law, the name Ōta Toyotarō was always at the top of the list. Thus, no doubt, I brought some comfort to my mother who had found in me, her only child, the strength to go through life. At nineteen I received my degree and was praised for having achieved greater honor than had any other student since the founding of the university. I joined a government department and spent three pleasant years in Tokyo with my mother, whom I called up from the country. Being especially high in the estimation of the head of my department, I was then given orders to travel to Europe and study matters connected with my particular section. Stirred by the thought that I now had the opportunity to make my name and raise my family fortunes, I was not unduly sorry to leave even my mother, although she was over fifty. So it was that I left home far behind and arrived in Berlin.

I had the vague hope of accomplishing great feats and was used to working hard under pressure. But suddenly here I was, standing in the middle of this most modern of European capitals. My eyes were dazzled by its brilliance, my mind was dazed by the riot of color. To translate Unter den Linden as "under the Bodhi tree" would suggest a quiet secluded spot. But just come and see the groups of men and women sauntering along the pavements that line each side of that great thoroughfare as it runs, straight as a die, through the city. It was still in the days when Wilhelm I would come to his window and gaze down upon his capital. The tall, broad-shouldered officers in their colorful dress uniform, and the attractive girls, their hair made up in the Parisian style, were everywhere a delight to the eye. Carriages ran silently on asphalt roads. Just visible in the clear sky between the towering buildings were fountains cascading with the sound of heavy rain. Looking into the distance, one could see the statue of the goddess on the victory column. She seemed to be floating halfway to heaven from the midst of the green trees on the other side of the Brandenburg Gate. All these myriad sights were gathered so close at hand that it was quite bewildering for the newcomer. But I had promised myself that I would not be impressed by such captivating scenes of beauty and I continually closed my mind to these external objects that bore in on me.

The Prussian officials were all happy to welcome me when I pulled on the bell rope, asked for an interview, and handed over my open letter of introduction, explaining to them why I had come. They promised to tell me whatever I wished to know once formal application had been received from the Legation. I was fortunate enough to have learned both French and German at home, and no sooner was I introduced than they asked where and when I had learned to speak so well.

I had already obtained official permission to enter Berlin University and so I enrolled to study politics whenever my duties might permit. After one or two months, when the official preliminaries had been carried out and my investigations were making good progress, I sent off a report on the most urgent matters, and the rest I wrote down in a number of notebooks. As far as the university was concerned, there was no chance of providing special courses for would-be politicians, as I had naively hoped. I was irresolute for a while, but then, deciding to attend two or three law lectures, I paid the fee and went to listen.

Some three years passed in this way like a dream. But there is always a time when, come what may, one's true nature reveals itself. I had obeyed my father's dying words and had done what my mother had taught me. From the beginning I had studied willingly, proud to hear myself praised as an infant prodigy, and later I had labored unremittingly in the happy knowledge that my department head was pleased with my excellent work. But all that time I had been a mere passive, mechanical being with no real awareness of myself. Now, however, at the age of twenty-five, perhaps because I had been exposed to the liberal ways of the university for some time, there grew within me a kind of uneasiness; it seemed as if my real self, which had been lying dormant deep down, was gradually appearing on the surface and threatening my former assumed self. I realized that I would be happy neither as a high-flying politician nor as a lawyer reciting statutes by heart and pronouncing sentence.

My mother, I thought to myself, had tried to make me into a walking dictionary, and my department head had tried to turn me into an incarnation of the law. The former I might just be able to stand, but the latter was out of the question. Up to then I had answered him with scrupulous care even in quite trifling matters, but from that time on, I often argued in my reports that one should not be bothered with petty legal details. Once a person grasped the spirit of the law, I grandly said, everything would solve itself. In the university I abandoned the law lectures and became more interested in history and literature; eventually I moved into the world of the arts.

My department head had obviously tried to turn me into a machine that could be manipulated as he desired. He could hardly have been very pleased with someone who entertained such independent ideas and held such unusual views. I was in a precarious situation. If that were all, however, it would not have been enough to undermine my position. But among the students studying in Berlin at the time was an influential group with whom I did not see eye to eye. They were only suspicious of me at first, but then they began to slander me. They may have had good reason.

Attributing the fact that I neither drank nor played billiards with them to apparent stubbornness and self-restraint on my part, they ridiculed and envied me. But this was because they did not know me. How could anyone else know the reason for my behavior when I did not know it myself? I felt like the leaves of the silk-tree which shrink and shy away when they are touched. I felt as unsure of myself as a young girl. Ever since my youth I had followed the advice of my elders and kept to the path of learning and obedience. If I had succeeded, it was not through being courageous. I might have seemed capable of arduous study, but I had deceived not only myself but others too. I had simply followed a path that I was made to follow. The fact that external matters did not disturb me was not because I had the courage to reject them or ignore them, but rather because I was afraid and tied myself hand and foot. Before I left home I was convinced I was a man of talent. I believed deeply in my own powers of endurance. Yes, but even that was short-lived. I felt quite the hero until the ship left Yokohama, but then I found myself weeping uncontrollably. I thought it strange at the time, but it was my true nature showing through. Perhaps it had been with me from birth; or perhaps it came about because my father died and I was brought up by my mother.

The ridicule of the students was only to be expected, but it was stupid of them to be jealous of such a weak and pitiful mind.

I used to see women sitting in the cafés soliciting for custom; their faces were heavily made up and their clothes were gaudy. But I never had the courage to go and approach them. Nor did I have the nerve to join with those men about town, with their tall hats, their pince-nez, and that aristocratic nasal accent so peculiar to Prussians. Not having the heart for such things, I found I could not mix with my more lively fellow countrymen, and because of this barrier between us, they bore a grudge against me. Then they started telling tales, and thus I was accused of crimes I had not committed and had to put up with so much hardship in so short a time.

One evening I sauntered through the Tiergarten and then walked down Unter den Linden. On the way back to my lodgings in Monbijoustrasse, I came in front of the old church in Klosterstrasse. How many times, I wonder, had I passed through that sea of lights, entered this gloomy passage, and stood enraptured, gazing at the three-hundred-year-old church that lay set back from the road. Opposite it stood some houses with the washing hanging out to dry on poles on the roofs, and a bar where an old Jew with long whiskers was standing idly by the door; there was also a tenement house with one flight of steps running directly to the upper rooms and another leading down to the home of a blacksmith who lived in the cellar.

Just as I was walking past I noticed a young girl sobbing against the closed door of the church. She must have been about sixteen or seventeen. Her light golden hair flowed down from under the scarf around her head, and her dress was spotlessly clean. Surprised by my footsteps, she turned around. Only a poet could really do her justice. Her eyes were blue and clear, but filled with a wistful sadness. They were shaded by long eyelashes which half hid her tears. Why was it that in one glance over her shoulder she pierced the defenses of my heart?

Perhaps it was because of some profound grief that she was standing there in tears oblivious to all else. The coward in me was overcome by compassion and sympathy, and without thinking I went to her side.

"Why are you crying?" I asked. "Perhaps because I am a stranger here I may be able to help you all the more." I was astounded by my audacity.

Startled, she stared into my sallow face, but she must have seen my sincerity from my expression.

"You look a kind sort of person," she sobbed. "Not cruel like him or my mother!"

Her tears had stopped for a moment, but now they overflowed again and ran down her lovely cheeks.

"Help me! You must help me from having to lose all sense of shame. My mother beat me because I did not agree to his proposal. My father has just died and we have to bury him tomorrow. But we don't have a penny in the house."

She dissolved into tears again. I gazed at her as she hung her head and trembled.

"If I am to take you home, you must calm down," I said. "Don't let everyone hear you. We're out in the street."

She had inadvertently lain her head on my shoulder while I was speaking. Suddenly she looked up and, giving me the same startled glance as before, she fled from me in shame.

She walked quickly, as if unwilling for people to see her, and I followed. Through a large door across the road from the church was a flight of old worn stone steps. Up these steps on the third floor was a door so small that one needed to bend down to enter. The girl pulled on the twisted end of a rusty piece of wire.

"Who's there?" came a hoarse voice from inside.

"It's Elise. I'm back."

She had hardly finished speaking when the door was roughly pulled open by an old woman. Although her hair was graying and her brow clearly showed the traces of poverty and suffering, it was not an evil face. She was wearing an old dress of some wool and cotton material and had on some dirty slippers. When Elise pointed to me and went inside, the old woman slammed the door in my face as if she had been waiting impatiently.

I stood there vacantly for a while. Then, by the light of an oil lamp, I noticed a name painted on the door in lacquer: "Ernst Weigert," and below, "Tailor." I presumed it was the name of the girl's dead father. Inside I heard voices raised as if in argument, then all was quiet again. The door was re-opened, and the old woman, apologizing profusely for such impolite behavior, invited me in.

The door opened into the kitchen. On the right was a low window with spotlessly clean linen curtains. On the left was a roughly built brick stove. The door of the room facing me was half open and I saw inside a bed covered with a white sheet. The dead man must have been lying there. She opened a door next to the stove and led me to an attic; it faced onto the street and had no real ceiling. The beams sloping down from the corners of the roof to the window were covered with paper, and below that, where there was only room enough to stoop, was a bed. On the table in the middle of the room was spread a beautiful woolen cloth on which were arranged two books, a photograph album, and a vase with a bunch of flowers. They seemed somehow too expensive for the place. Standing shyly beside the table was the girl.

She was exceedingly attractive. In the lamplight her pallid face had a faint blush, and the slender beauty of her hands and feet seemed hardly to belong to the daughter of a poor family. She waited until the old woman had left the room and then spoke. She had a slight accent.

"It was thoughtless of me to lead you here. Please forgive me. But you looked so very kind. You won't despise me, will you? I suppose you don't know Schaumberg, the man we were relying on for my father's funeral tomorrow. He's the manager at the Viktoria Theater. I have been working for him for two years so I thought he was bound to help us; but he took advantage of our misfortune and tried to force me to do what he wished.

You must help. I promise to pay you back from the little I earn, even if I have to go hungry. If not, then my mother says. . . . "

She burst into tears and stood there trembling. There was an irresistible appeal in her eyes as she gazed up at me. Did she know the effect her eyes had on me, or was it unintentional?

I had two or three silver marks in my pocket, but that would probably not have been enough. So I took off my watch and laid it on the table.

"This will help you for the time being," I said. "Tell the pawnbroker's man if he calls on Ōta at 3 Monbijoustrasse, I'll redeem it."

The girl looked startled but grateful. As I put out my hand to say good-bye, she raised it to her lips and covered it with tears.

Alas, what evil fate brought her to my lodgings to thank me? She looked so beautiful there standing by the window where I used to sit reading all day long surrounded by the works of Schopenhauer and Schiller. From that time on our relationship gradually deepened. When my countrymen got to know, they immediately assumed that I was seeking my pleasures in the company of dancing girls. But it was as yet nothing more than a foolish trifling affair.

One of my fellow countrymen—I will not give his name, but he was known as a mischief-maker—reported to my department head that I was frequenting theaters and seeking the company of actresses. My superior was in any case resentful that I was neglecting my proper studies, and so he eventually told the Legation to abolish my post and terminate my employment. The minister at the Legation passed this order on, advising me that they would pay the fare if I returned home immediately, but that I could expect no official help if I decided to stay on. I asked for one week's grace, and it was while I was thus worrying what to do that I received two letters which brought me the most intense pain I think I have ever suffered. They had both been sent at almost the same time, but one was written by my mother and the other by a friend telling me of her death, the death of the mother who was so dear to me. I cannot bear to repeat here what she wrote. Tears prevent my pen from writing more.

The relationship between Elise and myself had in fact been more innocent than had appeared to others. Her father had been poor and her education had been meager. At the age of fifteen she had answered an advertisement by a dancing master and had learned that disreputable trade. When she had finished the course, she went to the Viktoria Theater and was now the second dancer of the group. But the life of a dancer is precarious. As the writer Hackländer has said, they are today's slaves, tied by a poor wage and driven hard with rehearsals in the daytime and performances at night. In the theater dressing room they can make up and dress themselves in beautiful clothes; but outside they often do not have enough clothes or food for themselves and life is very hard for those who have to support their parents or families. It was said that, as a result, it was rare for them not to fall into the lowest of all professions.

That Elise had escaped this fate was due partly to her modest nature and partly to her father's careful protection. Ever since a child, she had in fact liked reading, but all she could lay her hands on were poor novels of the type lent by the circulating libraries, known by their cry of *"Colportage."* After meeting me, she began to read the books I lent her, and gradually her tastes improved and she lost her accent. Soon the mistakes in her letters to me became fewer. And so there had grown up between us a kind of pupil-teacher relationship. When she heard of my untimely dismissal, she went pale. I concealed the fact that it was connected with her, but she asked me not to tell her mother. She was afraid that if her mother knew I had lost financial support for my studies she would want nothing more to do with me.

There is no need to describe it in detail here, but it was about this time that my feeling for her suddenly changed to one of love and the bond between us deepened. The most important decision of my life lay before me. It was a time of real crisis. Some perhaps may wonder and criticize my behavior, but my affection for Elise had been strong ever since our first meeting, and now I could read in her expression sympathy for my misfortune and sadness at the prospect of parting. The way she stood there, a picture of loveliness, her hair hanging loose—I was distraught by so much suffering and powerless in the face of such enchantment.

The day I had arranged to meet the minister approached. Fate was pressing. If I returned home like this, I should have failed in my studies and bear a disgraced name. I would never be able to reestablish myself. But on the other hand, if I stayed, I could not see any way of obtaining funds to support my studies.

At this point, my friend Aizawa Kenkichi, with whom I am now traveling home, came to my aid. He was private secretary to Count Amakata in Tokyo, and he saw the report of my dismissal in the Official Gazette. He persuaded the editor of a certain newspaper to make me their foreign correspondent, so I could stay in Berlin and send back reports on various topics such as politics and the arts.

The salary they offered was a pittance, but by changing my lodgings and eating lunch at a cheaper restaurant, I would just be able to make ends meet. While I was trying to decide, Elise showed her love by throwing me a lifeline. I don't know how she did it, but she managed to win over her mother, and I was accepted as a lodger in their rooms. It was not long before Elise and I found ourselves pooling our meager resources, and managed, even in the midst of all our troubles, to enjoy life.

After breakfast, Elise either went to rehearsals or, when she was free, would stay at home. I would go to the coffee shop on Königsstrasse with its narrow frontage and its long deep interior. There, in a room lit by an open skylight, I used to read all the newspapers and jot down the odd note or two in pencil. Here would come young men with no regular job, old men who lived quite happily by lending out the little money that they had, and job-bers stealing time off from their work at the Exchange to put their feet up for a while. I wonder what they made of the strange Japanese who sat among them writing busily on the cold stone table, quite oblivious that the cup of coffee the waitress had brought was getting cold, and who was always going back and forth to the wall where the newspapers were hanging open in long wooden frames. When Elise had rehearsals, she would call in about one o'clock on her way home. Some of the people there must have looked askance when we left together, myself and this girl who seemed as if she could dance in the palm of your hand.

I neglected my studies. When she came home from the theater, Elise would sit in a chair and sew, and I would write my articles on the table by her side, using the faint light of the lamp hanging from the ceiling. These articles were quite unlike my earlier reports when I had raked up onto paper the dead leaves of laws and statutes. Now I wrote about the lively political scene and criticized the latest trends in literature and the arts, carefully com-posing the articles to the best of my ability, more in the style of Heine than Börne. During this time Wilhelm I and Friedrich III died in quick succes-sion. Writing particularly detailed reports on such subjects as the accession of the new emperor and the fall of Bismarck, I found myself from then on much busier than I had expected, and it was difficult to read the few books I had or return to my studies. I had not canceled my registration at the univer-sity, but I could not afford to pay the fees and seldom went to any lectures.

Yes, I neglected my studies. But I did become expert in a different sphere —popular education, for this was more advanced in Germany than in any other European country. No sooner had I become a correspondent than I was constantly reading and writing about the variety of excellent discussions appearing in the newspapers and journals, and I brought to this work the perception gained from my studies as a university student. My knowledge of the world, which up to then had been rather limited, thus became much broader, and I reached a stage undreamed of by most of my compatriots studying there. They could barely read the editorials in the German news-papers.

Then came the winter of 1888. They spread grit on the pavements of the main streets and shoveled the snow into piles. Although the ground in the Klosterstrasse area was bumpy and uneven, the surface became smooth with ice. It was sad to see the starved sparrows frozen to death on the ground when you opened the door in the mornings. We lit a fire in the stove to warm the room, but it was still unbearably cold. The north European winter penetrated the stone walls and pierced our cotton clothes. A few evenings before, Elise had fainted on stage and had been helped home by some friends. She felt ill from then on and rested. But she brought up whatever she tried to eat and it was her mother who first suggested that it might be morning sickness. Even without this my future was uncertain. What could I possibly do if it were true?

It was Sunday morning. I was at home, but felt somewhat uneasy. Elise did not feel bad enough to go to bed; she sat on a chair drawn up close to the small fireplace but said little. There was the sound of someone at the door and her mother, who had been in the kitchen, hurried in with a letter for me. I recognized Aizawa's handwriting immediately, but the stamp was Prussian and it was postmarked Berlin. Feeling puzzled, I opened the letter. The news was totally unexpected: "Arrived yesterday evening as part of Count Amakata's suite. The count says he wants to see you immediately. If your fortunes are ever to be restored, now is the time. Excuse brevity but sent in great haste."

I stared at the letter.

"Is it from home?" asked Elise. "It's not bad news, is it?"

She was probably thinking it was connected with my salary from the news-paper.

"No," I replied. "There is no need to worry. You've heard me mention Aizawa. Well, he's just arrived in Berlin with his minister. He wants to see me. He says it's urgent, so I'd better go along without delay."

Not even a mother seeing off her beloved only child could have been more solicitous. Thinking I was to have an interview with the count, Elise fought back her illness. She chose a clean white shirt and got out my *Gehrock,* a frockcoat with two rows of buttons, which she had carefully stored away. She helped me into it, and even tied my cravat for me.

"Now no one will be able to say you look a disgrace. Look in my mirror," she said. "Why so miserable? I wish I could come too!"

She straightened my suit a little.

"But when I see you dressed up like this, you somehow don't look like my Toyotarō."

She thought for a moment.

"If you do become rich and famous, you'll never leave me, will you? Even if my illness does not turn out to be what Mother says it is."

"What! Rich and famous?" I smiled. "I lost the desire to enter politics years ago. I don't even want to see the count. I'm just going to meet an old friend whom I have not seen for a very long time."

The first-class droshky that her mother had ordered drew up under the window, the wheels creaking in the snow. I put on my gloves, slung my slightly soiled overcoat about my shoulders without putting my arms through the sleeves, and picked up my hat. I kissed Elise good-bye and went downstairs. She opened the ice-covered window to see me off, her hair blowing in the north wind.

I got out at the entrance to the Kaiserhof. Inquiring the room number of Private Secretary Aizawa from the doorman, I climbed the marble staircase. It had been a long time since I had last been there. I came to an antechamber where there was a plush sofa by the central pillar and directly ahead a mirror. Here I took off my coat and, passing along the corridor, arrived at Aizawa's door. I hesitated a little. How would he greet me? When we were at university together, he had been so impressed by my correct behavior. I entered the room and we met face to face. He seemed stouter and sturdier than of old, but he had the same naturally cheerful disposition and did not appear to be concerned about my misconduct. But we were given no time to discuss in detail what had happened since we last met, for I was called in and interviewed by the count. He entrusted me with the translation of some urgent documents written in German. I accepted them and took my leave. Aizawa followed me out and invited me to lunch.

During the meal it was he who asked all the questions, and I who gave the answers, because his career had been in the main uneventful, whereas the story of my life was full of troubles and adversity.

He listened as I told him about my unhappy experiences with complete frankness. He was often surprised, but never tried to blame me. On the contrary he ridiculed my boorish countrymen. But when I had finished my tale he became serious and remonstrated with me. Things had reached this pass because I was basically weak-willed, but there was no point in laboring the fact now, he said. Nevertheless, how long could a man of talent and learning like myself remain emotionally involved with a mere chit of a girl and lead such an aimless life? At this stage Count Amakata merely needed me for my German. Since he knew the reason for my dismissal, Aizawa would make no attempt to make him change his preconception of me—it would do neither of us any good if the count were to think that we were trying to deceive him. But there was no better way to recommend people than by displaying their talents. I should show the count how good I was and thus try to win his confidence. As for the girl, she might be sincerely in love with me and our passions deeply involved, but there was certainly no meeting of minds—I had merely allowed myself to slip into what was an accepted practice. I must decide to give her up, he urged.

When he mapped out my future like this, I felt like a man adrift who spies a mountain in the distance. But the mountain was still covered in cloud. I was not sure whether I would reach it, or even if I did, whether it would bring satisfaction. Life was pleasant even in the midst of poverty and Elise's love was hard to reject. Being so weak-willed I could make no decision there and then, so I merely promised to follow my friend's advice for a while, and try and break off the affair. When it came to losing something close to me, I could resist my enemies, but never could refuse my friends.

We parted about four o'clock. As I came out of the hotel restaurant the wind hit me in the face. A fire had been burning in a big tiled stove inside, so when the double glass doors closed behind me and I stood outside in the open, the cold of the afternoon pierced my thin overcoat and seemed all the more intense. I shivered, and there was a strange chill in my heart too.

I finished the translation in one night. Thereafter I found myself going to the Kaiserhof quite often. At first the count spoke only of business, but after a while he brought up various things that had happened at home recently and asked my opinion. When the occasion arose, he would tell me about the mistakes people had made on the voyage out, and would burst out laughing.

A month went by. Then one day he suddenly turned to me.

"I'm leaving for Russia tomorrow. Will you come with me?" he asked.

I had not seen Aizawa for several days as he was busy with official business, and the request took me totally by surprise.

"How could I refuse?" I replied.

I must confess that I did not answer as the result of a quick decision. When I am suddenly asked a question by someone whom I trust, I instantly agree without weighing up the consequences. Not only do I agree, but, despite knowing how difficult the matter will be, I often hide my initial thoughtlessness by persevering and carrying it out.

That day I was given not only the translation fee but also my travel money. When I got home I gave the fee to Elise. With this she would be able to support herself and her mother until such time as I returned from Russia. She said she had been to see a doctor, who confirmed that she was pregnant. Being anaemic she hadn't realized her condition for some months. She had also received a message from the theater telling her that she had been dismissed as she had been away for so long. She had only been off work for a month, so there was probably some other reason for such severity. Believing implicitly in my sincerity, she did not seem unduly worried about the impending journey.

The journey was not long by train and so there was little to prepare. I just packed into a small suitcase a rented black suit, a copy of the *Almanach de Gotha,* and two or three dictionaries. In view of recent depressing events, I felt it would be miserable for Elise after my departure. I was also anxious lest she should cry at the station, so I took the step of sending her and her mother out early the next morning to visit friends. I collected up my things and locked the door on my way out, leaving the key with the cobbler who lived at the entrance.

What is there to tell of my travels in Russia? My duties as an interpreter suddenly lifted me from the mundane and dropped me above the clouds into the Russian court. Accompanying the count's party, I went to St. Petersburg, where I was overwhelmed by the ornate architecture of the palace, which represented for me the greatest splendors of Paris transported into the midst of ice and snow. Above all I remember the countless flickering yellow candles, the light reflected by the multitude of decorations and epaulets, and the fluttering fans of the court ladies, who forgot the cold outside as they sat in the warmth from the exquisitely carved and inlaid fireplaces. As I was the most fluent French speaker in the party, I had to circulate between host and guest and interpret for them.

But I had not forgotten Elise. How could I? She sent me letters every day. On the day I left, she had wanted to avoid the unaccustomed sadness of sitting alone by lamplight, and so had talked late into the night at a friend's house. Then, feeling tired, she returned home and immediately went to bed. Next morning, she wondered if she had not just dreamed she was alone. But when she got up, her depression and sense of loneliness were worse than the time when she had been scratching a living and had not known where the next meal was coming from. This was what she told me in her first letter.

Later letters seemed to be written in great distress, and each of them began in the same way.

"Ah! Only now do I realize the depth of my love for you. As you say you have no close relatives at home, you will stay here if you find you can make a good living, won't you? My love must tie you here to me. Even if that proves impossible and you have to return home, I could easily come with my mother. But where would we get the money for the fare? I had always intended to stay here and wait for the day you became famous, whatever I had to do. But the pain of separation grows stronger every day, even though you are only on a short trip and have only been away about twenty days. It was a mistake to have thought that parting was just a passing sorrow. My pregnancy is at last beginning to be obvious, so you cannot reject me now, whatever happens. I quarrel a lot with Mother. But she has given in, now she sees how much more determined I am than I used to be. When I travel home with you, she's talking of going to stay with some distant relatives who live on a farm near Stettin. If, as you say in your last letter, you are doing important work for the minister, we can somehow manage the fare. How I long for the day you return to Berlin."

It was only after reading this letter that I really understood my predicament. How could I have been so insensitive! I had been proud to have made a decision about my own course of action and that of others unrelated to me. But it had been made in entirely favorable rather than adverse conditions. When I tried to clarify my relationship with others, the emotions that I had formerly trusted became confused.

I was already on very good terms with the count. But in my shortsightedness I only took into consideration the duties that I was then undertaking. The gods might have known how this was connected to my hopes for the future, but I never gave it a thought. Was my passion cooling? When Aizawa had first recommended me, I had felt that the count's confidence would be hard to gain, but now I had to some extent won his trust. When Aizawa had said things like, "If we continue to work together after you return to Japan," I wondered whether he had really been hinting that this was what the count was saying. It was true that Aizawa was my friend, but he would not have been able to tell me openly since it was an official matter. Now that I thought about it, I wondered whether he had perhaps told the count what I had rashly promised him—that I was going to sever my connections with Elise.

When I first came to Germany, I thought that I had discovered my true nature, and I swore never to be used as a machine again. But perhaps it was merely the pride of a bird that had been given momentary freedom to flap its wings and yet still had its legs bound. There was no way I could loose the bonds. The rope had first been in the hands of my department head, and now, alas, it was in the hands of the count.

It happened to be New Year's Day when I returned to Berlin with the count's party. I left them at the station and took a cab home. In Berlin no one sleeps on New Year's Eve and it is the custom to lie in late the next morning. Every single house was quiet. The snow on the road had frozen hard into ruts in the bitter cold and shone brightly in the sunlight. The cab turned into Klosterstrasse and pulled up at the entrance to the house. I heard a window open but saw nothing from inside the cab. I got the driver to take my bag and was just about to climb the steps when Elise came flying down to meet me. She cried out and flung her arms around my neck. At this the driver was a little startled and mumbled something in his beard that I could not hear.

"Oh! Welcome home! I would have died if you had not returned!" she cried.

Up to now I had prevaricated. At times the thought of Japan and the desire to seek fame seemed to overcome my love, but at this precise moment all my hesitation left me and I hugged her. She laid her head on my shoulder and wept tears of happiness.

"Which floor do I take it to?" growled the driver as he hurried up the stairs with the luggage.

I gave a few silver coins to her mother, who had come to the door to meet me, and asked her to pay the driver. Elise held me by the hand and hurried into the room. I was surprised to see a pile of white cotton and lace lying on the table. She laughed and pointed to the pile.

"What do you think of all the preparations?" she said.

She picked up a piece of material and I saw it was a baby's diaper.

"You cannot imagine how happy I am!" she said. "I wonder if our child will have your dark eyes. Ah, your eyes that I have only been able to dream about. When it's born, you will do the right thing, won't you? You'll give it your name and no one else's, won't you?"

She hung her head.

"You may laugh at me for being silly, but I will be so happy the day we go to church."

Her uplifted eyes were full of tears.

I did not call on the count for two or three days because I thought he might be tired from the journey, and so I stayed home. Then, one evening, a messenger came bearing an invitation. When I arrived, the count greeted me warmly and thanked me for my work in Russia. He then asked me whether I felt like returning to Japan with him. I knew so much and my knowledge of languages alone was of great value, he said. He had thought that, seeing I had been so long in Germany, I might have some ties here, but he had asked Aizawa and had been relieved to hear that this was not the case.

I could not possibly deny what appeared to be the situation. I was shaken, but of course found it impossible to contradict what Aizawa had told him. If I did not take this chance, I might lose not only my homeland but also the very means by which I might retrieve my good name. I was suddenly struck by the thought that I might die in this sea of humanity, in this vast European capital. I showed my lack of moral fiber and agreed to go.

It was shameless. What could I say to Elise when I returned? As I left the hotel my mind was in indescribable turmoil. I wandered, deep in thought, not caring where I was going. Time and time again I was cursed at by the drivers of carriages that I bumped into and I jumped back startled. After a while I looked around and found I was in the Tiergarten. I half collapsed onto a bench by the side of the path. My head was on fire and felt as if someone were pounding it with a hammer as I leaned back. How long did I lie there like a corpse? The terrible cold creeping into the marrow of my bones woke me up. It was nighttime and the thickly falling snow had piled up an inch high on my shoulders and the peak of my cap.

It must have been past eleven. Even the tracks of the horse-drawn trams along Mohabit and Karlstrasse were buried under the snow and the gas lamps around the Brandenburg Gate gave out a bleak light. My feet were frozen stiff when I tried to get up, and I had to rub them with my hands before I could move.

I walked slowly and it must have been past midnight when I got to Klosterstrasse. I don't know how I got there. It was early January and the bars and tea shops on Unter den Linden must have been full, but I remember nothing of that. I was completely obsessed by the thought that I had committed an unforgivable crime.

In the fourth-floor attic Elise was evidently not yet asleep, for a bright gleam of light shone out into the night sky. The falling snowflakes were like a flock of small white birds, and the light kept on disappearing and reappearing as if the plaything of the wind. As I went in through the door I realized how weary I was. The pain in my joints was so unbearable that I half crawled up the stairs. I went through the kitchen, opened the door of the room, and stumbled inside. Elise was sewing diapers by the table and turned around.

"What have you been doing?" she gasped. "Just look at you!"

She had good reason to be shocked. My face was as pale as a corpse. I had lost my cap somewhere on the way and my hair was in a frightful mess. My clothes were torn and dirty from the muddy snow as I had stumbled many times along the road.

I remember trying to reply, but I could say nothing. Unable to stand because my knees were shaking so violently, I tried to grab a chair, but then I fell to the floor.

It was some weeks later that I regained consciousness. I had just babbled in a high fever while Elise tended me. Then one day Aizawa had come to visit me, saw for himself what I had hidden from him, and arranged matters by telling the count only that I was ill. When I first set eyes on Elise again, tending me at the bedside, I was shocked at her altered appearance. She had become terribly thin and her bloodshot eyes were sunk into her gray cheeks. With Aizawa's help she had not wanted for daily necessities, it was true, but this same benefactor had spiritually killed her.

As he told me later, she heard from Aizawa about the promise I had given him and how I had agreed to the count's proposal that evening. She had jumped up from her chair, her face ashen pale, and crying out "Toyotarō! How could you deceive me!" she had suddenly collapsed. Aizawa had called her mother and together they had put her to bed. When she awoke some time later, her eyes were fixed in a stare and she could not recognize those around her. She cried out my name, abused me, tore her hair, and bit the coverlet. Then she suddenly seemed to remember something and started to look for it. Everything her mother gave her she threw away, except the diapers that were on the table. These she stared at for a moment, then pressed them to her face and burst into tears.

From that time on, she was never violent, but her mind was almost completely unhinged and she became as simpleminded as a child. The doctor said there was no hope of recovery, for it was an illness called paranoia that had been brought on by sudden excessive emotion. They tried to remove her to the Dalldorf Asylum, but she cried out and refused to go. She would continually clasp a diaper to her breast and bring it out to look at, and this seemed to make her content. Although she did not leave my sickbed, she did not seem really aware of what was going on. Just occasionally she would repeat the word "medicine," as if remembering it.

I recovered from my illness completely. How often did I hold her living corpse in my arms and shed bitter tears? When I left with the count for the journey back to Japan, I discussed the matter with Aizawa and gave her mother enough to eke out a bare existence; I also left some money to pay for the birth of the child that I had left in the womb of the poor mad girl.

Friends like Aizawa Kenkichi are rare indeed, and yet to this very day there remains a part of me that curses him.

1890

Utakata no ki

A SAD TALE

LIKE *THE DANCING GIRL*, *A Sad Tale* deals with themes of madness and spiritual loss. Here, however, these themes, so personally expressed in the earlier story, are objectified and given a high literary gloss. The reader is no longer confined by the text to the interior feelings of the narrator but is given a tale that, for all its romantic language, deals with actual contemporary personages. Ōgai's ability to observe and to relate interior emotional states to historical events achieves early success in this instance.

The two figures he chooses for this purpose are quite different. One of them is mad King Ludwig II of Bavaria (1845–1886), famous as the patron of Wagner, whose increasingly perilous state of mental decay brought about his mysterious death during Ōgai's stay in Germany. The second is the young painter Harada Naojirō (1863–1899), who became a close friend of Ōgai and remained in close contact with the writer until his early death at the end of the century. At the time of this story's composition, Harada was still a young and talented artist with little reputation; soon afterwards, with the creation of his painting "Kannon on the Back of a Dragon" (1890) and other works, he was to become famous in Tokyo as one of the most gifted Western-style artists of the Meiji period. He serves as the model for the young painter Kose.

During his student years in Munich, Harada had close relationships with two persons who figure in the story. The first of them, Marie Huber, was a café waitress; Ōgai transforms her into the radiant Marie of the story and makes her the daughter of a court painter and a romantic and powerful figure of virtue capable of high artistic insight. The historical Marie is disguised and transmuted. The other character, mentioned by his own name, is Julius Exter (1863–1939), a young painter who, like Ōgai, became a close friend of Harada during their student days in Munich. Ōgai mentions in a later essay that he used Exter's real name in *A Sad Tale* because when the story was first published, he did not expect that anyone in 1890 would know the young artist's name. Exter, however, went on to become a professional painter in Germany, although not of the first rank. His elegant portrait of Harada as a student, rediscovered in 1980, provides a touching reminder of their early and enthusiastic friendship.

Whatever the borrowed materials that went into the composition of *A Sad Tale,* the final effect transcends them. Two romantic deaths of two idealists, King Ludwig and Marie, bound together as they are by the fragile links that connect them, project a powerful vision of the grandeur of life, and of art, to the Japanese art student Kose. As he observes the tragedy but does not participate in its development, Kose may qualify as one of Ōgai's first "bystanders," foreshadowing the kind of figure who will come to play such an important role in many of the stories to be written more than twenty years later.

THEY TELL YOU THAT THE STATUE of the goddess Bavaria, standing proudly erect in her chariot drawn by lions, was set here on the Siegestor, the victory arch, by the previous king, Ludwig I. Down below where the Ludwigstrasse bends away to the left stands a large building built of Triento marble—the Academy of Fine Arts, a well-known sight in the Bavarian capital. The head of the academy, Piloty, is famous at home and abroad, and many sculptors and artists gather here from the German states and even from Greece, Italy, and Denmark. Their lectures over, they crowd into the Café Minerva across the street and enjoy themselves chatting over coffee or some stronger drink. This evening the light from the gas lamps was reflected in the half-open windows as two young men, hearing the sound of noisy laughter inside, came up to the door.

Anyone could tell from his tousled dark brown hair and the way he tied his broad cravat at an angle that the one in front was an art student at the academy. He stopped and turned to his shorter, dark-skinned companion behind him.

"Here we are," he said, and opened the door.

The first thing they noticed was the tobacco smoke. Suddenly coming in from outside, they found it difficult to make out who was there. The evenings were warm at that time of year, but it seemed to be the custom to sit in all the smoke with the windows only half open. A general shout went up.

"Look. It's Exter! You're back soon! Still alive then?"

He evidently had many friends among this group. Meanwhile, the others were staring curiously at his companion who had come in behind him. He in turn, perhaps offended by their manner, frowned a little, but then suddenly seemed to change his mind and looked around with a little smile.

Having just arrived by train from Dresden, he noted the difference between the layout of cafés there and this one. Some of the round marble tables were spread with white tablecloths, presumably because the remains of the evening meal had not yet been cleared away. The customers were leaning on the bare tables and in front of them stood earthenware beer mugs, cyclindrical in shape and four or five times the size of a *sake* warmer, with bow-shaped handles and hinged metal lids. The coffee cups on the empty tables looked very strange, for they were turned upside down with their saucers placed on top and filled with lumps of sugar.

Although everyone wore different dress and spoke different languages, their long hair and untidy appearance gave them a kind of uniformity. That

TRANSLATED BY RICHARD BOWRING

27

they did not look utterly destitute, however, was due no doubt to their mixing in an artistic milieu. Sitting at a large table in the middle was one group which stood out as being more lively than the rest. All the other groups consisted only of men, but there was a girl at this center table. As her eyes met those of the young man who had just come in with Exter, both she and the newcomer seemed taken aback.

Perhaps it was because he was a stranger to the group. Perhaps it was the girl's good looks, which were more than enough to impress anyone meeting her for the first time. She was wearing a plain broad-peaked cap and her face was that of a sixteen or seventeen-year-old girl, but it bore a remarkable resemblance to that of a classical statue of Venus. There was a dignity in her actions that suggested something above the ordinary. As Exter slapped someone on the back at a nearby table and was talking with him, she called out.

"Nobody here has anything interesting to talk about. As things are, I wouldn't be surprised to see people slipping off to play cards or billiards, and I can't stand that. Why don't you bring your friend and come and sit down here?" she urged with a smile. The newly arrived guest felt attracted by her clear voice.

"Who wouldn't go and sit next to Marie!" said Exter. "Listen, everybody. This is Kose. He came along with me tonight to join our group here in the Minerva. He's an artist and has come all the way from Japan."

Having been thus introduced by Exter, his companion came forward to bow, but only the other foreigners got up to introduce themselves. The others remained seated as they returned his greeting. They were not insulting him—it was merely the custom among that group.

"You all know I went to see my relatives in Dresden," said Exter. "I met Kose there in the art gallery and we got to know each other. He said he wanted to study at our academy for a while, and so when he left I came back with him."

Everyone turned to Kose and said how pleased they were to meet someone from so far away. They all talked at once.

"We occasionally see Japanese at the university, but you're the first to come to the academy."

"As you've only just arrived, you won't have seen either the Pinakothek or the gallery of the Society of Fine Arts; but from what you have seen of South German painting elsewhere, what do you think of it?"

"What's your reason for coming here?"

Marie pushed them back.

"Wait a minute for goodness sake! Can't you see how confused he is with all of you asking questions at once? If you want to ask him, do it in a more orderly fashion."

"Oh! Madam is getting strict, isn't she!" they all laughed.

Kose started to speak in fairly good, though somewhat accented, German.

"This is not the first time I've been to Munich. I passed through here six years ago on my way to Saxony. On that occasion I only saw the pictures hanging in the Pinakothek and didn't manage to get to know anyone at the academy, because I was too intent on getting to the Dresden gallery, which was what I'd left home for. Mind you, the reason I have come here a second time and met you all is connected with something that happened then.

"I hope you won't find what I am about to say too naive. It was on the last day of Fasching. When I came out of the Pinakothek, it had just stopped snowing. Every branch of the trees along the middle of the road was covered in a thin layer of ice shining in the light of the street lamps that had just been lit. I was curious to see crowds of people milling about wearing fantastic dresses and black or white masks, and also the carpets hung out for show from the odd window here and there. I went into the Café L'Orient on Karlstrasse. I felt that even the ordinary dresses looked splendid, mingled as they were among all the different fancy-dress colors there. Everyone must have been waiting for dance halls like the Colosseum and the Victoria to open."

At this point a waitress, wearing a white apron below her bodice, came up holding four or five of the big mugs in each hand. They were full to overflowing with frothing beer.

"I'm sorry to keep you waiting, but I wanted to get you some from a new barrel," she said apologetically, passing them over to those who had emptied the mugs in front of them.

"Over here! Over here!" called out Marie and got the waitress to put one in front of Kose, who had not yet had a drink. He drank a little and then continued:

"I sat down on a bench over in one of the corners and was surveying all this bustle when the door opened and in stepped a scruffy Italian chestnut seller about fifteen years old. He was carrying a box under his arm, piled high with paper bags full of chestnuts. *'Maroni, Signore?'* he said in a self-assured manner. Behind him came a little girl who looked about twelve or thirteen. She was wearing a faded head-scarf pulled right down over her eyes; her little hands were red with the cold and were stretched round the edge of a shallow, openwork basket. In the basket lay bunches of violets beautifully arranged on top of layers of evergreen leaves. Violets were out of season then.

" *'Veilchen gefällig?'* she whispered. I still cannot forget how clear her voice sounded as she kept her head bowed low. They did not seem to be companions, so the girl must have waited until the boy came in and then taken the opportunity to follow him.

"I was immediately struck by their different appearance—the chestnut seller, insolent and slightly repulsive, and the gentle, sweet seller of violets. They both made their way through the crowd to the counter in the middle of the room. A big English dog belonging to a young man who looked like a university student had been lying on the floor, but it suddenly got up, arched its back, spread out its legs, and stuck its nose into the box of chestnuts. Seeing this, the boy tried to shoo it off and the frightened dog collided with the little girl behind. She cried out in terror and dropped her basket. The bunches of beautiful violets, their stems wound in tinfoil, glittered as they scattered in all directions, and the inquisitive dog trampled all over them, tearing them apart with his teeth.

"The floor was wet, as the snow on people's shoes had melted in the heat of the stove, and amid all the laughter and jeering her flowers were all ruined in the mud. The chestnut seller ran off as fast as he could, and the man who looked like a student just yawned and scolded his dog. The girl stared in disbelief. She didn't cry—perhaps she was so used to misery that she was unable to weep. Or perhaps she was so frightened and confused that she could not believe that a whole day's livelihood had just been destroyed. After a little while she listlessly attempted to pick up the two or three bunches that had escaped destruction, but just then in came the manager, who had been summoned by the girl at the counter. He was a red-faced, pot-bellied man with a white apron. Arms akimbo, he glared at her for a moment. 'I won't have any swindling little peddlers in here. Get out!' he shouted. The girl left without a murmur, watched by everyone in the place without a sign of pity.

"I threw a few coins onto the marble counter for my coffee, grabbed my overcoat, and rushed out. The girl was walking along sobbing to herself. I called out, but she didn't turn round. I ran after her. 'My dear child, let me give you money for the violets,' I said. Only then did she look up. There was a profound sadness in her beautiful face and in her deep blue eyes, and as she suddenly looked round my heart jumped. I left her speechless with surprise as I put the seven or eight marks that I had in my pocket on top of the leaves in her empty basket.

"I will always remember that face and those eyes. I went to Dresden and obtained permission to copy the pictures in the gallery. But no matter which one I turned to—Venus, Leda, the Madonna, or Helen—the face of the flower girl would somehow obtrude itself like a mist between me and the picture. In the end I began to doubt whether my painting would ever improve, so I shut myself up in my room on the second floor of my hotel and just lay there wearing out the sofa.

"Then one morning I suddenly felt a great urge to drive myself to the limit and try to transmit the figure of the flower girl for eternity. But I could not picture her either gazing in delight at the spring tides or enraptured by the sight of the evening clouds, and I felt it was inappropriate to portray her standing among Italian ruins with a flock of white doves flying overhead. My imagination placed her on a rock on the banks of the Rhine, a lyre in her hand and her voice full of tears. I stood in a little boat floating like a leaf in the waters below, my face turned toward her and my arms raised in an expression of unbounded love. Around the boat countless water sprites and nymphs sported in the waves. I've come here to Munich with this sketch in my case and have rented an atelier in the academy with the sole intention of planning with you how to finish it."

Kose had been completely absorbed in telling his story and when he finished his narrow Oriental eyes shone with emotion.

"What a beautiful story!" said two or three students.

Exter had been listening with an apathetic smile.

"Go and see his sketch. His atelier should be ready in a week," he said.

Halfway through the story Marie had flushed. Her eyes were riveted on Kose's lips and the glass she was holding once seemed to tremble. When he had first joined the group, Kose had been taken aback because she resembled the violet-seller; now as she listened to him with an intent gaze, he felt it must be her. Perhaps this, too, was a trick of his imagination. When he had finished, she looked at him for a moment.

"Haven't you seen her again since then?" she asked.

Kose suddenly seemed unable to find words to answer.

"No. I left for Dresden by train that very evening. But if you don't mind my saying so, there are times when you look exactly like my violet-seller and my picture of Lorelei."

Everyone in the group laughed loudly. The girl stood up.

"It seems that the link between the real me and you is this flower girl. Who do you think I am!" she said. Then in a tone that might have been either serious or mocking, she went on.

"I am the violet-seller and thus shall I reward you for your sympathy!"

She leaned across the table, took his lowered head in her hands, and kissed his forehead.

In the general stir the beer in front of her overturned and soaked her dress, spilling over the table in snakelike rivulets toward the others. Kose felt her burning hands on his ears, and had hardly time to feel surprised before her burning lips touched his brow.

"Don't embarrass him!" shouted Exter.

Everyone half stood up.

"What a joke!" said one, while another laughed, "This is terrible! Why should we be left out?"

The people at the other tables pressed round excitedly.

One of them who was sitting next to her stretched out his right arm and grabbed her around the waist.

"Hey! What about being nice to me?"

"What a rude lot you are!" she shouted back. "There's only one way to kiss you!"

She drew back and stood up glaring at them. Lightning semed to flash from her beautiful eyes. Kose sat there spellbound. She now resembled neither the flower girl nor Lorelei, but Bavaria on top of the Siegestor.

She picked up a glass that was next to a coffee cup someone had just finished with, and they saw her take the water into her mouth—then she spat it out in a stream.

"Outcasts! Rabble, all of you! You're all just the riffraff of art. If you study the Florentine school, you're a pale imitation of Michelangelo and Da Vinci. If you study the Dutch school, you're a mere ghost of Reubens and Van Dyck. And if you study our Albrecht Dürer, you are rarely anything more than a mere shadow of him. When you do manage to sell for a good price two or three studies hanging in the gallery, you all laud yourselves to the skies and give yourself names like the Pleiades, the Ten Masters, or the Twelve Apostles. How could Minerva's lips ever touch such rubbish! This cold kiss is all you'll ever get!" she shouted.

This speech, delivered as it was with a fine spray of water, was quite beyond Kose. He could only guess that she was expressing her hate and scorn for contemporary art. When he looked up into her face, he still had the strong impression that she resembled the goddess Bavaria. She finished her tirade, picked up her gloves, which had been soaked in the spilt beer, and marched out.

Everyone gave her menacing looks.

"You're mad!" said one.

"We'll get even with you for that soon!" said another.

Hearing this, she turned at the door.

"Why do you feel so hurt? Take a look at yourselves by the light of the moon. There's no blood on your foreheads—all I blew over you was water."

The party soon broke up after the strange girl left. On the way back Kose asked Exter who she was.

"She's called Fräulein Hansl. Models at the academy. There are those who say she's mad because, as you saw, she does behave a little strangely. And unlike the other girls she refuses to model in the nude, so some say she may be deformed. No one knows her background, but she's educated and somewhat out of the ordinary. As she doesn't sleep around, she easily makes friends with many of the art students. You saw what a fine face she has."

"I need someone like that for my painting. Could you ask her to come and see me when my atelier is ready?"

"All right. But she isn't your thirteen-year-old flower girl, you know. Don't you think a study in the nude would be a little risky?"

"You said she wouldn't model in the nude."

"That's what they say, but today's the first time I've seen her kiss someone."

Kose blushed, but they were near the Schiller Monument, where the street lights were dim, and his friend did not notice. When they reached Kose's hotel, they parted and went their separate ways.

It was a week later. With Exter's help Kose had been lent an atelier in the academy. On the south side ran a corridor, and the north wall was half taken up by a large window. All that separated the atelier from the next room was a canvas curtain. As it was the middle of June, many students were away and so there was no one next door. It was good to be without any distractions to prevent him from working. The girl had just come in and Kose was standing in front of his easel, showing her the picture of Lorelei.

"This is what you asked about. When you teased me about it, I wasn't too sure, but there are times when your face would be just right for this unfinished figure."

She laughed.

"Don't forget! I told you the other evening that I was the girl who sold violets, the original model for Lorelei!"

Suddenly she became serious.

"You don't believe me. I suppose it's only to be expected. Everyone says I am mad, so I expect you do too."

She no longer seemed to be joking.

Kose did not know what to believe.

"Don't torment me any more!" he burst out. "Even now I can still feel your burning lips on my brow. God knows how often I have tried to dismiss it as a casual joke, but I'm so confused. Unless you find it too distressing, you must tell me the real story of your life!"

He sat on the edge of the little table under the window, his chin in his hands. The table was strewn with old illustrated newspapers which he had just taken out of his case, tin tubes of the oils he used, and a rough Japanese pipe with a cigarette end in it. She sat in front of him on a rattan chair and began.

"Where shall I start? When I got the job of modeling at this academy, I was known as Hansl, but that's not my real name. My father was called Steinbach. He was once a favorite of the present king of Bavaria and was for a time a flourishing artist. When I was twelve years old, there was a party one evening in the Winter Garden at the palace and both my parents were invited. At the height of the festivities, the king disappeared. Everyone was worried and searched for him here and there under the large glass roof amid the luxuriant trees and flowers imported from the tropics. In one corner of the garden stood the famous statue of Faust and Gretchen carved by Tandardini.

"My father was approaching it when he heard a heartrending scream for help. Following the sound, he came to the door of a small pavilion with a cone-shaped roof made of gold. Gas lamps hung in the thick palms that surrounded the place. The light was shining in through the glass painted in many deep colors and he could just make out the weird dark shapes inside. A woman was fighting to free herself and the king was holding her back. What must my father have felt when he saw the woman's face? It was my mother!

"Stunned, he hesitated for a moment, but then cried out, 'Your Majesty! Let her go!' and knocked the king down. In that instant my mother ran off, but the king, who had been taken by surprise, recovered and started grappling with my father. How could he possibly stand up to the king who was so big and powerful? He was knocked to the ground and belabored with a watering can which was at hand. Ziegler, the Cabinet Secretary, remonstrated with the king when he heard of the affair and so expected to be incarcerated in the tower at Neuschwanstein, but a friend managed to save him from that fate.

"That evening I was waiting for my parents to come home. The maid came in to tell me they had arrived. I went out happily to welcome them back, but my father was carried in and my mother fell on me weeping."

For a moment she said nothing. It had been overcast since morning and now it started to rain. The raindrops pattered from time to time on the windowpanes.

"I read in the newspapers yesterday that the king had gone mad and had been moved to Schloss Berg by the Starnbergersee," said Kose, "but was he that bad even then?"

She continued her story.

"For some time now the king has shunned society and has been living in the country. He sleeps during the daytime and gets up at night. The fame he achieved in middle age when he overruled the Catholic parliament and allied with Prussia at the time of the Franco-Prussian War has gradually been eclipsed by rumors of his tyrannical rule. Although nothing is said about it in public, he tried to sentence both his Minister of War, Merlinger, and his Finance Minister, Riedel, to death for no reason at all. It was hushed up by the authorities, but everyone knew. They say that when he sleeps during the day, his retinue all retire, but he is often heard to mutter the name Marie over and over again in his sleep. Marie was my mother's name too. Perhaps his unrequited love for her made his illness that much worse. She looked a little like me and I heard that she was the most beautiful woman at court.

"Father soon fell ill and died. He had many friends and was generous and quite detached from worldly matters, so he left the family without a single penny. Then we moved to a rented room on the first floor of a tenement building at the north end of Dachauerstrasse. After we moved, mother fell ill. At such times one finds out who one's friends really are. Much suffering at that impressionable age soon turned me against people. By January the following year, at the time of the Karneval, we had used up all our money and sold everything. We couldn't afford to keep ourselves warm from one day to the next, and so I joined a group of young children and learned how to sell violets. It was thanks to your gift that mother passed her last three or four days in comfort before she died.

"I was helped to bury my mother by a tailor who lived on the floor above us. The poor orphan shouldn't be left alone, he said. It's terrible now to remember how happy I was when he took me in. There were two daughters who I saw were very choosy and liked showing themselves off. After I went to stay with them, I noticed that they had lots of visitors late at night. They drank a lot and ended up laughing, joking, and singing. There were many foreigners among them, and I even saw some Japanese students.

"One day the tailor told me to put on a new dress, but I was somehow frightened by the look on his face as he watched me with a smile. It was hardly the thing to bring joy to a young girl's heart. In the afternoon a strange man in his forties turned up and suggested a trip to the Starnberger-see. The tailor too urged me to go. I could not forget how I had loved going there with my father when he was alive and so I reluctantly agreed. They were full of praise. 'There's a good girl,' they said.

"My companion treated me gently on the way there and at the lake we got on a pleasure steamer, the *Bavaria* it was called. We went to the restaurant and he bought me a meal. He pressed beer on me, but I wasn't used to it and so refused. The steamer stopped at Seeshaupt, and he rented a small

boat suggesting we should go for a trip. It was getting dark and I felt helpless. I wanted to go back soon, I said, but he paid no attention and rowed
out onto the lake. As we went along close to the shore, we came to a lonely
place among the reeds and he stopped the boat.

"I was still only thirteen years old, and at first I didn't understand what
was going on; but then his expression changed and he looked frightening.
In desperation I jumped into the water. When I came to sometime later, I
was being tended by a poor couple in a fisherman's hut by the side of the
lake. I insisted I had no home to return to, and after one or two days I felt so
much at ease with the simple ways of the fisherman and his wife that I told
them my unhappy story; they took pity on me and brought me up as their
daughter. The fisherman's name was Hansl.

"And so I became a fisherman's daughter, but I was too frail to row boats.
I was employed as a chambermaid in the household of a rich Englishman
near Leoni. My foster parents, being Catholic, didn't like me working for an
Englishman, but it was due to the kindness of the governess there that I
learned to read. She was a forty-year-old spinster and had more affection for
me than for the pompous daughter of the house. In three years I had read
all the books in her small collection. I must have made many mistakes with
my reading and the works there were a rather motley lot. Knigge's *Über
den Umgang mit Menschen,* for instance, and Hufeland's *Die Kunst, das
menschliche Leben zu verlängern.* I almost learned by heart a selection of
Goethe's and Schiller's poetry; I also read König's *Deutsche Literaturges-
chichte,* examined photographs of the art gallery collections at Dresden and
the Louvre, and browsed through a translation of Taine's *Philosophie de
l'Art.*

"Last year, after the Englishman took his family back home, I thought I
might be taken on in a good household, but my background was not good
enough to enable me to work for the nobility there. I happened to be
noticed by one of the lecturers at this academy and became a model for him,
and this eventually led to my enrolling. But no one knows I'm the daughter
of the famous Steinbach.

"Now I mix with artists and have a very pleasant time. But what Gustav
Freytag says is absolutely true—no one behaves so badly as artists, so being
alone in the world I have to be on my guard all the time. Always trying to
keep them at bay has made me seem a bit eccentric, as you see. Sometimes I
doubt myself whether I'm sane. Perhaps it's a result to some extent of reading all those books at Leoni—but in that case, everyone who goes by the
name 'scholar' must be mad. The artists who abuse me and call me mad
should be sorry that they are not mad themselves, for what both Seneca and

Shakespeare said is obvious—one needs to be a little mad to become a great hero or a famous master. Just look at my breadth of learning! How sad to see people one would like to have mad remain sane! How sad to hear of a king who has no need of madness and yet becomes mad. There are so many piti- ful things that I cry with the cicadas by day and weep with the frogs by night, but no one has any sympathy. You're the only one I know who doesn't laugh at me, so don't blame me for saying whatever comes into my head. Is that a sign of madness too?"

The sky still looked unsettled but it had stopped raining. All one could see through the misted panes were the trees swaying in the academy garden. While she had been talking, Kose had felt a number of conflicting emo- tions. Sometimes he felt like a brother meeting his younger sister from whom he had parted long ago; then he was a sculptor standing alone in anguish by a fallen statue of Venus in a ruined garden; then he felt like an acolyte who is in love with a beautiful girl but has vowed not to sin. When she finished, his heart was pounding and he trembled. Hardly aware of what he was doing, he made to go down on his knees in front of her. She stood up suddenly.

"It's so hot in here. The academy gates will soon be shut, but it's stopped raining. I have nothing to fear with you. Let's go to Starnberg," she said, picking up the cap which lay beside her and putting it on. She clearly had not the slightest doubt that he would follow her. He went out meekly like a child led by his mother.

They hired a carriage at the gate and soon reached the station. It was Sun- day, but perhaps because the weather was bad, there were not many people returning from the countryside and it was very quiet. A woman was selling special editions of a newspaper. They bought one and saw a report that the king had moved to Schloss Berg. He had calmed down, so his doctor, Gud- den, had relaxed his surveillance. The train was full of people who were stay- ing at the lake to escape from the heat and were returning there after a shop- ping expedition to the capital.

Everyone was talking of the king.

"It's different from when he was at Hohenschwangau. He seems to be more at ease now. On his way to Berg, he asked for some water at Seeshaupt and bowed politely to some fishermen nearby," said an old woman in the local dialect as she sat there with her basket of shopping.

The journey took an hour. It was five in the evening when they arrived at Starnberg. It was only a day's walk from Munich, but they were aware of the nearness of the Alps and even in these cloudy conditions one could breathe more deeply. As the train wound to and fro, a gap suddenly opened up in the hills and they could see the large lake there before them. The station was at the southwest corner of the lake, and they could dimly make out the forest and the fishing villages on the east bank wrapped in the evening mist. The view south to the nearby mountains seemed endless.

The girl knew her way around, and Kose followed her, climbing up some stone steps on their right. They came up in front of a hotel called the Bayerischer Hof. Stone tables and chairs were arranged in the open, but as it had been raining that day, they were all damp and there were only a few people around. A waiter in a black jacket and white apron was muttering to himself as he lifted up the seats propped against the tables and wiped them dry. Suddenly Kose noticed a crowd of visitors sitting at a round table beneath a trellis entwined with ivy and vines that ran alongside the nearby eaves. Perhaps they were staying at the hotel. He noticed among them some students he had seen at the Minerva that night and made as if to go and talk to them, but Marie stopped him.

"You shouldn't mix with that crowd." she said. "Although I've turned up with a young man, they're the ones who feel embarrassed, not me. They know me. You'll see, they won't be able to go on sitting there; they'll have to hide."

The art students eventually got up and went into the hotel. Calling the waiter over, Marie asked whether the pleasure steamers were still running. He pointed at the scudding clouds. With such doubtful weather they had most likely stopped, he said. So she suggested to Kose that they should go to Leoni by carriage.

A carriage drew up and they got in. They passed the station and drove along the east side of the lake. Suddenly a squall came rushing down from the Alps and mist rose over the water. As they looked back the way they had come, everything slowly went gray and all they could see were the shapes of the roofs and the treetops standing out black. The driver turned round.

"Looks like rain. Shall I put the hood up?" he asked.

"No, don't bother," said the girl.

She turned to Kose.

"This is wonderful! Here is the lake where long ago I nearly lost my life, the lake where I was saved. You must be wondering why I brought you here. I drew you here because I felt that it had to be here that I should open my heart to you. How many years have passed since I was so humiliated at the Café L'Orient. Ever since then I have wanted to meet my savior once again! Oh, the happiness when I heard your story at the Minerva that night. Those art students are always talking such nonsense that I was rude and behaved outrageously—what a terrible impression I must have given. But if you don't raise your voice and laugh at the very moment of happiness, you will live to regret it one day."

She threw off her cap and turned toward him, warm blood surging through her marble veins and her golden hair blown in the wind like the long mane of a horse tossing its head.

"Today! Today! What use is yesterday? Tomorrow and the day after are mere useless words, mere hollow sounds!"

Two or three large raindrops fell on their clothes as they sat in the carriage. Suddenly it began to pour. As the spray was driven across the surface of the lake, whipping into them and striking Marie's flushed cheeks, Kose felt as if he were riding on air. She stretched forward.

"Driver! There's a tip to be earned! Faster! Whip her on! Faster!" she cried.

With her right hand around Kose's neck, she bent her head back and stared upwards. He laid his head on her shoulder, soft as down. As if in a dream, he saw again the goddess Bavaria on the Siegestor.

The rain became heavier as they came to the base of Schloss Berg, where the king was said to be living. As they looked back across the lake, the wind bore down in phalanxes creating a chiaroscuro effect—vertical lines of white rain in the heavier parts and black wind in the lighter. The driver stopped the carriage.

"Let's stop a minute. If you get too wet, you'll catch your death of cold. Besides, the carriage may be ancient but the boss will blame me if it gets too sodden," he said.

He swiftly pulled up the hood and then started the carriage again with a crack of his whip.

The rain fell ceaselessly and it began to thunder. The road led through the woods, and although the summer sun should still have been high in the sky in this region, the road under the trees was dark. The scent of the grasses heated in the sun and now moistened by rain penetrated the carriage, and they both drank it in greedily. In the intervals between the claps of thunder a nightingale sang its sweet notes again and again, quite unconcerned about the terrible weather. It was like a lone traveler singing as he trod some deserted path. Marie put her arms around Kose's neck and pressed close to him. Lit up by the lightning that flashed through the dark leaves, her face was laughing as they gazed into each other's eyes. The poignant couple had quite forgotten themselves, the carriage, and even the world outside.

As they came out of the wood and down a slope, the wind swept the mass of clouds away and the rain lifted. The haze over the lake cleared in a second as if layer upon layer of cloth were being peeled off. It seemed you could almost touch the houses on the far side. As they passed through the occasional shade of trees, all that was left of the storm were the raindrops being scattered from the branches by the wind.

They got out of the carriage at Leoni. On their left towered the Rottmannshöhe, where there was a stone plaque that read, "The best view of the lake." To their right was the inn facing the water; it was said to have been built by Leoni the musician. Marie walked along, both hands entwined around Kose's arm as if she were clinging to him. When they arrived in front of the inn, she turned around in the direction of the hill.

"The Englishman I worked for lived in a house halfway up. The fisherman's hut where the old Hansl couple live is only a hundred yards away. I came here thinking to take you there, but now I feel so agitated. Let's rest inside."

Kose agreed. They went in and ordered an evening meal.

"It won't be ready till seven. You'll have to wait another thirty minutes," they were told. The hotel only took in guests during the summer months, and as new waiters were hired each year, no one there knew Marie.

She jumped up and pointed to a boat moored by the jetty.

"Can you row?" she asked.

"When I was in Dresden, I rowed on the Carolasee in the public park. I'm not very good, mind, but if it's just you, I should be able to manage," said Kose.

"The seats in the garden are wet," said Marie. "But it's too hot inside. Row me round for a bit."

Kose took off his summer coat, gave it to Marie to put on, and sat her in the boat. He took the oars and rowed out onto the lake. It had stopped raining, but the sky was still cloudy and it was already dusk on the far shore. Perhaps because of the wind earlier, there were still waves big enough to slap against the rudder. They rowed along the side of the lake back in the direction of Berg and came to the point where the village of Leoni ended. A sandy path led gradually down to the margin of trees near the lake, and there was a bench by the water's edge.

The boat brushed against a clump of reeds and made them rustle. Then they heard footsteps on the bank and someone appeared among the trees. He was nearly six feet tall, wore a black overcoat, and held a closed umbrella in his hand. On his left, following a little behind, came an old man whose beard and hair were as white as snow. The man in front was walking head down, so his face was hidden under the broad brim of his hat. He came out from the trees and walked toward the lake. Standing there for a moment, he took off his hat and glanced up. His long black hair was combed back exposing a broad brow. Although his face was ashen, a piercing light shone from his sunken eyes. Marie was crouched in the boat with Kose's coat over her shoulders when she saw the man on the bank. Startled, she jumped up.

"It's the king!" she cried. The coat fell from her shoulders. She had taken off her hat and left it at the inn, and her flowing locks fell gracefully over the back of her white summer dress.

It was indeed the king out for a walk with his physician Gudden in attendance. The king stared at her enraptured as if she were some wonderful apparition; then suddenly crying out "Marie," he flung aside his umbrella and plunged toward them through the shallows. Marie too cried out and then fainted, collapsing before Kose could stretch out his hand to save her. Losing her balance from the rocking of the boat, she fell headfirst into the water.

The ground at this point shelved away only very gradually and so there was a mere five feet of water where the boat had stopped. But the sand at the water's edge turned to sticky mud further out, and the king struggled desperately as he sank deeper and deeper. At that moment the old man who had followed him threw away his umbrella and ran in after the king. Despite his age, he was still strong, and in two or three strides through the water he managed to grip the king's collar and tried to pull him back. The king was stuck so fast that his coat and shirt came away in the old man's hand. He clawed them away and tried yet again to drag the king back, but the king turned round and grappled with him. They struggled for a while in silence.

Everything had happened so quickly. Kose was just able to grab Marie's dress as she fell overboard, but she struck her chest hard on a stake hidden in the reeds and began to sink. He managed to drag her up and rowed back the way they had come, leaving behind the two men still struggling by the shore. All he could think of was how to save her life—he had no time for anything else. Rather than rowing to the inn, he carried on past it toward the fisherman's hut which she had said was a hundred yards further down. The sun had already set and on the shore the mass of oaks and elders merged together. The water formed an inlet, and in the evening darkness he could faintly see the white flowers of some water plants among the reeds. It was a pitiful sight—the body of the young girl lying in the boat, her tangled hair matted with mud and trailing water weeds. Just then, perhaps started by the rowing, a firefly flew out from the reeds toward the shore. Ah—it might have been the girl's soul slipping away.

After a while Kose saw a light from the hut, which had been hidden up to then in the shadow of the trees. As they approached, he shouted out: "Is this where the Hansls live?"

A small window just below the sloping eaves opened and a white-haired old woman looked out toward the boat.

"So the god of the lake has demanded another sacrifice. My husband was called over to Schloss Berg yesterday and he isn't back yet. If you want something done for her, you'll have to bring her here," she said quietly and was about to shut the window.

"It's Marie! Your Marie! She's fallen in the water!" Kose shouted.

Almost before he had finished, the old woman had left the open window and was rushing down to the jetty. She was weeping as she helped Kose to carry Marie back into the house.

There was only one room inside, half of it covered with a board floor. A small lamp, which looked as though it had just been lit, shone dimly over the stove. The colored paintings depicting the life of Christ on all four walls were covered in soot and very indistinct. They burned bracken to warm Marie and revive her, but she never regained consciousness. Kose passed the night sitting by the body with the old woman, lamenting this pitiless world in which things disappear and never return, like bubbles on water.

It was reported that, at seven o'clock in the evening of June 13 in that year of our Lord 1886, King Ludwig II of Bavaria had drowned in the waters of the lake. His aged physician Gudden had tried to save him, but he too lost his life and bore the scratches of the king's nails on his face. The turmoil in Munich on the following day, the fourteenth, at this terrible news was unprecedented. Black-bordered posters stood on every street corner announcing the death and crowds of people collected beneath them. Everyone fought to buy the newspaper extras which recorded the circumstances of the discovery of the king's body, together with various theories as to the cause. What with all the mustered troops in their dress uniforms and black-plumed Bavarian helmets, and the police rushing around on horseback and on foot, the confusion was indescribable. Although the king had not shown himself to the people for a long time, everyone was saddened by the news and many sorrowful faces were to be seen in the streets. In all the uproar, no one in the academy took any notice of the fact that the newly arrived Kose was nowhere to be seen. Only Exter was anxious as to his whereabouts.

The king's coffin was brought from Schloss Berg to the capital during the night. On the morning of June 15 the students at the academy who had been to see it arrive gathered at the Café Minerva. It was then that Exter suddenly wondered about Kose and went to his atelier. There he found him on his knees in front of the portrait of Lorelei. In three days he had utterly changed and looked terribly thin.

With all the rumors of the king's unnatural death, no one ever gave a thought to the fact that the daughter of the fisherman Hansl had drowned near Leoni at the same time.

1890

Fumizukai

THE COURIER

LIKE THE TWO EARLY STORIES that preceded it, *The Courier* combines elements of the high romantic style mixed with trenchant personal and social observation. In such a mixture, there is always the danger that a sense of disjuncture may result. Although the repertoire of romantic images employed here is slighter than in *A Sad Tale,* the young flute player who appears briefly in the text suggests the kind of poetic, melancholy figure worthy of habitation in the more fanciful sections of a novel such as *Wilhelm Meister* by Ōgai's beloved Goethe.

In many ways, however, this brief story can best be read as a psychological and spiritual portrait of Ida, the young German noblewoman who, in her decision to join the court as a means to escape a loveless marriage, becomes a feminine and objectified version of the narrator of *The Dancing Girl.* Both are forced to choose between duty and self-fulfillment. In such a context, even a figure like the shepherd boy seems integrated into the larger concerns of the tale, since his own sad experience contributes, at least implicitly, to Ida's poignant self-understanding.

The young military officer Kobayashi, like the art student in *A Sad Tale,* remains an observer who, while playing a relatively minor role in the forward motion of the story, nevertheless takes his important place as a listener and confidant, one who himself grows in self-understanding through his experience as a bystander.

Some of the background details found in the story—the military maneuvers, the glimpses of aristocratic life in Germany, and the court balls—were of course drawn from Ōgai's own experiences and lend authenticity to the whole. At one point in the narrative, Kobayashi finds himself watching the dancers in what seems to him an unusual form of social intercourse. That vision will surface again, two decades later, in his 1911 novella *Ghost Stories.*

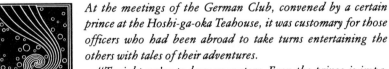 *At the meetings of the German Club, convened by a certain prince at the Hoshi-ga-oka Teahouse, it was customary for those officers who had been abroad to take turns entertaining the others with tales of their adventures.*

"Tonight we're to hear your story. Even the prince is impatient." Urged on in this way, Kobayashi, a young officer who had not yet made captain, took the cigarette from his mouth, flicked its ashes into a hibachi, and began his tale. . . .

The Saxon army corps to which I was attached was on its fall training maneuvers near the village of Ragewitz. The usual preliminary competitions were over, and it was time for the actual war games. After the defensive troops had been selected and had taken their positions atop a small rise, the offensive forces advanced from all directions, skillfully taking cover behind farmhouses, clumps of trees, and the contours of the terrain. It was a spectacular sight, and groups of local citizens had gathered here and there to watch. Reconnoitering with my field glasses, I discovered among the civilians a number of young girls decked out in velveteen bodices and small green hats that looked like saucers turned upside down and garnished with flowers. The girls on the hill just opposite me were especially pretty, I decided.

It was an unusually clear day in early September; the autumn sky was cobalt blue, the air so limpid that I could see every detail of that crowd, including a carriage filled with young ladies drawn up in the middle. The colors of their dresses blended well together, like a bouquet of flowers or a piece of brocade, and the sashes of the girls who were standing and the hat ribbons of those who were seated fluttered seductively in the breeze. The white-haired old man mounted beside them wore a green hunting suit with horn buttons and a light brown hat; he seemed to be someone of importance. A little further downhill a young girl on a white horse attracted my attention. She was elegantly dressed in a long, steel-gray riding outfit with a black hat wrapped in a thin white silk and had an air of refinement; although everyone else was milling about excitedly trying to get a glimpse of the jaegers emerging from the shadows of the woods, she never once looked around.

"Are you looking at someone in particular?" I felt a tap on my shoulder: it was Baron von Meerheim, a young officer with a long, carefully trimmed mustache, who was attached to the headquarters of my battalion. "That's

TRANSLATED BY KAREN BRAZELL

Count von Bülow's family. He's the lord of Döben castle. We're going to make his castle our headquarters tonight, so you'll be able to meet them." As he said this, Meerheim saw that the troops were closing in on our left flank, and he rode off. We hadn't been acquainted long, but he seemed like a good sort of fellow.

The attacking forces had reached the bottom of the hill and the day's maneuvers were ended. After the evaluations, Meerheim and I hurriedly followed the battalion commander to the night's lodgings, taking a causeway that wound through a pretty wheat field where old tree stumps still stood. The sound of running water from beyond a grove of trees indicated we were approaching the Mulde River.

The battalion commander was a man of forty-three or four whose hair was still dark brown, although his forehead was already creased with wrinkles. He was a simple man of few words, and when he did speak he qualified nearly every utterance with the apologetic phrase, "If I may say so." Suddenly he turned to Meerheim and said, "I suppose your fiancée is waiting for you."

"Excuse me, Major, but I don't have a fiancée yet."

"Is that so? Well, don't be offended. I thought, if I may say so, that you and Ida were engaged."

While the two of them were talking, we arrived at Döben castle. A long, sandy walk bounded on each side by a low iron fence compassing the gardens led to an old stone gate. Beyond the gate, surrounded by a profusion of white hydrangeas, stood the mansion, a tall building with whitewashed walls and a slate roof. To the south stood a tall stone tower evidently patterned after an Egyptian pyramid. As the liveried servant who had come out to greet us led the way up some white stone stairs, the light of the cinnabarred evening sun filtering down through the trees in the garden gleamed on the sphinxes couched on each side of the stairs. This was my first visit to a German castle, and I wondered what it would be like. I also wondered about the beautiful girl on horseback I had seen in the distance. It was all an unsolved riddle.

We passed through a number of rooms with vaulted ceilings and walls adorned with paintings of demons, god, dragons, and snakes. Lined up along the walls were immense trunks—they call them *Truhe*—and supporting the roof were rows of columns hung with carved animal heads, old shields, and weapons. At last we were led upstairs.

Count von Bülow, informally dressed in what appeared to be an ordinary suit with a dark jacket, was here with the countess. He knew the battalion commander and shook his hand cheerfully; when I was presented, he introduced himself in a deep, husky voice, and turning to Meerheim he said lightly, "Glad to see you."

The countess's heavy movements made her appear older than her husband, but her eyes revealed warmth and gentleness. She called Meerheim over to her, and while she was whispering something to him, the count said: "You must be tired after all today's activities. Why don't you rest a while?" And he had us shown to our room.

The room, which I shared with Meerheim, faced east. Directly below our window the Mulde River lapped up against the foundations of the building. On the opposite bank, behind some brush that was still green, the evening mist hung down over a grove of oak trees. There was a bend in the river to my right, and on the piece of land jutting out like a kneecap were two or three farmhouses and a black mill wheel silhouetted against the sky. To my left, another wing of the mansion overlooked the water, and as I was looking toward it, one of the balcony windows opened and three or four young girls crowded around and looked out. The rider of the white horse, however, was not among them. Meerheim, who had taken off his uniform and was about to go over to the washbasin, said, "That's the girls' room. Please close that shutter quickly."

That evening on our way to the dining room I remarked to Meerheim that there seemed to be a lot of young ladies in the house. "There used to be six," he replied, "but one of them married a friend of mine, Count von Fabrice, so there are only five now."

"Fabrice? Is he related to the minister Fabrice?"

"Yes, my friend is the minister's eldest son. The minister's wife is Count von Bülow's older sister."

When we were all seated at the table I saw that each of the girls was dressed so becomingly it was impossible to decide which was the prettiest. I looked curiously at the oldest girl, who was dressed completely in black, and I realized that she was the one who had been riding the white horse. The other girls seemed curious about the Japanese, and after the countess had admired my Japanese uniform, one of the girls said, "In that black uniform with black braid you look like one of the officers from Braunschweig."

The youngest daughter, a rosy-cheeked creature, was unable to contain her childish contempt and blurted out, "He does not!"

Attempting to hide their amusement, all the others attended minutely to the soup except the girl in black, who did not even bat an eyelash. After a minute, the youngest girl tried to redeem herself and said, "Anyway, since your uniform is black from top to bottom, Ida should like it."

At that, the girl in black turned and glared at her younger sister. Her eyes usually wore a faraway look, but when she gazed directly at someone, they revealed more than words ever could, and now her glare was a scolding, undisguised by her smile.

From the youngest girl's words, I gathered that this was Ida, to whom the battalion commander thought Meerheim was engaged. With this in mind I watched Meerheim, and sure enough, both his words and his actions indicated that he adored her; and Count von Bülow and his wife apparently approved of the match. Ida, tall and slender, was the only one of the girls with black hair. But it was in the eloquence of her eyes that her beauty surpassed that of her sisters. She had a few tiny wrinkles between her eyebrows, and her face seemed pale, but this was probably because of her black dress.

After dinner we went into an adjoining parlor filled with comfortable armchairs and sofas with extremely short legs. Here coffee was served. A servant brought in small glasses of several kinds of liqueur. The count and the battalion commander were the only ones to have any. "If I may say so, I'll take Chartreuse," the battalion commander said and drank a glassful in one gulp.

From a dark corner behind my back, a strange voice called out, "Say so, say so."

Startled, I looked around and saw a large wire cage with a parrot in it. It was mimicking the words the major used so often. "Oh, that awful bird!" the girls muttered, but the battalion commander laughed heartily.

"Let's go have a smoke and talk about hunting," the count suggested to the battalion commander, and led him off toward the library. I turned to the youngest girl, who had been eyeing me as though she wanted to talk to the strange Japanese. "Is this clever bird yours?" I asked with a smile.

"No, it isn't anybody's in particular, but I'm very fond of it. Until just recently we had several pigeons as well, and they grew so used to us that they followed us all around. But Ida couldn't stand that, so we gave them all away. This parrot hates Ida for some reason, but fortunately we still have it." Turning to the parrot she asked, "Isn't that so?"

The bird who was supposed to hate Ida turned, opened its beak, and croaked, "Isn't that so? Isn't that so?"

Meerheim was at Ida's side, apparently asking her something. She seemed reluctant to comply, but when the countess put in a word, she stood up abruptly and went to the piano. The manservant quickly put a light on either side, and Meerheim headed toward a small table beside the piano and asked if he could bring her some music.

"No, I don't need any," Ida replied. Her fingers slowly struck the keys, producing beautiful chords; as the piece became more complicated, her face flushed with excitement. Now the music was soft like the clinking of quartz prayer beads, so quiet that even the Mulde River seemed to have stopped flowing; then suddenly it burst forth with the clashing of swords and spears loud enough to arouse the castle's ancestors from their eternal dreams. The feelings that this young girl could not express in words and that ordinarily remained pent up in her narrow breast burst forth from her fine, slender fingertips. It seemed that the whole castle was floating on the waves of her music, and that all of us were being carried along, sinking, then bobbing up again. At the height of the melody, when the spirits of the strings lurking inside the piano had ended their individual complaints of boundless malice and were now crying out in unison, the uncertain sound of a flute arose from somewhere outside the castle and quaveringly tried to accompany Ida.

For a while Ida was so engrossed in her music that she was not aware of the flute, but when she finally noticed it, her playing became chaotic, and with a crashing chord loud enough to burst the piano, she stood up, her face even paler than usual. The girls looked at each other and whispered, "It's another stupid trick by the harelip." Outside the sound of the flute died away.

The count returned from the library and explained sympathetically, "We've grown accustomed to Ida's wild performances, but I'm sure you must be surprised."

With these sounds still ringing in my ears, I returned to my room unaware of my own movements. My mind was too full of what I'd seen and heard for me to sleep, and when I glanced over at Meerheim stretched out on his bed, I discovered he too was still awake. There were many things I wanted to know, but feeling hesitant I simply asked, "Do you know who was playing that strange flute music?"

The baron turned toward me. "That's a long story," he said, "but I can't seem to get to sleep either, so let's get up and I'll tell you about it."

We got down from our beds, which were not even warm yet, and went to a small table under the window where we sat facing each other and smoking. Outside I heard the flute music again; suddenly it broke off, then continued once more, like a young nightingale learning to sing. Meerheim cleared his throat and began his story:

"About ten years ago a pitiful orphan lived in the village of Brösen not far from here. His parents had both died in an epidemic when he was six or seven, and since he had a harelip and was very ugly, no one paid any attention to him. One day, nearly starved, he came to this castle begging for a crust of dry bread. At that time Ida was about ten: she pitied him and gave him something to eat. She also gave him her toy flute and told him to play it, but since he had a harelip he couldn't make a sound on it. Ida sobbed uncontrollably and cried to her mother, 'Have his terrible looking mouth fixed.' Her mother, impressed by the lad's gentleness, had a doctor fix his harelip.

"After that the boy stayed at the castle as a shepherd, never parting with the toy flute Ida had given him. Later on he carved himself a wooden flute and practiced diligently until he was able to produce quite a good tone without ever having been taught.

"When I came here on leave the summer before last, the whole family went out on a long ride together. Ida's white horse was so fast that I was the only one who could keep up with her. Suddenly at a turn in the narrow road, we met a loaded hay wagon. Ida's horse shied and reared up, and she barely managed to stay in the saddle. Before I could get to her, there was a shout from the tall grass at the side of the road, and this boy came flying out, grabbed the horse's bit firmly, and calmed it down. After this Ida realized that whenever the boy had some free time, he would follow her around secretly. She had some things given to him, but for some reason she wouldn't permit him to meet her in person. When they met accidentally she refused to speak to him. Realizing her dislike of him, he finally began to avoid meeting her, but continued watching from a distance. He even ties up a small boat under her window and spends the night in it sleeping on some hay."

By the time we had finished talking and returned to bed, the eastern sky was already faintly light. The flute music had stopped, but I couldn't get this Ida out of my mind. I pictured her on a horse which suddenly turned black. Since this seemed strange, I looked a little closer: the horse had a human head with a harelip. In my dream it seemed quite natural for Ida to be riding this horse, but when I looked again, what I had thought was Ida had a sphinx's head with half-closed, pupilless eyes, and the horse had become a lion with its two front paws together. On the lion's head was a parrot, staring at me and laughing.

Early that morning I got up and opened the window. The woods on the opposite bank were bathed in sunlight; a breeze rippled the surface of the Mulde River, and in a meadow near the water's edge a flock of sheep were grazing. Near them I saw a short boy with disheveled red hair dressed in a short green smock, or *Kittel*. He was engrossed in cracking the whip he held in his hand.

We had our morning coffee in our room. I donned my dress uniform, because at noon I was to go with the battalion commander to a hunting lodge at a place called Grimma where there was to be a banquet for the king, who had come to watch the maneuvers. The count lent us a carriage and climbed to the top of the stairway to see us off. I had been invited to this gathering, which was actually for generals and field grade officers, only because I was a foreigner; Meerheim remained at the castle.

Although it was out in the country, the hall was unexpectedly handsome; the dishes must have been brought from the royal palace, for there were sterling silver plates and fine Meissenware dishes. Although I had heard that German pottery was modeled on that of the East, I didn't think that the colors of the designs were at all like those in our country. I was told, however, that in the pottery collection at the royal palace in Dresden there are several Japanese and Chinese vases.

This was the first time I was presented to the king. He was a white-haired, kindly-looking old gentleman, and probably because he was a descendant of King John, the urbane translator of Dante's *Divine Comedy,* he was skillful at receiving people. He greeted me cordially and said, "Because we have met now, I'll be awaiting your return when Japan sends an emissary to Saxony." The king did not seem to realize that in our country people are appointed to such posts on the basis of their accomplishments, not because of friendships they might have established.

Among the one hundred and thirty or so officers gathered here was an old man of large build in a cavalry uniform. He was a minister of state, Count Fabrice.

Late that afternoon when we were returning to the castle we could hear the laughter of the girls before we reached the stone gate. The youngest girl, who had grown used to me, came bounding out to the carriage. "My sisters are playing a game of croquet, won't you join them?" she asked me.

The battalion commander said, "Don't spoil their fun. If I may say so, I'm going to get out of this uniform and rest a while."

I followed the youngest girl to the yard near the pyramid where the sisters were in the midst of their game. They had planted little black wire arches at various spots in the lawn, and, holding down gaily colored balls with the tips of their shoes, they would knock them sideways with a small mallet, sending the balls through the arches. The skillful girls rarely missed a stroke, but the clumsier ones howled when they missed and smashed their feet. I took off my saber and joined them, but no matter how many times I hit, the ball would never go where I wanted it to.

While the girls were laughing, Ida and Meerheim returned. With her fingers barely touching his arm, they didn't look like a very intimate couple. Meerheim turned to me and asked, "How was it? Was the banquet interesting?" Without waiting for a reply he walked over to the girls and asked if he could join them.

The girls laughed and said, "We're tired of this game. Where have you and Ida been?"

Meerheim replied, "We went across that rocky ledge to admire the view, but it can't compare with the view from the pyramid tower. Since Kobayashi has to leave with the battalion tomorrow and go to Mutzschen, why doesn't one of you girls take him to the top of the tower and show him where, way beyond the flour mill, you can see the smoke from the trains when they go by."

Before even her quick-tongued youngest sister could answer, Ida astonished everyone by saying, "I'll go." Like many people who don't talk much, her face turned bright red as soon as she blurted out these words. She started off quickly toward the tower, and I followed somewhat uncertainly. The other girls gathered around Meerheim and begged him to tell them exciting stories until suppertime.

There was really nothing so strange about Ida's volunteering to come with me. The stone steps were cut into the side of the pyramid which faced the garden, and the top had been leveled; anyone climbing the stairs or standing on the top could be seen clearly from below.

Ida almost ran to the base of the pyramid before she turned and looked back at me. I hurried to catch up and climbed the stone stairs ahead of her. She followed one step behind me, and as her breathing seemed short and painful, we stopped to rest often. We finally reached the top, which I discovered was bigger than I had imagined. There was a low railing around the edge and a large quarried rock in the center.

On the top of this pyramid, separated from the world below, I was now face to face with the girl whom I had seen for the first time yesterday on that hill near Ragewitz and whom I had since seen in my dreams and thought about in my waking hours. I was drawn to her by a strange attraction that was neither vulgar curiosity nor lustful desire. Below us, the Saxon plain we had come to view was indeed beautiful, but it could not compare with the lush forests and deep ravines I knew must exist in the heart of this girl.

She went over and sat down on the rock to calm her painfully beating heart, and her cheeks, flushed from the long climb up the steep stairs, glistened in the dazzling sunlight. Her eloquent eyes looked directly up at me, and although her features were not pretty in any conventional sense, she seemed even more beautiful than when she had played that strange, haunting tune on the piano, yet for some reason she reminded me of a stone figure carved on someone's tomb.

Her words came quickly: "I feel that I know you, and I want to ask a favor of you. I know that you'll think this is all very strange, since we just met yes-

terday and we haven't even had a chance to talk yet, but I'm not as distracted as this may sound. If you go to Dresden when the maneuvers are
over, you will probably be invited to the palace and to the minister's residence." She took a sealed letter out of her dress, handed it to me, and asked,
"Will you please give this to the minister's wife without anyone knowing
about it? Be sure that no one knows anything about it."

I knew that the minister's wife was her aunt, and that her sister too had
married into that family, so why should she ask for help from a foreigner she
scarcely knew? If she did not want anyone in the castle to know, she could
mail it secretly. Her behavior was so strange that I wondered if she was not
slightly mad.

All this was the thought of a moment, but Ida's passionately expressive
eyes seemed to be capable of reading people's thoughts, and she went on to
say, "You may have heard that the Countess Fabrice is my aunt. My sister
belongs to that family also, and as I don't want her to find out about this
either, I thought I'd request your help. If I were only worried about the people here, I could use the mails, of course, but even that would be difficult
since I so seldom go out by myself." What she said sounded reasonable, so I
agreed.

The rays of the setting sun shone like a rainbow through a clump of trees
near the castle gate, but the tower was already shrouded by mist rising from
the river as we descended. Meerheim had finished his stories, and the girls
were waiting to accompany us to the dining room, which was now a blaze of
lights. Tonight Ida was much more cheerful than yesterday, and Meerheim
had a joyful look about him.

The next morning we headed toward Mutzschen. In five days the fall
maneuvers would end and I would return with my battalion to Dresden,
where I hoped to visit the mansion on Seestrasse and carry out my promise to
Count von Bülow's daughter, Ida. Social contacts were limited in the winter,
however, and it would not be easy to meet such an important person, especially since a young officer's usual method of calling was to sign his name in
the register at the entrance and leave.

I was busy with battalion affairs until the end of the year. By this time
chunks of ice from the upper reaches of the Elbe were being tossed around
like fallen leaves on the waves of the river.

The New Year's celebration at the royal palace was a splendid affair. I
walked across a parquet floor so highly polished that it was dangerous and
paid my respects to the king, who was in an elegant uniform. Two or three
days later I was invited to a party given by the prime minister, Count von
Fabrice. After greeting the emissaries from Austria, Bavaria, and North

America, I waited until people had started their sherbet and then found an opportunity to approach the countess. I explained the situation briefly and handed Ida's letter to her.

In the middle of January I donned my dress uniform and went to the palace for an audience with the queen, along with some officers who were receiving promotions and appointments. We stood around in a circle until the queen was ushered in by a swaggering master of ceremonies, who then announced our names. The queen, attired in a dark-blue gown, spoke to each of us and offered her gloveless right hand for us to kiss. She was short, dark-haired, and by no means beautiful, but she had a gentle voice, and pleased those she greeted with such comments as, "And you are from such and such a family, which has served so meritoriously in France."

The court lady who had accompanied the queen remained at the door to the inner rooms. Erect, haughty, holding a closed fan in her right hand, she looked like a painting framed by the doorway. I casually glanced at her face: it was Ida. What in the world was going on?

The Elbe River flows through the middle of Dresden, and from a steel bridge that spans it I could see the royal castle, its windows more brilliantly lighted than usual, shining out onto the street. That night I had been invited to one of the balls from which I was normally excluded, and I was making my way through the throng of carriages along Auguststrasse. A lady descended from the carriage pulled up in front of the entrance, handed her fur lap robe to the attendant to put back inside, and, showing off her beautifully done golden hair and her dazzling white ermine stole, entered the palace without so much as a glance at the guard in full military dress who had helped her down. It took a while for each carriage to move on so that the next one in line could pull up.

Passing between two ranks of imperial guardsmen wearing busbies and standing with drawn sabers, I ascended the red-carpeted stone stairs. Along both sides of the staircase stood men dressed in deep-purple formal trousers and yellow woolen jackets trimmed in green and white. Their heads were bowed, and they stood without moving a muscle. Formerly each of these men had held a candle, but now the stairs and hall were lit by gaslight. In a large room at the top of the stairway, however, the flickering light of candles in traditional candelabra shone down on innumerable medals, epaulettes, and jewelry, and was reflected in the large mirror that hung among the oil portraits of generations of ancestors. Such occasions mark the ways of this world.

At the sound of the master of ceremonies' gold-tasseled mace striking the parquet floor, the velvet drapings over the doorway were noiselessly pushed

aside, a pathway was quickly cleared, and the guests—there were six hundred, I understand—all bowed from the waist while the royal party filed by
the gold-embroidered lapels of the officers' uniforms, high blonde hairdos,
and gowns cut so low they revealed the middles of the ladies' backs. The royalty were preceded by two footmen in lavishly curled perukes. Then came
Their Highnesses the King and Queen, the Crown Prince of Sachsen-
Meiningen with his wife, the Princess of Weimar and Schönberg, and finally
various important court ladies.

It was not an idle rumor that the ladies-in-waiting at the court of Saxony
were ugly. With my head bowed I covertly watched them pass: none of them
had really good features, most had lost the bloom of youth, and some were
actually wrinkled with age. Their low-cut formal gowns revealed chests so
skinny you could count every rib. The procession was almost over, and still
the person I was waiting for had not appeared. Then came a single young
court lady with an aristocratic bearing and dignified gait. Hoping it might
be her, I looked up. In front of me was Ida.

The royal party proceeded to one end of the room, and the ministers from
the various countries gathered around them with their wives. With a loud
drumroll the jaeger's regimental band that had been waiting up on a high
platform struck up a polonaise. Each man took a woman by the hand and
began to walk around the room. At the head of the line the king, in a military uniform, escorted the Princess of Meiningen in a scarlet gown; then
came the queen in a yellow silk gown with a train, accompanied by the
Prince of Meiningen. After about fifty couples had circled the room, the
queen went over to a chair marked with the royal insignia, and the king
headed toward an adjoining room where card tables had been set up.

At this point the real dancing began; I watched the guests, mostly young
officers with court ladies as partners, moving skillfully around the narrow
space in the center of the crowded room. At first I wondered why I did not
see Meerheim, then I realized that most of the officers who had been invited
were Imperial Guards. Curious as to what kind of a dancer Ida was, I
watched her with the feelings of a theatergoer looking at his favorite actress.
The only adornment on her pale-blue silk gown was a lovely fresh flower
pinned to her breast. As she moved around the crowded floor, the hem of
her skirt described a series of perfect circles. Her simple elegance outshone
all the gaudy, jewel-bedecked costumes of the vain aristocrats.

It grew late: the candles burned low and smoky, making the room dim,
and bits of torn paper and petals littered the floor. More and more people
headed toward the room where a buffet supper had been laid out. A lady
started to pass in front of me then turned, looked up at me with a face par-

tially hidden by a half-opened fan, and asked, "You haven't forgotten me already, have you?"

"How could I possibly forget you?" I replied, taking two or three steps toward Ida.

"Have you seen the pottery collection in the next room? There are some Oriental vases that have pictures of unfamiliar plants and animals on them. You're the only one I know who can tell me about them. Come." We went off together.

All four walls of the room we entered were lined with white stone shelves, crowded with vases from many different lands that must have been gathered by generations of collectors. Some were milky white, some emerald green, and others like bright, multicolored Chinese brocade. They seemed particularly beautiful against the shadowy walls. The other guests, familiar with the palace, did not pay much attention to them tonight. Occasionally we saw someone passing by to the buffet, but no one stopped in to look.

Ida sat down on a sofa with dark crimson figures of grass woven on a lighter background, taking care not to crush the graceful folds of her pale-blue gown, which were not the least bit wrinkled from dancing. Pointing obliquely to a vase on the middle shelf with her fan she began: "Last year already seems like the distant past. You must have wondered about me when I suddenly used you as a courier without explaining anything. I've never forgotten you even for a moment. You rescued me from a life of suffering.

"Recently I've been reading a couple of books about Japanese customs in which the European authors note with scorn that in your country marriages are arranged by the parents, and that consequently many couples don't know what real love is. Such scorn is ironical, for the same thing happens in Europe. Long friendships before an engagement are supposed to enable a couple to get to know each other before they decide whether to marry or not, but among the nobility marriages are arranged by one's superiors, and even though the couple may not be suited for each other, there is no getting out of it. After you have met so often that you can't stand the sight of one another, then you are married. That shows what a reasonable world this is.

"Meerheim is your friend. If I say anything against him, you are sure to defend him. Even I know that he is an honest, straightforward person, and it's certainly obvious that there's nothing wrong with his appearance. But never in all the years I have known him have I ever felt the slightest bit of affection for him. Sometimes I take his arm because he is kind, or just to keep up appearances in a relationship my parents approve of, but my dislike continues to grow so much that when the two of us are alone somewhere I'm usually so depressed that I end up making him sad. I make myself sick trying to put up with it. Don't ask me why. Who understands these things? People say that lovers love because they love. Maybe the same thing is true of hate.

"Once when my father was in a good mood I tried to discuss my unhappiness with him, but he seemed to know intuitively what I was about to say and interrupted me. 'It's unthinkable for people born to nobility to act with the selfishness common to the lower classes,' he explained. 'Personal rights must be sacrificed to the rights of heredity. Don't ever imagine that I've forgotten human emotions just because I'm old. Look at the picture of my mother hanging on the wall there. Her will was as stern as her face, and because she wouldn't put up with any nonsense, I missed a great many of life's pleasures. But I preserved our family's honor, which has not been stained by ignoble blood for several hundred years.' Instead of addressing me in his usual gruff, military manner, he spoke gently, almost tenderly, until my resolve was so weakened that I was unable to utter any of the arguments I had prepared to defend my case.

"There was no sense in talking to my mother: she never knew how to answer my father. Even though I was born the child of a nobleman, I am also a person. I can see through the disgusting sham of lineage and bloodline, and I want nothing more to do with it. It would have been too shameful for me, a woman of good birth, to have thrown myself into a vulgar love affair, but what if I stepped just slightly out of bounds? Wouldn't someone stand up for me? If I lived in a Roman Catholic country I could have become a nun, but that was impossible in Protestant Saxony. Then I thought of a solution. I would go to the palace which, like the Roman Catholic Church, understands rituals but not compassion, and let that become my tomb.

"My family is well known in this country and is closely connected with the currently powerful prime minister, Count von Fabrice. Theoretically it would have been an easy matter to make such a request, but in reality that was impossible for several reasons besides my father's stubbornness. By my very nature I do not like to share my joys or sorrows with others, nor to see everything in terms of love or hate, and I couldn't endure having my plans discussed here and there with some people admonishing and others encouraging me. I would resent it even more if Meerheim, who is so very frivolous, were to think it was all because of him and were to go around saying that I hated him and was trying to avoid him. Just when I was wondering how I could get a position in the palace without everyone knowing that I had requested it, you came to our country for a visit. I saw that you are a sincere person who could look at us impartially, as though we were just objects alongside the road. I secretly entrusted you with my letter to the Countess von Fabrice, who had already shown some pity for me. She didn't tell anyone about this, not even her family, and when there was a vacancy among the court ladies I was summoned to serve for a while. I was finally permitted to remain here because His Majesty desired it.

"A man like Meerheim, who simply takes the world as it comes, won't have much trouble forgetting about me and enjoying a long life. The only one who has been hurt by this is the boy who made me stop playing the night you visited us. Every night after I left he slept in his boat outside my window. One morning someone noticed that the door to the sheepfold had not been opened, and when they searched the riverbank they found his empty boat being battered by the waves. The only thing in it was his flute, lying on a pile of hay."

The clock was striking midnight as she finished her story, and the dancing had already ended. Since it was time for the queen to retire, Ida got up hurriedly and held out her right hand for me to kiss. Then she mingled with the guests who were crowded around the buffet table in the corner, and I was left with only an occasional glimpse of her pale-blue gown.

1891

II

SELF-PORTRAITS

OF THE ARTIST

1909–1915

OF THE TEN STORIES TRANSLATED HERE, some are mirrors, some reflections. They were written and published over a period of six years, from 1909 to 1915. In a number of them, Ōgai appears as himself or lightly disguised; in others, he creates a central character who, while resembling the author in some significant aspect, is nevertheless intended to reveal a life of his own. Although each of these stories is independently conceived in its own terms, there are subtle threads that link these various accounts together, so that when read as a group, larger themes and issues emerge.

After a silence of virtually two decades, Ōgai began writing fiction again in 1909. It is not that he had been idle since the composition of his first three romantic tales shortly after his return from Germany in 1888. He had been occupied as a critic and as a translator, rendering the novel of Hans Christian Andersen he so much admired, *The Improvisatore,* into Japanese, a project that took him, working off and on during his spare hours as he was forced to do, a period of nine years. He translated as well a number of Russian and German stories from German-language texts, as well as a body of German poetry and important plays by Ibsen, Hofmannsthal, and Wedekind. His work with the army involved him in campaigns during the Sino-Japanese War (1894–1895) and the Russo-Japanese War (1904–1905), and some of his war experiences found their way into his own experimental poetry. Still, given his literary beginnings and the rush of creative work in the decade or more that was to follow after 1909, this lengthy period seems a relatively empty one.

In many ways, this long artistic hiatus can best be summed up, in terms of Ōgai's inner life, as "years of exile." From the years 1899 to 1902, the writer was indeed virtually in exile, sent to Kokura on the southern island of Kyushu by his military superiors as a virtual punishment for his brash and independent thinking. In 1902, Ōgai was recalled to Tokyo; but neither that reprieve, nor his second marriage the same year, seemed to have brought him any sense of spiritual fulfillment. Indeed, the themes of many of these stories in this collection would suggest that this outpouring of fiction which began seven years later was to serve as a means for him to work out in print and on a broader artistic scale many of the personal difficulties he had himself experienced so acutely during the course of his middle years. In all these stories, the reader receives a powerful sense of the psyche of an artist struggling to express larger themes.

Four of the stories presented here were written in 1909: *Tsuina* (Exorcising Demons), *Hannichi* (Half a Day), *Hebi* (Snake), and *Kompira,* a novella named for the god worshiped at the famous Kotohira Shrine in Shikoku. In the course of these stories, Ōgai appears sometimes as himself, in *Exorcising*

Demons, or thinly disguised as Ono, a professor of Western philosophy, in *Kompira.* In *Half a Day,* written in a more satiric mode, he becomes Takayama, a literature professor. *Snake,* on the other hand, shows an experiment in dividing up the real personae who inhabit the story; there are elements of Ōgai in the narrator, in a doctor visiting in the provinces, and in the listless young master of the home in which he stays. The effect on the reader is as if the narrator were watching himself in a darkened mirror, one set at a certain angle from commonplace reality. Each story shows the author struggling, sometimes with more success than others, to discover the tone and structure needed to render in an artistically effective fashion the authentic sense of disquiet he felt within himself.

In the stories published a year later, in 1910, Ōgai's narrative strategies seem more aptly designed and crafted in terms of their suitability for the material to be presented. His ironic disguise as Kimura succeeds in making *Asobi* (Play) an effective mixture of wit and satire that has been much admired; and although Kimura does resemble Ōgai in certain particulars, the story does not depend on that fact for its success. In *Fushinchū* (Under Reconstruction), the protagonist becomes Watanabe, a Japanese military officer, but, as in *Play,* he exists apart from the author. Both stories are written in a laconic and finely honed prose that defies easy translation. *Dokushin* (A Bachelor) is closer to the historical Ōgai; here he disguises himself as still another Ono, and the brief story represents among other things an attempt, the first Ōgai was able to undertake in print, to exorcise the years in Kokura through writing about them in a more or less direct fashion.

The two 1911 stories are masterful and show Ōgai's increasing skill in clarifying the range of artistically suitable means available to him to write successfully about himself and his concerns. In one, *Mōsō* (Daydreams), he refines the form of direct personal narration used in *Exorcising Demons,* so that this later story becomes a virtual credo of his experiences and beliefs; in the second, *Hyaku monogatari* (Ghost Stories), he uses with considerably greater skill the device first explored in *Snake.* Here Ōgai plays the bystander, observing another who reminds him of himself, an uncanny double reflection.

The 1915 work, *Futari no tomo* (Two Friends), seems a perfect outcome of Ōgai's separation from the world that he observed. These two men he came to know during his years in Kokura are described, from the outside, with all the empathy and selective skill of a master writer. By now, as in his historical stories, Ōgai had perfected the means to use his self-acknowledged status as a bystander in order to describe others instead of himself. In his last great historical works, his models were resolutely external. Neither in their historical functions nor in their interior psyches, as recreated by Ōgai, did their concerns and their obsessions, as they do in these ten stories, come largely from within the consciousness of the author himself. *Two Friends* signals the end of a long and painful struggle for artistic, and human, self-definition, a process which, in turn, allowed for a new and final phase in the author's creative career.

Tsuina

EXORCISING DEMONS

STRICTLY SPEAKING, THIS BRIEF WORK is more a speculative essay than a piece of fiction, although there are several elements in the text, such as the description of the restaurant, that possessed sufficient symbolic freight to urge their reuse by the author in other more purely literary pieces as well. This brief account is valuable, however, in that it brings Ōgai, sardonic and lost in his own "night thoughts," into close contact with the reader.

In the final section of the text, Ōgai paraphrases Nietzsche on the twilight of art. There is more than an intellectual congruence between the two, however, in Ōgai's insistence that "the best things within us may be an inheritance of the sensibilities of an ancient time." Such a deeply felt impetus, expressed here in 1909, helps explain Ōgai's growing interest in history, a fascination that would result in the production of the magisterial historical accounts composed during his final period after the death of the Emperor Meiji.

THERE IS A SAYING IN THE WEST that if you give the devil a single hair, without fail he will depart with your soul.

It makes no difference whether a person is labeled innocuously as a chap who doesn't write, or spitefully as one who can't write. Either way, he has peace and quiet. There's not really a great deal of difference between these two labels.

As it happens, however, people do write. For example, they may write for the innocent, childish, and entirely sentimental reason that they feel moved to do so. Well, once it is said that someone writes, he is called upon to write from every direction.

How and what to write? I am exhausted when I return home from the government office. People usually have a drink at dinner and then cheerfully go to sleep until the next morning. But I turn the lamp low and sleep for just a while, with the resolution of getting up shortly. At midnight I wake up. My mind is a little recovered. I stay up from then until two o'clock and write.

Thoughts of the day are different from those of the night. It often happens that during the night I believe I have satisfactorily solved a problem I couldn't solve during the day, but when I reappraise this the next morning, it frequently turns out to be no solution at all. There is something unreliable about the thoughts of the night.

Among literary people, there are those such as Balzac who work at night. Lassailly, his sometime collaborator, was obliged to sleep in the early evening, and then roused at one o'clock in the morning. You still haven't broken your bad habit of sleeping during the night, Balzac is said to have told him. The night is for work! So here is coffee. Drink this, he said, and wake up and get to work. White paper was stacked on the table. Balzac, wearing his famous robe, dictated while pacing back and forth in the room. It is said that Lassailly was forced to transcribe what was dictated until seven o'clock in the morning. But Balzac didn't have to take care of government business from 8:00 A.M. to 4:00 P.M. When I think about this, my thoughts of the night seem even more unreliable.

Be that as it may, I sit at my desk, take pen in hand, and consider what to write.

In writing prose, we are told we should write about certain things in a certain way. Moreover, any creative work other than lyric poetry and drama

---

TRANSLATED BY JOHN W. DOWER

seems to be conceived of as some sort of literary prose. There are no such specifications in drama, but that appears to be because drama has been ignored anyway.

The injunction that one must write about certain things in a certain way is expounded as if it were a new invention. Thus it becomes almost a death sentence if a chap is accused of having retained the same style he used ten years ago.

Should it really be this way? Stendhal died in 1842. I wonder whether the things he wrote would ideally fulfill the requirements of these contemporaries who call for writing about certain things in a certain way.

If you take the view that everything in the world changes, then it is changing unceasingly, at every moment. If, however, you take the view that there is no change, then you have eternal immutability. Recently, words such as "shackled" and "liberated" have become fashionable, but strictly speaking, isn't it a shackled notion to insist that one should write literary prose about certain things in a certain way? I, with my "thoughts in the night," have concluded that what we call literary prose may be written about anything and in any style.

In a celebration such as Carnival, each year the elected king is paraded about, and when the festival is done he is cast aside without a second thought. Should this be the case also in a history of true literary development? Who was last year's king? Who is this year's king? When you think about it, people who want to cry certainly have something to cry about, but at the same time those who want to laugh have adequate reason to do so. Isn't that so?

I have written something supercilious. I didn't intend to write such a thing. But, so be it. Since I've already put it down, let it stand.

Strindberg has a play called *The Dance of Death*. As the curtain rises, the protagonist, a man named Edgar, is stricken by a heart attack and appears to be dead. His wife is delighted. Before the final curtain closes, he suffers a second stroke and does indeed die. Following his "first death," Edgar seeks after fame. He wallows in greed. This does not cease until his real death. This is the dance of the dead man. If you ask me to write things, isn't that like asking a dead man to dance?

I just had an idea and wrote "Shinkiraku," the name of the restaurant, where I had left space for the title of this piece. This struck me as a title which would have a certain magnetism when it was advertised. Nowadays, if you wish to attract attention when writing, it seems necessary to wear a slight tinge of scandal. On the other hand, there is the matter of this magazine's reputation. When I took this into consideration, I struck out the three ideographs for Shinkiraku and wrote the present title beside them. This will be taken a little more seriously.

I think I'd like to tell about the bean scattering ceremony which took place at the Shinkiraku restaurant in Tokyo's Tsukiji district. That I am able to relate this story to you now is due to the favor of Mr. M. F.

I thought of writing "dedicated to M. F." following the title. Since books are dedicated, why shouldn't it be all right to do this also with pieces written for magazines? Don't we often find "rights of translation reserved," "reprinting prohibited," and so forth, in magazines also? I refrained from this, however, out of pity for those gentlemen of the press who have resolved to employ only solemn expressions in describing me.

Mr. M. F. is a man whom I had met two or three times at literary gatherings. He invited me to the Shinkiraku at 6 P.M. last February 3. There was a postscript on the printed invitation saying that I should come because So-and-So had also been invited. I need not add that since it was me they were addressing, this certain So-and-So was not a woman.

The government office closed at four o'clock. I removed the documents with which I had been working from the table, placed them in the cabinet for confidential papers, and locked it. I put on my hat, fastened my sword, donned my cloak. I felt more animated than usual. The days on which I return straight home are rare. There are many dinner parties, and on some days I neglect two places to go to a third. The places I usually go to are all of a kind—places such as Kaikōsha, Fujimiken, Yaokan, Kogetsu, the Imperial Hotel, Seiyōken, and others. A step down from these there are places like Takaratei and Fujimirō. The Shinkiraku, however, is a rarity. Occasionally I go to such places as Tokiwa, Kotokiwa, and Hisagoya. But the Shinkiraku was an altogether unfamiliar world. I anticipated that going to the Shinkiraku would be like opening a door leading to a completely unknown place.

It was not that I thought there would be attractive women. When I look at the novels of the contemporary school of naturalism, the fantasies of the authors are always dominated by women, but I think that is just because of their youth. When one is close to fifty, as I am, sexual desires do not constitute the major part of life. I am not saying this just for the sake of appearance. What is the use of pretending?

It was only the fact that this was an unknown world that stimulated me. To give an example, it was like the feeling when one takes a penknife and cuts the pages of a book which he has never read before.

I left the office and got on the streetcar. Fine rain fell intermittently from a gray sky. I had provided myself with a book to read on the streetcar, but it is seldom possible to read on the tram after four o'clock.

I got off in front of Honganji Temple. Assuming this to be the general neighborhood, I headed in the direction of the moat, glancing at door after door as I passed by. There was a nameplate reading "Horikoshi" on a tidy house. We had met two or three times, and I thought: so this is where he lives. I zigzagged along, taking care not to muddy my boots.

At last I found the Shinkiraku. It was a house on the corner where the street joined the road running along the side of the moat. In front of the lattice door I looked at my watch. Ridiculously early. Since it was just 4:30, there remained an hour and a half before the engagement.

I entered the lattice door. The concrete floor inside had been freshly washed, and my muddy boots left an imprint. It irritated me. I apologized for arriving too early, and was led to the second floor.

It was a large corner room, with no veranda, which faced both east and south. On the west side was a *tokonoma,* and the north led to a stairway from the kitchen.

I seated myself in the southeast corner, intending to wait patiently until the time came.

The house was new. The *tatami* mats were new. There was not a single cigarette burn on the *tatami,* and I wondered if the guests who came here were especially well behaved. In any case, it was a pleasant atmosphere.

The maid brought in tea and cake. I liked the fact that she left without laughing or saying anything unnecessary. Her kimono too was a subdued color.

I drank the tea and ate the cake and then leafed through the book which I had brought, but did not feel like reading. I took out a cigar, bit off the end, and lit it by pushing the tip against a piece of charcoal in the brazier.

All around me it was hushed. The sound of rain clogs rose from the street by the moat. Built into the high and massive sliding doors by which I sat, at about the height of my elbow, there were two small movable panels. I opened one and looked out, but there was no one to be seen; apparently the person had turned into a side street. Everything had become gray; even the gaudy new Naval Memorial Museum appeared as if brushed over with gray. A solitary auto with no rider but the driver came from the direction of the Naval School and slowly made its way west.

I closed the panel. The lights came on. I smoked my cigar and looked around the room. In this large, airy, attractive room, I thought, nothing impedes the eye. There are no disagreeable hangings on the wall. Despite the inclusion of that inevitable relic, the *tokonoma,* the *kakemono* and flower arrangement are hardly conspicuous. It is a most suitable place to sit and eat delectable things and watch the geisha perform. One might say that this is Japan's architecture in these materialistic times.

A door opened in the northwest corner, diagonal to where I was sitting, and someone entered the room. It was a little, shriveled old lady, white hairs pulled back side-by-side and fastened in a bun. She wore a red sleeveless coat. Tucked into the crook of her left arm was a container, and without a moment's delay she walked into the very center of the room. Without kneeling down, she bowed to me in greeting, touching just the fingertips of her right hand to the floor. I stared at her in mute astonishment.

"In with fortune, out with demons."

The old woman began to scatter beans. The door on the north side opened and several maids flocked in and picked up the beans which had been scattered.

The old woman's manner was thoroughly lively and infectious. I perceived without asking that she was the mistress of the Shinkiraku.

In Nietzsche there is a passage concerning the twilight of art. Art is most deeply felt when the spell of death pervades it—as when people who have become old think back on the time of their youth and celebrate anniversaries. In Southern Italy there are people who hold a Greek festival once a year. The best things within us may be an inheritance of the sensibilities of an ancient time. The sun has already set. The heaven of our lives is lighted by the lingering glow of a sun which has already passed from sight. Art is not alone in this. It is the same with things like religion and morality.

After a while M. F. arrived. He was wearing a Western suit as usual and chatted with his right hand resting on the *tatami* behind him and body leaning to one side. Somehow he invariably gives the impression of being a person who, as the saying goes, "seeks out the ladies."

I told him of the bean scattering.

"Is that so? That's interesting. I shall have to make them do it again after the others have arrived."

Eventually the others came, all of them fat and prosperous. Carefully selected geisha flocked in, and seemed to outnumber the guests.

The repetition of the bean scattering ended without attracting much attention.

And that is the story. Let me add a bit more, however, to give the critics an opportunity to reinforce their accusations of pedantry.

The ceremony of exorcising demons originated long ago, but the scattering of beans probably came about after the Kamakura period. Interestingly, a similar custom was practiced in Rome. The Romans called dead souls *lemures* and held a ceremony to drive them away at midnight sometime during May. During that ritual they threw black beans behind themselves. In Japan we originally threw the beans behind us, but later changed to throwing them in front.

1909

Hannichi

HALF A DAY

ONE OF ŌGAI'S MOST TRENCHANT COMMENTARIES on marriage, *Half a Day* has often been interpreted as a dark sketch of Ōgai's own supposed marital difficulties with his second wife. It is doubtless possible in certain respects to accept this interpretation, but such a reading, by reducing the text to autobiography, reveals nothing of the piece's literary qualities. The ironic, often amusing, cartoons of marital discord the story provides have great merit in and of themselves. The sardonic mode in which the story is cast allows both for humor and rueful understanding. Each of the four characters—husband, wife, child, and "that person," the mother-in-law—are quickly and nicely sketched, and the battles that rage among them, however serious they may seem, move deftly toward caricature. Three women against one man: what is the poor fellow to do?

The story also contains a brief and poignant sketch of an old woman shelling beans, another powerful image that Ōgai was to carry with him and use again at the end of his touching historical story *Sanshō Dayū*, written six years later in 1915.

THEY HAD SPREAD THREE quilts side by side in the six-mat room and were sleeping with their seven-year-old daughter between them. The charcoal buried under ash in the brazier early that night had died down; a dim lamp shone faintly beside the man's pillow. A small case with a watch, a notebook, and other things inside had been placed nearby, and a Western paperback book lay open face down. Perhaps he had fallen asleep without finishing it.

It was 7:00 A.M., January 30. A harsh northwest wind was blowing, and now and again the shutters banged. One room away in the kitchen, the maid stirred and could be heard moving about. Awakened by the noise, the man opened his eyes.

The sliding paper door opening onto the back garden glowed dimly. At some time or other the maid had opened the shutters. The man turned and smiled at his sleeping daughter, whose round pink face was half-buried in the collar of her nightdress. He remembered that she had been dreaming and singing in her sleep during the night.

He recalled that this was the day commemorating Emperor Kōmei—he would have to join the others at the Palace Sanctuary by 9:30. He looked at his watch. If he went in his own rickshaw from here in Nishikatamachi to the Imperial Palace, he would not have to leave the house until 8:30. So, he thought, if he got up leisurely, there would still be time to wash and have breakfast.

Just then a sharp voice could be heard from the kitchen. "Do you mean to tell me the water hasn't boiled yet!" His wife immediately extended a slender white hand and pushed away the quilts. She had a habit of sleeping with her head under the covers. When she was a girl she heard of a thief who had broken into a house somewhere and been led to attack a woman by a glimpse of her beautiful face; from then on she slept with her face hidden. Yes, she had a beautifully proportioned face. The hair piled above her head, hair longer than herself when untied, was half undone; the pins and combs had fallen onto the edge of her black lacquer headrest, which was topped with a red cushion. Opening the large, dark eyes that seemed to occupy half of her pale face, she said, "Oh, that terrible voice. She's always waking Tama with it." She spoke in a loud, high-pitched tone that could be clearly heard in the kitchen.

The person who railed in the kitchen because the water was slow to boil was the mother of Dr. Takayama Shunzō, the head of the house and a uni-

TRANSLATED BY DARCY MURRAY

versity professor in the Department of Literature. Back in early Meiji times his father had ended up in Tokyo after a friend from his prefecture had helped him to get a minor official appointment paying fifteen yen a month, and ever since then his mother had saved for his education by skimping on food and clothes. It was entirely through her efforts that he eventually became what was then called a scholarship student. Once, in reply to his father's query about the cost of traveling abroad, his benefactor had said:

"I suppose you're thinking of saving enough to send your son abroad, but that is very risky. We Japanese are apt to have little idea of the value of money. Even if you were to save a bit of your salary by skipping meals, you couldn't send your son abroad; and supposing that by some miracle you could, what would happen if the boy were to die? If you starve your wife you fail in your duty. And surely you must give the younger children at least an ordinary education. Where will the money come from for that? With your income it's amazing that you're sending your son to the university at all. If you and your wife are set on it I won't stop you, but you're already taking risks. Taking a chance like this comes from the special Japanese custom of the parents being supported by the children. I can't vouch for its being a good thing. It certainly isn't a safe one."

It was in such circumstances that his mother had brought him up and enabled him to be what he was today. She was not the usual type of old woman who often has trouble sleeping at night. Even now, since her son commuted to the university and could not be late for lectures, she still got up every morning and took charge of breakfast herself. There had been one occasion when he had not had time for breakfast before leaving and she had grumbled about it for several days. That was why she scolded the maid about the water this morning.

His wife was a born sleeper, but not so easygoing as to really think it did not matter if he were late for his lectures. On mornings when she had to get up especially early, she rose to a musical alarm clock which played a phrase from the folksong "Takai yama kara," and woke the maids. His mother was more than likely up ahead of her, though. This was natural. His mother was an exceedingly strong-willed woman; when she went to bed at night she decided when she would get up the following morning, and invariably rose at that hour by autosuggestion. His wife, on the other hand, was extremely weak-willed.

The following incident happened just after their marriage. He was unsociable, detested parties, and loathed geisha; therefore, on national holidays and Sundays he would have a Kyoto-style lunch prepared, go to Dokanyama in the northern part of Tokyo with his mother, and opening his lunch on a stool in the teahouse, spend the day reading an anthology of Western poetry or some other book he had brought along. One day he persuaded his new bride to join them. She did not find his suggestion to her liking at all; she resigned herself to going, however, as she was still unsure of her place in the new household. When they got back and were alone she announced, "I don't like going with your mother, so please don't force me to do something I dislike." From then on whenever she complained she repeated the phrase, "Please don't force me to do something I dislike," again and again, like a refrain. His wife never did anything she disliked. She never did anything that required special effort or study. She did not have an ounce of self-discipline. This was a remnant of her girlhood days, when she had been pampered by her father, a chief magistrate. The slightest hint of some obligation produced three wrinkles between her beautiful long eyebrows. She even lacked the willpower to get out of bed when she was supposed to.

"Oh, that terrible voice. She's always waking Tama with it." When Tama heard her mother's voice—not the one from the kitchen—she abruptly thrust two plump little fists out, stretched sweetly, and opened those clear black eyes she inherited from her mother. Shunzō looked at Tama and said, "Are you awake? Yes? Oh, you're such a good girl." She turned to him, arms outstretched so she could be hugged, and laughed. His being able to speak gently to the child was one of the few rights he preserved; it had gotten to the point where it was difficult to speak at all, let alone gently, to someone like his mother. His wife firmly set her lips, now cracked and dry, and looked steadily at his face. She even felt like saying, "All right. Go on and say what you like to Tama. I've told you that woman's voice is irritating, and I don't like your not agreeing with me. Still, this time I won't say anything." Her lips were always cracked and dry from sleeping with her head under the covers. Since their marriage, his wife had never called his mother anything but "that woman." When he asked why she did not call her "Mother," her set reply was that she had married him to become his wife, not to become "that woman's' daughter." He, on his side, found it reprehensible for her to complain about his mother's voice loudly enough to be overheard; but if he blamed her for it there would be a storm—if he seemed to find fault even with something like that, there would be no peace in the house. So he kept quiet. Shunzō, his wife, and Tama had been living in this antagonistic atmosphere for seven years now.

The kitchen sounds had penetrated the next room where the three were lying. As one maid opened the shutters onto the front garden, another poured hot water in the next room. They heard more clattering in the dining room as his mother set the tables.

He got up. Tama frowned and began to fret because she wanted to go with him to wash her face. "Papa is getting up first—because I have to go to the Imperial Palace early today," he said gently. Then he said to his wife, "You'd better get her up and dressed." His relations with her were unpleasant, but the household kept moving because he at least spoke about necessary matters. By the time his wife was halfway up, he was out and into the other room.

He put on a crepe waistband, faded to dark gray, over a plain silk kimono and sat down. Outside the glass door, the frost covering the thin soil crackled here and there in the garden, where there was nothing left but branches as bare as deer's antlers. He poured water from the pitcher into a cup to gargle; then, pouring hot water from a pail into a metal basin, he brushed his teeth and washed his face. His routine was very systematic and orderly; when they were first married his wife commented that he looked as though he were performing the tea ceremony. Indeed, when he finished gargling he wiped his cup with a dry hand towel. After he finished washing he dumped the water into a bucket, wrung out the hand towel, wiped the metal basin, and placed the cup inside it. He wrung out the towel again and hung it on a rack. His toothbrush, comb, and soap were each set carefully in place on top of a small case. Exactly like the tea ceremony.

His wife donned a common silk *haori* in tea-colored striped print over her everyday kimono of double-knit tweed, dressed Tama in muslin with sleeves cut in the classical style, and came inside with her. By then he had finished his usual tea ceremony ablutions and gone to the dining room calling, "Tama, if you're ready, come and eat." Because it was a custom in their house for his mother to serve him and Tama and eat with them in the dining room, the cushion behind his wife's place was empty. She would eat in another room after everyone else had finished. And this was not just at meals—she would not sit in the same room with his mother. In the early years of their marriage, she would instantly get up and leave whenever his mother came in, but she eventually arranged it so that his mother could not get near him. He would leave each morning and often return after dark. If his mother came into their room in the evening to talk to him when he returned, his wife called it a sign of jealousy. To drive her point home she would say that once his mother had peeped into their room while they were asleep. Actually, Tama had been sick once and cried out during the night, so his worried mother had come in to check on her. Another time he had returned home and his mother came in to talk to him about something while he was in the bath. His wife said she had heard there were some servants who liked to take care of their master's bath, but it was strange for an old woman to want to do it. When his mother had some problem or need, she would come along the corridor outside their door, wait for what seemed an appropriate time, and then speak out; his wife would react by saying that she did not know what to do with this jealous woman always hovering outside their room.

It often happened that he was in the house on holidays, and when his mother came into the room his wife would get up abruptly and leave. Things got so bad that she would get up with an exclamation of disgust and slam the door. Finally, his mother could talk to him only while serving his meals. Of course, his wife could not be silent on that subject either. "Where in the world do you have a mother who wants to wait on her son?" she would jeer. If she had her way, the two of them would eat together with Tama, and she would not let his mother into the dining room; but he would not allow it. Though inevitably unsuccessful in his attempts to accommodate his wife and achieve harmony in the family circle, Shunzō used to say that this fortress, at least, must not fall, and so, no matter what, he would eat with his mother. Since Tama was a child and could not wait for her meals, she ate with her father and grandmother, and his wife was left to herself.

He finished breakfast quickly this morning. As he stood up he told his mother, "I have to go straight away to the Imperial Palace today." Tama had finished dressing and ran in, disappointed to see that her father had eaten; her mother's voice called from the back room, "Tama, bring your tray in here." At that moment, a maid came in to get trays for his wife and Tama.

The back room was his study. He did not like confined spaces and so had the largest room in the whole house. He did his work there, changed his clothes there, met his guests there. On his way from the dining room to his study, he asked whether the rickshaw was ready and listened for the driver's answer before going inside. The formal court attire his wife had laid out was there. He hated silk and silver brocade and it was no easy thing with his salary to pay out five hundred yen, so he had always arranged to be sick when his attendance at court was required; recently, though, he was somehow managing to come up with the sum. Since the maid had put the trays for his wife and Tama next to the brazier, he detoured toward one corner of the room so as not to stir up any dust near them, and put on the trousers of his outfit.

Tama ran toward him and, seeing him in his underwear, clung to his chest. "Your tray is all ready—hurry up and eat now." She sat down properly in front of it.

His wife had finished getting dressed and made up, and came in quietly; she seemed restless, for she balanced on her heels on a cushion, took up the tongs stuck together in the brazier, jabbed them into two separate places and, resting a hand on each, warmed her fingers. He could not help noticing the effect of the imported cosmetics she bought at Sekiguchi. Her face was now as fresh as flowing water. Even her cheeks, pale when she got up, were pink with rouge. She paid no attention to Tama eating her porridge; first she heaved a pained sigh and then, as he was putting on his inner jacket, said, "I'm going to take Tama and go away somewhere. I can't stand being within earshot of that irritating voice."

Shunzō stopped buttoning his jacket to take in this last statement. He was sick and tired of that "go away somewhere." She had said that once before and abruptly gone by herself for a stay at an inn in Yugawara. Having no idea of where she was, both his home and her family were in an uproar until a postcard arrived from the innkeeper, and her family sent someone to bring her back. On such occasions as this she always said she was going to take Tama with her. Her first reason was that "No one goes off and leaves a small child behind alone." Next she would come out with: "A child can't be left with someone who says she hates to take care of it, as 'that woman' did." By this she was insinuating that his mother had made a remark that taking care of Tama was a problem, because if she even let Tama catch cold while in her charge, there was no telling what verbal abuse she would be forced to endure. It was not true, of course. His mother loved Tama so much that she would greatly enjoy looking after the child were it not for the constraints she felt from her daughter-in-law. But he disagreed with such a reason. He was the one who made sure Tama did not catch a cold by not letting the fire go out in the brazier, and he was the one who would help her out of bed and take her to the bathroom when she could not wait any longer and just had to go; he would be uneasy if he let her go away with her mother. If asked, he would reply that the reason his wife wanted to take Tama with her was to have a hostage: if she just left alone, things would be too easily resolved; for if she just went off by herself in protest, that would be the end of it.

This morning too, with a look of "here we go again," Shunzō stopped buttoning his jacket and glanced at the clock in the alcove. 8:20. He clapped his hands for the maid. "Tell Matsukichi to put the rickshaw away because I won't be needing it, but to be ready to run an errand for me." As she was about to rise, he added, "Please serve Tama some rice." She dished out some, passed it to Tama, and left. With his jacket half-undone, he scribbled a report of illness to the Board of Ceremonies, took an identification pass from a drawer in his bureau, and summoning a maid, instructed her to have the driver take the letter. Tama ate up her rice and drank some tea she poured herself.

His wife slid her legs out from under her and stirred the fire in the ash-covered brazier with a pair of tongs. He quickly changed to ordinary clothes and sat in front of his desk. His wife brought the brazier to his side and faced him over it.

"Aren't you going to eat?" He spoke first.

"I'm not hungry."

"Do you really intend to go somewhere?"

"If I can take Tama with me, I'm going."

"I keep telling you that you are not to take Tama with you—isn't that clear? If you go by yourself, all right. But I'm not saying you can go anywhere. You can't just run off as before; I'll let you go to Zushi where your mother from Kioichō is staying." Her father, Mr. Han Naoto, a former judge by imperial appointment, had his home in Kioichō.

"Impossible. Both Father and Mother say that I just can't leave the child behind, and that if I can't take care of her, they will, even if they have to lose sleep to do it. In that case, I'm not going."

"Fine. And don't let me hear you say that my mother's voice shouldn't be heard."

His wife's trip had come to an abrupt halt. For a matter as trivial as this he did not have to give up attending the imperial festival. If it were a day he had to go to the university, he would not skip going. Were she to leave without a word, however, he would be in a fix afterwards not knowing where she had gone. He hated the idea of her taking Tama. Occasionally there were problems like this on ordinary days too, but at those times he took Tama and left her with his older sister, who was married to a professor of law and lived nearby.

They were silent for a time. Tama pulled out some Western magazines stacked in the alcove and looked at the pictures. The maid came in and glanced toward his wife. "You may take away the tray now; I'm not going to eat." This happened often and the maid knew what was going on. He told her to place a small brazier next to Tama.

He lit a cigar. It was his principle not to have liquor in the house; since he claimed he could not afford the luxury of keeping two women at the same time, tobacco was his only pleasure. As he did not, however, care for cigarettes, he bought Victorias at twenty for a hundred yen—expensive cigars were luxury items. Though after going abroad he said nothing had any true flavor except Havanas, he contented himself with Manilas for economy's sake. His wife, sunk in thought, was pulling at the dried, peeling skin on her lower lip. Tama was gazing intently at her pictures. Outside, the wind had died down and the sun's rays fell on the shutters. The room was hushed. Now and then the ticking of the clock could be heard.

"How could anybody have a voice like that!" his wife blurted out suddenly. "It's a holiday and you've decided not to go to the Imperial Palace and to stay home, but any minute now that voice will be calling from the dining room that it's time for lunch! It's going to drive me absolutely crazy."

He frowned. "What nonsense. Maybe Mother's voice isn't a particularly gentle one. She has a rather masculine nature, so her voice isn't very soft. But if it upsets you, it's just your nerves—just like when we were first married and you said the sound of the temple bell at Sakanamachi made you feel so lonely." The memory of a honeymoon that had been sweet flashed like lightning and suddenly vanished in the gloomy hearts of the husband and wife. Each time the bell had struck she had placed her cheek against his chest and said, "I feel so lonely when it makes that sound." This had given him an odd feeling and he had grown apprehensive about there being something wrong with her nerves. But he had thought again and had concluded that people's nerves were all different, that some had nerves as strong as factory pulleys, and others, nerves as sensitive as *koto* strings, and that someone whose nerves were set on edge by the sound of a bell, which meant nothing to ordinary people, should be pitied.

"No. An ordinary person's voice wouldn't upset me. But she's not an ordinary person. She's in charge of all the money, doesn't manage it well, and even wants to get control of you. The minute I'm not watching she's at your side. Does that seem normal to you? Does it? It makes me sick!" Her large, black eyes glistened.

"There you go again! If anyone heard you, they'd think you were plain crazy. Isn't she my own mother?" His voice became harsh. Tama glanced up from her book. It was the same old argument, and he was not so angry as he had been the first time. Even so, it got under his skin. It was like an old wound that had stopped hurting, but smarted again when someone touched it. Since the argument was not new, Tama was not in the least surprised and returned to her pictures.

"I don't consider your relationship with that woman like that of some adopted child taken in by a widow. She may be old, but she's young in spirit and she wants to act like somebody's wife. That's why she insists on managing the household accounts."

"Wrong again. It's just as I've always said. Managing the accounts is nothing at all. It's middle or lower class for a wife to handle them. In wealthy families they have a steward do them. Managing the accounts doesn't make you a wife, and not managing them doesn't mean you're not one. When we were first married you couldn't be trusted with the accounts. You had a bad habit of asking your father to buy everything you wanted. Living within a budget never occurred to you. Now you seem to have learned all about it. I might let you do the accounting soon, but I see no reason to deprive Mother of one of her only pleasures. If Mother were to say she wanted to give it up because it was becoming a burden to her, I would take it over myself first. Then if your present disposition gradually improved and we could talk reasonably, I might let you do it. But the way you are now, your attitude won't improve that quickly. Wouldn't it be better to make it possible for Mother, who's been handling the budget for so long, to say, 'Why, of course, in that case it can be handed over?' In other words, you should try to get her to let you take over the job naturally. It is wrong to act as if you were trying to capture an enemy's possessions in a war."

"It's not a matter of accepting a favor. After all, it's your salary, isn't it? I'm not saying the matter should be handled any old way. If you were to take charge, or if you consulted me, do you think that you would say that I'm not behaving in a wifely fashion? My mother in Kioichō never interferes with my brother's salary."

"That's different. Your father is wealthy and your brother's salary at the company is mere pocket money to him and his wife—so your mother doesn't care how they spend it. But with us there's only the money I make. Aren't we lucky Mother handles it so thriftily for us?"

"No. She's just interfering. It's your salary. Her husband was a petty official under the old system; they had absolutely nothing—that woman should be grateful if you did nothing but feed her. She's trying to grab something that's not hers."

"Now you're going too far. Who do you think paid my tuition and got me through the university?"

"She might have paid a little until you became a scholarship student. It's only right that a parent should do that. Isn't it by your own efforts that you earn the salary you do now? My brother had all his school expenses paid by my parents, and even had them send him to the West, but he didn't achieve a doctorate or anything like that."

"You can't weigh filial gratitude on the scale of whether they paid a minor or major part of the tuition. To give a little, my father might have had to struggle much more than your father did to give a great deal. True, your brother didn't get the highest degree. No matter how much parents pay tuition, it doesn't mean everybody becomes a scholar. Each person has his own bent. Besides, even the greatest scholar can't determine the extent to which a person is born successful or owes his success to the help of others. Being born successful might even be a matter of heredity. Can someone who succeeds by virtue of personal effort say he owes his parents nothing?"

"Go right ahead then. Just the same, I've never been told how much property we have or how your salary is spent. What would happen to Tama and me if you were to die?"

His wife had turned the argument in another direction. Clever little Tama was listening carefully; she had put down her book and was standing, a finger to her lips, her big beautiful eyes staring. She studied both her parents. She did not put her fingers in her mouth, for her father had taught her not to.

"You know our assets are negligible! Outside of the house, which we got with my father's money and the money I'd made before we bought it, our so-called real estate value is only five thousand yen. My yearly salary, together with my income from lecturing, is twenty-seven hundred yen. It's Mother's thrift that allows us to live as we do and provides you a clothes allowance of sixty yen every summer and winter."

"That's what you say. I don't see it so I don't really know. And I don't know what would happen to Tama and me if we were left to the mercy of that woman."

"Don't keep bringing Tama into this or she'll worry for no reason. I've made a will leaving you very well off, so neither you nor Tama will ever suffer." He looked at Tama, smiled, and turned up his nose; she came from behind her mother and he hugged her.

"How strange that I should finally learn about that will because the janitor in the notary public's office is the husband of an old woman who comes to Kioichō. I can only suppose it's worded to prevent any problems. My father says no matter how they're written, wills aren't completely reliable. Besides, isn't 'that woman' keeping the will?"

"No. Wills can also become invalid at times. It's a question of taking as many precautions as you can. I feel I've made a fair will. But I decided to make one because you've bitterly opposed Mother and she worries about what will become of her if something happens to me. This is utter nonsense. I haven't got any real property anyway, so a will is completely unnecessary. When my father was alive and all the children were at home, no one ever gave a thought to what would happen if one of us were to die, or what would become of the money. Our parents never worried about getting old and thought only about us children. And we found our happiness in studying hard to please them. Money was nothing to us. Our minds and our hands were our wealth. We all had to struggle together. Our house was filled with hope then—we were always laughing together." He held Tama close. "Tama doesn't know what it's like to hear her parents laugh."

His wife always blurted out what she had to say and then would stay quiet for a while. She was reticent by nature; when first married he had even remarked that it was a good point. Tama placed her cheek on her father's chest; she listened and watched him with half-closed eyes, breathing softly. The room was hushed once more. Now and then the ticking of the clock could be heard.

His wife played with the charcoal in the brazier, piling it up and then spreading it around, and was lost in thought. Her head was spinning. Thinking in an orderly fashion was beyond her, for he would assault her with logic; as she half-hysterically argued back and forth with him, she always felt like a checker piece about to be captured. Wondering how to escape her suffering, she remembered that right after their marriage her father had advised, "You can always come home if you find it unpleasant to live there." She wondered if it would have been better had she gone home earlier. Then again, she recalled that three months after her marriage, when she visited her parents with her husband, her mother had said, "You've never been one to take to others quickly; how did you become so close to your husband?" And so, somehow, she just could not have gone home then. Did she love her husband now? He was not handsome. At one time or another he had said, "Handsome men lose their looks with age, so it's better to be ugly like me." Another time he had said, "My face has been carved gradually by experience —it's not the one I was born with." Somehow she did not dislike him. She wondered what would happen if she changed husbands and the new one were nastier than the professor. And it might be difficult, the second time around, to marry a man whose position was as good as that of a university professor. If only his mother weren't there. If only she went somewhere else. Even to her sister-in-law's. No, they already had one mother-in-law—she couldn't go there after all. It would be better if she would just die. She wondered at the fact that she could think of such a thing without feeling any guilt.

While he had been hugging Tama with his right hand, the cigar in his left hand burned out unnoticed. Tama seemed comfortable and had not moved at all. A memory came floating up from the past about a wholesale granary on the road he took to the university. He had his own rickshaw, but when he was early he frequently walked to work for the exercise. Sometimes he walked because it was too cold to ride in the rickshaw. One day as he passed the granary he noticed an old woman in the shop. She was one of those old women whose white hair had grown yellow and whose hands were as wrinkled as crushed oil paper. She would place a fistful of small red beans in the flat of her hand and pick out particles of dust and shells. It had caught his attention and he stood there watching for a minute. Then he had begun to think. As the shop had a big pile of grain to winnow, there were a lot of husks. It seemed to be the old woman's job to take a handful of them at a time and, peering with her old blurred eyes, she would pick out the particles. But she was really superfluous, for a servant boy was shaking a large bamboo winnowing basket by her side. And yet for all that the old woman was wrapped up in what she was doing. Even though the shopkeeper evidently knew it was foolish, he never said a word about it. He had thought that was interesting.

After that, each time he passed the place, he would always take a discreet look inside. The old woman shelled beans every day. It really did seem that the shopkeeper never criticized her. He thought about the old woman now. His mother's managing of the accounts, about which his wife was so critical, did not have to be done by her. Perhaps it would be better if he took charge himself. But it would not be good for his mother to stop doing something she believed was beneficial to the house. If he were to take over the accounts he would be even less considerate than the bean seller.

His mother had said, "If I handed over the accounts to that wife of yours, I'd have to beg with bowed head any time I needed money. She came into the house and hasn't so much as made a polite bow since she toasted the parents and relatives on the wedding day. Whether she goes out or comes in, she has never given me a greeting. If only she weren't like that. I had resolved before your marriage to turn the accounts over to her and would have willingly done so long ago. Yet she never showed any inclination at all to manage them from the very moment she came here. Even now, my way cuts our expenses in half."

What his mother said was perfectly reasonable. At first he had gently reproved his wife, and only later turned to scolding her about being polite to his mother; but it did not work. If instead of giving in to his wife he took over the accounts himself, it would not make his mother subordinate to her, but it would be impossible to discuss running the house with his wife, who would not open her mouth. Naturally his mother was the thriftier one. She might well be more thrifty than he himself. And so of course she could not be compared with the old woman in the wholesale granary. He considered it better to leave things as they were.

His wife suddenly broke the silence. "She was born in the year of the *hinoe-uma* calendar sign—that's why." This referred to 1846, the year his mother was born. He used to joke that his mother was like a staunch heroic general because she was born the same year as the famed Meiji general Oku Yasukata. His wife, being superstitious by nature, was sensitive about this and felt that unless she downed her enemy, she herself would be vanquished. This was one more cause of her antipathy. She got this from her mother, who had been born and raised in Edo during the decline of the shogunate. That was also where she got her belief in the god of Kompira, as well. When a girl, she used to put on a purplish-blue *haori* and, from her residence in Kioichō, pass through Tamaike and visit the shrine at Toranomon. She looked so pretty that the geishas of the Akasaka area there used to say that this young lady in purplish-blue was their ideal of beauty.

Tama was tired of being hugged by her father and grew restless. "I'm going over there." Did she mean to go where her grandmother was living alone in the small room next to the storehouse by the back entrance, or to the servants' quarters? This question arose at the same moment in both parents' minds. He thought it would be nice if she went to his lonely mother. His wife thought the opposite. He kept silent. She did not.

"Where are you going?"

"I want to go to Grandma's room."

"You are not to go to such a person's room. Go and play in the servants' quarters."

Tama glanced at her father, made an expression of resignation, and went to the servants' room. Although he felt it was useless to say anything, he could not remain entirely silent.

"Say and think whatever you please, but why do you have to say 'such a person' right in front of Tama?"

"I say it because she is 'such a person.' She loves to stay at your side and talk, but hates to take care of Tama. She acts as if she's your wife. She manages the accounts. She's always at your side. She keeps trying to serve you during meals. She peeks in when you're taking a bath. She spies on us when we're in bed. She's a sex maniac!"

He restrained himself. If he said something, she would be angrier than ever. If she was not complaining about his mother managing the accounts, she was jealously complaining about his mother talking to him. He called the former the rational side of her argument, and the latter the emotional side. Curiously, her father was the first to suggest that her unwillingness to permit conversation between him and his mother was a sign of jealousy. Once after she had just been married, she went home for a visit and told her parents how she would get up and leave the room because she could not stand her husband and her mother-in-law talking to each other. Her father had declared, "That's jealousy." Her husband hated even to glimpse those people called "geisha," so there was no reason for her to be jealous of his doings away from home. Even when young servants or attractive maids were hired, none of his words or actions gave the slightest cause for jealousy. And so it seems that his mother became the object of her jealousy. There was a strange story about how the wife of a certain shogun was wildly jealous of his retainers; whenever this jealousy flared up, the shogun used to summon the highest among them to calm her down.

Even his old mother could not escape becoming the object of his wife's jealousy. He stared at his wife in silence, again seeing this new outburst as part of her emotional nature. When he was home and was subjected half the day to her speeches, which she would repeat over and over like a prepared script, his irritation would often increase and his head start to spin. He would no longer even feel like smoking.

At times like this his silence made her furious. She would close in on him with "Say something!" as her long, white fingers clutched at his wrist. Then she would declare war and threaten to cut off her hair or to cut her throat. Sometimes she would make her usual threat to take Tama and go away. And there were other times of fragile reconciliation just because they had touched. Now, because it was the aftermath of one explosion early in the morning, she did not even try to fight. It would be too difficult for her to introduce the problem of "going somewhere" a second time. Considering the time of day, and as things were different from the first couple of years of their marriage, she could no longer expect even those fragile reconciliations. As was to be expected, she remained silent. The room was hushed once more. Now and then the ticking of the clock could be heard.

As earlier, her head whirled with thoughts. Since leaving her husband was out of the question, she did not even consider it. And since bowing her head to his mother was also out of the question, she could not think of that either. Even when she occasionally said she was going away, she knew very well that things would be the same if she returned. At other times she would even venture something like, "I wonder whether it would be good for me to take up some lessons like flower arranging or the tea ceremony." The first time he had heard this he had half consented, saying that it really might be better if she put her mind to one or another of the arts, but he had been rather surprised at her idea. She had no real interest in art. She had none even as a girl. She had studied with a teacher of Japanese painting and with a *koto* master, but never had any real intention of painting pictures or playing the *koto*. Her idea of taking up something was to make herself up and ride back and forth every day in a carriage between Kioichō and the district where the drawing teacher and the *koto* master lived. That was what she meant by lessons.

When he had realized this, he asked why the waste of money? Now that she was married and did not have to mingle with avid devotees who were not very desirable acquaintances, would it not be better to take up walking? But he went a step further and rejected all palliative measures: "If you have any flaws at all, wouldn't it be better to correct them at their root? You do something and then hide it. That is irresponsible. If disease causes pain, cure the disease! I can't approve of some makeshift measure like killing pain with morphine." His wife reconsidered the matter of taking lessons. His suggestion that she take up walking instead of lessons was entirely unsatisfactory.

She had no interest in nature either. Once after they were first married he had brought flowers home to her, but she had not been delighted at all. He tried asking her, "Have you ever looked at the moon and let your thoughts wander?" She looked puzzled and just said, "No." It was no wonder, then, that walking did not interest her. Even when she was walking through town and saw things displayed in the shop windows, she did not find it interesting merely to look at them. She would turn away and say, "There's no point in looking if I'm not going to buy." There was every reason to expect walking would not suit her. But merely traveling to a lesson would, for she liked to decide on a certain destination and go along some route at her leisure until she reached it; in her experience there was no suitable means to this except the excuse of a lesson. Therefore, whenever her spirit demanded a palliative, the matter of taking some lesson was always raised. And the surfacing of this thought was proof that her mind had calmed a little.

Was there any other woman in the world like his wife? When the object of sexual desire veers in a strange direction, this is called perverse and is considered a sickness. Wasn't jealousy turned the wrong way also a sickness? Wasn't an abnormal reaction to another person's voice by itself a proof of sickness? These thoughts had been coming and going in his mind for a long time now. Once he had said to her, "I think something's wrong with you mentally." Later she returned from her parents and said that she had told her father; he had replied, "He had a nerve to say that! He has no competence to diagnose other people's psychological problems; only a specialist can do that."

He did not think she was a mental case. But weren't there borderline cases? If it wasn't a case of abnormality, how then could she be explained psychologically? How was it possible, in a country where rigid concepts like filial piety existed, to have a woman so unfeeling as to speak about her mother-in-law like that in front of her own husband? Even in Western thought, a person's mother was sacred—there wasn't a woman alive who believed it was all right to slur her mother-in-law in front of her husband. Not in any of the histories, not in a single novel or drama East or West, was there a woman like his wife! He wondered about this special product of the present age, which was changing each and every one of its values.

Meanwhile there was pattering in the kitchen. No doubt lunch was being prepared. Probably Tama would run in now and say, "Papa, it's lunch." Probably his mother would be leaving her lonely room for the dining room, to be hated once again.

1909

Hebi

SNAKE

LIKE *GHOST STORIES*, *SNAKE* USES A NARRATOR who resembles Ōgai himself, one who can form a bridge between the reader and the character he wishes to reveal. Both stories are extended character sketches of men with whom the narrator feels a powerful empathy. *Snake* piles layers of irony one upon the other. The setting, with the "harmony and tranquillity" of its traditional paintings and classical Chinese poetry and calligraphy, is at a far remove from the tortured thoughts of the protagonist, the young master. Suffering from fatigue and a terminal failure of will, he has been wounded by life and the demands of marriage. Ōgai gives us not an essay on marital relations but an account of the emotional colorings behind the ideas of a man who feels himself hurt by women.

The brief story takes up themes that appear elsewhere in the work of Ōgai at this time, in particular those tensions between daughter and mother-in-law that provide the major theme of *Half a Day*. The device of the snake is perhaps best seen as a literary experiment, later to be put to use in the 1911 novel *Wild Geese*, where the scene of the snake eating the caged birds is used to render the symbolic content of that narrative.

ON THAT SHORT SUMMER NIGHT I was gazing absently from the veranda upon a small garden of crowded stones and assorted trees planted thickly together—slapping at mosquitoes which flew annoyingly at my cheeks and wondering how I had ever come to lodge at such a noisy residence.

An earthen receptacle of mosquito repellent rested by the side of the cushion on which I sat. Blue smoke rose continuously from its apertures and drifted across the breezeless veranda, enveloping me completely, but still the mosquitoes came annoyingly at my face. During the evening meal I had drunk two or three cups of cheap *sake,* and I wondered whether it was the odor of this on my breath which attracted them. I would have been better off not drinking, but my throat was dry and so I drank without thinking. Now I regretted it.

When I was first shown here, we passed a number of other rooms on the way and I noticed that this house seemed to have a history, but comparatively few signs of people. Now the constant chatter of a woman's voice carried across several intervening rooms, never ceasing for a moment.

Her speech was terribly fast, and I could not distinguish the words. It was a rural dialect in which only the sound particle *nii* was clearly audible, appearing again and again, like the beads of a rosary, in the monotonous drone of her words. In Tokyo, people interject *nee* into their speech. This was a certain way-station in the mountains of Shinshū.

For some time I strained my ears listening, but couldn't hear anyone else's voice. The woman appeared to be chattering to herself.

When the old servant greeted me, he had said, apologetically, "We have a sick person and it will probably be noisy for you." It seemed improbable, however, that a sick person could chatter so.

Could she be insane?

Her words were not comprehensible, but judging from the tone of voice she seemed to be begging something of someone.

Far away the gong of a wall clock sounded. I took out my pocket watch; it was ten o'clock.

The moon was shining into the small garden. Its light was pale and milky. The rain which I had encountered the day before at the mountain pass had dried up in the sunshine of this day, but although the road was good, the moss in the garden was still wet. In the early evening the old man brought me here, saying "It may be a little cooler here," and at that time I observed a

TRANSLATED BY JOHN W. DOWER

large frog sitting motionless for long moments, occasionally opening his mouth wide and eating those detestable mosquitoes. I thought of him again, and looked over toward the stone water basin, but he was no longer there.

In the eight-mat room adjoining the veranda there was a *tokonoma* with a wide black-lacquer edge, in which was hung a blackish landscape in the Tokugawa *nanga* style. A poem by the Chinese T'ang poet Tu Fu was written in large, jagged characters on the sliding doors directly opposite, which were completely shut. I thought I heard a noise and, glancing toward the door, saw the phrase "harmony and tranquillity" just behind a dim lamp set in a bamboo stand. Then one door slid back and the same elderly servant entered, wearing an old and formal summer kimono.

"I've put your bed out over there. Anytime, if you want to sleep."

"I see. I don't seem able to sleep yet. Your speech is different from the natives, isn't it?"

"Yes," he replied, scratching his bald head. "When I was young I served as an apprentice in Tokyo, and so it may be somewhat different."

Gradually a hush had fallen over the interior of the house, and the woman's voice was more clearly audible than before. Instinctively I listened attentively, and the old man noticed this.

"I am very sorry indeed. It must be noisy."

The manner in which the old man spoke was not just an ordinary gesture, for he seemed truly apologetic, and consequently I in turn felt sorry for him. At the same time, however, the more I listened to him the more mysterious his manner of speaking became, and so, while I knew it would be indiscreet, I decided to ask what sort of a woman she was.

Not being aware of this, the old man touched just the fingers of his right hand to the floor and began to rise. Then, glancing at my face, he asked, "Can I do anything else for you?"

"Well, there's nothing special, but if you are not busy there is something I'd like to ask you about."

"No, I'm not busy. Please ask me whatever you will." He settled back in a kneeling position once again.

"But tell me. Around here you people probably don't stay up this late even in the summer, so are you sure it's all right if I keep you up talking like this?"

"Yes. Unlike the inns, we usually go to bed rather early in a place like this, but it happens that tonight I must take part in a mourning ceremony anyway."

"So. A mourning service. Then you must have had a misfortune recently."

"Yes. Tomorrow will be the twenty-seventh day since the master's mother died."

"I see. Then it must be a great inconvenience to have to take me as a guest when you are in mourning, and when, as you told me before, you also have a sick person here. It's truly unfortunate. But since I've already accepted your hospitality, there's nothing that can be done. Since it's a little cooler on the veranda, well, why don't you come over here and talk?"

"Thank you. No, it is a great honor that we were asked by the local government to be your host. Surely it must be inconvenient for you to be put up in such a place as this, but for us this is one way in which we can repay the blessings which we have received from the government."

As the old man was speaking, he noticed that the smoke from the mosquito repellent was becoming fainter and fainter. Taking a new wick from a small cupboard, he brought it over and replaced the old wick and sat down at that spot. Then, bit by bit at my questioning, he told me the following story.

The Hozumi family was once known as one of the three wealthiest families in the prefecture.

As one of the highest taxpayers in the land, it was expected that the predecessor of the present master would become a member of the House of Peers, but, pleading illness, he completely withdrew from public life at an early age. He was a great admirer of the late Tokugawa patriot and scholar Sakuma Shōzan, whose book *Seikenroku* (Reflections on My Errors) he kept by his side until the day of his death—a book in which there were "some sort of poems written only in Chinese."

In addition, the old master was a devotee of Buddhism. He felt that from his time on people would have to know about things of the West. But it would not do for them to become Christians. He had read some Christian texts and declared that they were all superficial and could not hold a candle to Buddhism. Thus, even to people like myself, he continually preached the virtues of Buddhism. It wasn't particularly complicated. All would be well, he said, if people simply did not forget their fourfold blessings: one's parents, the emperor, all living beings, and the Three Treasures, the Buddha, the Dharma, the Clergy. (So this was why the old servant had spoken earlier of "repaying blessings," instead of merely regarding my stay as a necessary duty owed the government.)

The predecessor's wife was truly a gentle woman who never disregarded a single thing her husband said. From myself on down, she was kind to the lower-class people who worked for her. It was this woman who died twenty-seven days ago. Her life was long, and every day until she died at the age of eighty she would give ten beggars twenty-five sen each; in recent years the district office took to investigating the poor of the area and sending them in turns to receive her gifts. Some of the young servants laughed at them behind their backs, calling them "the honorable guests of the venerable mistress," but there were none who would do anything which might hurt the feelings of those who came for alms.

It was a long and deep sorrow to the couple that for some reason they had no child; then, in 1868, the wife became pregnant at the age of thirty-nine. They rejoiced at this, but the obstetrician whom they called in from Nagano scowled and said he had never before taken care of a thirty-nine-year-old woman expecting her first child.

Despite this, the present master was born without complications. Around the time when elementary schools were first established in Japan, he was already known even to prefectural officials as one who did things well. At that time I myself was of a mind to become a merchant, and entered service with a wholesale dealer at Nihonbashi in Tokyo who did business with the old master. Ordinarily they did not employ people who had not begun an apprenticeship with them as a boy, but with the master as my sponsor I was made a clerk's helper.

Then came a time some four or five years after the Satsuma Rebellion when the wholesaler had realized great profits by selling provisions to the government. I had attained seniority in the firm and the proprietor was about to arrange a marriage and set me up in a shop of my own. Just then, however, the old master suffered a stroke and died suddenly at the age of sixty-four. His final, almost inaudible words, "From now on depend on Seikichi," were just barely understood by his wife.

Without a moment's thought I returned here to the country. Although the mistress was over fifty, the present master had only just entered middle school in Nagano. Ever since then I have held myself responsible for all affairs of the Hozumi house, and so, in the passing of all these years, I have remained unmarried.

The present master, who was regarded as a good child, gradually developed into a rather frail-looking youth. His record at school remained consistently good, and the old mistress took care to follow her late husband's wish that their son should by all means obtain a university degree. While attending middle school, the young master lived at a temple whose abbot had been a close friend of his father, and his return home for the summer and New Year's holidays was always anticipated with great pleasure by the old mistress.

Around this time, the present master began to suffer from a general malaise. If he studied excessively, he became dizzy. Often he fainted. At times this occurred even in the lecture hall, and he had to be accompanied back to the temple by a classmate.

Despite his weak constitution, he graduated from middle school with a respectable record. When he went to Tokyo to take the entrance examinations for the national high school, however, he failed several times, and because of this he gradually became exceedingly nervous. Realizing it was unreasonable to demand too much of him, he was prevailed upon by those around him to enter the private technical school at Waseda. From that time on he became resigned to his lot and studied very little.

Shortly thereafter, he became eligible for military conscription and took the examination for a year of volunteer service, but he failed to meet the physical requirements. During the year of the Sino-Japanese War he returned home as a Waseda graduate.

I regarded him as finally having become a man, and so little by little I began to consult with him about affairs of the household which previously I had discussed merely as a matter of formality with the old mistress. He showed not the slightest interest, however, saying "Seikichi, since things have been left in your hands, you just do as you have in the past." After that I observed him carefully, wondering if there weren't something toward which he showed enthusiasm. It was to no avail. He was considerate of his mother, who was then over sixty, and trusted me in all affairs of the house, and so to all appearances he was an exceptionally good master. But somehow I sensed a failure of spirit in him.

The most puzzling thing of all occurred the year after he returned from Tokyo, when, at the age of twenty-three, he accepted his present wife. In a family which was less wealthy than the Hozumi, but possessed nonetheless a name of long association in this district, there was a daughter who also went to Tokyo and returned after graduating from the girls' middle school there. It was said that once a native of Echigo saw this daughter and remarked that, although his prefecture was famous for its beautiful women, he had never seen anyone as beautiful as Otoyo. When Otoyo was small, the master would occasionally happen to meet her at affairs such as the festivals, and people often teased them by saying that Otoyo and Hozumi Chitaru would make a fine married couple indeed. Although there was no agreement between the two families, when Otoyo went to Tokyo for lessons it was even rumored that she did so only in order that she would not be inferior to Chitaru when they were married.

Her return from the capital when she was seventeen coincided almost exactly with that of the Hozumi heir. Then the rumors became so persistent that it appeared almost as if they would be obliged to get married. When the master was asked by his mother what he thought about the situation, he replied that it made no difference to him. Hearing such words from the modest mouth of a son who had survived the decadence of Tokyo without so much as a single mishap with women, the old mistress interpreted his response as an expression of pleased affirmation, and quickly set about arranging the affair. The girl's family was apparently already prepared for this. The go-between even reported to the Hozumi family that above all the daughter herself seemed to be expecting her.

After the formal meeting between the prospective couple had been held, newspapers as far away as Nagano mentioned the betrothal as an uncommonly excellent match. In the midst of all the praise, envy, jealousy, and general agitation which took place among everyone from relatives to complete strangers, only I, old Seikichi alone, felt something amiss in the young master's behavior.

This was because I found myself recalling that time when the proprietor of the wholesale shop first told me that he was going to find me a wife. I was already thirty-four at that time. Because I was working myself almost to death, the time had passed in vain when my heart would beat like a drum at the mere mention of a woman. I had settled down. But just hearing that I was really going to have a wife after all—and without even knowing who or from where—why, for two or three days I was so fidgety that I couldn't do a single thing right. It would have been all right if the master's reply, "It makes no difference," was in fact just spoken out of modesty, as the old mistress interpreted it, but to me even his attitude seemed to declare "it makes no difference." Affairs of the house made no difference. The matter of a wife made no difference. But only I seemed to think it should not be that way.

The wedding went off smoothly. Then came the next morning. The individual breakfast tables were set out. Up until this time the old mistress and the young master had sat beside each other at the place of honor at the head of the room. I had the privilege of eating in the same room. This had been our custom ever since the old master died. His final words had elevated me above the general run of servants, and so the old mistress had decided upon this arrangement. Although she was a widow, she was already over sixty;

thus she did not have to stand on ceremony. Among the relatives, there were a few picayune individuals, but even they did not reproach her for this. On that morning the master sat with his mother on one side of him and his bride on the other. The old mistress appeared pleased with the beautiful daughter-in-law she had received and conversed cheerfully with her son. The bride listened with bowed head and only picked at her food, and then she rose silently and left the room before the others. I had been observing her from across the room and thought that probably she left because she was shy. The old mistress and the master would have had the same idea.

At both the afternoon and evening meals, however, the same thing happened and only the bride left early. From the following day on, she appeared late to meals under the pretext of having had affairs to attend to. When the master finally asked her about this, she told him that she thoroughly despised her mother-in-law's stories. This was in reference to a habit peculiar to the Hozumi family. At mealtimes they were supposed to discuss some sort of exemplary deed or saying which had taken place in the neighborhood, a custom which had carried over from the previous master. These were stories which showed a face exactly opposite that of the newspaper scandals. When there were no such incidents, one of them would relate a story which they had heard or read in a book or such within the last few days. Because of this, whenever they read a book or heard a story from someone, they would look carefully and listen carefully for the seeds of such dinnertime conversation.

The master was perplexed. He realized that such stories of exemplary behavior could be boring to some people, but he could not understand why they should be unbearable to listen to. Even if they were irritating, there was no reason why one could not be patient. Puzzled by this, he asked his wife, and she apparently informed him she could not abide such hypocritical stories.

When the old mistress heard this, she became reticent and withdrawn. The natural human impulse when one is forced to be silent about a certain subject is to want to talk all the more. She suppressed this urge. This control became habitual, and she suppressed anything she might have wanted to say.

The Hozumi house became a house of silence.

I had heard the story up to this point when the sliding door through which Seikichi had previously entered, that on which the phrase "harmony and tranquillity" was written, once again opened quietly.

   As I glanced up, a dignified man of around forty entered, wearing a short black silk jacket over a dark kimono.

   He began to speak in a voice edged with nervous strain.

   "I am the master of this house, Hozumi Chitaru. Though you are my guest, I did not come out to greet you, Doctor, and now I appear suddenly in your room, so surely you must think I am a peculiar fellow. For about the last two weeks, however, I have been feeling entirely out of sorts, and so I was resting. When we received this request from the district officials at the directive of the provincial government, I thought of excusing ourselves, since we are in a period of mourning, but recently one misfortune has followed upon another, and this old man, who had become thoroughly despondent, suggested that perhaps if we accepted a famous scholar as a guest, we might hear from him something which could give us guidance. Therefore, although I felt it might be an imposition upon you, I accepted the request to be your host. It appears that Seikichi has been telling you various tales for some time now, and indeed our family has fallen into a wretched plight. A while ago I came into the next room. I know, of course, that a person of good upbringing shouldn't eavesdrop, but I hesitated before entering this room because it would seem very ill-bred to suddenly confront you after having failed to come out earlier or to greet you. As old Seikichi told you, I caused my mother much anxiety from the time I was small, and still I let her die in a cold house. I believe that I took care of my material obligations as well as possible, but as my mother entered her declining years, she lived an extremely lonely life because of my wife and me. In such a case, most people would say I should have divorced my wife, but that would not have been such an easy matter. Since a long time passed without my wife having a child, it might appear that I could have divorced her easily. Nowadays, however, we have a civil code, no? There was no one specific fault of which my wife could be accused. She was not kind to my mother. On the other hand, she was not particularly cruel. Even supposing I had tried to get a divorce, my wife, of course, would not have agreed. It was my wife's belief, even while passing day after day in such a way, that there would come a time when we would enter a happy life. With my wife's attitude such as it was, and there being no agreement between us, even if I had broached the subject, her relatives would not have accepted it. What reason could I have given? She doesn't talk much. What sort of a reason would that be? Such a reason would certainly not stand up in court. Moreover, there was also the matter of appearance. The Hozumi are an old family that is rather well known to the people of Shinshū. I did not want such family dissension to be discussed in the newspapers. Thus fourteen or fifteen years eventually passed under such circumstances. Old Seikichi, being a faithful man with exceedingly great power of perseverance, took care of the affairs of the house without a word, but I feel that in his heart he believes me to be either a coward or infatuated with my wife. I am most definitely not infatuated with my wife. If it is merely said that I am weak in will and action, that much I cannot deny. That can be explained by the fact that I have no settled view of life. Because I was sickly, I was unable to enter a university, but I have studied many subjects. If there were some sort of philosophy at the basis of my life and if I were able to sacrifice all other things to fulfill this, then somehow I would have been able to solve these problems. Not paying heed to what other people praise or deprecate; not caring if people die; indifferent even to my own death. If such were the case, then my problems could have been solved. Because that is not the case, now I waver. And so my mother finally has passed away. My wife has become insane. And I don't know what will become of me."

The master's bloodshot eyes peered intently at my face. I shuddered. Seikichi sat with arms crossed, head bowed. The clock sounded eleven times.

"Then, is it your wife whose voice I heard until a short while ago?" I asked.

"Yes. She is always like that until just before eleven o'clock. She goes on chattering in that way as if she saw a vision or something, and does not fall asleep until she is completely exhausted."

"I see. According to Seikichi's story, the unpleasantness in your house began when your wife declared she disliked those tales of exemplary deeds and sayings, but what really was the reason?"

"It's indeed idiotic. In my wife's opinion, there is no genuinely good person in the world. If there were such a person, he would either be the only one in a vast land or come once in a hundred or a thousand years, and it is hardly possible that such a one might exist among the people we actually know. Doing or saying good things is done with a purpose and serves one's own advantage. It's underhanded. Contrary to this, everyone desires to do what is bad. Since there is no need to broadcast these desires, however, it's better to remain silent. But if one does speak out, she said, and talks about the bad things, then they are speaking honestly and are being neither false nor underhanded. Because she made these remarks with a gentle face and lovely voice, they seemed ridiculous and I was perplexed. Then in the midst of this something curious happened.

"Last year or so a close friend from my schooldays in Tokyo dropped in at my place when he came to the hot spring, and he told me the following story. He had a wife, and they had many children. This wife was a wench who refused to acknowledge any authority at all and did not obey him in the slightest. Even when he told her that by behaving in such a way she wronged her parents or the emperor or the gods or Buddha or Christ, he could not persuade her to accept any of these as a guide. He concluded that somehow women who were products of contemporary girls' schools all seemed to have ideas which they had discovered among the anarchists or socialists. As I listened to him, I felt he was drawing a rather drastic conclusion, but when I reflected upon it a while, my wife did not admit authority either. Is it possible that present-day women fight against everything in a struggle for existence, just as if they were no better than animals? How in the world did such a thing ever come to pass?"

"If you let them be, they just become that way. Babies are egotistical by nature, no?"

"But why are they different from men?"

"Whatever you might say, men are rational beings. Previously you said that you do not have a settled view of life, but in spite of what you say, you are aware of the law of advantage and disadvantage which operates in society. If you make judgments only on the basis of selfishness, then you know you will lose your position. You would not accept dogma. You would not yield to a teaching based on negation. After calculating advantages and disadvantages, you would not do anything rash. Even among women, it's probably the same among those who are rational, but such women are few. If human beings just had a thorough understanding of the law of advantage and disadvantage, they would not do absurd things. People say that Christ's Sermon on the Mount is noble, but doesn't that also appeal to advantage and disadvantage?"

"To be sure. If something red catches a baby's eye, he'll grasp at it even if it's fire. In the same way, women push their desires to the fore and destroy themselves. Isn't that right?"

"Yes. That's about it. And so you prevent the baby from touching the flame, and let him cry. You do not treat babies as adults. Socialists and anarchists and the like err in trying to treat the dregs of society in the same way one treats rational human beings. This is where the problem of universal suffrage lies. Majority rule may be abandoned in the future if a good method is found to replace it. In a word, the very germ of the idea of equality is a blunder. Women too, since they cannot see very far, must be restrained by force from doing things which invite their own destruction."

"Do you really think so, Doctor? I've heard something to the effect that in Germany elementary school teachers are permitted to flog their students, and it is an accepted practice for husbands to whip their wives. But do you have no objections to this?"

I smiled to myself. "I'm afraid that even my opinions do not go quite that far. Some time ago someone in France wrote in the newspaper that the English system of flogging had had very effective results. On this occasion, George Bernard Shaw took the trouble to publish a contradictory reply. No matter what the circumstances, flogging is always an extreme measure and so it would be outrageous to set up a rule whereby a person might resort to the whip just because he is a teacher, or just because he is a husband."

"I see. But be that as it may, if I had had a will strong enough to enable me to strike my wife on certain occasions, then perhaps she, poor thing, would not have become as she is now. Ah, I pity my dead mother, but I truly pity my wife also."

The master brooded silently.

"Whatever was it," I asked, "that drove her to insanity?"

Old Seikichi, who had been kneeling with his arms folded, lowered his hands and drew closer. "As a matter of fact," he said, "it is almost embarrassing to say so, but when we heard that you were a doctor of science, we thought that if you stayed here we would try to ask you that very question. It was the evening of the first memorial service, seven days after the death. When the young mistress peered into the family altar while placing some incense, a large snake which lay coiled there raised its head and looked fixedly at her face. She shrieked, collapsed, and has been in her present condition ever since. We too were taken aback. Among the young people, there is one who handles snakes well and we had him catch it and take it to the fields and dump it. The master, who is familiar with recent studies, explained that snakes are acutely sensitive to atmospheric pressure, and so at such times as before a storm it sometimes happens that they leave their customary dwellings and enter human homes. The fact that it was in the altar was entirely a coincidence. But when we looked into the altar the next morning, the snake had returned to exactly the same place. This time I was far more startled than before. No matter what the cost, we had to prevent this from reaching the ears of the lower orders. Already on the previous evening, when the young mistress was stricken ill, it began to be whispered that this was a punishment for her alienation of the old mistress. If they learn about this, then I don't know what sort of things they will say, and thus since that time I have permitted no one to enter the room where the Buddhist altar stands. The truth of the matter is that I immediately discussed this with my master here, but he turned a deaf ear to me and said there was no need for either of us to have to handle such a loathsome thing; eventually it would leave of its own accord. I wanted to ask you about all this when you came, Doctor, although under the circumstances I am a little embarrassed and wonder whether I too might be called superstitious."

The master remained silent, a look of displeasure on his face.

"Is it still there?" I asked the old man.

"Yes. It has not moved."

"Really?" I stubbed out the cigar which I had been smoking during the conversation and stood up. "Then let me take a look at it now."

The old man led the way. As we entered the altar room I saw an elaborate Buddhist altar almost twelve feet wide, with innumerable candles standing upon it and joss sticks smoldering in a great bronze censer. The white memorial tablet in the very center would be for the recently departed person. When I peered over the sticks of incense, there, indeed, lay the snake.

It was a large, harmless reptile which appeared so extremely well nourished as to be obese. A stumpy tail stretched out more than five inches in front of its coiled body.

I glanced up at the roof of the altar. It had been constructed out of magnificent, wide Japanese cypress, but some time ago the wood had warped, and it had been left to age and darken just as it was.

The old man had seated himself and was mumbling the name of Buddha. The master, who had followed after us, walking like a somnambulist, stood behind me with a vapid expression.

I glanced over my shoulder at the old man and remarked, "There is a storeroom for rice near here, isn't there?"

"Yes. Just one room from here is a corridor which leads to the front door of the storehouse."

"It came from there. Animals are creatures of habit, and where they have settled once, they will settle again. Even if you throw them out, they return to their original abode. There's nothing mysterious about this. Anyway, I'll take this snake with me."

The old man's eyes opened wide. "In that case I'll call one of the young boys."

"No. Your precaution that the young people should not see the snake a second time is a wise one. Even I can catch a thing like a snake. I would need a stick if it were poisonous. With that you pin it down, roll the stick to the end of the spine, and seize it there at the base of the head. This one is harmless, and I don't need anything like a stick. Among my belongings there is a fish creel in which I received some trout yesterday. I'm sorry to trouble you, but would you please bring it to me?"

The old man fetched the creel at once.

I grasped the snake firmly by the tail, drew him out full length, and held him suspended in the air. The snake raised its head and wound around, twisting its body like a rope, but it could not reach my hand. I put it in the creel and shut the cover.

Just then the clock sounded twelve.

Before I left the next morning, I asked what sort of a doctor was looking after the master's wife, and they said that they had called one from Nagano but he was not a psychiatrist. Because they were such a prosperous family, I left the suggestion that they would do well to have her seen by a specialist brought from Tokyo.

1909

Kompira

KOMPIRA

PUBLISHED IN 1909, A YEAR AFTER THE DEATH OF Ōgai's own infant son from whooping cough, *Kompira* presents a vivid and moving account of the helplessness of science and the disengaged intellect in the face of death. The emotional impact of the children's illness that occupies much of the narrative is so powerful that a reader approaching the story for the first time may fail to reflect on how well the various portions of the narrative have been layered together, or to note how carefully Ōgai has prepared the ground early in the story for the harrowing descriptions of Hansu's and Yuri's decline. (Indeed, surely only a trained physician could have provided the excruciating medical details.)

Ono, the protagonist, who is a professor of philosophy, stops off at the area near the famous Kotohira Shrine on the island of Shikoku, not far from Takamatsu, but he fails to make a visit and pay his respects to Kompira (or "Kompira-sama," to use the honorific often applied), the deity worshiped there. His wife knows better. Ono realizes from his reading of Zola that even in such a "modern" country as France, superstition and a belief in the efficacy of prayer for health still exist in an advanced society, but he cannot bring himself to give much credence to such traditional beliefs. Yet once the illness of his children begins, he comes to see in his own rational attitudes a failure of nerve, a source of weakness. Here is another aspect of the bystander, portrayed here in terms of the immobility that can accompany too great an intellectual self-consciousness. The concept of "resignation," which figures ironically in so many of Ōgai's works composed during this period, here takes on more somber colors.

DURING THE WINTER HOLIDAYS, Doctor of Letters Ono Tasuku was asked to lecture on psychology in Shikoku, and after he completed the series of lectures in Takamatsu he traveled to Kotohira on January 10 and went to the Kotohira Kadan inn at the entrance to Mt. Zōzu.

One of the members of the group that invited him, a red-faced, portly middle-school teacher named Ogawa Hikaru, had done everything possible to take care of the professor, even going so far as to accompany him to Kotohira.

Since it was January, there were no other guests at the Kotohira Kadan inn. The professor was shown to a huge room of fifteen mats on the mezzanine. He put his small bag, which was filled with reference books and changes of clothing, in the big alcove, moved the sitting cushions from before the alcove away to one side, and lowered his thin body, loosely draped in a pepper-and-salt suit, onto one of the cushions. He spoke to Ogawa, who was sitting across the threshold in the next room where the fireplace and tea implements were.

"Say, my friend. Won't you come in here?"

"No, you must be quite tired."

"Not at all. You are the one who has gone to so much trouble. Of course it's not a simple thing to prepare a new lecture, selecting materials to use and devising where to put in something that will move the audience and keep them from getting bored. But since I go about it in such a haphazard manner, have no inherent wit, and am not good at speaking, I must have been a burden to you. For my part, I've gone to hardly any trouble at all, and certainly I've exerted myself less than those of you who were in charge of coordinating everything. Please. Please, come join me."

The professor repositioned a cushion on the other side of the hand-warmer for Ogawa to sit on. In the same manner in which he seemed stuffed into his slightly tight black Western-style suit, he brought his plump body awkwardly into the large room and squatted respectfully a long distance from the proffered cushion.

"There is still quite a long time before dinner is to be served, and since today happens to be the day of the month that a large number of local people are paying a visit to the Kotohira Shrine to honor the god Kompira-sama, perhaps you would like to join them. The mountain scenery is also quite pleasant."

"Hmm. Well, please sit here on this cushion and make yourself comfort-

TRANSLATED BY JAMES M. VARDAMAN, JR.

able. I think that rather than going to pay my respects now, I'll have a hot bath."

"Of course. That way you will be able to recover from your fatigue. I shall excuse myself and come again in a short while."

Ogawa left the large room and went downstairs. The professor removed his spectacles, wiped them with his handkerchief, put them in their case, drew toward him the table near the cupola window, and laid his glasses next to the inkstone box. In his own study, the professor laid his glasses in the exact same place. In the classroom, whenever he removed his glasses, he always put them next to the chalk box. From where he stood, he noticed that the *shōji,* the sliding paper doors, that led to the hallway from the next room were slightly ajar. He considered closing them, or closing the sliding door between the two rooms, and finally decided to close the latter.

Having done this, the professor seemed at ease. He took the pair of tongs and straightened out the charcoal in the brazier, carefully put the tongs together, and stuck them upright in the ashes. At least one of the tongs was supposed to be upright, and there was a proper place for them to be. It was always odd when he was talking with someone around such a brazier. If the other person stirred the ashes and placed the tongs in an odd place, the professor always reached out and put them back where they belonged. The other person would usually look at him in surprise and when he came up short upon realizing this, he always felt somewhat sorry for himself. On one occasion a new maid came to work at his home. When she brought in the brazier, the tongs were laid on their sides, more than half-buried in the ashes. The professor repeatedly rebuked her and made her fix them right. That particular maid was from Hachiōji. A long time thereafter he went to Hachiōji to deliver a lecture. When he arrived at his lodgings for the evening he noticed that the tongs had been laid down in the brazier, half-buried in the ashes. When he saw them, he said to himself, "so that's it," with sudden illumination.

The professor warmed his hands over the brazier and took a long look around. He noticed that although the room was newly built, there was a big hole in the *shōji* in the low bay window. He would have liked to have them immediately fix the *shōji,* but considering how dreadful it would be if an anecdote about how Professor Ono, who was only staying at an inn for one night, had the innkeeper repaper the *shōji* of his room were to appear in the newspaper, he restrained himself. Now that the *shōji* had attracted his attention, he suddenly stood up and opened it. As befitted a craggy mountain, above him red earth showed through at the base of the line of tall pines. The sky was clear and there was no wind, so it was not cold. He stood watching the view for a while, until the maid came in to tell him the bath was ready. He took his padded coat from his bag, changed out of his Western-style clothing, took out a small hand towel and soap, put his watch and wallet in the case, and went down to the bath.

When he came up from the bath, the barber he had requested had arrived. Whenever the professor came out of a bath at an inn, he was always troubled about where to put his wet towel. That day too he endured the disagreeable and hung the towel on the railing in the corridor. He was always saying that the biggest drawback to the Japanese inn was that there was no washbasin, although he was not one known for keeping himself especially neat.

He sat down in the rattan chair in the hallway for his shave. While the barber went to get hot water, the professor looked out the window. Below the railing, there was a strip of bare ground about six feet wide and then a cliff. Along the brink of the precipice, at intervals in the lawn were some small pines. Below that was a road wide enough for two rickshaws to pass one another with ease and along the road flowed a small stream. Across the stream was the back door of a lonely house, apparently a farmhouse. Beyond that were the rooftops of some houses and a cluster of trees, and above it all hung a silklike haze.

There was absolutely no one on the road below. The professor suddenly recalled his home in Tokyo. At about that time of the day his wife, who had probably left their baby son with the maid, would most likely be coming home from the public bath with their daughter, who was almost six. His wife had been hoping for a boy and now he was six months old. Already the baby had learned to recognize his father's face, and whenever the professor took the baby's small, still uncoordinated hand and said something, the child's round eyes would close into little half moons and he would stick out his tongue slightly and laugh. In the professor's eyes rose up the sight of his son's face.

The barber returned with hot water and began to shave his face. As he shaved his customer, the barber in a smooth Osaka dialect chatted on and on with no need of encouragement. He seemed to be something over fifty. When he had been younger he might have been either a youth proud of his masculinity or a shriveled-up lad. When asked if he was from Osaka, he replied that he was, but just as there were imitation "Tokyoites" throughout the country, there were imitation Osakans throughout Shikoku and Kyushu, so the truth of his reply remained uncertain. His monologue commenced with how few people came in January every year, moved on to the prosperous times when there were lots of visitors, and wound up with the divine favors bestowed by Kompira-sama. He went on about this marvel and that incredible actual occurrence, as he apparently did for all of his customers, fluently holding forth as if he were reading from the human interest page of the newspaper. For the most part, the tales were of seafarers who had encountered typhoons and been saved, but there were also tales of sick people recovering their health.

The professor had previously given some consideration to the matter of miracles, so he listened without great surprise. Given that pilgrims of all types and all ages from all over Europe descended upon the grotto at Lourdes, it came as no surprise that others believed in Kompira. Come to think of it, he recalled that his wife had paid a visit to another shrine to Kompira. His wife was the daughter of a family that was now retired and living in Kumamoto but had at one time resided near Kyōbashi, and she had graduated from the Kazoku Women's School, so she could read a newspaper without the assistance of phonetic glosses on the Chinese characters. When it came to arithmetic, she was superior to the quite inexpert professor himself. But it appeared that she had not been taught how to consider the rationality of things, so she was extremely weak when it came to reason. After they married, she had become friends with the wife of Professor Taka-yama, a fellow scholar who was their neighbor, and when their children became ill, the neighbor's wife would recommend that she go to pray at the Kompira shrine in Toranomon. And it was not an elaborate superstition. His wife went because the neighbor's wife went. She didn't go because she had given it much thought. However, if she had known that her husband would be coming so close to the head temple of Kompira, she might have asked him to bring back a talisman or something. These thoughts passed through the professor's mind as he listened to the barber.

Soon after the barber had left, the evening meal was brought in on a tray. Since he was not one to drink so much as a drop of *sake,* it took him no more than fifteen minutes to consume his dinner. As he ate, he pondered what to do next. When he had arrived at the inn, he had been planning to spend the night. It was not so much that he had decided to spend the night, but that he had not really given the matter much thought. He figured he would eventually make the decision, and it just worked out that he would probably stay. As he thought it over during the course of the evening meal, he began to feel that to spend the night for no reason was a waste. The professor's stingy temperament may also have contributed to his decision. He often rode trains to travel. Needless to say, he did so in order to save time. But to say that time was all he begrudged would not give full expression to his way of thinking. There was no doubt that he begrudged the expense of staying the night. Perhaps one could not censure a professor with a small income, who also did some writing in addition to teaching at a certain private college, for being that way, but at any rate one could not help but call him miserly. Yet if one excused him by saying that he did not accumulate the money he was so frugal with, then one could not heap great guilt upon him. Accordingly, the professor's miserliness contributed to a certain extent to his hesitation to stay overnight in Kotohira. It wasn't that he hesitated to spend the night just because he was averse to spending time and money for no real purpose. A deeper motivation lay concealed within him. It was a motivation that one could mention to his credit. The professor missed his wife and children back in Tokyo.

He asked the maid with the matronly hairstyle who had come to serve him what time the boat left. According to her, the boat left at seven in the evening and arrived in Osaka at five the next morning. The professor immediately asked her to bring his bill and arrange for a rickshaw.

The maid went downstairs to get tea, and when Ogawa overheard her say that the guest on the mezzanine would be leaving on the night boat, he returned with her upstairs. Ogawa was still in his suit and appeared to have not yet taken a bath. He sat stiffly on his rounded knees, strained to open his small eyes wide, and looked at the professor.

"I overheard, sir, that you are planning to leave without even spending the night."

"Well, I have no real reason to stay, and it appears that I have just enough time to catch the boat."

"I see. Actually there are several members of our group who live in this area, and we thought that if you were going to spend the night, we might get together this evening to talk with you, but I guess that can't be helped. Just a moment ago one of the members arrived downstairs and when he heard that you were planning to depart this evening he was greatly disappointed."

"Oh, really? But it's really useless because I'm no good at all at conversation."

"By no means. We are all grateful just to have you come."

The professor drank the tea which the maid had brought, poured another cup of tea, rinsed his chopsticks in it, and put them on top of the tray. While he was eating, he had spilled some soup, so he wiped that up, too. It wasn't that he practiced tea ceremony or some such. It was just that he disliked leaving food, so either he left a dish untouched or else ate it all up.

When the maid stood up to carry away the tray, he began to gather together his things and put them in his bag. Ogawa leaned forward.

"Can I help you in any way?"

"No, thank you. I haven't taken much out."

There really wasn't much. He put away the things he had taken when he went to the bath. If he took out the things he usually had in the compartment, he had only to put away the padded coat he was wearing, and that was all. He leaned on the brazier with his left hand and moved his body a little.

"If you'll excuse me, I'll change clothes."

"Oh, don't mind me."

Ogawa was nonchalant and made absolutely no motion of getting up. From his pocket he took out a pack of Asahi cigarettes, cut the seal, and lit one. The professor did feel uneasy about having someone around when he was changing clothes, but he seemed not to want the other person to notice his discomfort, so he went over to the clothes rack where his white shirt hung and began to change. Unaware of this, Ogawa smoked his cigarette.

"You know, you are leaving without going to Kompira at all."

His language had turned slightly less formal. When Ogawa met someone, he greeted them in an almost overly polite fashion, then gradually began to assume a more familiar tone. This was the man's singular nature, which made him treasured as a social being. It was certainly a means of approaching people. At one time, Ogawa had, because of this particular trait, achieved a certain success and had been brought up to Tokyo by some of the older men from the prefecture. There was something a little slow-witted about him, however, and he was incapable of observing others. He was not aware when he was annoying someone. This was apparently the reason for his drifting back to Shikoku. The more uneasy the professor became about Ogawa's presence, the more purposely and conscientiously polite he became to him.

As the professor tied his tie, he said, "Yes. It's not that I have any reason for not going. I'll go the next time I come, when I have more time."

"Nonetheless, they say that Kompira is a fierce deity, and if you leave without paying homage, it might bring ill fortune. If you were to stay overnight, you could come to our dinner party and pay your respects, too," he laughed.

"Well, it may be true that you all were expecting me, but I don't believe Kompira-sama has any expectations of my paying a visit."

"Even so, they say that the guardian spirit of a mountain always awaits, so what can I say? I've heard all kinds of legends about Kompira, but I wonder what really is enshrined there."

"You should ask Dr. Takakusu next time he comes. I've heard that the original word in Sanskrit, 'Kumbhira,' refers to a demon. The same word also refers to both a constellation and the crocodile. There seems to be no direct connection between them, but in view of the fact that mariners and others worship it, I have a feeling that it has some affinity with stars and crocodiles."

"Indeed! You must have studied Sanskrit as well!"

"I don't know a single word. I know just enough Devanagari to be able to look up a word in a dictionary with great effort."

"Really!" replied Ogawa, although he had no idea what he had just been told. Meanwhile, the professor had changed clothes, put his other clothes into his bag, picked up his glasses from the table, and put them on. Ogawa went with him downstairs.

As the evening clouds drifted in and lights began to appear here and there, two rickshaws arrived at the shipping agency. Inside the small building, there were so many people waiting for the lighter that it was hard to tell who were the passengers and who were the employees. Scattered everywhere were all sorts of baggage, so one stepped up from the dirt floor, where there was no room to stand, to the wooden floor where dirty straw sandals were strewn around. The maid was in a flurry, so Ogawa took over the job of guiding the professor as if it were his own business, going into a suitable vacant room, clapping his hands to call for service, shouting, and by various other means obtaining a brazier with embers flung into it. While the professor was warming his hands, Ogawa went to the counter to take care of things.

Although the embers in the brazier smoldered, there was no wind and the professor did not feel that it was cold, so he opened the six-foot-wide *shōji* leading to the veranda and sat there. People were constantly passing through the hall. The ones moving briskly were male employees and maids; the leisurely ones were passengers heading for the toilets. Among the latter were some going to the toilet still carrying large Kompira talismans on their backs. Watching them, the professor felt that at least the number of the obviously sick was fewer than at Lourdes.

Word came that the lighter would be departing before long. Ogawa boarded the lighter with the professor in order to see him off. He peeked into the professor's cabin, and when he finally took his leave, his language became once more respectful.

First-class passengers were fortunately few, and the professor was able to command a whole cabin. Thinking to himself that he would not have to perform some unskilled gymnastics in order to get to high places or sleep in a lower bunk and have to listen to the bed above him creak every time the passenger above rolled over in his sleep, he was relieved. Since it was not cold inside, he removed his overcoat and put it on a hook, then put his bag on what looked like a sofa. The long benchlike space was probably for a third passenger to sleep on when the first-class cabins were filled.

In a short while, the ship began to move. But the sea was so calm that it was hard to tell whether it was moving or not. Kompira-sama must not have been seeking to punish him for his negligence.

He sat down on the bench, took out his journal from his bag, and began to write in it with his fountain pen. First he wrote about having finished the lectures in Takamatsu. Then he noted that Ogawa Hikaru had taken him to the Kotohira Kadan inn and boarded the ship. Each item was two or three lines long. The professor's journal was always a rough outline, and whenever he read back over what he had written, it was devoid of any interest at all. Form with no content. Upon reflection, the professor's life itself also seemed dry and desolate.

The professor always looked back on the things he had done and worried about the mistakes. When he was to give a lecture, he always noted down on a scrap of paper what he was going to say and in what order, even noting here and there the main points, but then when he delivered the lecture, he was never able to breathe any life into it. That was his first worry. Somehow or other it all seemed like eloquence on paper. On top of that, despite the fact that when he was writing something on paper, his logic seemed elegantly executed, the connections were lost when he was speaking. When he recalled how he would hurriedly switch the order around and add things, he would fall into a bad humor. Finally, he worried about the places where he corrected himself, faltered, and paused. However, he attempted to vindicate himself by noting that those were all matters of form that didn't matter very much. At that point, he considered the content, in the preparation of which he had consulted a large number of reference books. He never merely arranged notes taken from these sources in a jumble. He always incorporated an adequate critique from his own position. Later, even when he read his shorthand notes, applying intellect to the whole conception, there would be no unjustifiable points. Despite all this, he was displeased that he had never felt he had moved an audience or made a strong impression on anyone. Not improbably his ideas had become only paper ideas. And further, the professor was dissatisfied with the grounds for his standards of judgment.

The professor had graduated from Bunka Daigaku, later the Literature Department of Tokyo University, in the middle of his class and had taken a position in a certain private university. Because he was a "man of intelligence," he made the university's department of philosophy his own and was soon sent abroad. When he was in Berlin, Nietzsche was at the pinnacle of his popularity. At the time, as a young scholar he had read Nietzsche with a certain amount of interest. However, young Ono was already too mature to join the ranks of the young men who idolized those eccentric views. He was unable to board the hot air balloon of the *Übermenschen* and rise above the rim of Decadence. Then when he rather ploddingly set about to do research in psychology, which was then flirting with natural science, the fact that literary critics such as Brunetière insisted that science was bankrupt impeded his cautious forward progress. He then threw himself down on the floor of his room on the second floor of the boardinghouse and became engrossed in the romantic literature of the "Blue Flower" school, which he had chanced upon. This was the reason that when Ono returned to Japan, one year before the death of Nietzsche, he brought back as a souvenir an article on the thought of romanticism.

Ono's souvenir from abroad was awarded a doctoral degree. The fact that Professor Ono had no philosophical viewpoint of his own was not particularly unusual, however, and could be surmised even from the origin of his doctoral thesis.

The professor put his journal into his bag and thought about the lecture he had finished that morning in Takamatsu. The original agreement had been that he would lecture on psychology for one week, so he had worked out his schedule based on Wundt's psychology. Therefore, today, the final day of the series, he had to deal with the soul. The argument became metaphysical and the professor's eloquence on the written page revealed its true character thoroughly. As he wiped his glasses, he became even more strongly displeased than normal.

He stood up and went out onto the deck. The wind from the ship's progress was strong, but the hull of the ship hardly vibrated at all. The various islands covered in gray mist sent the ship off and greeted its forward progress. He stood watching for a while, but becoming cold he went to the toilet, returned to his cabin, took off his coat, and got into bed.

He realized that there would be only a short time to rest before arriving in Osaka, so he wanted to go to sleep quickly, but considering the heavy weight of fatigue on his brain, he had a hard time dozing off. Somehow his own life seemed to have no content, and he felt unhappy passing himself off as a common philosopher just expounding the views of others. The sound of the ship's mechanical clunking reached his ears. His body was like the ship—loading and unloading varieties of thought, shuddering its way forward—but it all seemed to him to have no significance at all. He thought about his wife and children. There were, after all, things in this world such as love between husband and wife and felicity within the home and these were parts of human life. However, they were insufficient to fill up the void he felt within himself. Wife and child were merely bound to his own engine by rotten hawsers of convention. How dreary, how lonely, he thought, as he fell asleep.

The next morning there was a clamor outside his cabin, so he got up and put his coat on. When he opened the door, the deck was thronged with people. Before his very eyes were the buildings of the waterfront, and on a lighter plying the narrow space between the steamer and the shore, a boatman was cursing loudly. He quickly went back into his cabin and as he was washing his face the ship came to a standstill. They had arrived in Osaka.

He immediately took a rickshaw to Umeda, where he went to a tea shop. He requested that they buy him a ticket for the 8:30 express and then wrote a postcard to Ogawa in Takamatsu. "I am most grateful for your cordial hospitality during my stay in Takamatsu and for your graciously accompanying me all the way to Kotohira to see me off upon my departure. Fortunately Kompira has withheld vengeance and I have arrived in Osaka after a smooth voyage. I am now about to return home on the train. Please give my very best regards to the others as well." Having written the address on the card, he handed it to the young girl in the shop and she immediately ran out to mail it.

Whether that particular shop was a rest stop for passengers boarding the express he couldn't tell, but there were no other customers. At the counter an old woman sat alone smoking a cigarette. He had set his bag on the round table placed to one side of the earthen entranceway and stood nearby writing the postcard; then he went to the sunken hearth cut out in the dead center of the earthen floor and sat down on the wicker chair placed there. The firewood in the sunken hearth was covered with white ash, but it wasn't cold enough to want to stir up the fire.

A fellow, perhaps a working man, came up to the counter and was talking to the old lady. They seemed to be gossiping about someone they both knew, using lots of proper nouns, so the professor, who overheard them without really listening, had no idea what they were talking about. The girl who had gone to post the card stood a short distance away and looked at the professor, as if he were somehow unusual, but the old lady scolded her and she retreated in the direction of the back of the shop.

With time hanging heavily on his hands, he spoke to the old woman and went outside. He went to a plaza in front of the train station and for a while stood looking around, but the vicinity was deserted and only the occasional rickshaw with a passenger broke the quiet of the gray winter morning. On one road in the direction of Umeda-chō ran the Hanshin streetcar and it had stopped to pick up passengers. Turning into the apparently flourishing road lined with shops that went in the direction of Sonezaki and walking a short while, he could see little except a shop displaying a curtain with a plum blossom crest which sold millet cake.

The professor slowly wandered back to the tea shop. A man wearing a short coat, whom he had not seen before, handed the professor a second-class ticket to Shimbashi and an express ticket and told him that it was time. The professor paid his bill at the counter and when he went out, the same man went out ahead of him carrying his bag.

The compartment of the second-class carriage that the professor entered was quite full. One group was engrossed in eating something, even though it was perhaps only an hour since they had boarded in Kobe. Comparatively few spoke. Although there were the usual people sitting next to one another making themselves small, already this morning there were two or three men all stretched out. One had drawn his knees up, and in the place where he was stretching out both legs a lady with the hairstyle of a married woman had removed her wooden clogs and was sitting properly on her knees on the seat facing the window. The professor later discovered that she was the wife of the man who had his legs stuck out.

The professor was nearsighted to the degree that he preferred not to read on the train. He belonged to a *haiku* poetry association known as the Haku-jinkai, so he made it a point to think up *haiku* whenever he was on a train, but he was never able to accomplish one. That day was the same as always. After passing through Kyoto, the passengers fell silent and became like so much freight being carried by the train. Induced by monotonous nursery rhymes and other sounds, some began to doze off. At such times the professor always recalled the passage about the train in Zola's *Lourdes*. The story criticizes people for being wearisome, but he found such ennui interesting. The passage in which the train continues onward, where it is repeatedly described how the various hand baggage hung on ropes swings back and forth, had left a particularly strong impression on him. He admired the minuteness of detail, to the point of tediousness, of all of Zola's writings.

He began to feel sluggish of mind. When the train slowed in order to enter a station and then speeded up again after it had passed through, his body only felt it mechanically. This sensation was mixed with a certain unpleasantness, as if his body were being made sport of. From time to time, the steel-blue waters of Lake Biwa reflected in the train window, and after Sekigahara, the hillocks of gently sloped red earth lined with pines pressed in toward the train, then backed off, like a popular witty melody one has often heard, assaulting the dim consciousness, then in a flash completely disappearing. Occasionally pulled by whatever chain of images, he would recall his children in Tokyo. His imaginative powers were such that his children were clearly embodied right there before him. He was walking along Ginza with his daughter. She ran several yards ahead of him down the stone pavement, then turned around and laughed. Coming near an intersection, as soon as he told her to stop because it was dangerous, she would run ahead even faster and turn around and laugh. The maid stood outside the gate of their house holding the baby. Look at the child and say something, and the baby's eyes would grow narrow and the tip of his tongue would come out and he would smile. This smile was not merely that of pleasure. The Chinese have a word for it. They call it a "flattering smile." It is a social smile. To be sure, there were times when the baby smiled for such a reason. When the baby cried, the professor would gaze at his face and say something. The baby would immediately flash this regular smile, then immediately revert to his continuous crying.

When these fantasies arose, the professor almost always unconsciously sought to check them. Such daydreams, if given free rein, could lead to self-indulgence. It would be alarming if the muscles of his face were left to their own capriciousness of expression and he were to walk along the road with a big grin on his face.

As the train continued on near Nagoya, the professor went into the dining car. He always said that when he rode on a train for a long time he became queasy because of cigarette smoke. He thought that way because he himself did not smoke, and although it was not entirely because of smoke, he would get a headache. It was about time for the headache to set in, so when he went to the dining car, he began to feel better. He ate something and drank •ome Hiranosui carbonated water. He was a difficult person to please, for if just one part of a meal that was served to him was something he disliked, he would find the whole meal unsatisfactory. Fortunately no such item appeared.

In the afternoon, he put away his glasses, pulled his overcoat tightly around himself, leaned back against his seat, and closed and opened his eyes lazily. The same hour seemed to get longer and longer. Still, he refrained from yawning. He did not restrain himself because of others. In the sense of the expression commonly used that one respects oneself or one deludes oneself, he refrained from yawning in deference to himself.

Once the sun set, the passengers began to fidget. Repeatedly they would take out a watch and look at it, and every time the train passed through a lighted station without stopping, they would wonder whether perhaps it had been Hiratsuka or Hodogaya. Whenever he began to want to look at his own watch, he would reflect upon the fact that it was useless to do so, and end up not looking.

The train slowly came to a halt in the broad, sparsely lit, half-animated, half-desolate Shimbashi station. He returned to his home in Komagome in the especially cold Tokyo night.

From the postcard he had sent from Shikoku, his family knew approximately when he would be returning, but he felt it was a waste to send a telegram, so as a result they knew neither at what hour or even on what day he would come home. By the time the rickshaw he took from the station reached Nishikata, the house had already fallen quiet. The lady of the house brought a lamp from her own room into her husband's study. The maid took his bag and carried it to his study. His wife brought him a change of clothes, and said as she lighted the lamp in the study, "I thought you would be returning before too much longer, but I didn't know it would be this evening, so in a short while we were all going to go to bed."

"How are the children?"

"They are both sound asleep. The baby has been coughing a little since yesterday, but I have been keeping him as warm as possible, hoping he would get over it before your return. He just coughs every now and then."

"I see."

The professor did not give it much heed. His wife inquired whether he would like for her to heat the bath, but he said that wouldn't be necessary and asked her to just bring him some hot water for the washbasin, then washed himself and went to bed.

The following day was Sunday, January 12. The professor was looking through the mail that had arrived in his absence. His big-eyed daughter, Yuri, was delighted at her father's return and was romping about. His wife washed the baby's face and brought him in. She said that the previous night when he woke to be fed he coughed once or twice, but his color was good and he seemed to be in quite good spirits. The professor grasped his little hand and said, "Hansu, Hansu, what a good boy!" As he gazed at his son, the baby looked at his father's face for a while, then his eyes narrowed and his mouth rounded like it did when he drank milk, the tip of his tongue appeared, and he broke into a wide smile.

Professor Ono had given his children names that could be taken both as Japanese and as Western names. His daughter's Japanese name "Yuri" was for "Julie." He had named his son "Hans," or "Hansu" in Japanese. The origin of the name was Professor Ono's reading of a certain Chinese literatus who mentioned that his son-in-law was named Hansu. The professor simply borrowed the characters. Yuri loved fairy tales, and she had heard the German story of Hansel and Gretel from her father. When she heard that the baby would be named Hansu, she was delighted and said, "So then he can come with me to get rid of the old witch."

The professor asked his wife, "Is he drinking milk all right?"

"Yes, he's always impatient for it and gulps it down, and he is always fussy because it isn't enough for him. I wondered if perhaps I should increase the amount a little, so I asked Dr. Nishida, but he said that no matter how much you feed a healthy baby it will always want more, so it is not wise to give more than the prescribed amount."

This particular Nishida was an assistant of Professor Hirosawa at the university, and the Ono family always consulted with him in matters related to the children.

After noon the sky cleared and it was warm, so Yuri was in the garden playing on the swing. The professor sat on the veranda happily watching her in her peach-pink printed silk muslin coat, her beautiful thick hair fluttering as she swung so high that the rope stretched almost horizontally.

On Monday the professor went to the university for the first time in quite a while. He was responsible for teaching several levels of students and since he had to teach even language to the underclassmen, he went to the university every day. Almost half of the students who had gone home for the holidays had yet to return, so classes were quite deserted. He taught his classes in the aforementioned unsatisfactory manner and returned home in the evening.

His wife awaited him with a somewhat uneasy expression on her face.

"Dr. Nishida was here. He left just a moment ago. He says that the baby's cough seems spasmodic and although he can't say anything definite yet it would be best not to keep him together with Yuri."

"Hmm. Sounds like it might be whooping cough then."

"It may not be whooping cough, but it's best to be cautious. He says that there are a lot of children from the Hongō area in the university hospital. More precisely, he said he recommended putting the baby in the hospital and asked us to give serious consideration to the possibility."

His reserved, pale-complexioned wife opened her eyes wide like Yuri often did and looked at him as if hoping for encouragement. The professor knew nothing about medical practitioners, so he could hardly second-guess Nishida, who was a medical school graduate. At that point he did his best to hide from his wife as much as possible the uneasiness that was creeping up on him.

Their residence consisted of two separate buildings connected by a corridor, so they put Yuri in the professor's study, and his wife and baby moved across the corridor. The professor often went to the other part of the house to peek in. Whenever Yuri looked as if she might try to follow him, he would either humor her or scold her and go on alone. When he checked up on Hansu, he could see that the child would cough four or five times in succession and then wheeze between coughs. That's what Nishida referred to as spasmodic. However, he was still drinking milk in great quantities and had a good bowel movement. Except for the cough there was nothing unusual.

Four or five days passed in this manner. The professor worried about the children each day between the time when he left for the university and the time he came home in the evening. The baby's cough became progressively worse. The coughs came in tens, followed by hard crying. When the professor looked in on him, the child would always look at his father who would say, "Good boy, good boy," and then smile. Smile, and then start crying again. Administering the medicine was always easy. The child drank a lot of milk and whatever medicine one put in the glass milk bottle he would drink with no trouble at all. If one put powdered medicine on the nipple of the bottle, he would unconcernedly suck on that, too. At any rate, from all appearances it seemed that this small body was filled with vigor and strength.

When the professor was out, Yuri was left in her father's study accompanied unwillingly by the young maid to prevent her from following her mother around. She was extremely happy when her father returned home each day, but despite her young years she wore an expression of anxiety. When the professor told her that she must not begin coughing like her baby brother so she was not to go near him, she would gaze at her father's face and nod repeatedly.

There were only two maids in the professor's home. One did the cooking; the other was a young girl. The younger one had taken care of the baby until he got sick and she was the one who became Yuri's companion. As time passed, however, his wife was not getting enough sleep at nights, so it became necessary to call in someone else to give her some relief. In the professor's home, at such times they called on the services of a woman named O-ei. She was the daughter of a samurai family of the former Oshi domain and had once married, thanks to the professor's efforts. However, the man she married failed to pass the dental medicine examination he had aimed for and eventually ruined himself, so she had relinquished all rights and properties and separated from him and become a midwife. She was thirty-seven or thirty-eight, a woman of admirable character, and had an interesting face. There is a children's game called *fuku-warai*. On a piece of drawing paper are drawn the contours of a round-faced woman called O-kame. Children blindfold themselves in turn and place her nose and eyes within the contours on the paper. O-ei's face was cute, but as someone said, there was something about her eyes and nose that seemed as if someone who was blindfolded had placed them where they were. But that was when she was younger. Gradually, as she grew older, there congealed in her face the expression of a very resourceful, strong-willed person and absolutely nothing odd remained. This woman came to stay in the house and take turns looking after the baby during the night.

Although the patient was a mere babe, the detached sickroom was a rather serious affair. Even when the child was not sick, just feeding him sterilized cow's milk required a complex nursing bottle. On top of that, they had brought in an inhalator, which they used with the baby repeatedly. When they did not have him on the inhalator, they put a metal basin on the brazier to humidify the room. When it was time for milk they gave him a variety of medicines mixed with it. It was hardly an easy thing to do. His wife was doing her utmost and it would have been hard for an ordinary nurse to have done as well. The only one who could have done it was O-ei.

At any rate, while all this was going on, it became the twentieth of January. When the professor came home from school, he was informed of a detestable new development. Yuri had coughed. It had been only once or twice, but that was how it had been with Hansu in the beginning. The professor did not have the courage to contradict the alarm in his wife's manner of speaking. Yuri herself was frisking about, however, boisterous as always, and that was at least some consolation.

Supper appeared. Leaving the baby in the care of O-ei, the other three members of the family sat down to eat. "Oh, rolled cabbage!" Yuri said as she took up her chopsticks. It was her favorite vegetable. She took one bite, then started coughing. She only coughed three or four times, but for some reason she fell over on her back on the floor, as if she had been struck by lightning, her tightly clenched fists pressed against her chest, and started to cry. "What's the matter?" asked her mother as she embraced Yuri and raised her up. By that time the coughing had already stopped, but Yuri said she did not want to eat anymore and simply cried softly. Neither husband nor wife felt like eating either, so they immediately took Yuri to the study, fixed a bed for her, and put her in it.

His wife said that she would give Yuri some milk and went to prepare it. The professor stayed at his daughter's side. She was not in very good condition. This perpetually energetic child was sleeping exhaustedly, like one who has endured a long illness. His wife brought in the milk she had prepared and tried to get Yuri to drink a little. But Yuri was not interested in milk.

The professor's wife mentioned that Nishida was planning to come the next day anyway and, thinking that there might be something he could do for Yuri, she sent a neighborhood rickshaw man to get him. While she was talking, Yuri at last finished drinking the milk, but then the coughing came, and the crying, and finally she vomited all the milk she had just drunk. She was crying as before with her fists clenched tight against her chest. "Now, now, it'll be all right," said the professor, trying to comfort his daughter. But in his heart he was feeling just the opposite.

After it had grown dark, Nishida, the medical school graduate, arrived. While he was examining Yuri, the father and mother were at her side, having left the baby completely in O-ei's care. The tapping of the chest and stethoscope examination done, Nishida was taking her temperature when the professor spoke.

"How is she?"

"Well . . . ," Nishida said, in thought, and then Yuri coughed again. When the mother made as if to rub her back, Yuri complained. It seemed as if it was painful to be touched. Her mother straightened the thermometer and gently held it in place.

Nishida continued, "It's whooping cough."

"It came on much faster than in Hansu's case. Why do you think that is?"

"I'm not sure. At any rate she's quite a bit older, so the prognosis for her is probably good."

"I guess you're right. She's bigger so she can undergo any kind of treatment. Aren't there some special measures that can be taken?"

"I'm afraid the only way is to treat the symptoms. So far no one has discovered a medicine that is especially effective in treating whooping cough, so they let it run its natural course and just treat the symptoms."

"Isn't there some type of new medicine or something?"

"Well, yes, there's Pertussin, and then there's Tussol, but they still have low efficacy, and doctors like Dr. Hirosawa are not using them."

"Is that so? I say this without partiality toward Hansu or Yuri, but since Yuri is already this big, I hope you will do everything possible for her. If there are new medicines, whether or not they have been clearly shown to be effective, as long as they are not obviously harmful, please have her take anything that might be good for her."

"All right. I will inquire about new medicines, too."

Nishida took out the thermometer, looked at it, and said she had no fever. He then gave instructions to Mrs. Ono to take care of Yuri in the same way she was doing with Hansu, wrote out three prescriptions and handed them over, then thought for a moment.

"I really do think it would be preferable to put them both in the hospital."

The professor considered this for a moment, then replied that he would prefer to engage a nurse and try caring for them at home.

Saying that he would inquire about new medicines, Nishida went out to use a phone at the home of one of the neighbors. The professor hired a rickshaw for going to get the medicine. His wife prepared compresses. They brought the inhalator from Hansu's room and had Yuri use it. In the meantime, Nishida returned. At the pharmacies in the Hongō area, he said, there were no new medicines that the university did not regularly administer. He said that he had at long last located some Pertussin at Shiseidō. The professor immediately sent the rickshaw man to Shiseidō in Ginza.

After Nishida departed, saying that he would come again the next day, the professor moved the desk from his study to another room and had Hansu moved in together with Yuri. Once it had been diagnosed that both had whooping cough, it seemed that putting them together in the study, the largest room in the house, would make for less trouble. Although Yuri had for a long time been wanting to see the baby, when she was laid down near him at last she did not have enough energy to be glad. Fortunately, eating the rice gruel that her mother had fixed and brought in somehow agreed with her.

The study, which faced south, became a virtual hospital. On the east side of the north-facing room to which the professor's desk had been moved was a small room that opened on the corridor. In this room was stored all the paraphernalia that the patients might need. The professor and his wife spread bedding, one in the study where the children slept and one in the north room where the desk had been put, and they took turns napping in one room and taking care of the children in the other. They did this because in the study, even if they lay down tired, they really could not fall asleep.

The following day when the professor returned home from the university, the nurse had come. She had been born in the Sakaha area and was an acquaintance of O-ei's. She was not very formal and seemed a sensible woman. Her name was Fujie. Since the nurse had arrived, O-ei went out to make the rounds of her various clients. Reasonably enough, when she came home in the evening, she said that she had given each family the telephone number of the professor's neighbor in the event that they should suddenly need her assistance in a delivery.

The condition of the two patients did not change. Although it was the twelfth day since Hansu had begun coughing, he had not grown thinner but was plump and there was strength in his voice when he cried. He drank milk

vigorously, as usual, and his stool was normal. Yuri had commenced coughing only the day before, but even her appearance had changed, like that of
someone seriously ill. She accomplished all of her excremental functions on
a chamber pot and made no effort to get out of bed. The professor avoided
looking at Hansu, but whenever Yuri coughed in pain he comforted her as
best he could. His wife asked him, "Why don't you pay the least attention
to Hansu?" He answered, "Because he's too young to be comforted," but
actually it was because he could not endure to see the baby try to smile even
in his pain when someone spoke to him.

In the evening O-ei returned. His wife said that they should leave things
to Fujie that night, go to sleep in the detached section, and from then on
take turns, but there had developed a certain customary way of doing things
and, saying it would be just for that night, sure enough she ended up staying with the children.

The professor was still worried on the twenty-second but went to the university anyhow, and when he returned home everything was much the same.
To the professor, neither Yuri, who had been in bad condition from the
onset, nor Hansu, who had been sick now for a long time, seemed to be getting the least bit better. He just thought it would be fortunate if they did
not grow worse.

"The baby," his wife said, "has been sick for thirteen days now, so there
are less than ninety days remaining. Yuri has still a full hundred days to go,
so I feel sorry for her." The professor replied that one could see things that
way, but even though the illness was, in Japanese, called the "hundred-day
cough" that meant it was a long illness and did not necessarily take one hundred days to run its course. He said this out of a desire to offer comfort, but
his voice did not convey his intention.

The professor noticed a piece of red flannel material on the edge of the
futon pulled up on each child and asked his wife about them.

"What are those red pieces of cloth?"

His wife answered, looking briefly at the nurse, "I realized that you
would be displeased, but those are pieces that have been offered in prayer to
Kompira."

Having said this and paused, she went on. The neighboring Professor
Takayama's wife realized that Yuri had not recently gone to play with
Otama, one of her friends, so she had come the day before to pay a visit. The
lady had recommended that she go to offer a prayer to Kompira. Since it
had been morning and Fujie had not yet come, she could not leave things,
but Mrs. Takayama had kindly offered to go instead. The pieces of cloth that
she had prayed over had been delivered that very morning.

At the outset, his wife said she knew she might be scolded, but at such times the professor said nothing. Somewhere or other he had read a metaphor about robbing a beggar of his rags and not having silk to give in exchange. Whatever the superstition, one has to offer some superior belief to replace it. Since he did not have such within himself, he could not scold her. And yet to nod and say he approved would have made him feel that he was surrendering his grounds as a scholar, and at other times he would have laughed or poked fun. On the surface, her way of speaking had made it seem that she had been induced by someone else and had simply no way out. But when he perceived that in actuality she half-believed and half-doubted and that there was a certain degree of hope attached to these pieces of cloth, he felt sympathy with her, and that day he neither laughed nor made fun. The professor listened in silence.

She continued, prefacing her comments by saying she realized she was still just rambling on. She said that on the tenth, the day the baby had begun coughing, she had had a dream. She said that in her dream she had taken the two children with her to the public bath and that somehow or other they had both fallen into the bath and drowned. Out of their minds with the shock, she and the maid, carrying the limp children in their arms, went to the house of Dr. Futoi, who lived right next door to the bathhouse. He was a doctor that they had in reality gone to every now and then when one of the children had caught cold or something. In her dream the doctor had accepted the children, told the women to wait a while, and carried the children into the back of the house. They waited a long time and at length a sliding door opened and out came Yuri. Following her came the doctor carrying in his arms the baby who was stiff as a board. "Your daughter," the doctor explained, "was big enough that she was able to come back to life, but the baby was not." When she woke up and thought about the dream, she recalled that in the afternoon of that very day, when she had taken the children to the bath and was washing the baby, there was a child nearby who was coughing a lot. After they had returned home, the baby had started to cough.

She continued, "It's such a trifling, but Dr. Nishida is such a kindhearted person that I even mentioned my dream to him. According to him, we can't let either one die, so he couldn't say whether mine was a dream that prophesied the truth or one that prophesied the opposite."

As one might expect, the professor listened quietly, but in his heart he had an odd feeling. There was no doubt that since dreams are bound by neither time nor space, one could see any kind of dream. But the dream she had had was one that might have been fabricated by an old-style novelist.

On January 10, he had arrived at Kotohira and had gone into an inn at the foot of Mt. Zōzu, and when Ogawa had tried to persuade him to spend the night and pay a visit to the temple of Kompira-sama the next day, he had made a point of departing without going to the temple. On that exact day the baby had gone to the bath and started coughing. That was to say, the baby had caught a cold at the bathhouse, but there had been at the bath a child with what seemed to be whooping cough, and the baby had since developed the illness. On top of that, his wife had seen a dream that very night which prophesied that Yuri would come down with the same illness. It was even a dream of disaster, involving water in which they drowned. In the modern day if one were to write such things in a novel, unlike the tales of retribution of a century earlier in which no one would raise a stir about such bothersome foreshadowing, the author would be in great trouble. His wife, when she read at all, only read books by popular writers such as Ozaki Kōyō and Kosugi Tengai. After graduating from school, she never looked back over history or geography, so fortunately she did not realize that on his way to Kōchi he had to pass through Kotohira or that Kotohira was the head temple of Kompira. Anyhow, he would not mention to her anything about the events at Kotohira.

That night, since they had let the nurse sleep during the daytime, O-ei went to the detached room to sleep. Yuri accepted the gruel that evening well and her coughing was relatively mild. The baby continued with no change.

A day later, on the twenty-fourth, when the professor came home from the university, things seemed changed—melancholy, but agitated. Everyone was speaking in a lower voice than usual. Yet everyone seemed to bustle about more than usual. The professor had no idea what was going on, but his heart palpitated. When he entered the children's sickroom, Yuri was breathing harshly and with great discomfort. Since she had collapsed in pain in the midst of dinner on the twentieth, her cute face had exhibited a pained expression without cease. One almost wanted to say that pain was engraved on her face. The engraving seemed one layer deeper.

The professor wondered what was going on, but he was afraid to voice his questions and have to hear the replies, and since even his throat tightened, he just stood there in silence. Finally, his wife, with a gloomy voice, began to describe the changes in the children's respective conditions. Nishida had said that Yuri's breathing had grown worse and when he examined her more carefully he said there was a slight touch of bronchial pneumonia. Her temperature was thirty-eight degrees centigrade, which was low for pneumonia. Nishida also examined the baby carefully. He seemed to have the same symptoms. His temperature was over thirty-nine degrees centigrade. Nishida changed the medicine for both of them and said that since Yuri was older he could apply a mustard plaster to her chest. They had just removed that and applied a damp compress. Sooner or later, Nishida said, they should have Professor Hirosawa take a look at the children, too. Nishida himself had gone home for the time being, but had said he would come back later to spend the night.

The professor peeked at the baby, and sure enough the child was breathing rapidly. To the uninformed eye, there was no great change. He then took a quick look at Yuri. Between coughs, the regular breaths had become clearly more rapid and one heard a constant harsh vibrating sound. It sounded like a wheeze. Seeing that in addition to the pain which had until then appeared on her face she could not breathe comfortably even between coughs, he knew that she must really be in pain, and an unendurable feeling came over him. Yuri had been dozing, but while the professor was watching her intently she opened her eyes. "It hurts now," he said, "but it will be better soon, so let's be patient, let's be patient." With a tormented look on her face, Yuri nodded. "I feel so sorry for her," his wife said, "because she is so well behaved." His wife could not hide the tears in her voice.

That night they brought bedding into the neighboring room on the east side and had Nishida sleep there. The man was quite unreserved, and telling them to wake him if there was any change, he lay down and promptly fell asleep. Even at that, they both felt reassured.

The following day, the twenty-fifth, was Saturday. The professor came home at noon and from then through Sunday the twenty-sixth he watched the condition of the two children. The baby's temperature rose to forty degrees centigrade. Still his appearance changed hardly at all. He drank his milk well, and when he defecated he would make a little grunt as he put strength into his legs and produced a firm stool. Even when he cried, there was strength in his voice and he cried vigorously. It almost struck the uneducated eye as strange that the child was seriously ill with whooping cough complicated by pneumonia. In contrast, from the very first day of illness Yuri had worn a single expression that the professor had felt was engraved with pain, but now there was swelling in her face, her uncommonly big eyes had grown narrower, and she no longer seemed the same child. Her face was not all that had changed. Her voice, too, was entirely different. When she was in pain, she would sometimes say one word at a time, tending toward voiced sounds with long drawn out vowels. Naturally it was hard to catch what she was trying to say, but she did not say anything particularly unfamiliar, so one could usually understand her. But there was one sad occasion when they misunderstood her. On Saturday night, when the professor was at her side, Yuri said something. The nurse had understood her to say that she wanted to relieve herself and had slipped in the bedpan. Yuri was normally a long-suffering child, but as a result of her illness she had lost her staying power, and unable to bear any more, she broke down into tears. After some cajoling they got her to say again what she wanted. What she had said was that she wanted "something." When she was well and said she wanted "something," they would give her something she liked, such as a chocolate with cream in it. But that time when they gave her one, she was disappointed that it didn't taste good, and left it half-eaten.

On Sunday, when the professor's wife was writing to her mother in Kumamoto to notify her about the children's illness for the first time, Professor Hirosawa dropped in for a short while. He said that he had heard all of the details from Nishida, looked at the children briefly, said something to Nishida, and left.

During the following week, the two children's critical condition continued unabated. If one had plotted the progress of their illness on a curved line, that line would have been generally upward, and once up, it would have continued along with no downward movement at all. All the while, there were minor fluctuations in both children—the right side of the chest would be worse than the left one day, the bad place would be spread more widely or more narrowly another day. In any circumstance, the baby's temperature every afternoon was fixed at forty degrees centigrade, and although Yuri had little fever, she could hardly conceal her continued pain. Neither child's cough improved at all. Their two small bodies seemed to be fighting illness just as hard as they could. The baby stopped demanding milk, but once it was offered he would drink heartily as always. Gradually he began to leave some milk in the baby bottle, however, which he had previously drunk dry. His stool was normal. They fed Yuri rice gruel a little at a time, to keep her from spitting it up, and when she started coughing they would wait a while until they thought she was all right and then give her a little more. Meanwhile they would make her some milk and assorted flavors of soup which she was not very fond of, and give that to her a little at a time. Her face had become swollen with dropsy, and it remained swollen.

January came to an end and the first of February arrived. It was Saturday and the professor again came home from school early and watched the children through the next day. By that time, Yuri's normally beautiful big eyes had not only become smaller, they had become bloodshot. He had been told that it resulted from the severe cough. The coughing certainly worsened. Just before the coughing started, she would cry, and once it commenced she said her whole body would become painfully itchy. Whether she tried to scratch or stroke, there was a compress on her chest, so she could not move as she wished. After Nishida examined the baby, and after he examined Yuri, as well, he wore a silent, displeased expression on his face. In addition to the medicine he had been giving, he also injected the baby with Digalen. He said it was because the baby's pulse had grown a little weak. Whenever the baby felt the sudden prick of the needle, he would respond by kicking his legs out straight, just as he did when he had a bowel movement. His legs remained appealingly plump. Every time Nishida examined the two, their mother would ask again and again, "How are they? Will one of them survive?" Nishida always appeared rather distressed and prevaricated.

It was the morning of the fourth, two days after Sunday. O-ei said that she noticed the baby seemed a little swollen. The professor, who had been occupied in washing his face, replied, "Let me have a look," and went in to see. Although it was already twenty-six days since the onset of the illness, the child had not lost enough weight that anyone would notice. When he turned over the child's chubby hand and looked at the palm, the tendons and muscles that were always visible had disappeared and the skin was stretched flat. He then looked at the child's feet. He looked at the child's face. If one looked carefully, even a nonspecialist could detect a swelling all over the baby's body. The baby remained pudgy to that day without losing weight and ultimately swelling had appeared.

Though anxious, the professor went to the university. When he arrived home in the evening and went in to where the children were, the baby was not there. He was startled and his wife said, "We put him in there," pointing to the small room where Nishida had been sleeping. He thought the child had finally died, as he had expected it might, but that was not the case. It had simply been ascertained that the baby *might* die. Just as in a large hospital ward they put screens around patients that have been given up on, the baby had been moved to the adjacent room.

The professor went to see the baby. While she prepared the baby's milk and put on the nipple, O-ei grumbled that Nishida had muttered to himself, while he was administering the shot of Digalen, that it was really not worth causing the baby any more pain. As always, the baby was noisily downing his milk. The swelling had not increased since the day before and his face was as cute as always. His eyes were clearly open. For this reason the professor could not help thinking that the mark of death had not been placed upon the child. Perhaps O-ei had intuited his thoughts. "But he has been taking only half of the milk," she said. The professor abruptly turned his back on the baby and went to where Yuri lay.

His wife asked where they should have Nishida sleep that night, so he had bedding brought and set out with his own in the north room. Through the night there was no change in Yuri or the baby's condition that warranted wakening Nishida.

The following day, the fifth, was the day Hansu finally died. The professor in his stubbornness had gone to the university. While he was out, he was later told, Nishida had administered camphor both by injection and internally, and as he left he said, "He will hold out until the professor returns." O-ei, who was again that day at the baby's side, called to the professor's wife, who was at Yuri's side, "The baby cannot be saved," at the very same instant that the professor was removing his shoes in the entrance. The professor stood as he had arrived—still wearing his hat, glasses, and overcoat—before the light-blue *futon* with whitish crane-and-tortoise design which had for a long time enwrapped small and great pains, and watched the last breath feebly escape from the just now paled lips of the charming face from which even such a dread illness had not been able to take away the charm.

O-ei was silent and her eyes were cast down. His wife called, "Hansu. Hansu." But she suppressed her tearful voice, so as not to be heard by Yuri in the next room. Although the professor had contemplated how very sad it would be if his son were to die, he was shocked at how exceedingly shallow and insignificant his grief now seemed. It was as if he felt none of the deep sorrow he had expected. He felt simply that his sense of empty loneliness was somewhat sharper than usual. At the same time, the scene in the room struck him with vivid, objective, dreadful clarity. On the brazier, which emanated only a weak heat since they had neglected to add more charcoal, lay a metal basin. Faint traces of steam rose like entangling threads from the murky water that had been boiling. There were various medicines for internal use and others for injection lying on several trays. There was also a bottle of Digalen in a cardboard box which had just been opened. The child had been unable to keep the nipple of the baby bottle in his mouth since that morning and so some of the milk remained in a small teacup. O-ei had soaked a piece of bleached cotton cloth in it and then given it to him to suck. On top of a small wooden trunk were piled several of the baby's diapers. Pale O-ei gazed down upon the chubby face of the baby who seemed as though he were merely sleeping peacefully. The face of his wife was red from weeping. And he himself stood nearby. He saw them all so clearly and with cool indifference as if they were merely characters on a stage. He felt intensely displeased to see himself standing there as if he were a mere bystander.

He spoke to his wife.

"I have a little idea, so please leave the baby just as he is."

The professor hurriedly put on his shoes and went out of the house. He headed to the home of a sculptor named Ishida whom he knew well, who lived below the bridge at the foot of the slope below Nishikata-machi. Ishida was seated at dinner with a drink in his hand. "Well, well, this is quite a surprise," he said with a smile in greeting. Hearing the professor's tale, however, he straightened up in an instant, for he realized how great the pain must have been that had driven the professor to come to him. The professor asked him to make a death mask. Ishida had his assistant carry the container of plaster of paris and cloth and walked home with the professor. Hansu's face seemed as if he were alive, so the professor thought a mask could be made to look just that way, but when the mask was completed, because the lips remained open due to the mouth being overstuffed with cotton, it was a pitiful image.

They changed the baby into a black crepe outfit with the family crest, which he had worn at the time they took him to the shrine, and laid him down on a hurriedly sewn together muslin *futon*. They lost no time in placing a candlestand and an incense burner at the foot of his pillow and smoke rose from the incense sticks.

The following day, the sixth, the professor went to the university. He had taken care of his classes automatically as he usually did, so he had gotten through them without difficulty. Until the preceding day he had been troubled in the depths of his mind. But on this day, though there ought to have been some anxiety concerning Yuri, who was now alone, and sorrow about Hansu, who was no longer alive, unexpectedly there was neither. He merely felt that his mind was empty, as if it had become a void; he no longer felt even the worry he had felt the previous day. He had until then said nothing at all to anyone about his children's illness and he thought to himself that probably no one noticed any change at all in his speech or deportment.

At the normal time of day, the professor returned home abstracted. He came in from the entrance and when he passed by the room where the baby's remains were, one of the *shōji* was open and he could see the bedding in the shadow of the screen. One of the students he had become friendly with sat dressed in *hakama* along the side of the room, turning over the pages of a magazine. He was probably being sure that the incense did not stop burning.

The professor came to the north room, and out of the study where Yuri lay came his pale-faced wife. She rose as she spoke.

"I had the funeral people put the things they brought in the detached rooms. Mr. Makino will come this evening and go to the crematory."

This Makino she spoke of was an old man who had been a steward in the household of the lord of the professor's former feudal domain. The professor nodded in silence. He then went to glance into Yuri's room, but it seemed that there had been no change.

The professor was in the main room eating dinner when Makino came. Makino was a punctilious old man with graying hair. He brought the paraphernalia from the detached part of the house into the study where the lifeless child lay. On the plain wood table he placed a white cotton cloth, had the mother get out the child's photograph and put it right in the middle, then aligned it with the low table which had the candlestand and incense burner. He was ready to lay the baby in the small casket. The professor had hastily finished dinner and when, together with his wife, he went in to witness the final moments, she looked at her husband and at Makino and said, most awkwardly, "I'd like to hold him just once more."

"Of course."

It was Makino who spoke. The professor nodded silently. His wife, self-conscious as a young girl, gently picked up the baby, pressed him to her breast as she had when he was alive, kept him there for a short while, then without a word put him back down on the *futon*. The young student, who until then had been observing all of this, thinking who knew what, abruptly excused himself and ran out. The polite professor hurriedly went to the entrance to see him off, but he wasn't in time. Old man Makino picked up the lifeless body of the child from where she had put him down, and when, in her stead, he put the baby into the casket, tears shone on his wrinkled, dark-red cheeks. When Makino had the men he had brought with him carry out the coffin, his wife opened the door of the room and from there she watched the paper lantern of the small party until it disappeared in the distance.

On the seventh, the professor went to school, but his anxiety over how Yuri was doing came and went through his head as it had before. His mind had recovered enough that he could be worried. When he forgot for a moment what had happened to the baby, he tried to deny the fact that he had died, and was struck by a lonely, uncomfortable feeling.

When the professor returned home and went into the room where the desk had been put, Yuri was continuing to cry in a voice that was singularly lower than ever before. He quickly took off his overcoat, threw it down, threw his hat on top of that, and slid open the door. Yuri's face was in such pain that it was almost too much to look at, and there intermittently escaped from her mouth, which seemed stretched open at the corners, an indescribable cry. One look at her face and what he had until that day thought to be the extreme countenance of pain no longer seemed that way.

His wife, who was at the child's side, finally raised her head. Her face was even more pale and her eyes all the larger.

"She has really put up with a lot. A little while ago when it was really bad she did this to my arm."

His wife rolled up her sleeve and showed her arm to the professor. Welts had been raised on her upper arm. Carried away by the pain, Yuri had scratched her mother.

"What did Nishida say?"

"He said it's uremia. Whatever, it's quite . . . ," she stopped in mid-sentence, looking at Yuri and falling silent. Her eyes were tearful. Through the period of a month that the two children's illness had continued, in this weak female breast, which had embraced incomprehensible suffering, the only request she had made was that Yuri, being older, might survive. Her body had fallen into the abyss of suffering and it clung with all its might to that hope like a drowning woman to a floating branch of a tree. There could be no doubt, moreover, that her mysterious dream had encouraged that hope. And now was the moment that this woman's cramped, thin fingers were reluctantly beginning to release their grasp on the floating branch.

The professor stood looking intensely at Yuri and as he did her crying became intermittent and changed to rattle-suffused rapid breathing. Yuri opened her eyes slightly, stared off into space, and said, "Look. A bug is coming." She frowned and made as if to shoo it away. When his wife in displeasure looked around the room and said, "There aren't any bugs in here," the professor made motions of swatting at something and said, "I'll drive them away. Out with you!" The professor had once taken care of a certain male relative who had developed a severe case of typhoid fever, and he had seen the man talking in delirium. But the man had never said such things. The professor thought that it might be what are called hallucinations or optical illusions, so he pretended that he could see them in order to comfort her.

Nishida came after it grew dark, and the professor asked him to step into the room on the east side, thinking he would ask about Yuri. Smoke from the incense hung over the table upon which lay the urn wrapped in white cloth that bore the ashes that had been brought back from the crematory, together with the photograph. Stirring up the coals in the brazier in one corner of the room, the professor looked at the other man and asked simply, "How is the situation?" For a moment Nishida was silent. When he answered, it was simple and in a deliberate tone. "It does not look good."

"The uremia?"

"Actually there is no assurance about that. That really bad spell this afternoon seemed to me to be caused by a headache. And it seemed to me at the time that her arms cramped. I sort of mumbled something to myself about how it might be uremia, and your wife heard what I said. With uremia, there is usually a real spasm or incessant vomiting or the like."

"In that case, when you say it doesn't look good, what makes you think so? Has she developed a fever?"

"Her temperature has remained low. Today she had only thirty-eight degrees centigrade, for some reason the area of the lung that has the inflammation has not shrunk, and the heart is a cause for concern. After all, we've been using digitalis off and on for a long time now."

"Hmm. In any event, please do whatever you can for her as long as there is any hope."

"Of course. Perhaps you should have Dr. Hirosawa come tomorrow and look at her."

"If you think that would be best, I will speak to him."

"That won't be necessary. I can ask him to drop by on his way to work tomorrow. He is a person who dislikes formalities."

"In that case, please do ask for us."

Their conversation ended there.

That evening they changed Yuri's compress while the professor was in the room, so he saw her naked body for the first time in a long while. He felt all the more keenly astonished. The place where her legs, which looked like thin stems of hemp, connected with the angular bones of her pelvis looked just like a plucked chicken, so it appeared as if her dropsy-swollen face were somehow connected at the neck to another child's body. She had been having compresses for so long that she had developed a red rash on her chest and back. It must have been itchy every time the coughing started. Unable to stand there looking, he turned his eyes away.

The eighth was a Saturday. It was the day Dr. Hirosawa was coming by, so the professor returned home after noon, wondering what had occurred. He hurried into Yuri's room and saw that his wife's face was pale and her eyes swollen and rimmed with red. He called her to the next room and questioned her in a low voice.

"What did Dr. Hirosawa say?"

Tears rolled down her cheeks.

"There's nothing that can be done to save her. He said it might be one day or maybe two."

"Hmm."

Words failed him. His wife went on.

"I don't know why it is, but although I felt so sorry about the baby, the feelings I had weren't yet so strong. But when I think about what it would be like if Yuri were to die, it is just unbearable. Next year she is supposed to start school. What would it be like, after it's all over, to look at the letters of the syllabary or pictures she had drawn with a pencil? And then there are all the memories of various occasions that one could hardly keep from recalling. Or remember how last year when we went to the exhibition how she darted on past us, and then turned back and smiled. . . . To remember such things later would be so heartrending I just don't know if I could bear it."

His wife sobbed convulsively. The professor spoke as if he had struck upon something.

"I wish I could tell you not to talk such nonsense, but in reality I have the same feeling. In any case, in contrast to the baby, there are so many memories remaining. There are her little straw sandals with red thongs in the entrance. There are things in every room, like dolls and little pieces of clothing. When the time came to hear that she was not going to make it, I just could not endure to see those things. One looks at those sandals and thinks that she'll never wear them again. One looks at the dolls and knows that she'll never walk around carrying them again, either. Each time it happens, it strikes a nerve. While she is alive we ought to cherish to the utmost every single hour and minute, but we should also collect together every single reminder scattered here and there and put them away as soon as possible. It would be best to hide them away in a place we never look into."

The professor actually felt what he said, but mixed in was also a slight stratagem. He was considering it one way to confer on his wife a mechanical task to carry out, as a way of diverting her attention.

In fact, she immediately did begin to gather together Yuri's things. And of her own accord she called in O-ei, had her go in to Yuri, and she herself walked around the house collecting together all the things the professor had referred to as "reminders."

The professor went out to the main room, and just as he was eating dinner old man Makino stopped by, having finished his work at the residence. He came by intending to assist with the preparations for the baby's funeral. The professor sent Makino home, saying that he wanted to think things over and that he would do it within a few days. Within two or three days Yuri would be ashes, too. He thought they could then inter both children at the same time.

Curiously, that night Yuri slept peacefully. She coughed occasionally and that woke her up each time, but she went right back to a sound sleep. The professor concluded that it was because she was so exhausted.

The next day, Sunday, the professor did not leave Yuri's side from morning on, but contrary to expectations, there was no change in her condition. In the morning when the nurse started to change her compress, Yuri as always put on a pained expression.

Watching close by, the professor thought for a moment, then said, "Let's leave it off for a while." Fujie, the nurse, was of an obedient nature and withdrew her hands. His wife stared at the professor's face. Abstracted as she was, even she realized immediately that since there was no hope left there was no reason to cause Yuri any more irritation.

Yuri mumbled something. When her mother asked what she had said, Yuri said very clearly, "If we leave off the compress, I won't get better." The professor and his wife started. At the same moment a dreadful feeling brushed past their hearts, as if they had done some evil deed in secret and been found out. Yuri really disliked the compresses and in the beginning she had fought having them applied, so they had told her that if she did not have them she would not get well. So when she realized that they were going to stop the compresses, she wanted them to put one on. The professor had the nurse apply it.

Whether or not it was because he had heard the doctor's verdict, Nishida did not appear even in the afternoon. Yuri had had only milk in the morning and as always ate a little gruel. After she had eaten, she said, "I want something."

"I'll give you some mandarin orange," said her mother. She peeled the rind and removed the strings from the segments. When Yuri took a segment, she carefully removed the few remaining strings of skin.

Watching the way Yuri used her hands, her mother spoke to the professor. "She has that much strength."

As might be expected, his wife had spoken in defense of Yuri's life. While the professor thought her notion was no more than that of a novice, he was unable to restrain her from a certain hopefulness.

In the afternoon, after Yuri coughed, she spit up a lot of something that looked like foam. "Oh dear," her mother said. Fujie wiped it up with a gauze, saying, "This is the first time that so much has come up."

It was time for the evening meal. O-ei prepared rice gruel in a small wide earthenware pot and brought it in. "The fire in there is down, so I've brought it in here," she said, handing it to the nurse. The nurse took it, removed the basin of water used for humidifying the room from the brazier, and put the pot in its place. Yuri said something. The professor was unable to catch what she said.

"Hmm? What did you say?"

Yuri fretfully repeated the same thing. The nurse by her side translated for her.

"She seems to be saying 'beef and onions'."

The professor had been unable to understand at all. He looked at Yuri and asked, "Do you want to eat beef and onions? Is that it?"

Yuri nodded. The professor and his wife looked at each other. They were astonished. The professor thought carefully for a minute. And when he spoke, there was a certain decisiveness in the tone of his voice.

"All right. We'll get you some beef and onions."

He quickly sent someone off to a Western-style restaurant nearby called Paradise. He sent instructions to grind up some top-quality roast and fry it like steak and add a side portion of tender onions sauteed in butter. The professor did not believe in the superstition of the red cloth attached to the top of Yuri's *futon*. That did not mean, however, that he had completely believed in the scientific restricted diet the doctor had prescribed. He knew nothing about health care or medical treatment, so he did what the doctor said. But he did not have absolute faith in it. So this morning he had attempted to stop the compresses. From the commencement of her swelling, her urine had decreased in quantity, and these days she was even diagnosed as possibly suffering from uremia, but the entire time, Yuri's stool had not changed at all. Since the doctor had given up on her surviving, however, even though it was beef and onions that she wanted, he saw no reason in automatically sticking to the restrictions. It was not that he had given no consideration at all to whether beef and onions would be all right. He had just quashed his doubts by telling himself that it would just be a bite or two.

The professor went back to Yuri and told her, "I sent out for it right this minute, so you wait just a little while." Yuri nodded once more. His wife watched his behavior in amazement. Of course, she understood he was letting her have it because, after all, she was going to die. But even though she realized that, and although Yuri had been given up on by the doctor, still there might be some way to save her, so she wanted to protect her from any possible risk at this point. But her heart was so exhausted that she just watched in feminine opposition, unable to put will into action. The nurse undoubtedly disapproved, but as a result of her own submissive nature she simply deferred to the professor and watched him silently.

After a while the beef and onions arrived. The professor called to O-ei, who had gone to the back door to help, and instructed her to warm the plate of food. The lid of the earthenware pot of gruel that had been placed on the brazier was bubbling up and down so the nurse removed the lid.

O-ei appeared and offered Yuri some of the gruel with the meat and onions. Yuri asked for a bite of each in turn. In the end she had eaten a third of the beef and although the portions of gruel had been small, she had asked for seconds. Her appetite was bigger than it had been for a long time.

Having let her eat, the professor was a little anxious about what would happen when she finished, but even when she coughed, she did not spit anything up and she seemed to digest the food all right. Later when Nishida came to stay the night, no one mentioned the beef and onions.

That was the beginning of Yuri's recovery from illness. From that time forward she improved day by day. Therefore, they quietly held a funeral for the baby. Finally on the tenth of March, Yuri, who had once seemed to have lost the use of her legs, was able to sit up in her bed and play with the toys that her mother brought out from the wicker trunk where she had hidden them away.

No matter how wise he may be, every doctor makes mistakes. In response to these events, the professor's wife told the wife of the neighbor, Professor Takayama, how her dream had portended the truth, and from then on the god of Kompira was worshiped even more devoutly by the women of both households. It would be better, however, if the would-be philosopher Professor Ono were not to become a devotee as well.

1909

Asobi

PLAY

PLAY IS A LOOK AT ŌGAI THROUGH THE WRONG end of a telescope. Casting himself as Kimura (a character who will later appear in *The Dining Room*), Ōgai belittles his own personal accomplishments in order to highlight those aspects of contemporary society he sets out to satirize. Within this framework, therefore, the important writer becomes a hack and the high government official is no more than a small cog in a large and uncomprehending bureaucratic machine. Kimura faces piles of documents, both at home and at work; his work is never done, and his only recourse is to treat everything as though it were a game. He takes refuge in fantasy, somewhat in the same fashion described, many generations later, and for different purposes, by James Thurber in "The Secret Life of Walter Mitty." Thurber's gentle satire, however, possesses a whimsy quite different from Ōgai's withering satire, which is written with great economy and is aimed directly at himself, his superiors, and modern Japanese society in general.

Kimura is a bit like Charlie Chaplin on the production line in the opening scene of *Modern Times;* both can no longer envision any meaningful role for the individual, and both use their own respective brands of acerbic wit to express their ironic visions of contemporary reality.

Kimura was a civil servant.

One morning he awoke at six as was his custom. It was the beginning of summer. It was already light, but the maid had refrained from opening the shutters of his room. Through the mosquito netting, the room where he slept appeared lonely in the light from a small lamp.

Automatically his hand searched around his pillow, feeling for his watch. It was a rather large nickel-plated one like those the Postal Ministry bought for its conductors. As always the hand was pointing exactly at six.

He called out, "How about opening the shutters?"

The maid came in, drying her hands, and opened the shutters. As it had for days, a light rain fell from the ashen sky. It was not hot, but the dampness of the air was palpable on his face.

The sleeves of her cotton kimono tucked up snugly with a sash, the maid slid the shutters back one by one into their storage compartment. Loose strands of hair clung to her forehead with sweat.

He thought to himself, "Another one of those days when it's hot just to move!" It was seven or eight blocks from the house he rented to the streetcar stop. It might seem cool enough when he left the house, he thought, but by the time he reached the stop, he'd be sweating.

Out on the veranda as he washed his face, he remembered the documents he had to hurry and give his section chief that morning. The chief usually appeared around 8:30, so as long as he was there by eight everything would be all right.

Then with a rather cheerful expression on his face, he peered up at the gloomy, gray sky. Someone who didn't know Kimura would have wondered what Kimura found so amusing.

While he was out washing his face, the maid had quickly folded the mosquito net and put away the bedding. He walked back through the room and into the living room.

Two low tables were drawn together at a ninety-degree angle, a cushion for sitting on the floor before them. He sat down and struck a match for his morning smoke.

When Kimura worked, he divided his tasks into things that required immediate attention and those that could wait until he had time. He always made a clear space on one of the tables and then brought to it the things he had to do immediately. Once he had disposed of this urgent business, he

TRANSLATED BY JAMES M. VARDAMAN, JR.

137

moved on to the next part of the pile. The stack was always piled high. Things were piled high according to urgency, the relatively urgent things placed on top.

Kimura picked up the *Hinode News* beside the cushion and spread it on top of the empty table. He opened to the seventh page—the literary section —and read, blowing ashes from his cigarette off over the other side of the table. His expression was still cheerful.

From the other side of the sliding door came the furious sounds of duster and broom. The maid was quickly cleaning his room. The sound of the duster was particularly harsh. Kimura often complained to her about it, but a day or so later she was back doing it the way she always had. It seemed to him that she didn't use the end with the strips of paper, but used the handle end for dusting. Kimura called this "instinctive clean- ing." She was like a pigeon sitting on an egg. If you traded the egg for a round piece of chalk, it would still sit there quite oblivious of the result, but faithful to the action. The maid did not seem to be think- ing of the purpose of dusting, but was simply beating for the sake of beating.

Though the maid cleaned "instinctively" and had a wagging tongue, she was hardworking enough, so Kimura was satisfied. He said she had a "wag- ging tongue," using the phrase of some romantic novelist, because after her employer left for work she customarily made the rounds of the neighbor- hood to chat.

Kimura read something and frowned. Generally whenever Kimura put the newspaper down, he either wore an extremely apathetic expression or else he frowned. What he read was either mediocre or biased. Or, if that were not the case, Kimura would find it unfair. In that case it would seem better not to read at all, but, all the same, he would continue to read. He would read, first with an indifferent expression, then with a bit of a frown, and then soon become quite cheerful again.

Kimura was a man of letters.

A government employee, he was engaged in trivial, time-consuming, mindless work, and though his head was already balding with age, he had absolutely no influence whatsoever. As a man of letters he was known to some degree. Oddly enough, though what he wrote was hardly worth men- tioning, he did have a reputation of sorts. But that wasn't all. Once he had gained a name for himself as a writer, he had been transferred to a provincial office and promptly forgotten, like someone who had died. It was only after he had begun to go bald that he was transferred back to Tokyo, and consequently recovered his position as a writer. His career had been one of many turnabouts.

It would be a misrepresentation to say that the displeasure Kimura felt when he read the literary column resulted from self-interest, that is, that he was disgruntled when he was criticized or happy when he was praised. Regardless of who was under examination, he felt it unjust when insignificant points were attacked and points of some consequence were belittled. He felt the injustice more keenly, of course, when he himself was directly involved.

Roosevelt walked the earth preaching, "Where you see injustice, fight!" Why didn't Kimura fight? Actually, in his early years he had fought vigorously. But now he was a civil servant and he wouldn't be able to write at all if he engaged in controversy. After his comeback, and despite his lack of talent, he had eschewed debates and devoted himself to writing.

In that day's literary column he read the following: "In literature there is tone. This tone is built upon 'situation.' What this is, however, remains unclear. The works which appear in the magazines Kimura is associated with and the works of Kimura himself all lack this 'situation.' "

In short, that was all that was written in the article. The writer offered several illustrations of what he meant by "situation," but none of them were especially good. Kimura felt sure that no good writer would be pleased with the examples.

Kimura couldn't really understand what the article was all about. He had no idea what "a tone built upon a situation" meant. He had read a considerable number of books on both philosophy and art criticism, but he could make no sense out of the phrase. Certainly, there was in literature an element that might be described as "undefinable." That was conceivable, but what was "situation"?

Hadn't it been written since ancient times that in drama, or whatever, character exists in time and place? Isn't that what might be referred to as "situation"? The Austrian playwright Hermann Bahr wrote that the aim of ancient literature was to create a dramatic tension from sudden, rich changes in the action. Could "situation" be any different from what Bahr described? Kimura simply failed to understand what could possibly be constructed over and above these specific elements.

Kimura was not a particularly self-assured person, but, on the other hand, he did not feel that his inability to comprehend the article was due to any lack of intelligence on his part. Actually, he felt a little sorry for the columnist. And looking at the samples of works that the writer had cited, he felt somewhat disgusted.

But Kimura's frown was soon replaced by a cheerful expression. As it was his bachelor's habit to put everything in its place, he carefully folded the newspaper and put it on a corner of the porch. If he left it there, the maid would use it to clean lamps with and sell the rest to the ragman.

This has been dwelt on at length, but actually it all occurred in the few minutes in which he smoked his cigarette.

As he was snuffing out his cigarette in the abalone shell he used as an ashtray, something interesting occurred to him and he smiled to himself. On the side table were piled ten or so bundles of what looked like manuscripts. He moved over where he could see them.

They were manuscripts which had been sent in to the *Hinode News* and which the paper had asked him to read.

When the *Hinode News* had invited contributions to a prefectural writing competition, they had asked him to be a judge. He already had so much work that he hardly had time to breathe and he really had no time to spare for the manuscripts. Even if he were able to manufacture time, it would only be enough for a smoke and no one likes to do an unpleasant task during a break. It was doubtful whether even one of the ten manuscripts submitted might be in any way interesting.

He had taken on the job of reading them in spite of himself.

Kimura was often criticized on the third page of the newspaper, usually with a phrase about "the offenses against public decency committed by the Kimura group." Even when a theater had put on a Western play which he had translated, this phrase was used. The play itself was an extremely innocuous work published in Vienna and Berlin, where censorship was quite strict, and even performed in the theaters.

But that was what the writer on page three wrote. Kimura was unfamiliar with the circumstances of the newspaper, but he was certain that the literary opinions of the publisher extended as far as page three.

What he was just reading was different. In the literary column, even if a writer signs his column, the opinions are published without any explanatory note, in the same way that political editorials are published. So one could take it as a statement of the publisher's literary viewpoint. The fact that Kimura's work had no "situation" and the works which appeared in magazines he edited had no "situation" meant, in the opinion of the columnist, that Kimura did not understand literature. Why then was a person who didn't understand literature entrusted by the same publisher with the responsibility for refereeing manuscripts? What would happen if he selected a manuscript which did not have "situation"? Would the writer escape criticism? He imagined that neither the winner nor he himself would escape.

It was bad enough being called a dilettante, in the worst sense of the word, and being treated like one, but it was too much to then have to read such uninteresting manuscripts. Anyway, wishing to be free from the chore of digging into them a while longer, he moved the stack to the chest.

Again, it has taken a long time to write this, but it all happened in a moment.

In the next room, the sounds of "instinctive cleaning" had ceased, and the door slid open. Breakfast appeared.

Kimura ate his breakfast of bean soup and potatoes. After breakfast and a cup of tea, he felt his back beginning to sweat. After all, he thought, summer is summer.

Kimura changed clothes and put an unopened pack of Asahis into his pocket. In the entranceway he found his lunchbox, umbrella, and nicely polished shoes.

He put up his umbrella and plodded out. The road to the streetcar stop was narrow and lined with houses, so the number of shopkeepers who greeted him was fairly well set. He paid close attention as he walked. Some people showed a liking for him and greeted him. No one seemed to hold any animosity toward him.

Kimura would try to read the minds of those who spoke to him. Perhaps they thought that anyone who wrote novels and such was a bit strange. They may have thought him eccentric and perhaps felt somewhat sorry for him, but they seemed friendly enough. At least that is what their expressions seemed to convey. This didn't displease him, nor did it make him feel especially happy.

Just as he had few detractors in the neighborhood, he had few enemies in society as a whole. There were only those who acted friendly, if somewhat condescendingly, and those who were indifferent.

In literary circles, this was not always the case. Kimura preferred to be simply left alone. He wished that people would deal with what he wrote and that his works would not be criticized because they were misread. And then deep in his heart he hoped that a few people would read his works and feel just as he felt.

After he had walked half the way to the streetcar stop, Ogawa came out of a side street. Ogawa worked at the same office, so about one time in three, they would happen to meet along the way.

"I thought I left a little early this morning," said Ogawa, tilting his umbrella and coming alongside Kimura.

"Really?"

"Aren't you always earlier than I am? You seemed to be deep in thought when I saw you a minute ago. Are you working out the scheme for some major work?"

Kimura was always amused when someone asked such questions. He maintained his cheerful expression and said nothing in reply.

"Someone wrote an article in *Taiyō* magazine recently saying that your disciplined life at the office and your literary life were inconsistent, that there was no way they could be reconciled with one another. Did you see that?"

"It probably means that literary works which offend public morals are incongruous with the duties and regulations of a civil servant."

"Come to think of it, there was something about offending public morality, but I didn't take it that way. I thought it simply meant that there was an inconsistency between literature and government service. Government is something which deals with current affairs and is only temporary, but literature remains forever. Governments belong to one nation, but literature belongs to mankind." Ogawa was a real talker, and though Kimura always thought him obnoxious, he tried not to let it show. As if seized by some uncontrollable passion, his companion hit his stride. "But you've probably read what Roosevelt has been lecturing on everywhere. If things were to go the way he says, politics would not be something for only the present or for only one country. If it were ennobled still more, politics would become great literature. Wouldn't that conform with your ideals?"

Kimura thought the idea foolish, but stifled a desire to frown.

They soon came to the stop. As always in the suburbs, the trains going to the center of town in the morning and returning to the suburbs in the evening were full. They stood under the red signpost, their umbrellas side by side, and two trains passed before they could get on.

They hung onto the straps. Ogawa seemed not to be finished talking.

"What do you think of my view of literature?"

"I don't agree," Kimura replied reluctantly.

"In what way do you disagree?"

"I just don't agree. When I want to write, I write. Well, it's like eating—when you want to eat, you eat."

"Instinct, huh?"

"No, it's not instinct."

"Why not?"

"It's done consciously."

"Hmm," replied Ogawa, making an odd face. He said no more until they got off the streetcar.

Kimura parted from Ogawa and went to the door of his own office. He hung his hat on the hat rack and stood his umbrella in the stand. There were only two or three hats in the rack.

The door was left open and bamboo blinds were hung up. He passed by the office boys dressed in their white uniforms and went to his desk. Those who had already arrived were fanning themselves, not having settled down to work yet. Some went so far as to say "Good morning" and others nodded a greeting. Everyone looked pale and unhealthy. That was to be expected. There was no one who didn't get sick at least once a month. Except Kimura.

Kimura took the damp documents from the stained gray cabinet marked "important documents" and put them in two piles on his desk. The short pile was business which had to be dealt with that day. On the very top was a file of papers to which was attached a red slip that looked like a tongue sticking out. That was the urgent matter he had to hand to his chief that morning. The tall pile was work which could be tended to later. In addition to his normal work allotment there were documents from other bureaus that he had to proofread. They were in the stack of documents that were not immediately pending.

Kimura took out the documents, put them down on the desk, sat in his chair, took out his conductor's watch, and looked at it. Still ten minutes before eight. It would be another forty minutes before the chief appeared.

He took his time getting settled and always worked steadily. When he worked, he always wore a cheerful expression. His feelings at such times are difficult to describe. Whatever he did, he was like a child at play. The work of the bureau was no laughing matter. He realized clearly that he himself was going round and round like a small cog in the huge machinery of government organization. Conscious of that he nevertheless did his work as if he were at play. His cheerfulness was the way his attitude exhibited itself.

When he finished one job, he smoked a cigarette. At such times, Kimura's imagination became mischievous. He thought about the division of labor and how monotonous some jobs were for the unlucky. And yet he felt no reason to complain. Nor did he hold fatalistic notions about being bound to his fate. He occasionally thought of quitting. But what would happen after he quit? At present he wrote at night beneath the light of a lamp. He tried to imagine doing the same thing from morning to night. When he wrote, he felt like a child playing its favorite game. That didn't mean that there weren't some difficult times. In every "sport" there was some obstacle to overcome. He also knew that art was nothing to laugh at. He knew that if he were to hand the instrument he held in his hand to a true master, he could produce a work that would move the whole world. Even as the thought passed through his mind he fell into a "playful" mood. The French

politician Gambetta's troops once lost their zeal prior to an offensive. When
Gambetta gave the command to sound the charge, the bugler blew reveille
instead. Italians have this playful frame of mind even when they stand on
the border between life and death. Anyway, for Kimura doing anything was
a kind of play. Nonetheless, though it was all play, he certainly preferred
doing that which he was interested in to that which was boring. But if he did
what he enjoyed from morning to night, surely it would become monotonous and he would grow tired of it. Even this trivial job had at least helped
to break the monotony.

What would break the boredom of a writer's life if he were to quit his job?
There would be social life and travel. But that would require money. He
wouldn't want to look at social life in the way that one might watch someone catching fish. In order to savor the pleasure of "vagabondage" as Gorky
did, one would have to have Russian heritage. Well, perhaps being a parsi-
monious bureaucrat was better. Thinking of things this way didn't bring on
any special pangs of despair.

Once his imagination had become quite wayward and he had even had
dreams of war. The bugle played the charge! How exhilarating to charge forward, one's eyes looking up at the flag raised high. Kimura had never really
been ill, but he was short and thin so he had not been taken by the military
conscription. Therefore he had never been to war. But he recalled hearing
people say that what is called a "heroic assault" was often in reality crawling
along on all fours behind the shelter of sandbags. That dampened his
enthusiasm somewhat. He couldn't deny the fact that if he were placed in
that sort of situation he would probably crawl along in the trench, too. The
bravery and exhilaration grew pale. Then again even if he were able to go to
war, he might be enlisted in transportation and have to transport goods. If
he were put in front of a cart, then he would pull. If he were put behind a
cart, then he would push. But that would have little to do with heroism or
exhilaration.

Another time he had a dream about an ocean voyage. How pleasant to
cross the sea, enduring waves as high as the deck! Or to plant the country's
flag on polar ice! But it occurred to him that there was probably a division of
labor even in that. He awoke from his dream with the thought that he
would probably end up as a stoker in the engine room of the ship.

Having finished one bit of business, Kimura pushed that bundle of documents to the other side of the desk and took another bundle from the tall
stack. The first was ruled Japanese paper, but this was Western paper, ruled
with purple lines. It stuck to the palm of his hand. It felt the way it would

feel if one picked up a bamboo clothes pole, not realizing that there was a slug clinging to it.

By that time five or six of his colleagues had come in and all of the desks were occupied. Shortly after the signal for eight o'clock and the beginning of the workday, the section chief appeared.

Before the chief even had time to sit down, Kimura brought him the red-labeled documents. He stood back and watched his superior leisurely remove the documents from the portfolio, take the cover from the inkstone case, and prepare some ink. When he had finished, he casually turned to Kimura. He was a doctor of law, three or four years younger than Kimura, with firm-set eyes and nose, gold-rimmed spectacles, and a shrewd-looking face.

"The matter you told me to take care of yesterday." Kimura stopped in mid-sentence and handed over the documents. The chief took them and gave them a cursory glance.

"Fine," he said.

Feeling as if he had just put down a heavy burden, Kimura went back to his desk and sat down. Documents which did not pass inspection the first time never seemed to make it through without some hitch the second time around. They had to be amended three or four times. Meanwhile the chief would be rethinking various parts, so that what he had originally said would gradually be altered. Ultimately it would be completely out of his hands. That was why he was glad when documents were accepted the first time through.

When he sat down, tea was served. Without having to say a word, the office boy brought a cup of tea at eight when he arrived at work and, when there was work, another cup at three o'clock. The tea had color, but was tasteless. Lees settled in the bottom of the cup. After tea Kimura would always settle down and work steadily without a break. In dealing with the shorter stack of documents all he had to do was occasionally check them with the register, so he made rapid progress. There were times when he had finished three or four items without a break. What he had finished he would stamp "approved" and have the office boy take them wherever they should go. Some he took straight to the section chief.

Meanwhile other documents would be brought in. Those labeled in red he would deal with immediately. The others he would put at the bottom of one stack or another. He would treat telegrams like red-labeled documents.

In the middle of his work, he suddenly felt hot. He glanced out of the window. The ashen sky was now filled with dark, purplish clouds.

When he looked at his colleagues, their faces bore extremely tired expressions. In most cases their chins hung down, making their faces seem somewhat longish. The damp air in the room felt heavy and seemed to press down on one's head. Even at times when it was not so hot, during business hours when he went to the toilet and came back in from the hallway, the stale smell of cigarette smoke and sweat seemed as if it would smother him. But summer was better than winter when the stoves were lit and windows were shut. Kimura looked around at the others, grimaced for a second, and quickly regained his cheerfulness before setting to work again.

In a little while it thundered and a downpour began. The rain struck the window, raising an awful noise. Everyone in the office stopped working and looked out the windows.

"It sure was muggy," said Yamada who sat at Kimura's right. "At last we have a shower."

"Uh-huh," replied Kimura cheerfully looking in his direction.

Yamada looked at Kimura and, as if he had suddenly remembered something, lowered his voice and whispered, "You're really making headway with your work, but you seem to be amused by it all."

"That's not true," answered Kimura calmly. He had been told the same thing over and over. One might go so far as to say that his expression, speech, and behavior made people say such things. The previous section chief had called Kimura frivolous and had disliked him altogether. Even in the literary world, critics condemned him for not being "serious." He had once been married, though they had unfortunately separated. His former wife's most common complaint, which came out whenever they had a row, was "You're always making fun of me!"

Kimura's attitude was neither serious nor frivolous. His wife was no Nora, as in Ibsen's play, but the "playful" attitude with which he approached everything probably made her feel unpleasantly like some doll or plaything.

For Kimura this attitude was an irrepressible part of his character. One young writer who was on visiting terms with Kimura had told him, "Somehow or other you seem to lack the major characteristic of modern man—a nervous temperament." But Kimura didn't seem to feel that was particularly unfortunate.

The downpour was followed by a drizzle and there was no letup in the heat. Since some of them lived too far away from home to return for lunch, around 11:30 or so they went into the lunchroom to eat their box lunches. Kimura would work up until the noon signal, then eat his lunch by himself.

Two or three of his colleagues went into the lunchroom and the phone

rang. The office boy answered, listened for a moment, asked the other party
to wait, and came to Kimura.

"It's someone from the *Hinode News* asking to speak with you."

Kimura went to the phone. "Kimura speaking. What can I do for you?"

"Mr. Kimura? Excuse me for calling you, but when do you think you will
be able to look at those manuscripts?"

"Well, I'm quite busy these days, so I won't be able to get to them right
away."

"I see." The other party seemed to be thinking about what to say next.
"I'll check with you later on then. Thank you."

"Goodbye."

"Goodbye."

A trace of a smile skimmed across Kimura's face. Deep inside he knew
that those manuscripts would not be coming down from the top of that
chest for some time to come. Had he been the way he used to be, he'd have
brought on an argument by saying something like "I've made up my mind
not to fool with those manuscripts." His manner had become much milder,
but there was still some measure of spite in his smile. Despite this stubborn,
malicious streak, he was still not Nietzsche's modern man.

The signal sounded. Everyone took off their watches and wound them.
Kimura took out his conductor's watch and did the same. His colleagues
who had already put their documents away left in a group. Kimura and the
office boy were the only two left. Kimura slowly put his documents away in
the cabinet, went to the lunchroom and leisurely ate his box lunch, then
boarded the sweaty, crowded streetcar.

1910

Fushinchū

UNDER RECONSTRUCTION

A PERFECT LITTLE STORY, *UNDER RECONSTRUCTION* captures in a succinct and telling way a number of themes that inform so many of the writings from this period in Ōgai's work. Each aspect of the narrative indicates some phase of lives and a society that are "under reconstruction," ranging from the fading relationship between the German woman and the Japanese official, to the condition of the restaurant in which they have their dinner, indeed to the whole nation of Japan itself. In this emotional environment, youthful enthusiasm has been left behind. "We are in Japan," Watanabe remarks drily, refusing a kiss from his German dinner companion. In one sense, the tale might be considered as an ironic pendant to the romantic situation created in *The Dancing Girl*, an imaginary conversation between two youthful lovers here grown older, more self-assured, and more weary of the world.

Under Reconstruction can profitably be read in conjunction with *Exorcising Demons*, published a year earlier in 1909, where Ōgai himself serves as protagonist. Some effective descriptive passages are first sketched there, then later adapted and used with great economy to establish the mood and setting of this present story.

IT HAD JUST STOPPED RAINING when Councillor Watanabe got off the tram in front of the *kabuki* playhouse. Carefully avoiding the puddles, he hurried through the Kobiki district in the direction of the Department of Communications. Surely that restaurant was somewhere around here, he thought as he strode along the canal; he remembered having noticed the signboard on one of these corners.

The streets were fairly empty. He passed a group of young men in Western clothes. They were talking noisily and looked as if they had all just left their office. Then a girl in a kimono and a gaily colored sash hurried by, almost bumping into him. She was probably a waitress from some local teahouse, he thought. A rickshaw with its hood up passed him from behind.

Finally he caught sight of a small signboard with the inscription written horizontally in the Western style: "Seiyōken Hotel." The front of the building facing the canal was covered with scaffolding. The side entrance was on a small street. There were two oblique flights of stairs outside the restaurant, forming a sort of truncated triangle. At the head of each staircase was a glass door; after hesitating a moment, Watanabe entered the one on the left on which were written the characters for "Entrance."

Inside he found a wide passage. By the door was a pile of little cloths for wiping one's shoes and next to these a large Western doormat. Watanabe's shoes were muddy after the rain and he carefully cleaned them with both implements. Apparently in this restaurant one was supposed to observe the Western custom and wear one's shoes indoors.

There was no sign of life in the passage, but from the distance came a great sound of hammering and sawing. The place was under reconstruction, thought Watanabe.

He waited awhile, but as no one came to receive him, he walked to the end of the passage. Here he stopped, not knowing which way to turn. Suddenly he noticed a man with a napkin under his arm leaning against the wall a few yards away. He went up to him.

"I telephoned yesterday for a reservation."

The man sprang to attention. "Oh yes, sir. A table for two, I believe? It's on the second floor. Would you mind coming with me, sir."

The waiter followed him up another flight of stairs. The man had known immediately who he was, thought Watanabe. Customers must be few and far between with the repairs under way. As he mounted the stairs, the clatter and banging of the workmen became almost deafening.

"Quite a lively place," said Watanabe, looking back at the waiter.

TRANSLATED BY IVAN MORRIS

"Oh no, sir. The men go home at five o'clock. You won't be disturbed while you're dining, sir."

When they reached the top of the stairs, the waiter hurried past Watanabe and opened a door to the left. It was a large room overlooking the canal. It seemed rather big for just two people. Round each of the three small tables in the room were squeezed as many chairs as could possibly be fitted. Under the window was a huge sofa and next to it a potted vine about three feet high and a dwarfed plant with large hothouse grapes.

The waiter walked across the room and opened another door. "This is your dining room, sir." Watanabe followed him. The room was small—just right, in fact, for a couple. In the middle a table was elaborately set with two covers and a large basket of azaleas and rhododendrons.

With a certain feeling of satisfaction, Watanabe returned to the large room. The waiter withdrew and Watanabe again found himself alone. Abruptly the sound of hammering stopped. He looked at his watch: yes, it was exactly five o'clock. There was still half an hour till his appointment. Watanabe took a cigar from an open box on the table, pierced the end, and lit it.

Strangely he did not have the slightest feeling of anticipation. It was as if it did not matter who was to join him in this room, as if he did not care in the slightest whose face it was that he would soon be seeing across the flower basket. He was surprised at his own coolness.

Puffing comfortably at his cigar, he walked over to the window and opened it. Directly below were stacked huge piles of timber. This was the main entrance. The water in the canal appeared completely stationary. On the other side he could see a row of wooden buildings. They looked like houses of assignation. Except for a woman with a child on her back, walking slowly back and forth outside one of the houses, there was no one in sight. At the far right, the massive red-brick structure of the Naval Museum imposingly blocked his view.

Watanabe sat down on the sofa and examined the room. The walls were decorated with an ill-assorted collection of pictures: nightingales on a plum tree, an illustration from a fairy tale, a hawk. The scrolls were small and narrow, and on the high walls they looked strangely short as if the bottom portions had been tucked under and concealed. Over the door was a large framed Buddhist text. And this is meant to be the land of art, thought Watanabe.

For a while he sat there smoking his cigar and simply enjoying a sensation of physical well-being. Then he heard the sound of voices in the passage and the door opened. It was she.

She wore a large Anne-Marie straw hat decorated with beads. Under her long gray coat he noticed a white embroidered batiste blouse. Her skirt was also gray. She carried a tiny umbrella with a tassel. Watanabe forced a smile to his face. Throwing his cigar in an ashtray, he got up from the sofa.

The German woman removed her veil and glanced back at the waiter, who had followed her into the room and who was now standing by the door. Then she turned her eyes to Watanabe. They were the large, brown eyes of a brunette. They were the eyes into which he had so often gazed in the past. Yet he did not remember those mauve shadows from their days in Berlin. . . .

"I'm sorry I kept you waiting," she said abruptly in German.

She transferred her umbrella to her left hand and stiffly extended the gloved fingers of her right hand. No doubt all this was for the benefit of the waiter, thought Watanabe as he courteously took the fingers in his hand.

"You can let me know when dinner is ready," he said, glancing at the door. The waiter bowed and left the room.

"How delightful to see you," he said in German.

The woman nonchalantly threw her umbrella on a chair and sat down on the sofa with a slight gasp of exhaustion. Putting her elbows on the table, she gazed silently at Watanabe. He drew up a chair next to the table and sat down.

"It's very quiet here, isn't it?' she said after a while.

"It's under reconstruction," said Watanabe. "They were making a terrible noise when I arrived."

"Oh, that explains it. The place does give one rather an unsettled feeling. Not that I'm a particularly calm sort of person at best."

"When did you arrive in Japan?"

"The day before yesterday. And then yesterday I happened to see you on the street."

"And why did you come?"

"Well, you see, I've been in Vladivostok since the end of last year."

"I suppose you've been singing in that hotel there, whatever it's called."

"Yes."

"You obviously weren't alone. Were you with a company?"

"No, I wasn't with a company. But I wasn't alone either. . . . I was with a man. In fact you know him." She hesitated a moment. "I've been with Kosinsky."

"Oh, that Pole. So I suppose you're called Kosinskaya now."

"Don't be silly! It's simply that I sing and Kosinsky accompanies me."

"Are you sure that's all?"

"You mean, do we have a good time together? Well, I can't say it never happens."

"That's hardly surprising. I suppose he's in Tokyo with you?"

"Yes, we're both at the Aikokusan Hotel."

"But he lets you come out alone."

"My dear friend, I only let him accompany me in singing, you know." She used the word *begleiten*. If he accompanied her on the piano, thought Watanabe, he accompanied her in other ways too.

"I told him that I'd seen you on the Ginza," she continued, "and he's very anxious to meet you."

"Allow me to deprive myself of that pleasure."

"Don't worry. He isn't short of money or anything."

"No, but he probably will be before long if he stays here," said Watanabe with a smile. "And where do you plan to go next?"

"I'm going to America. Everyone tells me that Japan is hopeless, so I'm not going to count on getting work here."

"You're quite right. America is a good place to go after Russia. Japan is still backward. . . . It's still under reconstruction, you see."

"Good heavens! If you aren't careful, I'll tell them in America that a Japanese gentleman admitted his country was backward. In fact, I'll say it was a Japanese government official. You are a government official, aren't you?"

"Yes, I'm in the government."

"And behaving yourself very correctly, no doubt?"

"Frighteningly so! I've become a real conservative, you know. Tonight's the only exception."

"I'm very honored!" She slowly undid the buttons of her long gloves, took them off, and held out her right hand to Watanabe. It was a beautiful, dazzlingly white hand. He clasped it firmly, amazed at its coldness. Without removing her hand from Watanabe's grasp, she looked steadily at him. Her large, brown eyes seemed with their dark shadows to have grown to twice their former size.

"Would you like me to kiss you?" she said.

Watanabe made a wry face. "We are in Japan," he said.

Without any warning, the door was flung open and the waiter appeared. "Dinner is served, sir."

"We are in Japan," repeated Watanabe. He got up and led the woman into the little dining room. The waiter suddenly turned on the glaring overhead lights.

The woman sat down opposite Watanabe and glanced round the room. "They've given us a *chambre séparée*," she said, laughing. "How exciting!" She straightened her back and looked directly at Watanabe as if to see how he would react.

"I'm sure it's quite by chance," he said calmly.

Three waiters were in constant attendance on the two of them. One poured sherry, the other served slices of melon, and the third bustled about ineffectually.

"The place is alive with waiters," said Watanabe.

"Yes, and they seem to be a clumsy lot," she said, squaring her elbows as she started on her melon. "They're just as bad at my hotel."

"I expect you and Kosinsky find they get in your way. Always barging in without knocking. . . ."

"You're wrong about all that, you know. Well, the melon is good anyway."

"In America you'll be getting stacks of food to eat every morning as soon as you wake up."

The conversation drifted along lightly. Finally the waiters brought in fruit salad and poured champagne.

"Aren't you jealous—even a little?" the woman suddenly asked. All the time they had been eating and chatting away. She had remembered how they used to sit facing each other like this after the theater at the little restaurant above the Blühr Steps. Sometimes they had quarreled, but they had always made up in the end. She had meant to sound as if she were joking; but despite herself, her voice was serious and she felt ashamed.

Watanabe lifted his champagne glass high above the flowers and said in a clear voice: "Long live Kosinsky!"

The woman silently raised her glass. There was a frozen smile on her face. Under the table her hand trembled uncontrollably.

It was still only half past eight when a solitary, black car drove slowly along the Ginza through an ocean of flickering lights. In the back sat a woman, her face hidden by a veil.

1910

Dokushin

A BACHELOR

TWO ACCOUNTS OF ŌGAI'S LIFE in the town of Kokura on the southern island of Kyushu appear in this volume, *A Bachelor* and *Two Friends,* both composed in retrospect. Ōgai lived in Kokura from 1899 to 1902, assigned there by higher officials in the army with whom relations had become increasingly strained, among other reasons, because of Ōgai's insistence on using the advanced medical methods he had observed in Europe. He was sent to Kyushu to serve as the chief medical officer for the Twelfth Division. For Ōgai, now cut off from the intellectual life of the capital, this assignment represented a virtual exile. Whatever the range of feelings he underwent during this time, however, only certain aspects of the experience entered into his later writing on the subject. In both *A Bachelor* and his later story *Two Friends,* the sense conveyed is more one of calm and a certain resignation than the bitterness that sometimes creeps into his private correspondence during these years.

A Bachelor, published in 1910, six years after Ōgai's return to Tokyo and his remarriage, makes at least a minimal attempt to treat his predicament in a fictional way. The protagonist (however much he may in certain ways resemble the author) is named Ono, here pictured as a friend of a pleasant group, culled from the local intelligentsia, exchanging stories with them in a genial fashion on a cold winter night. That same coldness, however, seems to pervade the emotional life of the protagonist, who is divorced and cannot seem to warm to the idea of a second marriage, despite pleas from his friends and a letter from his grandmother describing a possible candidate.

Whatever the disguise, the resemblance between Ono and the author is striking. The other figures who appear are modeled as well on real acquaintances he developed there. One of the characters, the Zen priest "Neikokuji-san," will appear in the second story of exile, *Two Friends,* under his real name. The priest is a diligent student of Buddhist texts, as indicated by references to *The Commentary on the Great Wisdom Sutra (Daichidoron)* and the Buddhist dictionary *Hōon-jurin*, both composed in classical Chinese and dating back to the T'ang dynasty and before. The glimpse that this brief story offers of Ōgai's life during the period provides not only a sense of his mental state during those years but also a general reflection on the ambiguous merits of a life spent alone.

WINTER IN KOKURA is not really winter. A cold wind blows off the sea to the northwest, grazes a corner of western Honshu, whisks the withered leaves off the mandarin orange tree onto the sand of the garden, where it rustles them about for a short time before sweeping them under the veranda. On such days everyone closes up their homes in the early evening.

Before one is hardly aware, it begins to snow. Occasionally one can hear the bell of the *denbin* man making chopped steps as he races by. A stranger to Kokura would not know what a *denbin* man is. The *denbin* or "convenience circulation" is one of two customs which were imported from the west to Kokura but remain unknown to Tokyo. At the foot of the Tokiwa Bridge in Kokura stands a round pillar. On it are posted advertisements. Written on red, blue, or yellow paper in large, rough characters are notices for newly opened shops and entertainments like plays and exhibitions. Of course, there is only this one pillar and then the stone wall in Daimon-machi where these advertisements can be posted, and since Kokura is a town that requires few advertisements anyway, most of the bills are handwritten rather than printed. Although they are done by hand, there are none as tasteful as the posters one sees in Paris. At any rate, it is remarkable that such advertising pillars exist at all. This is one of the two customs.

The other is the aforementioned *denbin*. Heinrich von Stephan, the first chief of the German Imperial Postal Service, was born in a police state and the postal network was so ingeniously laid throughout the land that there should have been no inconvenience in the sending and receiving of mail. Mail by post in our country, however, requires sometimes a matter of days and sometimes a matter of months. For business that has to be accomplished the same day, the postal service is insufficient. For a rendezvous, where one must agree on where to meet the following day, the postal service would suffice. But for some sudden emergency where one must agree on where to meet on that very evening, the post is inadequate. In such a situation, some people would send a telegram. Yet this would be carrying things a little too far. On top of that, the formality of a telegram delivery would be entirely lacking in taste. At such a time one would surely wish to have an errand boy. These *denbin*, who wear a cap with their company's badge, stand at every crossroads, ready to deliver a letter to anyone in town, to carry home bothersome purchases that one has made along the way, to do any such errand. In

TRANSLATED BY JAMES M. VARDAMAN, JR.

exchange for the letter or parcel, one receives a slip of paper with the official stamp of the delivery service. It involves no uncertainty at all. In Kokura these delivery boys are called *denbin*.

The story of the messengers has become unintentionally long. On winter evenings in Kokura, when all is quiet outside, one can still hear the quick-tempoed ringing of the errand boys' bells.

And then one can hear the gentle voice of a woman passing by calling out melodically, "*Karintō!* How about some fried dough cakes!" With the deep-fried sugar-coated treats in a tin container, the kind one uses for collecting vegetables, slung over her shoulder, she walks the streets with a small paper lantern selling her goods.

The errand boys and the *karintō* seller come around throughout the year, so in summer it is the sidewalk fortune-tellers and others that one is con-scious of hearing, rather than the errand boys' bells and the *karintō* seller's voice.

On such evenings there are probably those who warm themselves with a charcoal brazier. But it really is not that cold.

The next morning the washbasin may be frozen over. For this ice to remain more than two days, however, is most unusual. The wind changes by the third day at the latest. The snow and ice then melt away.

2

It was a snowy night in Kokura.

Two guests gathered at the home of Ono Yutaka in Shinuo-machi. One was the president of the court, a man with graying hair named Togawa. The other was Tomita, the head of the municipal hospital, who after graduating from Tokyo University had come to this area and was saving up money for going abroad. He had almost gathered together enough money for his expenses and was saying that before long he would hand over his duties to a young doctor named Kitagawa and depart. Dr. Tomita was past forty, but his close-cropped head was not yet streaked with gray. One brief glance at his plump, ruddy face was enough to tell you that he liked his *sake*.

The master of the house, who led an extremely simple bachelor's life, had his maid Take go out to buy *udon* noodles, boil them in the kitchen, and serve them with *sake* to his guests. When he served tea, he would have the maid go out and buy baked sweet potatoes, saying they were better than the well-known *tsuru-no-ko* cakes. At the Tokiwa Bridge crossroad, where the corner turns at Kyō-machi, there is an old man with a towel wrapped around his head, tending a small iron cauldron and calling out, "Hot! Hot sweet potatoes! Get them while they're hot!" Although the master himself did not drink, when he offered *sake* to his friends he always had the maid buy his favorite noodles. The noodles came from a shop two or three doors down from the sweet potato seller's cauldron, where the faded, dark blue shop curtain bore the name Bunroku.

The master only partook of the noodles, and with a happy smile replacing his normally indifferent expression, he watched his two guests as they drank. The conversation was quiet and confidential. Only from time to time did Tomita's laughter become loud enough to break the general mood. It was close to the Asahi-machi entertainment district, so occasionally one could hear the sounds of *shamisen* and drum, but the sounds were quite faint and not at all noisy.

Take came from the kitchen to offer another helping of noodles.

Tomita shook his head. "No, I can't eat any more. I've had plenty of noodles. If there were a mistress of the house here, I wouldn't sit here drinking *sake* with noodles."

With this as the spark, they commenced a lively debate on the subject of being single and being married. This was hardly the first time that the men gathered in the room had taken up that topic.

It had been already two years since the master of the house had become chief director the the Imperial Coal Mining Corporation and come to Kokura. Within that time the fact that Ono lived alone had become well known throughout Kokura and consequently often became a topic for discussion.

Had the master been living without any woman in his life at all? Tomita was one of those who had been worrying about that.

"In Kokura," said Tomita, "there doesn't seem to be anyone who has attracted your attention. I thought there might be someone across the straits in Bakan and rather zealously inquired around, but the results were negative."

"You went to quite a lot of trouble," said the reserved Togawa, looking at the master's face.

The master merely grinned.

Tomita was slightly intoxicated, and at length the force of the arguments turned directly toward the master.

"With our host living this way, it's dangerous because of the women around here."

"What do you mean?"

"Something could start with some woman at any time."

"It makes me sound like some kind of Don Juan, doesn't it?"

Togawa felt sorry for the master, and half-unconsciously attempted to shift the conversation in another direction. And in his innate taciturn manner he began to tell an odd story.

3

Togawa hunched over holding both hands over the brazier.

"Now, the single life is undoubtedly something that most people would have a hard time pulling through blamelessly. I have a classmate named Miyazawa. This fellow graduated and was immediately assigned to his first post in Shibata, in Niigata. You probably have an idea what kind of place I'm talking about. He rented a small house near the courthouse and took a maid. His colleagues continued to encourage him to take a wife, but he simply would not do it. People kept asking themselves why he didn't get married. Finally they convinced themselves that it must be because he was miserly. Now I have known him from the time we were schoolboys and I can tell you that he's not stingy. He's not a man of strong enough will to hoard money. He is the kind who is moderate in all things and unable to take a plunge in anything. He was probably convinced that on his salary as a legal clerk he couldn't support a wife and children. Anyway, the land is the land and snowy nights like tonight continue for days and days. Miyazawa was alone in his room reading. The maid was in the next room, one wall away, sewing. Miyazawa yawned. The maid suppressed a yawn. Apparently this went on for a rather long time. Then one night a blizzard came up and outside the storm shutters the wind was whistling. Occasionally the bamboo in the garden would brush against the shutters like a sweeping broom. Around ten o'clock the maid brewed some tea and brought it in, commented on how bad the weather was, and then hesitated for a moment. Miyazawa told me that he himself was unable to bear the loneliness any more, and imagining that she must be lonely, he told her that it would not bother him if she were to bring her needlework in and do it in his room. She gladly brought in her sewing, made herself small in one corner of the room, and resumed her work. From that time on, the maid would occasionally come into his room saying that there would probably be no visitors coming that evening."

Tomita broke out in a laugh. "Togawa, you are a real novelist. That's pretty good."

Togawa laughed as well and scratched his head with some embarrassment.

"No. Actually Miyazawa later came to regret everything and he told me about it in great detail. That's why my tale has become inadvertently long. Let me abridge the rest. I'll tell you one more specific detail, though. It's this. One night, after the maid had said good night and retired to her own room, Miyazawa was unable to get to sleep. From beyond the wall he could hear the maid sighing as she tossed and turned. He said that after a while the sighs gradually became bigger and became moans as if she were in pain. In spite of himself, Miyazawa asked her if she were all right. I'll just say that much and then I really will omit the rest."

Tomita's voice took on an exaggerated tone.

"Hey. Now wait a minute. While you are about it, don't just cut the story short. Tell us the rest. It's quite interesting."

His voice grew even larger.

"Say, Take-san. You should listen carefully to this."

The master, who had been smiling abashedly the whole time, scowled.

Togawa continued, "I'm at a loss with Tomita breaking in all the time. Anyway, from then on the maid was no longer just a maid. Miyazawa regretted things immediately. Even someone like me realizes that since one's office is one's office, detection would be a serious matter. But the maid, who until then had been rather modest, gradually began to use makeup and wear rather bright-colored clothing. Indefinably it became obvious to others. Miyazawa was anxious. In the end he paid a visit to her parents and told them that in due course he would make her his wife. He provided compensation and was able to get off the hook for the time being. He thought that he would be able to figure something out in the meantime, but her parents were in earnest and there was nothing he could do. Miyazawa was quite destitute, but he contrived a scheme to cut himself free by means of money. Her parents, however, would take nothing beyond the set compensation. They had their hearts set on what he had promised and would not accept anything else. Ultimately he took her as his wife and to this day he is still married to her. Now they are living respectably in Tokyo, but be that as it may she is an uneducated woman, so Miyazawa has his troubles."

Tomita avidly sipped at his *sake* and made sport. "Is that it? What an anticlimax! If that's the story, I shouldn't have praised you so much."

<h1 style="text-align:center">4</h1>

At that moment from the front door came footsteps and then the sound of someone stamping snow off his clogs. The master's large pet dog Jean contemplated barking, then gave up and sniffed loudly. Take slid open the door and said something.

In a moment a priest wearing deep yellow robes and with a half-grown

beard came in. Looking at everyone, he bowed deeply and apologized profusely for coming by so late, then put his folded bundle on the right and sat
down between Togawa and Tomita.

He was a Buddhist priest of the Sōtō Zen sect and known to everyone as
Neikokuji-san. Neikokuji was a temple in Kaneda-chō near the railroad
tracks which for a long time had been without a priest. Most of the descen-
dants of the samurai for the former Kokura domain who had supported the
temple had returned to Toyotsu, and the temple had lost its priest. The walls
of the main hall of the temple, which seemed like a wayside shrine, only
enlarged, had been for the time being covered up with waste newspaper and
the priest had recently taken up residence there.

The master seemed delighted and called in the maid.

"If there are any more noodles left, could you heat up a bowl for Neikokuji-san? He must be quite cold."

Togawa put the brazier with which he had been warming his hands in
front of the priest.

Neikokuji-san smiled almost continuously. The gaunt-faced priest faced
the master and told him the following story.

"To tell the truth, this morning when I went out to beg for alms, I happened to notice a pile of splendid books, part of the *Commentary on the
Great Wisdom Sutra,* at a used book dealer in Tate-machi. I thought it quite
odd that such books would be in an incomplete set. Then as I came this way
and was going along Nishiki-machi toward Tanga Bridge, I passed another
used book store and they too had a similar pile of those volumes. Beside
that, there were others such as *Hōon-jurin* and that sort of thing. Between
the two stores there must have been a complete set of the *Commentary.*"

The master put in a word. "So someone purposely broke up the set when
they sold it?"

"I believe you're right. And I have a reasonably good idea of where they
came from. Since they are the kind of volumes that one would like to refer to
once in a while, and since if they were left as incomplete sets they would end
up as wastepaper, it would have been most regrettable to have left them
where they were. I have spoken with the priest in charge of Tōzenji temple
and asked him to purchase the volumes and keep them. I dropped in this
evening to let you know about his, just in case you might wish to consult the
volumes."

"That's most kind of you. I may even stop by and have a look on my way
home from the office tomorrow. Please help yourself to the noodles before
they cool off."

The priest began to eat. Before long, Take came out to offer him another helping. While waiting for the next bowl to be brought out, the master called Take.

"Clean up a little and fix us some tea, will you? And slice off some of the Bakan *yōkan*. Oh, wait, don't take away that *sake* bottle next to Tomita."

"Oh, no. Can't let this get away," said Tomita, locking his hand like a shrimp's tail around the bottle. He then spoke to the master.

"Really, your broad reading and vast knowledge are a wonderful thing, but I can't understand why someone who is involved in the sciences like you are would be reading books on Buddhism. Shouldn't one leave Buddhist writings to the priests?"

Neikokuji-san continued to smile as he slowly ate his noodles.

The master answered, "It's perfectly natural for you to think that way. If someone who is not a doctor were to read medical books, it wouldn't be of much help and might even cause harm. But books on Buddhism are different."

"I wonder. It's odd enough with you being single, but on top of that to take refuge in the Three Treasures of Buddhism is more than one can bear."

"You're going to take up the attack on bachelorhood again, are you? In my way of thinking, you too have put faith in the Three Treasures."

"Even if it looks that way, I don't really know what the Three Treasures are."

"You believe in them, even if you don't know what they are."

"You really ought not try your hand at such sophistry."

When the master spoke, it was in an ambiguous way, as if laughing about the subject yet as if in earnest.

"Not true. You are the one who is talking about science. That's also a kind of law. Among your colleagues there are some venerable learned figures that everyone respects. They are 'authorities.' They are all buddhas. And you are all priests. And somehow or other you are trying to outdo the ones who went before you. It's called 'overthrowing the authorities.' 'Scold the buddhas and berate the founders,' as they say."

Neikokuji-san ate his *yōkan* and drank his tea, smiling as always.

5

Tomita's eyes fixed and he looked at the master.

"Another lecture. You listen to a little story and suddenly you realize that you have been taught something. It's painful, you know."

He frowned a bit and went on.

"I see. One is treated to *sake*. One is dumbfounded, however, when the accompanying snacks are noodles. But then to be forced to listen to a lecture on top of everything is really a bit much."

The master chuckled to himself. "Who is the one who started attacking Buddhism?"

"Well, if the sermons come to an end, I won't speak ill of Buddhism. But I won't keep from laying into the life of the bachelor. If you go to Minomura's house, the dishes served with *sake* there are quite different. Oume-san sits in front of the *tokonoma* and assiduously and solemnly feeds Tomita as if by divine command. Such being the case, the gastronomic delights of mountain and sea are lined up in front of him."

"I don't understand. Who is Minomura? And why are you boasting so much about this woman named Oume-san?"

"Of course I'm boasting. If you go in and sit down before the *tokonoma* in the seat of honor, they say that your wish is their command, and Minomura withdraws far off to the other end of the room and prostrates himself."

"Who is this Minomura?"

"He's the one who opened the pediatric clinic along the way to the shore. They say that one day during the mourning period after his first wife passed away, someone brought a large sea bream and left it at his house. Minomura was greatly astonished and he went around the neighborhood asking everyone and making a big fuss. Miss Oume, who was at that time still the maid, was most nonchalant about the matter. She said that it was a gift from Inari-sama, the god of the harvests, and immediately proceeded willy-nilly to prepare it for Minomura. This was the beginning of the wonders and occasionally there were possessions by Inari-sama. There was even a divine oracle that he should marry Miss Oume—pronounced, of course, by Oume—and when Minomura had made the preparations for the wedding, she asked him with an expression of great surprise where his bride was to come from. It appears that I myself utter divine decrees, so there is an oracle that I am to be feasted."

"A strange woman indeed," said Togawa, cutting in.

"What? I'm not just saying this because I am treated to a feast, but she's a pretty good wife. The children who stay in the hospital all become attached to her. They say she really watches after everyone well. It's just that from time to time there are these divine revelations."

Neikokuji-san and the master had exchanged glances with that continuous smile on their faces as they listened. Then the priest abruptly got up and said, "Good night." And he left without even a word of farewell.

The priest was always casually coming and going like that.

The wind whistled. Take brought in a kettle and poured hot water into the teapot. "The sky has cleared completely," she said.

"It's about time we were taking our leave, too," said Togawa.

A broad grin came to Tomita's broad face. "I just don't seem ready to go home yet. After the withdrawal of our teacher who has made the single life a matter of vocation, I still have to launch one final offensive. Minomura is the same way. I don't presume to know why Inari-sama went so far as to select Oume, who had been the maid, as an oracle, or to penetrate the mysteries of the divine decrees. But I do know that the fact that he was able to find a second wife so quickly was certainly fortuitous for Minomura. He has not suffered inconvenience for a single day. The husband is fortunate and so are the guests."

The smile on the nonchalant face of the master never faded, no matter how much Tomita babbled in his cups.

Togawa looked meaningfully at the master. "Sorry it has gotten so late. Come on, let's say good night."

Making a move to get up, without actually standing, he repeatedly pressed Tomita. "Come on, you too. It's time for us to go home. We understand you now. We get your point."

At length Togawa managed to drag Tomita out with him.

Tomita tottered a bit on the way to the entrance of the house, shouting in a loud voice, "Hey, Miss Take. I was expecting another bottle of warm *sake,* but I'll save it for the next evening."

The master went out to see them off. He whispered to Togawa, "Shall I have a rickshaw called?"

"There's no need to do that. We're going the same way, so I'll go as far as his gate. Good night."

6

After the two guests had left it became suddenly still. The drums from Asahi-machi had ceased some time earlier, and the previously inaudible sound of the ocean reached him now.

Take came out and was clearing away the *sake* and tea things. Ono looked at her without really being conscious of it, and suddenly he attempted to regard Take as a woman.

She was short, her hair was thin, and her eyes were different in size. When she first came into service, she was thin and pale and seemed somehow meek. But after a while, she gradually filled out and her cheeks became plump. Her womanly charms had declined to a considerable degree.

The place where she stayed was near Kokura, and her elder brother operated a small pub in Hakata. The brother had encouraged her to come to help with the pouring of *sake* rather than as a kitchenmaid, saying that he would quickly make arrangements for her to get married. She was in Hakata for a while, but the customers were all seamen, and a rough lot at that, so she grew scared, ran away, and returned home. She was an unusual maid, upright and thinking always of the master's best interests. But it was hard to regard her as a woman. Even though he now tried to do so, it was next to impossible. He just could not feel that she was a member of the opposite sex.

He watched her finish cleaning up, then rise and withdraw, and without thinking he smiled. As he considered his own coolness, he fell to wondering.

Gradually his feelings turned strangely defensive and something within him called forth a desire to search within himself for some concealed feelings for the opposite sex.

Within Ono's imagination there floated up the time when a Buddhist mass was held in Kokura for those who had died in wartime. The brother high priests from the Honganji temple had come for the occasion, so around the pavilion where the ceremony was held thronged men and women of all ages. After Ono had taken his seat in the section for invited guests, the spectators gradually poured in, and a farmer's daughter with hair coiffed in the Shimada style came and squatted between his knees. She smelled of face powder and hair oil. He had been listening to the speech of someone or other, but midway it became only so much noise. For a short while his heart was entirely possessed by his organs of vision, which looked at the decorative silk band on her Shimada chignon, and by his olfactory sense smelling the fragrance emanating from her hair and skin. For that moment certainly Ono was a slave to his physical senses. As Ono recalled the experience, he again smiled unconsciously.

Ono would be forty that year. His separation from his former wife had taken place a long time before. His grandmother in Tokyo had been extremely anxious about his going off to Kokura alone, and every time she wrote to him it was about considerations for taking a new wife. That very evening a letter had arrived from his grandmother, but since he had been expecting guests, he had left it unopened on the top of his desk.

The lamp had dimmed, so Ono turned up the wick and opened the envelope. The polite, delicate, elegant old-style calligraphy of the letter brought to his mind the face of his grandmother with her horn-rimmed spectacles.

The year-end is rapidly approaching and I am looking forward to your coming to Tokyo within a very short time. As I wrote in my earlier letter about the Inoue's daughter, Mrs. Tanida had requested that I meet the young lady. Mrs.

Tanida and I went to Ueno and I have just returned. Mrs. Tanida and I arrived first and when Tomiko and her mother arrived, and when Tomiko with her elaborate Taka-shimada hairstyle stepped down from the rickshaw and I saw her for the first time, I was taken aback. I was just astonished that such a beautiful person could exist in this world. Even a misogynist like you, if you were to see her, could hardly remain unimpressed. Having met her only this once, I can say nothing about her personality, but she is certainly intelligent. Only one thing about her struck me as unusual, and that is that during the hour we relaxed at the tea shop, Tomiko did not laugh even once. At exactly the time we were there, two westerners were in the shop and because they were unable to communicate there were a number of amusing moments. Mrs. Tanida uses English quite well, so she was called upon to act as an interpreter. Tomiko's mother and I were both amused, but each time we laughed, Tomiko did not laugh at all. As I wrote before, she has been in an unfortunate situation, so it is only natural that she would be somewhat different from other young women her age. Whatever, I do hope that you will come to Tokyo at the earliest possible moment to see her for yourself.

Respectfully.

P.S.   Seijirō and his wife have asked me to send you their best. The cask of Kikkoman soy sauce we ordered from Ishizaki should already have arrived.

Having read the letter, he lit the portable candlestick that Take had put by the side of his desk, picked it up, blew out the lamp and stood up. Then he went to get into his cold bed to sleep alone, and perhaps to dream.

1910

Mōsō

DAYDREAMS

HALF MEMOIR, HALF REVERIE, *DAYDREAMS* IS perhaps the closest Ōgai came to providing a full sketch of the way in which he saw himself. The eloquence of the text is apparent throughout. The author's own sense of himself as a bystander, an "eternal malcontent," here receives its most succinct formulation. In 1911, nearing fifty, Ōgai may have felt the need to compose such a work in order to provide himself with an assessment and a summing up, a stern glance backwards, one without illusions, at all he had attempted to do, be, and accomplish. Yet that assessment was hardly complete, for much of his best writing was to follow.

It would be a mistake, however, to read this work merely as an artless attempt at autobiographical confession. The central portion of the text is written in the first person, but the story is framed by a description of the narrator as an old man (Ōgai is never named) living the life of a recluse, a device well known from such celebrated classic Japanese literary texts as Kamo no Chōmei's *Hōjōki* (An Account of My Hut), written in the thirteenth century. In 1911, when *Daydreams* was published, Ōgai was in no sense retired from the world. He was exceptionally busy with his governmental work and his various writing projects. The old man thus represents rather an extended mental self-image, a literary persona. Many of the memories and reflections pondered over by the narrator can be taken as autobiographical, but layers of literary arrangement and adjustment are nevertheless central to the author's compositional strategy. The text, trenchant and moving, conceals as it reveals.

BEFORE HIM LIES THE OPEN SEA. The sand cast up by the waves has formed small hillocks, creating a natural defensive barrier. It is this kind of formation that is meant by the word "dune," a word that originated with the Irish and Scots but which is now commonly used throughout Europe. Thin red pines grow in clusters on these dunes. They are still fairly young.

The white-haired old man gazes out to sea from a room in his small house, which has been built surrounded by the pines in a small clearing cut for the purpose. He built it before his retirement as a kind of country retreat and so it only has two rooms and a kitchen. He is sitting now in the six-mat room, which faces east and commands a full view of the sea.

From where he sits all he can see are the endless waves, because the outer ridge of the dunes, interlaced and crisscrossed with pine roots, falls away almost perpendicular, interspersed here and there with the occasional hollow; but in actual fact between the dunes and the water's edge there flows a small river with a sandbar. The river meanders somewhat before it flows into the sea, so just under the ridge fresh water mixes with salt. In the low-lying areas behind the dunes are scattered here and there the houses of the local fishing and farming community; the man's house is in fact the only one to be built on the dunes themselves. The story goes that a fishing boat was once flung up the beach in a storm and landed in the pine branches, so the local people shun the area and will not live there.

The river is the Ishimigawa; the province, Kazusa; the sea, the Pacific.

Autumn is approaching and the old man has just been for a stroll over the clean sand under the pines shrouded in a light morning mist. He has finished his breakfast, prepared for him by his old servant Yasohachi and has just this minute sat down.

Stillness all around. No human voice; not even a dog barking. All he can hear is the quiet, dull, leaden sound of the waves in the morning calm, like the pulse of the universe. The orb of an orange-yellow sun about a foot in diameter emerges from a point dead ahead, where the sea meets the sky. He gauges it in relation to the horizon, and so it gives the impression of rising with great rapidity. Watching it, the old man starts to think of time. He thinks of life and then of death. "Death is the only true source of inspiration for philosophy, its guardian spirit (Musagetes)," Schopenhauer had once written. The old man remembered these words. Yes, you could put it like that. But then you could hardly think of death without also considering life. To think of death was to contemplate life coming to an end. Most people

---

TRANSLATED BY RICHARD BOWRING

who had written about such things claimed that the thought of dying became of increasing concern the older one got. Casting his mind back over his own experience, he came to a somewhat different conclusion.

I was still only in my twenties, a time of life when one reacts to every external stimulus with instinct pure and simple, when one still retains an inner strength of purpose as yet unbowed. I was in Berlin. Wilhelm I was still on the throne, lending to that barbaric-sounding word *Deutsch* a sense of dignity and hence threatening to upset the existing balance of world power. The Social Democrats, not yet subject to the kind of demonic suppression practiced under the present Kaiser Wilhelm II, yet suffered under some pressure in the natural course of events. On the stage, Ernst von Wildenbruch was capturing the imagination of the student youth with his plays about the ancestors of the Hohenzollern.

During the day I would study in the lecture halls and the laboratories with the other students, all full of enthusiasm. Occasionally I even felt excited at my own ability to work so deftly, outdoing those Europeans, who always seem slightly clumsy and heavy-handed no matter what. In the evenings I would go to the theater or the dance hall, then while away the time in coffee shops and end up strolling home under the lonely light of the street lamps just as the sweepers in their horse-drawn carts were beginning their rounds. There were also occasions when I stopped off on the way.

So I would arrive back at my rooms. I say rooms, but it involved opening the entrance door to a tall tenement building with a large and cumbersome key, climbing three or four stories, striking match after match, and eventually arriving at the door to a small *chambre garnie*. A high table and two or three chairs; a bed, a chest of drawers, and a shelf. Nothing else. I would turn on the light, get undressed, turn off the light, and lie down.

It was at times like these that a feeling of loneliness would come upon me. Normally, all that would happen would be that vague images of home and family would come to me and I would fall asleep in the midst of such visions. Nostalgia is not a very deep form of human suffering. There were times, however, when I could not get to sleep at all. I would get up again, light the lamp, and try to study. Sometimes I became totally involved and lost myself in my studies all night. Near daybreak, once sounds of life began outside, I would take a short nap. It is easy to recuperate when you are young. There were times, however, when I simply could not settle to any work. Full of nervous energy and mentally alert, I found it irritating to open a book and follow in the tracks of another's thoughts. My own thoughts would take their own course. Here I was, studying medicine, the most "natural" of the natural sciences, devoting my life to an exact science, and yet somehow I felt a hunger of the spirit. I thought about life. Was what I was doing really enough to fulfill that life?

What had I been doing all my life? I had been toiling away at my studies as if constantly whipped on by something. I believed I was building myself up so that I would be able to be of some service, and it was just possible that such an aim might in future be fulfilled to some extent. But I felt that all I was really doing was emerging onto a stage to act out some part like an actor. I felt that something else must exist behind this role I was performing. I was under so much pressure there was no time for it to awaken. Studying as a child, studying as a student, studying as an official, studying abroad; it was all just this act. However much I longed to wash off this painted mask of mine, come down from the stage for a moment, and think about myself in peace; however much I hoped to catch a glimpse of that something behind it all, I kept on performing role after role, the director's whip at my back. That this role was life itself was unthinkable. Surely what lay behind was real life. Yet while I kept on hoping and praying that this something would wake up, it would always subside back into sleep. The strong feeling of homesickness that I felt at such times—like the action of the waves on water-weed always echoing back to its roots despite the fact it has been carried far away—that certainly did not feel like an act performed. No sooner would this impression raise its head than it immediately withdrew again.

And then at other times, on those nights when I could not sleep, I sometimes worried whether I might not perhaps end my life still playing on the stage like this. One could never know whether one's life would be long or short. Just about that time one of my fellow countrymen studying there caught typhus and died in the hospital. Whenever lectures permitted, I would go and see him at the Charité. They allowed me to see him lying there on the other side of the glass partition of the ward for contagious diseases. As his temperature was over forty degrees, they told me, he was given an ice bath every day. As a medical student, I worried whether ice baths might not be dangerous for a Japanese and I tried discussing it with others; but once he had been admitted to the hospital, they said, it would not really be possible to interfere with his treatment, and besides, even if they did mention it, it was doubtful whether anyone would take any notice. And so I just had to observe from the sidelines. Then one day I went to visit him only to find he had died the previous night. When I saw his face, I was deeply moved, and it suddenly occurred to me that I too might fall prey to some disease and die here like this. From then on I often thought about how it would be to die here in Berlin.

At such times, the first thing to come to mind was how sad my parents would feel waiting there at home. Then I thought of others who were close to me; in particular my curly-haired young brother who was so full of affection. When I left he had only just begun learning how to walk, but now the letters from home were full of how he would never stop asking when big brother was coming home. How sad he would be if they told him that his brother was never coming back.

And, too, I was a student abroad and it would be such a waste if I died without making something of it. When viewed in the abstract like this, it felt little more than a cold sense of duty, but when I thought more carefully about what each person actually meant to me, I experienced, of course, the same pain of longing, the same emotional reaction as I had toward my immediate family.

So thoughts of all one's multifarious social ties crowd in at random and come eventually to rest on the individual self. The self is a joining up of threads drawn together from all directions, and death is its unraveling.

Ever since childhood I have enjoyed novels, and having learned other languages I now read foreign novels too, whenever I have the time. Without exception the extinction of the self is always seen as the greatest, the deepest, agony of all. But if the self just ceases to be, how can that be agony? If one died by the sword no doubt there would be a momentary sensation of physical pain, and if one died of an illness or from drugs, one would feel the pain of suffocation or convulsion depending on the symptoms of the illness or the nature of the drugs; but there is no suffering merely because the self is extinguished.

In the West they say it is in the nature of barbarians not to fear death. Well, perhaps I am what they term a barbarian. And yet I recall when I was young my parents constantly impressing upon me the fact that because I had been born into a samurai family, I had to be prepared to commit suicide. I remember thinking then that this might well involve some physical pain that would just have to be endured. Well, then, perhaps I am a "barbarian." And yet I cannot agree that Western attitudes are always the right ones.

This is not to say that I am totally indifferent to the loss of the self. How annoying to have this thing we call the self disappear forever, without ever having known or even tried to think about what kind of thing it was while it did exist. Such a pity that would be! Sad to live one's whole life "living like a drunkard and dying like a dreamer" as a Chinese scholar once put it. And yet, in the midst of such remorse and such regret, there also lies an acute emptiness of the spirit. One feels an indescribable loneliness, which turns to anguish, turns to pain.

Often had I suffered thus on sleepless nights in my lodgings in Berlin. At such times everything that I had done from birth began to seem superficial and pointless. I became convinced that I was indeed just acting out a role on stage. Fragments of Buddhist and Christian ideas, that I had either heard from others or read in books, would float into my mind in no particular order, only to fade away again; fade away and bring no solace. I would search through all the scientific facts, all the scientific deductions that I had studied, to try to find something that might bring some consolation. This too was in vain.

It was one such night. I suddenly decided to read some philosophy and then could hardly wait until the morning. I went out and bought Hartmann's book *The Philosophy of the Unconscious*. This was the first time that I had dipped into philosophy. Why Hartmann? Well, at the time his work was at the center of heated discussion. It was the first great synthesis, they said; so much so that his philosophy was mentioned in the same breath as the railways as being among the greatest inventions of the Nineteenth Century.

It was his "three stages of illusion" that brought home to me the comforts of philosophy. Hartmann propounds these three stages of illusion in order to prove that happiness is an impossible goal for humanity. In the first stage, humanity hopes to achieve happiness in this life. He lists youth, health, friendship, love, and honor, and then destroys each illusion one by one. Love and similar emotions are basically pain. Happiness lies in severing the roots of sexual desire. By sacrificing this happiness, humanity can contribute a little toward the world's evolution. In the second stage, happiness is sought after death. Here one must first accept as a premise the immortality of the individual. But the individual consciousness is destroyed at death, and the core of the nervous system severed. In the third stage, happiness is sought in a future world process. This presupposes that the world develops and evolves. But however the world may evolve, old age, death, pain, and misfortune will never cease. The nervous system will become even more sensitive and so the pain will be felt all the more. Pain will increase with evolution. So a full examination of all three stages, beginning, middle, and end, shows that happiness is eternally unattainable.

According to Hartmann's metaphysics, the world is constructed as well as it could be. But if one then went on to ask whether it should or should not exist, the answer would be it should not. That which causes the world to be he named the Unconscious. But there was no point in denying life, because the world would continue to exist. Even though present humanity might be utterly destroyed, another human race will arise at another occasion and repeat the same process. On the contrary, mankind should affirm life, entrust itself to the world process, accept pain gladly, and await salvation.

I shook my head at such a conclusion. But I was strongly drawn to his idea of destroying illusion; it appealed to me very much. Then, seeing that Hartmann himself confessed that his theory of the three stages of illusion had come to him from a reading of Max Stirner, I turned to Stirner. I then went back even further to Schopenhauer, said to be the ultimate source of the philosophy of the Unconscious.

Reading Stirner one had the impression that he was saying the same thing as Hartmann, only Hartmann wrote as a gentleman and Stirner like an anarchist. In the end all that remained after the destruction of every illusion was the self. The self was the only thing in this world on which one could rely. Push this argument to its logical conclusion and anarchy is the only possible conclusion. I shuddered at the thought.

Schopenhauer was Hartmann minus the theory of evolution. Not only would it be better if the world did not exist, it was in fact the worst of all possible worlds. The fact that it existed at all was a blunder. It was simply that the quietude of nothingness had been mistakenly disrupted. The only solution was for the world to return to this quietude through a conscious act. Each individual was a separate blunder and should preferably not exist. To desire the immortality of the individual was to try and immortalize the mistake. Yet even though the individual is destroyed, the species we call humanity will always remain. This indestructible element he called the Will, in the broadest sense of the word, and this Will was in opposition to Representation, which was mortal. Precisely because this Will existed, nothingness was not an absolute but only a relative negation. His Will was the same thing as Kant's "thing-in-itself." Suicide might well be the best way for the individual to return to nothingness, but nevertheless the species, the thing-in-itself, would always remain. So all one could really do was live on until death came naturally. Hartmann's concept of the Unconscious was a slightly different version of this concept of Will.

I shook my head all the more.

So passed three years of study abroad. And then, while my mind was still agitated in this way, like an object not yet in equilibrium, the time came for me to leave that cultured land, so conducive to the pursuit of learning. I do not only mean teachers. The books that were my constant companions were never very far away and could invariably be found just by going to the university library; and when you wanted to buy them, there was none of the bother of having to wait months and months for them to arrive. Such was the convenient land I had to leave behind.

I longed for home. I longed for home as the beautiful familiar land of my dreams. But I also regretted that I was returning to a land that was not yet equipped either for the kind of serious scientific research I had to undertake or for the opening up of new fields within that discipline. I venture to say "not yet." A certain German, who has lived in Japan for a long time and is said to know the country inside out, has stated not only that such necessary conditions are lacking for the moment but that they will never arise in the Far East. He claims that the atmosphere to nourish the natural sciences does not exist here. If this is in fact the case, then such establishments as the Imperial University and the Research Institute for Infectious Diseases will never be anything more than transmitters of the results of research done in Europe. This same kind of attitude can also be found in the play *Taifun*, which was all the rage in Europe in the wake of the Russo-Japanese War. But I still venture to say "not yet." I refuse to believe that the Japanese are a race of such hopeless incompetents. I have always felt, ever since those earliest days, that the time will come when the fruits of scientific research carried out in Japan will be exported to Europe.

So, with a backward glance at that land where the atmosphere was so conducive to the development of the natural sciences, I set out for the native land of my dreams. I had to leave, of course, but it was not simply out of a feeling of duty that I left. The balance of my desires, with a land of so many conveniences on the one hand and my homeland on the other, definitely inclined toward the latter, despite the fact that a gentle white hand was pulling softly on the cord from which the former hung suspended.

The Siberian railway was not yet completed, so I returned across the Indian Ocean. Even on a short one-day trip the way back always seems shorter than the way there. My journey took forty or fifty days, and yet I had the same impression. In contrast to the past, when I had set out full of hope for an unknown world, the voyage back seemed both short and lonely; and as I lay back in my wicker deck chair, I thought of the presents I had in my trunk.

In my branch of the natural sciences I was not bringing back merely the results of my research; I was returning with seedlings which I intended should grow in the future. And yet the climate to nourish them did not exist at home, at least not yet. I was worried lest they wither away and die. I was overwhelmed by a fatalism and a dull sense of foreboding. Nor was I carrying in my trunk a philosophy bright enough to break through this gloomy darkness. All I had was the pessimism of Schopenhauer, Hartmann, and the like: a philosophy that considered it would be better if the phenomenal world did not exist at all. Not exactly a complete denial of evolution, but certainly an evolution toward an awareness of nothingness.

In Ceylon I was sold a beautiful bird with blue wings by a man with a red-checkered cloth wound round his head and loins. When I came back to the ship carrying the cage, one of the French sailors made a strange gesture. *"Il ne vivra pas,"* he said. That beautiful blue bird did indeed die before the ship reached Yokohama. It too was an ephemeral souvenir.

I was received with great disappointment by my friends in Japan; and not without reason, because to return with my attitudes was unprecedented. Those before me had pulled their wares from their trunk and shown off some new trick or other, their faces bright with anticipation. I, on the other hand, did exactly the opposite.

In Tokyo the debate about reconstructing the city was at its height, and the smart set said they wanted to put up those buildings the Germans call *Wolkenkratzer,* skyscrapers that you find in America on Block A or B. I argued to the contrary that the more people live in a confined space such as a city the higher the death rate, especially among children. Rather than taking all those dwellings that were now built side by side and piling them on top of each other, it would make far more sense to improve the water supply and the sewerage, I said.

Then there was a committee which wanted to impose restrictions on building, arguing that we should try to standardize the heights of eaves in Tokyo and thus achieve a beautiful ordered look. I argued that houses lined up like so many soldiers on parade were not at all attractive. If we really wanted a Western style, we should, on the contrary, forget about the height and rather allow each particular form of architecture to have its own style of roof. It would be better to build the fine spectacle of a random mixture of styles as in Venice.

There was also a debate over improving the Japanese diet. They wanted to stop people eating rice and make them eat lots of meat instead. I advised them that it would be better to leave the Japanese diet as it had always been, because rice and fish were so easy to digest. Not that one would prevent anyone from raising cattle and eating meat as well, of course.

There was a similar debate about reforming the spelling system. Some wanted to make us write lines of classical poetry in accordance with modern pronunciation; I insisted that every country had its own system of accepted spelling: the traditional spelling should be retained.

So it turned out that whenever people tried to reform things, I advocated the status quo. I was thus driven into the company of conservatives. Later it became popular to return from abroad as a conservative, although for very different reasons. I think I must have been the first.

Then what of the natural sciences I had studied? Soon after my return I entered a laboratory for a year or two. I worked steadily, intent on providing a solid basis for my conservative views. Proper research would be bound to show that the Japanese, who had developed quite satisfactorily over thousands of years, did not lead so irrational a life. It was self-evident. But when it came to progressing a stage further and setting up new research on new foundations, promotion and other circumstances conspired to remove me from laboratory work. It was farewell to the natural sciences.

I had of course many friends who were far abler than I in this field. Because they stayed and still battle on for the cause, the fact that I was excluded is no particular loss either for the state or for mankind. And yet I feel sorry for those who carry on the struggle. There is no atmosphere and so they gasp for air like divers working under high pressure. There is as yet no satisfactory Japanese equivalent for the word *Forschung* (research): proof that the right atmosphere does not exist. Society does not yet feel the need to express this concept with clarity. It is hardly anything to boast about, but I myself gave the scientific world such coined words as *gyōseki* (results) and *gakumon no suiban* (encouragement of learning), yet there is still no simple, easy way of expressing the idea of *Forschung* in Japanese. The vague word *kenkyū* is not really appropriate. Mere reading and study of books is *kenkyū*, is it not?

Even after such experiences, my mind remains as before, chasing visions of the future and ignoring present realities. What is this phantom we seek, even while we know our life to be already on the downward path?

"How can a man come to know himself?" Goethe once wrote. "Never through reflection. Perhaps through action. Try to do your duty and in the end you will know your own true worth. What is your duty? The demands of the here-and-now."

To see the demands of the here-and-now as one's duty and then to carry them out: this is the exact opposite of ignoring present realities. Why is it that I seem incapable of putting myself in such a position? To be able to treat the demands of the day as the whole of your work you must know they will suffice, and that I cannot do. I am an eternal malcontent. Somehow I am fated to be misplaced. Somehow I cannot bring myself to see a gray bird as if it were a blue bird. I am lost. I wander in a dream; in a dream and searching for a blue bird within that dream. I ask why, but can give no answer. It is a simple fact, a fact of my consciousness.

And so I descend the final slope of life and know that at the bottom lies death. I am not, however, afraid of death. They say the older one gets, the stronger one's fear of death. But I feel no such fear. As a youth I had a passionate desire to solve every problem that lay in my path, before reaching the destination we know as death. But this desire has gradually lessened and lost its intensity. It is not that I am blind to insoluble problems that lie across my path; it is not that the problems I see I consider to be insoluble; it is merely that I have lost that sense of urgency.

It was about then that I came to hear of the theories of Philipp Mainlaender, and so read his "Philosophy of Redemption." Mainlaender accepted Hartmann's three stages of illusion, but then he said it was unreasonable to first of all destroy people's illusions and then tell them to affirm life. All was indeed illusion, but death made a nonsense of the whole matter in any case, so you could hardly tell people to pursue such illusions. First of all man catches sight of death in the distance and turns his back on it in fear. Then he gingerly skirts around it in a wide circle. This circle gradually gets smaller and smaller, until eventually he flings his tired arms around the neck of death and looks it straight in the eye. And in the eyes of death he finds peace. Having argued this far, Mainlaender himself committed suicide at the age of thirty-five.

I myself have no fear of death, nor have I Mainlaender's "death wish." Neither in fear nor in love with death, I simply walk down the final slope.

Knowing I could not solve this puzzle, I had lost the sense of urgency to do so; but I could not simply discard it without a second thought. Having little taste for entertainment and having nothing you could really call a vice, interested in neither *go,* chess, nor billiards, and bereft of my test tube once

I had left the laboratory, I would occasionally go and see a painting or sculpture, or listen to some music. Mostly, however, when I was not fulfilling the demands that each day happened to put upon me, I was reduced to reading books.

In the process of destroying all human happiness as mere illusion, Hartmann also claimed that man suffers aftereffects somewhat akin to a hangover from almost everything he thinks makes him happy. Only art and learning are free from such effects. This is precisely what I found myself concentrating upon. The avoidance of painful aftereffects was not so much a calculated decision as a natural distaste for such things.

I read avidly. When I left the laboratory the type of book I read changed drastically as a matter of course. Ever since my years in Europe I had subscribed to complete sets of fifteen or sixteen different specialized scientific journals such as *Archive* and *Jahresberichte*. But when I realized that I would no longer be working in a laboratory, I found I had no need to refer to detailed records of experiments and the like. These journals were really the kind of thing you would expect colleges and libraries to buy rather than individuals, but I had brought back many thousands with me, partly because I was unsure exactly how much the government would allow me for journals, and partly because I had no idea where I might be working. I decided now to keep two or three annual reports, the most convenient references for the history and development of certain sciences, and give the rest to the Military Academy. I would buy books on philosophy and literature instead, I decided; and these I read whenever time permitted.

Now, however, I read in a very different way from when I had hungrily devoured Hartmann for the first time. As I considered the words of famous men in the past and in the present, I felt like a man standing at the crossroads who looks coolly at the faces of passersby. My gaze was detached, but I did stand there and occasionally raise my hat to them. There were many, both past and present, who were worthy of respect. I raised my hat, but I was never tempted to leave the crossroads and follow in their footsteps. Many teachers have I met, but not a single master.

There were times when my gestures were misinterpreted. At the very moment I returned from my scientific studies abroad, there was this question of the Japanese diet. In stating my case, I applied standards based on work done by Voit, a recognized authority of the time. I was then accused by a senior colleague of being a Voit worshiper. No, I replied, that was not necessarily the case; I was just using his defenses to attack the enemy on this occasion. He was not impressed. But I had only used Voit as a convenient authority. Exactly the same thing happened when I once dared to voice an opinion on artistic matters and used Hartmann's aesthetics as the foundation for discussion. Some young hero argued that because Hartmann's aesthetics came from his philosophy of the Unconscious, one had to believe in the philosophy before one could use the aesthetics as a basis for criticism. Of course Hartmann's aesthetics were closely tied to his own view of the world, but even if you severed this link completely, his system of aesthetics was still the best to date, the most original. All I was doing was raising my hat to him as one contemporary authority in the field of aesthetics. Much later, excellent proof was provided that Hartmann's aesthetics could stand independently of his view of the world. Open any book on the subject written later than Hartmann, and you will find they all talk of the "modification of the Beautiful." You will not find this phrase before Hartmann, because he originated the idea. Everyone takes it for granted now and never even mentions him; they ignore him.

Be that as it may, the man at the crossroads has met many a teacher, but not a single master; and he also came to realize that metaphysics, no matter how cleverly constructed, is no better and no worse than a single piece of lyric poetry.

And then, to my ears, weary of metaphysical edifices, reminiscent of the complex harmonies of church music of the Dutch school, came the odd fragmented melodies of certain aphorisms.

I had not been able to accept Schopenhauer's *Quietive,* that sedative which tried to destroy the will to life and make people enter a state of nothingness; but now something whipped me out of my soporific state. Nietzsche's philosophy of the superman. This too, however, was intoxicating wine rather than nourishing food. With keen pleasure I saw his dismissal of the passive altruistic morals of the past as the morals of the common herd. I was also delighted to see him not only describe the socialist view of universal brotherhood as the morality of a stupid, foolish crowd who rejected all privilege, but also revile rampant anarchists as dogs barking in the streets of Europe. I could not, however, seriously accept his rejection of the conventions of the intellect, his argument that the will to power lay at the root of all culture, nor the way he made a figure such as Cesare Borgia the classic model for a ruler's morality, a man who never thought twice of using poison or the dagger for the sake of his clique or himself. Moreover, to eyes that had seen the closely argued ethical theories of Hartmann, even the Revaluation of All Values lost some of its novelty. And then what of death? The Eternal Recurrence brought no consolation. I felt some sympathy for the emotions of a man who could not bring himself to write of Zarathustra's final hours.

Somewhat later I also investigated why Paulsen's work was so popular, but I could find no sympathy for his eclecticism and thus left such trends of thought untouched.

≈

In this small hut, built some time ago as a country retreat, just large enough to sit in, the old man has only the barest of necessities, like a Buddhist recluse. But every wall is covered with shelves and every shelf filled with books. Although he seems quite cut off from intercourse with the outside world, parcels of books arrive from Europe. He has arranged for a notary to have control of his financial affairs, small though they be, and the greater part of the interest from his estate is sent to some bookshop in Europe.

He is getting on in years but still has eyes as sharp as any Negro. He reads old books as most people visit old acquaintances, and he reads new books as most people go to market and meet new people. When he tires of reading, he walks over the dunes and contemplates the pine groves, or he goes down to the shore and gazes at the turbulent sea. He satisfies his hunger with a plate of vegetables prepared by his servant Yasohachi.

Apart from books, the old man plays with his small magnifying glass, studying the little flowers he brings back from the dunes. He also has a Zeiss microscope with which he examines minute creatures to be found in drops of seawater. There is also a Merz telescope through which he can study the stars on cloudless nights. Odd pastimes which serve as reminders of earlier scientific study.

Even since moving here, however, he has still been unable to rid himself of that age-old feeling that he is chasing a vision. Musing on times gone by, it occurs to him that perhaps the only people who are really entitled to be dissatisfied with the demands of the present are men of genius. If he had been in the position of having made a great scientific discovery or having produced a great idea, or a great work in philosophy or the arts, would he not now have felt a certain satisfaction? But this was beyond him; hence he too was bedeviled by a sense of unrest.

Seeds sown in the heart at youth are not easily uprooted. The old man, who now regards all philosophical and literary movements with a certain amount of skepticism, still takes an interest, albeit indirect, in the work of scientists, that patient work of building, heavy stone on heavy stone. Many years have passed since the Catholic editor of the *Revue des Deux Mondes,*

Brunetière, prophesied the bankruptcy of science, but science is still with us. In the midst of the pointlessness of much of man's endeavor, science is surely one of the things that has the greatest future.

Consider how it now seems possible to prevent and cure disease, the greatest scourge of mankind, with the aid of science. Vaccination prevents smallpox. With the aid of artificially cultivated bacilli and the serum of animals implanted with those bacilli, it is possible to prevent typhus and to cure diphtheria. Even with such a terrible disease as the plague, the virus responsible has just been isolated and prevention is a distinct possibility. Leprosy too: the virus at least is known. And in the case of tuberculosis, although tuberculin has not had the success that was at first anticipated, there is at least some clue as to its prevention. And with malignant tumors such as cancer, we may soon discover how to prevent them now that we can transplant them into animals. Recently they have found a cure for syphilis in Salvarsan. Nor is it beyond the bounds of possibility that life itself may be prolonged indefinitely, as prophesied in the optimistic philosophy of Elias Metschnikoff, who invests such hope in the future.

So the old man spends the rest of his days, already numbered, neither in fear of death nor in love with death, but with the sense of a dream unfinished. Sometimes his reminiscences reveal the traces of many years in an instant, like a long, long chain, and at such times his keen eyes stare out over the distant sea and sky.

This is an odd scrap jotted down at just such a moment.

1911

Hyaku monogatari

GHOST STORIES

GHOST STORIES, WRITTEN IN 1911, remains one of the classic statements in which Ōgai reveals his attitude as a "bystander." The narrator, presumably the author himself, attends a foolish party in which an old-fashioned game of telling ghost stories is to be played. When he meets the host of the evening, so restrained and withdrawn, the protagonist suddenly has the eerie feeling that in this strange mirror image he has met "an old friend in a strange land." This sense of recognition provides a genuine chill and perhaps serves as the only real "ghost" observed during the evening. The extended play of observation and reflection that constitutes the texture of the narrative makes this story one of the most satisfying of Ōgai's shorter works written during these years.

A number of real people inhabit the narrative. Some, like the celebrated novelist Ozaki Kōyō (1867–1903), center of his celebrated writer's group the Kenyūsha (Society of Friends of the Inkstone), the scholar Yoda Gakkai (1833–1909), and the translator of French drama and fiction Osada Shūtō (1871–1915), were well known to Ōgai's readers. Descriptions of others, like the host Shikamaya himself, were based on real persons living at the time but here transmuted into fictional characters to serve the larger purposes of the narrative. Shikamaya, incidentally, is called on several occasions "the Kibun of our time"—a reference to a famous merchant of the Tokugawa period, Kinokuniya Bunzaemon (1665–1734), a profligate whose life and adventures were chronicled in various popular *kabuki* plays.

AS I REMEMBER, IT WAS A DAY in the year when, for some reason or other, the Sumida River festival was pushed back well toward autumn. As a certain number of years have gone by, it may be that my memory has become a bit hazy; on the other hand, it may be precisely because of such reasons that the whole incident, blurred and muddy though it may be, remains so brightly colored and thus has been rolled into a corner of the storehouse of my memory.

It was, of course, the first time in my life that such a thing had happened to me. Nor did I expect that such a thing would occur again. Thus I might describe what follows as a once-in-a-lifetime experience. The occasion was my visit to a gathering of the *hyaku monogatari,* "a hundred tales."

I know well enough that in fiction no explanations are provided, but here I flatter myself, as perhaps would anyone, in thinking that if a tale such as this were to be translated into any of the European languages, then, when it joined the literature of the world, readers in other countries would doubtless have difficulty in fathoming its meaning; they would be convinced that the writer had created something altogether preposterous. Therefore, I have decided to begin my tale with an explanation. The "telling of a hundred tales" requires that a large group of persons be gathered together. A hundred candles are set up and lighted. Each person in turn tells a ghost story, at which time one candle is extinguished. Then, just as the hundredth candle is put out, a real ghost will actually appear. Or so it is said. The effect must arise from some sort of stimulation to the nerves, as when a fakir cries out "Allah! Allah!" and lowers his head, so that a vision of his god might suddenly appear.

The one who tempted me to join this gathering was my friend the amateur photographer Shitomi. He was always well groomed, and indeed his clothing and belongings showed him to follow the latest fashions. Once, when he saw me attempting a playscript, he made the following remark. "Somehow, in the things you write, there is something a little out of the ordinary. It would be a good thing if you actually *saw* a play from time to time." I believe he said this to me out of kindness, but I don't think he realized that his remark threatened to destroy whatever I had that was mine to contribute. In any case, my theatrical experiment was to end as one, and I achieved no sort of success whatsoever; still, those who followed me began to compose one "awkward experiment" after another, so that the appearance of our theater has changed considerably. Perverse as he was, Shitomi had no idea that one might surpass the age in which one lives; nor did he wish to

TRANSLATED BY J. THOMAS RIMER

understand. Our relations, which had never been very deep, have since been discontinued; nevertheless, I still envy him that life of his, in which he could enjoy whatever was proffered for his use before his very eyes. On the whole, it could probably be said that Shitomi was at that time the most perspicacious of all those young gentlemen of the Tokyo downtown quarters.

It was during the afternoon of the day before the river festival that Shitomi came to see me. Why not come along, he said. Before the festival, a boat will go upstream, he informed me, past the Kuroda and Chūō sections of the city, then on up the river, to the place where the "tales of a hundred candles" will be held at Terajima.

"Why not come along?"

"Who is the host? I don't really have an invitation, so is it really all right that I come?" I asked him.

"Oh, of course. The man who is giving the party is Mr. Shikamaya. You know the one. He's got a lot of money. There are sure to be some who won't turn up, so if you come along, no one will mind at all. Knowing you, though, I suppose you'll insist that it's not the morally correct thing to do. I met Shikamaya two or three days ago, and I told him about you. He said that I might bring you as my guest. I am perfectly willing to go with you, but I had to go off on some other business, so I will leave before you do, if that is all right with you."

As far as I was concerned, the time and the place could be managed, and I had no other business at hand just then. So, with a certain amount of curiosity as to what all of this might be about, I went off accordingly to the boathouse at Yanagibashi at around half past three.

The weather was a bit humid, but as there was a light breeze blowing from the south, the day was quite endurable. The boathouse was constructed on a portion of the riverbank that has since been removed, just across from Kamesei. I believe it used to be called the Masudaya. Because of the importance of the occasion, the boathouse had apparently been reserved, and near it throng after throng of people were crowding about. The guests were pushing into the upper and lower floors alike, into whatever rooms they could find. I was guided upstairs, where I managed to get a look across the room. There, in the midst of a mass of male faces I did not know, I saw sitting my white-bearded friend Yoda Gakkai, dressed informally in a gauze silk *haori* with a splashed blue pattern. In front of him sat an overdressed, somewhat plump young man who was speaking with him in a respectful fashion. I greeted my friend, then wedged myself in at a slightly distant spot. The breeze from the river blew past the bamboo blinds, so that, despite the crowding, it was not all that hot.

As I listened to Mr. Yoda and his partner chatter on for a time, I realized

that the young man was in fact an actor who performed with the Sōshi Theater Company, known for its stagings of political dramas. Responding to Mr.
Yoda's thoughts, he said something to the effect that "surely, from now on,
actors will doubtless have to do a lot of reading concerning all sorts of
things."

I sensed such an extraordinary lack of harmony between his own attitude
and the subject of reading that, although in a sense I was interfering in their
conversation, I couldn't help laughing to myself as I sat by the side listening
to them. At the same time, I culled up an amusing recollection of my own
on the subject of reading. At some moment or other a while back, I was
watching a *kabuki* actor in the performance of a domestic drama. The actor,
who was playing the part of the young protagonist, one of those of the type
whose good looks are for sale, had the line, "So, I'm supposed to 'do reading,' then . . . ," at which point he pulled a bookstand toward him while a
flirtatious young woman managed to bring around some thin tea. The hypocritical youth did not appear as though he had much interest in books and
was quite prepared to employ such an artifical word as "do reading," a term
coined in this country from Chinese characters; now I found this unintended
humor duplicated still again, this time away from the stage.

Then I suddenly became aware of something else. The matter of feigned
airs and hypocrisy did not apply only to this discussion between the actor
and Mr. Yoda alone. The whole large group assembled on the second floor
said very little, but when they did manage to mutter something or other,
they all appeared to dissemble. Each and every one of them had been
invited here as guests; yet it was as though they had come together by chance
in a carriage or on a ferry, for between them they found no points of common interest. Now and again, when they did manage to say something to
each other, their words never extended beyond pleasantries concerning the
weather. Their conversation went in fits and starts, like a watch which,
shaken when wound, ticks for a few seconds and then stops again. In a
moment, the original silence would quickly return.

I thought to speak a bit with Mr. Yoda, but I could think of nothing but
empty remarks myself, so I said nothing at all. I looked at the faces of all
those assembled there. Each was thinking of things that pertained to him
personally. They had all been gathered to participate in this "tale of a hundred candles," but this pastime in itself represented a legacy from another
age. Even to define this occasion as a legacy was perhaps to go too far; the
game itself was long dead, and only the empty name remained. Objectively
speaking, perhaps, a ghost was a ghost, but even such illusionary subjectivity
created during past centuries by the insertion of such empty stuff had now
disappeared completely. Tales of a hundred ghosts such as those were now

replaced with the *Ghosts* of Ibsen. Such old things could thus no longer hold any power of attraction. They did not possess the force to prevent all those guests from thinking only about their personal interests.

A kind of assistant appeared while I and the others were vaguely standing about. He guided us to the boat itself. There were five or six roofed pleasure boats tied up at the wharf just by the boathouse. Crowds of people were climbing up and down the stairs in order to board them. In the midst of all this, I caught a fleeting vision of a red sleeve of printed silk muslin, accompanied by the shrill voice of one who might be importuning a friend while serving *sake*. "I want to go on board with you! Over this way!" Yet in fact most of the guests were men, and there were only a few women mixed among them. I could not figure out at all where Shikamaya the host might be. Nor did I meet my friend Shitomi.

Even though the doors on the second story of the boathouse were thrown open, the guests, packed into the room, were suffering from the heat; but once the boat started off, it became delightfully cool. The boats to be used for viewing the fireworks had not yet set sail, so the surface of the water was surprisingly uncrowded. The boat I boarded was propelled by a stalwart rower of forty, with a face like an ivory *netsuke* carving soiled from too much handling; he looked extremely serious in his work, using his arms and legs like a gymnast in order to manipulate the oars. As this was Shikamaya's affair, it was clear that he could expect to receive an ample gratuity, yet he did not look particularly pleased. He looked as though he wanted to say something like "do any fool thing you want to; as for me, I'll get by just rowing this boat."

I sat cross-legged on the thin matting and, taking off my straw hat and pulling out my handkerchief to wipe the sweat from my forehead, I looked over at the faces of the others seated in the boat. Persons from the various rooms in the boathouse had been mixed together before leaving the boathouse in order to board, and so there were many faces I had not seen before. Mr. Yoda had apparently gone on another boat; in the end, I realized that I recognized none of these faces. And each of those faces I could not recognize seemed, just like those I had observed on the second floor of the boathouse, to be in a daze, as if each person were altogether lost in private thoughts.

The boat had been provided with food and drink, but, as on all the other boats, perhaps because there was no detailed plan on the part of the host as to how such things were to be distributed, this hospitality was spurned, and no one urged the *sake* along. As was the custom on such occasions, the guests uttered a polite refusal of what was offered, all the while scowling at each other. Eventually, a red-faced man of about fifty, who wore over his unlined, tightly woven silk kimono an outer jacket of thin gauze, said, "Well, what about it, all of you? After all, this has been prepared especially for us." Saying this, he took a *sake* cup in his hand; in turn, hands reached from everywhere to do the same. Then they took up the chopsticks. Eating and drinking began with great aplomb. Still, the conversation never progressed beyond niceties concerning the weather. "What do you think about that? If this beautiful summer continues on like this, the rice will come out fine." "Absolutely. But if the rice sells too cheaply, that might bring some sort of downturn." "Oh, that's unthinkable! Heaven forbid!" Such was the level of the conversation.

From where I was sitting, I could look directly at the stern of the boat that was being rowed along just in front of us. There were two people serving *sake* there. Near them was a man with a closely cropped head, wearing a *hakama* with empty crests, of a roughly woven simple fabric, but with no outer jacket. He appeared to be a *nō* actor and was joking about the *sake,* as he bantered on with the servers, who were cackling back at him.

The boat moved on upstream toward Nishigashi; until we reached this side of Umayabashi, each time we passed the sluice gates of one of the big storehouses, the flowing tide brought floating on the surface of the stagnant water bits of straw, wood shavings, umbrella frames, even the contents of emptied chamber pots. In the midst of all this, and seeming not to mind, a seagull was pitching about in the waves. From a point at the bank of the river at Suwachō, the boat moved toward the middle of the river. At a point above Azumabashi, a large clump of people stood watching the river. There were some students among them, and just as our boat passed under the spot where they stood, they roared out "Stupid fools!"

The place where the boat finally pulled in was, I believe, in the vicinity of Mokubaji. Unluckily, the breeze had stopped altogether; the reeds growing along the bank never moved at all. Over on the bank on the other side, the atmosphere seemed saturated with humidity. The ash-colored air rendered indistinct the outlines of the houses built there at Hashiba. From the bottom of the embankment to the edge of the water, at a spot crisscrossed by a tiny path, one boat after another landed; and while the tiny sandals worn by the servers were easy to identify, it was impossible to pick out each set of the ordinary low clogs worn by most of the guests.

Those who were earnest descended with bare feet and looked around for their own clogs, while others carelessly picked up any old thing they could find and went off. There were even some who lazily chose some fairly new-looking footwear and impudently made use of them. I saw that there was nothing to be done and so waited until after the others in order to put on an old pair of wooden clogs that had been left behind. Then I realized that they were very difficult to walk in, since they were unevenly worn down from so much prior use. From what I learned later, the host had heard about the mixup in footwear; he then had sent to each guest as a gift a new pair of sandals. But in my own case, he must somehow have felt that the gesture was somehow improper, so he evidently never did make such a gift to me.

Presumably there had been someone there to guide the guests when the first boat arrived. As one boat pulled up, those on board would put on the wooden shoes provided, but before they could reach their destination, the next boat would arrive at the dock. The passengers would then climb up on the embankment, follow along the tiny path, and then cross through the rice fields, seeking out a certain villa at Terajima. The line formed by the clusters of the arriving guests would continue, then break off; yet even when the path remained occasionally empty, the new group following along was never far from the sight of those who had gone on ahead. I too stumbled along on my worn-down clogs over those paths through the paddies and by the country hedges until reaching the spot that represented the object of our journey.

The residence was a small one, very much like the ones I had seen along the way. The house was surrounded by a tall hedge with a roofed gate. Once inside, I caught a glimpse of the entrance hall to the age-blackened building, but in front of it ran a path bordered on left and right with a low hedge of Chinese hawthorn that served as an outside face; granite stones were spread about there at intervals. The person whose back happened to be in front of me made his way safely to the entranceway. Just as he was about to enter, from a break in the hedge to the left, two of the assistants for the evening suddenly emerged, whispering together. Grabbing each others' hands, the two girls said, pulling in their necks, "Oh, it was so scary!"

"What's going on?" I asked them. Both of them looked at me disrespectfully, as if to indicate that I must be some sort of fool who understood nothing; then, with extremely inhospitable expressions, they walked ahead right into the entrance. I suddenly was reminded of a foolish anecdote. In ancient times there was a great lord who wished to remain impassive at all times. He therefore decided that he should practice learning not to smile. Thinking about this, I realized that I did not possess the necessary enthusiasm to ascertain the real reason why these girls felt afraid, and, moving a bit to the side through a hole in the fence, I went on inside and looked around.

There, in a space set toward the back, was a small storeroom that might usually have been used for flowerpots, even brooms. It was already becoming a bit dim in the shade, and it was difficult to see into the depths of the shed. Peeping inside, I could just make out the life-sized figure of a ghost constructed of reeds or some such materials, dressed in a white kimono, long flowing hair hanging down the back. This was the figure already assembled for the storyteller to bring out; he would move among the guests with this figure after lowering the lights. Thinking that I had now a proper foretaste of the "Tale of a Hundred Candles" which would follow, I felt as though I had been made a fool of, and I withdrew.

When I stepped up into the entranceway, I saw in the small space ahead of me two men standing and whispering urgently together. "How are we going to manage this? We told the people on the boat they must bring our candles along. The ones on the stands are all we have." Such was the general tenor of their conversation. They were apparently meddling in some backstage business. They paid no attention to me standing there and went on inside. Another man came out as if to replace them, peered around, and then went back inside without saying a word.

Wondering what I should do next, I remained quietly where I was for a moment; then I noticed that to the right a light was shining behind the paper sliding doors, and I could hear voices there. I went off to look in that direction. The room was fourteen mats in size, and the southern portion faced a garden in which were arranged such things as a pruned pine tree, a large three-legged lantern, a small pond, and so forth. There were upwards of twenty people packed in the room. As in the boathouse and on the boat itself, no one seemed to have very much to say. Into whichever face I might look, I found revealed no intensity, no sign of anticipation, not even any curiosity.

Just as I entered the room, a fairly elderly man with a long beard and wearing a roughly woven short traveling coat was saying, "Those mosquitoes are certainly terrible!" The young man next to him replied, "It's that big striped variety. As soon as the lights come on, they'll go away." The voice was familiar to me, and when I looked at the speaker, I realized that it was my friend Shitomi. He discovered me at precisely the same moment.

"Ah! So you got here after all. You haven't yet met Mr. Shikamaya, our host. Let me introduce you."

With these words, Shitomi pushed on through the crowd, saying, "Excuse me, excuse me . . ." and, forcing a space between the guests with the palm of his hand, he moved away from the entrance toward the latticed window. I followed behind him quietly.

At a spot by the latticed window where Shitomi was heading stood a man whose appearance was quite different from that of the other guests. Although the room was filled with people, the space surrounding him was empty; indeed, when I had first entered the room, I had taken cognizance of that fact. He appeared to be about thirty years old. His face was long and pale, and it seemed some time since his hair had been cropped. Over some sort of unlined summer kimono of a muted pale blue with sober stripes, he wore a *hakama*. He sat slouching slightly forward. His eyes were a bit bloodshot, as though he had spent a sleepless night. He hardly looked around at the guests but rather stared stiffly, directly in front of him. Nearby sat a young woman, apparently in charge of escorting him. She remained somewhat behind him. She was dressed as well in extremely conservative taste. She had taken pains that her *obi,* her sash clip, and her kimono made of light crepe, in the popular fashion, would attract as little attention as possible; indeed, the fundamental tone of gray she had chosen was most unusual for a young woman of about twenty. She was of medium height and build, with an appealing round face. Her hair was bound up in a butterfly coiffure. Down her back she wore only a hairpin with a small piece of red coral as decoration. A stray lock from her refulgent hair lay across one cheek of her tilted head. She was a lovely young woman; there was nothing sharp about her, no conspicuous aspect, nothing striking. From the moment I observed the pair, I had the sense that her presence at the side of this man was like that of a nurse at the side of her patient.

My friend Shitomi led me to him. When he introduced me by name, the man looked at me for an instant, then only returned a polite and silent bow. Shitomi then moved away to talk to someone or other that he knew, while I went off in the direction of the veranda. While looking up at the evening sky, now streaked with thin clouds, I thought about this man Shikamaya I had just met.

For a long time, the society columns of the newspapers had referred to him as the "Kibun of our time" because of his profligate extravagances. And indeed if today's "Tale of a Hundred Candles" was to serve as any example, it could surely be said that his gesture was a bold and curious one that showed an indifference to the situation and manners of our time.

From the beginning, my curiosity as to what would be done when calling people together to participate in such a "Tale of a Hundred Candles" was somewhat abetted by my curiosity concerning the nature of the man who would conceive of such a plan. It is certainly true that I had already begun to sketch out in my mind this Shikamaya in a fanciful way; and when I tried to imagine what sort of man he might be, I would have found it impossible to say. Still, if I were to speak plainly, if I were to have concluded that the host of such an affair as this was indeed some sort of lunatic, I would have imagined him to be of the manic-depressive type. I would never have imagined him to be the grave sort of individual I saw before me now. A long time after this event occurred, I happened to read a novel by Maxim Gorky entitled *Forma Gordeyev,* and I would have have been surprised if, like Forma, Shikamaya had grabbed at one of his guests and thrown him into the Sumida River.

In fact, just what kind of man was he? I knew that he certainly had a complex family background. I saw his name in the papers, and rumors about him circulated by his various friends had certainly reached my ears. I had taken no interest in any of these matters, and therefore had never gave them the slightest thought. Yet the man before me now had, for some reason or other, become full of cares; there could be no doubt at all about that aspect of his behavior. Most men full of woe fall into desperation, and should they sink into profligacy, they seek out strong sensual pleasure; as a result, they apparently dull their consciousness. It is such people as this who risk assuming the manner of a manic-depressive. Yet Shikamaya seemed somehow different. What could be at the root of his melancholy appearance? Those bloodshot eyes, in fact, might well have been caused not by a late night of drinking and profligacy but by a night of thinking and reflection, during which an ordinary and peaceful sleep could well have been impossible. Indeed, if one took a guess, perhaps the host of this "hundred candles" knew very well indeed, and from the beginning, that the whole affair was foolishness. His guests may well have come running out of greed for his food and drink. Or, suppressing their rational faculties in a haze of superstition, they may have been moved to come through a credulous sense of fearful curiosity. Perhaps he was looking at this whole situation in a malicious, indeed a demonic fashion through those very bloodshot eyes. Even after such a thought floated up, then disappeared, the more I thought about it, the more intriguing the evening's host became as my object of study.

While I was observing this Shikamaya, in order to ascertain just what sort of man he might be, I gave no less attention to the woman who accompanied him.

It was widely known all over the country that Shikamaya's most intimate friend was the geisha Tarō. All the more impressive was the fact that she was considered to be the most beautiful geisha in Tokyo. When my friend the novelist Ozaki Kōyō posed for an informal picture with his head on his hands, it was widely recognized as a posture in the manner of Tarō. Everyone said that it was her picture that was being spread around everywhere. Thus when I remembered this incident concerning Kōyō, I realized that I was not seeing this geisha for the first time.

The incident had taken place two years before, as I recall. I was attending a party at the Kogetsu Restaurant. My friend Kōyō and his colleagues from the Kenyūsha made up a majority of the guests. The night was cool, and there were plums and daffodils blooming in the *tokonoma*. It had grown very late, and by the *hibachi* Kōyō, using his arm as a pillar, had fallen asleep. Kōyō was, however, the sort of man who often only dozed, so I am not sure whether he was actually asleep or not. When I looked casually over toward the *tokonoma*, I saw my friend the translator Osada Shūtō, who dressed in a crested kimono of *habutae* silk (unlike the others in the group, who generally wore stripes). He was leaning on the ornamental wooden post of the *tokonoma* talking to a young geisha sitting in front of him. She had a rosy lovely face, well rounded in the chin. She was seated with her body slightly bent, speaking in a quiet fashion in a sober voice, very much in the manner of a young girl. With her hair bound up in a Shimada coiffure and her plump cheeks, she was absolutely charming. When I asked her name of someone sitting nearby, he answered me in surprise, "You mean, you don't know Tarō?"

Since that time, I thought that she must be no ordinary geisha; seeing her today, the difference was remarkable. She was no more geisha-like on this occasion. The earlier innocent girlish quality had by now disappeared. That smiling face, always framed in modesty, which she had before shown so readily, was now hardly to be seen. Still, keeping herself so beautifully groomed as she did, and choosing her clothing with such consummate tact, why was it that now there seemed to be nothing of the geisha about her? Might it be said that she now appeared more like a wife, one who possessed a superb sense of style? No, that supposition was not altogether correct either. My first impression on entering the room still seemed to pursue me. An accidental glance had told me that she appeared to be serving as a nurse to her patient. Such had been my quick impression.

While I stood musing on the veranda, in the room behind me the candle stands were being placed about. This was a period when electric light was not yet available, and gas lamps had not yet found their way to a spot like Terajima. But the fact that ordinary lamps were taken away on purpose and replaced by candles constituted part of the special effects needed for the evening.

After these candle stands were placed about, a huge tub was carried in. It was piled full of *sushi* to eat. The old man who was dressed in his short traveler's coat exclaimed, "Oh, what a good idea!" The young man next to him commented that "this tub seems just like the kind you wash a dead body in!" Then small buckets with ladles thrust inside them were carried in.

Vapor arose from the liquid inside. The same young man cried out, "a bucket to offer holy water to the Buddha!" Into these "holy buckets" were dangled bags of rough cloth filled with tea, soaking in the hot water.

At that moment I saw the man of whom I had caught an earlier glimpse standing in the doorway, the one who was evidently in attendance in order to provide service for the guests. Now, seated in the middle of the room, he began calling out, "Just a moment, honored guests," words that he pronounced as an opening greeting. He was sorry that the preparations had taken so long, but now, for those who might care to eat something simple, boxed dinners were prepared so that those wishing them should come to the adjoining room. Everyone present ate the sushi and drank the tea.

Shitomi brought me some food served up on a piece of paper. Crouched on the sill of the veranda, I ate. "There will be tea soon. All these buckets are brand new," he told me, as if to provide some sort of excuse; then he went off to find some. Even if I had not heard this sort of apology, there was nothing sufficiently unusual about these containers to have set my nerves on edge.

The only time I managed to take my eyes off this couple (doubtless she was not yet his wife, so I would like to call them a couple) was when I turned away from the room to look into the darkening garden, wishing to ponder over my own observations. But when looking into the room, I could find no way to take my eyes off the pair. Even though their guests were busy eating and drinking, the two of them remained absolutely still, without moving at all. Sitting slightly forward, so as not to crush the pleats in his formal dress, the host spoke with no one, his eyes still fixed directly in front of him. Tarō drew near him; she showed no boredom nor, whatever might happen, manifested no smile. Occasionally, however, she would look across at his face as though to gauge his temper.

Leaning on a wooden post where the paper doors had been pushed back, I crouched on the lintel and, filling my mouth with a piece of *sushi* rolled in seaweed, I made a pretense of looking outside; but in fact, I did not cease to observe Shikamaya's appearance. I myself, both by natural inclination and personal custom, have always had a tendency, wherever I may go, to become a bystander. When I lived in the West, I came to know a very open-hearted older scholar. He was possessed of an incurable disease and thus had gone through life without a family. It was therefore not surprising that he had never learned to dance. Once when the subject came up, one of those present explained to me the importance of dancing for reasons of social intercourse and urged me to take some lessons. Another, however, made the observation that dancing represented the remnant of a barbarous age, and with an exchange of peculiar anecdotes, attacked the art of dancing and all the vices that accompany it.

All this time, the older man sat quietly listening. Eventually he said, "You know, of course, of my physical condition, so it is not surprising that I myself have never danced. When I, who cannot dance, look on those who have this skill, they appear to me somehow not as men but as gods; I can only open my eyes wide with astonishment as I watch them." When the old man said this, the faint shadow of a smile played over his face, and it was a smile that contained nothing of disdain or ridicule.

I thought deeply, deeply, over my own attitude of the bystander which has been with me since I was born. I possess no incurable illness. Yet I am one fated since birth to be a bystander. From the time when I first began to play with other children, and even when I grew to adulthood and made my way in the world, and with every kind of person in society, I have never been able to throw myself into the whirlpool and enjoy myself to the depths of my being, no matter what kind of excitement may have been stirred in me. Even though I have made my appearance on the stage of human activity, I have never played a role worthy of the name. The most I have achieved has been the position of a supernumerary. And indeed I have felt most like myself when I had no need to mount that stage and, like a fish in water, could remain at ease among the bystanders. With these feelings, I watched Shikamaya, and, as I did so, I realized that I felt as though I had met an old friend in a strange land. I felt as though one bystander had recognized another.

I knew nothing of Shikamaya's former life. In his youth, when he inherited so much wealth, what sorts of ambitions did he nourish, what sorts of exertions did he undertake? There had been no one to tell me these things. Still, quite a lot of time had passed since he had become intimate with the world of geisha and had gained the nickname of "the Kibun of our time." Indeed, I doubted that Shikamaya was born, as was I, to be a bystander. Nevertheless, he had surely now become one.

How had this situation come about? Had something like an organic defect appeared, such as the one possessed by my doctor friend in the West? Such was not the case. Then Shikamaya must somehow or other have received some sort of intangible wound, one which could not be cured. Was it this that made him a bystander? If such were the case, why was Shikamaya playing host to such a party as tonight's? There were already widespread rumors about his bankruptcy. As his name had been identified as a profligate for some time now, so perhaps his personal life had indeed been such, for all I knew. If so, then perhaps his hosting a party of this kind represented some force of habit that remained from his prideful former way of life, at that moment when he defied so many upon his suddenly becoming a rich man. He might have therefore given in to this habit, continuing to behave as he had before. Perhaps now he observed the traces of his former glory through the eyes of a bystander just in the same way as a writer, for example, observes the work he has created through the eyes of a critic.

Then I found my thoughts turning to Tarō. What kind of woman could she be? If rumors of Shikamaya's bankruptcy could have reached even me, living as I do in virtually a different world, then it was surely impossible for a woman of her apparent sagacity not to be aware herself of the situation. Why did she not abandon this man, surely to expire soon, just as vermin would leave a dying body? Indeed, what was Shikamaya's temperament at this time? Was he not a bystander? If he were truly a bystander, a woman would not be likely to choose him to be her partner. This is because she could not take any real interest in the pleasures of daily life at the side of such a man. Then what had actually happened? The image of a patient and his nurse floated again into my mind. Still, if this woman were to give her life as a nurse who might expect no reward, while all the time placing at the center of her own existence the care that she provided, then she could only be seen herself as a victim. If she were linked to him by any chains of duty as a wife, then she would be bound up in the kind of curse described in Ibsen's *Ghosts*. Such would constitute a different issue. If she were urged on by the desires of carnal love, that too would raise a different set of questions. Yet even if such a situation might appear to be the real one, there were still some reasons for doubt. I looked again at the possibilities: if it were not a question of money, nor of the joys of life, nor duty, nor love, then I became all the more astonished at her powers of self-sacrifice.

As I was thinking over these matters, I found still in my hand the paper with a bit of sliced ginger left over from the *sushi* I had been eating while staring vacantly at the couple. At that moment, one of the men assisting with the party came up to the host and whispered something into his ear; Shikamaya, who until now had remained as motionless as a doll, suddenly got up and left the room. Tarō followed along inside after him.

A few moments later, my friend Shitomi came over to where I was sitting. Squatting down on the lintel, he said, "Professor Yoda, now that he has eaten his supper there in the other room, says that he would prefer to go home without waiting to hear the ghost stories, so Shikamaya has gone to see him off. The heat has gone down, so they are going to close up the sliding doors and ask everyone to come in here, even though the place is rather small, so that the storytelling can begin."

When I first saw Shikamaya, I noticed at once his melancholy expression; and then, watching him as I sat, never taking my eyes away from him for an instant, I first had a strong feeling that he had set out to make fools of us. That initial feeling grew sharper; at one instant I even found his look demonic. Yet now that feeling, at the moment when my friend Shitomi told me that Shikamaya was going to see off Mr. Yoda, had somehow softened. Now I told Shitomi that I was thinking of getting ready to leave myself. When I first heard about the "Tale of a Hundred Candles," I was curious as to what such an event might be, just as I had a considerable curiosity as to what kind of man Shikamaya the host might be; yet now, as I was largely satisfied on both points, my desire to hear these old ghost stories told by the entertainer hired for the evening had faded completely. Nor did Shitomi attempt to persuade me to remain.

There was no occasion for me to bid the host goodbye in any ceremonial fashion nor, happily, were there any others I knew among all the other guests assembled. I got up silently and put on the same old battered wooden clogs I had worn when the boat had landed in the first place. I casually strolled away from the now haunted house.

Until my eyes adjusted to the dark, I found it difficult to walk along the path that ran through the rice fields. In the shade of the grasses that grew beside the path, the crickets began to chirp faintly.

Two or three days later, when I met my friend Shitomi, I asked him, "What happened after I went home?" This is what he told me. "You left at exactly the right time. After listening to the stories for a bit, I suddenly realized that Shikamaya wasn't there. When I asked, it turned out that he had doubtless gone upstairs with Tarō, put up a mosquito net, and gone to sleep. Shikamaya is not the kind of person who would purposely set out to act in any rude fashion, but he is indifferent. So this is just the sort of thing he's likely to do."

I thought to myself that those who are truly bystanders doubtless do make fools of others, to a certain degree.

1911

Futari no tomo

TWO FRIENDS

PUBLISHED FIVE YEARS AFTER *A Bachelor* in 1915, *Two Friends* dispenses with the fictional mode altogether. Ōgai was now in his mature phase and was engaged in writing his historical narratives and stories. In the present account, he was to turn his subtle techniques of commentary and description that proved so effective in bringing alive the Tokugawa period or ancient China to use in describing two friendships he had developed during his four years of exile in Kokura. His friend F was not described in *A Bachelor*, but the Zen monk who appeared briefly in that story as Neikokuji-san now assumes his real name (or, more properly, real nickname) of Ankokuji-san.

Ōgai's technique employed so successfully in the historical stories, where he uses selective description as a means of delineating character, is put to good use here as he traces certain details in the lives of his two Kokura friends. Each detail helps sharpen the contrasting images of these two men, but subtle resemblances are suggested as well, so that the fact of the pair's later meeting in Tokyo emerges naturally as part of the total design of the narrative. Here Ōgai again plays the bystander, watching the two of them, first apart, then together. The account is spare but extremely touching in its rendering of the characters of these two men who, each in his own way, loved learning and thus came to respect one another.

I LIVED IN KOKURA IN BUZEN for nearly four years. It was October of my first year there. I had spent a lonely summer in the house in Kajimachi which I had rented at the height of a long rainy spell in June. The summer lingered and warm days continued one after the other. I returned home from the office after four o'clock every day. Occasionally when I sat in the ten-mat room, the honeybees which the owner of the house kept would come buzzing around the eaves. The road in front of the house was wide enough for two rickshaws to pass one another with ease. From the house on the other side of the road, I could hear the humming of a spinning wheel twisting thread. The woman spinning thread was a one-eyed old maid who worked at my house the day my regular maid took off.

One day when I came home from the office, I opened a book on psychology written by the German philosopher Wilhelm Wundt, which I had been reading and had left on the desk. I read half a page, but couldn't get interested in it and put it down. Listening to the usual sound of the spinning wheel I became lost in thought.

The maid came in with the name card of someone I didn't know. I asked her what sort of person he was and she replied that he was a young man wearing Western-style clothes. I told her to show him in and in a moment he entered the room.

He seemed barely twenty, jovial and quite unreserved in disposition. I later realized that what had given me this impression was that, as a result of his mixing with many foreigners, without being aware of what was happening, he had lost the customary Oriental reserve.

After the introductions were finished, I asked why he had come to see me. His name was F. His reply was most unusual. Like myself, he was from Iwami. I was born in Tsuwano in the domain of the Kamei clan, but F was from the so-called "*daimyō*-owned" lands controlled by the Tokugawa shoguns. He said that he had decided at an early age to study German and had gone to Tokyo to study. He had registered in several different schools and had studied under various teachers, but at present none of the schools or instructors satisfied him. He had also become acquainted with a large number of Germans. But just as there are few Japanese who have a systematic understanding of the Japanese language, his German acquaintances were not well versed in their native language either. He had then tried looking at German written by Japanese and at various translations from German by Japanese, but he found that they were full of errors. Of these, however, F

TRANSLATED BY JAMES M. VARDAMAN, JR.

198

said that he had concluded that I wrote German the most freely and translated most accurately. Nevertheless, since it appeared that my life in Tokyo was exceedingly busy, he had not approached me. Then I had moved to Kokura. At that point he had taken the trouble to follow me from Tokyo. From now on he would be in Kokura, he said, and wanted to study German under my tutelage.

I was astounded at F's great self-confidence and at his tremendous overestimation of me. I listened to what he said, and for a while I looked at him in silence. Thinking back on it later I regretted having considered the thought, but at that moment I began to think that he might be a lunatic.

For the time being, I replied that he was overestimating me. I was not as good as he thought. But setting that matter aside for the time being, was he really so fluent in German that in the whole city of Tokyo there was no one who could teach him? He must forgive me, I said, but I certainly doubted that was true. Having said this, I took up the Wundt volume that was on my desk and put it in front of him. I told him that the book was a little too specialized and was not completely suitable for testing one's ability in German, but that if he didn't mind, I wanted to have him read a page or so and explain to me in Japanese what it was about. I added that I had novels and magazines in German if he preferred.

F took the book from me and looked at the title. "It's psychology," he said.

"That's right. Can you read it?"

"I think I can. I've heard about this volume, but I have never actually seen it before. When I was researching *Pädagogik,* I decided that I simply had to start with psychology, so I have looked a bit at books on psychology. Where shall I read?" As he spoke, he thumbed through the book and came to a chapter toward the end entitled "Die Seele," "A Chapter on the Soul."

"Read a little there and explain it," I said.

F somewhat sheepishly read five or six lines. His voice was lowered, but his pronunciation was clear. He read smoothly and I could understand everything that he read.

"That's enough," I said. "Tell me what it says."

F interpreted the meaning of the technical terminology without much difficulty.

Again I was surprised. F was no lunatic. No wonder he had such self-confidence.

"If you can read that well," I said, "then we are rather evenly matched."

"That's not true. As time goes by I will have questions," he replied.

I had found out that F was not simply bragging. Everything else, however, was in doubt. I decided that most of these things would work themselves out as time passed. But there was one thing I had to know very quickly. That was about his living arrangements—how he was situated.

"If you mean that you want me to advise you in your studies of German, I won't say that I won't advise you. But how do you intend to support yourself here in Kokura?" I asked. F was silent. I immediately pressed on straight-forwardly. "Do you have any money?"

F couldn't maintain his silence. "I used all the money I had to buy the train ticket from Tokyo," he said. "If I ask my parents, I might be able to get some money, but that doesn't help me at the moment. Would you allow me to stay with you for the time being?"

These words had a great impact on my evaluation of him. Although his evident scholarship in German dispelled my doubts that he was crazy and made me raise my estimation of him, these words caused me to lower my estimation of him again. Of course, I don't mean to detract from a man's ability simply because he is poor. But since F, who had not one coin to his name, had come all this way to see me and had paid me a compliment a moment ago, I couldn't help wondering whether his compliment was flattery or sheer sycophancy.

If the desire to pursue knowledge was accompanied by a desire to live off of me, then his motives for coming to me were compromised. If so, given the assumption that there are almost no motives for human behavior that are completely pure, one could hardly help doubting that there was some degree of impurity in the motives that had pressed him to do what he did.

Of those who had called on me to ask to study with me, there had been no one with F's competence. From that perspective F was a marvel. Of those who had come to me as prospective students hoping to receive room and board from me, however, there had been many who had no money to call their own. From that perspective F was no different from the average young man with certain aspirations. I have often had the experience of dealing with such people. In such matters it is good to use a little discretion, taking into consideration the one part of the person that is a marvel.

I never give money to such people. This is one of my guiding principles in dealing with them. I told F that he was very good at German, but that was all I knew about him. Knowing only that, I could hardly consider the possi-bility of his living in my home. I told him I would introduce him to a close friend who ran a boardinghouse. He could lodge and board there on my credit. During that time I would look for a position for him. For a person of his ability, there were several places I might inquire. If things went well, then he could settle accounts with the boardinghouse himself. If things didn't go well, or if he couldn't get money from home, then I would only take care of his boarding expenses. Beyond that I could promise nothing. I asked if that suited him.

What I offered seemed to differ from what he had hoped for, but in the end he agreed to my proposition. He probably figured that I would either accept his proposition or else completely refuse him. Since my reply was neither an approval nor a refusal, he must have been unprepared for what I had said. Though he didn't seem particularly grateful, in the end he agreed to my terms.

I sent a messenger for one of my subordinates and gave him careful instructions. I had him take F to a boardinghouse named Tatsumi. The Tatsumi, located near Kokura station, was where I had stayed when I first arrived in Kokura. The landlady was a widow in her forties who doted on a Japanese spaniel. I entrusted F to this prudent, understanding woman.

The reason I said there might be a position for F was that right at that time there was a youth group in Kokura that was looking for someone who could teach German. I immediately spoke with the person in charge of the group and requested that he engage F. So it worked out that I did not have to pay the Tatsumi account.

F came to visit me almost every day. Our discussions never digressed from the German language, but he didn't ask me very difficult questions. Satisfied with his newly acquired position, he was enthusiastically researching ways to teach beginning German-language students and asked me for advice. As I listened to him, I gradually came to realize a major difference in our respective understandings of German. I realized that each of us had strengths and weaknesses. He was well versed in grammar. He could give a detailed analysis of a sentence. At times he would surprise me with technical words I didn't know. However, he composed in German in the same way a Japanese scholar might write Chinese in a Japanized form. I pointed out that a German would not say things in such a fashion. When he remained unconvinced, I pulled out the paperbound edition of Goethe that I used to carry even when I was traveling, or perhaps some other volume, to prove my point. This kind of interview was rather interesting, so I looked forward to these occasions as much as he did.

On Saturdays and Sundays when the weather was good, I invited F to take walks with me. Since Kokura is such a small town, even walking from one end of town to the other didn't amount to much of a walk. So sometimes we walked along the seashore to Dairi or took the train toward Kashii. Even though he had no particular time to read, he always carried a German book in his pocket. It was usually the Goeschen volume on epistemology or ethnology, or the like. When asked why he did this, he replied that he simply enjoyed reading whenever he did have time. He was a person with a strong desire for learning.

Two or three weeks passed. I wondered what kind of life he was leading, so on my way home from the office one day I visited the Tatsumi boarding-house. At that very moment that landlady was chasing a small dog away from the gate. "I have a hard time because my spaniel is a female and all kinds of dogs come around." "Damn you! Damn you!" she scolded the dog, which kept looking back as it walked away. Her own spaniel looked on indifferently from the reception desk inside.

"How is F doing?" I asked.

With a smile she replied, "He's a rather peculiar character, but after all it's you who is looking out for him."

"You mean it's because I'm looking out for him that he's peculiar? Now that's hard to take. In what way on earth is he peculiar?" I asked, sitting down in front of the reception desk.

"No, I mean he's a very nice person. It's just that now, even when it has gotten cold in the mornings and evenings, he reads with a blanket over his head," she said, offering me a *zabuton* to sit on.

"Oh, dear. I wonder if he's short of funds," I said, as if to myself.

"No. Not too long after he moved in, he told me that he had received some money and he went ahead and paid his account up to the end of this month." Since it was already November, apparently F had paid with the money he had received from the youth group the month before.

I decided to see him and went up to the second floor. In the Tatsumi house the first-class guests were put in the detached room in the back. The second-best room was a room on the second floor of the main house facing the central garden. Then there was a small room with intricate latticework on the windows which faced the road in front. This room was not used for guests. Saying that he would prefer the cheapest room, F settled in the latter room.

"F, are you in?" I called. He opened the sliding door from within. Sure enough he was wearing a flannel shirt with his summer kimono over it. The latticework blocked the sun and there at the foot of the gloomy window was an old writing desk. That was where he sat. We sat facing each other across the small *hibachi* in which glowed a small briquette of charcoal.

What caught my eye immediately was an empty Ebisu beer case on the other side of the desk which he had turned on its side and was using as a bookcase. Three large volumes were quite new. The gold lettering on the leather binding shone from inside the dimly lit box. I tilted my head in order to read the gold letters.

"It's the small Meyer edition," said F.

"I see. They've really put out a nice volume. The one I have is a two-volume set."

"That's the old one. I saw this one when it first appeared at the Nankōdō Bookstore and ordered it through the mail."

"Even though the title says 'Concise' it really takes up a lot of space. Why did you go to the trouble of ordering it?"

"Why? Well, when I'm teaching, I'm asked for the explanation of personal names and place names. I'd feel helpless without a book like this."

F and I talked about encyclopedias, discussing the merits and demerits of Meyer and Brockhaus and how they differ from Larousse and the Britannica in the way they are compiled. We also talked about the current trend of popular novels becoming more like scientific books. We talked on until the lamps came on, and then I went home.

When I got home, I had the maid take an old, lined kimono over to F's place. I realized the reason he had paid fifty days' lodging and bought the *Konversations-Lexikon,* completely using up his monthly wages, was so he wouldn't thoughtlessly waste money on things like cigarettes.

I had felt that F was not without certain expectations and ambitions in our relationship, so from the beginning I maintained a certain distance between us. But as our acquaintance evolved, that distance gradually shrank.

This was in part a result of my recognizing that he was devoted to scholarship enough to buy books even if it meant scrimping on food and clothing. But that certainly wasn't the only reason. From the first day we met I was aware that he had a profound knowledge of German. From that point of view it was clear that he was a lover of learning.

The major reason that the distance between us shrank lay in my discovery that he had almost no knowledge whatsoever concerning the opposite sex. Perhaps this was a misjudgment on my part. But even now I find it hard to believe that I was deluded concerning him.

I'm sure that he wasn't without secrets. And I don't believe that he never told a lie. But he didn't seem like the kind of person who would deliberately tell a lie. He seemed to be the type who wouldn't go to the trouble of put-

ting words together in order to make up a falsehood. Anyone is welcome to
sit down with me and purposely lie to me. I immediately have a strong reaction. This is my instinct. Because of this instinct, I am not easily fooled by
others. Time and time again with one glance I have been able to see through
an impostor who has duped a great number of people.

On the other hand, I am pleased if an irresponsible person, an amoral
person, or a person who has been judged untrustworthy by the world will sit
down with me and frankly reveal himself. For many years I have associated
with such people without resisting them in any way.

As I said before, I felt F expected something of our relationship and I
treated him accordingly. Yet in all our conversations, there was never anything that caused me to react negatively toward him. He spoke impulsively.
When he opened his heart to me, he occasionally did so without reserve.
From time to time what F told me left me completely perplexed. But I
always listened and found what he said to be rather amusing.

Since we saw each other every day and sometimes had the whole day
together, our conversations began to go beyond German and philosophy.
One day I told him the following story. I was known by many people in the
area because of my position. They also came to know F. To look at us one
might have thought we were brothers. Once when I went into the Tokumi
variety shop on Hondori, the shopkeeper told me that my brother had also
been in the shop. I wondered who he was talking about. When I asked, I
found that he was talking about F. I explained that although we were from
the same region of the country, we were not related at all. At that the shopkeeper seemed to put on an incredulous look and said, "Really? But you
look so much alike!" I looked at F and asked him if he thought we
resembled each other.

F replied that the aphorism that there is sometimes a resemblance
between total strangers often seemed to be true. Then he told a story about
the night he stayed in Onomichi. He was put up in a room on one side of
the second floor which surrounded the central garden. The guest on the
other side of the garden had called in a large group of geisha and they were
making a great uproar. Unable to bear the tedium in his room, he went to
the hallway and looked over to the other side. Across the way a geisha came
out, put her hands on the handrail, and looked in his direction. The geisha
called another geisha from the room. The two of them whispered and
looked in F's direction. He had felt it was all right for him to look at them,
but he didn't like being looked at, so he returned to his room. The clamor
from the other side continued well into the night. He got into his bed and
while thinking just how noisy the *shamisen* sounded, he fell asleep. After he

had been asleep a short while, he thought he heard someone come into the room and he awoke. When he opened his eyes, he found that the geisha he had seen earlier was sitting at his bedside. Startled, he got up. "What are you doing here?" he asked. "I have something to ask you," she replied. He got up and folded up his bedding. Then he asked her what she wanted to know. She explained that she was one of the group of geisha in the room on the far side who were spending the night. She said that she was a local girl who had had one brother. Her brother had left home and she didn't know where he was. A while ago when she saw F from the other side of the garden she immediately thought he might be her brother. Many years had passed since they had been separated, but every day she thought about seeing her brother again and was quite unable to forget him. So she had come to his room. When she saw F, she immediately thought of rushing to him, but since she was being watched, she resisted her impulses. If she were mistaken about him, she hoped that he would forgive her. But if she saw someone who she thought was her beloved brother and let him go away without saying anything to him, then she was sure to regret it for the rest of her life. Would he please tell her who he was? F answered that she was, unfortunately, mistaken. He told her that he was from Sekishū and that it was his first visit to Onomichi. He said that it shouldn't become known that she had come to his room and that she had best return quickly.

I was quite interested in listening to F's story. From my own perspective, I felt it would have been extremely ironical for F to resemble a complete stranger. When the geisha came to his bedside, just like Inuzuka Shino in the story by Takizawa Bakin, who was visited in the middle of the night by his fiancée Hamaji, he put his bedding in order and listened guardedly to her "business." He listened seriously to her story to the very end, all the while maintaining a respectful distance. When F finished telling his story, I fixed my eyes on his face searching in vain for some expression of irony.

F told me exactly what the geisha had said, taking her for her word. I was astonished. Then I said, "Japanese women are bold, but in a gentle way. Had she been a Western woman, she probably would have been aggressive. Had that happened—and since you were like Wilhelm who hadn't the courage to thrust Philene away—you would have fallen victim to her charms."

When I said this, it was his turn to be astonished. He had been admonished by some Westerner not to read novels, but even he knew about Goethe's *Wilhelm Meister* and Schiller's *Geisterseher.* Later as I listened to him, I discovered that he had suddenly understood everything, almost as if he had undergone an operation for cataracts.

Since that event occurred, I paid close attention to F's speech and conduct concerning the opposite sex. And I learned that he had absolutely no experience whatsoever in that field. He did not regret his lack of food and clothing. He suppressed his sexual desire. He was different from the average person who entertains certain ambitions. At any rate, I thought him remarkable. I made no further efforts to prevent the gradual shortening of the distance that I had tried to maintain in my relationship with him in the beginning. Perhaps my judgment was faulty. But to this day I don't believe he deceived me.

December came. I had been in Kokura six months and F had been there for three months. I had begun to take French lessons and was going to a missionary's home in Bashakumachi every evening after dinner.

This had a considerable influence on my relationship with F. This was because when he did come to see me, I would talk about French. "French is probably interesting," he would say, "but instead of having a superficial understanding of two languages, I would rather understand one language in depth." "That's certainly one way of looking at it," I replied. But what I really meant was that I didn't agree. He surmised as much. And he probably felt somewhat hurt. Moreover, a natural loss of interest entered his frequent comings-and-goings. He stopped coming every day and began coming every other day. Then he began to come once every three days. Metaphorically speaking, we lived our lives like two parallel lines which are quite far apart in the beginning, for a while closely approach one another, and then remain separated by a short distance.

F supported himself as a German teacher. I was a bureaucrat taking French lessons on the side. We met now and then and talked without reserve. Between us an ordinary friendship had materialized.

The following year came. At the beginning of April, F came saying he had to return home because his father was ill, and asked if I would loan him money for the trip. I asked how much he needed and he replied that twenty-five yen would be enough. I gave it to him. I no longer regarded him as a person who wanted to be dependent on me. Neither of us ever brought up the subject of that money again. I didn't expect him to return the money, and it was not his disposition to be scrupulous about such matters. I realized that this part of his character was neither dishonest nor brazen. In our long friendship this was the only material thing he ever troubled me for.

Before long F returned and took a room in Torimachi. He resumed teaching German just as he had done before. One day during the summer I vis-

ited him and was treated to a lemon drink. Toward the end of the year the
landlord of the Kajimachi house suddenly raised the rent, so I moved to
another place in Kyōmachi, from a house where I could hear a spinning
wheel to one where I could hear a drum. Kyōmachi was on the backside of
Kokura's geisha quarters, so I constantly heard the sounds of *shamisen* and
drums. F visited me at that house often.

Another year came. I was my third year in Kokura. F left for Yamaguchi
where he had been invited to teach at the Yamaguchi Higher School.

In March the following year I was transferred back to Tokyo. At the time I
left, I had been in Kokura for four years.

I went to Kokura without a wife and returned to Tokyo married. But my wife
wasn't the only person who followed me back. There was also a Buddhist
priest, who was still young at that time, who was referred to by my household as Ankokuji-san, since he served at the Ankokuji Temple.

From the time I moved into the Kyōmachi house in Kokura, Ankokuji-
san had come to see me daily. Every day I would come home from the office
to find him waiting and he would stay until dinnertime. During that time I
would read and explicate a German introduction to philosophy to him. In
return he would instruct me on the Yuishikiron, the Buddhist doctrine that
matter is a form of mind. After seeing Ankokuji-san off, I would eat dinner
and go to Bashakumachi to study French with the missionary.

Because of the close relationship we developed, among the many acquaintances and colleagues who came to the station to see me off when I left
Kokura, the person who seemed most to regret my departure was Ankokuji-
san. An acquaintance said to me half-jokingly, "When you leave, Ankokuji-
san will be miserable."

True enough, Ankokuji-san couldn't bear to sever our ties. He turned his
temple over to someone and abruptly left Kokura. He then came to Tokyo
and moved into a boardinghouse across from my house at the top of Dangozaka. Originally there was a cliff in front of my house which was contiguous
with a plain that continued as far as Nezu. On that cliff there was a small flat
place no larger than the proverbial "cat's forehead." Back in the days when
Nezu was a geisha quarter, there had been a small secondary house on that
plot, where the retired owners of the famous Yahatarō had lived. Later
someone had bought the land and demolished the house. Then, by building tall supports up from the bottom of the cliff, they constructed a wide
two-story house whose eaves matched those of my house. My house had

commanded a fine view, but because of that two-story house it became rather gloomy. The lodging house Ankokuji-san moved into was that two-story house.

After returning to Tokyo, my life became quite busy compared to my life in Kokura. Although Ankokuji-san had taken the trouble to come, it was not possible for us to exchange knowledge as we had done before. Just as I was regretting the situation, F appeared and took a room in the same lodging house. He had relinquished his position in Yamaguchi and had come to Tokyo with the intention of living there.

It was decided that F would take my place in reading and explicating the volume on philosophy to Ankokuji-san. F's manner of dealing with a foreign language, however, was different from mine. I dealt with both colloquial language and literary language from an overall point of view. F, however, would not be content without grammatically analyzing each word. I had opened Raphael Koeber's introduction to philosophy and started explaining from the very first word. On top of that, I had tried to translate using as much Buddhist vocabulary as possible. Since Ankokuji-san was entirely capable of lecturing on the Yuishikiron, he had understood that as well as an ordinary person would have understood Fibel's primer or a textbook. F would not consent to following the aforementioned procedure and proceeded to train Ankokuji-san in grammar. Having to direct his energy in an entirely different direction, Ankokuji-san was completely perplexed.

A short time passed, when F was employed at the First Higher School in Tokyo. Since the school was near their lodging house, however, F and Ankokuji-san's relationship remained unchanged.

Since I had returned to Tokyo the cherry blossoms had come and gone, and the warmth quickly gave way to heat. When I went up to the second floor and looked at the lodging house across the street, I could see that the second-floor windows were left wide open there also. There were a large number of rooms, so I couldn't see F or Ankokuji-san's rooms. But I could see the room of a young woman student. On her balcony were hung a kimono with a red neck-lining and a maroon *hakama*. There was also a woman's undergarment with red sleeves slovenly thrown over. In the evening the owner of these various garments sat on the balcony in a gay summer kimono cooling herself. On one occasion I had to turn my eyes away when I unexpectedly saw her changing clothes after coming home from somewhere. Before long, she had become a familiar face, but I never heard her name nor had any way of knowing where she was going to school. She was neither beautiful nor ugly, nor was there anything about her that would attract a person's eye. As the boarders in the house across the street came and went, I paid attention to the disappearance of people I had come to recognize and to the appearance of new boarders. Nevertheless, F and Ankokuji-san stayed. And the woman student I could see from my second-story window also stayed.

Over a year went by and my second summer since returning to Tokyo arrived. One day Ankokuji-san came to tell me that in midsummer he was going to go home for a while. He had turned the temple in Kokura over to someone else, but he had relatives living in a small place on the Hōnshū line of the Kyushu Railway. He was going there to pay a visit.

After Ankokuji-san left, a person in my household heard a rumor. The rumor was that the Buddhist priest, Ankokuji-san, had gone to Shikoku on an errand for F on his way back to Kyushu. The errand he had undertaken was to visit the parents of the young woman student living in the boarding-house. F had secretly become intimate with the girl, but ultimately things had developed to the point where they could no longer conceal the matter and they had decided to get married. The parents in Shikoku would not consent to the marriage. So F had asked Ankokuji-san to go there to persuade them.

When I heard the story, I said, "If Ankokuji-san is acting as a messenger in this marriage proposal, that makes F a feudal lord, doesn't it?" remembering how priests often served in such capacities. Had it not been F, the unreserved egoist, and Ankokuji-san, who was occupied with learning and virtue, who had little knowledge of the ways of the world, but whose heart was made of gold, this situation could never have materialized.

Ankokuji-san's sincerity moved the stubborn country parents and the girl was allowed to marry F. The two of them took a house in Koishikawa.

≈

Another year passed. The war with Russia broke out and I left for the front. F saw me off as far as Shimbashi station and gave me a Russian grammar written in German. This volume and a Russian-German dictionary I had bought at Nankōdō would be quite handy while I was in Manchuria.

Among the letters I received in Manchuria was one from Ankokuji-san.

He wrote that he had fallen seriously ill and had therefore abandoned the study of German. He was going somewhere near the Boshū coast to convalesce. I immediately dispatched a letter consoling him. It was the longest letter I have ever written. I wrote, somewhat metaphorically, that one should not believe that what the world called an "incurable illness" was really "incurable" and that in aspiring to have peace of mind one should not give in to illness. I suspected that Ankokuji-san's struggle with language was what had brought on this illness. I felt thoroughly sympathetic just imagining how much a person, no matter how easily he was able to follow even complex logic, would be afflicted if he were to have to mechanically learn grammatical rules.

Two years later, after our victory in Manchuria, I returned home to find that Ankokuji-san had already returned to Kyushu. He had taken over as a priest of a temple in the middle of the mountains near Kokura.

F still lived in Koishikawa and worked at the First Higher School. His life and mine were so busy that neither of us had time to visit the other. On occasion I would exchange a few words with him when we met on the train on the Sugamo Mita line, but never more than that.

And then four or five years later I unexpectedly received word of F's death. He had died suddenly of cancer of the pharynx.

1915

III

THE DEMANDS

OF THE DAY

1910–1912

≈

How may one come to know oneself?
Never by contemplation, but only by action.
Seek to do your duty, and you will know how
it is with you. And what is your duty?
The demands of the day.

≈

ŌGAI'S FAVORITE QUOTATION FROM GOETHE, the great German writer for whom he maintained an enormous respect throughout his life, took on a terrible poignancy during the period when an increasingly authoritarian Meiji government began to respond with sharper harshness to the increasingly complex social situation in the country. Much of the controversy swirled around the activities of Kōtoku Shūsui (1871–1911), a distinguished socialist, widely respected throughout the world, whose adherence to these supposedly "radical" doctrines set up unwarranted fears in high government circles over the dangers of anarchism, socialism, and communism. Eventually, Shūsui was implicated in a plot to assassinate the Emperor Meiji; the group of conspirators was tried secretly, and Shūsui and others were put to death in 1911. The unwarranted execution of Kōtoku Shūsui, and the dark atmosphere that surrounded the whole incident, came as a profound shock to many Japanese writers, artists, and intellectuals who were working for a more liberal atmosphere in which to pursue their own vision of a modern Japanese society.

Ōgai, by now an army bureaucrat of high standing himself, was certainly no socialist. Nevertheless, his whole upbringing, background, and, in particular, his scientific training gave him a deep conviction of the need for patient understanding and rational inquiry concerning any new set of ideas. The uninformed and autocratic gestures of high government officials, including many of his colleagues, were deeply repugnant to him. His response was to speak out in a series of fictional writings in order to underscore his conviction that rational understanding must precede action, whatever that action might be.

The three works that follow, *Chinmoku no tō* (The Tower of Silence), *Shokudō* (The Dining Room), both written in 1910, and *Ka no yō ni* (As If), published in 1922, constitute a representative sampling of the works Ōgai composed during these years that set out to reflect more or less directly on these issues. In many ways, these brief pieces were meant to instruct their readers, and the fictional gloss he provides may seem too slight for their contents. This criticism, however, overlooks the fact that, in the nineteenth century, such quasi-fictional didactic or philosophical writings were fairly commonplace. This was the case both in Japan, where a book like Nakae Chōmin's *Three Drunkards* had already attained the status of a classic, and in the West, where ideas were often composed in the form of dialogue between fictitious characters; at the end of the nineteenth century, such writers as George Bernard Shaw and Oscar Wilde, among others, used such devices.

The essential artistic question posed by such works is that of finding a satisfying means to blend art and ideas. In one sense, this was a quest pursued by Ōgai throughout his entire creative life, one that he was perhaps to answer best to his personal satisfaction only in his late historical writings. In these three earlier works written before the death of the Emperor Meiji, where Ōgai comes closest to a direct and pointed commentary on his vision of "the demands of the day," he plays more the role of teacher rather than artist. For many Japanese readers, however, the moral passion that informs these writings gives them an important place in Ōgai's various literary experiments undertaken during these years.

Chinmoku no tō

THE TOWER OF SILENCE

THIS BRIEF WORK, WRITTEN IN 1910, serves as a dark cartoon sketched to satirize the attitudes prevalent in government circles concerning the reading of "subversive books." Ōgai, who believed deeply that rational understanding must precede any intelligent action, portrays the government's attempts to examine "dangerous" material as a futile gesture of moral impoverishment. Progress can come only through intelligent debate; the alternative is intellectual and spiritual death. The use of the Parsi community's towers where the dead are disposed of provides an effective framework for Ōgai's critique.

The main issue behind the polemics of the piece concerns the distinction that Ōgai wishes to make between knowledge and belief. One can have an intellectual knowledge of a system of beliefs, Ōgai was convinced, without necessarily subscribing to those beliefs themselves. This idea, expressed here in terms of "foreign books," moves into a deeper realm of controversy in the conflict between knowledge and religious belief that informs *As If,* written two years later.

A TALL TOWER SOARS into the evening sky.

Crows gathering at the top of the tower seem just about to fly away when suddenly they begin to caw excitedly.

Separated from the flock of crows, two or three seagulls dart back and forth about the tower. Their intermittent crying signifies their dislike of the restless, flapping behavior of the crows.

A weary horse, pulling a heavily laden cart, draws up at the foot of the tower. What is it hauling to the tower? Something to be sold from the cart?

As soon as one cart leaves, another arrives. So many objects are being carried into the tower.

Standing on the beach I survey these events while the tide, slowly rising, washes against the stone wall at the edge of the shore. The carts pass by in front of me as they travel to and fro from town to tower and back again. Riding in the driver's seat of each cart sits a man wearing a soft, mouse-gray hat with the brim bent over downcast eyes.

I can hear the monotonous lazy clippity-clop of the horses' hooves and the dull clash of pebbles against the wheel rims.

I continue to stand on the shore until the tower seems painted gray against a gray-colored sky.

As I walked into the brightly lit lobby of the hotel I noticed a man sitting in an easy chair, his crossed legs clothed in broadly checkered woolen trousers. His head was flopped back as if he had fallen asleep while reading his newspaper. Yesterday as well, I had encountered the same long-legged man in the same place looking as if he had slipped out of a canvas by the Western-style painter Yanagi Keisuke.

"Anything interesting happening?" I called out.

Without changing the position of his hands on the newspaper spread out before him, Long Legs glanced lazily to one side for a moment. "Nothing at all!" he declared, more to the newspaper than to me. Then, momentarily, he added in a tone of displeasure, "It seems two or three chaps have packed empty coconut shells with explosives again."

"Ah yes, the revolutionaries."

I picked up some matches that were lying on the marble table, lit a cigarette, and sat down in a chair.

A short while later, Long Legs put his newspaper on the table. His face

---

TRANSLATED BY HELEN M. HOPPER

wore a bored expression. I spoke to him again. "I just came back from looking at that strange tower. Do you know the one I mean?"
     "You must mean the one on Malabar Hill."
     "What sort of tower is it, anyway?"
     "That's the Tower of Silence."
     "What are they carrying into the tower from those carts?"
     "Corpses."
     "Whose corpses?"
     "They are members of the Parsi clan."
     "How come so many of these people die? Has there been an outbreak of
something like cholera?"
     "They are murdered. Whenever another twenty or thirty are killed, it is
reported in the newspaper."
     "Who murders them?"
     "Their fellow Parsis kill them."
     "For what reason?"
     "They kill the chaps who read dangerous books."
     "What kind of books?"
     "Books about naturalism and socialism."
     "That's a strange combination, isn't it?"
     "You think books on naturalism and those on socialism are different?"
     "I suppose so. But I still don't really understand. Do you know the names
of any of these books?"
     "The details are all written down here." Long Legs grabbed the paper
which he had put on the table and spread it out in front of me. I picked it
up and began to read. Sitting back in his easy chair, Long Legs affected a
look of boredom.
     The article headlined "The Parsi Clan's Bloody Battles" immediately
caught my eye. It was a fairly factual account.

Young members of the Parsi clan were taught foreign languages, and so, as
time went by, they began to read Western books. English was the most
widely used language. However, they started to communicate a little in
French and German as well. This group of young people began to create new
forms of literature. These were primarily novels that were publicly acclaimed
under the rubric of naturalism both by the authors themselves and by their
friends. You couldn't really say that this was the same sort of naturalism proclaimed by Zola in his *roman experimental*, but then you couldn't say that it

wasn't, either. In any event, the very best artists within this movement were attempting to escape convention and return to nature.

One feature of these naturalistic novels which caught the public's attention was their destructive rejection of all convention without any attempt to construct something positive in its place. In a word, this sort of thinking led to the practice of nihilism and a denial of the possibility of enlightenment. The result was that anyone who said anything the least bit positive had to be considered either an old-fashioned fool or a liar.

The next thing that caught people's eye was that these novelists took great pains to describe impulsive lives, especially regarding sexual desires. While these novels were devoid of the dark, strong colors that characterized their predecessors in the West, it is not too much to suggest that those writers who achieved some success were not very reserved in their writing.

From the standpoint of the public, two of the most conspicuous features of these naturalistic novels were, first, that the naturalists preached new and modern ideas, and second, that they called themselves new and modern men.

Meanwhile, one by one these novels were banned. It was believed that such negative thoughts disturbed peace and order, and that descriptions of impulsive lives corrupted morals.

At exactly the same time there arose in the country a movement of revolutionaries, and among a group who were caught carrying coconut-shell bombs were a few members of the Parsi clan. They were identified as anarchists. Then a *propagande par le fait* group was apprehended. Immediately, publications that had any connection whatsoever with socialism, communism, anarchism, and the like were classified under the rubric of socialist books and prohibited as disruptive of peace and order.

Novels as well were mixed in with those publications that were prohibited. These were works that contained true socialist ideas; works of naturalism were categorized differently at this time. Soon after, however, novels could no longer contain either naturalism or socialism.

When the fire to consume naturalism was accidentally fanned by the winds destroying socialism, the list of works prohibited under the heading of naturalism was gradually extended. No longer was it limited just to novels. Plays were banned. Lyric poems were banned. Essays were banned. Translations of foreign works were banned.

From that point on, naturalism and socialism were sought in every written phrase. People began to scrutinize every "man of letters" or literary artist, wondering whether he might be a naturalist or a socialist.

The world of the literary artist became a world of fear.

At this time someone within the Parsi clan invented the phrase "dangerous Western books."

Dangerous Western books conveyed naturalism. Dangerous Western books conveyed socialism. Translators related verbatim what was in the dangerous material. Those who wrote their own books simply imitated Westerners and thus created dangerous material out of copied imports.

The ideas disrupting our peace and order are the ideas transmitted by dangerous Western books. The ideas breaking down our traditions and customs are the ideas transmitted by dangerous Western books.

It was by an act of the god Angra Mainyu that the dangerous Western books crossed the ocean.

It was the reading of dangerous Western books that caused the killings.

To such an end, two pogroms were unleashed within the Parsi clan. And so at the top of the Tower of Silence the crows are feasting upon a banquet.

Brief biographies of those killed were printed in the newspaper along with the names of who had read what, who had translated what, and a list of the titles of the dangerous Western books.

I was astonished to read all this.

It is true that those who pore over the works of writers like Saint-Simon or translate Marx's *Theory of Capitalism* are doing the bidding of the socialists, and those who introduce Bakunin or Kropotkin are proselytizing for the anarchists. Just the same, readers and translators do not necessarily believe in the doctrines they propound. To the extent that they do not directly nod their heads in agreement, there is insufficient reason for making damning accusations.

If it is true that translating books by authors such as Casanova or Louvet de Courvay corrupts public morals, then, even though such works are valuable from the perspective of a history of civilization, one need only say that translating them would be ill-advised.

But you do not call for the withdrawal of such works as so-called dangerous Western books.

Those who dislike certain articles by the Russian writer Tolstoy because the Anarchist Party used adaptations from some of his works, such as *My Religious Faith* and *My Confession,* in their manifestos are surely not being reasonable. Among all the world's novels and plays there is not one single work which does not contain some sensitive section in it. That is dangerous. If in the victorious battles in *War and Peace* it is the brave foot soldiers and not the distinguished generals and their staff who win the war, then the danger is in the concept of individualism which underpins this point of view. Pressing this issue a little further, one might be suspicious of just how many years the Old Count's pristine life-style can survive if the reason he can get only simple food is that the meat he desires is not available on his estate.

In *Crime and Punishment* Dostoyevsky depicts a protagonist who commits a murder saying that no one can possibly expect him to let a greedy old hag with no useful role in society keep her money. So he too is no respecter of private property. This too is dangerous. In any case, this man's writings are no more than the insane ramblings of someone having an epileptic fit. Gorky spurned public order simply by writing about his yearnings for the life of a vagabond. This too is dangerous. In actuality, during his lifetime he resigned his membership in the Socialist Party. In admiration of Stirner, who founded individualism, Artzibaschew published many novels with revolutionaries as heroes. This is dangerous too. Moreover, his body became so wracked with consumption that his mind became deranged.

We turn now to French and Belgian literature. In regard to the writings of Maupasant, Count Tolstoy has objected that evil must be met with evil. If this is true, then there is no point in writing anything, for writing is then without ideals; it is amoral. It is as dangerous as shooting off firearms without taking aim. In the end the Frenchman killed himself in pursuit of wild delusions. The Belgian Maeterlinck writes adulterous plays like *Monna Vanna*. This is extremely dangerous.

The Italian writer D'Annunzio has boldly traced sexual lives in his plays and novels. In *Death City* he even wrote about an incestuous love affair between a brother and sister. If this is not dangerous then there is nothing dangerous in the world.

Then there is Scandinavian literature. Even Ibsen is called an enemy of our people because he manifests the concept of individualism in his works. Strindberg wrote about a count's daughter who gave herself to her father's valet. This supposedly represents the conquest of democratic ideals over aristocratic ones. Hasn't it been suggested over and over again that Strindberg went truly mad? These days he would be exposed and more than a little disgraced. In any event, this is dangerous.

What about English writers? A glance at Wilde's masterpiece *Dorian Gray* shows us the extent to which man's fundamental nature is horrifying. One might just as well call this a textbook for teaching man to commit secret crimes. To that extent it must certainly be dangerous. Of course, the author had previously been convicted of sodomy. As for Shaw, the hero of his play *The Devil's Disciple* is sympathetic to the obsolete. Isn't that dangerous? And what's more, his writings argue the case for socialism.

Here are two examples from German literature. In *The Weavers* Haupt-
mann has workers attack the house of a factory owner. Wedekind, in his
work *The Awakening of Spring,* has a middle school pupil participate in an
illicit sexual liaison. There is nothing more dangerous than either of these.

In brief, this is the sort of atmosphere in which the butchers of the Parsi
clan declared Western books dangerous.

If one were to look at literary art anywhere in the world today from the perspective of the Parsis, it would be considered dangerous to the extent that it
has some merit and is not regarded as mediocre.

That is to be expected.

Works of art that are recognized as valuable are exactly those that shatter
convention. A work that continues to peddle its wares within the orbit of the
conventional is mediocre. When we look at art with a conventional eye, all
art appears dangerous.

Art manifests itself impulsively, for it lies hidden in the depths and
behind the surface of the facts. Just as a painter can create by laying down
permanent colors, and a composer can create by manipulating the musical
scale, so can literary artists fashion impressions with sentences. Subscribing
to an impulsive way of life is natural. One cannot subscribe to a spontaneous
life without being impulsive sexually as well.

Because this is the essence of art, there are many times in which an artist,
especially a genius, cannot possibly live within the constraints of the real
world. Goethe was a provincial privy councillor in his youth. Immediately
after Disraeli entered the cabinet, he gave many hot-headed speeches and
generally conducted himself in an unrestrained manner. The only exception
to this behavior involved policies related to imperialism. George Sand and
Eugène Sue, in association with Leroux, issued communist propaganda, and
the three men Freiligrath, Herwegh, and Gutzkow became associated with
Marx and wrote articles for socialist magazines. Just the same, literary historians cannot conclude that these activities impaired the value of the works of
these artists.

It is the same with the pursuit of knowledge.

Knowledge, too, advances by breaking down convention. Knowledge will
die if it is constrained by the customs in any particular era or country.

Knowledge of the highest order, psychology, changes profoundly in turn
from contemplation to will, from will to drive, and from drive to mental
action. And that forces a change in ethics. It forces a change in metaphysics.
Schopenhauer thought it better to call this a "philosophy of drive." Think-

ers from this tradition include Hartmann and Wundt and, in addition, Nietzsche, who wrote *Aphorismen*. Schopenhauer's other-world philosophy, which does not recognize growth, gave birth to Nietzsche's this-world philosophy, which preaches a superman theory.

What can we say about these learned men? Hartmann and Wundt are exceptions to the general rule. While they were useless in their early years, Hartmann contributed to society in later years and Wundt grew old while working as a university professor. Schopenhauer disowned his parents and was a bigot who used abusive language toward any university professor who displayed confidence in the government. He was neither a filial son nor a loyal citizen. Nietzsche had a strange mind. No one tries to conceal the fact that he gradually went insane.

If we consider art dangerous, then we ought to consider the pursuit of learning all the more dangerous. Hartmann concentrated on the keen arguments of Max Stirner, who held anarchism to be the successor to the radical left faction within the Hegelian school. Hartmann's conclusions were different, however, for he examined three stages of illusion in his philosophy of the unconscious. If you reexamine Nietzsche's *God Is Dead* and Stirner's *God Was a Ghost,* you will have to conclude that they are obsolete. This is not the case, however, with the superman conclusion.

Both art and the pursuit of learning must be seen to be dangerous if you look with the conventional eye of the Parsi clan. Why is this? In every country and every age, crowds of reactionaries lurk behind those who walk new paths awaiting an unguarded moment. And when the opportunity arises they inflict persecution. Only the pretext changes, depending upon the country and the times. "Dangerous Western books" is no more than such a pretext.

On top of the Tower of Silence on Malabar Hill the banquet of the crows is in full swing.

1910

Shokudō

THE DINING ROOM

THE DINING ROOM, LIKE THE TOWER OF SILENCE written in 1910, presents another fictional attempt to capture a sense of the tensions between the government and Japanese intellectuals over the importation of "dangerous information." In this story, Ōgai makes use of his character, perhaps his alter ego, named Kimura, who served as the protagonist of his earlier story *Asobi* (Play). Here Ōgai sets out to instruct his readers concerning the crucial distinctions between "good" and "bad" socialism. Kimura provides his lunchroom colleagues with a basic historical account of movements and events as yet little written about in Japan. Toward the end of the story, he refers as well to the dangers of martyring men who risk imprisonment, even execution, on the basis of what appears to be slight evidence. A year later, Ōgai's concerns were to be justified, for Shūsui did indeed lose his life.

KIMURA ENTERED THE GOVERNMENT agency's dining room.

It had a papered ceiling on which the rain leaking through the roof had drawn strange yellowish-brown shapes; its once-white walls had turned a rat-gray hue streaked with shades of light and dark; one glass window had paper stretched over just that part which one might peep through from the hall; there was dirt of some kind or other saturating the wood grain, and the floorboards looked ash-colored when dry but the color of india ink when soaked. This was how the room looked. There was a glass window in the center of the room which was thickly layered with dust. Since the glass had completely lost its transparency it had not been necessary to stretch paper across it. The stretched paper had probably been placed over the other window by an inventive official at a time when one could still see through it clearly.

The long benches and long tables were made of a white wood. They looked stuck together as if they were stage properties. Usually the benches were placed on top of the tables with their legs sticking straight up in the air; since it was almost time for lunch, however, they had been taken down. Because the remains of previous meals were only roughly wiped away, this furniture was turning the color of thin india ink, just like the floor.

The entire office staff had clamored loudly for an outlay of money, but in the end frugality won out and the entire place was left looking poverty-stricken.

Responding to the clang, clang of a hand-shaken copper bell as if to a starting gun, the staff impatiently filed out of their offices as one man and formed a queue. Prepared meals were available in the dining room, but more than half of the employees brought lunch from home. Both the men dressed in Western style and those wearing the traditional *hakama* carried their lunchboxes with them in one hand. They had brought with them every possible size and shape of lunchbox, each one tied up in a colorful *furoshiki*.

If you had looked across the room at the men lined up in their long queue, you would have wondered if they hadn't been selected for their similarity, for they all had the same pale, thin faces. Some were just past twenty and some were nearing fifty, but not one healthy face could be found among these anonymous office workers coming into the dining room. Once in a while you might have wondered whether that one did not appear to be plump, but then you realized he actually had the sickly look of someone swollen with dropsy.

TRANSLATED BY HELEN M. HOPPER

Although Kimura was senior to most of this group, he took a seat at the edge of the table which was nearest the wall and furthest from the entrance and the dining room's serving window. In sumo wrestling lore, this was the place for the god of the poor.

Even though he had the same thinness, the colleague across the table, Inutsuka, who had wide round eyes and light brown coloring, appeared a clever sort of fellow. Because he had been employed as the bureau chief's spy, so it was said, he had already achieved a salary which eclipsed Kimura's.

Everything that Inutsuka heard was told straight away to his chief. Whenever someone was summoned to the bureau chief to receive a reprimand, what he heard usually resembled very closely what Inutsuka had already said to him. There was a general feeling that it was Inutsuka's scoldings which one heard from the chief's mouth.

Inutsuka always ate the catered lunch. This was the same twelve-sen lunch which everyone was served, but he had brought a separately cooked side dish from home as well. And so, like a treacherous gambler using loaded dice, he produced his own lunchbox as if to stamp a mark of mystery on the catered lunch.

Kimura habitually took his lunchbox out of its *furoshiki,* carefully folded the cloth, and put it into his left trouser pocket. Then, just as he was taking off the lid to his lunchbox and picking up his chopsticks, Inutsuka spoke.

"Well, they've finally made the activities of that terrible gang public!"

Although he didn't seem to be saying this to Kimura, since Inutsuka's face was momentarily turned toward him Kimura paused, his chopsticks in midair, and said, "You mean the anarchists?"

A quiet-mannered man called Yamada, who was sitting on Kimura's left, slipped in a word. It was said that this man could not tell a poison from an antidote. Somebody or other told Kimura that since Yamada spoke without thinking and could not conceal his real feelings, Kimura might just as well sit down, cross his legs, and relax with a cup of tea when he conversed with Yamada. And so this Yamada said, "How absolutely astonishing! I never thought that such an event could occur in Japan! What on earth is all this about?"

Inutsuka replied as if he were giving a lecture. "There is no why or wherefore. In the eyes of this gang there is neither god nor nation. Consequently, whether they become assassins, whether they kill other people, what does it matter to them? There's no logic to it. There's no way of knowing what sort of obstacle the people chosen as murder targets represent. Except for that ambiguous reason, there doesn't seem to be any explanation at all. A short time ago I learned from the bureau chief about an incident which happened just about fifteen years ago. A chap in Paris called Émile Henry hurled a bomb into a police station killing five or six people. Shortly after that he hurled another explosive into a coffeeshop killing two and injuring about twenty. Before that fellow was executed he spoke in his own defense. He asked, what could be better than throwing bombs? Since society lumps together and persecutes all anarchists, we lump together and fight against all the rest of society. What constitutes a sacrifice of innocent people? There isn't anyone living in society today who is able to eat good food and sleep in a warm bed who has not wrung these out of the blood and sweat of the workers. And so he concluded that it was all right to throw bombs anywhere. The effect, that of announcing a monumental principle, is the same whether you aim at kings or presidents, he said."

"That's the talk of a desperate man," Yamada said.

Smiling, Inutsuka said, "In any case, because this was a gang formed by people from various desperate causes, we could call anarchism the grandest desperation of all."

Because there were signs posted here and there on the office walls which said "Walk Quietly!" dining room conversations were conducted softly as well. Consequently conversational groups consisted of just two or three, and rarely did anyone from a distant seat break in.

"When on earth did such criminal activities get started?" Yamada asked, staring at Inutsuka.

"It's no use asking even the scholarly Kimura about that," replied Inutsuka looking straight at Kimura, who had been listening silently to the conversation.

"Ah yes, that's so. I haven't yet tried to investigate that particular issue. But I do know about the godparents of both anarchism and nihilism." Kimura spoke slowly, in a voice softer than other people, as he always did when he was thinking something over. Whenever he spoke to Inutsuka he spoke more politely than to any of the others. For his part, Inutsuka quite disliked this man Kimura, who exhibited both self-respect and an impression of distancing himself.

"Is nihilism something different from this, then?" Yamada asked.

As if he thought the conversation was becoming complex and he might get into difficulty, Kimura answered reluctantly in his customarily soft voice.

"Since people have not yet agreed just exactly what nihilism is but they have decided on a concept to represent anarchism, they have had to use the one word for both concepts."

Inutsuka asked, "Who, then, are the godparents?"

"About sixty years ago, in 1849, Proudhon proclaimed 'I am an anarchist' and then wrote 'I do not recognize kings and sovereigns; I do not accept the restraint of human will.' You immerse yourself in all sorts of literary magazines, Inutsuka, so I'm sure you'll bear me out on the fact that nihilist was a coined word that first appeared in Turgenev's novel *Fathers and Sons,* which was published about fifty years ago, in 1862."

"Then there isn't any doubt that anarchism came first, is there?" Yamada said.

"That's right. At the time Turgenev wrote his novel, however, Bakunin had not returned to Russia with his concept of anarchism. And after the expression 'nihilism' came into wide use, its meaning changed completely from that expressed in the novel. That is just like the word 'snob,' which has changed in meaning completely from the time it was first introduced by Thackeray. After Bakunin returned to Russia, Turgenev no longer expressed the sorts of youthful ideas he had voiced in *Fathers and Sons,* but rather those expressed in his novel *Virgin Soil.*"

"Well informed, aren't you?" said Inutsuka sarcastically.

"I'm just drawing a little attention to literary history. Matters of the world are understood indirectly through literature in much the same way that light is reflected." Kimura's response sounded both modest and defensive.

"If that's the case, then you must think that prohibiting the sale of books stops that light, which is a bad thing."

Kimura fixed a sharp eye on Inutsuka's face. Every time he heard the sort of thing that Inutsuka just said he felt as if he had been quietly pecked by the beak of a bird or pricked by the point of a bamboo skewer. And so he said the following: "Well, if someone acts as a result of seeing the light, then, extinguishing that light is probably effective. However, since I believe that freedom of discussion is important, I simply deplore the ever-widening use of book banning. Of course, I do realize that from a political standpoint it isn't possible to eliminate this practice altogether."

"Isn't that the sort of thing that flourishes in countries like Russia?" Yamada asked.

"They use the 'caviar' method for that sort of thing," Inutsuka said smiling through a sneer. No doubt this word, too, he had heard from his supervisor.

Yamada stared in puzzled astonishment.

Seeing the look on Yamada's face, Kimura took pity on him and explained the foreign term this way: "They censor printed materials which are imported from abroad by smearing them with printer's ink. They probably use the term 'caviar' because they blacken things out. This year, however, they have started to cut out sections with scissors and confiscate whole items. The caviar method destroys one side but cutting ruins both sides. When they confiscate, everything is totally lost."

Yamada smiled innocently.

For a little while they ate in silence, but then, appearing to have something weighing on his mind, Yamada spoke again. "Do you think that groups like that might be on the increase?"

"Increasing in both number and size!" Inutsuka said as he snapped off an especially thick piece of pickled radish with his sharp, white front teeth.

Turning an uneasy face toward his neighbor on the right, Yamada said, "Say, Kimura, what do you think?"

"In the first place, thanks to our national character, if the authorities skillfully grasp the tiller of state, they can probably prevent such increases. But depending on how this is done, it could accelerate the growth even more. You might ask what sort of people would be candidates for these groups? There are all sorts of contemptible people who would qualify, aren't there? One example would be political henchmen."

Here and there people were drinking tea or leaving their seats.

Kimura took his *furoshiki* out of his pocket and began to wrap his empty lunchbox in it.

Picking his teeth with a toothpick, Inutsuka said to Kimura, "Hey, why don't you stay and relax a bit!"

Kimura, who had just stood up, sat down again and poured himself a cup of tea.

Yamada remained with the other two. As if urged on by earnest intellectual curiosity, he put forward this question: "Actually, I've been wondering about the history of anarchism, and recently I even tried to read a discussion about it by several scholars which appeared in a certain magazine, but I didn't understand one bit of it. So, godparents aside, what sort of people shaped this doctrine?"

Inutsuka said, "After all, it's been around for fifty or sixty years so its history shouldn't be difficult," and then, looking straight at Kimura, he added, "In all probability, you know it."

Kimura grimaced, thinking what a nuisance this fellow was. Then he quickly mended his attitude and answered. "Well, yes. Though I haven't studied this specifically, it is in the mainstream of modern thought and so I have a rough idea about it. It is generally recognized to have begun when Max Stirner, who died about fifty years ago, 1856, espoused radical individualism. Next came Proudhon, who died about forty years ago, in 1865. Leaving aside the question of whether he or Kropotkin should be called the father of anarchism, we can say with certainty that Proudhon was its godfather. The first one to actually practice anarchism was Michael Bakunin, who died about thirty years ago, 1876. The next one, and the one who is best known here, is Peter Alexejevich Kropotkin, who fled to London. He was born more than seventy years ago, in 1842. Of the rest, we probably need to consider just one more, a man called Tucker, who is in America."

His attitude once again cool, Inutsuka commented, "Know a lot about it, don't you!"

Yamada, who had been listening earnestly, opened his mouth once again. "Generally speaking, what sort of people were those few who had the greatest minds?"

Leaning his right elbow on the back of the bench, Kimura propped up his head and, with a somewhat bored look, continued speaking. "Stirner's primary influence was on the history of philosophy and so it is a pity to lump him together with those called anarchists. He was a lecturer at a gymnasium in Berlin under his real name, Johann Kaspar Schmidt. When he published his famous *Individual and His Property,* he did not use his real name because the discussion in his book was so very radical. These days, however, it is available in a cheap edition and everyone reads it. Proudhon was the son of a poor man of Besançon, and in his youth he worked at such jobs as typesetting. Gradually he worked his way up to membership in the Paris Assembly. He was not a great scholar. Like Stirner he idolized Hegel, but in later years he confessed that he had never actually read any of Hegel's works.

"Unlike Stirner, who formulated original arguments with sharp logic, Proudhon usually did no more than expand upon opinions already expressed by others. Even his famous phrase 'property is theft,' was stated by Brissot twenty years before Proudhon was born. In truth, it would probably be more accurate to call Proudhon a debater. Next we have Bakunin who was born into a noble family of Prjamuchina, a town situated midway between Moscow and Petrograd. He became an artillery officer. But because he was a rebel by nature, he eventually fled the military ranks and traveled throughout Europe promoting rebellion. Besides being exiled in his own country to Siberia, he was locked up in prisons all over the continent. The strike by the watchmakers in Jura, which was the biggest disturbance counted among anarchist party incidents, was incited by him. He died of heart disease while he was in Bern, Switzerland.

"The next anarchist, Kropotkin, was born the son of the prince of Smolensk. During his youth he worked as a valet at the imperial palace. Later he became a cossack cavalry officer and was sent to Siberia, where he lived and worked for five years before trying to transfer to Manchuria. It was at this time, it seems, as a result of his contact with a wide variety of people, that he became an anarchist. Next he entered Petrograd University and studied geography. It is said that he considered the map of Asia which he published at the age of thirty his most valuable scientific accomplishment. He went to Jura, too, and then to England, where he was obliged to work part time as a geographer. Finally, I should mention the American, Tucker, though he was not much more than a translator of Proudhon and is not very significant."

After Kimura had been silent for a little while, Inutsuka said, "Don't they say that Kropotkin's daughter was really gorgeous?"

"Yes, the kind of woman who is filled with much compassion for humanity," Kimura answered and then fell silent again.

As if suddenly remembering something, Yamada spoke. "Some say that since this gang seems eager to be executed, maybe it would be better not to execute them after all. What do you think of that idea?"

Blowing a puff of smoke from his Shikishima cigarette, Inutsuka said with a smile, "Well, yes. Since they want to die, I suppose we ought to force them to feed on delicious delicacies in prison so that they will live long lives." Then, turning toward Kimura, he said, "Since the chaps who have been executed up to this point are known as martyrs, you could say that they have been especially honored, couldn't you?"

Kimura said, "Ravachol, Vaillant, Henry, Caserio," as if reading from a list, and then he added, "Of course, these names are used in a way that publicizes their cause extensively."

"Well!" Inutsuka exclaimed and threw his burning cigarette butt in the ashtray. At this signal, all three get up from their seats.

The dining room custodian, who had already straightened up the other places and was waiting, removed the ashtrays and teacups which had been in front of the three men, swished his scrubbing cloth in some water, and began to wipe the table.

1910

Ka no yō ni

AS IF

AS IF IS OGAI'S MOST SUCCESSFUL dramatization of the clash of ideas in fictional personalized form. In this story, he perhaps comes closest to combining his intellectual concerns and his sense of personal anguish regarding the disparities he had come to experience between his impulse to seek out the truth of politics and history and the growing government repression he now saw developing in contemporary society.

The title refers to an important work of German philosophy, *Die Philosophie des Als Ob* by Hans Vaihinger, published only the year before the composition of Ōgai's story. An English translation of this important work, entitled *The Philosophy of "As If,"* incidentally, was published in 1924, and the book had considerable currency for some time in British and American philosophical circles. The fact that within the space of a few months Ōgai had obtained the book so quickly from Germany, mastered its contents, and recast some of the author's crucial arguments in his own terms suggests the passion with which Ōgai viewed certain of the issues involved.

In one sense, the story can be read as a discussion between two Japanese who had lived abroad. In a larger sense, however, the latent tension between the protagonist Hidemaro and his father can be understood as a sort of extended metaphor between European-trained intellectuals, such as Ōgai, and the paternalistic Japanese state, which, while perhaps tolerating the sort of "high-class idlers" represented by Hidemaro's friend the painter Ayakōji, who symbolizes the fine arts, looked with increasing suspicion upon those intellectuals, typified by Hidemaro, who had begun to question the thickening clusters of myth and history propounded by the authorities of the Meiji state in order to solidify nationalistic sentiments among the general population.

What moves this story from the realm of an essay to that of an artistic statement is the passion with which it is written. Hidemaro not only sees the issues clearly; his whole being is placed in a state of psychic tension by them.

In this regard, he resembles the protagonist of Natsume Sōseki's 1912 novel *Kōjin* (The Wayfarer); Ichirō, when his old friend tries to console him by acknowledging his high-strung sensitivities over the changes coming too quickly to Japanese society, cries out: "You are not truly frightened. The fear you say you feel is only theoretical. My fear is not the same. I feel it in my heart. It is alive, a throbbing sort of dread." Here, both Ōgai and Sōseki are responding to the rapid and disquieting shifts they sense in their society, and the anguish of their characters, in turn, is a reflection of the tensions felt by their authors as well.

"How can one live without thinking?" says Hidemaro to his genial friend Ayakōji. In many ways, it is this ability to think and ponder on the deeper issues of society and history that will push Ōgai ever closer to the historical mode of the works to be written after the death of the Emperor Meiji and the suicide of General Nogi, which occurred later in 1912, the same year as the publication of *As If.*

THAT MORNING WHEN YUKI, the parlor maid, brought in the charcoal for the brazier, the viscountess, with a worried expression on her face, said to her, "The light was on in Hidemaro's room last night, was it not?"

"Oh, was it? When I went there some time ago to start the gas stove, the light was out, and he was smoking in bed."

Yuki recalled her momentary surprise when, entering his room, she saw the glowing end of a big cigar, now bright and now dim, in the silent darkness, and how she had almost screamed, although this was by no means a new experience for her.

"Is that so?" said the viscountess. And with the same worried expression, she watched the maid put the charcoal into the large square brazier, arrange the snow-white ashes prettily around the fire, and leave the room. In this house gas was used even in the kitchen, but the viscountess always warmed herself by charcoal fire, her excuse being that gas was too hot for her.

In every bedroom the electric lights burned all night, but as Hidemaro invariably turned his off before he retired to sleep, his parents knew that he was still up and reading if they saw his room illuminated. Therefore, the viscountess, awakening at night, felt anxious about her son if she saw a light emerging from the window of his foreign-style room.

Hidemaro entered the College of Literature after his graduation from the Peers School. At the college he specialized in history and graduated with honors. He intended to make the writing of a history of Japan his lifework, but he did not care to begin it without thorough preparation, and so for his graduation thesis he selected as his subject "King Kani Shika and the Compilation of the Buddhist Scriptures" and wrote about that. What induced Hidemaro to choose this was the fact that the life of King Asoka was in doubt and no one had made King Kani Shika the subject of research. Hidemaro had never made any special study of such topics, and he encountered many great difficulties at every turn; he concluded he could never form a clear and correct judgment without some knowledge of Sanskrit. He went to see Dr. Takakusu and received from him a few elementary lessons, but such a study cannot be learned quickly. As Hidemaro's knowledge of the language increased little by little, the difficulties increased as well. He persevered and

---

TRANSLATED BY GREGG M. SINCLAIR AND KAZO SUITA

233

managed somehow to bring his thesis to a conclusion, but he himself was quite dissatisfied with the result; for style, however, though simple and unadorned, it was unique among the theses handed in.

While working on his paper, Hidemaro lost some of his vitality, although he did not become noticeably ill. His face grew pale and his eyes strangely bright. He had a very narrow circle of acquaintances, but he grew still more exclusive. All the members of Viscount Gojō's family from the viscountess down were much concerned over his health and wanted to call a physician. Hidemaro would not hear of this; he denied that he was ill. When Dr. Aoyama called, the viscountess asked him privately for advice. The physician looked surprised at the question.

"Is Hidemaro sick? I cannot advise until I've examined him. Hmm! Did you say he refused to consult a doctor because he wasn't ill? Maybe he's right. I know many young students. Those who are good scholars at all look like your son just before and after they graduate. I attend the graduation ceremony every year, and I notice that nearly all the students who graduate with honors and step forward to receive the imperial prizes of watches look like Hidemaro and make one fear they will faint away. They usually come very near to being nervous wrecks, but they don't break down. They get well as soon as they graduate."

The mother thought this was sound wisdom. She suppressed her apprehensions and endeavored to make herself believe that her son would soon recover. When Hidemaro was not before her, she repeated to herself the doctor's thought word for word and tried to believe, "What he said is true. Hidemaro cannot be ill. He is all right. He will be himself again." Just then Hidemaro would appear with his face pale, say something in a listless way, and sink into silence. If she addressed him, he would reply in a gentle tone but only because it was his duty to say something. It seemed to her that her words rebounded from him just as an arrow rebounds from a bronze statue; and then she would feel that the castle she had erected with Dr. Aoyama's words as the foundation was falling, and she would begin to worry once more.

Hidemaro went abroad immediately after his graduation. One of his classmates, who had graduated with honors and received the imperial prize of a silver watch, though his marks were only slightly better than Hidemaro's, was to be sent to Europe by the Department of Education, but the government could not afford to send him until the student now abroad returned. While the honor student waited for his appointment, Hidemaro was sent to Europe by his father, Viscount Gojō. The nobleman was comparatively wealthy, and he could afford to let his son live the ordinary student life in a foreign country without any discomfort to himself.

Hidemaro recovered much of his vitality when it was decided that he should go abroad; and it was evident from the letters which he wrote home on his way to Berlin that he took an interest in the sights around him. He wrote about the dark-skinned boys he saw in a certain port in India, who swam like fish deep down in the water to recover the silver thrown to them; about the polyglot band of women with stereotyped smiles who played on various musical instruments at Port Said; about his impressions in Marseilles when he walked along a European street for the first time; how he stopped at a store where no lies were told and bought something which had only one price; how when about to leave the store with the article he was told by the storekeeper that a gentleman need not walk about with a bundle and that it would be sent to his hotel; and how when he returned to his hotel he found the article already there; about his feeling of surprise in Paris when he went to the opera with a young nobleman of his acquaintance and they were accosted by an elegant lady, and his friend replied brusquely that they did not speak French; and how he understood the situation when his friend, noticing the puzzled expression on his face, said so loudly that he feared the woman might hear, *'Tout ce qui brille, n'est pas or'*; and about his first impressions of Berlin, describing them even to the minutest detail.

His parents were amused by the letters. The viscount bought an atlas of the world and gave it to his wife; and he marked the atlas with a pencil whenever he received letters or telegrams from his son, and explained to her where Hidemaro had arrived or where he was passing.

Hidemaro remained in Berlin three years. The last year was the three-hundredth anniversary of the founding of the university and the occasion for a celebration under President Erich Schmidt. Hidemaro joined the procession and with a torch set in a kind of sword hilt paraded with the others around the streets.

While in the university, he wrote to his father each term about the subjects of the lectures he planned to attend. Among the lectures were those on history itself—such as "The Italian Renaissance" and "The Causes of the Reformation"—and those on abstract history which might be called "First Principles of Historical Study." There were lectures also on "Ethnological Psychology" and the "History of Myths"; on the "Place of Pragmatism in the History of Philosophy"; on the "History of Literature," such as "Fried-rich Hebbel," which a certain assistant professor had read; and then quite apart from these were lectures on "Ecclesiastical History" and the "History of Dogma."

Each term was like the others, and the viscount, who had never made a specialty of any branch of learning, could not determine what some of the lectures were about. However, he concluded that his son was pursuing a very heterogeneous line of work. He had not sent his son to the university and Europe to enable him to become proficient in a special profession; he wanted him only to acquire a certain amount of knowledge which would enable him to have opinions about things when he succeeded his father and became one of the supports of the imperial family and to do the work that his position in life required him to do. He wished to have his son better edu-cated than the average person; and he was of the opinion that his son could study any subject he desired.

In one letter from Berlin, Hidemaro wrote about several scholars. He praised the speeches and writings of Schmidt. He also discussed the work and influ-ence of the theologian Adolf Harnack. That he attached special importance to this man was shown clearly by his constant references to him; he could not wait until he returned home to tell his father about him; he wanted to make his father comprehend immediately what he felt. A certain enthusiasm was evident in his words, especially when he wrote about the three-hundredth anniversary of the founding of the university and described Harnack as the central figure of that splendid festival. He discussed in terms of eulogy the relations between William II and Harnack, and stated that they were exem-plary, in that the emperor trusted the scholar and the scholar contributed to his own branch of service in a sacrificial manner, at the same time serving his emperor and his country. In order to clarify the foundations of Harnack's work, Hidemaro sketched the life of Harnack's father, Theodosius, and the history of the development of the Protestant religion.

The viscount wondered why his son wrote so enthusiastically about Harnack but never with the same enthusiasm of his own specialty, history; and he read that letter very carefully over and over again. He tried to grasp its salient points. The gist might be given as follows: politics concerns the people; the politician must therefore attach importance to religion, which even now influences the masses. The German government has to manage its power very carefully, so that the northern and southern regions with their different religions may not clash. In diplomacy, Germany cannot ignore the pope, who retains a profound influence even though he has lost a good deal of his former authority. Therefore, in order to govern Germany, the government must control the Catholic South without giving offense and must try to make it progress in civilization in the Protestant spirit of the North. For this task the monarch must stand on a sure religious foundation. That foundation is based upon the Protestant theology. The scholar who represents the Protestant theology of the day is Harnack. Although placed in such a significant position, Harnack never trims his theological views to accommodate the government, and the emperor never tries to force him to do so. Therein lies the strength of Germany, which enables her to spread her wings proudly to the world. It is on account of this, too, that William II can go about in the city of Berlin in an automobile with his adjutant and without his guards, visit an exhibition without previous notice, or go to a shop to make his purchases, in an age when socialist democrats are rampant.

Compare this with Russia. The Russian government leaves the orthodox church to stagnate, "covers the church with some silk-cotton," and rules the people in a way to suggest they are fools. If the people who are treated like fools wake up just a little they become extreme anarchists. Therefore, the czar cannot go about without policemen in mufti standing along the street like pickets in a fence. One need know no theology to believe in a religion. Even in Germany only those who intend to become ministers study theology; and at first glance theology seems unnecessary for the layman. Indeed, theology is unnecessary, but only for the masses who are uneducated and whose intellects are not developed. To the educated, theology is essential. Properly speaking, the educated do not have what in religion is called "faith." Even if you tell the educated people who are without faith that they should worship God and the Gospels, they cannot do so. When they do not believe in any religion they gradually cease to see any need for religion. Such people have dangerous ideas. There are some who have dangerous ideas in reality who pretend to have faith, and who make believe they see some necessity for religion but really do not see any necessity. Truly, there are a great many such persons. Now in Germany there is such a thing as a Protestant theology which is the result of a thorough study of the history of dogma and the church; an educated person may examine if he wishes this religious doctrine which has been cleared of all superfluities by specialists. If one examines it, one comes to see the need for religion even if one does not believe in religion. Healthy thinkers appear. There are a great many in Germany who have this viewpoint. Hence it is that the strength of Germany rests on theology. Hidemaro meant this when he praised Harnack.

The father could grasp the main points of the letter.

The viscount, who had lived in an age of such books as Fukuzawa Yukichi's *Conditions in the West* and translations of Dutch geography books, who could manage very well with translated books and had educated himself to be able to speak among the nobles, had no knowledge of anything spiritual, except that gained from attending lectures on the Analects of Confucius as interpreted by the Neo-Confucian school. But he had a clear head, and he examined himself introspectively after he had read his son's letter. The religion mentioned in the letter was Christianity, and the God mentioned a Christian God. He had nothing to do with God or with Christianity. The graves of his ancestors lay in a certain Buddhist temple where periodic services were held for them. But his father had broken with the temple at the time of the restoration and had become a Shintoist. The family had nothing to do with Buddhism thereafter, and now the viscount recognized only the spirits of his ancestors. There was a shrine on the premises sacred to their memory, and their spirits were worshiped with due ceremony. But did he really believe the spirits of his ancestors existed? Whenever he observed their anniversaries he always recalled the words of Confucius, who taught that the spirits should be worshiped as if they really existed. After examining himself he concluded that he did not believe they existed; nor did he act as if they existed. Rather it seemed that he only tried to act as if they existed. If so, he was among those who did not believe in any religion but who saw the need for the kind of religion of which his son had written. No! No! It was not that. What his son meant was that one should know something of theology and should realize that a certain amount of religious doctrine was necessary, even though, after thinking it over rationally, one did not believe in it.

Viscount Gojō had never read any books on Shintoism, nor did he know if there were any books on the subject which he could read. Still his position was not that of an uneducated person who has faith and believes instinctively in the existence of some Divine Being, and who never has a doubt about it. When he observed the festivals to his ancestors, he merely went through the form. Even if he endeavored to think that the spirits of his ancestors existed, it was an "empty endeavor." No! No! There could be no such thing as an empty endeavor. It was impossible. If there were there was nothing to do but believe that the faith of uneducated persons descended to their children to a certain extent. Such a conclusion could be arrived at only after he admitted, as his son had admitted, that knowledge destroyed faith. Was this so? It might well be. One who had received a modern education could not regard mythology and history as one and the same thing. However superficially a man might study, he was obliged occasionally to ponder how this world was made, how it developed, how mankind came into being, and how mankind developed. Such thoughts did not allow the thinker to regard mythology as fact. The moment the line between mythology and history was clearly drawn, the existence of the spirits of one's ancestors became doubtful. When a man arrived at this conclusion, were there not terrible dangers lying in his path? What were the masses of people thinking on such questions? Did they not think it at all strange that men of today regard as false the belief in the existence of spirits which men of old held to be true? Did they not think it somewhat strange that all religious observances have become empty forms? Did they think it right to have mythology taught to children as history, and did they not think it ridiculous to have children taught a mixture of the two, while they themselves clearly distinguished between myths and historic facts? Did they not evade the issue by observing the festivals and such, according to the customs of society, and by being indifferent as to whether or not these customs, the relics of the times when people did believe in the existence of spirits, should continue for long or should totally disappear? And without any qualms of conscience at the falseness and without considering the effect of such teaching upon the minds of their children, did they not pretend to believe in things they really disbelieved?

His son, Hidemaro, said he recognized the necessity of religion, although he had no faith. The necessity of recognizing that necessity was the last thing to enter the minds of the people. They were indifferent and never thought about the possibility of recognizing the necessity of religion now, or of recognizing it in the future without regarding myth as historic fact and without believing in the existence of the spirit. It was quite likely that the majority of educated people had thoughts like these. Of course, there were men outside this large group of indifferent people who did try to change this state of affairs. Such men were those who, as described by his son, taught men simply to believe in God and the Gospels. And then there were men who echoed this thought. These were imitators, according to his son. Turning to the opposite class, the father knew from experience that there were men who had lost their faith entirely, who had come to see no necessity for religion, and who confessed the fact honestly. His son called such men dangerous thinkers, but those who attempted to ferret out dangerous thinkers in Japan did not get very far. No instances had been recorded of men of this kind arrested on the charge of breaking the public peace or contaminating public morals; but even if men had been arrested on these charges, would it not have been difficult to condemn them? Was this not beyond the power of men? If so, an inquiry into such matters might be more dangerous than the indifference of the masses. Had not his own son thrust his head into a dangerous topic? Might it not be that his son had lighted upon this while pursuing his special studies, had become uneasy, and so had written to his father? Or was it that the son did not consider this a question of great importance?

Viscount Gojō formed some such opinion after reading his son's letter and weighing his own mind and reflecting on society at large; but he did not believe he could reach a satisfactory solution by an exchange of letters with his son on the subject. The father knew also that the time of the son's return was approaching, and he decided he might as well wait until then; therefore when he wrote he did not enter into any religious discussion but simply stated that he had understood what the son had written and desired him to cultivate a wholesome way of thinking and try to become the kind of man who is of great service to the state. Hidemaro never knew how much his father understood of what he had written.

Hidemaro had the habit of telling his friends or writing them his thoughts at various times, but he never attempted to make his correspondents understand fully what he meant or to persuade them to his own way of thinking. Rather, he felt a sort of satisfaction in making his own thoughts stand out clearly before him while he talked or wrote about them. Thus his thoughts received a new stimulus and went further afield. Even if his father had written a very careful answer to his letter, therefore, Hidemaro might not have replied satisfactorily to his father on the same question.

Hidemaro's health, which had been the subject of solicitude by his family before he left on his journey, seemed to have improved very much; the letters which he wrote home at frequent intervals were full of life; and a certain nobleman, an intimate of Hidemaro when in Germany, who came to see the parents, told them that although Hidemaro studied very hard, still he found time to play billiards or to go skating, and that in the pension which Madame So and So maintained for ladies and gentlemen of the upper classes, the young borders were so fond of the younger Viscount Gojō that they declared they did not enjoy their first nights at the theater unless he were present. The old viscount and viscountess were delighted to hear such good news of their son, and they looked forward to his return and expected to see him a strong man.

Hidemaro came home with a great number of books toward the end of his last year. There had been something of the boy about him when he went away, but his three years in Germany had made a man of him, given his complexion a healthy color, and put some flesh on him. To the observant eye of his mother, however, who had been impatiently awaiting his coming, there was an unnaturalness in his manner of talking. It is true that after his graduation and previous to his departure she had noticed that he looked preoccupied and talked absently with people, but she expected this listlessness to disappear before his return. She fancied that in this respect she found him exactly the same.

Many of his relatives and friends who went to Shimbashi to greet Hidemaro on the day of his arrival returned with him to his house, where the viscount entertained all callers with a light dinner and with *sake*. After they had gone, father and son conversed together.

The viscount sat on the floor, dressed in *hakama*, and smoked his pipe. The wrinkles about his eyes indicated his pleasant humor. He said simply, "How do you feel?"

"Oh," answered Hidemaro, looking at his father's face.

His mother fancied there was no difference in his manner now than when guests were present; it was still reserved.

The viscount remained silent for a while, expecting that his son would say something more; when he believed he would not, the father continued, "You've brought home many books, I understand."

"Yes, quite a number; I thought I should need them in my work here. They're books I don't read but only refer to."

"I see. You must be impatient to begin your work."

Hidemaro seemed to hesitate a little. "I thought about it a great deal while on the boat, but I'm afraid I cannot begin work immediately." And he looked up thoughtfully.

"There's no hurry. You don't have to sell what you write or work for a degree," said the viscount; and after a moment he added, laughing, "A degree wouldn't be unwelcome, though."

The viscountess, who had been listening, now began to talk to her son. Hidemaro answered her gently. It was then she got her first impression that Hidemaro talked without being interested and only because he did not wish to be impolite. Consequently, after her son left the room, the viscountess remarked to her husband, "I can see he's very much improved in health, but I cannot help thinking he's strangely absorbed when he talks."

"That's simply because he has become a man. A man must not speak out everything that comes to his lips, as my lady does."

"Oh," and she opened her eyes more widely. Though she was well on in her forties, the viscountess had lovely bright eyes.

"Don't be angry."

"I'm not angry," she answered with a smile; but there was less heartiness in her smile than in Hidemaro's words.

≈

Nearly a year had elapsed since the homecoming.

New Year's came, and Hidemaro celebrated it at home for the first time after his long absence. He had had court rank confirmed on him, and he had to be a little ceremonious, though not so much so as his father. Hidemaro put on his new ceremonial clothes and went through the ceremonials with apparent willingness.

"What is New Year's Day like in Europe?" asked his mother.

Hidemaro smiled amiably. "There isn't much festivity. The students go to the restaurants on New Year's Eve, and they wait for the new year, with a liquor called '*bowle*,' which consists of champagne, wine, sugar, and soda water, mixed and heated with sliced lemon in it, all ready for them. When the clock begins striking, they pour the liquor into glasses, clink them with a shout '*Prosit Neujahr!*' and drink. After walking about the streets, laughing and joking, they go home. On New Year's Day they don't get up until noon; the doors of most of the houses in the city aren't open during the day, and there is very little noise. In short, they have all their festivities at Christmas and seem to forget New Year's Day."

"But there is some ceremony at court, I think."

"Yes, so I've heard. People are received in audience at two o'clock in the afternoon."

Thus he would explain the manners and customs of Europe if someone questioned him; he never volunteered information.

February and March, the coldest months in the year, passed. "I think it must be much colder there?" asked his mother.

"They have what is called 'slippery ice.' During the coldest weather they have comparatively warm nights when the top of the snowdrift melts, but it freezes in the morning. The branches of the trees appear glazed. The sidewalks of the street called Unter den Linden become like uneven mirrors and are so slippery as to make walking difficult; and laborers sprinkle them with sand from baskets carried under their arms. It is the coldest season of the year, but it isn't so cold as in Russia, where people who go out walking have their noses frozen. In Berlin, no house is without a fireplace, and no man goes about without furs, so the cold isn't much felt. In Japan, people seem to shiver with the cold in winter, living as they do in summer rooms and clothed as they are in summer dress."

Spring, the season of the cherry blossoms, passed. When his mother asked him if there were cherry blossoms in Europe, Hidemaro replied, "In a cold country like Germany, spring comes all of a sudden and different flowers bloom all at once. The Germans have an expression, 'beautiful May.' There are some cherry blossoms, but people regard cherry trees as the trees which bear cherries, and they don't go out to look at the blossoms. In the village of Stralau, about a mile from Berlin, there are many cherry trees along the bank of the river Spree. I remember going there once with some Japanese students in Berlin to see the blossoms. While we were there, some girls who worked in the carpet factories walked by, and they wondered what we were doing under the trees."

The hot summer passed. In reply to his mother's question, "What did you do on such a day as this in Berlin?" he answered, smiling, after thinking a moment, "This is the most uninteresting season. Everybody goes traveling. Young girls go to Switzerland and climb high mountains. Those who stay behind have very little to do to take up the time, so they go to concerts given in restaurants in the parks, and they stay there until midnight enjoying the cool breezes. It is much nearer the North Pole, so when men go home to bed it is already getting light outside the window."

By and by autumn came. "In Europe, the cold season comes earlier, and we cannot enjoy such autumn weather as this," said Hidemaro, smiling pleasantly at his mother.

Such talks were confined to the dining table; except when eating, Hidemaro spent all his time shut up in his foreign-style room. The books he brought home from Europe were so numerous that the bookcases could not hold them; shelves had been built in around the walls and were filled with books. Thin green curtains covered these shelves and served as a sort of ornament to the room. The walls were now doubly thick, and the room became much darker than before. At the same time it became very quiet, admitting little noise from without. When the bright autumn sun shone clearly overhead and everybody went out of doors, Hidemaro shut himself up in his quiet retreat and read books; he never left his desk. The desk was covered with green cloth and half of it was brightened by the light which fell slanting through the window on the left.

While many have thought that the autumn was unusually warm, chilly rain fell now and then. The gas stove in Hidemaro's room had been lighted for several days. Hidemaro rose early and went out on the veranda which extends into the garden; he noticed that the ground was covered with large yellow paulownia and small red maple leaves. Even the stone steps leading from the veranda into the garden were gay with leaves. The *yatsude,* their broad dark-green leaves wet with dew, lined the stone wall and raised here and there white stalks with white blossoms, resembling branched candlesticks. The sunbeams from a slightly cloudy sky fell over them, and two or three sparrows hopped and twittered.

For a time Hidemaro gazed at the birds. Presently he yawned, stretched himself, and took a deep breath. All the while his arms hung limply at his sides. He returned to his room, went to the washstand, and washed with the warm water Yuki had brought. He put on a sack coat. Since his return from abroad he always wore foreign clothes.

His mother came into the room. "Today is Sunday, and your father won't get up for a little while yet, but I'm going to have breakfast; won't you come, too?" She threw a sidelong glance into her son's face and added, "You sat up late again last night. I've said this time after time, and I must say it again: when you returned from Europe you were very healthy, but since then you've studied so hard your face has become quite pale."

"Well, there's nothing the matter with me. I don't get out often, and so I don't get sunburnt, you see," he answered laughingly, and left the room with her.

The mother felt that his laughter had pierced her bosom. She knew intuitively that Hidemaro had formed this habit of laughing lightly in order to deceive his companions, although he himself was probably unconscious of the deceit.

By the time they had eaten breakfast, the sky, which had been slightly cloudy at daybreak, had cleared up, and sunbeams gleamed over the many objects in his room. The sun gilded the edges of the window curtains and the sides of the bookcases and fell in broad bright bars across the table, making the inkstand glitter and giving momentary life to the arabesques of the carpet. Where the sun's rays passed, the air looked like leaves turned yellow and minute specks danced.

Hidemaro did not like to have the room very warm; he closed the damper a little, and sank into a rocking chair, a cigar in his mouth.

To explain briefly Hidemaro's state of mind at this time, we can only say that he was bored. But what bored him was not the ennui of vulgar men who yearn for some low stimulus; he felt oppressed by the task which slept inside him. It was a pain inflicted on him by his latent energy. The old Chinese heroes were grieved to see their calves grow fat from inaction. Similarly, though he looked thin and pale to other people, he was conscious of his powers and was afraid that his brain might atrophy. It was for the purpose of exercising his mind that he read books on philosophy. His father, not so pessimistic regarding Hidemaro's health as his mother, once said to him at the table, "You're out of harmony with the world," and smiled meaningly. Hidemaro smiled his customary smile and replied, "I'm not a malcontent." It seemed to Hidemaro that his father suspected that he entertained extremely liberal ideas; that was a mistake. Nevertheless, Hidemaro believed that his father, because he was a man, understood one phase of his mind more correctly than did his mother.

When Hidemaro remembered those words of his father, he recalled also another remark of his. One day at dinner his father said, "I don't want to have people believe that men descended from monkeys." Hidemaro had started. Of course he did not wish to put his name under Haeckel's and say that the "Anthropogenesis" was Hidemaro's own confession; but his father's words implied something incompatible with his own thoughts. Surely his father did not believe the myths of uncivilized times were historical; but he might think that if one nonchalantly asserted that myths were not history, an important something in human life would begin to crumble, and materialistic ideas would pour into society as water rushes through a leak into a ship, eventually to sink it. Hidemaro concluded that his father thought so and had fallen unawares into the same hole that stubborn men and more thinkers who hide behind masks fall into.

So Hidemaro hesitated to clear up his father's misunderstanding. Hidemaro's conscience insisted that myths were not history; and he thought that even if he did state that fact, the important something wrapped up in the myth would be well protected, just like the pit in a piece of fruit; and he believed it was every man's as well as every scholar's duty to acknowledge the truth of the statement and cling to it.

Hidemaro felt that there existed a narrow but deep gulf between his father and himself. At the same time he noticed that in their conversations his father would assume the attitude of a man who wanted to lift the lid from a box in which he suspected something dangerous was hidden and who would draw back his hand. On such occasions Hidemaro would feel provoked and then sorry for his father; and he would feel that he must be lenient and keep his father from touching the dangerous thing. Hidemaro preferred to have him suspicious of the contents of the box rather than have him remove the lid, see goblin forms in broad daylight, and be frightened at mistaking for poison what was not.

Small wonder that Hidemaro thought in this way. After the intelligent viscount, his father, had read the letter in which Harnack was mentioned and did not reply to it, he often turned over religious questions in his mind when he could not sleep at night. The more he thought, the more he was inclined to believe that those questions were very difficult to handle and it was dangerous to touch them. Therefore, he did not want to have his son go far into such problems, but preferred to direct his attention to other fields, if such a thing were possible. This being the viscount's opinion, he never referred to religious questions, but he observed secretly how deep they struck root in his son's mind.

This was the reason why the conversation between father and son ever since the latter's return from Europe a year previous resembled two hostile armies encamped opposite each other, both of which sent out scouts who at each encounter simply exchanged long-range shots. They did not crash into each other; at the same time they did not come to a peaceful understanding.

The white ashes of the cigar in Hidemaro's mouth had not fallen for some time, but at last they fell and scattered over the carpet, leaving small scaly particles on his vest as he leaned back in the rocking-chair. Whenever he found himself doing nothing, as now, he felt oppressed from within by the sense of the pressure of work and from without by the air of tension in the house.

"Shall I read?" Hidemaro asked himself. He could not begin a history of Japan, which he conceived to be his lifework, without making clear the line dividing myth and history. Perhaps he ought to investigate mythology scientifically, and then write of the beliefs in it in the form of a history of dogma, and also of the priesthood that taught people these beliefs in the form of an ecclesiastical history. If he did so, the doctrines and the means of propagating ancestor worship would not be exposed to any special danger even as the histories of dogma and the church had not endangered Protestantism. When he thought this much at least would be easy to accomplish, he fancied he saw before his mind's eye the clear and well-written accounts. As soon as he had finished them he would be able to begin the history itself with a clean conscience. The unsuitable environment which prevented him from commencing the work he already saw accomplished first made itself felt when he began to prepare for his return from Berlin, and gradually it assumed distinct proportions in his mind, just as some vapors begin to crystallize around a particle of dust and grow larger and larger. This was the dark lump which filled his mind and obstructed the development of his chosen work; and so he shut all the "veins on his creative side" and engaged himself in reading as a kind of mental gymnastics. It was strange how he could concentrate when once he began to read; he did not feel the oppression of work or the air of tension in the house. And this was the reason he was always reading books.

"Shall I read?" he asked himself again, rising from the rocking chair.

At that instant he heard a knock at the door. Yuki came in after waiting a time for Hidemaro's answer. She was a pretty girl, with a small face, sparkling lacquer-black eyes, and a narrow, high, and slightly turned-up nose. At the time Hidemaro returned from Berlin she was unaccustomed to foreign ways, and she would kneel on the floor to close the door and would address her young master with her hands on the carpet. This surprised him, and he taught her smilingly how to act in foreign rooms. She remembered well whatever he taught her, and she followed his instructions as though she had long been used to such manners.

Hidemaro's face lighted up as he stood with his back to the fire and looked at Yuki. The erotic side of his nature had lain dormant hitherto, but I may say that when he saw her face he felt happy then for the first time in this humdrum though peaceful house.

"Mr. Ayakōji has come, sir," announced Yuki, turning her round eyes toward Hidemaro's face just as a little bird in a cage turns to look at a man. Whenever she had an opportunity to speak to her young master she almost heard a joyful shout in her bosom. She worshiped Hidemaro without knowing why.

Just then the door which she had closed carefully was unceremoniously opened from the outside, and a man about as old as Hidemaro and dressed in a foreign suit of brown velvet came in, almost running. He put his big ruddy hand on Yuki's shoulder and said, "I say, don't look so long at your master's face that you forget to announce me."

Yuki blushed a deep red and escaped without a word. She did not look at Ayakōji.

Some lines appeared upon Hidemaro's forehead which were imperceptible except to observant eyes, and then vanished so quickly that even the most observant could not have noticed them. His expression became very serious.

"Please don't joke foolishly in my house."

"Well, I'm surprised to get scolded as soon as I come in. Isn't this fine weather? Your father would learnedly call it "autumnal serenity." Maybe the season is already winter, but in transitional times like these the days are sometimes autumnal and sometimes wintry. We can regard today as autumnal. There are some sharp wintry elements lurking in the concerns of it. It's both sad and pleasant, just as we might feel when we look at the sun shining brilliantly just as it is setting. It is, so to speak, like a beauty no longer youthful. Perhaps you're the only fellow in the wide world who stays at home like a mole and reads. However, some praises are due you because you weren't sleeping on your desk."

Though Hidemaro had a grave expression, he did not seem bored as he looked at the talkative Ayakōji. Briefly, this man had the appearance of a boyish leader of a gang of rowdies. His hair, cut rather long, was brushed straight back from his forehead and bristled like that of a wild boar as represented by Japanese artists. A sarcastic smile played about the corners of his rather sloping eyes. Two deep lines like parentheses enclosed his wide mouth.

"Don't stare at me so," Ayakōji went on. "Very likely you despise me in your heart. It's all right. You're the *roi* and I'm the *bouffon;* in German it's *Hofnarr,* the court jester. Do you treat me as one?"

Hidemaro burst into involuntary laughter. "Why should I despise you?"

"Why did you scold me as soon as I came in?"

"Oh, I beg your pardon." And he opened his cigar case and offered it to his friend, and added almost to himself, "But I felt your remarks might poison another's daydreams."

"You're too sentimental," said Ayakōji, as he took a cigar.

Hidemaro struck a match.

"Merci," said Ayakōji and lighted his cigar.

"You like a warm place," remarked Hidemaro, and he pushed a chair in front of the stove.

Ayakōji put his hand on the back of the chair but did not sit down immediately. He glanced around and his eyes fell on the thick paper-covered book which had been left open on the table since the previous night. Beside the book was a tortoiseshell paper knife. "You're plodding away at a big book again," he said, looking at the other's face; and then he sat down.

Ayakōji and Hidemaro were members of the same graduating class of the Peers' School. When Hidemaro decided to continue his studies in the university, Ayakōji wished to be an artist and he began to attend an art school at Tameika; later he went to Paris, while his friend still attended the College of Literature. When Hidemaro stayed for a few days in Paris on his way from Marseilles to Berlin, Ayakōji looked after him. Together they walked along Champs Elysées, went to the Théâtre Français and the Gymnase Dramatique. Ayakōji even ordered some suits of clothes for his friend to wear in Berlin.

Ayakōji lived, as it were, only with his eyes and ears. He did not regard even art very seriously, but his clear head always yearned for knowledge. After both returned to Japan, he came often to see his friend, although his visits were seldom returned, in order to find out what books Hidemaro was reading and to think seriously about them, notwithstanding the fact that outwardly he used to laugh at him.

Ayakōji now walked to the table and turned over the cover of the book. *"Die Philosophie des Als Ab.'* What a peculiar title!"

Just then Yuki brought in an oval nickel tray with a tea-set on it. She placed a small table in front of the stove, put the tray on it, glanced at Ayakōji while pretending not to do so, and then left the room. Would Ayakōji say something to her? If he did, would it be something embarrassing? What would he say? Yuki felt like listening. This time, however, he kept silent.

Hidemaro turned the cups right-side-up and poured tea into them. "Shall I put in some milk?" said he, turning to his friend.

"Not so much as you did the other day. What does *'Als Ab'* mean?" asked Ayakōji as he sat down by the stove.

"It means *'comme si.'* We might say, 'as if.' The author takes up a singular point and discusses it. Oddly enough it explains my own philosophy, it seems to me, and I was very glad to read it. I sat over it until three o'clock this morning."

"Until three?" Ayakōji's eyes bulged out. "How? Where does he explain your philosophy?"

"Well," began Hidemaro, and he thought for a while. He had read six-or seven-tenths of the book which comprised nearly one thousand pages, and he considered how best to give a synopsis of what he had read. "First of all, we must define the word 'fact.' A judge examines every bit of evidence in a case and then renders a decision, and people regard his summary as the statement of the true facts. This, to my mind, is the commonest acceptance of the word 'fact.' Now 'fact,' in this sense, doesn't exist. True, it's called 'fact,' but since it has passed through the mind of man it has become modified and arranged, as some scholar has put it. It has been idealized, so to speak, unconsciously. It has become an untruth. Therefore, we must establish another meaning of the word.

"A novel, for instance, tells falsehood in that it narrates events as so many facts; but the novelist never believed they were real occurrences; he was conscious they were made up, and he passed them on as such, and they have life in themselves; they have worth. Sacred myths, too, now common among men, were brought into being by the same process. But there's a difference between myths and novels, and it's this: the former insisted they were authentic. Now when you paint pictures, however faithful you may be to the objects you portray, you cannot make your pictures the objects themselves. You paint, conscious all the time your paintings are untruths. Everything that reveals the souls of men, all that has value, comes from just such 'untruths' brought into consciousness. This, and this alone, is our second meaning of the word 'fact.' This idea of seeing two kinds of fact was first expressed by Kant, and it is one and the same thing as that which is now repeated in a much more popular form by the philosophy of pragmatism and the like. This much must be said before coming to the main point, if I am to make myself clear to you."

"All right. Never mind the word. Even I can understand that. My paintings are not the things painted, but one of them sold at the exhibition this year, so I'm sure it has some value. And so I don't object to regarding my paintings as real; but how about *'comme si'*?"

"Just wait a minute. We examine the foundations of every branch of science man knows anything about. Consider mathematics, the most exact of sciences. There we discover point and line. However small we make a point it still has magnitude; however fine we draw a line it still has width. The edge of a board, however well planed, still has dimensions; its corners are more than points. A point or line in the abstract sense doesn't exist. It is one of these conscious lies; but unless we think as if there were such a thing as a point or a line there would be no geometry. I say, as if. Consider the natural sciences. Matter doesn't exist. Substance is said to be composed of atoms; those atoms don't exist. Unless we think there is substance and that it is composed of atoms, however, we cannot measure atomic weights, and there would be no chemistry. Take the mental sciences. Liberty, immortality of the soul, duty, all these do not exist, but unless we think as if they do exist there would be no ethics. These are called ideals. We knew long ago that there was no such thing as free will, as the law calls it; but unless we think as if there is free will the penal code would be meaningless. Most of the modern philosophers regard the world as relative and not as absolute. Still they think as if the absolute existed. In religion, again, Schleiermacher long ago stated that he regarded God as if He were the Father. Confucius centuries ago said that when we worship the spirits of our ancestors we should do so as if they were really with us; that means that we should worship them as if their spirits really did exist. Now we have examined religion as well as all branches of human knowledge and have seen that they are established on something which cannot be proved as real. That is to say, 'as if' lies at their foundations."

"Wait a moment. You say I'm talkative, but once you start talking you go along at a gallop, and I cannot follow you. Well, I begin to see what that monster, 'as if,' really is. But wait. Let me have another cup of tea, and let me think it over, because my conception is rather vague yet."

"I fear the tea is lukewarm now."

"It's all right. If a provable fact called Yuki comes in, my thoughts will become entangled. You mean, although there are many facts lying around us, they are of no use; when we want to connect them in our thoughts we must get something for a foundation, whether we will or no, and that foundation is, according to what you say, 'as if.' Is that what you mean? All right. For my part I leave such a monster alone, or if I do think about it at all, I don't speak about it." Ayakōji stated this positively as he drank the lukewarm tea at a gulp.

Hidemaro frowned. "I don't speak about it, either. As for you, you can paint pictures and leave your thoughts unspoken; but I've studied in order to speak. I must think. If I were to think and not give utterance to my thoughts in a straightforward way, I should have either to say nothing or to invent some lie. Then my philosophy would be lost."

"But, my friend, when you say that you've studied in order to speak, you mean that you want to write history, don't you? Why not begin to write without regard to whether or not this monster is at the foundation, just as I do when I paint pictures?"

"That's impossible. Before beginning to write, I must distinguish myths from facts. Perhaps you will ask, why do you distinguish them? Why not leave them mixed together? My answer is: histories cannot be written as you paint pictures, 'catching hold of one moment.' "

"Then you mean it's all right in my pictures because the monster is hiding, but it isn't right in your history because the monster comes into view?"

"That's about it."

"How cowardly are you! What if it did come into view?"

"I should be labeled a dangerous thinker. I don't care what men say; I can fight them. But what I am afraid of is that my father won't agree with me."

"You're still more cowardly. I solved such differences long ago. When I became an artist, my father gave up on me, and now he treats me as a 'high-class idler.' It's different with you. Your father gladly agreed to your idea of becoming a historian. You graduated from the university. You went abroad without the difficulties I had to meet. You've simply postponed the quarrel. You can solve the same question now which I solved five or six years ago, and then you can write your history as you please. I see no other way."

"But I think I may be able to manage the matter without a quarrel. I seem to see a peaceable understanding before my eyes so near I almost think I've but to reach out my hand to grasp it. And I don't wish to make a mess of our relations in my hurry to snatch a solution. So I just procrastinate and get called 'coward' by you." Hidemaro heaved a sigh.

"Well, but how do you propose to persuade your father?"

"I only want him to understand that my thoughts are not dangerous."

"But how will you go about it? Imagine that I'm your father and rehearse to me what you will say to him."

"I really cannot say," said Hidemaro as he rose and began to pace the room.

The veranda on which the sun had shone was now shaded by the roof. The clear autumnal sky reflected on the glass doors of the veranda as blue as sapphires; but it looked a little dull when seen through the window. The quiet of Sunday in the hilly part of the city gave to the fairly large garden the air of a place in the country. Suddenly a motor car ran noisily on the other side of the brick wall which enclosed the garden, and then quiet reigned as before.

Hidemaro continued. "Well, it's this: that 'as if' which you've called a monster each time isn't a monster at all. Without it, there would be no science, no art, no religion. Whatever has worth in life is centered around 'as if.' I bow my head reverently before it, just as men of old bowed their heads before the one or more gods who they believed existed and who they supposed had personality. My reverence isn't fervent, but it's a feeling serene and pure. With morality, it's the same thing. I grow indignant whenever I see such plays as Ibsen's that treat duty as a monster, a ghost, knowing that this cannot be proved as fact. A certain destruction of duty may be inevitable, but does nothing remain? At the foundation is 'as if,' indisputable though intangible and very slight of form. Man should act as if duty existed. I intend to act that way. That man descended from the monkey is a question of fact, and men undertake to prove it as fact, and so it's a hypothesis and not 'as if;' still, the fundamental idea of evolution is 'as if.' We cannot help thinking as if living things evolved. I look forward to the future of mankind; I look back as if the spirits of my ancestors exist, and I worship them. I walk along the path of virtue as if duty exists, and I go on seeing hope for the future. So, practically, I'm just the same as very ignorant, very obedient peasants living in out-of-the-way places. The only difference is that my head is a little clearer. I'm just the same as an obstinate and upright believer in the gods or the moralists. The only difference is that I'm not so stubborn. Don't you see that there's nothing safer, nothing less dangerous, than my thoughts? God isn't a fact; duty isn't a fact. We cannot but admit that now. But if we glory in that discovery and blaspheme, if we trample upon duty, then real danger begins for the first time. We should try to repress not only such actions, but also such thoughts. When such dangerous men appear we realize that it would be impossible to turn the world back to the time when people sincerely believed in the kingdom of heaven and in the dictum that the earth is stationary and the sun moves around it. To accomplish that, we should have to demolish universities and make the world dark and the people ignorant. That would be impossible. There's no other position than mine, which reverences 'as if.' "

Ayakōji, who had been smoking and listening with a peculiar smile that doubled and tripled the parentheses around his mouth, here knocked the ashes from his cigar into the ashtray and rose.

"No good," he said summarily, and turned his back toward the stove. He looked coolly at Hidemaro as the latter strode rapidly up and down before speaking.

Hidemaro stopped and gazed into the other's face. On Hidemaro's pale countenance there was a faint flush around the eyes, and there shone in them a kind of light like the fire of fanaticism. "Why? Why is it no good?"

"It's easy enough to see why. Nobody could be induced to think as you do. The peasants believe that the spirits of their ancestors, with triangular pieces of paper on their foreheads, come back to their houses at the summer *bon* festival. The moralists, on the other hand, think that somewhere up in the heavens is a sort of electric powerhouse from which emanates duty, and that their teachers transmit that electricity to them, and thanks to it they live and move through life. Men worship and follow because they see some tangible object before them. Do you suppose that if I were to give a man a picture of a nude woman which I painted he would be induced to remain unmarried or go to questionable places? Your 'as if' assumes that he will."

"Then, what do you think? Do you think ghosts come back walking on their legs, or do you think that you are electrified?"

"Not at all."

"Then, what do you think?"

"I don't think at all."

"Can you live without thinking?"

"Well, I don't mean that I don't think at all, but I try to think as little as possible. I leave difficult questions alone. I needn't necessarily meddle with them when I paint pictures, you see."

"Suppose you were in my place and had to write a history, what would you do?"

"I'll never have to write a history; I'll have to be excused from that." The smile vanished from his lips and was succeeded by a cool, almost unamiable, expression.

Hidemaro stood, quite exhausted, with his hands hanging limply, and then he smiled in his turn. "I see. Each person attends to his own affairs and leaves such questions alone. I did unwisely when I selected my profession.

It's easy enough to do my work without distinguishing clearly or by dissembling, but if I want to do it honestly, earnestly, I see I am hemmed in on all sides. It was my misfortune to choose such a profession."

Ayakōji's eyes flashed like steel that instant. "If you are hemmed in, why don't you break through like soldiers on a charge?"

Hidemaro again flushed around the eyes. He spoke in a low tone and in the manner of a child addressing a grown-up. "Is there no hope of my doing my work without quarreling with my father?"

"No, no," said Ayakōji.

He approached the stove seemingly desirous of warming his broad back, and stooped over a little, his hands clasped behind him. Hidemaro stood a few paces off, his thin slender body straight as a young growing bamboo. They looked into each other's eyes and remained silent for a time. The stillness of Sunday in the hilly part of the city reigned around them.

1912

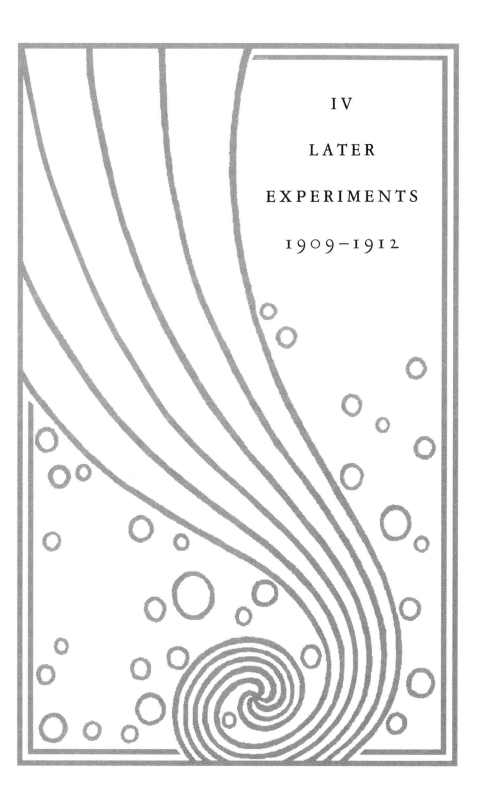

IV

LATER

EXPERIMENTS

1909–1912

DURING THE YEARS FROM 1909 to 1912, Ōgai was writing in a variety of literary forms, from the speculative essay to the modern drama. The six brief works in this section constitute a sampling of works illustrating Ōgai's continuing inclination to investigate new literary possibilities.

Although the themes he pursues in these works are not altogether dissociated from those elsewhere that mirror directly his own developing self-awareness, they involve, on the whole, an enlarged set of concerns, sometimes intellectual, sometimes formal and stylistic. They show as well the author's continued fascination with contemporary developments in European art and literature. And experiments though these may be, the fragments of the uncompleted novel *Kaijin* (The Ashes of Destruction) in particular show the hand of a master writer in the process of commencing a chilling literary experiment.

Kinka

THE GOLD COIN

WRITTEN IN 1909, *THE GOLD COIN* is one of Ōgai's most successful brief stories, presenting as it does such an amusing portrait of the disfigured Hachi, a lovable rogue who loves to drink and sets out to find enough money to satisfy his desires. Hachi's life is a hard one. He cannot read; he has no money; he has a difficult wife. Still, he is described with considerable sympathy by Ōgai; and although Hachi may resemble in some way the figure of the outsider looking in who inhabits a number of Ōgai's more somber works, any darker implications of such elements are set aside here and the humorous purposes of the narrative dominate.

Indeed, it is Hachi's good qualities that save him. Like the actress Hanako in the story written the following year, the real nature of Hachi's inner temperament can be recognized by the discerning despite what appears to be an unsuitable exterior. The army officers instinctively understand his real innocence and thus release this amateur thief; what is more, they see their own self-indulgent servant as another kind of culprit, one less deserving of forgiveness.

Nicely planned and executed, *A Gold Coin* is unproblematic and easy to read and enjoy. Of the stories in the present anthology, it perhaps conforms best to the notion of the well-knit short story as understood by readers and writers alike in the late nineteenth and early twentieth centuries.

HACHI, STILL WEARING HIS OLD PLASTERER'S JACKET, which had been turned inside out, remade, and patched time and time again, looked somewhat lost as he stood there in the light from the ticket gate at the Wakinosaka exit of Sendagaya station. It must have been about eight o'clock in the evening. Things were really most confusing. He was dying for a drink and the agony of not being able to get one left him almost paralyzed with indecision.

Fantasy drew a picture for him in his mind's eye. Standing in the corner of a kitchen was a large wooden bucket filled to overflowing with clear water, and water was trickling down into it from a rubber tube attached to a tap. Floating on the surface were two or three small tubs. A shelf had been hung above the barrel and on it stood a glass upside down. The glass seemed to be bang in front of his nose, and he was just on the point of stretching out a hand to pick it up.

He couldn't just stand around like this forever; even he realized that much. But then where on earth could he go? Normally the answer would be home, a tenement he had just moved into: the thin shingles were new and leaked, but the rent was cheap. But there lay the enemy that really frightened him. It was all right arguing with your mates, because no matter who got beaten up at least somebody won. But that wasn't the case with the enemy holed up there under the shingles. No matter how often you fought, there was never any outcome. Up would go the war cry, up would come the lump. Then down it would go. Up would go the war cry again and up would come the lump again, and down it would go again. Just like Sisyphus and the rock: no matter how often you pushed it up, it always rolled back down. The only time Hachi could steel himself to face the enemy was with a belly-ful of drink. When the drink ran out he couldn't face it. It was like they said: no foe as fierce as the old woman.

He stood there listless. The darkness around him gradually deepened and the raindrops that fell from time to time from the gray sky felt chilly on his bald patch. A train pulled up at the station. A group of three army officers came out through the gate and walked toward him talking loudly among themselves. No one else seemed to be getting off and the train left almost immediately. As they walked past him, the man in front brushed the sleeve of Hachi's jacket with his cape. Hachi had never been called up because he was disfigured with a large scar running from the corner of his right eye to

TRANSLATED BY RICHARD BOWRING

his temple, the result of having been burned as a boy. As a result he knew
next to nothing about army ranks. But the stout, square-faced man in front
looked about forty and was probably either a colonel or a lieutenant-colonel;
that much he did know. And his bars were neither red nor green, nothing
conspicuous, so he was probably in the artillery. He marched past without so
much as a glance. The two behind both had red bars: one had a florid complexion and was unusually tall; the other was well set and had stern features.
Both seemed to be about the same rank as the man in front. They looked
straight at him as they passed. The stern-looking one gave him a hard look.
Just like the police, confound him, thought Hachi angrily, then fear gained
the upper hand and he looked away.

Still deep in discussion, the three men turned up toward the new estate.
Halfway up the hill the road became pitch dark, but they obviously knew
their way and skillfully avoided the puddles. From behind he could see the
glint of their spurs. Almost unconsciously, he started to follow them. He too
knew this road like the back of his hand.

They crossed the tracks twice and eventually turned in through an impos-
ing black gate; above the doors of the gate hung one of those signs sold by
the Tokyo Electric Light Company: "Arakawa" it said, although Hachi
couldn't read it. A servant emerged from the guard hut to the left of the
gate and gave the customary greeting. It appeared that the square-faced
man was the master of the house, for he led the way. The porch to the house
was lit by a standing lamp. Two little boys, one about twelve or thirteen, the
other about eight, ran out of the house and grabbed their father. The other
two men seemed to be frequent visitors and said something nice to the children. All three then took off their capes, hung them on hooks on a beam,
and went inside. The servant carefully arranged the visitor's boots on the
stone step at the entrance and then carried his master's boots back to the
guardhouse. He came out again immediately and closed the main gate.

Hachi had been watching these goings-on standing in the rain on the
other side of the road by a fence, a fence made of cryptomeria wood bound
with vines. When the servant came out to close the gate, Hachi found himself shuffling off down the muddy road again. But once the gate was shut,
he came to a halt. Just where he had stopped he noticed another small gate;
it too had a glass lamp hanging over it. It belonged to the house opposite
the Arakawa mansion, the house with the fence. He took shelter.

The guardhouse and the adjacent stable of the Arakawa mansion were
built close to the road, and the rest was all enclosed by a black wooden
fence. As he stood gazing, the window in the guardhouse, which had been

dimly lit until now, suddenly went black, and a few seconds later the servant opened the small side door of the main gate, put up an umbrella, and disappeared in the opposite direction.

So where to go? The question presented itself for a second time. Why not see what was inside the black fence? He may have thought that the idea had occurred to him on the spur of the moment, but of course there was more to it than that. His subconscious had been at work for some time and had just come up with an answer. He had been standing around at Wakinosaka with not a clue where to go. When the officers passed by, he had simply followed them. He had sensed a kind of connection between them and himself, so that when they finally disappeared into the mansion, Hachi felt as if he had suddenly lost something he needed. When the servant appeared, it was as if some barrier had been erected which interfered with whatever relationship it was that tied him to the officers. When he saw the servant leave, it was as if that barrier had been removed. And then, lurking at an even lower level than these subconscious feelings rising to the surface one by one, lay the intention to steal something. The underlying intention rose out of his unconscious at precisely the same moment that he decided to make his way through the fence.

He cut across the road and approached the large black gate. He tried the small side door; it opened without a sound. He went inside. Suddenly there was an almighty clatter and a thump. Startled, he grabbed the door behind him; but it was only the noise of a horse settling down on its bed of straw. He took his hands away from the door again and looked around. To the right of the entrance porch as he faced it was a bamboo fence which seemed to enclose a garden. He could just see the tops of what looked like two or three cypress trees. He passed in front of the guardhouse and went round to the left. As he came to the end of the stable, he saw a light on in the kitchen of the house and he heard women's voices. The wife and the maid were busy, it seemed. In the light from the window he could just make out a bamboo thicket stretching from the end of the stable to the boundary with the neighbors over on the left. He took stock of the situation for a while. Then, taking off his clogs and leaving them under the eaves by the stable wall, he crept into the bamboo. Coming to where it met the neighbor's fence, he crossed through the area lit up by the light from the window. The rain was fairly heavy and drowned any noise as he trod over the squelchy mass of leaves.

He came to the far end of the thicket. From here he could see an eight-mat room from which the screens had been removed. The light shone out onto the hedge of small prickly orange bushes that formed the boundary with the fields at the back, and raindrops caught in the spider's webs glistened. The master of the house and both guests had changed into something more comfortable and were sitting near the veranda, the smaller man watching the host and the florid one play *go*. The air was heavy with the smoke from mosquito repellent which rose from a black, square firebox forming part of a foot-warmer similar to one Hachi had at home. The man watching would replenish the firebox from time to time, scooping up some insect powder from a tin by his side with a small Chinese spoon. All three had glasses of beer beside them. There was a bucket on the ground just by the veranda keeping some bottles cool, and from time to time the small man would refill the glasses. As soon as an open bottle was finished, he would put the cap back on again and stand it upside down on the ground against the side of the house. Funny thing to do, thought Hachi.

The thicket was dense, but still the rain came dripping in through the leaves. Standing there in the wet, his jacket sticking to his back, Hachi felt very uncomfortable. He looked around and spied a large black bush just where the side fence met the back hedge; a camellia perhaps. He went over and squatted down underneath it. Here it was dry at least. No sooner had he settled down, however, than he felt a mosquito bite him on the face and legs. His instinct was to slap, but he knew he must keep quiet and so rubbed the bites instead. Somewhat contemptuously the insect flew off, only to return again immediately. Hachi sat there rubbing first his face and then his ankles in turn.

The wife brought something out from the kitchen. It was evidently some pickles for the men.

"That's very kind of you," said the small man, taking the bowl from her.

Her husband turned round.

"Have you put up the mosquito net in the six-mat room?"

"Yes."

"How about the children?"

"I've put them to bed in the smaller room."

"Good. I don't think we'll need anything else, so you and the maid can go to sleep."

"Then if you'll excuse me, I'll say good night."

The florid man had picked up a *go* stone and was concentrating.

"It must be very inconvenient for you to have to put us up so often like this," he said.

"It's no trouble at all, I assure you."

Hachi could hear all this clearly. The wife went back into the kitchen. After a short pause, he heard the kitchen door close, then the sound of various screens being opened and shut. Then silence. A clock struck. He counted: ten o'clock.

The host seemed to have lost. He pulled out a large handkerchief that he had wrapped round his open neck for comfort and wiped the sweat from his brow, laughing loudly. The small man was his next opponent. The host got up and looked outside. It seemed to Hachi as though their eyes met, but of course there was no way he could be seen in the thicket. Hachi was not in the least bit scared; on the contrary, the man looked a good sort. He pulled a beer bottle out of the bucket, took off the cap, filled the three glasses, and then drank his own in one long swig. Hachi instinctively felt his mouth start to water.

The next game of *go* seemed to be taking a lot longer than the first. The small man gave it careful thought and took his time over every move. The host looked on for a while, then got up, went to the middle of the room, and lay spread-eagled on the floor cooling himself with a fan. It was a quiet scene. Only the click-click of the stones at very long intervals could be heard in the rain.

Since he had crawled in under the bush, Hachi had managed to avoid most of the rain and he could feel his jacket drying of its own accord. It was getting late but was still as muggy as ever, so that the coolness against his skin was in fact very welcome. The only problem was the wretched mosquitoes. Surely it was time they stopped playing, he thought, but progress seemed to be slow. The gap between clicks kept on getting longer and longer. The small man replenished the repellent and folded his arms again deep in thought. Suddenly the host gave a loud snort. The small man got up, went over, and shook him.

"You'll catch cold if you fall asleep," he said.

"Oh! Asleep, was I?" said the host, springing up. The short nap seemed to have revived him and he came over to the side of the board full of spirits.

"Haven't made much progress, have you!" he said.

The florid man leant back and looked up with a smile.

"Long way to go yet," he said. The small man turned his attention to the board again. He was obviously determined not to play casually. The clock struck eleven.

Squatting under the camellia bush, Hachi watched them patiently. In fact he was a fairly placid type and found no difficulty in waiting. "Wait and hold your ground!" had been an order you often heard during the Russo-Japanese War. Well, Hachi could wait and hold his ground with the best of them. Only when the beer was slipping down their throats and his mouth started to water did he find it difficult. That was the worst bit. He toyed with the idea of creeping over the end of the veranda, crawling underneath it to where the bucket was, and taking a bottle back with him. But even he had to admit this was a little foolhardy. Besides, even if he succeeded in getting one, how on earth would he get the cap off? Men who had enlisted and gone to war had stories of knocking off the tops of bottles with their bayonets to drink the stuff the Russkies had left behind, but unfortunately there wasn't anything handy; not even a stone. And in any case breaking a glass bottle would be noisy. No, it just couldn't be done, he told himself. And then, for some strange reason, he found himself forgetting what he was squatting there for in the first place. He started cursing the rain, thanking his lucky stars for the camellia bush, and hoping that it might stop raining, just overhead anyway; hardly the thoughts of a serious burglar.

Neither man seemed to be winning the game. The beer flowed freely; the host in particular seemed to be drinking a lot. Having got through a fair amount, he obviously felt the need to relieve himself and went to the toilet. It was at the end of the veranda furthest away from Hachi. Hearing the man clear his throat, expectorate, and then urinate made Hachi want to go too.

As the urge came on, it occurred to Hachi how unfair life was: the man wanted to go because he'd been drinking; but Hachi hadn't had a drop! Things were getting desperate, but if he did it here he might be heard. As luck would have it the rain had eased off a little and that would make it all the more obvious. What the hell could he do? He racked his brains and finally came up with the idea of doing it against the stem of the bush. Even then he occasionally strayed off the mark and made a splash, giving himself a bit of a scare. Luckily no one seemed to notice.

Then another thought came to him. He remembered hearing that before breaking into a house burglars often left their "calling card" before going in. No time like the present! But it was no good. Now the author considers it may well be that some burglars defecate and then cover up the results with a washtub in order to cast an evil spell, but there is probably a more fundamental reason for such behavior. When they enter a house to steal, an attack of nerves sometimes causes an involuntary contraction of the bowels, just as students are sometimes taken short before their exams. Some of the soldiers who attacked Nanshan during the Russo-Japanese War had defecated in the millet fields while under enemy bombardment. It had been written up in the newspapers as an act of courage, but that too was undoubtedly an attack of nerves. Hachi's mental processes had become so dulled that he felt not the slightest bit nervous. As a result, he felt no need to defecate.

He heard the clock strike twelve. Soon after, the game came to a close.

This time it seemed the small man had won. The florid one smiled, running his fingers through his close-cropped hair. The host got up as if he had just thought of something.

"Half a minute," he said. "It's my turn next. But the beer's run out, so I'll just get a substitute."

He brought out a bottle of cognac and three small glasses from a cupboard beside the alcove and put them down by the side of the board. The bottle had been opened, but it was still quite full. The small man picked it up and examined the label.

"Substitute my foot! This is the real thing!" he said, and filled the three glasses. The florid man picked his up, had a sip, and savored it. The host sat down opposite the small man, took his glass, and drank it off in one gulp.

"That's how cognac should be drunk!" he said.

"Just a moment," said the small man, and he took his beer glass out onto the veranda to rinse it in the bucket. Then he poured some warm water into it from a small kettle on the tea tray and mixed it with the cognac.

They settled down to play. As usual the small man deliberated over every move, whereas the host could hardly wait until his opponent's hand was off the board. The one played very cautiously, sipping his watered-down cognac; the other slapped down his pieces without thinking and drank the cognac neat. But no matter how fast he played, his opponent needed to give it all his concentration. So time passed.

After a while the florid man, who was looking on, gave a sudden laugh.

"You've had it now!" he burst out, and a little while later the host gave up.

"When you lose, lose thoroughly: that's my motto!" he said and began to clear the board. "When you lose, lose thoroughly! Well, time to turn in."

"It'll be hot under the mosquito net, I shouldn't wonder," said the small man, putting the stones away. The host didn't seem to be unduly concerned.

"Well. It should be all right if we leave the shutters open a bit."

He got up and pulled the shutters out from the recess in the wall, while the others slid them to, leaving a one-foot gap between each pair. The three of them left the cluttered room as it was and fell asleep under the net that had been hung in the next room. The clock struck one.

Hachi emerged from the thicket and crept up outside the room where they were sleeping to spy out the land. A light still came from the eight-mat room, but the room with the mosquito net was pitch black. At first he could hear someone using a fan, but it soon stopped and he heard snoring. He could distinguish the snores of the host and the florid man, and after a while he was also able to make out the regular breathing of the small man. All three, he now knew, were asleep.

Now that he was actually standing right outside the shutters, he felt a little different. Yes, he was scared. He began to sweat again under his clothes, already damp from the rain; he sweated most profusely down the line of his breastbone. It may have been close in the thicket, but he hadn't felt as bad as this. And yet he was determined to get into the house soon. He was dying for a drink and could think of nothing else. Get in and get a drink. Not that he wasn't going to steal something at the same time, but it was hardly his major concern: more a result of having become a burglar. A drink: that was what drove him. The idea of stealing was little more than a face-saver.

He came to where the bucket was lying outside the shutters. The main room had been left open and the lamp was still there with the wick turned down low. But there was a thick screen dividing this room off from the six-mat room where the men were sleeping. He listened to their breathing for a while and then stepped up onto the veranda, squeezing sideways through a gap in the shutters. Realizing that if anyone inside the net happened to wake up now they would see him, he quickly slipped past the *go* board and into the main room. He had been walking on leaves in the thicket and on moss in the garden so his feet were fairly clean. The only traces he left were some wet patches on the veranda.

The first thing to catch his eye was four or five beer bottles lined up on two trays. They were probably empty, but he picked them up to make sure. As he thought, not a drop left in any of them. Then he tried the cognac bottle which was down beside the *go* board. There were still seven or eight measures left in it. He filled a beer glass and took a swig. It was a little strong to be sure, but the warm tingling sensation as it slipped down his throat to the pit of his stomach felt so good that he drank the whole lot off in three mouthfuls; after the third his insides were so warm he half expected to see steam rising from his rain-soaked jacket. He poured out the rest of the cognac, but left it standing there. Need a little breather before I drink that, he thought.

Brushing away the mosquitoes that were slowly gathering, he looked around. It was rare to come across a room as tastelessly decorated as this one. Instead of a scroll in the alcove there were two large artillery shells surrounded by a jumble of books and magazines. On the cross beam hung a large frame with a sample of calligraphy which read: "Advance to the Ninth Heaven." It was in the hand of some field-marshal or other, but then Hachi couldn't read it anyway. A collection of black and red ink bottles, brushes, pens, and pencils were wedged into an open inkstone box on a low table that was pulled up against the alcove. There was also a set square and a pair of dividers doing duty as paperweights on top of some Japanese writing paper and some Western graph paper, possibly a manuscript. Apart from that, there was the *go* board, the firebox with the mosquito repellent, the beer bottles, and the empty bowl of pickles; little else.

Outside the shutters Hachi had felt nervous and somewhat scared, but now he calmed down again. This was probably due to the cognac which was gradually having its effect. The fact that three large men, army officers at that, were asleep in the next room, only a screen's width away, didn't seem to bother him at all. But that didn't prevent him from wondering just what might happen if they did happen to wake up. Cut him down with a saber? Shoot him with a pistol? But where were their swords and things? Perhaps they had taken them into the bedroom with them? In this supposition he was correct. The host, Colonel Arakawa, always kept his uniform and his sword with him when asleep. He had once been fairly easygoing about it, in the habit of leaving his uniform lying around for his wife to clear away, but then he had seen something that made him decide to keep it by him at all times, even when asleep. The florid man, Colonel Annaka, and the small man, Lieutenant Utsunomiya, who were staying the night, approved of this habit of his, and neither of them would let their uniforms out of their sight, at home or abroad.

That "something" for Arakawa had been shortly after the battle of Mukden in the Russo-Japanese War when the troops were stationed at Cheng Tu. Stages had been erected here and there, and the men had been encouraged to put on shows so they wouldn't get bored. One day he had gone over on business to General Oku's headquarters and had stayed the night there. There was a show going on there too, and when the evening meal was over they all went over to see it. It was a cold evening and everyone watching was wrapped in furs. Hardly anyone had come with his sword. But then the general himself had put in an appearance. He was the only one to wear his sword, and while watching the play he just loosened the catch that held it and pulled it up beside him. This made a very deep impression indeed on Arakawa. He was reminded of an anecdote about the wars long ago between Kai and Echigo. It told of a samurai who had gone to play a game of *go* at a neighbor's house totally unarmed. A quarrel had erupted and he had been taken unawares. When his lord heard about it later, he was ordered to forfeit his stipend. Arakawa was most impressed by the general's prudence and thereafter never let his sword from his side under any circumstances.

Hachi devoutly hoped that they wouldn't wake up. Cut down or shot; either way it wasn't a very pleasant prospect. But he was not fully aware that his whole life actually hung in the balance. It was all just a possibility. Somehow he couldn't bring himself to believe it would actually happen.

The cognac had begun to have quite an effect. Hachi liked his drink, but that didn't mean he could hold it. In particular, the older one got the less one could take. Until he reached his thirties, there had been no problem, but now he was getting near forty and he found he just couldn't hold it like he used to, although he liked it just the same. His head drooped a little, but feeling like another drink he took another swig of the cognac left in the glass. This time it did seem a little too strong. He diluted it with some water from the kettle and tried another sip. Yes, that was much better. So down the hatch it went. The clock struck two.

Startled by the sudden noise, Hachi came to his senses a little. Mustn't forget one's duty as a burglar! Must steal something! He had another look around, but nothing in particular caught his eye and he didn't have the willpower to go into another room and search there. The muscles on his face began to slacken and his scar made it seem as if his eyes were sunk in a kind of grimace. Once again he was almost on the point of forgetting he ought to steal something. This won't do at all, he thought, making a determined effort. He sat down cross-legged on the floor, his hands on his knees, and straightened his back.

"Hmm, a fine fool they're making me look," he mumbled to himself and had another look round.

This time his eyes alighted on a drawer in the table in front of the alcove. He stood up and slouched over to it. On his feet he had the strange impression that he was floating on air, but he returned to normal once he was ensconced in front of the table. It was made of some kind of hardwood and was sturdily built with real brass fittings on the drawer. Reaching out, he pulled at it. It opened smoothly.

It was mostly filled with a pile of discarded letters, some in envelopes and some without. Some had Western writing on them and there were also a few picture postcards. Pushing the pile of letters to one side a little, he found a collection of beautiful, small lacquered boxes in one corner. He opened them but they were all empty, empty medal boxes. In the other corner was a fairly large box made from some shiny red wood, and on top of that lay a small silver box with a chrysanthemum crest in gold, and what seemed like a purse of green leather with silver inlay. At the sight of these, his eyes lit up.

He brought the three objects out onto the matting and tackled the large red box first. It was full of brass implements of various sizes: geometry instruments in a mahogany case. Next he opened the silver container with the crest. It was a cigar box which had been given to Arakawa as a gesture of thanks by a certain imperial prince who had been at Saint Cyr with him. Lastly Hachi opened the leather pouch that looked like a purse. From the moment he picked it up he realized it contained something heavy that jingled. He wasn't too sure what it was, but he had high hopes.

That it was a purse of sorts there was no doubt. It was square and made of green leather. The rim, hinges, scaled pattern corners, and the initial letter A inlaid in the center were all made of silver. Arakawa had been to France and had bought it in Paris as a curiosity. It had a flap top and you opened it by twisting a small silver knob.

Hachi managed to twist it open with his clumsy, gnarled fingers. The inside was padded with material and two or three coins were lying in each fold. They were of various sizes, some big and some small, and most of them silver. None of them seemed to be the usual ten, twenty, or fifty-sen pieces one normally came across. What did catch his attention was a fairly large gold-colored coin which shone brightly. This lot would do, he thought, picking them out one by one with his stubby fingers and stuffing them into the apron pocket of his jacket.

He was somewhat relieved now that it was all over. It was time to be off. But just then what should catch his eye but the glass of watered-down cognac that he had left unfinished. It would be a pity to leave it, so he tried another swig. But this time it didn't taste half as good. Somehow he preferred the kick he had got after the very first drink. He poured some cognac straight from the bottle into one of the smaller glasses lying around and knocked it back. That was much better; he felt it penetrate all the way down.

He had felt nervous while searching through the drawer, but now he felt relaxed and very lethargic. He put his left hand out onto the matting. The snores from the next room which he had been listening for with such apprehension gradually seemed to fade away. He rested his left elbow on the floor. His eyelids felt heavy. Because of the mosquitoes and because he knew he mustn't fall asleep, he just managed to force open his drooping eyelids. But they were so very heavy. Opening and closing his eyes like this, he did in fact drop off a number of times and became quite oblivious to the snores next door. Occasionally he would open his eyes with a start, either on the point of snoring himself or being bitten by a particularly vicious mosquito.

There is an episode in a book by Anatole France where some shipwrecked sailors get onto the back of a whale basking in the ocean and start to gamble. In a sense Hachi was taking no less of a risk by nodding off now. He lay there dozing on and off for about thirty minutes, unaware that the clock had struck three. But even a short nap can prove surprisingly refreshing, so when something finally did occur to wake him properly, he no longer felt sleepy. Perhaps he had been startled by one of the men next door talking in his sleep or turning over on his mattress. As his eyes opened he was dreaming in a kind of half-sleep; in fact he was right in the middle of a dream. As far as he could recall, he was, as usual, in trouble with his boss, Kuma. What on earth was the reason this time? Oh yes. It had something to do with those gold and silver coins he had just taken. Yes, now he remembered. Kuma was pressing him for the train fare he had borrowed, and as usual he stuck his hand in his pocket to pull out what he thought were some copper coins. But he brought out the gold one instead. It had given him quite a shock. Kuma looked at him with a strange glint in his eyes.

"Nice haul you've got there!" he said.

Hachi was at a loss for words and in a bit of a tight spot when all of sudden something startled him and he woke up. He found himself putting his hand into his pocket and fumbling around for the coins. Both his apron and his jacket were quite dry now. Yes, the coins were definitely there. He pulled out the first one that came to hand to look at it; it was the bright gold one, about the size of a one-sen copper. He couldn't suppress a grin.

By now he was fully awake. Looking outside, he noticed that it was already getting light. The rain seemed to have stopped without his realizing it. He got up. His dizziness had gone, but fear suddenly returned and he longed to escape, fly if possible. He left the lamp dying, its wick burnt low, and crept stealthily out through the shutters.

The dawn air felt cool on his face. The raindrops caught in the spider's webs in the hedge were still shining like pearls and there was a low mist over the thicket. He shivered. He felt like relieving himself, but realized it was out of the question and so went back the way he had come. The clogs he had taken off and put down by the stable that evening were still there and after some hesitation as to whether to carry them or not, he put them on. In the stable the horse was clattering its hooves. He looked at the guardhouse but the servant didn't seem to be around. Coming across a box for the horse's dung, he took the opportunity to relieve himself. Some people passed close by, chatting to each other as they pulled their carts; they were probably on their way to market.

He had been listening carefully for sounds in the street outside, but no one was passing by the mansion, so he put his hand to the small side door.

Suddenly it opened from the outside and a man stepped in. They came face to face and for a split second both stood there dumbfounded. The servant had slipped off to Shinjuku without permission and so had tiptoed the last few blocks. It was he who broke the silence first.

"Who the hell are you?" he whispered.

Seeing that the man was slow in reacting, Hachi tried to slip past him and out the door. But the servant instinctively dropped his umbrella and grabbed Hachi by the elbow.

"Help! A burglar!"

The two of them struggled. Being a little out of sorts because of the drink, Hachi was at a disadvantage. Taikichi, the servant, a pale thin man whose nose, chin, and cheekbones jutted out from his sunken features, was not very strong either. But even dogs fight better on their home turf. Holding the gate shut with his back against it, he gripped Hachi by the elbow with both hands and refused to let go.

"Sir! Help! A burglar! Help!" he shouted louder this time.

The wife, who had been sleeping in the small room near the front of the house, had heard his first shout and hurried through to tell her husband. He got up, glanced around him, decided against the army sword by the bed, and picked up instead a wooden sword he used for practice. He went out to the entrance porch. Both guests followed him without bothering to change, but each carrying a sword. The three of them arrived at the porch just as Taikichi let out his second shout.

Arakawa quickly sized up the situation. The one who appeared to be the burglar was not carrying a weapon of any kind and didn't seem to be resisting in the slightest. The colonel looked a little disappointed.

"That's enough! It's all right, let him go!" he said.

Taikichi released his hold and Hachi stood there cowering.

The colonel turned to Taikichi, who was still standing with his back to the gate looking a trifle awkward.

"What's he taken? Was he in your room?" he asked.

"Well, sir."

"Come on, out with it, man! How did you catch him?"

"Well, you see, sir, he was trying to get out just as I was coming in, so I bumped into him."

"What! Been to Shinjuku again, have you, you sly dog! So you really don't know whether he's stolen anything or not, do you!"

At this juncture the colonel's wife came out of the house.

"I've just had a look round and those European coins have been taken from the drawer in your desk," she said. "I don't think anything else has gone."

"I see," said the colonel. Then, evidently trying to suppress a smile, he turned to Hachi.

"You there! Did you take the money from the drawer?" he asked.

Now that he knew escape was impossible, Hachi felt quite unconcerned and hadn't the slightest intention of trying to hide the coins in his pocket. Indeed, he had taken a liking to the master of the house from the very beginning; there was something generous about his large square face. It was almost as if Hachi had followed him and come in to burgle his house partly because of it. For some reason he couldn't quite fathom, the colonel was stern when scolding the servant for his nocturnal outing but looked kinder when questioning Hachi about what he had taken: he was rather impressed by this. Suddenly he plunged his right hand into his pocket and brought out a fistful of coins. He placed them on the ground and looked up.

"Very sorry, sir," he said.

Hachi had that ugly scar by his right eye and showed the indelible traces of a dull, monotonous life, but there was nothing menacing about him at all. Realizing this, the colonel relaxed even more.

"First time, I suppose," he said.

"Yes sir, first time."

"I thought as much. Don't try it again, do you hear?"

Annaka and Utsunomiya came over to look at the coins that Hachi had put down and knelt down without paying him the slightest attention. Hachi, of course, was hardly in a position to appear threatening; Taikichi meanwhile was crouched behind him bending his head and on the lookout.

"They're all foreign ones."

"Yes, I collected them while I was abroad. I did have a pound, twenty francs, and twenty marks, but I changed them all when I needed the money. These little silver coins are all that's left."

"But there's a yellow one among them, isn't there?"

Utsunomiya gave a laugh. "It's yellow right enough, but it's only a sou!" he said, holding it in his hand.

"So it is!" chuckled the colonel. "A sou. The large sum of five centimes. I kept it because it was so clean and new. If you don't use them and just put them away, they stay clean forever, don't they?"

"But there's a rumor that the French are going to do away with copper coins and replace them with small aluminum ones," said Utsunomiya. "This sou should soon be pretty rare." As an intelligence officer it was his duty to read foreign newspapers.

Annaka showed him the Spanish piaster and the Portuguese tostão, asking him what they were. Hachi listened without understanding a thing they said, but he did grasp that the yellow coin was not gold. He couldn't help feeling a bit disappointed that he had brought it out at that particular moment.

Confident that he had been rather smart, Taikichi turned to the colonel.

"Shall we hand him over to the police, sir?" he asked.

Hachi glowered at him.

"You keep out of this!" said the colonel. He turned to Hachi.

"It's all right, you can go. But you're not to steal again, you understand." Hachi said nothing. He bowed to the colonel and, casting a sidelong glance at Taikichi, left through the side gate.

From a house nearby came the clatter of shutters being opened and then the sound of someone clearing his throat.

1909

Hanako

HANAKO

HANAKO WAS THE STAGE NAME adopted by a young Japanese actress who appeared with success in America and Europe early in the century and drew the attention of the great French sculptor Auguste Rodin in 1906. Ōgai read of their encounters in the Japanese press and wrote this brief tale, published in 1910. By including the use of the Baudelaire text, Ōgai, in the short space he gave himself, managed to make a profound point concerning the differences and subtle correspondences between the outward and the inner natures of a human being. Ōgai's creation of the two major figures who inhabit the story, Rodin and Hanako, are masterfully sketched, and it seems altogether appropriate that Kubota, a Japanese medical student, should be the one to link the two.

Rodin, the supreme artist, can see beneath the surface; the possession of that ability in turn helps to mark him as a superior man. The theme of the superior man appears in a muted and humorous way in *The Gold Coin* and, in its more openly Nietzschean dimensions, in the play *Masks*.

Auguste Rodin came into the studio.

The spacious room was filled with sunshine. This Hotel Biron was a luxurious building, originally erected by a certain rich man, but later it became a convent of the school of the Sacred Heart and remained so until a short time ago. Perhaps in this very room the nuns of the Sacré Coeur called together the girls of the Faubourg Saint Germain and taught them their hymns. Just as little birds cry out from their nest on seeing the mother approaching, so the little girls, standing in rows and opening their mouths, may have sung.

Those cheerful voices no longer may be heard.

But another sort of cheerfulness is reigning in this room, a different life is dominating. It is a voiceless life, but though voiceless, it is magnificent, pulsating, cultured.

There were several lumps of gypsum on each of several tables. The master is accustomed to begin several works at a time, and to work on them intermittently, according to his mood, until complete. As various plants bloom at the same time, so certain of his works grow, like things in nature, some rapidly, some slowly. This man has a tremendous perception of form. His works are growing before his hands touch them. This man has a tremendous power of concentration. The moment he begins a work he is able to assume the attitude of continuing a work begun some hours before.

With bright face Rodin looked over the numerous half-completed works: that face with a broad forehead, a nose that seemed to have a joint in the middle; a white, ample beard that crowded about the chin.

There were knocks at the door.

"*Entrez.*"

A deep, powerful voice, unlike that of an old man, vibrated through the air of the room. The man who entered the door was a lean fellow about thirty years of age, with dark brown hair, and a Jewish cast of countenance.

He announced that he was bringing Mademoiselle Hanako as he had promised.

Rodin did not change his appearance either when he saw the man entering or when he heard the words.

Once when a chieftain from Cambodia was staying in Paris, Rodin saw a dancer whom this chieftain had brought, and he felt a kind of attraction for the flexible movements of her long slender limbs. The *dessins* taken in haste are still in his possession. Rodin—believing, as in that case, that every person has something of beauty, a beauty to one who discovers the point—had

TRANSLATED BY TORAO TAKETOMO

heard that a Japanese girl, called Hanako, had been on the stage at the Varieté for several days. Through a mediator he asked the man who had charge of Hanako to bring her to his house.

The man who had come was the manager, the impresario.

"Let her come hither," Rodin said.

It was not merely from lack of time that he neglected to show him to a chair.

"I have brought an interpreter with us," the man said, as if to learn his humor.

"Who is he? Is he a Frenchman?"

"No, a Japanese who works at L'Institut Pasteur. He heard from Hanako that she was called to you, and desired to come as interpreter."

"All right. Let him enter also."

Instantly two Japanese, a man and a woman, entered the room. Both of them looked peculiarly small. The manager, who followed and closed the door, was not a tall man, but the two Japanese reached only to his ears.

Rodin's face wrinkled about the eyes, wrinkles which seem to be carved at the inner corner, when he looks at things intently. The wrinkles showed at this time. His gaze moved from the student to Hanako, and stayed there a while. The student saluted, and grasped the right hand Rodin offered, the hand on which each sinew stood on the surface, the hand that had created *La Danaïde*, *Le Baiser*, and *Le Penseur*. And, taking out a card on which Kubota, M.P., was written, he delivered it to Rodin.

Rodin glanced at the card, and said:

"Are you working at L'Institut Pasteur?"

"Yes, sir."

"Have you been there for some time?"

"Three years, sir."

"Avez-vous bien travaillé?"

Kubota was surprised. He had been told that Rodin says this as a habit. Now, these simple words were spoken directly to him.

"Oui, beaucoup, monsieur!"

At the moment he said this, Kubota felt as if he were swearing to be diligent for life.

Kubota introduced Hanako. Rodin looked down as if to comprehend her with a glance of the eye, and he saw the small, trim body of Hanako from the unbecomingly dressed hair in Takashimada style to the tips of her feet in white *tabi* and Chiyoda sandals, and he reached forth and took the tiny but robust hand.

Kubota could not but feel in his mind a sort of humility. He wished that he had a finer person to introduce to Rodin as a Japanese woman. His feeling was not unreasonable, for Hanako was not a beauty. She had appeared in the European cities as a Japanese actress, but the Japanese themselves knew nothing of such an actress. Kubota knew nothing about her either. Moreover, the actress was not a beauty. It might be too severe to call her a servant. She did not seem to have worked especially hard, for her hands and feet were not hardened. But even at her bloom of seventeen, her appearance would hardly rank her as a chambermaid. In a word, she was no more presentable than a nursery maid.

Unexpectedly, Rodin's face showed a glow of satisfaction. He was pleased with Hanako: healthy; no sign of indulgence in leisure; firm, elastic flesh, well developed by proper exercise—characteristics that were vividly shown in the face, short from forehead to chin, in the bare wrists and gloveless hands, and in the thin skin which showed not a particle of fat.

Hanako, who was already accustomed to European manners, took the hand of Rodin with an amiable smile on her face.

Rodin offered chairs to both of them, and said to the manager:

"Please wait for us a while in the parlor."

After the manager was gone, they sat down.

Offering the uncovered box of cigars to Kubota, Rodin said to Hanako:

"Are there any mountains or sea at Mademoiselle's home?"

Hanako, as is common among the women in such a profession, had a regular stereotyped story of her life, which she told to persons whenever she was questioned. Just as in the case of the little girl in Zola's *Lourdes,* who relates the miracle of the recovery of her injured feet in the train, her story became, through frequent repetition, like the composition of the routine storyteller. Fortunately, the unexpected question of Rodin upset this ready-made plan.

"The mountain is at a distance. The sea is close by."

The answer pleased Rodin.

"Did you ride on junks frequently?"

"Yes, sir."

"Did you row yourself?"

"No, sir. I did not row as I was still small. My father rowed."

A picture came into Rodin's imagination, and he became silent for a while. Rodin is a man who is often silent.

Rodin said abruptly to Kubota:

"I presume Mademoiselle is acquainted with my profession. Would she be willing to remove her clothing?"

Kubota reflected a moment. Of course he did not wish to be instrumental in causing a woman of his own country to bare herself before another man, but he did not object to daring it for Rodin. There was no need on his part for reflection; his hesitation was due to doubts as to what Hanako would say.

"Anyway, I will speak to her."

"If you please."

Kubota addressed Hanako in this manner:

"The master has something to consult you about. I think you understand that he is the peerless sculptor of the world and models the shape of the human body. This is the point about which he wishes to consult you. He wishes to know if you will oblige him by posing for him in the nude for a few moments. What do you say? As you see, he is an elderly man, not far from seventy; moreover, he is such a fine gentleman. What do you think?"

Thus saying, Kubota looked attentively into Hanako's face. He was wondering whether she would be overcome with shame, or affect airs, or blame him.

"I will," she replied frankly and naively.

"She consents," Kubota told Rodin.

Rodin's face shone with pleasure, and rising up from the chair, he took out paper and chalk, and said to Kubota as he laid them on the table:

"Will you stay here?"

"The same thing is sometimes necessary in my profession," said Kubota, "but it might be unpleasant to Mademoiselle."

"Then, will you wait there in the library? I shall be through in fifteen or twenty minutes. Light a cigar, if you like."

"He says he will be through in fifteen or twenty minutes." Saying these words to Hanako, Kubota went out through the door shown him.

The small chamber into which Kubota stepped had entrances on either side and only one window. Bookcases were on the wall opposite the window and on the other walls that constituted its wings.

Kubota stood a while reading the titles on the leather bindings of the books. This was a collection which had been assembled rather by chance than intention. Rodin was by nature a book lover, and it is said that he was always carrying a book in his hand even in his young days of misery, when he was roaming the streets of Brussels. Among the old dusty books there must be some of varied memories and brought here with purpose.

As the ashes of his cigar were about to fall, Kubota walked toward the table and dropped the ashes in the ashtray.

And, wondering about the books on the table, he picked them up to see.

On the furthest edge of the table, leaning against the window, was a book which Kubota took to be the Bible, but, on opening it, he found that it was the *édition de poche* of *La Commedia Divina.* The book aslant was one of the works of Baudelaire.

Without any idea of reading, he opened the first page, on which there was a treatise entitled "The Metaphysics of the Toy," and, wondering what was in it, he all at once began to read.

The treatise opened with this memory, that when Baudelaire was a little boy he was taken to a certain demoiselle who had a room full of toys, and told he might have his choice. After a child has played with a toy for a while, he is possessed to break it. He wonders what there is beyond the thing. If it be a moving toy, he wishes to search after the origin of the impulse. Hence the child goes from *physique* to *metaphysique,* from science to metaphysics.

As it was only four or five pages, Kubota, becoming interested, read through to the end.

Then there was a knock; the door opened and Rodin's white-haired head peeped through.

"Pardon me. You must be tired."

"No, sir, I was reading Baudelaire."

Saying thus, Kubota entered the studio. Hanako was already dressed. Two *esquisses* were lying on the table.

"What of Baudelaire were you reading?"

" 'The Metaphysics of the Toy.' "

"The same idea pertains to the human body—that the form is not interesting simply because it is a form. It is a mirror of the soul. The inner flame, showing transparently through the form, alone is interesting."

As Kubota looked timidly at the *esquisses,* Rodin said:

"They must be hard to understand, as they are so rough."

He continued after a moment:

"Mademoiselle has an exceedingly beautiful body. She has not a particle of fat. Each muscle rises on the surface like the muscle of a fox terrier. As the fibers are tight and thick, the size of the joints is made the same as the size of the limbs. They are so firm that she could stand on one leg while the other is stretched at a right angle, like a tree that has its roots thrust deep in the earth. This is different from the Mediterranean type with broad shoulders and loins, and does not resemble the North European type with broad loins, but narrow shoulders. It is the beauty of strength."

1910

Sakazuki

CUPS

WRITTEN IN 1909, THIS LITTLE PROSE FANTASY is generally regarded as belonging to a group of works intended by Ōgai to serve as a muted protest against those Japanese writers who, in developing a movement in consonance with European naturalism, tended to emphasize the sordid and the sexual in their works. Ōgai's main attack on these writers came in his own trenchant *Vita Sexualis,* written in the same year. *Cups,* rather than a protest, appears instead as a small experiment composed in the style of an alternative and anti-naturalist variety of European writing that had attracted Ōgai's interest—in this case, that of the Belgian symbolist dramatist Maurice Maeterlinck, the celebrated author of *Pelléas and Mélisande.* During this period, Ōgai was busy translating another of Maeterlinck's famous dramas, *Le Miracle de St. Antoine.* In visual terms, Ōgai's little prose poem resembles a mural by the French artist Puvis de Chavannes, one set in Japan.

A CLEAR SPRING BUBBLES FORTH by the path ascending from the hot springs inn to Tsuzumi waterfall.

The water has accumulated to form a convex surface at the top of the well crib. The overflow spills down all four sides.

Green, beautiful moss covers the exterior of the well crib.

It is a summer morning.

The mist which shrouded the woods until now still remains, in tatters, in the tops of the trees which surround the spring.

Several people appear to be approaching from the inn, climbing the path which ascends by the side of a crystal-voiced mountain stream.

They draw near, talking gaily all the while.

Their voices resemble the twittering of a flock of small birds.

They are obviously all children, obviously girls.

"Come on! You're always falling behind."

"Wait! It's hard to walk with all these loose stones around."

Lagging behind, pushing ahead, the young girls come, all alike with their hair washed and tied with wide red ribbons that look like butterflies fluttering together.

The sleeves of their white-and-indigo hot springs' kimono too are fluttering, and on their feet they wear identical red-thonged sandals.

"I'm first."

"Say, that's not fair!"

Pushing to be foremost, they swarm toward the spring. There are seven.

All appear to be eleven or twelve years old. They are too much of a size to be sisters. All are pretty, and rather coquettish. They are probably friends.

What thread joins these seven little coral beads? Who brought them to the hot springs inn?

Breaking through the drifting white clouds, through the tops of the trees, the light of the morning sun traces a rough, striped pattern on the edge of the spring.

Some of the bright red ribbons glow.

One of the girls inflates the pod of a ground cherry which she has been holding in her mouth and throws it into the center of the well, where the water has accumulated to form a convex surface.

It circles around and around and then flows over the edge of the crib.

TRANSLATED BY JOHN W. DOWER

"Oh! It falls off right away. I was wondering what would happen."

"Of course it falls."

"Did you know before that it would?"

"It was obvious."

"You're lying."

Mockingly, she strikes out at the other. Her indigo sleeve flutters.

"Let's drink quickly."

"Oh, now I remember. We came here to drink."

"Did you forget?"

"Yes."

"Goodness."

Each girl reaches into the bosom of her kimono and takes out a cup.

Pale light glances from seven hands.

All are silver cups. Large silver cups.

Just then the sun breaks fully through, and the seven cups glitter even more. Seven silver snakes dart around the spring.

The silver cups are identical, and each is inscribed with two ideographs.

They are the characters for "Nature."

They are written in a strange style. Is it that of some particular school? Or is it original?

By turns they dip water from the spring and drink.

Pouting bright red lips, puffing out pink cheeks, they drink.

Whirring sounds emerge from various places in the grove. The cicada are trying out their voices. When the white clouds are scattered and the sun flourishes, their voices will make the mountain tremble.

Now a solitary girl comes up the path and stands behind the others.

She is the eighth.

In stature she is taller than the others. She appears to be fourteen or fifteen.

Her yellow-gold hair is tied with a black ribbon.

From her face, close to amber color, peer eyes as blue as the cornflower. She gazes with endless wonder upon the world about her.

Only her lips are faintly red.

She wears a gray dress with black piping.

A Western child born in the East? A Eurasian?

The eighth girl takes a cup from the pocket of her skirt.

A small cup.

From where could such ceramics come? It has the color of molten rock that has cooled after flowing from a pit of fire.

The seven girls have finished drinking. The concentric circles made as they dipped their cups have disappeared on the surface of the spring—disappeared into the spring, which has welled up to form once again a convex surface.

The eighth girl, making her way between sleeve after indigo sleeve, approaches the crib of the well.

For the first time, the seven become aware of this one disturbing their harmony.

Then they notice the small blackened cup she holds in her amber hand.

They've never dreamed of such a thing.

Seven pairs of bright red lips gape open, speechless.

The cicada shrill and shrill.

For a long interval the voices of the cicada are the only sound.

Finally, one of the girls speaks:

"Do you want to drink too?"

Her voice is suspicious, and edged with displeasure.

The eighth girl nods silently.

Then another girl speaks:

"Your cup is an odd one, isn't it? Let me have a look."

Her voice is suspicious, and edged with scorn.

Without a word, the eighth girl extends her cup, the color of lava.

The small cup is separated from her amber hand, her sinewy fingers, and passed from one plump and pinkish hand to another.

"My, what a funny, drab color."

"Even so, do you think it could be porcelain?"

"Isn't it stone?"

"It looks like it was picked out of the ashes of a fire, doesn't it?"

"Or dug up from a grave."

"From a grave, how nice."

Laughter tinkles from seven throats like little silver bells.

The eighth girl lets her arms hang limply by her sides. Her eyes, cornflower blue, look at nothing.

One of the girls speaks again:

"It's a silly little thing, isn't it?"

Then another:

"Oh yes. Impossible to drink from such a thing."

And another:

"Maybe you want to borrow mine."

A sympathetic voice.

Then she extends to the eighth girl her large, sparkling silver cup, inscribed with the ideographs for "Nature."

The lips of the eighth girl, which have remained sealed until now, part for the first time.

"Mon verre n'est pas grand mais je bois dans mon verre."

It is a melancholy and yet penetrating voice.

"My cup may not be large," she replied, "but I drink from my cup."

The seven girls glance at each other with innocent eyes.

They don't understand the language.

The arms of the eighth girl hang limply by her sides.

There is no need to understand the language.

The manner of the eighth girl expresses her will and leaves no room for misunderstanding.

The girl draws back her silver cup.

She draws back the large shining silver cup on which "Nature" is inscribed.

Another girl returns the black cup.

She hands back the little cup dark as lava that has cooled after gushing from a pit of fire.

The eighth girl calmly dips a few drops of water from the spring and moistens her lips, faintly red.

1909

Sanbashi

THE PIER

IF *CUPS* RESEMBLES A PUVIS DE CHAVANNES MURAL, *The Pier,* written a year later in 1910, is an impressionist sketch in which each detail is highlighted and juxtaposed against others in order to create a surprisingly vivid evocation, that of an impending sense of loss. Details of the ship, the cabin, the workmen, the passengers, all contribute to the total effect produced, but they all represent themselves and are not described with any emotional coloring; it is the author who assembles the mosaic and hence creates through juxtaposition the total effect aimed at the reader.

The models for a brief piece of this kind may have come from modern European poetry, which Ōgai continued to admire, or from contemporary impressionist and post-impressionist Western art, which Ōgai knew well and appreciated highly. In this context, the work, brief though it is, seems a surprising success.

Along with *Hanako, The Pier* was one of the first works of Ōgai to be translated into English: both appeared in a 1918 anthology entitled *Paulownia,* published in New York.

THE PIER IS LONG—LONG—

The rails of four railroads cut straight and obliquely the beams of the iron bridge on which the long and short cross-beams are like the bars of a xylophone on which children play. Through the cracks of the cross-beams, which almost catch the heels of shoes and wooden clogs, here and there the black waves are shown, reflected on the white flashes of sunshine.

The sky has cleared into a deep blue. On the inside of the train where she was sitting with her husband departing today, she did not think the wind was blowing.

When leaving the rickshaw, in which she rode from the station of Yokohama, and standing on this pier, she found that the wind of the fifth of March was still blowing as if to bite the skin, fluttering the skirts of the Azuma coat.

It is the Azuma coat in silver gray, which she loosely wears on her body, that carries the child of her husband, who is starting today, this day which is not far from the month of confinement.

She came with her hair in the Western style. Her boa is of white ostrich. Holding the light green umbrella with tassels, she walks along, surrounded by four or five maidservants.

The pier is long—long—

The big ships are anchoring on the right and the left of the pier. Some are painted in black, some in white.

The anchored ships are making a fence for the wind. Every time she leaves the place where there are ships, a gust of wind blows and flutters the skirts of her Azuma coat.

Two years ago, immediately after he was graduated from the Department of Literature, the count, her husband, had married her. It was during the previous year that she gave birth to her first child, a princess like a jewel. At the end of the year the husband became a master of ceremonies at the court. And, now, he is departing for London, charged with his official duty.

In his newly made gray overcoat, flinging the cane with its crooked handle, her husband is walking rapidly along the pier. The viscount, who is going with him, and whose height is taller by a head than his, also walks rapidly beside him, clad in a suit of similar color.

The French ship, on which her husband is about to go abroad, is anchoring at the extreme end of the right side of the pier.

A stool, like that which is used to repair the wires of a trolley, is stationed on the pier, and from it a gangplank is laid across to the bulwark.

TRANSLATED BY TORAO TAKETOMO

While walking slowly, she sees her husband and the viscount, his companion, crossing the gangplank and entering the ship.

The group of people looking after them are standing, here and there, on the pier. Almost all of them are those who came to bid adieu to her husband and the viscount. Perhaps there are no other passengers on this ship about to sail who are so important and are looked at by so many people.

Some of them are going to the foot of the stool on which the gangplank is laid, and stop there to wait for their companions. Some of them are standing at the place, a bit before the stool, where the blocks and ropes are laid down.

Among these people there must be some who are intimately known to her husband, and some who know him but slightly. But, standing under this clear sky, they all seem dejected; or is it only her fancy?

The pier is long—long—

Following slowly after them, unconsciously she looks off to her right where there are many round windows on the side of the ship. The faces and chests of women are seen from one of those round windows. Three of them are from thirty to forty years of age; all with white aprons on their chests. They must be the waitresses of the ship. Supposing them to be the waitresses who wait on the passengers of the ship, on which her husband is aboard, she feels envious of even those humble women.

There is also a woman at the bulwark, looking down on the pier, who wears a big bonnet with white cloth and carries a small leather bag in her hand. Two big eyes, as if painted with shadows, are shining on her wrinkled face above the large nose, like a hook. She looks like a Jewess. She also must be a traveler who is going on this ship. She is also envious of her.

The pier is long—long—

At last she arrives at the foot of the gangplank. Cautiously she carries her body, which has the second infant of her husband under the Azuma coat, and descends onto the deck of the big, black-painted ship. She hands the umbrella to a maidservant.

Led by the people who have come to say farewell and were already on board, she goes back along the bulwark toward the prow. There are rooms for passengers at the end of the way, the numbers of which increase from twenty-seven to twenty-nine.

The viscount is standing at the entrance and addresses her.

"This is the room, madam."

Peeping into the room she finds two beds, under which the familiar packages and trunks are deposited. Her husband is standing before one of the beds.

"Look it over, madam. It is like this."

This is the room; she must look through it carefully. During the long,

long voyage of her husband, this is the room where her dreams must come and go.

A man, who looks like the captain, comes, and, addressing her husband in French, guides him to the saloon of the ship. She follows her husband and the viscount and enters the room.

This is a spacious and beautiful saloon. Several tables are arranged, each bearing a flower basket. . . . Gradually the people who came to say farewell gather into the room.

By the order of this man, who looks like the captain, a waiter brings forth many cups in the shape of morning glories; and, pouring champagne into them, he distributes them among the people. Another waiter brings cakes, like those which are brought with ice cream, piled on a plate in the form of a well crib, and distributes them among the people.

The people who received the cups go one after another, and stand before her husband and the viscount, wishing them a happy voyage, and drink from the cups.

Sitting on a small chair beside the table, she is waiting for the time when the congratulations are at an end. During his busy moments, now and then, her husband lifts his eyes to her.

However, there is no more to be said to her before so many people. Also, there is no more to be said to him, before so many people.

The bell rings. Having bidden farewell to her husband and to the viscount the people are going out, one after another. She also follows them, saluting her husband and the viscount.

Again crossing the dangerous gangplank, she descends to the pier. She receives the light green umbrella from the hand of her maidservant, and raises it.

Her husband and the viscount are standing on the bulwark, looking in her direction. She is looking up at them from under her umbrella. She feels that her eyes, as she looks up, are growing gradually larger and larger.

Again the bell rings. A few French sailors begin to untie the rope from the gangplank. A Japanese laborer wearing a short workman's coat is standing on the stool like that which is used in repairing the trolley, preparing to draw down the gangplank. Hanging on the rope of the wheel, pulled by the man in the coat, the gangplank at last leaves the bulwark.

The noon cannon of the city of Yokohama resounds. With this as a signal, the ship, from the hold of which for some time a noise has been issuing, silently begins to move.

The elderly Europeans, who seem to be a married couple, are standing at the bulwark. They are talking about something of a jolly nature with a white-haired old man who is standing on the pier, with one of his feet placed on an apparatus, to roll the ropes, which looks like a big bobbin. They do not seem to regret the parting.

It looks as if the ship is moving. It looks as if the pier is moving. There seems to be a distance created by parallax, between the place where her husband and the viscount are standing and the place where she is standing. She feels her eyes growing larger and larger.

Some of the people who are looking after them are running to the end of the pier. She cannot do such an immodest thing. Suddenly something white waves at the bulwark. It is a handkerchief waved by the hand of a woman who wears a big bonnet decorated with a white cloth. A tall man stands at the end of the pier, in red waistcoat and tan shoes. A white handkerchief waves from the hand of this man as well. This also must be a parting in human life.

These two persons set the fashion, and the handkerchiefs are waved here and there. White things are waving also from the people who are looking after the group surrounding the count. She also grasps the batiste handkerchief which she has brought in her sleeve, but she cannot do such an immodest thing.

When the ships seems to have left the pier, it turns its prow a bit to the right. The place where her husband and the viscount were standing has disappeared at last.

Still she can see a boy about fifteen or sixteen, standing at the stern, in a blue, cold-looking garment like a blouse. What mother is waiting for him in France? Or has he no parents? What is he looking at, standing by the rail at the stern?

Slowly she turns her feet and walks among the maidservants surrounding her.

The pier is long—long—

At the place where the black-painted ship was anchored, until a short time ago, the water is glittering like the scales of fish, as the tiny ripples reflect the pale sunshine.

1910

Illustration accompanying the publication of *Kamen* (Masks) in the magazine *Subaru* (The Pleiades), April 1909.

Kamen

MASKS

FOR MUCH OF HIS CAREER, Ōgai took an interest in the Japanese theater. When he first returned to Japan in 1889 after his years in Europe, his fascination was naturally with the *kabuki* and other forms of drama then being composed and performed. At that time, he experimented with writing dramas for this medium. By the end of the century, a powerful interest among Japanese intellectuals in the contemporary European drama of ideas had developed; indeed, Ōgai contributed much to this enthusiasm though his translations of Ibsen, Strindberg, Wedekind, and other dramatists then considered extremely avant-garde even in European terms. Many of Ōgai's translations were performed on the stage in Tokyo.

This work as a translator also led Ōgai to experiment himself with the composition of modern dramas. *Masks* is one of several short plays written by him at this time and the only one given a contemporary setting; the others, somewhat in the style of Maeterlinck, draw on history and legend for their characters and setting. Ōgai wrote *Masks* in 1909, and it was given a professional production during the same year.

Masks is a play about death and human resolution. As Ōgai uses Baudelaire as a point of reference in *Hanako,* he uses Nietzsche in *Masks.* Still, the play is not merely a didactic exercise. The urgency of the need for self-understanding—and self-concealment—are articulated as well here as in any of his semi-autobiographical stories written during the same period. It has been suggested that, like Dr. Sugimura, Ōgai himself knew that he was infected with tuberculosis but had decided to go forward as though there were nothing wrong with him. True or not, the play, with all its ambiguities, seems propelled by authentic concerns; *Masks* is an experiment, perhaps, but on the whole a successful one.

CHARACTERS

SUGIMURA SHIGERU, *doctor of medicine*

YAMAGUCHI SHIORI, *student at Bunkadaigaku (former name of Tokyo University's Literature Department)*

MRS. KANAI, *wife of a professor at Bunkadaigaku*

ENDŌ TŌRU, *bachelor of medicine, assistant to* DR. SUGIMURA

SAKICHI, *gardener*

SANTA, *gardener*

MIYO, SAKICHI *'s wife*

TWO NURSES

TWO HOUSEBOYS

LARGE NUMBER OF PATIENTS

SCENE

Reception room of DR. SUGIMURA *'s residence in Surugadai. Wood-frame Western-style room. Large table and several chairs. On the table is a tray with cigars, matches, and so forth. Door to stage right leads to the doctor's office. Door to stage left leads to the patient's waiting room and examination room. Window between the two doors. Couch in front of the wall near the right door. Between the window and the door on the left is a fireplace in which a fire is burning. Clock on the mantle. No flower arrangement.*

The curtain opens. MRS. KANAI *is seated on the couch, her eyes cast down, worrying about something. Her hair is swept back with a chignon at the back. She wears an overcoat with an attachable fur neckpiece. Muff. White* tabi *with red-thonged slippers from the patients' waiting room. About thirty years of age.*

After a moment, a NURSE *comes into the room from the door to the left.*

NURSE: We're sorry to keep you waiting. The doctor says to tell you that he will be with you in a moment.

MRS. KANAI: Thank you. The waiting room was so crowded that I realized

---

TRANSLATED BY JAMES M. VARDAMAN JR.

this would be an imposition, but there is a certain matter that I simply have to consult the doctor about.

NURSE: It's always like this on mornings when the doctor doesn't go to the university. So he always sees people with urgent matters between patients. If you will wait a short while, please.

(NURSE *exits door on left.* MRS. KANAI *takes out a pocket watch and looks at it, then stands and looks out the window. The* DOCTOR *enters following the* NURSE. *Closely trimmed mustache. Pince-nez. Black suit. Forty-eight years old.*)

DOCTOR: My, I'm sorry to have kept you waiting.

MRS. KANAI: *(Bowing.)* Not at all. I must apologize for making such an unreasonable request.

DOCTOR: Mr. Yamaguchi came in a few days ago.

MRS. KANAI: Actually, that's the matter I came to consult with you about. I heard that he asked for a sputum examination and that he would be coming for a consultation today at ten o'clock, so I was wondering about his condition. His complexion is healthy and there doesn't seem to be any change in him at all, but if by chance it is something like tuberculosis, I know that it isn't curable, so I came to inquire. What seems to be the situation?

DOCTOR: I see. With your permission, I think I'll have a smoke.

(*He picks up a cigar from the table, then takes out a small knife from his inside pocket and leisurely snips it.*)

Well, please do have a seat.

(*He moves the chair for her.*)

MRS. KANAI: Thank you. *(Sits.)* Shiori is a dutiful younger brother, and our mother in Wakayama has only him to depend on, so she is looking forward to his returning home during the summer holidays. Yesterday a letter came from Mother. She wrote that she hadn't had even one letter from Shiori recently and was greatly concerned that perhaps something had happened. Shiori says that at the end of the year he caught a cold while he was traveling and it had just hung on. He says that it will go away when spring comes and has been going to the university every day as if nothing at all were the matter. But he has a bad cough and it has lingered on so long that even my husband has noticed it.

DOCTOR: *(Lights his cigar and sits.)* Indeed. No, it's not a simple bronchial inflammation.

MRS. KANAI: *(Eyes glistening.)* Really? Then what might it be?

DOCTOR: He hasn't the slightest fever and there doesn't seem to be a major cause for concern, but on the other hand we can't take it too lightly.

MRS. KANAI: Is it tuberculosis?

(There is a knock at the door to the left.)

DOCTOR: Come in.

(NURSE enters. She stops in the doorway, looks at the DOCTOR, and waits.)

DOCTOR: *(To NURSE.)* There are no new patients, are there?

NURSE: No, sir, the rest are regular patients.

DOCTOR: In that case, please tell Dr. Endō that it's all right for him to take care of them as he thinks best.

NURSE: Yes, sir. (NURSE *exits.*)

DOCTOR: *(To MRS. KANAI.)* You must pardon me. At this clinic I don't normally give out the names of illnesses, but since you are not an ordinary lady, and since it would be improper to cause you needless worry, I will tell you. To be truthful . . .

(She earnestly observes his expression.)

Actually, the year before last he developed pleurisy, and he never fully recovered. There still seems to be some adhesion.

MRS. KANAI: Now that you mention it, one day when it was quite cold he did say that his chest was hurting. Is that what you were referring to a moment ago as pleurisy?

DOCTOR: Yes. The pleura are not bad enough to be diagnosed as pleurisy, but the bronchi are in somewhat bad shape. If I were to try to give the illness a name, I guess I'd call it chronic bronchitis.

MRS. KANAI: So then it's not tuberculosis?

DOCTOR: No. However, given the condition, tuberculosis frequently develops, so one cannot take the situation lightly.

MRS. KANAI: I see. I understand completely. To tell the truth, my husband felt that since Shiori is such a sensitive type, if he had a sputum examination and the results showed that he did have tuberculosis. . . . Well, he was afraid that Shiori would be greatly disheartened when you told him. Anyway, my husband told me to come and inquire about the situation before Shiori himself came this morning. That is why I imposed on you, even though I knew you would be very busy. Shiori says that he is very busy because he will graduate at the end of this year, but since there is no way to substitute for his health, if you think it advisable, we can have him take a leave from the university. For the sake of his health, perhaps we should have him move out of his boardinghouse. Shiori says that his boardinghouse is a good place for studying, but we have considered having him move in with us.

DOCTOR: Hmm. I see nothing wrong with letting him postpone his graduation one year. *(Pause.)* Really, it's still rather cold, isn't it? *(He places his cigar in the ashtray, and puts the charcoal in the scuttle into the fireplace.)*

MRS. KANAI: Tokyo certainly is cold. Mother says that she had enough of Tokyo's winter weather on one occasion, and no matter how we try to persuade her she won't come again. And I have a feeling that Komagome is even a little worse than other areas. Still, this morning there were frost columns in the garden. At home, when I comment on how cold it is, though, my husband always laughs and says that if I think this is cold I would never be able to survive in a place like Berlin.

DOCTOR: *(Standing by the window.)* That's certainly true. Berlin is much colder. Then again, the facilities are quite different. When people go outside, they wear thick overcoats. When they're inside, there is a fireplace. And not just the kind that the French use in order to be chic.

MRS. KANAI: *(Gets up from her chair.)* Well, I shall be excusing myself. I apologize for troubling you so long when you are so busy. *(Goes to the couch where her muff is. The clock on the mantle strikes ten o'clock.)* Oh my, it's already ten.

DOCTOR: Mr. Yamaguchi will be here any minute. He'll be coming by streetcar, so although it wouldn't do for you to leave together, you can certainly wait a little.

MRS. KANAI: *(Stands. Stretches her right hand toward the table.)* No, I came by streetcar, too. Since the streetcar came into operation, it's just too cold to go anywhere by rickshaw.

DOCTOR: I've told Kanai that he ought to get a horse-drawn carriage, but he's the type of person who just won't listen at all.

MRS. KANAI: It's not that he *won't,* but rather that we *can't.* He says that he wishes he had taken up medicine instead.

DOCTOR: Ha, ha, ha. He says that only because he has no idea what it's like to be a doctor. People like myself are quite envious of those who can simply spend their time reading. That room *(points to the door on the right)* becomes more full of books with the arrival of each ship, but I have no time to read them.

(There is a knock at the door on the left.)

Come in.

(YAMAGUCHI SHIORI opens the door on the left and enters. Handsome young man, twenty-four or twenty-five years old. Appears bright. Pale

*complexion but stout physique. University uniform. Elegant letter "L" on
collar. University cap with cockade. Does not greet the* DOCTOR, *but is
astonished when he sees his* SISTER.)

YAMAGUCHI: Sister! What are you doing here?

DOCTOR: Mrs. Kanai came because she is concerned about your health.

YAMAGUCHI: (*To the* DOCTOR.) Please excuse my rudeness. It was just so
   unexpected.

MRS. KANAI: (*To her* BROTHER.) There's no way of making excuses to
   someone as old as you are, but when I heard that you had requested
   the sputum examination, I came to see about the diagnosis.

YAMAGUCHI: (*To his older* SISTER.) Ha, ha. How thoughtful of you. In all
   probability this is a result of Professor Kanai's typical cautiousness,
   telling you to do this.

MRS. KANAI: How awful of you. You make it sound as if I'm not concerned
   about you myself.

YAMAGUCHI: That's not what I meant. (*To the* DOCTOR.) She's always like
   this. My sister claims she's inept at social intercourse, but she is quite
   glib of tongue.

DOCTOR: (*To* MRS. KANAI.) Why don't you take a seat. (*To* YAMAGUCHI.)
   If you are going to quarrel with your sister, at least be seated first.

(The three sit around the table. YAMAGUCHI *puts his cap on the table.)*

YAMAGUCHI: (*To the* DOCTOR.) Just because I cough once or twice is no
   reason to trouble you, but Professor Kanai and my sister were so
   insistent that I gave in and made the request.

MRS. KANAI: Because you are so kind, in spite of ourselves we come to you
   about any little matter at all.

DOCTOR: Please do so. When you give it serious thought, there is really not
   a single illness that you ought not have a doctor look at. (*To* YAMA-
   GUCHI.) It would be careless to neglect a cough like you have had

these two months. Anyway, there are several things I'd like to talk with you about, so stay a little while.

MRS. KANAI: *(Stands.)* There are several places I would like to drop by on my way back, so I'll excuse myself.

DOCTOR: There's really no reason to rush off, is there?

MRS. KANAI: Well, there are a few things my children have asked me to pick up, and I really must be home by noon.

DOCTOR: *(Stands.)* Well, if you are sure.

MRS. KANAI: *(To* YAMAGUCHI.) Now, Shiori, you be sure to listen carefully to Doctor's advice.

YAMAGUCHI: I will. And I'll come by your house this evening.

(She does not move toward the couch, where her muff is. The DOCTOR *quickly picks it up and hands it to her.* YAMAGUCHI *stands.)*

MRS. KANAI: *(Receives the muff.)* Thank you. Goodbye, then. *(Turns as she starts to leave.)* I'm sure that you must be very busy, but we do hope that you will come to Komagome to visit us once in a while.

DOCTOR: I'll call on you some time before too long.

*(*MRS. KANAI *opens the door on the left and exits through it. The* DOCTOR *and* YAMAGUCHI *turn toward each other, look at one another, and turn serious.)*

YAMAGUCHI: Doctor, what is the situation? There are periods of two or three hours when I don't cough at all, but at night when I sleep on my left side, it makes a puffing sound. It's just like blowing into a small tube which is filled with water. It's different from the rough rattling sound I had when I had pleurisy. Apart from that there are no other symptoms.

DOCTOR: Uh-huh. The area where you say there's a puffing sound is getting worse. It seems that there is a constriction. You have done as I told you, haven't you?

YAMAGUCHI: I put on a flannel. I carry medicine in my pocket when I go to the lecture hall, and I take it as prescribed. But I don't stay home from the university.

DOCTOR: And that's a problem.

YAMAGUCHI: *(Earnestly.)* But, Doctor, it's imperative that I graduate this year.

DOCTOR: All right, have a seat, won't you? *(Sits.* YAMAGUCHI *also sits.)* Perhaps it's careless of me to have a smoke with you here suffering from bronchial problems. *(He takes out a cigar, clips it with his small knife, and lights it.)*

YAMAGUCHI: Not at all. The student lobbies are always dark with smoke.

DOCTOR: That's precisely the reason why I think that going to school isn't good for your health. Your sister is also hoping that you will take a leave from school.

YAMAGUCHI: Of course she'd think that. People always think such things when it involves someone else. Take my sister herself. When she's at home she's always deferring to Professor Kanai's mother, and the only time she goes out is when she's on an errand such as going to ask a favor of a teacher at school, or buying textbooks and supplies. As much as she enjoys music, she ought to do things like go to the concert that is being held at the music school today. After all, Professor Kanai is always receiving complimentary tickets. Today's program includes three pieces by Chopin. I definitely intend to go.

DOCTOR: You should, you should. It's different from going to the university, so I don't oppose that at all. Whenever there's something wrong with some part of the body, the most important thing is to keep from becoming emotionally strained.

YAMAGUCHI: I realize that, too. But when I think about the situation back home in Wakayama, it would be even more distressing to me to stay home from classes. Compared with that, it is far and away easier to attend lectures at the university.

DOCTOR: Hmm. This has become considerably difficult from a psychological point of view. What would happen if, say, you continued going to the university, but your health didn't hold up and your life itself were endangered? You would have to seriously reconsider the situation, wouldn't you?

YAMAGUCHI: *(Eyes glistening.)* Is my illness really that serious? Doctor, was there something wrong with my sputum?

(From the door to the left can be heard the voices of a LARGE NUMBER OF PEOPLE. *At once, the door opens and* ENDO TORU, *the assistant, comes in. Mustache. Over Western clothing he wears linen work clothes that look like a surgical gown. About thirty years of age.)*

ENDO: Doctor, please come. We have a patient who is in critical condition.

DOCTOR: What's the problem?

ENDO: It seems to be internal bleeding in the abdomen.

(From beyond the door which the ASSISTANT *has left open there are shouts such as "It's too late," "He's dead.")*

DOCTOR: Why did they bring a surgery patient to this hospital?

ENDO: You don't understand. It's one of the gardeners who came to plant trees in the grounds here. He fell from some kind of scaffolding onto a standing stone and apparently struck his abdomen pretty hard.

(A NURSE *appears from beyond the door. From beyond the door two or three male and female* PATIENTS *peer in.)*

NURSE: *(To* ENDO.*)* The pulse is quite weak.

ENDO: I see.

DOCTOR: Have they brought him into the waiting room?

ENDO: They brought him into the waiting room on an emergency stretcher.

DOCTOR: *(Stands.)* We can't leave him among the patients. There must be patients in the examination room, too. Well, I guess there is nothing else we can do but bring him in here. Don't let them jolt the stretcher.

NURSE: I'll tell them.

(NURSE exits. The DOCTOR discards his cigar in the ashtray, then ponders something. YAMAGUCHI stands looking at the door. Immediately two HOUSEBOYS enter carrying SAKICHI the gardener on a stretcher. SAKICHI is a robust man, twenty-five or twenty-six years old. Printed workman's coat. Eyes drowsy, mouth open wide. Breathing faintly. FIRST NURSE enters accompanied by SECOND NURSE. FIRST NURSE takes SAKICHI's pulse. SECOND NURSE brings in the box of examination apparatus. Another gardener, SANTA, enters following the NURSE. Crouches down along the left side. About the same age as SAKICHI. Printed workman's coat. LARGE NUMBER OF MALE AND FEMALE PATIENTS push in the door to peek. Four or five actually enter the room.)

DOCTOR: *(To YAMAGUCHI.)* If you'll pardon me, would you wait in there *(pointing to the door on the right)* a little while? *(To everyone.)* I'll ask that everyone who has no business in here go to the waiting room. The nurses can stay. *(To SANTA.)* You stay, too, please. *(YAMAGUCHI opens the door to the right and exits through it. HOUSEBOYS and PATIENTS exit from the door on the left.)* *(To ENDO.)* Close that door, please. *(ENDO closes the door on the left.)*

FIRST NURSE: There is almost no pulse.

ENDO: *(To DOCTOR.)* He's been unconscious since they brought him in.

DOCTOR: Uh-huh.

(Quietly kneels at the side of the stretcher, removes the unfastened workman's waistcoat, looks for a moment, presses gently, taps very gently with his fingers. ENDO kneels alongside.)

At any rate, let's administer an injection of camphor.

(SECOND NURSE *removes syringe from the emergency box and hands it to* ENDO, *who gives the injection.*)

(*In a low voice.*) We have no facilities for a laparotomy, and there's not enough time to take him anywhere else.

(*Covers with the waistcoat, and stands quietly.* ENDO *also stands.*)

SECOND NURSE: (*Watching* SANTA *intently.*) He has opened his eyes.

SANTA: (*Moving toward* SAKICHI*'s head.*) Pull yourself together!

DOCTOR: (*To* ENDO.) His house is in Sugamo, I believe.

ENDO: A telegram has already been sent.

DOCTOR: Good thinking. How about the police?

ENDO: An officer was here. I explained the circumstances and he said that he would leave matters to us. He said that if we need anything to get in touch with them.

DOCTOR: All right.

SAKICHI: Ahh! It hurts!

DOCTOR: (*Drawing close.*) The injury is pretty bad. Is there anything you want to say?

SANTA: (*To* SECOND NURSE.) Can we give him some water?

DOCTOR: No water. (*To* SAKICHI.) Have you regained consciousness? Is there anything you want us to know?

SANTA: (*Tearfully.*) Can you hear the gentleman? If you want to tell us anything, say it.

SAKICHI: There's nothing. (*Pause.*) O-miyo.

SANTA: What about O-miyo?

SAKICHI: She's young.

SANTA: She's young.

SAKICHI: She'll manage somehow. *(Pause.)* Augh, it hurts!

(Everyone falls silent for a minute. Clock strikes eleven. Beyond the door to the left comes the sound of LARGE NUMBERS OF PEOPLE *whispering.)*

FIRST NURSE: Breathing has stopped.

*(*ENDO *silently kneels, lifts the waistcoat, presses his right ear to the chest; after a moment he replaces the waistcoat and stands.* ENDO *and the* DOCTOR, *without saying a word, look at each other.)*

SANTA: *(Wiping his eyes with a towel. In tears.)* Is he gone?

ENDO: Yes, he's passed away. *(To* NURSE.*)* There's a blanket in the examination room. Please bring it in and cover him.

(The NURSE *nods, opens the door on the left, and exits.)*

We have to inform the police. We can conduct the postmortem examination here.

DOCTOR: Yes. Do whatever is necessary. You did a fine job. And if it wouldn't be too much to ask you to attend to the other patients . . .

ENDO: Of course, I'll be happy to. *(To* SANTA.*)* You come, too.

*(*ENDO *and* SANTA *exit via left door. Coming in the opposite direction the* FIRST NURSE *enters carrying a white blanket. Covers* SAKICHI*'s body.* DOCTOR *sits down, folds his arms.)*

FIRST NURSE: Is there anything else?

DOCTOR: No, so please attend to the patients in the other room.

FIRST NURSE: Yes, sir.

(FIRST NURSE exits via door on left. The DOCTOR leisurely stands up and goes to tap on the door on the right. YAMAGUCHI opens the door from the other side and enters. He has paled and his appearance is changed. He turns his back to the DOCTOR as he steps toward the stretcher. He looks at the body covered by the blanket. The DOCTOR stands, constantly watching YAMAGUCHI's movements.)

DOCTOR: Yamaguchi, my friend.

YAMAGUCHI: *(As if being awakened from a dream, he turns toward the DOCTOR with his head drooping.)* Yes. *(Pause.)* I'll go now.

DOCTOR: Uh. *(Pause.)* You saw the memorandum on my desk, didn't you?

YAMAGUCHI: I apologize. It was face up on the desk and I unintentionally looked. I noticed my name written in large roman letters and looked at it without really meaning to. "Diagnosis positive." *(Agitated.)* Doctor! I have tuberculosis, don't I? *(Pause. Places both hands over his face.)* Aah! *(Pause.)* I don't want to let you see my weakness. I've frequently wondered whether it might not be that. But I always ended up denying to myself that such a thing could happen. And in addition to that, there were your—at the risk of seeming impolite—words of consolation giving me encouragement. I confess that at this moment my mind is in utter chaos. I can't think clearly at all. You have probably decided to say something to comfort me. But right now my mind is in no condition to respond at all. *(Again conceals his face with both hands.)* Aah! *(Turns his back to the DOCTOR and looks at the stretcher.)* If one is going to die, it's most fortunate to die in an instant. Doctor, you said that the area that is getting worse is small. If that gradually enlarges and one lung is destroyed . . . if the infection does not spread to the other lung, then one won't die. And for that to happen would take at least a year. A year has twelve months. A month has thirty days. One day has twenty-four hours. Each hour is divided into minutes; and the minutes, into seconds. Every second a small drop of poison will be injected into my heart. How much poison will my heart have to take from this moment onward? I cannot imagine that pain. *(Pause.)* I'm sorry to have said such cowardly things. I'm quite ashamed of myself. I shall take my leave now. I'd like to be alone until I can become accustomed to this new reality. *(Picks up his cap from the table, bows to the* DOCTOR, *and walks toward the left door.)*

DOCTOR: *(Not batting an eyelash from start to finish, he has watched* YAMAGUCHI's *movements. Now he speaks forcibly.)* Yamaguchi. (YAMAGUCHI *turns around.*) Wait a minute. I'll calm your anxieties for you in an instant.

*(*YAMAGUCHI *steps back slightly, stands still, holding his cap.)*

You said that you weren't interested in hearing words of solace. That's as it should be. You are not in danger of hearing a sham lecture about how philanthropy is impossible without turning away from declared love and preaching morality without giving money to one who has announced his poverty. *(Pause.)* I won't become loquacious. I want to show you something. Why don't you put your cap down and sit down over there.

*(*YAMAGUCHI *sits down, his head bent. The* DOCTOR *quietly opens the door to the right and goes in. In a moment he brings out a microscope specimen case and one microphotograph and puts them on the table. He goes back and brings out a microscope, turns his back to the audience, stands between the table and the stretcher, turns the microscope toward the window, and sits. He throws off his pince-nez and examines the oil immersion apparatus. He pulls the case toward himself, takes out four or five thick-paper slide clips, selects one, takes out one slide, and affixes it to the microscope. He places the photograph next to it and speaks to* YAMAGUCHI.*)*

Look at this.

YAMAGUCHI: *(Halfheartedly.)* All right. *(Stands and exchanges places with the* DOCTOR.*)*

DOCTOR: First take a look at the labels attached to the photograph and the slide. The photograph is dated October 24, 1892. The slide is dated today. (YAMAGUCHI *looks at the labels.*) Now look at the slide. (YAMAGUCHI *looks into the microscope.*) You can see the bacteria. The scattered filament-like ones are *Mycobacterium tuberculosis*. They appear red against the blue field. It's called Ziehl-Neelsen carbolfuchsin stain, and that's pretty much the way it's done these days. (YAMAGUCHI *compares the two. The* DOCTOR*'s tone of voice turns serious and deliberate.*) Whose tubercle bacilli do you think those are in the photograph? *(Pause.)* They're mine.

YAMAGUCHI: *(Astonished.)* Does that mean that you have tuberculosis, too?

DOCTOR: No, as you can see, I'm quite healthy. However, at one time I did have tuberculosis.

YAMAGUCHI: Does that mean that you recovered from it?

DOCTOR: Well, let me tell you about that. The October 24, 1892, written on the photograph is one of the most memorable days of my entire life. It was just after I returned from abroad. In those days I was frequently catching colds and I had phlegm, but I didn't pay it much attention. October 24 was a Monday and I had two lectures in succession. When I returned to the lecturers' room, it felt like there was a warm ball rising up my throat. In the room there was a glass microscope plate, so I spit it up into there. It was a clot of blood about as big as the tip of my thumb. I was greatly shocked. No matter how you look at it, there is absolutely no way that blood will come from a healthy lung. *(Pause.)* So I decided to examine the clot, but I really didn't want anyone to find out about it. I felt like I held my fate in my own hands. However, there were other professors coming in to chat, students were coming in with questions, and there just wasn't a free moment. I fixed the clot so that it wouldn't dry out and locked it away. Finally on the third of November I took it out and stained it. It was a horrible sensation. The following day I put it under the microscope and there it was, beautifully stained. That's the photograph there. *(Emphatically.)* That day for me was like today is for you. Do you know what I did after that? *(Pause.)* Take a seat and hear me out. (YAMAGUCHI *sits. The* DOCTOR *sits, obviously looking at* YAMAGUCHI *and speaking forcefully.*) For seventeen years, until I told this to you, I have never told this to a soul. *(Relaxedly.)* And from what motive has this silence come? I'll leave that judgment up to you. It may be selfishness. In that case why did I tell you this? It may have been foolish to tell you.

(YAMAGUCHI gradually appears to be moved, and his eyes glisten. At the same time, since he seems to entertain some doubts, he looks at the DOC-TOR as if trying to solve an enigma.)

Have you ever read Nietzsche?

YAMAGUCHI: I've only read *Beyond Good and Evil,* after being stimulated by Professor Kanai's lectures.

DOCTOR: I see. Well, even there he mentions again and again the idea of masks. He says that what we refer to as the Good is merely following the same course of action as the common herd of humanity. Evil is when one attempts to destroy those attitudes. We ought not to concern ourselves with Good or Evil. He writes that he wants to stand aloof from the common herd, to strengthen his resolve and place himself high above them in an aristocratic position of lonely eminence. Such eminent beings wear masks and those masks are to be respected. What do you think? Do you respect my mask?

YAMAGUCHI: *(In high spirits.)* I understand. I won't tell anyone a thing about my tuberculosis, either. My worries are, in reality, not worries about myself. When I thought about how my mother in Wakayama would grieve if she were to hear about this, I was dumbfounded. What I can tell no one else I also cannot tell my mother. In exchange, Doctor, you won't keep me from attending lectures, will you?

DOCTOR: *(A faint smile appearing on his face.)* No, I won't stop you. *(Pause.)* As a medical doctor, I should forbid you to attend classes. And I should order you to move to your sister's house. But that would be what I would prescribe for one of the common herd. In your case, however, I'll allow you to do whatever you want. In the meantime I'll do my best to prevent your disease from endangering those around you . . . *(pause)* . . . and we shall cure you. I will do everything within my power, and we will stand together beyond Good and Evil.

YAMAGUCHI: I thank you from the bottom of my heart. From this day forth I will never say I am fatherless. *(Pause.)* But *(somewhat anxiously)* it's no laughing matter. Recovering from tuberculosis is quite exceptional, isn't it?

DOCTOR: Nägeli has reported that there is evidence of prior tuberculosis in almost every cadaver.

(There is a knock at the door on the left.)

Come in.

(The FIRST NURSE *opens the door and enters. She leaves the door open.)*

FIRST NURSE: (*Looks back over her shoulder, then speaks to the* DOCTOR.) The gardener's wife has come from Sugamo.

DOCTOR: I see. *(Stands.* YAMAGUCHI *also stands.)*

FIRST NURSE: Madam.

MIYO: *(From behind the door.)* Yes.

(Sakichi's wife, MIYO, *enters. Gingko-leaf coiffure. New silk padded kimono with replaceable neckpiece. Also new coat with replaceable neckpiece. A formal apron. White* tabi *with red-thonged indoor slippers. Eighteen- or nineteen-year-old beauty. Eyes are reddened but she sheds no tears.)*

(To the DOCTOR.) I am greatly indebted to you for your kindnesses.

DOCTOR: It was truly an unfortunate occurrence. His condition was such that I'm afraid there was nothing I could do for him.

MIYO: Not at all. Even though he died from injuries, at least he was able to pass away at your residence, so I have no regrets. *(Looking at the stretcher, to the* NURSE.) Is that him?

(The NURSE *nods, goes to the head of the stretcher, kneels, and turns back the blanket so that just the face is visible.* MIYO *kneels.)*

Thank you for your kind treatment.

*(*MIYO *looks briefly at the face, wipes her eyes with the sleeve of her underkimono. The* DOCTOR *and* YAMAGUCHI *watch the woman's move-*

ments ceaselessly. The DOCTOR *removes his wallet from his inner pocket and places it on the table. He also removes a sheet of paper from his pocket. From his wallet he takes out several ten-yen bills, wraps them in paper, writes something on it in pencil, and puts it on the table.* MIYO *pulls the blanket back up and quietly stands. The* NURSE *also stands.* MIYO *speaks to the* DOCTOR.)

I . . . I have asked Santa, who came with him, to help, and I would like to receive the body. A moment ago I spoke with the doctor in there, and he said that arrangements with the police have been completed.

DOCTOR: I see. *(Picks up the money wrapped in paper.)* Madam, I hope that you will accept this small token of my condolences.

MIYO: *(Hesitating slightly.)* It would be rude of me not to accept it then. *(Takes it.)* Thank you very much. *(Inserts the bundle into her obi, bows, and moves toward the door.)*

FIRST NURSE: *(To* MIYO.) Please let me go for you. There should be a wagon waiting.

MIYO: That would be very kind.

*(*NURSE *exits through the door. She soon returns with* SANTA *and a* HOUSEBOY. *The two pick up the stretcher and exit through the door.* MIYO *speaks to the* DOCTOR.)

Again, thank you very much for your many kindnesses.

(She bows to the DOCTOR, YAMAGUCHI, *and the* NURSE, *then exits following the stretcher.)*

DOCTOR: *(To* NURSE.) Ask them to prepare the wagon.

FIRST NURSE: Yes, sir.

*(*NURSE *exits. Outside the door on the left it is finally quiet.)*

DOCTOR: *(To* YAMAGUCHI.) How about that—that woman's composure? *(Pause.)* There is certainly something in people who are moved by mere instinct that resembles the nobler class. There couldn't be many ladies among the common herd who could carry it off like that.

YAMAGUCHI: That's the truth. I had a high opinion of her as well.

DOCTOR: When you recover from your illness and are ready to take a wife, you ought to give some thought to that.

YAMAGUCHI: There's absolutely no way that I would ever marry someone who is the instinctive type.

DOCTOR: That goes without saying. *(Pause.)* I discovered my illness in October seventeen years ago, and from that December on, no matter how many times I have examined myself, the results have always been negative. But I kept thinking to myself that I'd wait a little longer, a little longer, and inadvertently I have remained single. Another reason, however, is that I have never found the ideal woman. Kanai and his wife always poke fun at me for being so strange.

YAMAGUCHI: My sister even mentioned to me that it is strange.

DOCTOR: They don't understand the mask, so of course they think that way. *(Pause.)* Or perhaps . . . *(He looks intently at* YAMAGUCHI.) Maybe you think that my history of tuberculosis is just an improvisation, and that it is just a mask in that sense. What do you think?

YAMAGUCHI: *(Thinking briefly.)* Well . . . Sir, whatever meaning the mask may take, there is no difference in my feeling of gratitude.

DOCTOR: How skillful you are with words. *(Pause.)* Today I'll go with you. We'll have lunch at Seiyōken, then we'll listen to Chopin. You certainly won't refuse me, will you?

YAMAGUCHI: Hardly. I do intend to go.

(There is a knock at the door on the left.)

DOCTOR: Come in.

(The HOUSEBOY *who previously carried out the stretcher enters.)*

HOUSEBOY: The wagon is ready.

DOCTOR: Good. (HOUSEBOY *exits. To* YAMAGUCHI.) Just a moment.

(He opens the door on the right and exits through it. He immediately puts on his overcoat and hat. He brings in his gloves and cane, leans his cane against the couch, and places his gloves on the table. He raises the tube of the microscope with the adjustment knob, removes the oil from the oil immersion apparatus with a piece of leather. Picks up his gloves and cane. In the meanwhile, YAMAGUCHI *picks up his own cap from the table.)*

Well, shall we?

(He walks toward the door at left. YAMAGUCHI *follows cap in hand. The noon cannon sounds. The clock strikes twelve. The* DOCTOR *and* YAMA-GUCHI *stop still.* YAMAGUCHI *places his cap under his left arm. Both remove their watches from their pockets and wind them. Curtain.)*

1909

Kaijin

THE ASHES OF DESTRUCTION

THE ASHES OF DESTRUCTION, published in 1912, is the fourth and last of Ōgai's novels. As all are now available in translation, English-language readers can make extensive comparisons among the various texts. All were composed within a relatively short length of time. Written in 1909, *Vita Sexualis* (translated by Ninomiya Kazumi and Sanford Goldstein), Ōgai's satire on naturalism as a literary movement, provides a fascinating glimpse into elements of his own psychic life. The fact that its publication was censored caused Ōgai, not surprisingly, considerable discomfort and dissatisfaction. The novel which followed, *Seinen* (translated as *Youth* by Shoichi Ono and Sanford Goldstein in the present volume), offers a different set of insights into the contemporary cultural life of Tokyo and Ōgai's ideas concerning the nature of creativity. *Gan* (translated by Ochiai Kingo and Sanford Goldstein as *Wild Geese*), a tale of repression and renunciation encapsulated in a romantic plot, was published in 1911 and has remained one of Ōgai's most popular works, both in Japan and abroad. *The Ashes of Destruction* was begun in 1911, and the first brief nineteen sections were published in the following year, but the work was never completed.

Reading what exists of the text indicates at once the author's growing mastery in combining incident, ideas, and descriptions to advance the larger purposes of his narrative, although the larger plot lines remain unclear. Whatever inadequacies in literary technique the other novels may occasionally show, the sections presented here are the work of a master. The gray and nihilistic world of Setsuzō, the protagonist, are skillfully, indeed chillingly, rendered in a variety of strategies ranging from emotionally fraught incidents, such as the breaking of the flute, to powerfully suggestive interior monologues.

The themes presented by these fragments are not unfamiliar in the context of other works of Ōgai written at this time. Loneliness, resignation, the need for masks, a dissatisfaction with the restraints of society, a sense of spiritual fatigue, all are reflected with an unfailing certainty of touch in these pages. Here, however, these issues are now touched with peculiar emotional and sexual overtones—as though, to borrow an example from the visual arts, a scene depicting a stroll through the streets of Meiji Japan were to be redrawn in the style of Edvard Munch's *The Scream*. The romantic veneer of *Wild Geese* has disappeared completely.

In such a context, the work of Tayama Katai and the other writers of the naturalist movement, who wrote novels in which they confessed to sordid sexual peccadillos, seem tame indeed compared to the sort of dark and Dionysian imagination unleashed here by Ōgai. If the twisted emotions revealed in these fragments actually represent to any great extent a fictionalized record of the true state of Ōgai's self-understanding at the time, then it is no wonder that the novel remained unfinished, for here he has opened up a frightening region of his psyche. Perhaps the only way to bring a halt to such revelations was to stop writing the work altogether. Given the artistic control shown in these pages, however, it seems unlikely that Ōgai had abandoned, either willfully or not, his usual sense of restraint. What he says here, he surely wanted to say, and in precisely these terms. These terms, in turn, may have caused him to abandon the work.

It is not clear to literary historians why Ōgai, after publishing these opening sections, failed to continue. Some have suggested that the implications of the death of the Emperor Meiji in the same year so shook the author's own patterns of thinking (as it did those of many other writers) that it sent him veering off in another literary direction, which it most assuredly did. The suicide of General Nogi Maresuke, who followed the Emperor Meiji in death, became the occasion for many writers to take stock of their own situation, and the state of the nation as well. Natsume Sōseki wrote *Kokoro*, arguably his finest novel, on the subject; the younger Akutagawa Ryūnosuke was to ridicule the same event in his 1921 story *Shōgun* (The General). Ōgai, seeking a historical parallel for the attitudes he sensed in Nogi's decision, composed *The Last Will and Testament of Okitsu Yagoemon*, the work that began his own long series of historical stories and accounts. He would never again look inside himself in any such direct fashion.

FOR ONCE, SETSUZO LEFT THE HOUSE EARLY. A strong
wind had been blowing in the hot August sky since the
night before. Just as the sky had seemed about to clear, it
became locked in by a grayness through which black clouds floated. The
printed announcement said Hinode-chō in Zōshigaya, but he had no idea
how far it was to Gokokuji, so when he left his house in Sashigaya, he abandoned the thought of transferring from the Mita streetcar to the Otsuka
train and instead hired a rickshaw at Hakuzanshita.

Cutting across a corner of Koishikawa, going up and down from one narrow street to another, the fiftyish man pulling the rickshaw was sweating at
the nape of his neck, but there was a breeze so Setsuzō did not feel hot. In
fact he was much cooler than when sitting in his house which was halfway
down the slope from Katamachi.

Setsuzō's mind was blank. He was not even conscious of the fact that he
was riding to a funeral in a rickshaw. Passing along places where there were
buildings, he was unaware even of the various shops doing business. In some
places it was barely possible for a rickshaw to pass between hedge and brick
wall. Some places where the road had been damaged by the torrential rain a
week or so earlier had still not been repaired. They passed an intersection
with a police box. The white-uniformed policeman looked haughtily at Setsuzō, but he paid no attention. The time was long past when he would have
thought such a person pitiful, and the time he would have thought such a
person a fool was even further in the past. It had been a long time since such
reactions had even occurred to him.

After many twists and turns they finally came out of a narrow road in
Otsuka Nakama-chō, crossed Ōdori, and went down a slight slope to Gokokuji Temple. He had read something in the paper about the temple having
been moved and wondered what had been done, but nothing seemed to
be different. The gate on the path that led to the tomb of Toyoshimaoka
was closed, but a man in a livery coat was sweeping inside the little side
gate.

From Gokokuji on, he stopped frequently to ask for directions. At the
foot of a small bluff he passed a paper mill which appeared abandoned. On
top of the bluff was a wooden frame, all that remained of a small house.
Stray squash seeds had apparently fallen in the surrounding plot of land
where they had sprouted. They had put out runners over a wide area and
were now covered with yellow flowers.

TRANSLATED BY JAMES M. VARDAMAN, JR.

A little further along the right side of the narrow road was a rice mill. On the left across a fairly wide field was an area planted with saplings of some kind of tree, all carefully arranged and spaced as though it were some sort of afforestation experiment. The trees were all bending in the strong wind and some had been snapped off or uprooted.

Continuing on, he came to another area lined with houses, and before long, at a place where some tombs lined the side of the road, at the corner of a path leading off to the right he saw a small wooden sign with the name Honryuji Temple written on it. It had been set up for those who were coming to the funeral this morning. The area was known as Asahide-chō.

Turning off at the sign, he saw a path paved with oblong hewn stones leading down a long line of scattered cedars. The road had apparently been hastily repaired on account of the funeral; green branches were laid across the puddles. It looked exactly like the roads the army engineers would quickly repair for gun carriages and military supplies during maneuvers.

Deciding there was no reason to ride in the rickshaw down such a road, he alighted. Because everything had been swept quickly and carelessly in preparation for the funeral, the moss which grew along the road in the dampness created by the row of tall cedars had been uprooted in places, and the red earth showed through. Setsuzō walked along on the stones. The rickshaw man followed behind, pulling the rickshaw beside the stone walk when there was space enough and with one wheel on each side of the walk when it became too narrow.

Near the temple gate on the right side was a stone post with the words "Glory to the Sutra of the Lotus of the Supreme Law" engraved on it. The man left his rickshaw there and wiped away the sweat. As Setsuzō passed through the gate, he looked around. It was quite spacious. Between the gate and the steps of the main hall was a large garden covered with a layer of moss. The wind played with the newly fallen leaves, blowing them here and there over the moss. The *shōji* of the main hall were closed. At a table which had been set up to the right of the entranceway several men were receiving those who came to attend the funeral. Setsuzō took a step inside the entrance and looked at the men, but he recognized neither the young man seated at the table nor the middle-aged men talking together behind him. Nonetheless, Setsuzō greeted them.

"People still haven't arrived yet." The announcement said that the hearse would leave the house at seven, and so Setsuzō had left his house right after seven, too. It had taken him forty minutes, but since the procession would start from Harajuku, it would take almost two hours to reach the temple.

"That's right. It should take about two hours," replied the fortyish-looking man. He wore a splash-patterned unlined kimono and silk gauze *haori*, and either because he was pockmarked or because he was just naturally that way, the man had a confused expression on his plump face.

"I see. From one end of the town to the other," he said, taking out his watch and looking at it.

"We got up at four o'clock and came here," said the man in the kimono. Setsuzō went out through the entrance and strolled toward the temple gate. From the entrance he passed under the eaves to the front of the main hall, walked up the steps, and sat down on the veranda.

To the right of where he sat, in the opposite direction from the entrance-way, was the graveyard lined with tombstones of various shapes. It was divided into sections by hedges, and here and there were standing stupas, some old, some new.

The wind tossed the leaves on the moss-covered garden. There were not too many of them, only ten or twenty tattered leaves, mostly oak or Chinese parasol, swirling about in the wide garden and rustling in the wind.

Since there was still no sign of the mourners, Setsuzō took a piece of paper out of his sateen bag, a bag like the ones students carry, and with a fountain pen began to write something. He wrote a line, then put his elbow on his knee and looked at the leaves dancing in the garden. After a few moments he wrote another line. In this way he continued writing little by little.

After a short while, a small boy of about ten, dressed in a workman's backless waistcoat with a short shirt over it, came sneaking out from behind the main hall. At first he stared at Setsuzō from a distance, but then gradually came closer. Eventually he came to the place where a mulberry seedling had been planted under a rainspout from the roof. It had flourished and sent out several graceful branches. Here the boy discovered a grasshopper on a leaf and slowly reached out to try to catch it. The grasshopper flew down to the moss in the garden. The boy approached it stealthily, but the insect flew off again. Each time it flew about six feet, so when the boy had chased after it several times, it had ended up in the graveyard and was no longer to be seen. When it had finally disappeared, the boy turned back to Setsuzō. Occasionally looking around to take stock of the situation, he inched toward him. Finally he came to where Setsuzō was sitting and began to inspect the area around him curiously.

Although aware that the boy was gradually approaching close enough to touch his very sleeve, like the dog warily circling Faust in ever narrowing circles, Setsuzō remained indifferent. His attitude at that moment was such that it would be better to say that rather than watching the child's behavior, he allowed the child's actions to be reflected in his eyes.

He could not decide whether the boy was from some poor family in the neighborhood, the child of the temple caretaker, or what. His clothes looked like something he had been given to wear at some local festival years before. The dark blue had so completely faded that it looked like the pale indigo of the clothing issued to prisoners in the army, and it was quite dirty in places. He was naked from the waist down and tanned dark by the sun. His face had a vacant expression and his mouth hung wide open.

For a moment the child studied Setsuzō, then finally, looking as if he intended mischief, put his hand on the panama hat which Setsuzō had placed on the veranda. It did not seem as if he had originally planned to touch it. He had only wanted to feel it.

At that moment Setsuzō stopped writing, turned, and glanced at the boy. Setsuzō's expression seemed frightening to the child, who quickly pulled back his extended arm and retreated a few paces. Gaping in wonder, as if he had seen something incredible, he stood there briefly looking at the profile of the man once more writing and paying him no attention. Finally the boy wandered over to a stack of cedar logs that had been cut up after the trees had been blown down by the heavy winds, sat down, and began to hum to himself.

The wind was still blowing the leaves about the garden. The area inside the temple gate was quiet and there was nothing to distract Setsuzō from his writing. In this way a considerable time passed.

By and by, another boy, wearing a white *yukata,* came out of the main hall behind Setsuzō and without a word walked over to the stack of logs where the other boy was and sat down beside him. At the same moment a rickshaw pulled up to the temple gate and a mourner got out and went in the direction of the entrance.

Mourners then began to trickle in. Children gathered around the pile of cedar logs and mothers with babies on their backs joined them in conversation. One of the children walked along a cedar log balancing himself as if it were a tightrope, but then slipped off. One woman with a baby on her back said to another, "That's the way it goes. Even brand new clothes are ruined like that, so it doesn't seem worth the trouble." The other woman replied, "Mine are just the same." For all that, the mud-splattered *yukata* hardly seemed new.

The lower branch of a large cypress stretched protectively over the cedar logs. One of the children swung from the branch like a long-legged monkey, shaking it, as the wind shakes the treetops.

The children and their parents assembled around the pile of logs had probably come to beg for alms at the funeral, like hyenas. Yet still they wanted to talk as if they always dressed their children in new clothes.

Gradually the number of mourners increased. They began to come through the temple gate in twos and threes, then came in an unbroken stream. For the most part the mourners were men, with only an occasional older woman, perhaps because they had to come so far to attend the funeral.

Almost everyone entered by the regular entranceway. An attendant took their footwear and handed each person a wooden chit in exchange. One young man, a houseboy perhaps from his appearance, did not go in but strolled through the garden to the graveyard where he sat down on a stone basin in front of a tomb.

Since Setsuzō had occupied the steps in front of the building early, no one presumed to challenge him. The temple became more animated, however, and Setsuzō gave up writing, put the paper back into the bag, and aimlessly watched the people walking from the gate to the entrance.

It was already past nine-thirty. The *shōji* behind Setsuzō opened and a priest came out. He stood under the bell that hung at the corner of the porch on the side toward the entrance and took the wooden bell mallet from the pillar where it hung. Setsuzō turned and looked inside the hall. The right side which had been set aside for mourners was already full. Glancing over the rows of faces that could be seen from outside, he recognized no one.

It occurred to Setsuzō that it had been eight or nine years since he had left the home of the Mr. Tanida for whom they were holding the service today. Since that time the old man had left government service and become a businessman who was neither successful nor unsuccessful. "Since then the family and I have had absolutely no contact whatsoever," he mused, "so it's not really surprising that I don't know any of the people here this morning. It's only natural."

However, just as he was about to turn around after glancing over the assembled crowd, his attention was caught by a face that seemed vaguely familiar in the front row of mourners on the central aisle opposite the dais facing the space for the officiating priests. But then as he looked again, the fiftyish, yellowish wrinkled face reminded him of no one in particular.

Feeling foolish, he turned away. At that moment the man with the wrinkled face, so short that his *hakama* seemed to trail behind him, got up and walked over to him. When he stood up, the familiar look returned to his face and Setsuzō immediately recognized him as Makiyama. Earlier when Makiyama had been conversing with the person next to him, Setsuzō had recognized something in his smile that reminded him of the man in his forties he had once known, but when he had stopped smiling the face became again an aged mask that Setsuzō no longer recognized.

Smiling, Makiyama came out to the veranda.

"Yamaguchi, what a long time it's been! You're looking well as usual, but you've changed quite a bit so it took me quite a while before I was sure it was you. You know, the people who are in charge of the funeral arrangements either have forgotten all about you or do not know you at all. I just happened to be there when they were making up the list of people to be notified and felt that you really should be told. Your address was easy enough. I just called up the editorial office of that newspaper that published your articles and asked. Since I'm getting along in years I don't read anything very deep, so actually I haven't read your pieces, but I always think of you when I see your name."

Makiyama looked curiously at Setsuzō again and Setsuzō smiled pleasantly.

"That was very kind of you. Thank you for doing that. What kind of illness was it?"

"A stroke."

"How old was he?"

"Four years older than me, so he was exactly fifty-eight."

"You seem quite healthy yourself."

"Thanks for saying so. I'm headed into my second childhood."

Makiyama stood up and returned to his seat. From behind, the hem of the blue-tinged *haori* and that of the fine, greenish pin-striped *hakama* fell almost on the same line. This was due to the fact that Makiyama was not only short but also walked with a stoop.

The man whom he had first spoken with as he passed through the entrance came around the outside of the hall to the steps and told Setsuzō that as the procession was due any moment would he please go inside. Setsuzō put on his hat and went to the entrance of the hall. Those who had already arrived had gone in, so the entrance was empty and there were only ten footwear tags left over in one corner.

He went into the hall and stood at the back along the wall. The heavy-set man told him there were vacant places in the front. In fact, some person of status had seated himself near the dais and since everyone had therefore kept a respectful distance there was a big section of vacant seats. Except for those spaces, the temple was filled.

Setsuzō unceremoniously headed straight for the vacant places, put down his hat and bag, made himself comfortable, and looked around at the dark interior of the main worship hall.

The procession arrived. As the priest in the corridor struck the bell, the coffin was carried in. The members of the Tanida family filed into the spaces reserved for relatives on the opposite side. In the seat of honor as the chief mourner sat Jirō Tanida, whom Setsuzō had met just once. At that time the man's name was still Nogawa and he was a student in the humanities department. Although he had not yet graduated, out of a sense of duty to his elderly mother he acquiesced in becoming the Tanidas' adopted son-in-law and Setsuzō saw him on the day he came with the go-between to the Tanidas. It had been two years previous to that date that Setsuzō had left his own country home, been taken in by the Tanidas, and had begun to go to school in Mita.

"You must be eager to see the new son-in-law," he had said to Hatsu, one of the maids, "but I'm not. Too many people just get in the way on a day like this, so I'm going out for a walk." He had slipped on his high *geta,* and just as he was about to go out of the gate, two rickshaws pulled in. As Jirō, in his university uniform emblazoned on the collar with the literature department emblem, stepped down from the second rickshaw, Setsuzō, going through the gate, caught a glimpse of his face. The marriage of Jirō and the Tanidas' only daughter, Otane, was held a mere ten days thereafter, but Setsuzō was no longer living in the house. Now, however, the bashful student whom Setsuzō had seen nine years earlier somewhat awkwardly getting out of the rickshaw was quite mature. Perhaps as a result of the rough and tumble of life, his forehead was now etched with several deep wrinkles. Setsuzō watched him for a while, but Jirō, whom he had met only that once by accident, seemed not to recognize him and simply looked outside past him.

Next to Jirō sat Otane, small, dressed in white, with her hair done up very simply as befitted the occasion. She walked into the hall with downcast eyes and sat looking at her knees, glancing neither in Setsuzō's direction nor anywhere else. When Setsuzō left the Tanida home she was just sixteen. Young apprentice geisha from Akasaka, who became friends with her at the flower arrangement teacher's at Shinsaka-chō, were the first to proclaim her the most beautiful girl they knew. In the rickshaw going to the Kazoku Jogakkō, a school for girls of the upper classes, at the top of Mitsuke, the apprentice geisha and young geisha she passed along the way would turn to one another and say, "That's the Tanida daughter." Everyone knew about her. Now she must be twenty-five. Buried beneath her abundant hair, the complexion of her small pale face was so white and fair that one could almost see the healthy blood flowing underneath the skin. Yet one could not call it a healthy face. The features of her lowered face reminded one of a flower vase that is much too fine to be used for everyday purposes. It was a touching beauty. Setsuzō's gaze had rested on Jirō's face only for a moment, but rested upon hers for quite a long time. Then after turning to look at the people outside, he turned back to her.

On Otane's lap, half-hidden by her sleeve, with hair braided, sat her nine or ten-year-old daughter. She had been born somewhat less than nine months following the marriage and there had been considerable worry around the household that she might be somewhat delicate, but contrary to expectation she had grown up with no problems at all. For whatever reason, no other child was born to them. During all that time, while Setsuzō had had no contact with the Tanidas, their family had not increased beyond this one child, Minako.

Among those attending the funeral who were not relatives of the deceased there may have been people who had visited the house when Setsuzō was living there, but such a long time had passed that he recognized no one. The old man Makiyama had suggested that those who made the funeral arrangements did not know Setsuzō, or maybe it was actually that there was no one there whom he had known when he lived with them.

The priests entered. The chief priest took his place in front of the central lectern, and when the other priests had taken their respective places at the double row of desks the service began. There was not the slightest solemnity in either the priest's features, the gestures of his hands, or the words that he chanted. There was undoubtedly little difference between the sentiments of the pallbearers employed by the undertaker who had brought the coffin and those of the priests who, with resplendent surplices draped across their shoulders, sat like automatons moving their hands and exercising their tongues. There had been a time years ago when Setsuzō, faced with such a poor spectacle, would have had to exert tremendous effort not to rush forward and punch every one of those tonsured heads. At other times such a scene would have irritated him so greatly that it became physically painful. Neither closing his eyes nor covering his ears would help and heedless of being stared at by everyone in the assemblage, he would jump to his feet and flee home. But now he could sit calmly and watch the priests. Just as he watched indifferently the day laborers who carried the coffin with no more respect than they would have for soil and rocks, so too he coolly observed the priests mechanically chanting to send forth the soul of the departed.

Seated opposite Setsuzō, with his back to the places reserved for relatives, was a priest of about twenty who intoned the sutra together with the other priests. As his mouth opened wide, his longish pallid face with its sunken cheeks seemed wistful, as if hungering excessively for something. Almost all of his even, pure white teeth showed. His jaws opened and closed as he read the phrases of the sutra in broken rhythm. He was chewing the sutra. The clicking of his teeth was, like the background noise that accompanies the sound of a voice in a phonograph, faint but unmistakable. Setsuzō's senses were concentrated on the priest's teeth for a fairly long while. Watching the teeth and listening to the sound they made gave Setsuzō a kind of sensual pleasure.

Before long the offering of incense began. Jirō went first. Otane, who had yet to raise her eyes, was next. Her eyes still lowered and holding Minako's hand, she rose and went forward.

Just as Otane was helping her daughter offer incense at the altar, Makiyama stood up and bending forward tiptoed past the rows of mourners and squatted down at Setsuzō's side.

"Since you were kind enough to come, shall I introduce you to the younger Tanida? He's quite a fine person."

"I would like very much to meet him, but is now a good time to do so?"

"By all means. It will be quite a while before the relatives finish offering incense and when they're done the others will begin and it won't do to crowd the aisle."

"Then shall we go now?"

They conversed hurriedly in whispers. Makiyama stood up first and, still crouching over, stealthily crossed in front of the dais toward the other side. Setsuzō followed him looking to neither side and seeming to pay respect neither to the dais nor to the head priest. As the two approached, Jirō looked at them inquiringly. Makiyama squatted down in front of Jirō and Setsuzō kneeled next to him.

"This is Yamaguchi," said Makiyama.

"Oh really," replied Jirō, turning to Setsuzō.

"I'm Yamaguchi Setsuzō. I was greatly indebted to your father. I was deeply saddened to hear of his death."

"Yes. He was still quite healthy. He collapsed at Yudono and that was that. It was a shock."

His expression frank and open, Jirō spoke without reserve. At that point Otane, who seemed drained of all strength, returned holding Minako's hand. She first looked curiously at Makiyama, but when her gaze moved to Setsuzō she seemed to receive an instant shock. Her already pale face became one shade paler, and even her lips were drained of color. Her whole body shuddered convulsively, but instantly she seemed to try to make a conscious effort to regain control of herself. She stood staring wide-eyed at Setsuzō, as if she had forgotten all about returning to her seat. When Otane had shuddered, she had unconsciously jerked Minako's hand, surprising her. The child instinctively looked at her mother and then followed her mother's gaze so she too stood staring at Setsuzō. Setsuzō sat transfixed by the glare of the two women, the mother's eyes glowing with anger, the daughter's startled eyes seeming to ask who he was that had caused such a violent reaction in her mother, but the muscles of Setsuzō's face moved not at all. The mysterious tension that locked the three of them together lasted only a few seconds, and neither Jirō nor Makiyama had any inkling of the variety or strength of the emotions that were ignited and almost as quickly extinguished inside Otane. She gracefully returned to her original place and drew Minako toward her.

"I'm Yamaguchi. It has been a long time. I'm sorry about your father." Before she could say anything, Setsuzō quickly stood as if a reply was not to be expected under the circumstances and headed back to where he had been sitting.

"After the mourning period is over do come by," said Jirō after Setsuzō had already turned away.

"Thank you. Some day I shall," Setsuzō replied over his shoulder, not slackening his pace as he returned to his place.

The closest family members had finished offering incense and although over half of the relatives remained, several of the funeral organizers came to the distinguished person who sat alone in the front, expressed their appreciation for his kindness in attending, and invited him to offer incense. Then they made the same invitation to the others.

When the man who first received the invitation stood up, Setsuzō saw the crest of the family of a famous *daimyō* on his *haori*. He had been sent to represent the Tanidas' former feudal lord. Actually the reason Setsuzō had left his country home to come to Tokyo was that his grandfather and Tanida's father had become quite close when they served the domain together in the capital. As a result of this long-standing friendship, when all the domain officials returned home following the abolition of the fiefs in 1882, Setsuzō's father had asked Shigeru Tanida, at that time a brilliant young government official, to look after his newborn son Setsuzō when he became old enough to leave home and go to Tokyo for training.

Soon thereafter Setsuzō unceremoniously picked up his bag and hat, offered incense, and left the temple. As he was putting on his footwear, people began pouring out of the hall with footwear tags thrust out, putting the liveried attendant in quite a flurry.

The children and mothers with babies strapped to their backs who still stood around the veranda of the temple seemed not to have received anything in the way of alms. These people made an outward pretense of coming to the funerals out of curiosity, but hoped to get something out of coming. But today, as sometimes happens, their dreams disappointed, they would return home empty-handed.

Scattered clouds still floated in the sky and the wind had not stopped, but it looked as though there would be no high wind. Setsuzō returned the way he had come. Several rickshaws carrying mourners from the funeral proceeded together as far as Otowa and then turned in different directions.

Rocked by the rickshaw as it passed along the deserted street, Setsuzō quite indifferently recalled the time he had spent in the Tanida home, as if it had happened to someone else, without sorrow, without remorse.

2

It was at the time when the Boxers had encircled Peking, where the various nations maintained legations, and Japan along with several European countries sent a combined force to the rescue. Extra editions of the newspapers came out several times a day claiming that contact with Peking had been established or that it had been broken.

Setsuzō arrived in Tokyo for the first time and settled in the Tanidas' residence in Harajuku. At that time the master of the house, who was quite accomplished in the Chinese classics, was working as a secretary in the Cabinet. Other than going to his office, he rarely went out except to lecture at the Shibunkai, and so he had virtually no direct contact with the outside world. When he was at home he sat at the red sandalwood desk and read. "I'm slowly going farsighted, but fortunately I don't read Western books, so I don't need glasses," he said, smiling in his usual way. He enjoyed *sake,* so when he had a drink at dinner he took a long time over it. At the time Setsuzō arrived, it rained almost every day and was quite humid. In the evenings, when Setsuzō looked in, the master would be having an evening drink while his wife cooled him with a fan, pouring his *sake* for him and listening to him read the news of the allied troops in the newspaper. Sometimes he would drink while reading a book. Or he would put before him an outline of an epitaph someone had asked him to write and in turn pick up his *sake* cup and the red-correction brush he used for revising the draft. Still his wife did not seem the least bit bored. The embodiment of serenity, she devoted herself to taking care of the needs of her husband and tending to the clothes and hair of her daughter who attended a school for upper-class girls. Everything else she left to the maid, Fuyu.

Setsuzō came from the country where despite the low cost of living it was hard to make ends meet and where each day was a struggle, so when he first encountered this idyllic scene, he was astounded that such an easy way of life was actually possible. He felt sorry for his parents at home. He envied the Tanidas on his parents' behalf rather than on his own. Since he was not yet twenty, having a family and settling down was still far in the future and so he did not envy them himself.

Setsuzō was given the room closed off by *fusuma* across from the entrance. In it he put his desk and was free to spend his time there. The room had not been used at all. When you came in the entrance, passed through that room and turned left, you came to a drawing room decorated in Western style. If you turned right, you came to the servants' quarters and the kitchen. Walking straight through the room from the entrance, you came to a wide corridor. To the right this corridor led to the family's rooms and through glass-fitted *shōji* on the left afforded a view of a garden planted with small pines. In this way, except for those who came in and out of the back door, everyone who came passed by Setsuzō's room, but he hardly ever had to answer the door. That was because a young student from the Tanidas' country home acted as a sort of houseboy, spending the day in the servants' room until they retired for the night, greeting guests at the door, and running errands. Only rarely did Mrs. Tanida ever call Setsuzō, and usually when she did call, it was only to run an errand such as buying some cakes.

Except for the book he was reading and a notebook, there was nothing on his desk. Everything else that he had brought from home was stored in a small closet between his room and the servants' room. Even if he stepped out for just a moment, he always cleared his desk and put everything in order. Beside the closet was a small door which connected to the servants' room, but because the houseboy reached the entrance through a door that opened from the kitchen veranda whenever he had to go out on an errand, hardly anyone ever used it.

Despite being at the corner of the hallway, there were not many people coming and going, so the room was quiet enough for study. At the beginning, when he was going around investigating various schools and came home in the middle of the day for lunch, he worried that the room might be too dark because of the width of the corridor and the depth of the projecting eaves that allowed little direct light to come through the windows. But once he settled on a school, the maid Hatsu made him a packed lunch to take with him. Thus, since he was gone from early morning until dark, his qualms about the darkness of the room disappeared.

Within a week Setsuzō had become completely accustomed to the place. At night he wrapped his legs in a blanket to keep from being chewed by mosquitoes and read beneath the electric light, feeling as if he had made the place his very own.

3

Setsuzō had attended school for only ten days when the summer vacation
began. Mr. Tanida and his colleagues were taking vacations in turn, so he
went off to his office in Marunouchi only intermittently. Throughout the
house the sole topic of conversation was the rebellion in China. Special editions of the newspapers came out frequently, but there was little favorable
news. No matter what the news was, the nations all seemed to be hostilely
facing off and keeping their distance from one another. Peking was under
siege and everyone was anxious about the members of the Japanese legation
who were no doubt in dire straits. Nonetheless it was not the same as during
the Sino-Japanese War when no one, regardless of his profession, could keep
his mind on his work due to these great worries. Now people went about
their daily tasks doing little more than commenting on the sad state of
affairs in Peking and spreading rumors.

Setsuzō read at his desk which he placed in the space that was always open
between the entranceway and the glass-fitted *shōji* along the back garden.
The garden was quite large; part of it was grass-covered, and in the center an
artificial conical-shaped mountain had been constructed. The "mountain"
was also covered with grass. The outer edge of the garden was thick with several varieties of trees and during the day cicadas in those trees filled the air
with ceaseless waves of droning.

Even in the grounds of the school in Mita was preserved part of a garden
that had been laid out in the Edo period. Despite the fact that it was on an
elevation and there was no water, small stones were arranged in the shape of
a pond, and trees pruned both round and square were planted with deliberate disregard to evenness of height. It was not much different from the residences of samurai families at home. But the garden of this house was so
peculiar he decided to ask the houseboy, whose name was Saitō, if he knew
anything about it. Saitō replied that it was supposed to be that way and
explained the history of the garden.

Saitō had come to the Tanida family in the midst of the reconstruction.
Mr. Tanida disliked cramped little gardens and wanted a spacious country-
style garden which could be left to grow somewhat naturally. The house had
been built in a field, so he wanted to leave the weeds and horsetail to grow
naturally. His wife, however, put up a stiff resistance and finally had the garden planted with grass while the trees that had stood by the residence were
planted around the grass in the garden. The mountain had been made by
piling up the earth that had been excavated for the house foundations.

Though the place where Setsuzō sat was left wide open, there was almost no breeze. That was because the family rooms had been built with the garden on the south side, and from his room the garden was to the west. Occasionally a breeze would blow through. When it came from the entrance, it was hot; when it came from the garden, it was cool. In exchange for the darkness of the room at the times when it rained all day, the width of the corridor and depth of the eaves proved to be blessings in that the hot late afternoon sun did not shine in to where he sat.

Seated at his desk in the heat of the afternoon, Setsuzō would sometimes become a little sleepy, and when he raised his eyes from the open book in front of him to see if the leaves of the trees in the garden were moving, Otane, the daughter, would pass by in the corridor. She wore a gay summer kimono, red-sashed, with white *tabi* on her small feet, and her hair was braided in two long strands down her back. Otane was on summer vacation, as well, and when the time came for her parents' afternoon nap, she would get restless and wander all over the house.

In the beginning she would pass along the corridor going toward the Western-style room without a glance in Setsuzō's direction; then she would return. First she would turn her head to the right and look at the garden as she walked along. Upon her return, as expected, she would look at the garden to her left. She walked at a normal pace, neither too fast nor too slow. Then she began to steal a glance at Setsuzō as she passed by. Later she began to walk by, laughing, her big eyes shining brightly, or run by unceremoniously. Sometimes she would pass through Setsuzō's room, go to the entranceway, stand and look at the rickshaws passing by outside the gate, and return toward the corridor. At such times she would smilingly nod to Setsuzō and then leave. There were also instances when she dropped the rubber ball she had been carrying, chased it all over the room, picked it up, and left.

One day Otane stealthily crept up behind Setsuzō and looked over his shoulder at the book which lay on his desk. Setsuzō pretended to be unaware of her and went on reading.

She stood behind Setsuzō and said, "Mother said I could come to your room as long as I didn't bother you."

"Is that right?" Setsuzō turned around for the first time.

A mischievous imp danced in her eyes, but she stood modestly still, holding a small lacquer box in her hand. Setsuzō started to turn the book he had been reading face down.

"Oh, no. Don't stop studying. If you do, Mother will scold me." She came near the desk, sat down, placed the box in front of her, and took the lid off the box.

Setsuzō looked curiously to see what the box contained. Inside was a large collection of small pieces of cloth. Otane took them out one by one, laid them out on the *tatami,* and separated them according to color and texture. Breathing quietly she seemed completely absorbed in her task. Her thin, almost transparent fingers deftly and restlessly picked up and put down the red, blue, and purple strips.

Setsuzō had assumed that she had come to his room because she wanted him to join her in something, but since that did not seem to be the case, he resumed reading. After reading a few more lines, he looked at her out of the corner of his eye. He could not help feeling intrigued by the graceful, resilient movement of her small fingers as if he were watching some natural phenomenon. He realized that he would be asked to do something together with her.

4

Thereafter, once the household had turned in for an afternoon nap, Otane regularly visited his room.

Sometimes she brought a doll and dressed and undressed it. Other times she brought a rubber ball and bounced it. The sound of the ball bouncing on the *tatami* greatly irritated him. But the sight of her agile figure bouncing the ball high in the air, spinning completely around, and bouncing the ball again in midair amused him and revived his spirits.

As the long summer vacation progressed, Otane gradually became less reserved. She was not much of a talker, so he was not bothered by chatter. But from time to time she was boldly mischievous. One day he unintentionally fell asleep with his head on his desk. It was about two o'clock on an extremely hot and humid day when there was not even a breath of wind and the cloudy sky seemed to press down heavily on his head. Setsuzō very rarely slept at his desk, but this time he fell sound asleep. Suddenly a noise woke him with a start. It must have been a cart or something going along the road outside the gate. He raised his head and with his right hand rubbed his left wrist which had "gone to sleep" under his forehead. When he stretched his back, the desk moved on its own with a jerk. The right leg of the desk struck his leg. "What's this?" he wondered. He pulled away from the desk only to have the desk follow along behind him at an angle. At that very moment, the laugh Otane had tried to suppress exploded. When he looked, he could see only her eyes and the top of her head in the shadow of the pillar at the corner of the corridor. Her forehead, eyes, and bangs were shaking from her giggles. Figuring that she had played some trick on him while he was asleep, he looked down and saw that the trailing end of his waistband had been tied to the right table leg.

5

In August the combined forces made rapid advances, and finally on the fourteenth and fifteenth they succeeded in reaching Peking and rescuing those who had entrenched themselves in the legation. When the confirmed report appeared in the newspaper special edition, Mr. Tanida was extremely pleased. He invited Setsuzō and Saitō in for evening drinks.

He had drunk a great deal more than usual and his nearly bald pate was bright red. "Excellent! Truly excellent! Now the Europeans will not be able to question the might of our army," he said, drink in hand. "My dear," his wife said anxiously, hoping to stem the rate of his imbibing, "you've already had twice as much as you usually have." But to one who is intoxicated, this caveat has the opposite of the desired effect. "Well? There's nothing wrong with that once in a while," he replied and went on drinking.

Setsuzō drained his *sake* cup. He left as Saitō was telling Mrs. Tanida the details of the entrance into Peking which were in the paper, and quickly returned to his own room. He sat at his desk, his brows knit, and fell into thought.

In his heart he understood how Mr. Tanida and his wife and Saitō felt, but for some reason he could not join in their delight. There was no denying that he had felt the same uneasiness, suspense, and sense of danger in the long period from the start of the siege of the legation until that day and that he too had breathed a deep sigh of relief at the resolution of the crisis. However, at the very moment of relief, he felt a dreadful emptiness, as if he had seen the climax of a play and then just stepped out of the theater. At the same time he could not help noticing an unbridgeable gulf between himself and those who never tire of dissecting every fragment of information thrown out by the papers. For some reason or other, everyone seemed to him like a ruminating animal. They irritated him so much that he could not help but feel contempt for them.

That was not all. The master's evening drinks had recently begun to get on his nerves. When he first arrived, he had opened his eyes in astonishment at this strange scene of household peace. But his irritation grew worse day by day. The alcohol was poured on top of the unclouded satisfaction of the accomplishments of that day's work at the office. That *sake* was a tribute to the accomplishments of half a lifetime of mechanically adding rhetorical flourishes to other people's ideas and feeling never the slightest qualm of conscience. That evening drink was the paradise of the mindless. Setsuzō grew to want to curse that paradise.

At such times he had often picked a fight with someone or assaulted someone without motive. That he had broken off relations with every single friend when he was at school back home and that he now had not one friend to exchange letters with was due to this quirk. If someone was doing something interesting, he would approach him. But before long he would grow tired of him. Very often it was because he became bored with what had first attracted him. While they were friends he was kind and conciliatory. Then when that friendship broke off he was cruel and inconsiderate. The time he had shocked someone the most was with a middle-school friend named Izumi. Izumi was quite skillful at playing the flute and took great care of a flute which he said had been in his family for a very long time. He kept it in a brocade case whose original design and color had long since become unrecognizable. Once in a while, when Setsuzō got bored, he would go to Izumi's house and ask him to play a little on his flute. He would sit leaning against a pillar, rest his elbows on his raised knees and his chin upon his elbows, and listen while Izumi played. This continued for quite a while.

One day he went to see Izumi and found he was not at home. Izumi's room was carefully tidied and the flute was on the desk. Out of the blue Setsuzō took the flute, still in its case, grasped one end in each hand, and tried to break it against his right shin. The flute refused to break, so he put it on the broad stone step that led to the garden and stepped on it with a garden clog. With a crack the flute splintered. At that very moment Izumi returned home. Setsuzō looked at him as if he were not even there. Without a word, with long steps he strode out of the house. Completely stunned for a moment Izumi stood there as if he had seen some mysterious midday dream. For Izumi the broken flute in his hand was proof that it was not just a bad dream. Even among Setsuzō's many unaccountable actions, this breaking off with Izumi was to outsiders the most incomprehensible, and it was the main cause of his losing the sympathy of those around him. The same feeling he had had when he broke Izumi's flute welled up in him as he watched Mr. Tanida enjoying the peace of his small, innocent household, but he stopped himself from doing or saying anything cruel and simply returned to his room.

It had not been his will that had suppressed it. At times like those when he had broken the flute, Setsuzō had absolutely no ability to control his actions one way or the other of his own will. Even he was amazed that he had been able to stop himself on this particular occasion. It was because without his realizing it his disposition had changed.

6

When his parents first requested the Tanidas to take him in, they had sent a letter which read in part, "Though it will undoubtedly cause you great trouble because of his rough country upbringing, we humbly request that you take him under your tutelage so that his willfulness can be reformed and he may be made to make some small contribution to society." The Tanidas had read his father's letter and speculated about what uncouth character they should expect. Contrary to their expectations, however, Setsuzō upon arrival appeared gentle in speech and behavior. They were both surprised and relieved.

For a while they were concerned that some bad habit of his would surface, but none did. Mr. Tanida wondered off and on whether the father's letter had been overly humble or whether Setsuzō had really been unruly as a child, but had grown out of it and settled down somewhat.

Mr. Tanida once asked his wife, "What do you think of Yamaguchi?"

"Well, he was so amiable when he first arrived that I thought we would be able to get to know him rather easily, but he seems hard to get close to. He hasn't overstepped the bounds of propriety in any way, but, on the other hand, he doesn't seem to be able to open up and speak frankly about things either. But he is certainly not a disagreeable sort."

"That's all right. They say a wise man's relations should be light like water, so don't be too persistent with him."

"All right. How is he doing at school? I heard you talking with him about that the other day."

"He doesn't seem incapable, but he says he can't manage to do all of his subjects properly. I asked what he seemed to be best at and he said writing. I suggested that he try writing classical Chinese, but that was a big mistake."

"Why? What did he say?"

"He was quite clever. He said that his writing was in modern Japanese. If he was going to write some 'foreign' language, he would rather write in some European language, rather than in a classical style. Isn't that something? He just came right out and said that even though he knows I write in the scholarly Chinese style."

"But that was an awful thing for him to have said to you. You should have said something."

"But there is some truth in what he said," her husband replied with a laugh.

Whenever his wife felt he was too kind for his own good, she took it almost like a direct insult and fell into a bad humor, but normally this would not last long. On this occasion, however, she turned moody and fell silent.

7

Setsuzō occasionally indulged in introspection and was always astonished by how fleeting was his interest in things around him and by the weakness of his desires. Looking backward, his previous interests were even shallower and his desires less ardent than he had thought them earlier.

Even in his life at school, he had felt from the very beginning no interest in his courses, but because he did feel some competitiveness toward his classmates, he realized a certain pleasure when he excelled, and from that came his motivation. Even in his relations with friends, he felt no more than a random impulse to go to visit a friend on his own. That was why he had gone to Izumi's house to hear him play the flute. In those days he had not thought that there was any difference in his own sensitivity to things and that of other people.

It was just that after continuing with something for a while, it suddenly became tedious. He began to curse all the teachers at the school he attended. On such days when a teacher asked him a question in class, he would either ostentatiously refuse to answer or fling back some defiant reply and stare fixedly at the teacher. He experienced a sort of pleasure when the teacher showed some sign of worry, anger, or other emotion. When he severed relations with a friend, it was on such a day that he did it. The friend with whom he had theretofore been close could suddenly become infinitely repugnant, like a plate filled with fishbones or the dirty brown sauce left after stuffing oneself that one wants quickly to clear away. Before anyone could remove it, he would want to throw it away somewhere so that he would never have to set eyes on it again. It made no difference how much he hurt the friend.

He had indeed had such gray days.

But looking back on the past, it would be safe to say like the philosopher that all human events are trial and trouble, and pleasure is that moment when they momentarily abate, so there was some pleasure on the days that were not gray.

This emotional state began changing, without his being aware of it, at about the time he came to Tokyo. Previously his actions on the gray days occurred without warning, like a thunderbolt that comes and goes in an instant, but now the muddiness of the gray had become clearer and instead had infiltrated the ordinary days. In the past he had simply acted without thinking, but now on a gray day he was aware of it, like the aura an epileptic is said to feel on the day that a seizure may occur. "Here it comes again," he would say to himself, and this gave rise to a margin of self-control, room to direct his own conduct. In exchange for this, he lost the pleasant feeling and alleviation of suffering that he had earlier felt between gray days.

Setsuzō had awakened. Everything had become clearer and more conscious than before.

At the same time he noticed a wide psychological gulf between himself and others. Or rather, he thought he noticed it. Others were apt to be positive in their daily lives, such that, even though there were differences in temperament or in point of view, they were affirming something. But he was unable to assimilate himself in that way. Every time he saw people affirming something, he would consider them fools, deluded and unfortunate.

Once he had in this way reached the conclusion that being positive about things was a delusion and that everyone was a fool, his language and behavior became more gentle and deferential. He tried not to let people see his scorn. Generally those who wear a mask of stoicism as they pass through life want something from others. The mask is worn to gain something and no sacrifice is spared to obtain it. Setsuzō, however, wanted nothing. He just wanted to conceal his inner self.

What was surprising was how it affected those around him. Others looked at him with a degree of respect tempered with awe. People could hardly imagine that he affirmed nothing and respected nothing, so they mistakenly imagined that what he sought was something infinitely greater and more noble than most people sought. He was seen as a so-called man of great ambition. Before he knew it, he found a group of devotees growing up around him. Saitō had once said he was remarkable. Only Mrs. Tanida felt instinctively something cold and sinister deep inside Setsuzō.

8

Even the thought of going to school in such heat was unbearable. But in due course by September when school restarted there was a cool breeze blowing. Otane began school at the same time as Setsuzō's classes started.

One day, Otane came home from school and told her mother that she was being bothered by a boy who lay in wait for her almost every day on the way to school and "took liberties" with her, accosting her by name. "It is so unpleasant, I don't know what to do." The phrase "so unpleasant" was one she had heard an older girl at school use and had come to use herself. Somehow or other it didn't sound as if being teased by the boy was what had given rise to her using the expression.

Mrs. Tanida, who was quite aware that her daughter was immature, treated Otane as a child in all respects, so she did not take her seriously when she said this unknown boy had been "taking liberties" with her. "There are lots of boys like that," she told her daughter, "so no matter what he says, just ignore him and look the other way." In any case, she thought, he was probably some child on his way to school who was only being mischievous.

Several days later Otane complained again. "I don't pay any attention to him at all, but he says all kinds of things."

"What do you mean by 'all kinds of things'?"

"No matter how many times he calls my name, I don't look in his direction at all. Today he came right up to the rickshaw and told me I shouldn't ignore him like that."

"Really? What a thing to say! He's really impertinent and mischievous, isn't he? But even if you try to reply, you're no match for a boy, so you had better keep on ignoring him."

That was all their conversation amounted to, but Mrs. Tanida did feel anxious, so she called the man who pulled the rickshaw.

The man who took her daughter to school was from the same association as the man who took her husband to work. This second man, named Kisaburō, was quick-witted and alert, but Seikichi who took her daughter was older and somewhat absentminded.

Seikichi's replies to Mrs. Tanida's questioning were rather vague and noncommittal as usual. Come to think of it, he said, there was a student who sometimes greeted and spoke to her daughter. He seemed nicely dressed, perhaps from some good family, and a little younger than Yamaguchi. He had thought the young man was an acquaintance. He said no more than that he had not felt that the boy had said anything especially rude.

After listening to what Seikichi said, Mrs. Tanida thought for a moment and said, "My daughter says she doesn't know that boy, so from now on be more careful and try not to let him speak to her."

Seikichi was a man of a rather unkempt appearance who seemingly out of laziness let his graying hair grow long and his salt-and-pepper beard grow out somewhat from his squarish face. With an expression of shock, he looked at the mistress. "Really? You mean she doesn't know him? If he says something next time, I'll give him a good scolding." Seikichi bowed several times and left.

9

In the same area in which the Tanidas lived was a man by the name of Makiyama who made a decent living by helping people buy and sell land.

When the Tanidas bought their present residence, he handled things for them, and thereafter whenever there was anything to be done at the district office, Makiyama always went in the Tanidas' stead.

There was a reason for his working in faithful service to the Tanida family.

It all came about at the time Mr. Tanida was considering buying land in Harajuku. As they were talking together Makiyama suddenly asked about Tanida's religion. Mr. Tanida replied that he was a member of the Nichiren sect of Buddhism. In that case, Makiyama said, they were of the same sect and when he inquired further he heard the following story. Tanida's grandfather had been a merchant, but his father was fond of studying and pursued Confucianism and, as a result, was granted samurai status. That was the origin of the rarity of the household of a Confucianist belonging to the Nichiren sect. Makiyama also handled the affairs of a religious group that worshiped both Shintō gods and the Buddha, and since he prevailed upon Mr. Tanida at least to put his name on the roll and make a contribution, he was especially kind in all his dealings.

Makiyama's son attended the Tokyo Middle School in Kojimachi. One day after he came home from school, he told a strange story at dinner.

"Father, you know that Aihara? Well, this morning on my way to school along the road behind Zenkoji, I saw him standing at the corner of that narrow road. I figured he must be up to no good, so I slowed down and watched him. A rickshaw came past me from behind and just as it turned the corner Aihara walked up to it and said, 'Good morning, young lady.' I wondered who was riding in the rickshaw, and when I looked, it was the Tanidas' daughter. Why do you suppose she knows a fellow like him?"

Momentarily stunned by their son's tale, the Makiyamas laid down their chopsticks and looked at each other.

"This is terrible," said his mother, all in a flurry.

"But even Mitsu wouldn't take notice of such a young girl," his father replied.

"I don't know about that. He's such a bad boy it's hard to know what he might be thinking. She's big for her age and looks fifteen or sixteen, and besides, she's strikingly beautiful."

"Well, that may be," his father said, deep in thought.

Mrs. Makiyama asked her son, "What did she do in the midst of all that?"

"I was so busy watching Aihara that I'm not positive, but it didn't look as though she said anything at all."

"I see." Mrs. Makiyama took her husband's rice bowl and refilled it. "My dear, before any trouble arises you had better go to the Tanidas immediately and tell them to be careful. There's no telling what might happen if they are off their guard."

Her husband poured tea over his rice and ate hastily, thinking about what it would be best to do. He seemed to hit upon something and at long last replied.

"All right. Leave everything to me. I'll fix matters so that nothing will happen."

10

Aihara Mitsutarō, of whom the Makiyamas seemed so afraid, was the only son of a widow who lived on a back road in Aoyama Minami-cho and managed, with a small sum of money, to live without working.

This widow, who was called Motoko, had been married to a man who owned one of the shops lining the side street that ran from Aoyama to the cemetery which sold branches of *sakaki* and star anise which visitors would take to the graves. When her husband died, she sold her share in the store and now lived alone with her son, doing no particular work. On the surface she appeared to be an elegant retired widow, but the rumor going around the neighborhood was that, to be blunt about it, she lent money at exorbitant interest and did other unkind things.

Her son Mitsutarō was seventeen. Although he seemed to be an ordinary student, he was a conspicuously handsome youth. He always took great care of his appearance and dressed so that he could easily be mistaken for a young gentleman of the upper class. He was enrolled at the same school as the Makiyama boy, but he tended to be absent a lot and his grades were appalling.

Among his classmates at school, he was known as Omitsu. He had no close friends in his class and at recess whenever Aihara approached a big group of chatting students, as if by previous agreement they all fell silent.

That he came to be called by this feminine nickname was not simply due to his being pampered by his mother and growing up effeminate. Actually at the time when his parents were still living near the cemetery, Mitsutarō was a little girl in red ribbons. In elementary school he was a girl called Aihara Omitsu, who was learning to sew.

Aihara Omitsu became Aihara Mitsutarō through legal proceedings to amend the family register. He had gone to a university-affiliated hospital for a medical examination. At the time, some news agency picked up the story and it appeared in various newspapers. The headlines said "Girl Becomes Boy" and the lengthy article that followed concluded by inquiring whether this was to be viewed as auspicious in the life of society. Surely no newspaper reporter would be foolish enough to tie a natural phenomenon to the state of society. Or was it only a witty remark? Was there some meaning behind it? Probably not. In the past the words "auspicious" and "inauspicious" were sometimes used when reporting some natural calamity, and then they came to be used for anything mysterious or marvelous. A writer writes without thinking. A reader reads without thinking. To assume that there must be some thought or meaning hidden in the background is evidence of the reader's deviousness and narrowmindedness.

That was all that appeared in the articles, but there was an external motivation that had prompted Omitsu's undergoing the examination and becoming a male. Omitsu had one close friend and they did everything together. They kept aloof from others and consulted with each other about every little thing. This friend began to come to Aihara's house when the widow was away. About the time of graduation from upper elementary school, it became apparent that they were not simply close friends. Finally one day the widow came home earlier than she was expected and encountered a situation that would not occur between a girl and a girl. Once she had become aware of them, there were things about Omitsu's body that made her put two and two together, so the mother had a professor at the university look at Omitsu. She had entered elementary school as Omitsu, but he received his graduation certificate as Mitsutarō.

Mitsutarō had become a boy. But he still preferred the company of girls and the various rumors were unending about his writing a letter to such and such a girl or holding hands and becoming friendly with some girl at the exit of a storyteller's hall. At that time words like "juvenile delinquent" or "lady-killer" had not become fashionable or used in the newspapers, but it was not entirely unreasonable for the Makiyamas to worry when they heard that Mitsutarō had been talking to the Tanidas' daughter.

II

When Makiyama heard that Aihara had been following the Tanidas' girl, he had spoken to his wife as if he knew what to do, but actually he did not have any specific plan. He had just decided that if he talked to Setsuzō, something would work out.

That evening, when it began to get dark outside, it became a little humid in the house, so Setsuzō went out to the gate and squatted down watching several children playing in front of a similar gate that stood in front of the house of the army general across the road. The remains of the gate house across the way had been made into a stable where two horses were kept. Inside it was quite cool. The stable keeper seemed to be putting down litter for the horses to sleep on and giving them something to eat. Setsuzō could hear the man calling to the horses and the sound of their hooves on the wooden floor. Even in the evening there was almost no one hurrying through the back streets around there.

Along came Makiyama, his striped summer *haori* tied loosely, and walking with mincing steps, his chest thrown out. Except for some ceremonious occasion he never wore a hat. When Makiyama saw Setsuzō, he stopped and bowed.

"It's still pretty sultry, isn't it? Your garden is full of shrubs, so you must have lots of mosquitoes these days."

"Not really. It was too soon to turn on the lights, so I came outside." Setsuzō stood up to stretch himself, not out of deference to Makiyama.

Makiyama made as if to go in the gate. "If you have a moment now, there's something I'd like to talk to you about."

"Well, if it won't take too long, we can talk out here, can't we?"

Setsuzō strolled along the wooden fence of the Tanida residence, almost completely ignoring Makiyama.

Makiyama followed along. He told how his son had discovered that a boy was following the Tanidas' daughter around. He explained that the boy's name was Aihara and that there was a plethora of rumors about him.

"Oh, is that what you wanted to talk about? I heard from Saitō that some boy was up to mischief, but I didn't know what his name was. What was it you wanted to talk to me about?"

Somewhat at a loss for words, Makiyama went on hesitatingly.

"Well, it's about him. Actually we thought we should say something to Mr. Tanida and warn him to be more careful, but there has been no particular incident to point out and besides her mother would have to be involved, too. As I said before, this boy seems to lead a rather disreputable life and it isn't inconceivable that he could cause the family some trouble. According to our way of thinking, the most expedient way would be to catch Mitsutarō and give him a firm talking to."

"Hmm." Setsuzō was silent for a moment, then he turned on his heel and headed back in the direction they had come from. They were in front of a row of stores with a rickshaw stall and a kitchenware shop hemmed in by residences. With a comprehending look, Setsuzō said to Makiyama who had also turned back, "That's exactly what the rickshaw man promised to do when Mrs. Tanida told him to watch out for him. Saitō has known the man for a long time, however, and he says the man isn't the type to say anything at all, even to a houseboy. I thought it would be good to have Saitō go, but as you say, nothing has actually happened and since I didn't want to interfere, I didn't say anything."

"To be sure." Makiyama nodded and continued, "Mitsutarō isn't that old, but he's rather too much of a rascal for Saitō."

Setsuzō let out a short laugh. "Aha! So you are suggesting that I go to talk with him?"

Makiyama was evidently embarrassed. "Well, actually I thought I would consult with you and see if you would."

"If he's as odd as you say he is, I'm tempted to have a look at him for myself. Anyway, let me think it over."

"Yes. Please do. Actually I hadn't thought of asking such a favor of you. I just thought I'd ask your opinion."

"I'm afraid I'm not very resourceful myself. Surely he wouldn't be violent, so it's either leave him alone or teach him a lesson."

They arrived back at the Tanidas' gate.

"Well, please do give it your consideration." Makiyama bowed a polite farewell to Setsuzō and returned along the road he had come from, where lights were beginning to be turned on here and there.

Setsuzō's saying that he wanted to see this boy was not far from the truth. Among the lectures he attended at Mita was one in aesthetics. The lecturer was terrible, quite unbearable to listen to. He would read some biased volume, one that would only be read in Japan as a curiosity, and then say the most extraordinary things in his lectures. The aesthetics course was divided into two terms, the first term being the history of aesthetics. Only that morning Setsuzō had heard that according to someone's interpretation the beauty of the human body tended toward either masculine beauty or feminine beauty, but that "pure" beauty did not exist. "Pure" beauty existed between the extremes. Therefore, beauty was to be sought among hermaphrodites, who were neither men nor women. The lecturer disagreed, saying that beauty should be sought in different places depending on the thing involved, but he nevertheless gave a serious introduction to what physical structure would make this person neither man nor woman, and at the same time both man and woman. The lecturer had apparently even consulted medical textbooks, but Setsuzō thought his explanation utterly ridiculous. Setsuzō's already minimal respect for scholarship was diminished even further and he felt that a profession whose main activity was to look up such things in a book and then convey them to others was the height of absurdity. As he listened to Makiyama, he felt he had discovered an actual case of what he had heard about in Mita and his curiosity was piqued by the possibility of seeing just what such a person would look like and how that person would behave.

Although he had no deep interest in much of anything, he was often stirred by curiosity. He always listened to his lectures and read his books looking for holes in the logic. After parting from Makiyama, he went back into the house and sat down at his desk. He opened the book he had left unfinished and looked at it, but his curiosity was roused less by the contents of the book than by the story he had just heard about this hermaphroditic boy Aihara. He began to reflect. I've been thinking for a long time about writing, but until now I haven't been able to get hold of anything to write about. Whenever you hear the critics, they say you shouldn't place too much importance on what you write about, but pay attention to how you write about it. But still it's difficult to judge readily how much a writer's success is due to how he writes and how much is due to what he writes about. Perhaps Gorky became a great writer at one bound at least half because no one had ever written about the life of vagabonds before. And such novelists here in Japan as Kōda Rohan and Ozaki Kōyō write about extraordinary events from their respective viewpoints. Hirotsu Ryūrō's *Cross-Eyed Den* describes the sexual activities of an idiot and it was given a favorable reception. Who knows? Someone may well one day become a success by writing about sadism and abnormal sexual desire. Perhaps I should write my maiden work about this hermaphrodite. In any case, he wanted to see this Aihara, even if it was only to see his face.

After a while, he muttered to himself again. "Even plot becomes foolish." The leading lights of criticism burn incense before the altar of authors who write about commonplace events and condemn those whose works are interesting. But no matter how extraordinary the plot is, that by itself does not make it "interesting." For them to confess that they think something is interesting on the basis of the plot alone is almost the same as confessing that they cannot appreciate art. Typically of Setsuzō, the prospective writer who is sensible and writes from his head, he tried to imagine the destination of the road he had to travel step by step. It was no more than a desire to satisfy the sense of his own power and at such times he always laughed scornfully at himself, never making any serious plan or project. Therefore he had still not made even a childish attempt at writing.

12

When Setsuzō awoke the next morning, Makiyama's tale came immediately to his mind. It was not because he was being asked to do something that he had listened to Makiyama. Nor did he want to punish the fellow who was following Otane around. The idea of coming across this Aihara fellow came and went in his mind as he brushed his teeth and ate breakfast. When someone walking down the street points out the red glow in the sky and says that there is a fire, the passerby looks up and turns and walks in that direction. Makiyama was simply the one who did the pointing.

Wrapping his books and notebook in the sateen wrapping cloth that students carried at that time, Setsuzō left the house. He always looked to see whether the rickshaw that took Otane to school was at the gate or not, and if it was he would hurry a bit. But this morning the rickshaw was waiting at the gate and the man was sitting on the floorboard vacantly smoking a cigarette. Dropped at his feet were a burnt match and the butt of a Tengu cigarette that Saitō was always being scolded about. Seeing this, Setsuzō set out more leisurely than usual, thinking about something, but not sure himself about what. Having walked a few yards, he realized that, contrary to his normal habit of turning right after going out the gate and cutting through the temple grounds to Aoyama, he had turned left. He clearly recalled the place where Makiyama had told him Aihara accosted Otane and consciously strode off in that direction. Remembering that the first class of the day was that of a Chinese classics professor named Sakaya, and that the second period was free, he decided he would not miss anything important, so he walked off enjoying the freedom of being able to go where he wanted.

Passing through the residential quarter and walking for a while through an area with houses on both sides of the road, he could already see a corner where the road slanted off to the right. That was the place Makiyama had described. Setsuzō noticed as he passed that the corner house was one of the picture postcard stores that were so popular at the time, with an upright frame about the size of a paper screen holding rows of samples. Just opposite it was a small barbershop in the outside curve of the road. Setsuzō's eyes came to a halt on the short barber in the white coat standing as he worked.

Even while he was still some distance from the corner, he had noticed a boy standing by the sign outside the postcard shop. Whenever someone approached, the boy would walk a block or so and then turn around and return to his position in front of the sign. Setsuzō saw him and realized that he was the one. He was wearing a light gray pepper-and-salt student uniform. Setsuzō estimated that Aihara was much shorter than he was.

It was still early so not many stores were open yet. Only the barber was already at work. The sun shone in through the half-open door and as if floating in the yellow-tinged blue air was the barber, mysteriously clad in a white blouse-like garment, cutting the hair of the man in the chair. One somewhat older man who looked like a shopkeeper lay stretched out on the bench reading his spread-out newspaper. As Setsuzō gradually approached the shop, he could hear the busy snip of the scissors clipping hair.

Without giving it much thought, Setsuzō abruptly went into the barbershop. The barber glanced around quickly, not missing a stroke with his scissor hand. The customer reading the newspaper sat up. "You'll have to wait," the customer said, apologizing instead of the barber. Setsuzō nodded wordlessly and sat down next to him. He sat toying with the parcel of books on his lap, nonchalantly looking out of the window, as if waiting for one or even two hours would be no problem. The barber snipped away earnestly and the other customer went back to reading his paper.

Setsuzō was not particularly observing the boy looking at the sign in front of the postcard shop, but on whatever part of his retina the boy's image fell, he missed not the slightest movement. The boy was, needless to say, Aihara. He had been aware of Setsuzō's approach, but once Setsuzō turned into the barbershop, he seemed to pay no more attention to him. He stood there in front of the shop intently gazing in the direction Setsuzō had come from.

Aihara seemed handsome enough. His brow was hidden by the visor of his cap, but his face glowed pink in the somewhat cold morning air. His face was smallish, with slightly prominent cheekbones. Never looking for long in one direction, his eyes moved restlessly from place to place. Unconscious of what he was looking at, he occasionally glanced at the barbershop. Whenever he did, Setsuzō was always staring vacantly over the roof of the house opposite the shop at the threads of smoke rising and disappearing into the blue sky.

All of a sudden, in the direction from which Setsuzō had come, came a single rickshaw racing at top speed around the corner, breaking the morning stillness. Instantly both Aihara's and Setsuzō's eyes were riveted in the direction of the rickshaw.

13

When the rickshaw came around the corner, Aihara suddenly and nimbly jumped to the side of the rickshaw fender as if pulled to it. He removed his hat and said, "Good morning, Otane." No reply. That was all. Her face was turned down so far that the brim of her big straw hat was almost vertical. The rickshaw man pulled on with an air of perfect nonchalance.

Aihara's actions could be considered laughable, nothing more than those of a harmless youth. Purposely to wait around every morning just to do something so foolish would seem silly to anyone else. Just as Saitō had suspected, Seikichi felt that there was little that could be done about Aihara's pranks. He was not afraid of Aihara, but neither did he want to stir up trouble unnecessarily. If he accompanied Otane safely to the top of Akasaka Mitsuke then he had fulfilled his responsibility. There was no point in starting a fight with a young man for no real reason. If this young fellow tried to inflict some harm on his passenger, then he would probably flee pulling the rickshaw behind him.

As he sat on the bench of the barbershop observing the situation, a scornful smile came to Setsuzō's face. Neither the shopkeeper-like fellow reading the newspaper on the bench next to him nor the barber busily trimming away seemed to have noticed what happened on the street at all. The industrious barber was probably so busy thinking of how much he could make for trimming one head and shaving one face that he had no time to pay any attention to what Aihara did every morning out on the street. Were that not the case, Aihara might long ago have chosen to express his homage to Otane in a different place.

Aihara ambled in the direction the rickshaw had gone.

"I'll come back on my way home," Setsuzō said as he left the shop.

"Please do," the barber replied, but Setsuzō ignored the reply and followed along behind Aihara a dozen or so steps.

Just in front of a shabby ice dealer, who in the winter became a baked potato vendor, Setsuzō called to Aihara.

"Say!"

"Are you speaking to me?" Aihara said, turning around. When he spoke, one could see delicate, almost mouse-like teeth and part of the gums between his thin lips.

Setsuzō walked on Aihara's left side so close that their elbows rubbed.

"There is something I want to ask you about. Come over there with me."

"Do you know me?" Aihara's expression betrayed nothing other than suspicion. Instinctively recognizing a certain hostility in Setsuzō's attitude and being an obstinate person by nature, Aihara's tone of voice served notice that he was prepared to stand his ground and not give in to anyone.

"Yes, I do," he replied and walked briskly on.

Aihara did not turn to look at Setsuzō directly, but rather looked at him out of the corner of his eye. When it occurred to him that that cold eye had probably been observing him since Setsuzō went into the barbershop, he was horrified. Moreover, Setsuzō's stony, masklike countenance devoid of all human emotion left him more and more uneasy. The desire to get away from this fellow by some means or another gradually grew within him. What would he do if Aihara just dodged him and made his escape? Surely he wouldn't chase after him, catch him, and beat him up. Thinking such things, he suddenly looked around him and realized that their rapid progress had brought them north of Aoyama Dori and as far as the corner leading to the cemetery.

Setsuzō silently turned at the corner and Aihara meekly followed him. Aihara hated this side street and never came this way, because it reminded him of the days when he had played there dressed in a kimono with a red muslin sash. Here was the house where he used to live. The large earth-floored room was swept clean and there were star anise and cut flowers piled up on the memorial shelf that was attached along one wall. Although different people were living there now, it almost seemed as if his mother in her maidenly coiffure might at this very moment be in the kitchen waiting to come running out and scold him for picking the flowers on the shelf. In the very instant that he recalled his mother's coiffure, he remembered another coiffure, and his eyes moved timidly from the right side of the road where he had lived to a tea shop on the left-hand side. That was where Kii-chan, a girl he had gone to elementary school with, lived. She had just recently taken a husband and he had once seen her wearing a red silk hair ornament as do young brides. Kii was the first woman to make Aihara aware of his masculinity. When he had seen her the other day on the street in Aoyama, sho looked at him with a queer, mocking expression that had left him ill at ease. She looked at him in the way one animal that is satiated with food might look at another, starving, animal. Aihara looked at the tea shop hoping that the red silk hair ornament might be there, but it was not. Her mother stood at the counter talking to some man who looked like a merchant.

When they reached the place where funeral services were held, it appeared that there was a funeral today also. The name of the bereaved family was written on a piece of paper stuck to the square glass pane of the door. A receptionist dressed in a thin *haori* stood at the desk. Both in front of the window and in the street stood several funeral attendants with rather bored expressions on their faces.

Setsuzō walked on quickly. Aihara, marveling at himself, kept up the pace, as if he were completely devoid of will.

Walking along, Setsuzō could see Aihara's pale pink ear. The cheek and neck around the ear were so white that it seemed as if they were covered with white face powder and this pallor turned bluish as it approached his hairline. There was a kind of softness in the skin from his face to his neck. But as a woman he would be no beauty. Setsuzo thought to himself that in a Western hairstyle his face would look like any ordinary girl student's.

They walked along the fairly wide path that traversed the cemetery. The path was bordered on both sides by low hedges of Chinese hawthorn and over the hedges one could see a wide variety of tombstones arranged in no apparent order. The sounds of a locust chirring came from somewhere, and then it was joined by several others. With an audible beat of wings, a locust flew from a nearby crepe myrtle and everything became silent.

Suddenly Setsuzō said, "Let's sit down over there," pointing to a narrow branch road on the east side where the morning sun shone on the low hedge casting netlike shadows on the red earth. He could have been a friend getting ready to tell his closest friend something important.

Aihara looked in the direction in which Setsuzō pointed. Along the small crosspath five or six yards away was a large new tombstone enclosed by a new white wooden fence, and placed in front of the fence was a low granite basin.

Setsuzō sat on the edge of the basin, took out from his pocket a pack of Cameo cigarettes, which at the time were being imported in great quantities from America, lit one, and offered one to Aihara.

"I don't smoke. Just what is your business with me?" Aihara stood facing Setsuzō.

"Come, have a seat," he replied, moving a bit to one side.

Aihara hesitated, then sat down on the edge of the basin.

"I hate beating around the bush, so I'll make it simple." Setsuzō smoked his cigarette and glanced at Aihara out of the corner of his eye. Just like a friend making idle conversation, Setsuzō continued in a relaxed manner. "I hear you have been waiting around every morning to say hello to the Tanidas' daughter, like I just saw you do. I want you to stop doing that."

Aihara took a quick look at Setsuzō, but when his fidgety eyes met Setsuzō's calm gaze which held some deeper meaning, they quickly turned aside. Aihara had expected something like this. But that should have been the conclusion of the conversation. Surely there should have been some scouting out of the terrain and then a showdown before the decision was made. It was like awaiting a bold frontal attack, only to be attacked by surprise from the rear. He was speechless for a moment. Awake in the still windless morning air, he had fallen into a trance. The morning sun, bearing the strength of summer, kissed the leaves of the cypress which stood in front of the graves before them, and the faint quivering made the eye rove here and there. The more he thought about how he should react and then what attitude to assume, the more distressed he became at his indecisiveness and the more confused became his train of thought.

"You like her, don't you?" Setsuzō probed again.

In any event Aihara had to do something. "I don't quite understand. Just who are you to be telling me what to do? What's so unusual about saying hello to someone I see on the street all the time? What's wrong with that?" He grumbled on and on to himself, but in a final, sharp outburst he said, "I don't understand!" As the sharpness of his own voice reached his ears, he became greatly emboldened. A brute force which until then had lain asleep below the threshold of his consciousness was awakened by this cry and raised its head.

"Humph," replied Setsuzō, as if exhaling through his nose. "Guess I'm a bit late in explaining, but my name is Yamaguchi. I'm a student boarding with the Tanidas. For the time being, it doesn't make much difference whether your actions are improper or not. I don't like complications. Just tell me, will you stop, or won't you?" He threw his half-smoked cigarette on the ground and shifted the tied-up bundle from his left knee to his right knee.

"How rude!" Aihara spoke even more shrilly, almost shouting, and stood up. His eyes, which slanted upward at the corners, seemed moist and they stared fixedly at Setsuzō. His thin lips lost their color and trembled. With a deep breath, he drew up his miserable shoulders and swaggered a bit. Although Aihara had only a folded notebook stuck in the left pocket of his cloak, at that moment he thrust his right hand into his trouser pocket searching for something.

Setsuzō warily observed Aihara's conduct. His extreme composure, neither angry nor intense, had the effect of restraining Aihara. Had Aihara been a fool with blind brute strength, he might have been able to strike Setsuzō at that moment. As chance would have it, Aihara was sensible. From the very beginning, he had felt intimidated by Setsuzō's height and sturdiness and, as Setsuzō had given him absolutely no opportunity to make use of his usual tricks, he was disheartened, and a look of suspicion returned to his face. Aihara's usual course of action was to use intimidation, making use of others' nervousness and lack of composure. Applied to timid young boys and to even more defenseless girls, it had brought repeated success. What he gripped in his pocket with his right hand was a weapon of intimidation—a small, unloaded pistol.

At almost the precise same instant, Setsuzō calmly began to speak and Aihara removed his hand from his pocket.

"Don't get angry. All I want to know is whether you will honor my request or not."

"And just what do you intend to do if I don't?" Although Aihara's tone was more relaxed, his eyes flashed sharply.

"I haven't thought about that yet. I'm just asking." As Setsuzō indifferently delivered this undiplomatic, almost inane reply, a smile crossed his face. It was not a smile of scorn, but seemed intended only for himself.

For the third time, a trace of suspicion came to Aihara's face. In his heart sprang up feelings of slight fear mingled with respect.

"You're a strange fellow."

Setsuzō laughed out loud. "Yes, maybe I am. Maybe I am, but leave the Tanidas' daughter alone. They say she's not even a woman yet." As he spoke, he repeatedly pushed over and then set upright the bundle which was on his lap.

Setsuzō's concluding statement satisfied Aihara's self-respect and in that moment he realized he had found a felicitous opportunity to withdraw from the conflict. Aihara suddenly felt as if a cool, gentle breeze were playing about him from head to toe. The ancient Chinese philosopher Chuang-tsu says that if a man crosses a river and an empty boat bumps into his, no matter how hot-tempered he may be, he will not be in the least angry. That may be the attitude of the sages, but there was something very similar in Setsuzō's own attitude.

"I'll quit," said Aihara, suddenly.

"At that moment they heard the sound of small stones being ground by the wooden *geta* of some people who had turned down the small lane where they were. Two women were coming to visit a grave. The first to appear was a slender woman dressed in a black crepe *haori*, whose white complexion and simple Western manner of doing up her hair lent her an air of awesome beauty. Following behind her was a maid carrying star anise.

Aihara looked sharply at the first woman. Setsuzō glanced indifferently at the same woman as he got to his feet, turning quickly back to Aihara. "Well, thank you. My apologies for being so rude. Goodbye." He set off toward the path which ran through the middle of the cemetery. Aihara followed after him, and when he passed by the woman, he stared right at her. The woman turned her face aside.

When Setsuzō reached the main path, he doffed his hat slightly and again said good-bye. He turned off to the left.

"Goodbye. Your name is Yamaguchi, right?" Aihara made the same gesture as he turned in the opposite direction, the one they had come from.

"That's right. Yamaguchi," he said over his shoulder, walking off with long strides toward the south.

Aihara stood for a moment watching Setsuzō's retreating figure, took one more look in the direction the woman had gone, then casually turned toward Aoyama.

14

When Setsuzō set out walking alone once more, Aihara's sharp white, mouse-like teeth and the constant movement of his eyes, never settling on one place, unconsciously came to his mind. And accompanying that image was a ticklish, exciting sort of unpleasantness. From the moment Aihara had said he would quit, Setsuzō had felt himself become strangely friendly toward him and he felt this disagreeableness even then. He wondered why. Aihara seemed to be showing off and parading all the time. He would show a flash of temper. He would show his amiability. A man who makes it his business to seduce women has to be that way. And Aihara was not entirely conscious of doing it. It had become a habit and his expression had become almost a reflex. From a woman's point of view, there was nothing so conspicuous as to make his mannerisms unpleasant. Of, course, the kind of women whom Aihara dealt with would not feel it. At the same time, one would have to entirely detest and anathematize the deceiver, the deceived, and anyone who witnessed the event, and to become righteously indignant.

From Kasumi-chō to Higakubo, purposely choosing the narrow back streets, Setsuzō continued walking, thinking about nothing in particular. Although not as intense as at the height of summer, the rays of the sun which shone from the cloudless sky were dazzling. Setsuzō neither perspired nor grew tired. He was still full of a healthy strength which had not diminished at all since his childhood—an obstinacy which, in order to repel any external challenge, had never even once lapsed into relaxation or self-indulgence. Even though he tried to imagine the way Aihara lived, it was as if he were trying to imagine the life of a completely different species of animal, and he could not detect any point in common, nor sympathize with him. Following women around. Just like a dog, he wanted to jeer. Setsuzō lived a completely stark existence. People like Aihara lived an existence entirely of outer clothing. It occurred to Setsuzō that if there were splendor in that, then this life was cheap and superficial—like paint. However, it was impossible for Setsuzō, once some such thought had entered his mind, to hold out and not try to imagine both sides of the coin. Once he saw one face of a coin, he had to turn it over to see the other. Wait a minute. Maybe he was being foolish. He tried ridiculing himself. Maybe they had meat and skin and all he had was bones. That was so contradictory to his own present physical sensation that he laughed to himself.

Upon arriving at school, he discovered most of the students were amusing themselves on the athletic field because the lecturer for rhetoric, which followed his course on the Chinese classics, had failed to appear. Among the students were some who received large allowances from their families and they had gone to the Western-style restaurant directly across from the school in order to drink tea. Others had gone to neighboring classrooms partly for fun. Normally at such times, Setsuzō went to the applied chemistry laboratory. For the students who lacked a basic knowledge of chemistry, there were partly popularized lectures without special apparatus, but the lecturer of this course attempted a variety of experiments with the rudimentary equipment and paltry chemicals which were provided. Occasionally he would bring a chart he had drawn himself, pin it up on the blackboard, and give an explanation. At other times he would even buy chemicals for experiments with his own money. He made an eccentric hobby out of seeing how much he could teach absolute beginners with little or no equipment. He was bald despite his youth, disproportionately tall, and jocular, and his name was Kudō. No matter what lecture Setsuzō heard, he would search out the metaphysical principles in it and was unable to avoid making some sarcastic criticism of them. But Kudō's lecture was always too much for him, because Kudō was merely describing and pointing out facts. His lectures never lapsed into dullness.

Today, however, the period was already half over and there was no other lecture he wanted to sit in on, so Setsuzō went to a place where he could view the sea. His eyes rested on the water, from the battery where the surface sparkled like silver in the sun's rays to the muddied ashen-gray water off the coast where sailing vessels plied their way. At such moments, if someone among his classmates appeared and tried to strike up a conversation, he would respond sociably, but he would never initiate a conversation himself or become so involved in a topic that he would carry it on at much length. Even in a brief exchange, a perceptive fellow would detect any number of expressions which artlessly destroyed commonplace feelings or "illusions," and later that fellow would recall them and feel ashamed that his own experience and training were insufficient. Some people go on chattering as they wish, completely ignoring the other person, among them each and every human being continually subservient to the natural impulses toward nourishment and procreation. Carrying on tedious, vulgar discussions, they think they are smashing the mask of hypocrisy, like pirates talking about plunder among themselves. On these occasions, when such a person trapped him and began to talk, Setsuzō would suddenly fall silent. The person would be startled, and when he came to notice that Setsuzō's vacant stare, which seemed to be fixed imperiously on something of absolutely no value, was actually settled upon his own face, he would begin to feel uneasy and turn to retreat. Today, Setsuzō was of no mind to catch birds in his net, and no bird of any kind came to be entangled.

In the reflection of the sun on the scaly waves just in front of the battery, Setsuzō noticed a gull, gleaming silver, taking flight, then suddenly returning to the water. Close up, the bird was a dirty ashen gray, but then he remembered that it was that bird, the one which revealed that momentary brilliance. Everything beautiful and good in the world was just a momentary sparkle, which on closer examination turned out to be an ugly gray. Always to write about the bright aspects of life was to describe an evanescent brightness, but to write of the dark side of things was to express the reality. Even writers who tend to look at the brighter side of life try to write about the unusual, don't they? Ordinary life is meaningless and worthless, so they seek out the transitory flash of brightness. The writer who sees the dark side of life recognizes the true value of the gray and commonplace. Among them are some who eulogize that grayness like a woman who adores clothes for their chic and elegance. Some caressingly describe the grayness with a kind of voluptuousness.

He himself was not dazzled by the momentary splendor, nor did he abandon himself to the grayness. He acknowledged no values. He was impartial and disinterested. If he were to write something, it would be more disinterested than anything anyone had ever written. He would write pages of unparalleled balance. People would, of course, probably call his writings "heartless." Nonetheless, as he was thinking how he could find nothing to write about, he again recalled that fellow Aihara whom he had met that morning. For some reason or other, he did not appear to amount to much. He would have to get inside Aihara, project his own feelings inside him, and set them to work. It would require that he set his own feelings in concert with Aihara's but it seemed that such points of contact were quite rare. When they had parted, thought Setsuzō, he had had the feeling that Aihara wanted to get to know him better. If Aihara were to take steps in that direction, would he respond to them? Maybe they would be able to discover some elements for contact between them. But in order to write a work of literature, to get the impetus to write something, to *have* to write, certainly required finding a great number of common elements. Discovering sufficient factors in this instance seemed extremely unlikely.

There might be partial truth in the theory that literature is constructed by the impetus of instinct, but those who hold that that is all are going too far. That may be so with a work of literature which has few restraints, like a novel, but when it comes to writing a play, instinct alone would not be enough to carry it through. Of course, it would be necessary to use an outline as a means for "administering" those impulses, but depending upon the subject, for the time being, he could take the first step by making an outline, then later fill it out with what he could obtain from his own experience. His considerations would move from one point to another and never stop.

The bell rang. Students who had scattered here and there, basking in the sun or indulging themselves in idle chat, each headed toward his own classroom. Watching the others, Setsuzō followed after. In his heart, he realized he had just engaged in an unprofitable exercise, and a smile rose to his face.

15

Even since he had entrusted Setsuzō with the task of rescuing the Tanidas' daughter Otane from the net which had been thrown about her, Makiyama had been continually uneasy. In the evening of the day following their conversation, and again the next evening, Makiyama had hoped he would by chance meet Setsuzō as he strolled past the Tanida residence. But both times Setsuzō was not to be seen. Being both frank and timid by nature, Makiyama let his uneasiness get the better of him and at last, on the third day, he manufactured some excuse and, peeking in the Tanidas' entranceway, was told that Setsuzō had gone out for a walk.

"Surely he wouldn't just leave the matter as it stands, after I begged him so earnestly," he thought as he returned to his own gate, arriving at the same moment as his son Shigetarō came back from school.

When he saw his father, Shigetarō came quickly up to him. "Father, I have something very interesting to tell you." His eyes sparkled with the excitement of what he had learned and his enthusiasm in passing it on.

"What is it?" his father asked, passing through the gate in front of him.

Drawn into the house by his father, Shigetarō looked up at his father, pouting. "Very interesting. Very interesting," he repeated as he made false starts at removing his sandals, stepping on the other footwear already in the entrance.

"What is it? Now calm down and tell me." Makiyama spoke as if in admonition as he sat down in his usual place. Since his mind was still full of Aihara and he supposed that the interesting story his son was so eager to tell had nothing to do with Aihara, Makiyama was in no hurry to hear what it was.

"What's the meaning of leaving your hat and schoolbooks lying around like this?" said Mrs. Makiyama as she came into the room. Noticing the glitter in Shigetarō's eyes, she sat down.

Shigetarō threw his hat and books aside and began to tell his story. "Everybody at school has been talking about it today. That Yamaguchi who lives with the Tanidas is really something. Aihara gave in to him completely. Everyone calls Aihara "Miss," but I always call him "puffed-up Aihara." When I get a little bit bigger, I'll never back down from someone like that who isn't strong or anything, but everybody is afraid of the looks he gives them and they stay clear of him. But Yamaguchi got the better of him, yes he did. And you know, it was me who told Father about what had happened, and he asked Yamaguchi to do something about it, so I told everyone how I had been responsible for the whole business, how Yamaguchi was a friend of my father's."

His father waited impatiently for him to get to the point. "Who cares about that! Just what did Yamaguchi do to Aihara?"

"Oh, that?" Finally Shigetarō got around to telling what had occurred. "Aihara had been waiting for the Tanidas' daughter and when her rickshaw appeared, he stood right in front of it and said, 'Young lady, when will you favor me by complying with my desires?' The rickshaw man crouched cowering by his vehicle. Then all of a sudden, Aihara took her hand. At that moment, Yamaguchi, who had been sitting in a nearby barbershop, pretending to read a newspaper, but actually keeping an eye on the scene in the street, came flying out of the shop, grabbed Aihara by the arm, and whispered in his ear, 'Come with me.' Then he walked off quickly, pulling Aihara behind him. Completely nonplussed, Aihara wondered where he was being dragged off to. Finally, they reached the road in Aoyama and turned down a side street in the cemetery. With Aihara's elbow in his grasp, so he couldn't break away, Yamaguchi walked along nonchalantly so no one passing by would notice anything amiss. Aihara walked as if in a trance. When they reached the middle of the cemetery, Yamaguchi released his grip on Aihara's arm.

"At that instant, Aihara felt as if he were waking from a dream and he exploded in anger. With a determination born of emergency, he pulled out the pistol he kept in the right pocket of his trousers and pointed it at Yamaguchi. 'My name is Aihara,' he said, 'and you owe me an apology. You may be stronger than I am, but I'm just as brave. Now apologize. At once, or I'll shoot.' In a flash, Yamaguchi flew forward and smashed the arm that was holding the pistol. The pistol dropped to the ground. Completely self-possessed, Yamaguchi said, 'We've got some things to talk over. I want you to stop speaking to the Tanidas' daughter.' Seeing Yamaguchi's stance, Aihara gave in. 'Even the haughty Aihara will submit to you. I was wrong, so please forgive me. I completely resign myself over the Tanida girl,' said Aihara most politely. 'You will, huh? said Yamaguchi. 'I've been rude myself, so please accept my own apology.' 'Not at all, it's been my pleasure to meet someone like you.' Aihara put out his right hand, and Yamaguchi reached his own out to shake hands. For a moment they silently looked into each other's eyes. When their hands parted, a tear appeared in Aihara's eye. 'Please think of me as your little brother,' he said. Yamaguchi nodded silently. As Aihara stooped over to pick up the pistol, he said, 'The Machine cannot prevail over the Spirit, can it?' "

<h2 style="text-align:center">16</h2>

When Shigetarō finished, Mrs. Makiyama's eyes were wide open, as they were whenever she was surprised by something. "Why, that's frightening. Shige, you be careful yourself. What with even students carrying around pistols and things like that, there's no telling who might end up with what kind of injury. Isn't that so, dear?" she said, looking at her husband. "Isn't there some way to keep children from carrying around pistols?"

"Of course there's a regulation concerning such things," he replied. His educator instincts, regardless of the subject at hand, never let an opportunity to educate the members of his household slip by without comment. "Merchants are required to fill out a report on who bought what kind of firearm or ammunition and when. In all probability, Aihara is carrying a pistol for self-defense which he bought using his lenient mother's name. That doesn't mean that every student is walking around with a pistol in his pocket."

"Well, that may be true. Our Shige is the type who doesn't like violence, so it's all right, but if we're not careful, there's no telling what might happen."

Shigetarō, listening somewhat elatedly, as if he held his parents in contempt, inserted a few words into the conversation. "If you go around trembling all the time, saying that things are dangerous, you won't be able to do anything. You won't even be able to play football, if you play it half seriously. You just can't stop and think about the danger."

"See what I mean," said Mrs. Makiyama, her eyes meeting her husband's.

"A man has to do things even though it is dangerous; he just does not have to go out and look for danger. 'Deporting oneself with abandon' it's called." Shigetarō's father dredged up a quotation he had heard someone use somewhere.

≈

It was the same day that the Makiyamas' son had come home from school and related to his parents so admiringly the deeds of the hero. Mrs. Tanida became worried when her daughter failed to return from school at the normal time, and she went out to the front gate to wait for her.

In the distance, she recognized the hair ribbon of her daughter riding homeward in the rickshaw. As always, her shoulders appeared pitifully narrow and delicate, and her chest, which had, until recently, been entirely boyish, was just beginning to fill out. With her slender frame and the summer kimono she was wearing, yellow with auburn and brown stripes, highlighting her unadorned, extremely white complexion, she attracted from far away the admiring stares of passersby. Her mother was justifiably proud of her daughter every time she looked at her. The particular weave of her kimono was not a customary one for the general public, but many of the students at that upper-class girls' school wore it. When the heat began to lose its strength and most people changed to flannel or serge, the imperial princesses, who did not wear such materials, put on this special yellow Hachijo weave. The other students became accustomed to it and began wearing it themselves.

The rickshaw came closer and closer, but the girl did not notice her mother waiting for her at the gate. It was not at all that she was putting on airs; it was just that whenever she went out for a walk, she never looked around her, but always looked straight ahead, and this habit made her seem most genteel.

At first, her daughter's face had seemed one white blur, but now Mrs. Tanida could distinguish the eyes and eyebrows. The splendid beauty of her daughter's features was such that, even though she was completely aware of them, they struck her afresh each and every time she saw them. The instantaneous impression they created defied the memory's recollection. Feeling this, a smile came to her face. At the same moment, her daughter finally noticed her standing there and broke out into a joyous smile.

The rickshaw stopped at the gate and Otane got out.

"Why are you so late today?" her mother asked.

"I don't know. I thought I was coming home at the usual time. Today our teacher finished lecturing early and spent the rest of the time telling us all kinds of interesting things. Perhaps that's what made me late." The daughter who was awaited so impatiently by her mother was extremely easygoing.

Carrying her bundle of school things, Otane virtually bounded into the entrance of the house. Her mother followed behind, but was stopped by Kisaburō, the rickshaw man, who was wiping the sweat from his face and neck with a small cloth. "Madam," he said quietly, "about that, uh, young man you were worrying about earlier. Well, it seems that he has finally disappeared. I didn't see him anywhere today."

"I see. That's fortunate. All the same, keep up your guard and be careful," she said. Then she followed her daughter into the house.

That was the first time anyone in the Tanida household had heard about Mitsutarō's having given up waiting for Otane and teasing her on her way to school. However, Mrs. Tanida had not paid too much heed to the rickshaw man's comment. The fact that a student greeted her along the way had not seemed to be such a dreadful thing in the first place, and, after all, just because he had not shown up on that particular day did not necessarily mean that he had given up his continued mischief altogether. In fact, as she turned her attention to dinner preparations, the rickshaw man's comment was the thing furthest from her mind.

That evening after sunset, Fuyu the maid came in after answering the door to tell Mrs. Tanida that Mr. Makiyama had come and wanted to speak with her. "Please show him in here." "He's in Yamaguchi's room right now," Fuyu said as she went out to convey the mistress's message.

In a moment, Makiyama walked in. Mrs. Tanida immediately noticed something different in his bearing, something different from the times he came with mundane subjects like taxes to discuss. In his behavior was something more ceremonious and something out of harmony with his normal attitude. However, he did not seem to be bringing a matter which warranted anxiety or worry. Rather, he had the expression of someone coming to announce some felicitous news.

At any rate, Mrs. Tanida recognized a difference and she was eager to discover what he knew. But it was not easy to get Makiyama to reveal his business when he came before a social superior. First, he casually commented on the weather. Next followed a long, drawn-out conversation resulting from his commenting with relief that it had grown cooler, and then moving on to expressing condolences for the suffering they were enduring due to the continued presence of striped mosquitoes in their house, a fact which he had learned from Yamaguchi. Then he brought up an item or two from the political page of the newspaper, and another from the social columns. Finally, just as his listener thought the preliminaries were over at last, he would straighten his posture anew and inquire about the health of the members of the family. This could never be omitted, even though they might have met and talked about everyone the previous day. Of course, at that point his listener would at least have to make some general inquiry about the members of his family.

At first, Mrs. Tanida sought to include some comment in her responses to his inquiries which would obviate further preliminaries, but this ended in complete failure, so she resigned herself and listened calmly. It was extremely irritating, but there was not sufficient willfulness within her to cause her to reveal her mood.

At length Makiyama came to the topic of concern. Needless to say, it was the negotiations between Aihara and Yamaguchi which he had heard about from his son Shigetarō. He endeavored to relate the details in just the right sequence, in order to have the greatest effect possible, revealing a certain element of pride.

Recalling what she had heard from the rickshaw man, she pricked up her ears in spite of herself. She was particularly stirred by the mention of Aihara's carrying a pistol.

"What a wild one he must be! Then it's an even greater wonder that he agreed with Yamaguchi."

"It certainly is. Nowadays people can't do such things. I considered a variety of possibilities, but decided there was nothing to do except ask Yamaguchi's help."

"I can't tell you how grateful we are to you. We have been inadvertently lax in this matter. Why, we had no idea how dangerous the situation really was."

She was deeply happy and even went so far as to serve Makiyama some cakes from Fūgetsudō, which someone had brought as an expression of appreciation for her husband's correcting a manuscript. When Makiyama left, he seemed entirely changed from when he arrived. His unprecedented success had made him elated.

From that time onward, Setsuzō was treated deferentially by the Tanidas. He was still addressed with the honorific, but the tone of voice was different. Furthermore, the word endings used in conversations with him became inconspicuously more polite. One day after Setsuzō returned from school, Mrs. Tanida passed by in the hall and saw him eating his meal. She quickly returned to her room and called the maid.

"When Mr. Yamaguchi has his meals, O-Hatsu doesn't seem to be serving him. Why is that?" asked Mrs. Tanida.

"Mr. Yamaguchi always says it's not necessary to go to such trouble. And O-Hatsu is quite busy, anyway."

"That may very well be true, and when she is busy, we'll have to ask him to serve himself, but in general she should serve him. And one more thing. Mr. Saitō takes meals with the rest of you, but you should also serve him as much as possible. After all, he is a student, too." The preferential treatment extended to Yamaguchi affected even Saitō.

In the manner Setsuzō was treated kindly, but he did not become more familiar with the head of the house or his wife. He was, in a manner of speaking, treated with awe. If one may turn the expression "keep one at a respectful distance" around, in this instance one wanted to say that he was respected because he was kept at a distance. The Tanidas maintained the fixed distance between themselves and Setsuzō, but took great care in all their dealings with him.

Setsuzō knew that the reason the Tanidas were treating him so well was because of what Makiyama had told them. Then this occurred to him: Makiyama's tale had been a bit exaggerated and Setsuzō wondered whether the master or his wife would renew their expressions of gratitude. And then, when he tried to imagine the situation, he felt a ticklish, unpleasant sensation. The way things stood, nothing would come of it. It seemed they had no intention of expressing their gratitude in words, but rather they expressed it in deeds. They were conventional in whatever they did, and this was a perfect example of that trait.

By the time Setsuzō realized this, about twenty days had passed since the incident in question. It was already the beginning of October. One day, upon arriving home from school, he noticed an unfamiliar object on his desk. It was a large inkstand. It was made so that one could insert red ink and black ink side by side, and there was a groove in front in which one could lay a pen. It was such a large thing that it would fit only the largest of desks, but even in such a place, it was too big for practical use. But the body was silver, inlaid with gold, and the craftsmanship was superb. Setsuzō was wondering why this inkstand was on his desk, when he looked at it even more closely and saw, on the hinged lid of the jar for ink, a symmetrical design on the circumference to right and left and in the middle two individual letters: S and Y. At the instant he saw those letters, he realized that the inkstand was his, and, furthermore, that it was a gift to thank him for what he had done in the "incident." He noticed someone stirring in the hallway behind him.

17

Turning around and seeing the mistress behind him, he said, somewhat
flustered, "Mrs. Tanida?" Regardless of the situation, Setsuzō had never
revealed a loss of self-control to any man. But when he suddenly had to
speak to a woman, he felt as if he were under surprise attack by some adversary. This quirk was not the result of a form of respect for women. Therefore,
whenever he exhibited this confused state of mind to someone, he later felt
dissatisfied with himself. He had once mulled over the probable cause of
this reaction and had concluded finally that it was a physiological response.

Mrs. Tanida wore an expression of pleasure as she came in and sat down
across the desk from Setsuzō.

"We ordered that for you quite some time ago, but it wasn't delivered
until today. My husband said that something which you could use for years
to come would be best, but he wouldn't make any concrete suggestions. I
was really in a quandary. I finally asked him what he would be most pleased
with if he himself were receiving something and he replied that he would
probably be happy with an inkstone. I reminded him that you always write
with a pen, rather than a brush. He thought for a moment, then suggested
an inkstand. Well, that was as far as it went, until someone who works at the
design department of the Bijutsu Shōkai in Kyōbashi came in order to have
some manuscripts corrected. My husband asked if there wasn't something
they could do. The man replied that an inkstand would be fine and that it
could be made as elegant as one desired. So we asked him to order it from
Bijutsu Shōkai for us. What do you think, Mr. Yamaguchi? Do you like it?"

Setsuzō smiled appreciatively. "I see. I don't have any likes or dislikes,
but this is truly an elegant piece. I don't really know what I could have done
to deserve it." Having said that, he felt again that ticklish, unpleasant sensation and was most uncomfortable. He had responded in the only way possible and was uninterested in hearing her answer.

Mrs. Tanida responded without hesitation. "Don't you remember? Why,
this is our way of showing how much we appreciate all the trouble you took
in helping Otane."

"Really? But that was nothing at all. However, I certainly do appreciate
this." Setsuzō thought of nothing else besides bringing the conversation to
as rapid a conclusion as possible.

"We wanted to find something you would like, but really we were not
sure what to choose," she added, rising from the desk.

≈

At about that time, Setsuzō began to recognize a certain student at school. Setsuzō guessed that the boy was a year or two younger than himself. The boy did not appear to have any close friends and he was always off by himself, reading a novel tucked inside an exercise book. He seemed bright enough, but rather aloof, his eyes shifting constantly from place to place. On one occasion he was walking about the school grounds staring up at sky, when some acquaintances called his name. He answered in a great flurry, as if he had been wakened from a dream or as if his soul had been called back from some great distance. "What an odd fellow," Setsuzō had thought, and thereafter he remembered the student's face.

After two days of cold rain, the sky cleared and became a bright, deep blue. As he often did between classes, Setsuzō walked out to the grassy area where he could view the sea. He stood all by himself looking at nothing in particular and thinking about nothing in particular. The student came up nearby, and throwing out his legs sat down on the slightly damp lawn. From his sateen wrapping cloth he took out the novel which he carried with his exercise book and began to read. As he removed the book from his bundle, Setsuzō absently looked at the cover. He recognized it as a novel by Izumi Kyōka which was published by Shunyōdō.

After reading a mere two pages, the fellow stuck his finger in the book to mark his place, closed it, and looked around. Setsuzō felt the student's gaze come to rest on him and as he turned in that direction their eyes met.

"Do you ever read novels?" the fellow asked unexpectedly. From his appearances, he seemed entirely naive. The question had occurred to him and he had merely asked it.

"Are you asking me?" Setsuzō replied, looking at him as if trying to read his mind.

"Actually, for a long I've been thinking that a person like you probably reads novels."

"A person *like me?*" Setsuzō continued looking at this unusual character before him.

"Well, you just seem different from the rest," he explained, putting the volume back in his bundle. He turned around to look at the large group of their classmates who were raising a clamor on the school ground.

Setsuzō smiled unconsciously. "So, since I'm an odd fellow, I probably read novels, is that it?"

"I didn't mean it that way."

As if to head off the boy before he could say anything else, Setsuzō added, "Yes, I do." His language turned abruptly rough. It was his nature to throw off polite language as one would throw off dangling, uncomfortable clothing, at one's earliest convenience. Of course, this attitude included a certain contempt for the other person.

"Is that so?" The fellow was evidently pleased. He quickly pressed on. "What do you think of Kyōka?"

"Are you among his admirers?" Setsuzō parried, withholding his own opinion.

"Yes, I like him very much," replied the questioner eagerly. "How about Rohan?" he added, seeming determined to extract a clear opinion of approval or disapproval this time, since his previous question had been dismissed.

Setsuzō felt a bit irritated, but answered casually, with the same feeling of internal strain he felt whenever he was forced to wear a tight kimono. "I read a comparison of the two in some newspaper. I like Kyōka, but I also like Rohan, so I cannot say which is better. It seems reasonable to me that I am unable to choose between them. The day is past when people considered Rohan the finest poet. At present everyone is claiming Kyōka is the best. That will pass, too. Look. From this day forth a variety of people will by turns be nominated for the seat of honor. And the heralds will take the hand of some new poet, waiting just below the horizon for the time to make his appearance. They will proclaim him the best in the land by aiding his debut. They say that the French literary world selects the 'poet-king' and it's done just that way. Poets who have come to be viewed as hackneyed elect the up-and-coming poets. In France, reasonably enough, a poet-king must pass away before a successor is chosen, but in Japan the poet royalty falls out of favor before death overtakes them."

"Do you really think so? Kyōka is the only one I find overwhelmingly interesting."

"I agree that he is interesting, but before long you'll find other writers interesting, too."

"Hmm, I wonder. My appreciation of art is like romantic love and it seems that I can go on adoring one thing forever."

A smile rose to Setsuzō's lips. "What? Don't you realize that love is not such an exclusive emotion?"

The fellow's eyes widened in astonishment and he looked at Setsuzō, wondering how to express himself. "Well, then, what should I call it? A religion? Even doctrines hold that there is one particular truth."

Setsuzō replied, as if to head off the fellow, "I don't believe in doctrines, but to me, Kyōka is interesting."

The student's eyes opened wider than before, but just as he was about to say something, the bell rang. From his kimono sleeve he took out a calling card, handed it to Setsuzō, and walked away.

On the card, in small characters, was printed the name Ikeda Hishitarō. Setsuzō glanced at the card, slipped it into his own kimono sleeve, then he too walked off toward the classroom.

18

It was evening of the day of his conversation with Ikeda. In the Tanidas' garden the insects were chirping. Everyone in the back of the house was already fast asleep, but Setsuzō was undecided whether he should turn in or not, so he made a pillow out of a stack of four or five books and lay down at his desk. From the time he had come to live in the house, there had been no set time by which he was supposed to go to bed, but from the beginning he had refrained from staying up late at night. One night he had stayed up until one o'clock reading a book when he had heard footsteps in the hallway. "Still awake?" the master of the house had asked. "Yes," he had replied. The master had said nothing more and simply walked off down the hall, but Setsuzō was worried that he might return, so thereafter he made a point of being in bed before midnight. However, once the preferential treatment began, and before he himself was completely aware of it, he began to lie down in the evening and fall fast asleep. Then he would wake up around twelve and read for two or three hours. On other nights when he was not particularly sleepy he would read until one or two in the morning without an evening nap beforehand. Every now and then the mistress of the house would comment on his having stayed up late the previous night, but there was never any trace of censure in her voice. There was a limited number of lamps in the household and it was all right to leave all the lights on all night, so no matter how late he stayed up it was no economic burden upon the family. The only thing the master did not approve of was going to sleep with a night lamp on. "It's a waste of heavenly gifts," he said. So they turned the lamps out before retiring.

Setsuzō was no daydreamer. Even this evening, stretched out on the floor, his mind did not indulge in aimless, foolish imaginings. He had once realized that fact about himself and decided that a person like himself who could not indulge in fancy could never become a poet. Again tonight he was lying down without a thought in his head. Suddenly he noticed the sounds of insects and discovered that there was a swarm of countless insects singing in the night. Exactly in the way one is able to distinguish a soprano from amongst a chorus of singers, one particular insect voice became more conspicuous than the others. Listening unconsciously, it seemed that this one insect was the only one singing. The only sounds he could hear were the ticking of the clock which hung on the wall one room away and the singing of the one insect.

For a while, his mind was blank, his ears trained on the sound of the insect, but unexpectedly his conversation about novels with the fellow Ikeda at school that day came to mind. At the same time, deep in his heart that long-lived yearning to write something reasserted itself. Actually it had been quite some time since that "something" had begun to take tentative shape in his mind. He had no desire to imitate the sorts of model to be found in the contemporary literary world. He wanted to withdraw from the periphery of mere criteria of reality and give full play to his fancies. Within these fancies, in a roundabout way, he did not intend to abandon reality. He had gradually grown able to read English more easily, and when he read Poe, he felt that a guide was showing him the way he had to take. And he also felt that this predecessor was looking down on him from some high place, laughing at the danger and recklessness of his undertaking. Today, Setsuzō, whose habit it was to speak arbitrarily and think as he wished, had contradicted the ordinary logic of address and chain of thought in his conversation with Ikeda. Setting aside his conversation as mere talk, in his mind he was in addition borrowing light from a different direction to shine upon his scheme. That is, in what he was about to write, he would have to borrow from Kyōka's delicate figurative language and follow his emotions.

Abruptly deciding to try to write at that very moment, Setsuzō sat right up, opened the notebook he had bought for taking notes at school, and began to write. The pen flowed so easily, he marveled despite himself. The words in his mind seemed to obstruct the succeeding words while he was writing, but once they had poured themselves out on paper, the next words welled up in his mind. One would think that what was being written had a life of its own and acted as it wished—that he was passively observing it all happen. Later, when Setsuzō had become recognized for his writings, and had undertaken work which had to be completed by certain deadlines, squeezing out one line at a time despite his mood, he recalled that evening and it seemed like a dream.

Setsuzō had still not thought of a title. He left space for one at the top of the page. He had contemplated the general plot construction for quite a long while and had attached the words "Newspaper Country" to it, like some kind of cipher. He vacillated between replacing that with a more appropriate title, should one occur to him, and leaving it as it was, since an artless title might be best after all.

"Newspaper Country" was a bitter satire. If this work were to include within it a glowing ardor, however, the satire would be all the more biting. Looking at things more broadly, there were certain passages which only Setsuzō, cold as ice, could produce.

Setsuzō had been strongly influenced by a piece in Poe's collected works entitled "The Devil in the Belfry," and in writing "Newspaper Country" he described the condition of the country without embellishment, as if he were writing a purely geographic description. He wrote guilelessly and without artifice, and, passage after passage, it became a venomous satire.

In this country one is not allowed to own anything except newspapers. The citizens of the country can be divided into three categories: the people whose actions become the subjects of the stories in the newspapers, the people who gather the topics and write about them for the newspapers, and those who buy the newspapers and read them. Of course, sometimes the person who is the subject of an article also writes the article and then reads it. A person who does certain things so that he will be written about may not like the way another person handles the story, so finally he decides to write it himself. He has it published. Of all the citizens who read the article, the one who is the subject of the story and who then wrote it is most exultant. Furthermore, the people whose business it is to collect news and write about it may also become the subject of the news. No, one probably ought to say that it is the aspiration of every writer to turn from writing to doing. But when that does not occur, he grows increasingly desperate and begins to write. Needless to say, it is the one who writes who is the most zealous reader. If another person writes well, it is to that person's glory, and if he writes poorly, it is to that person's shame, but he himself cannot but read his own writings without becoming enthusiastic. There are stories which are read lovingly only by the writer himself because no one else has read them. Furthermore, a person who reads newspapers for his own benefit may at the same time be both the subject of the news item and the one who wrote it down. It is remarkable that there are people who have nothing to do besides read, but they decide that even they, if they put their minds to it, can do anything—if they want to write, then they, too, can write.

The citizens of Newspaper Country are divided into these three groups by these vague demarcations; nevertheless, the distinctions may not be ignored. The reason is that if one wants to group all of the things which exist in disorder in the universe, one is obliged to make use of any distinctions which are available. Every "classification" is like that. Linnaeus' plant taxonomy is that way. And Blumenback's human races. Anyway, it is a fact that all the citizens of Newspaper Country can be divided into these three groups. No one exists outside these three. Absolutely no one.

Examining first of all the group of those who generate stories, we find one small group called politicians. They are the elite of society. Some are born into it, and others work their way up into it. The stories they generate become the second page of the newspaper. Actually what appears in the paper is the exact opposite of what they do. The positive comes out negative. The negative comes out positive. This is natural, and while this relationship is maintained, the politicians wear an air of satisfaction. When, at times, plus and minus match up perfectly, they laugh and applaud in delight. If, by coincidence, the relationship is reversed, they screw up their faces in displeasure. And they demand and receive a retraction. This method of generating stories is far from new. The constitution of Newspaper Country was only recently established, but this method existed prior to that.

In earlier ages, when there were no newspapers, there was an annually published volume of the names of politicians and their positions, a "Who's Who" similar to the Book of Heraldry of Japan (which, in the Edo period, listed all of the *daimyō* names and such things as their lineages and castle residences). In those days, a certain politician discovered that what was written about him was incorrect and he had it changed. They say that another, more prestigious politician said that such a book *ought* to be at variance with the facts, that it was supposed to be the exact opposite. He wondered how there could be someone foolish enough to have it corrected to conform to fact. How could one afford to have the reality of one's position written as it actually was? The eminent politicians of the past are just like those of today. They purposely have the opposite of the truth published on the second page of the newspaper. Since they seem to be so carefully hiding the truth, one may think that the hidden truth is really very important, but it is not the least bit significant. It is really nothing at all. They possess the merit of having the positive written as negative in the newspaper and they enjoy the benefits of having the negative written as positive. Other than that, there is no value at all. Politicians become politicians in order to generate topics for the second page. If the papers do not write anything about them, what is the point in going to the trouble of becoming politicians? That is the reason it is superficial to think that reporters who follow politicians about trying to curry favor with them seem obnoxious. If the reporters did not follow them around, their political life would become nonexistent. To make the reporter appear bothersome is one trick the politician uses in order to make the reverse of reality come to the surface. It is precisely the same as the voluptuary who says that women are a nuisance.

The vast majority of those whose actions fill the papers devote their entire energy to generating stories for the third page of the paper. These people are the most vigorous in Newspaper Country, and also the most foolish. They can see only one side of everything and they simply do not think about the repercussions of their actions. If they want something that happens to belong to someone else, they take it. If another man's wife is pretty, they make advances. If they detest someone, they attack him or kill him. And when they take action, they take the most direct method. When one thinks of "taking measures," one usually sees some sequence of actions, but there is absolutely no sequence in the methods this group uses. What they do is a single "act." Even politicians will take things, if they want them, but they will give first and take later, in order of some kind. By pushing here, they make something give there. This is especially true in having the paper write the exact opposite. Just as the group that generates topics for the third page can only see things from one angle, in the things they do there is no front and back. And the newspaper writers describe them just that way. The third page of the newspaper is plain objective description.

Those who generate the stories for the third page on rare occasion generate stories for the second page as well. This occurs when they act not independently, but as a group. As a mass. As a throng. Even a crowd can think, but its visual realm is still narrower than that of an individual and sees only one side of everything. The energy with which such a crowd acts of one accord is uncontrollable, like an act of God. Long ago in the cities of Japan, there were cases of looting the stores of rice merchants. And in the countryside, there were peasant rebellions. In France, there was the destruction of the Bastille. In Newspaper Country, the people go on strike. When this appears in the newspapers, it is included as an exception on the second page, just as it happened. Unfortunately concentration on particulars has not been discovered yet, so naturally all of the events are described in plain style.

19

The majority of writers for the newspapers are failures. They attempted to become politicians, but failed. In the age when there were no newspapers, these people wrote what were called "essays." Others made copies of them and handed them around for pleasure. In those days, men of letters still maintained their integrity. They confessed that literary work was not their specialty, but they were unfortunate and therefore they composed essays. By "unfortunate" they meant that they were "unemployed," and by "unemployed" they meant that they could not find a patron. The people who write for newspapers today openly despise that attitude as a slave complex.

"What's this?" they seem to say. "Do people think we will let someone employ us? We are not the type to be used by others. *We* make use of other people. At the moment the times are not suitable for us to rise and rule. The foolishness which the authorities are perpetrating is most appropriate for the world as it is now. We will make a record of that nonsense. For the most part, we'll just ridicule and let it go at that, but if things get worse, we will attack with the pen. Today's politicians are like the Ainu in Hokkaido or the aborigines of Taiwan. They are destined to gradual extinction. It is pitiful, but what we are writing in the newspapers is a history of their downfall."

To begin with, this is the tone of the usual writing in the papers. However, the politicians can always find a means to alter that tone. That is, they let the writers get hold of a little bit of money, or else let them closer into the fold of politics. Even when they ridicule the politicians, deep in their hearts they are grateful that politicians exist, so, if they are allowed even a brief glimpse into the inner workings of the government, they are even more grateful than if they receive some money. If they are given such a glimpse, the actions of the authorities, which heretofore have been portrayed as so much foolishness, are transformed into benevolent government which has developed from farsightedness. Factions which until then had been cruelly execrating one another become close-knit groups which must flourish for all eternity.

And yet, not all of those who write for newspapers are failures. There are lots of men with half-witted faces, dressed in velvet clothing or with long hair, who become like painters who do not paint or sculptors who do not sculpt. They do not bear the mark of Cain, but you can tell them at a glance. They lack a sense of honor, exhibit a dreadful arrogance, and advertise themselves. Noticing that such men are saying and doing the same things, some people would assume that their capacity for united action must be tremendously powerful. However, once one discovers that they are precisely like two atoms which repel one another so that they never under any circumstances unite, and that whenever any two of them gather together they quarrel among themselves, never allowing room for compromise, one can see that they are exceedingly independent. Unlike the politicians whose factions are composed of lineage, the capacity for united action which these men possess comes from a unity based on something like an enterprise trust, which is founded upon mutual advantage and which completely tramples upon everyone who is not a cohort. They bicker among themselves, but when it comes to facing outsiders, they build and defend an impregnable fortress around themselves. Newspaper writers, who are constituted from among these failures, entrench themselves within their newspapers like the powers of the world. They are like the believers of Catholicism who, although scattered around the world, act in conjunction with one another though the same spirit. These people are called "writers." A person who knows little of the situation in Newspaper Country might suppose that a "writer" creates poetry, composes novels, and writes plays, but nothing could be further from the truth. Such things can be done without forming alliances. One could almost say that you cannot do such things if you form alliances. If a person who writes such things, draws pictures, or carves sculptures may be compared to an ordinary woman, a "writer" is like a geisha. Just as there are geisha who have children, there are exceptions, but the "writers" are all barren.

These unfruitful "writers" enlist two or three others who can produce to some degree, carry them around like a portable shrine and, with a narrow gauge abstracted for their works, measure all other works and reject them as lacking something. Even if there are some points of similarity between these authors whose works are being held up for examination, each writes from his own individual character, so the authors are never the same. And if there are point of similarity occasionally, they do not form the foundation for an "ism" or anything else. The works of these authors have currency even without a hallmark, so it is worth pondering whether such creative writers ought to be grateful to the newspaper critics who support them.

Newspaper writers are roughly composed of these two types, and these types apply to virtually every youth as well as those bureaucrats pretending to be politicians and those who generate the stories for the third pages of the newspapers. From childhood, before they could even read, these newspaper writers carried around and played with magazines which had the word "youth" somewhere in the title, and by the time they started elementary school they were imitating the newspapers and magazines and making their classmates read them. At first, they wrote each character one by one, just like typesetting. Then gradually they began to copy their materials on mimeograph machines. The next step was to insert imitation of illustrations. Even here, in the germ of newspapers, were abundant falsehoods, malicious gossip, and self-serving debates. From the age when children pinch the cheek of the child in the next seat and secretly try to trade the food which they bring to school in their lunchboxes, only to be scolded by their teachers, the genius of these future "writers" has already asserted itself.

In this way, the "writers" who expound on the front pages of the papers can be distinguished from the others. Though what they write may be crowded off the first pages and relegated to a special supplement of the Sunday paper, if what they write is short enough, it will appear on the front page. In addition, there are those who write for the third page, but even if they are one and the same, the "class" is lower. The third-page variety is nothing more than a faithful, objective chronicling of who did what, when, where, and how in which black is black and white is white. However, in the middle of the article, the "writer" has to take a moralistic stance, either lauding or deprecating. Some critique is jammed into each and every article. Every fable has its final moral point, and these critiques and morals seem as if they are typeset in advance. When, on rare occasion, a pun is used, it is entirely predictable. Once in a while, some variation is used but it is an established variation. In other words, the reporters who write for the third page avoid at all costs revealing their shallow knowledge and must write in an entirely conventionalized manner. Women are by definition "beauties" and love is always "infatuation." Regardless of the subject, they are forced to arouse public indignation and denounce the events as scandalous. Christ said that men ought not to judge other men, but the columnists of the third page judge everything and everybody. No matter what kind of person he seizes upon, regardless of the person's education and lineage, he will entrap that person in every possible way and sit in judgment upon him. Perhaps that is the way of Confucian moralizing.

The third kind of person in Newspaper Country is the reader. The reader does absolutely nothing other than read the papers. It is his entire life. One may say that those who generate the stories which find their way into the newspapers include both young and old, that generally those who write for the papers are almost always young and that those who read the papers are either older people or young people who are old beyond their years. Just as they nourish their bodies with food, they nourish their spirits with newspapers. However, it may not be appropriate to use the word "spirit" in reference to them. "Spirit" somehow seems to imply something flowing, something difficult to capture. But the "spirit" of the newspaper reader, if not exactly in solid form, has viscosity like ointment or thin rice gruel. The molecules in it do not move easily. What rare movement does occur always occurs in one direction. The judgment of the newspaper writer invariably coalesces with that movement. If no judgment is provided, the reader has to make one on his own. That is as painful for the reader as it is for a cripple who is told to walk. The reader, for his own part, wants by all means for the writers to stand in his stead and think for him. And that consideration should always walk the same path and arrive at the same destination. "Disgraceful!" and such are among the most familiar destinations. Because of these people, a new, unprecedented conclusion about an event is unendurable. A change in appraisal is strictly taboo. For that reason, the newspapers which come out anew every day never age. The reader's satisfaction and pleasure rest in thinking that since old things are eternally new, those who read them are also new.

What testifies most clearly to this relationship is a column called "historical tales" which always appears in the papers of Newspaper Country. There are papers in countries besides Newspaper Country, but there is nothing like "historical tales," nothing even close. Long ago, before there were newspapers in Newspaper Country, book lenders carried around copied manuscripts of these stories in light-blue wrapping cloths tied on their back. Eventually these copies were turned into paper for sliding screens or standing screens, tanned papers, wicker clothes boxes, or the backing for cheap leather satchels, disappearing without a trace. Then, after movable type was created, they became printed books which can still be found in the stores of the main streets of the land.

The papers take these stories of family strife, which can be bought for a pittance, and cut them up into small pieces, publishing them continuously for a half year or so. When the conclusion is reached, it is perfectly acceptable to start all over again from the beginning. There is no difficulty with this because by the time the conclusion appears, the beginning has been completely forgotten. If they are afraid of the rare reader whose memory is good, all the publisher has to do is to use two or three different tales and repeat them in the same sequence. In other countries, an editor may use scissors and paste, but in Newspaper Country, at least when it comes to filling up the column in question, such materials are unnecessary. As long as a tale is preserved in typeset form, and as long as the paper is not worn and torn, it can be used repeatedly ad infinitum. For the reader, it is new. It is new because yesterday and today are different.

In this way Setsuzō divided the citizens of Newspaper Country into types and wrote about them in the manner of a description in natural history. The format was occasionally like a number of short sections, almost "studies," strung together, and in such a plot they did not seem dry or dull, but they still did not seem to form a short story. In Setsuzō's estimation, it made no difference whether the categorizations and so on were novelistic, because he intended to use that as a foundation for writing something else. The categorization of the citizens took longer than he had thought it would, and still no end was in sight. At last, dawn approached, and thinking to himself that it was better to have even a little sleep than none at all, Setsuzō lay down in his bedding.

He closed his eyes for a while, but curiously enough his mind was clear and he could not fall asleep. What he intended to write about floated up into his consciousness: the politics of Newspaper Country. A powerful politician would appear and in a kind of coup d'état attempt to abolish the newspapers. This politician would want a correspondent to report everything to suit the politician's aims and would exhaust every means, legal and otherwise, persuasive and demanding, trying to accomplish that. Still, he would be unable to leave the reporting to the correspondent without anxiety. At that point, he would sacrifice the pleasure of the times when he was lauded by the newspaper and abolish the papers. The effect of this prohibition on everyone—other politicians, newspaper writers and readers—could be of infinite variety. There would be not a few opponents of the continuance of newspapers among the politicians, but among the writers and readers one and all would oppose the prohibition. One could write quite interestingly about all the flurry this would cause. Among the possibilities were two or three conspicuously interesting events which formed in his mind like paintings, almost demanding that they be put on paper immediately: a conversation between a certain group of people, a certain disturbance on the street, and fragmentary, yet coherent, details brought forth in dense brilliance. As his mind pursued these scenes, his consciousness gradually faded, and before long he fell into a deep sleep.

1911–1912

V

SEINEN

YOUTH

Seinen

YOUTH

I

PUBLISHED OVER A PERIOD OF TWO YEARS in serial fashion, from March 1910 until August 1911, *Youth* spans much of the period covered by the second part of this collection, "Self-Portraits of The Artist." The book represents Ōgai's attempt at writing his own sort of *Bildungsroman*, or "novel of self-discovery," as the German term is sometimes translated, and in certain ways his conception surely owes something to the work that served as a model for so many later endeavors: Goethe's *Wilhelm Meister's Apprenticeship*, published in 1796. Yet while Ōgai's decision to compose such a work may suggest his attraction to this overwhelming model provided by his favorite European writer, he was evidently driven to write the book as well by the example set by his younger colleague, the brilliant Natsume Sōseki (1867–1916), whose own novel of youthful discovery of the interior life, *Sanshirō,* was published in 1908, the year before Ōgai began writing *Youth.*

Sōseki himself figures as a minor character in *Youth,* where he appears in the guise of the writer Hirata Fuseki, whose talk on the purposes of literature and the intellectual life so excites Ōgai's protagonist Koizumi Junichi. Junichi, like Sanshirō, is a young man coming from the provinces to Tokyo in order to experience the excitement of the great world he was convinced would lie before him.

Youth represents Ōgai's attempt to capture the way in which wisdom and maturity can come to the young. These concerns spill over into all his works of this period; themes that appear elsewhere in Ōgai's work at this time, notably his emphasis on self-recognition and resignation, are central to the concerns of this novel as well. Indeed, *Youth* is perhaps best read in conjunction with *Vita Sexualis,* an account from another point of view of a young man's coming to maturity, written the year before, and *Gan* (Wild Geese),

published in 1911, in which Junichi's friend and mentor Ōmura seems here
to be recast as Okada, the young medical student bound for Germany.
Indeed, a number of characters in other stories appear on the periphery of
Youth. Professor Takayama, for example, bears more than a passing resemblance to the protagonist of *Half a Day*.

The concerns taken up in *Youth* are of two sorts. Both involve the need to
find a means to make the leap, however painful, from youth to maturity.
That authentic maturity which Junichi, and thus Ōgai the author behind
him, attempts to seek out must possess two aspects, one intellectual, one
emotional. In the few months allotted his development in the novel, Junichi
achieves both.

To achieve intellectual maturity represented a complex process in a society
as rapidly changing as Meiji Japan. Junichi arrives in Tokyo hoping to
become a writer. With his thirst for Western knowledge, fired by his study of
French while still living in his home province, Junichi now finds himself
thrown into a diverse world of intellectuals seeking to establish themselves
within the parameters of a new universe of imported ideas, notably those of
Ibsen and Nietzsche. Given these heady possibilities, it is no wonder that
Junichi (as did Ōgai) finds the writings of the so-called Japanese naturalists,
caught up in picturing the details of their own narrow emotional lives, vapid
and worthy of little sustained admiration.

Still, the realm of ideas, however exciting in and of itself, is difficult for a
young person like Junichi to internalize. In the midst of one exciting discussion, Junichi's mentor Ōmura tells him that "it's the privilege of young men
like us to say whatever we feel like saying without weighing each word on a
scale." To seize upon those ideas in order to make them serve the development of one's own inner life, however, is a more difficult task. Ōgai
attempts, in this ambitious novel, to show how this challenge might best be
undertaken.

Maturity involves, moreover, an understanding of one's own physical and
emotional needs and drives. In the course of the novel, Junichi comes to
know this aspect of himself as well. He has important encounters with three
women. The first is with Oyuki, the charming young girl who lives near his
rented house. The second is with Ochara, a geisha he meets at a party he
finds otherwise unpleasant. Together these women represent Ōgai's sense of
the bifurcated nature of the traditional views taken of Japanese women.
Oyuki is the innocent girl, fresh and spontaneous; Ochara, the sophisticated
and professional purveyor of female charm. Junichi can understand the
attraction of both models but succumbs to neither. It is surely the third
woman who gives Junichi the jolt he needs in his journey forward.

Given Junichi's deep desire to become a man in the spirit of a new and liberated age, that jolt comes through his encounter with Mrs. Sakai, the widow of a famous professor and, in her way, a new woman of the sort that Ibsen put on the stage in his plays. It is not by happenstance that the two meet at the sensational Tokyo premiere in 1909 of Ibsen's *John Gabriel Borkman* (the first professional production of a modern play in Japan and staged, incidentally, in a translation prepared for that occasion by Ōgai himself). Indeed, Mrs. Sakai bears more than a little resemblance to Mrs. Wilton, one of the characters who is attracted to a young man in the play, Erhart; as he follows her abroad "to the south," so Junichi follows Mrs. Sakai to Hakone hoping to find his infatuation returned. For Junichi, Ibsen's drama which has so fascinated him in the theater now serves as an implicit model for what he believes to be the nature of his own attachment to this elegant woman. Eventually he realizes that she is merely hiding behind her own mask, an image that pervades other works of Ōgai written during this period. Ōgai attempts to synthesize, and with some success, both Junichi's intellectual and his sensual responses to Mrs. Sakai in his depiction of this one central relationship, where ideas and emotions are combined.

II

Whatever the significance of the novel for its contemporary readers at the end of the Meiji period, *Youth* reveals at least three points of great interest to us as readers now, more than eighty years later. In the first place, Ōgai's famous position as a "bystander" allows him to describe in absorbing detail a specific and highly charged sense of time and place. The novel has long been cited as a crucial source of information concerning the intellectual, social, and artistic attitudes of the period. The accounts of the first staging of Ibsen in Tokyo, the emotional tenor of student discussions, the shifting tonalities of a geisha party, the look and feel of the countryside, the city streets, even the train stations, are evocatively captured in the novel. Ōgai's text is often cited by Japanese scholars when attempting to locate an authentic account of the atmosphere prevalent during the period in which the novel takes place. The novel includes as well a number of characters whom Ōgai expects his readers may recognize. Hirata as Natsume Sōseki has already been mentioned; others include Junichi's friend Ōmura, who may be partially modeled on the brilliant doctor, playwright, and novelist Kinoshita Mokutarō (1885–1945), himself a student and already a successful critic and author at the time. Critics have pointed out that the novelist Ōishi Roka, whom Junichi meets early in the novel, resembles the well-respected writer Masamune Hakuchō (1879–1962). Then, too, there is Mōri Ōson, a satiric rendering of Ōgai himself. But *Youth* is not focused on these characters. Their inclusion in the body of the novel provides incidental pleasures, but they perform their functions in the larger scheme of the narrative without reference to whether or not the reader can recognize the originals on which they are based. Indeed, aspects of Ōgai's own personality reveal themselves through the attitudes expressed by many of these same characters, each of whom may espouse concerns central in one way or other to the totality of the author's conception.

Second, a reader in our time cannot help but be struck by the terms in which Ōgai posits the development of real maturity. In the case of Junichi, the trajectory is from passive narcissism to self-understanding and self-control. In the early sections of the novel, Junichi is dependent: emotionally on women, intellectually on his confidant Ōmura. This dual dependency creates within Junichi's psyche a writer's block; despite his deep desire to become a creator himself, he cannot find any authentic way in which to express himself and articulate his concerns. When, at the end of the novel, he arrives at a powerful and chastened understanding of his own emotional state, he finds the strength to shed his dependencies, both emotional and intellectual. At that moment, he is able to express himself as a writer for the first time.

Central among the lessons to be learned by Junichi is the need for conscious determination. Midway through the novel, Ōmura gently chides Junichi, who has as yet been able to write nothing:

> They say a man of letters makes quite a coup. But this compares art to gambling, to tossing down a pair of dice. Apparently one can become a popular writer or a best-selling novelist by mere chance. But apart from the problem of being censured these days, when one can express one's thought freely, there's no fear that a worthy work will go unnoticed by the perceptive. So you neither have to hurry nor hesitate. Once you're determined, you can start writing at any time.

At the end of the novel, after he has realized that his romantic infatuation with Mrs. Sakai is without significant meaning or foundation, Junichi achieves that sense of determination. And, precisely at that same moment, he finds himself spontaneously treated as an adult. Before his personal epiphany, he had entered his inn at Hakone as a fearful, timid adolescent whom none appeared to respect. Now, on the first day of the new year, itself a powerful symbol for fresh beginnings, he emerges as a mature man. "The innkeeper's wife came to offer thanks. What she said to him as she bowed with her hands touching the floor just outside the threshold of the room sounded quite respectful." Such respect is new; and, in Junichi's (and Ōgai's) terms, it is deserved.

Junichi comes to maturity because he finally comes to realize that, in order to create, he must truly seek within himself. Intellectual ideas and emotional relationships can feed the self and help it to grow, but true inspiration must spring from within. In one sense, this conviction may be read as a critique by the author of those writers during his period who chased after the latest imported ideas merely in order to copy them, but Ōgai's own convictions lay much deeper than any such critique suggests. Junichi decides to look into the past and write down in contemporary language a legend told him by his grandmother. (She is, in fact, a figure of some importance in the novel; she never appears but is referred to throughout with affection by Junichi.) By writing this kind of story, Junichi seeks to integrate his own cultural past with his particular contemporary understanding. Indeed, such was the path to be chosen by Ōgai himself a year later in 1912, when he began the composition of his own historical stories, a task that would occupy him in one way or another until his death in 1922. In a sense, *Youth* presents the reader with Ōgai's justification in advance for what was to become his own final choice of a compatible mode of literary expression.

The third element in Ōgai's novel that retains its fascination concerns the author's various strategies to surmount the challenges involved in trying to integrate the play of ideas into the text of a work of fiction. It might be observed, at the start, that the British and American literary traditions find little praise for any such attempts to blend philosophy and literature. Our innate prejudices against such a synthesis often give the novels of writers of the stature of even a Thomas Mann the reputation of being overloaded with abstractions. The German tradition, on the other hand, thrives on such alliances. The European model for all such novels of self-discovery, Goethe's *Wilhelm Meister's Apprenticeship,* is filled with discussions of ideas that can take up many pages, most notably the sections on Shakespeare's *Hamlet.* Ōgai thus possessed what he well might have deemed satisfactory precedents.

Then, too, Ōgai was justified in his portrayal of the ways in which students and other intellectuals sat and discussed ideas during these years. In this sense, those sections of the novel given over to such conversations can well be read as selective and sensitive reportage. Everyone in the book wants to talk, and talk on, about the intellectual currents then sweeping into the mental world of Japan, a nation itself in a new period of "youth," when stale ideas were being reexamined and often cast away by the intellectual classes. In that sense, Sanford Goldstein, the cotranslator of the novel for this anthology, showed great perception when he suggested in his notes accompanying the draft version of this translation that "the title of the novel might best be rendered in English as *Young Men,*" since "Ōgai has given us in these sharply focused portraits of youth a sense of what it was like to be a young man in Meiji Japan, the world opening up to foreign influences in literature, art, philosophy, and even psychology and sociology."

Nevertheless, on the surface, these discussions may not always appear, in and of themselves, to advance in any satisfactory way the larger purposes of the novel. Ōgai himself is quite aware of the disparity between ideas and actions, since this issue represents one of the larger themes of the novel itself. As old Professor Takayama remarks to Junichi concerning his own youthful adolescent pranks: "It's quite wrong to think students will behave morally if we force them to read the Analects of Confucius." Since Ōgai is aware of the need to combine a discussion of ideas with the advancement of the story, one cannot help but admire his often ingenious attempts to seek some credible means to do so. The scene in which Junichi tries to hide from Ōmura the calling card of Ochaya the geisha, which has been stuck in a book of Maeterlinck the two are discussing, represents one such device; Junichi's reflections on the deferential behavior of her students to their teacher Takabatake Eiko (based on the historical figure of Shimoda Utako [1855–1936], a leading champion of women's education in modern Japan) constitute another. Ōmura's discussion of Weininger's classification of women helps prepare Junichi's responses to Mrs. Sakai and the other women he encounters in the course of the narrative. His choice of a book to borrow, which includes the text of Racine's drama *Phèdre,* in which an older woman develops a passion for a younger man, is an apt symbolic choice. Junichi, however, does not read it, a signal perhaps that he will not develop a genuine relationship with Mrs. Sakai. Then there is the mysterious sequence describing Junichi's dream, the explication of which may indicate something of Ōgai's interest in the workings of the psychological mechanisms he had learned to appreciate through his readings of European research in these areas.

Nevertheless, there is little doubt that for many readers nowadays, those passages devoted to intellectual debate will on first encounter prove undramatic and therefore troubling, despite the fact that for Ōgai and many of his contemporaries, the clash of excitement these ideas produced was palpable and real. To the perceptive reader, however, some of that conviction may still come across. Then, too, a careful reading, and rereading, of the text will indicate that these debates do not represent an intrusion of merely undigested material into the course of the narrative. The nature of the debates shifts as the book moves forward, and at each level Junichi reaches toward a new and more inclusive level of self-understanding. In this sense, then, these intellectual discussions are intended to form an integral part of the whole. We learn from our mind as well as from our body, Ōgai would say, and he attempts to chronicle thoroughly both such means.

Finally, there is another way to view the accomplishments of Ōgai in this novel, one suggested in a series of telling remarks made concerning *Youth* by the great modern Japanese critic and philosopher, Watsuji Tetsurō (1889–1960). Himself a disciple of Natsume Sōseki and the author of such central works in modern Japanese intellectual history as *Fūdo* (A Climate), Watsuji maintained an admiration for the work of Ōgai in general and *Youth* in particular. In discussing the nature of that interest in the course of an essay written in 1952, he makes an important point:

> *Youth* was being serialized in the journal *Subaru* while I was around twenty-one or twenty-two. I read the novel, fully aware that its subject matter dealt with my own generation. Yet there was no erudite youth such as the protagonist among any of my acquaintances. Looking back, it now seems clear to me that for his novel Ōgai used such effective materials as his mental state when returning from Kokura to Tokyo, his study of the French language while in Kokura, and his fresh interest in the French literary arts. Therefore, his protagonist, supposedly a young man of our own age, possessed the precocious emotional responses of a literary master well into his forties. Nevertheless, it must be said that since Ōgai set out to picture a young man, the results did not seem unnatural, even though his protagonist exhibited such responses. This fact stands as proof that when Ōgai himself was young, he possessed the same sorts of precocious responses. [Watsuji Tetsurō, "Ōgai no omoide," in *Watsuji Tetsurō zenshū* (Tokyo: Iwanami shoten, 1963), vol. 20, p. 460]

Watsuji is able to observe, and to appreciate, the textual layerings of fact and fiction that give the narrative both its peculiar fascination and something of its moral urgency. Watsuji recognizes that *Youth* represents a construct, one in which Ōgai wishes to share crucial insights with his readers, who, in reading the book, can borrow the author's powerful intellectual authority in order to share in them. Thus acknowledging the construct helps create the pleasure involved in reading and understanding the text.

All art, of course, is in some sense a construct. If our own desire, so important in the British and American traditions, to maintain the primacy of mimetic imitation makes a novel like *Youth,* based as it is on other artistic principles, occasionally difficult of access, the force of Ōgai's own spiritual and intellectual concerns, recast in the multiple disguises provided by virtually every character in this novel, cannot but make *Youth* a compelling statement of what it meant to seek the highest level of truth about one's society and oneself during the years that Ōgai wrote his novel. In that sense, the author's authentic moral passion makes *Youth,* whatever may seem in our eyes to be its incidental flaws, an estimable contribution to modern Japanese literature.

I

KOIZUMI JUNICHI LEFT HIS INN on Shiba-Hikage. Despite the map of Tokyo he had with him, he kept bothering people about directions. At a Shinbashi streetcar stop, he caught a car for Ueno, and he somehow managed to make the rather complicated transfer at Suda to another car. He finally got off at Third on Hongō, turned right from Oiwake along a road bordering the First Higher School, and reached his destination, the Sodeura-kan, a boarding-house just up Omotesakaue in front of Nezu-Gongen Shrine. It was eight in the morning around the twentieth of October.

There the street forked into a T-shape. The Sodeura-kan was just at the spot where the street leading uphill from Gongenmae was cut at right angles by the road he was walking along. The painted wooden structure, looking like an oversized matchbox, seemed an imitation of a Western-style building. Above the door frame at the entrance were several resident nameplates.

Junichi stopped and scanned the names. The name he was searching for he easily found, Ōishi Kentarō, second or third from the top. A fifteen or sixteen-year-old maid, a red sash crisscrossing her turned-up kimono sleeves as she held a mop in one hand while cleaning the wooden floor at the entrance, asked him, "Who is it you've come to call on?"

"I would like to see Mr. Ōishi."

Having just arrived from the country, Junichi replied in the Tokyo accent he had picked up in reading a novel. He had uttered each word with deliberate care as if reciting an unfamiliar foreign language. That he was able to come out with an acceptable response pleased him.

The pert and precocious girl standing there holding a mop found that the eyes of this fair-complexioned young man reminded her of a chick just out of its shell. He was dressed in a lined kimono with a Satsuma splashed pattern, a Kokura *hakama* skirt, and a *haori* coat with the same splashed pattern. The fabric of his brown hat was soft, his *tabi* socks dark blue, his wooden clogs made in Satsuma. Though dressed the way ordinary students were, everything he had on was new. No one would have thought him someone from the country who had arrived at Shinbashi only the night before. The girl continued looking at Junichi in a friendly way.

"So you've come to see Mr. Ōishi?" she said. "But it's not a good time. He doesn't even get up before ten. You see, he eats breakfast and lunch together. He gets back at two or three in the morning, so he sleeps all day."

TRANSLATED BY SHOICHI ONO AND SANFORD GOLDSTEIN

"Well, I'll take a short walk and come back."

"Yes, that would be much better."

Junichi began walking toward the slope in front of Gongen Shrine. Every few steps, he took from his kimono sleeve the minutely folded road map and marched on while looking at it. Along the way he passed men dressed like government officials, university students in their square-shaped caps and high school students in their rounded ones with the usual two white lines sewed on, elementary school children, and girl students, all streaming toward Hongō. Turning right to Imasaka Lane, he couldn't see a single soul. On his right was the outer fence of the First Higher School and on his left a church partially under construction. A rickshawman who had come out of a shabby-looking house near the church asked Junichi if he wanted a ride. Ignoring him, Junichi found himself on a wide beautiful road lined with mansions surrounded either by mud walls or hedges.

Since no one other than Junichi was walking along this wide road, he felt invigorated, as if the morning air had tightened the roots of his hair. He kept thinking of Mr. Ōishi's daily life he had just heard about from the girl. He could clearly picture Ōishi, whom he had come all the way from the country to see. What Junichi had heard from the girl in no way marred the image he had of him. Instead of ruining that image, the girl's remarks seemed to sharpen it even more. The mixed feeling of awe and fear Junichi had harbored of Ōishi was given added clarity.

Junichi reached the top of the slope. Though difficult to tell from his map, this fairly wide slope formed a clumsily curved S-shape. At the top Junichi stopped and looked ahead.

Beneath the gray cloudy sky he could see the same gray color, and yet that gray color seemed to be steeped in an atmosphere both clear and transparent. Between Mukōgaoka Hill, where he stood, and Ueno Hill in the distance, clusters of houses could be seen. He felt he was seeing as many houses there as he could in his entire hometown. As he stood for a while staring at this view, he took a deep breath.

Descending the slope, he entered the gate to a shrine on his left. He walked along a granite path to the sanctuary of Nezu-Gongen Shrine. The rhythm of his clogs, which sounded like a chevron-stone Chinese musical instrument, pleased him. An antiquated fence surrounded the inner precinct behind the Zuishin-mon Gate, where wooden sculptures of warriors had been installed, their paint peeling and discolored. In a room in his grandmother's house in his village was a colorful print on a folding screen. He didn't know which shrine had been depicted on the screen, but the fence he was now seeing reminded him of the one in the print. Sitting on the veranda of the shrine was a girl with a towel around her head, a baby on her back under her padded short coat. She seemed cold huddled there. Since Junichi did not feel like offering a prayer before the shrine, he passed through another small gate and turned left. A ditchlike pond confronted him, and on a small hill he saw a thicket of trees with yellowish leaves mixed in among evergreens. Disgusted by the dirty muddied water in the pond, bubbles here and there on its surface, he left in a hurry by a back gate. He entered a narrow road called Yabushita. In front of a row of houses, each with a lattice door, were unattended carts for selling merchandise, so sometimes he had to turn sideways to get by. To his right was a dilapidated and uninhabited tenement, all boarded up. He passed it, thinking it the type of structure dubbed a "three-by-four-yard" house. Next to it was a roofed gate on which a wooden nameplate, "Irokawa Kunio's Villa," had been nailed. Since the name was unusual, he recalled seeing it in a newspaper, remembering it as the name of a Diet member or some such person, and Junichi continued on his way. Next to it was a rather dirty villa and then a house, perhaps owned by a gardener. On a hill to his left were some tall trees whose branches had been trimmed in a rough and careless way. He passed, thinking the spot a backyard of a large residence in need of repair.

As he climbed a gentle road to its flat top, whose right side formed a cliff, he could see rows of residential roofs stretching as far as Ueno Hill. As he casually looked to the left and saw a house surrounded by a bamboo fence, he was attracted by a nameplate on its gate that read Mori somebody or other, and he thought it perhaps the home of Mōri Ōson. Momentarily he glanced over its low fence.

He felt that Ōson, although a wizened old man, seemed like someone who would lose his composure if he mingled with innocent young men, a man who was always grumbling and nasty, a man who wrote novels and plays the way a surveyor measures land with a rod and tape. The mere thought that Ōson would be making a sour face on waking and would now be finding fault with the charcoal fire in the kitchen made Junichi shudder, and he left the gatepost.

As he turned right at a crossroad after descending the slope, he found to his right and left small stalls displaying chrysanthemum figures and wares. On an elevated stand at each stall a man was sitting tailor-style, more reminiscent of a slave dealer or a pickpocket as he brandished an illustrated program or something like it and kept noisily calling out to passersby, the way a ticket agent at the theater back home might have done. Since it was early morning, few people were passing, so that Junichi in going by was an easy target from both sides of the road. He wanted to look at some of the chrysanthemum figures which could be viewed outside the stalls, but he couldn't bring himself to stop. Instinctively he quickened his pace and turned right onto a wide street.

He took out his watch and glanced at it. It was still only 8:30, too early for Ōishi to be up, and Junichi turned toward Ueno Hill along a bystreet he had come upon. The narrow passageway had dirty tenements on both sides. There were shops selling salted rice crackers and kitchenware and the like. Because some of the storeroom doors of these shops were half-open, he had to walk sideways to pass. As the gutters were not built on an incline, the water was stagnant, fallen trash at the bottom. Pale and emaciated children were seen loitering around, almost as if they had no energy to get into mischief. Junichi felt he would never find such a miserable and pathetic area in his hometown.

While following the winding road, he crossed a wooden bridge over a small river and came to a district where rice fields occupied half the space, the other half with scattered houses newly built looking like disposable lunchboxes. Painted in large letters on a side of one of these houses was a sign that read "Musical Instrument Factory." He looked at it in surprise, no such sign likely in his hometown. As he continued on, he felt Tokyo was enormously different from the country.

Suddenly he took a road running along a graveyard and came to the bottom of a slope leading to Yanaka. The road reminded him of one in the country. The sun, which had been hidden behind gray clouds, now appeared, all at once shedding its yellowish and lonely yet warm light. He wondered if he should climb to the top and look over part of Ueno. He decided not to, afraid he might be late for his appointment.

A while back he had noticed a figure, possibly a student, coming down the slope. When the person came near, they instinctively exchanged glances.

"Well, if it isn't Koizumi!" the other called out.

"Seto? I didn't expect to see you. I'm really surprised."

"I'm the one who ought to be surprised. When did you get in?"

"Last night. Are you still going to art school?"

"Yes. I'm just on my way back. Our model didn't show up because she was ill. So I'm thinking of visiting a friend at Komagome."

"Do you have that kind of freedom?"

"Art school, you know, is different from middle school!"

Junichi felt his friend had put one over on him. Seto Hayato had been his classmate at middle school in Y City.

"I can't help being ignorant. I don't know a thing about art schools," Junichi said, conceding without the least bit of sarcasm. Seto himself felt sorry for him. Actually, under the pretext of an upset stomach, Seto had skipped school after taking advantage of his teacher's visit to an art exhibition. Seto, in fact, felt uncomfortable when he looked at Junichi's face with its clear black eyes, something in them like an incarnation of idealism.

Just then a somewhat winsome girl passed, perhaps seventeen or eighteen, apparently on her way shopping, her hair arranged in a low pompadour, her kimono quite ordinary. She passed so close to them her kimono sleeves almost touched them. In passing, she looked at Junichi as if boldly revealing in her look an attraction for him. As for Seto, he kept staring at her well-developed body, but apparently flustered, he turned his eyes toward Junichi.

"Where you going now?"

"I've just come from trying to see Roka, but I was told he doesn't get up until ten, so I've been wandering around the area."

"You mean Ōishi Roka? I hear he's awfully blunt. I guess you still want to be a novelist."

"I'm not sure I do."

"You come from a wealthy family, so you can do whatever you like. Do you have a letter of introduction or something?"

"Yes. After you left for Tokyo, a new teacher, Tanaka, came to our middle school. I met him at an alumni gathering. He once visited me at my home. Since he graduated from the same school as Mr. Ōishi, I asked him for a letter of introduction."

"That should do it. I simply thought it would be bad to suddenly drop in because I hear Ōishi's a hard man to approach. It's almost ten now. I'll walk you part of the way."

Both of them headed back along the narrow side street, crossed the wide deserted road, went over the wooden bridge above the small river Junichi had previously passed, and came to the large thoroughfare of Sendagi-shita. Quite a few vehicles, apparently on the way to chrysanthemum exhibitions, came along one after another from the direction of Aisome Bridge. Leading the way, Seto turned west into a side street where a painted post displayed the name Idei Hospital, the writing a strange mixture of a *kana* syllabary and a Chinese character. Junichi followed him.

"Where are you staying?" Seto asked as if suddenly remembering.

"At an inn on Hikage-chō."

"Well, let me know once you get settled."

Seto took out his name card, wrote down the address of his boardinghouse on Dōzaka, and handed the card to Junichi.

"Here's where I live. You thinking of becoming one of Roka's pupils? They say he's quite active, writes lots of stuff."

"Don't you read him?"

"I rarely read novels."

They arrived at Yabushita. Seto stopped there.

"I'll say goodbye. I suppose you know the way?"

"This is the road I took a while ago."

"Well, see you one of these days."

"So long."

They parted company, Seto heading for Dangozaka, Junichi for Nezu-Gongen.

2

The room on the second floor had eight mats. The sunlight, streaming in through two Western-style windows facing east, fell against an opposite wall adorned with wallpaper. The Sodeura-kan boardinghouse had apparently been built originally for foreigners, Chinese students for example. A while back the room had been occupied by two students from India, the two idling away the time by sitting on long rattan chairs. The floor, then covered with a cheap carpet, was now laid with *tatami* mats. The rattan chairs left behind by those students had been placed under the window facing south. A large desk whose legs had been sawed off a little had been artlessly placed between the two windows facing east, a slight distance from the papered wall. When asked by a friend why the desk had not been set by the windows, the present occupant of the room had replied there was no sun if the window curtains were drawn whereas the light was blinding when they weren't. Once the maid had caught him drying his hands on the white cotton curtains, and she reported the incident to the landlord. When he came in to complain, the occupant turned the tables on him, reprimanding him, much to the landlord's astonishment, that it was high time the curtains were washed. The room's occupant was none other than Ōishi Kentarō.

Ōishi had just returned from washing up. Legs crossed tailor-style on a calico cushion as he puffed on a Shikishima cigarette, he drew close to him the charcoal brazier on which a small steaming teakettle had been placed. A maid brought in his meal on a tray. Near the soup bowl he found a calling card. He picked it up, read the name, and silently looked at the maid's face.

"I told him you were about to eat," the maid said, "and he said he would wait. He's downstairs now."

Without replying, Ōishi nodded and began his meal. While eating, he spread out the *Tōkei* newspaper near his cushion and started reading the serialized novel on the front page. It was his own work. Though he usually finished proofreading his story while at the newspaper office, he always read

the columns each morning, word by word. And he read them quite rapidly
at that. He also looked over the supplement, which he was in charge of. The
supplement dealt almost exclusively with literary criticism put out by no
more than four or five reporters, the criticism focusing on the works of two
or three leading authors. Ōishi himself was one of these two or three chosen
few. When he finished his meal, the maid stood up, the tray in one hand,
the earthen teapot in the other.

"May I bring in your guest?" she asked.

"All right. Show him in."

Ōishi had responded without even looking at the woman. Though he was
quite blunt and never attempted any jokes, she was being exceedingly
polite. That was because Ōishi gave her twice as many tips as any other
lodger. And the reason the landlord had backed down without a word on
the curtain incident was that not only did Ōishi pay his rent punctually, he
sometimes offered to pay a month in advance because he said paying by the
month was a nuisance. As for money matters, not a single person in the
Sodeura-kan could compete with Ōishi, yet in clothing and other respects he
was quite modest, frugal. True, the coarse silk padded kimono he wore and
the white crepe waistband were reasonably new, but not only did he sleep in
this outfit, he also appeared everywhere in it unless the occasion called for
Western-style clothing.

After he finished the *Tōkei* and began skimming through the literary columns of two or three other papers piled up beside him, the visitor entered.
Twenty-two or three, he looked like a student. Dressed in a padded striped
kimono and a Kokura *hakama* skirt, he wore no *haori* coat. His name card
had indicated he was a reporter for *New Trends in Thought*. Actually most
serious newspaper reporters dressed in this way nowadays.

"I'm Kondō Tokio."

Despite his sharp sunken eyes and pointed nose, the man had something
informal and attractive about him as he introduced himself.

"I'm Ōishi."

With these words Ōishi looked up at the man even while continuing to
hold the newspaper he was glancing through. He seemed to evoke the feeling: If you have something to say, say it quickly and be on your way! And yet
Kondō still retained the same little smile on his face. Apparently he had no
expectation that Ōishi would put aside the newspaper. Perhaps the visitor
thought Ōishi, whose photograph appeared in all newspapers and magazines, had no need to mention his own name at all, yet he had done so possibly because he wanted to be polite.

"Might I, Sensei, ask an opinion of you?"

Finally Ōishi let the newspaper fall.

"I'd be delighted if you could let me have your views on contemporary thought."

"I've nothing special to say about that."

"But, Sensei, you could talk about the heroes in your novels or their frame of mind. Many people argue about your novels from several angles, but I've no idea what you think. Just some aspect of your views will do. We young men would be overjoyed if you'd give even a clue."

Kondō kept urging him. Just then the maid brought in another calling card and a letter of introduction. Ōishi merely glanced at the signature, Tanaka Akira, and the words written on the envelope: "Brought by Koizumi Junichi." Ōishi put down the envelope without so much as opening it.

"Fine. Tell him to come in," Ōishi said to the maid.

Kondō pressed him even further. "How about it, Sensei? I really do beseech you."

Junichi, who had been waiting at the foot of the stairs, came up immediately. Seeing Ōishi with a guest, Junichi bowed to them from a slight distance away and waited. Since he had hurried on his walk back, his face was slightly flushed. His clear dark eyes were fixed on a world totally unfamiliar to him. The moment Ōishi noticed those bright eyes fixed on him, he felt his face brighten in spite of himself. And he said to Kondō, who kept looking intently at him, "I try to write into my novels whatever I have to about my characters. Other than that, what's there to say? Nowadays it's too troublesome for me to read long essays. What in the world does anyone say about the characters I create?"

For the first time Ōishi had said something substantial. But if he let Kondō comment on what the critics said about his novels, he himself would inevitably have to respond either in the affirmative or negative. Because he had been distracted by Junichi's innocent, unaffected look, Ōishi realized he had suddenly let the reins slip from his hands, but already it was too late.

"Usually the critics say something that goes this way: What you write are your own true confessions. They admire the serious attitude you take in making these confessions genuine. They say it's similar to the attitude taken by people of the past, for example Aurelius Augustinus or Jean-Jacques Rousseau."

"I'm flattered. But not only do I not read the critical essays of contemporary scholars, I don't read those written by past writers either, because it's too much trouble. Saint Augustinus sowed quite a few wild oats in his youth, completely reversed his attitude after he turned to Christianity, and made his confessions after he became a 'fanatic' monk. As for Rousseau, he had an affair with a woman he couldn't call wife, and when their child was born, he was at a total loss as to how to raise it. He placed it in an orphanage and later made his confessions, but originally he was quite straitlaced. When he worked for the legation in Italy, didn't he get all distraught when he was taken to a place that had beautiful women and he couldn't perform? The characters I write about lead a loose life too. They buy prostitutes. Do these critics say that's admirable?"

"Oh, yes, they say it's admirable. All your heroes buy prostitutes, but because they admit to it quite naturally, the critics call your men serious in thinking about their actions."

"Well, does that mean fellows who don't buy prostitutes are deficient in having a serious frame of mind?"

"Well, I guess there are some narrow-minded fellows who don't buy them. Or there are some who do buy but try to fool others by pretending to be innocent. Such men remain shallow in their inner lives. They're unable to judge the true value of art. They can't write novels or anything. They've nothing to repent about. They've nothing to confess. So it can be said they can't have a serious attitude about anything."

"I see. Then are you saying that no one can understand the value of art or create novels unless they are not innocent or not deceptive?"

"Well, no one can affirm whether there are godlike men or not. But the object of literary criticism is not godlike men but men as human beings."

"So you mean all human beings, all real men, buy prostitutes?"

"My dear Sensei, please don't make fun of me."

"I'm not making fun of you," said Ōishi, not batting an eyelash, at ease in his cross-legged posture.

The wall clock in the office below began its clamor, like the sound of something scorching in a pot, endlessly pealing out its loud sound that it was twelve noon.

"I'm afraid I've disturbed you too long," said Kondō as if suddenly remembering. "I'll drop by again."

"Bye. I won't see you off since I've kept this other guest waiting."

"Please don't bother," said Kondō, standing and leaving.

For a while Ōishi, a gentle look on his face, stared at Junichi before saying, "Sorry to keep you waiting so long. You haven't eaten lunch yet, have you?"

"I'm not hungry."

"When did you have breakfast?"

"At 6:30."

"What? Can it be that an energetic young man like you doesn't want lunch at noon even though he ate breakfast at half past six? You're lying, aren't you?"

Ōishi's tone of voice was rather harsh. Caught off balance by this sudden remark, Junichi felt flustered, but he did not avert his eyes from the other's face. He had felt flustered not only because he thought it wrong to have given such a perfunctory reply out of mere politeness, but also from feeling that Ōishi ought not to have so suddenly reprimanded him for making that kind of specious remark.

"I'm sorry. It's not true that I don't want anything to eat."

"I like the way you confess so honestly," said Ōishi, laughing. "The food here's not that good, but have lunch on me. But you'll have to eat alone since I had my breakfast less than two hours ago."

The ordered meal was soon brought in. Having learned his lesson, Junichi began eating without reserve. Ōishi, while smoking, observed him with interest. As he ate, Junichi's thought seemed to take the following path: "I felt this Ōishi person was quite a peculiar character, but he's even more eccentric than I imagined. If he had remained silent after his guest left, I could have told him why I came. At least he should have asked me why before he let me have lunch. But since he didn't, I couldn't find an opportunity. He hasn't even bothered to open the envelope of the letter of introduction that was handed him a while ago, much less read it, and he hasn't even asked me what I want. Instead, he suddenly offers a meal to a complete stranger. I've never known or heard of anyone like him. He really is the strangest person."

On the other hand, Ōishi had a quite simple reasoning of his own: "It's obvious from his facial expression that Junichi is one of those young men who admire me. I can tell just from glancing at the writing on Tanaka's envelope where the boy is from. An admirer from Y Prefecture. That's all I need to know about the attributes of this Junichi who's devouring his lunch before my eyes. There's no more to say, is there?"

The lunch finished, the maid took away the tray and proceeded downstairs. Suddenly Ōishi stood up and, after taking his *haori* coat from a closet, said while putting on the coat, "I'm going to my office at the newspaper, so come see me again. But don't come at night."

Ōishi picked up some documents from his desk and stuffed them into his kimono sleeve. From a wall rack he took his fedora hat and put it on. In a moment he was descending the stairs. Junichi, totally stunned, grabbed his own cap and followed.

3

The day after his first visit to Ōishi, Junichi left the inn he was at to find a new place to live. He was so tired of lodging houses after his visit to the Sodeura-kan that he wanted to rent a small house in some quiet area. After parting from Ōishi in front of the Sodeura-kan the previous day, Junichi, before returning to his inn, had stopped off at an art exhibition sponsored by the Ministry of Education. For some reason, Ueno had made such a good impression on him at the time that on this day he went directly from Shin-bashi to Ueno.

As he found himself standing before the gate of Ueno Museum, he pon-dered for a while whether he should go to Negishi or to Yanaka, which he had passed the day before, but since he thought it better to find a place con-venient to visiting Ōishi, it seemed natural to head for Yanaka. Turning the corner on which the Art School was located, he walked from Sakuragi-chō to the cemetery of Tennōji Temple.

It was another fine and windless day. Stepping on fallen gingko leaves scattered on the stone pavement as he moved along, he read some of the names of persons unknown to him engraved on the various-sized gravestones, and he sauntered over to Hatsune-chō. He found him-self on a wide street with few passersby, small houses surrounded by hedges lining the street. He was attracted to one of these houses, its wicket gate made from twigs, a For Rent sign on a gatepost of natural wood.

Junichi stopped before the gate and looked in through the hedge just as an elderly woman with white hair came out from the neighboring house whose entranceway had a good many flowerpots arranged there. She started speaking to him. She told him the house for rent had been built by her hus-band, a gardener who wanted to live in it when he retired and handed his other property over to their married son. But at seventy or so, her husband died while the son was off at the war.

Consequently, she had rented the house to an artist who painted in oils. The house had been left vacant when the man had moved to Kyoto the month before. He was a bachelor, so she had brought over his meals from her late husband's home next door. She said she would not mind doing the same for the new occupant if he was single, for she could then use the extra income.

Junichi was quite pleased with the woman's honest simplicity and tidy appearance. She herself was instantly taken with Junichi's gentle and refined manner. "It's all right," she said, "if the renter wishes to live with a friend, but I prefer, if I had my way, to have someone like you live in the house alone."

And saying, "Well, at least take a look at it," she opened the wicket gate. Reminded of his grandmother back home who was now hard of hearing and walked bent over, Junichi was surprised by the robustness of this elderly woman. They went into the house together. Though she had said the house had been built ten years ago, there wasn't the slightest evidence it needed repair. Hearing her say that taking care of this house and keeping it clean was her job, Junichi couldn't help feeling the truth of her assertion. Its best room was four-and-a-half mats in size, a stone washbasin set at a bend in a row of garden steppingstones. Beyond a door that faced west and looked like the entrance to a tearoom was a corridor polished mirror smooth, the corridor leading to a six-mat room. Adjacent to this room was a kitchen.

Until this moment Junichi had associated a tearoom with something gloomy, something unpleasant. His house in the country had one which a feudal lord was supposed to have once visited. Even after the weather turned the room cold, mosquitoes could be found in it, the room always making him feel cramped, suffocated. Even though this room in the rented house had been modeled after a tearoom, it had somehow taken on a bright quality. This was perhaps due to its miniature entrance to the south and its window to the east looking out onto a small garden facing the wide street.

Even before Junichi realized it, he had agreed to rent the house. After walking around it outside, he stood on a large Kurama rock set just in front of the miniature entrance.

"Can I move in this afternoon?" he asked.

The old woman, who had been plucking some small weeds among the moss beside the garden washbasin, said, "Of course. I don't mind at all. As you can see, I clean every day, so the house can be moved into at any time."

Between this house and the gardener's next door was a low bamboo fence, and Junichi could see just ahead where he was standing a thick cluster of bush clover whose flowers were no longer in bloom. Beside the bush clover were about ten lengthy stalks of dahlia, red ones and yellow mixed together at the height of their second flowering.

As Junichi found himself attracted to these flowers permeated with a bluish glow from the sun, there suddenly appeared between the dahlia and the thicket of bush clover the head of a girl whose hair was swept up into a chignon bound with a wide cream-colored ribbon.

Following Junichi's glance and catching sight of the girl's face, the old woman said, "Oh, it's you, is it?"

"You've a guest?" the girl asked, her smile radiant even without waiting for a reply to her question. And then she disappeared behind the bush clover thicket.

After promising he would move in that afternoon, Junichi hurried out the house gate. As he passed the gardener's residence, he looked at the spot where the dahlias were blooming, but since the path turned right with four granite rocks arranged in a row at that point, he could see no further than the planted bush clover.

4

The seventh day after moving to Hatsune-chō happened to fall on the Emperor's Birthday.

The night Junichi moved in, he mailed a postcard to Seto, who lived so close that Junichi thought he would visit right away, but he hadn't yet showed up.

As for Ōishi, Junichi had dropped in twice and told him he wanted to be a poet or a novelist. Fearing Ōishi would rebuke him by saying that poets were born so that one could not be a poet even if he tried, Junichi, nevertheless, took the plunge and bared his mind. But Ōishi made neither a favorable nor unfavorable comment about it. "You can't practice poems," he said. "You can't study how to write them. All you can do is simply write them by yourself. Of course, if you want to imitate the style of ancient literature, you may have to practice their sentences and such, but I myself can't do it. My own work may have numerous inappropriate words in it, but I pay no attention to that. After all, it's the brain, the mind, that's important. In any event, writing's not very remunerative."

When asked what he thought about this last point, Junichi said, "Since I'm an only child in a wealthy family, I don't have to earn a living."

"If you don't have to struggle to make a living," Ōishi said laughing, "you'll have lots of free time. But that means you'll have few chances to be stimulated, so you'll probably stray from the path of success if you're not careful."

Ōishi's words were so vague Junichi felt somewhat disappointed. But on thinking about them after getting home, he realized it was wrong of him to have expected something else from Ōishi since there was no other way in which he could have responded. Somehow, though, Junichi felt lonely, felt helpless. While sitting at the Chinese desk, one of the pieces of furniture the landlord-gardener had once managed to collect for this room, Junichi tried to write something but found his brain empty, that brain which Ōishi had said was all that mattered. Junichi did not know what to write. He wasn't sure whether or not what he had experienced or felt since coming to Tokyo really existed. Even what seemed to exist was all jumbled, something he could not put into order. Everything seemed so absurd he finally put down the pen he was holding.

On opening his eyes on the morning of the Emperor's Birthday, Junichi found the orange-colored sunlight streaming onto his pillow through a small opening in the door facing east in his four-and-a-half-mat room. Particles of dust seemed to be dancing energetically in the air. The clock he picked up by his bed indicated the time was six.

Remembering how he had gone to school in his hometown to worship the emperor's portrait on this holiday, Junichi suddenly thought of going to the Aoyama Military Drill Grounds. But on second thought he decided against it, for he felt it would be tedious to see soldiers on parade.

Before long the old woman brought in his breakfast. While eating, he heard a gentle voice calling her. Junichi's eyes followed those of the old woman to where the voice came from, the south entrance outside toward the dahlia flowers. And in the same place he had seen that girl's head on the day he had rented the house, he saw it again. Again he viewed that cream-colored ribbon, and those wide-open eyes reminded him of those of a deer he had once seen on visiting Miyajima. He had had only a glimpse of her that other day, so he had completely forgotten her. But on suddenly seeing her, he felt as if unawares he was already on friendly terms with her. Perhaps her image had unconsciously filtered in and out of his mind.

"Oh, it's nice of you to look in," said the old woman. "Yasu has gone shopping at Dangozaka, but she'll be back soon. Why don't you come over here?"

"May I?"

"Of course, of course. Please come around from there."

The girl's head again disappeared behind the bush clover thicket.

The old woman told Junichi that the girl was the daughter of Nakazawa, president of a bank, and that she lived in a villa nearby. The old woman's daughter-in-law Yasu, who had once worked at the villa, was a very good friend to the girl.

Before long Oyuki, Nakazawa's daughter, came round to the back door and walked over the garden steppingstones to the front of Junichi's room.

"This is Mr. Koizumi, who has just moved in," the old woman said. Oyuki made a silent bow and stood there gazing at Junichi. Her kimono and *haori* were of coarse dark-colored silk, her scarlet silk undergarment slightly visible under the arm opening of her long kimono sleeves.

Putting down the teacup he had been drinking from, Junichi, also silent as he bowed, found himself reddening. Oyuki, however, remained quite calm. She stood there, her posture so straight she looked as if she were almost forcing herself to bend backwards. Junichi found her posture so oppressive that it was almost as if she were challenging him to fight. He felt he ought to say something, but the words failed to come. He lifted his teacup and took a gulp.

"You used to come often to see the oil paintings, young miss," said the old woman to help him out. "Mr. Koizumi likes books, so you ought to visit him often and ask about them. You like to hear about books, don't you?"

"I don't read much," Junichi said. But the minute he had said that he felt his remark was quite stupid. Wondering if he had hurt Oyuki's feelings, he looked to see if he had. However, she continued to smile at him.

Yet her smile made him feel all the more uneasy, for he somehow felt that smile revealed her contempt for him. And yet he felt he deserved to be looked at in this way.

He thought he had to somehow regain his honor, and he mustered the courage to say, "Please, won't you sit down?"

"Thanks."

With her right sandal on one of the garden steppingstones, she raised her left sandaled foot onto the Kurama steppingstone whose grain looked something like hemp leaves, and gracefully twisting her body in its long student *haori,* she sat at the edge of the veranda entrance to the room.

It was proverbial that the Emperor's Birthday was usually favored with fine weather. And just as the proverb went, the sun suddenly began to shine. Dazzled by the winter sun, Oyuki turned her profile toward Junichi. Her face reminded him of Manet's Nana in profile as the model held a large eyebrow brush and stood in front of a mirror. He had seen the painting in a book on a history of modern art he had found in his hometown. He thought Oyuki's face resembled Nana's narrow, though a little too handsome, face. That impression was perhaps due to Oyuki's gentle bangs slanting from right to left on her forehead, bangs as big as the little finger of a hand. Her large eyes under those bangs seemed dazzled by the sun even though Junichi's were not.

"You don't look like a man from the country," she said.

Laughing, Junichi felt his face turn red. Aware he was blushing, he found he was angry at himself. Besides, he felt it was rude of her to suddenly level that criticism at him, and he thought to himself that this was what people have called "the thorn in beauty."

The old woman stood up to leave, carrying out the rice tub. For a while Junichi and Oyuki remained silent. Suddenly he felt the very air was stifling.

Beyond the hedge he saw a rickshaw running toward Tabata, the passenger it carried a man in an overcoat with a fur neckpiece. Until the old woman finally returned to clear away his tray, Junichi had been unable to utter a single word. As she looked at them, the old woman said, the tray and earthen teapot in her hands, "My, the two of you are quiet," and she headed toward the kitchen.

A sparrow flew down from a branch of a camellia tree to the garden washbasin.

The bird's sudden appearance miraculously loosened Junichi's tongue.

"Look! A sparrow's drinking some water."

"Be quiet," said Oyuki.

He stood and went over to the entrance. Suddenly the sparrow flew off. Oyuki glanced at him.

"See? You made it fly away!"

"Oh, it would have done that even if I hadn't come over."

Junichi was aware he had finally been able to speak out, yet he had the feeling he was like an actor badly mouthing his lines.

"You're wrong!" Suddenly her way of speaking gave him the impression she was becoming more friendly. A while later she said, "I'll come again," and flashing her big eyes at him, she went off, her Chiyoda sandals pattering along the garden stones.

5

Junichi picked up the French journal lying on his desk. Though the foreign language at his middle school had been English, he had gone every night to study French at the Protestant Episcopal church in his hometown. At first, just reading the textbook, one used at the well-known Gyōsei School, had been beyond him, but in about a year he had managed to read with considerable ease. That was why he had asked Reverend Bertand to introduce him to a bookstore in Paris. Later the shop had sent him some catalogs, and he had been able to order new books directly from the bookstore. He had even been able to have journals sent to him.

The page of the journal he happened to open to was about the Italian painter Segantini on his deathbed in 1899. The man was dying in the country, dying in a kind of hovel near a glacier. There was no longer any heat from the fireplace. The artist was on the verge of death, and though his internal organs were about to cease to function, the artist had asked that the windows be opened, and he continued to gaze at clouds drifting across the peak of the glacier. Lost in thought, Junichi closed the journal.

Art, he felt, ought to be like that. What he ought to write about was a present-day society as visible as the Alps. And yet he was being tossed about in this Tokyo whirlpool, this metropolis he had dreamed of when he had been in his hometown. No, that was not so. It would have been all right if he were being tossed about. Had he not merely been clinging to vines along the shore instead of doing what he ought: being tossed and hurled about? Had he been living in any real sense of that word? What if Segantini had never once opened a window, had never once gone outside? If so, his life in the mountains would have been a total waste.

Junichi felt that many people from his prefecture were now leading active roles in Tokyo. In fact, the world now seemed ripe for those from Y Prefecture. When he had left home, there were those who had said they would introduce him to ministers of state, yet all these offers he had declined. That was because he could not have cared less about these bigwigs, no matter how great or powerful they were. He had thought he could do without them for another reason. He felt that one could not get acquainted with another person through letters of introduction. And even if one did become acquainted with someone through such letters, the groundwork had been laid by something ordained, something prearranged. Letters of introduction might accidentally help achieve such encounters. Should a door be opened, one ought to step in. And if that door is closed, merely pass by it. That had been his philosophy. And that was why he had accepted Tanaka's letter of introduction and no one else's.

There could be no doubt that he himself was in Tokyo, and yet could he understand Tokyo if he remained as he was? Was it not true that the life he had led back home was the same he was now leading? If it was the same, that would be all right, and he could bear up under that life. Some of the friends who had finished middle school with him had come to Tokyo to take the examination for high school. Some were now college students. And others, like Seto, were at art school. Still others had gone out into the world to find jobs after their graduation from middle school. As for himself, even though he had graduated with honors from middle school, he had continued his study of French by remaining at home for a while. That had been due to ambition and confidence. He had wanted neither a bachelor's degree nor a doctorate. Nor could he think of any job he wanted. His family was wealthy, and each of its members could live comfortably even if someone else managed their property. And so he had decided to become a writer despite the objections of his relatives.

After he had made this resolution, he had asked his French teacher, Reverend Bertand, a good many questions on various aspects of literature.

Though the man had lived in Paris, he knew nothing about literary movements. When Junichi asked him about the Bible, something you'd expect
the reverend to have read, he did not regard it as a magnificent piece of literature. And in trying to ask him something about the Bible, Junichi found
that not only did the man not regard it as a piece of literature, he had apparently not even read it with any kind of enjoyment. Without even trying to
thoroughly study the complicated annotated versions of the Bible written
from the viewpoint of the church, he had merely kept the Bible on his book-
shelf. His only reading each day was from a newspaper published in his own
country. The only thing that interested him was maintaining the balance
among the world powers or diplomatic problems that occasionally appeared
in the newspaper. Not that he had some secret political mission to perform.
He was probably one of those men that Europeans and Americans call "cof-
feehouse politicians." Apart from this kind of reading, he had a small collection of medical texts he had brought with him to the Orient, texts read for
the purpose of treating his own illnesses. He suffered, for example, from
chronic headaches, his long brown hair covering his scalp, and he had some
kind of nasty disease around those hips of his which he concealed under a
black garment that resembled an old-fashioned *talar.* Apparently he treated
these ills in his own way. Since he was this kind of person, he would change
the subject whenever the topic of literature or art was brought up. In the
final analysis, Junichi thought, the only thing his teacher had done was to
act as an intermediary between him and the Paris bookshop.

Absorbed in these reflections, Junichi pictured before him the clumsily
built and badly painted church that stood on sodden ground in the middle
of a rice field on the outskirts of his hometown. When he passed through
the red painted gate on which a wooden plate black with age was inscribed
"Protestant Episcopal Church," he would see two flowerbeds bordered with
tiles. In one bed were lilies, in the other cosmos. Both flowers brought forth
buds in the spring, both varieties continuing their stunted growths, the frail
lilies appearing in early fall, the frail blooms of the cosmos later in the same
season. Among these flowers the cosmos stalks stood lean and lanky, their
carrotlike leaves wrinkled, curled.

At the rear of this garden stood the dilapidated painted church with its
pseudo-Gothic gables, the church where Junichi had gone to learn French.
Except for the few young men who had come to study the language, no one
came to visit no matter how long one waited. Reverend Bertand lived alone
in the fairly large empty structure except for a decrepit old man who served
as cook and caretaker, and so the place was littered with dust, rats running
around everywhere even in broad daylight.

Reverend Bertand would be sitting at a large desk he said he had bought in Nagasaki and on which were piled in disarray some books with the era, eighteen fifty something or other, inscribed on the bound leather covers, which were so dirty it was difficult to tell if the books had originally been red or black. Left on a plate near these books would be some half-eaten sausages and pieces of cheese, Reverend Bertand too lazy to carry the leftovers to the kitchen, scraps of old sheets of *Le Figaro,* the French newspaper, covering them. A cat with black stripes on its tawny fur would leap up on the piled books and with its back sloping like an incense casket would begin sniffing at the sausage. Sitting on a grandfather chair draped over with the fur from a Hokkaido fox someone had given him would be Reverend Bertand, his hand running from the back of his long brown hair down over to his broad white forehead, Bertand again dressed in the same imitation *talar* in black. He would always do the same thing, whether it was summer or winter. The only difference was that in winter, pine for the fire would be smoldering in the iron stove in a corner of the room.

One day Junichi had arrived at the church thirty minutes early for his lesson, and he had talked with the Reverend Bertand about various subjects. Since his teacher had asked him what he wanted to become, Junichi had answered quite frankly, *"Un romancier."* Bertand repeated his question two or three times, and then, his face strangely transformed, he lapsed into silence. Since he had not once ever thought about the subject of novelists, he had apparently been confused on how to respond. He seemed to be as astonished as he would have been if Junichi had said, "I'm going to migrate to Mars."

Junichi had been so immersed in these memories he had hardly glanced at the magazine he was reading. He suddenly realized the charcoal in the brazier the old woman had kindled for him that morning had already turned into small white embers. He quickly added more charcoal, and his cheeks puffing in and out, he repeatedly began fanning the fire with his breath.

6

Junichi passed the entire morning of the Emperor's Birthday indulging in these reflections. While he was eating the lunch the old woman had brought to him, Seto Hayato dropped in. Since Junichi had written his name on the small wooden plate that Chōjirō, the old woman's son, had planed and sanded and hung for him on the gatepost of the house, Seto had not had any difficulty in finding the place. Now sitting opposite Junichi in the small sunny room, Seto looked quite different from his former appearance in their hometown. When Junichi had met him at the foot of Yanaka Slope, this difference was not perceived, probably because Junichi had paid more attention to Seto's facial expressions than to his voice and actual features. Seto's face, which had once taken on an oily sheen, was now dried, parched, and now, when he spoke, wrinkles appeared around the corners of his eyes and mouth. Junichi felt his landlady, despite her elderly years, had a more healthy glow than Seto.

"Quite a fancy home you've found," Seto said.

"Do you think so?"

"What do you mean with your 'Do you think so?' Some say you're an innocent young man, but actually you're shrewd, sly. Most guys that rush in from the country get lost and confused in Tokyo, but you go around visiting this and that person's place by yourself. You can even find and rent a house on your own. You look like you've lived in Tokyo one hundred years!"

"Well, you know that there was no Tokyo one hundred years ago."

"That's just what I mean. That's the side of your personality fools can't see through. You're too clever!"

Repeating "You're too clever!" a number of times, Seto seemed to fancy himself Junichi's good friend. And then he added, "I'm free this afternoon, so I'll take you anywhere you want. We could go to an exhibition in Ueno or take a stroll in Asakusa Park. One thing we might do is go to the Young Men's Club I often attend. Most of its members are aspiring writers and a few are painters. It's quite a serious kind of meeting, and they usually invite authorities giving lectures. Today, Fuseki's coming. He belongs to a school of writing different from Roka's and others, but Fuseki's so famous more people than usual are expected."

As far as paintings were concerned, Junichi disliked viewing them with other persons, for he wondered if he could understand the paintings under his own powers. As for Asakusa Park, he didn't feel it worth the trouble, for every so often in the newspapers he had understood that the park was a waste of energy. As for Fuseki, he had heard some people say Fuseki was a little behind the times, but he was considered to be the most learned of all novelists at present. Junichi wanted to see what Fuseki was like. So he decided to ask Seto to take him to the club.

They both left Hatsune-chō and walked leisurely along Ueno Hill. In front of the Ueno Art Museum several horse-drawn carriages had pulled up to let off passengers to view the exhibition. Parked in front of the entrance to the Seiyōken Restaurant near the Tōshōgū Shrine was a splendid automobile.

"Turner's paintings have included trains, but I have yet to hear of a famous painting of an automobile," said Seto.

"I'm not sure about that, but I do think the automobile's mentioned in quite a few written works."

"Has anyone written a great novel on automobiles?"

"Several have appeared in novels and plays, but only because cars are used in them. About the only good story I know of with an automobile is a short piece of Maeterlinck's."

"Really? What in the world does an automobile cost?"

"Five or six thousand yen, I hear. Better ones cost more than ten thousand."

"Well, if it's that expensive, I wouldn't be able to buy one even if I devoted my entire life to painting."

With these words Seto rudely threw down the butt of his Asahi cigarette toward the feet of some pedestrians streaming along. He smiled bitterly. When he smiled, his face took on an ugly look.

They came to Hirokōji. Streetcars with the national flag placed crosswise in twos at the very front of the car kept coming, but all the streetcars were crowded. Seto pushed his way through a waiting crowd and boarded one, so Junichi had no choice but to follow. They transferred at Suda-chō and got off at Nishiki-chō. Turning into a side street, they came to a place opposite the Kanda Ward Office with its red brick exterior. Seto suddenly stopped.

In this area all the wooden houses were shabby. Under the eaves of one of these houses was a paper poster pasted to a wooden frame, the kind often placed in front of bookstores. At the top of the signboard the word DIDASKALIA was written horizontally in roman letters, and beneath it written vertically in Chinese characters were the words "November Meeting."

"This is it. Let's go upstairs."

Kicking off his Satsuma clogs where other clogs and shoes had been thrown down in disorder, Seto went up the front stairs. As Junichi followed, he glanced to his right. Sitting behind a latticed counter was a pale young man about twenty years old with his hair cropped short. He was talking with a big ruddy-faced woman standing at a small door that probably led to a kitchen. With her kimono sleeves tucked up by a sash, she had rolled up the bottom of her kimono so that part of her gray discolored undergarment was visible above her knees. Saying in a loud voice, "Please come right in," she glanced briefly at them and then continued speaking to the man, her voice so hoarse it reminded Junichi of a chirping grasshopper.

The large room upstairs was quite dirty. In front of a wall at one side were a table and chair. On the table were some Chinese barberry twigs in a vase whose leaves were in various places, to use the expression the poet Kyūkin liked for dead leaves, "dried and curled," probably because they had long been kept in the vase. Beside the vase was a pitcher filled with water alongside an empty glass.

About fourteen or fifteen people were sitting on dirty floor cushions around two or three braziers. Scattered here and there were more cushions laid out as if in anticipation of the arrival of more guests. Most of these people wore blue *haori* coats with a white splashed pattern and Kokura *hakama* skirts, and mixed in among these were others wearing university or high school uniforms.

The conversation was quite animated.

The moment Junichi came upstairs, he heard someone in one of the groups near the entrance say in a loud voice, "At any rate, it's no good thinking life and art are two different things."

While wondering about the speaker who had been exaggerating what was so obvious, Junichi expected, even rather hesitantly, that Seto would introduce him to someone, but Seto had noticed at the far end of the hall somebody he could comfortably talk to, hurriedly walked in the person's direction, and then excitedly whispered something to him. Junichi, feeling isolated, pulled over a cushion and sat down close to a group near the entrance to the room.

The group continued talking without seeming to pay the least bit of attention to Junichi, whom no one knew. Their topic focused on Fuseki, who was going to lecture that afternoon. One of the speakers, who looked older than the others, said, "At any rate, he's succeeded as an artist. By that I don't mean he's made a real dent on the world. I mean he's significant in the history of literature. Besides, he's learned, scholarly. They say that among the short stories in his collection are some he wrote about the Western style of life that are so un-Japanese they sound as if a Westerner wrote them."

Then the man who had spoken earlier in that loud voice said, "Scholarship and special knowledge have no value in themselves. It seems to me that a successful artist is one who arranges puppets cleverly and lets them dance, perform. Not that I admire that kind of success. I detest such clever arrangements. It seems to me he lets them dance in whatever way they wish and conceals his own egoistic self behind them, all the while sneering at the enjoyment of the spectators. And that's what I mean by saying life and art are two separate entities." The person expressing this view was a skinny man wearing spectacles for nearsightedness, his loud voice incongruous with his appearance.

A man sitting near this speaker cut in rather hesitantly: "Still, don't you think he quit teaching in order to unite his life with art?"

"That I doubt," said the bespectacled man, flatly rejecting the possibility.

Another man who looked fairly intelligent and who had remained silent until then turned to the hesitant speaker and said, "But the mere fact that Fuseki has stopped teaching shows he's more like an artist than Ōson, who still works for the government, don't you think?"

The topic suddenly shifted from Fuseki to Ōson.

Junichi had been interested in Fuseki and had read some of his works, but he had only looked at Ōson's translation of Hans Christian Andersen. Junichi could not understand why Ōson had taken the trouble to translate that boring story even if only to kill time. Since Junichi had already lost interest in Ōson, he no longer listened to the conversation, indulging instead in his own thoughts.

The conversation, however, became more and more animated, and their laughing voices mingled with the other sounds in the room.

"Ōson seems worried his writing will be called sarcastic or affected, and he himself wrote that it is. But it's really sad that his confessions about his writing were themselves criticized as being sarcastic and affected," said the intelligent-looking man. Junichi happened to hear him laugh with the other men in the group.

Hearing this remark, Junichi snapped out of his reveries, thinking to himself: "If a man defends himself against the criticism of the world, he'll end up either ridiculed or viewed as being sarcastic and affected. A man who tries to defend himself against these criticisms is perhaps a fool, and he'll probably be sarcastic and affected. Or possibly he may be so indifferent to criticism that he observes himself objectively. No one could hand down a psychological judgment on anyone without knowing that person's character."

From the back of the room Seto called out, "Koizumi!" When Junichi looked back, Seto had already left the place where he had sat and was now sitting opposite another man, a brazier between them, the man seated at a child's desk in a corner of the room on which papers were piled haphazardly.

Junichi got up from his seat and went over to Seto. He saw a one-yen bill and some coins lying beside the papers on the desk. Junichi paid the seventy-sen fee for the meeting.

"The money's for admission to the meeting and for the meal," Seto explained, and turning to the man sitting behind the desk asked, "Are you serving any cakes today?"

Before the other could respond, the ruddy-faced maid Junichi had noticed before came in carrying a big tray heaped with bean-jam cakes, each cake individually wrapped, and she started handing one to each person.

After handing out the cakes, she went about placing at various spots large earthen containers filled with coarse cheap tea.

While Junichi still sat near the desk of this man collecting fees and while still holding a cake in his hand, he heard someone call out, "I say, Seto!" Seto stood and moved off in a hurry. The person who had called out, his hair long, his face pale, was the same one who had shouted to Seto when he had first come into the room. Again Seto began whispering something in an excited manner.

Gradually the room filled, and inevitably all approached the desk to pay their fees. Junichi returned to his former seat. It was so close to the entrance that the cushion he had set there had not been taken by anyone. Just as he was about to sit down, he overturned a half-filled cup of tea. He was somewhat embarrassed. "Oh, I'm sorry," said Junichi, taking out a handkerchief from his kimono sleeve and wiping the *tatami* mat.

"The *tatami* would be quite surprised!" said the man whose tea had been spilled. He looked at Junichi's handkerchief. Bought at a shop on the Ginza, it was an expensive one made of Flanders batiste. This man, who had been leaning against a pillar and listening quietly to the others from the start, had occasionally stolen a glance at Junichi. Sturdy of build, he was wearing a university uniform, an insignia inscribed with an M on the stand-up collar of his school jacket.

The student's remark was so strange that as Junichi looked at the speaker, Junichi was himself more surprised than the *tatami* mat would have been.

"Are you a painter too?" the man asked.

"No, not at all. I've just come to Tokyo from the country. I've not really been doing anything."

With these words Junichi handed his name card to the student. Muttering "I wonder if I brought mine," the student fumbled around in his pocket and finally handed his small card to Junichi. It read Ōmura Sōnosuke.

"I'm going to be a doctor," Ōmura said, "but I like literature, so I often come to these meetings. What foreign languages have you learned?"

"A little French."

"And what books are you reading?"

"I've only read a little of Flaubert, Maupassant, Bourget, and *le Belgique* Maeterlinck."

"Can you read them fluently?"

"Well, Maeterlinck's plays I can, but essays give me a lot of trouble."

"What do you mean by trouble?"

"I find it difficult to catch the main points."

"That's my trouble too."

With these words Ōmura smiled faintly, but it was a warm smile that had not the slightest trace of scorn. As a young man who was easily moved, Junichi felt Ōmura could be somebody to rely on. When Junichi had met Ōishi, whom he admired because of his novels, he felt Ōishi was just as he had imagined he would be, yet Junichi couldn't help feeling he was standing in front of a jagged rock. Ōmura, on the contrary, seemed quite different, even though Junichi knew little about him. If he was a medical student, he probably knew German. And possibly French. Though these were conjectures made on the spur of the moment, Junichi felt he could rely on Ōmura for help. Junichi thought Nietzsche had once said something like "I'm a railing in a stream by the shore," and Junichi couldn't help feeling this Ōmura was the railing he himself might grab onto with his hands. And this thought of Junichi's, revealed in his large eyes, communicated itself to Ōmura.

At that moment a voice called out from the stairs below, "Everyone, Hirata Sensei's arrived." Hirata was Fuseki's family name.

7

A man, perhaps the secretary of the club, led Fuseki up the stairs and into the room. Junichi kept looking at Fuseki, wondering what kind of person he was.

Fuseki's black woolen suit looked somewhat worn from long use. He was of medium height, pale, yet a lively and ironic expression was on his face. People said that, like Ōson, he had a rather perverse disposition, often characteristic of an adopted child, yet Junichi felt Fuseki's appearance didn't give that kind of impression. His slight reddish mustache, not treated with oil, was twisted up at its ends. It occurred to Junichi that a mustache turns reddish in one's forties before it turns gray and that a Japanese with a mustache didn't look good until he was in his forties.

Noticing Ōmura by the entrance, Fuseki called out to him, "Have you been able to write anything yet?"

"Nothing good enough to show you."

"Don't be afraid to bring out your work. Now we can publish anything quite freely."

"Too much freedom can cause lots of problems."

"I suppose," said Fuseki. "Even if we have freedom, ideas don't come that easily."

Though Fuseki's tone was gentle, his words made a strong impression on others. The reason for this strong impression was probably due to the miraculous energy behind his thoughts and his ability to use exactly the right expression.

He walked over to a seat near the treasurer's desk and, sitting tailor-style on a cushion, took out a small-sized cigarette and began smoking just as the secretary went over to the table and began his introductory remarks on Fuseki.

Then Fuseki walked sluggishly toward the table, waited a while for everyone to quiet down, and started slowly. It sounded as if he were carrying on an ordinary conversation.

"You've asked me to speak on Ibsen. Actually I haven't thought much about him. What I do know about him is perhaps the same as you already know. It's hard to listen to something you're unfamiliar with. It's far more comfortable to listen to something you already know. I see you all have your cakes, so feel free to eat while listening at your ease."

That was the tone Fuseki began with. He did not make the slightest effort to animate his voice. Nor was his speech "eloquently ineloquent" in the fashion of Miyake Setsurei's speeches, which had gained so much popularity. Yet Fuseki seemed similar to Setsurei, whose speeches Junichi had read in abbreviated form. Although Fuseki's voice was quite monotonous, these two speakers both made at times quite clever and witty remarks without much effort.

For a while Fuseki's words continued in this vein; then the following point was brought out. "At first, Ibsen was Norway's little Ibsen, but after turning to social dramas, he became Europe's big Ibsen. When he was introduced in Japan, however, he again reverted to the small Ibsen. No matter what comes to Japan, it turns into something small. Even Nietzsche became small in our country. And so did Tolstoy. Something occurs to me that Nietzsche once said: 'At that time the earth became small. And then everything on earth became even smaller.' The last race of human beings will be dancing with superb nimbleness and flexibility. 'We've discovered real happiness,' this last race will say, their eyes blinking. The Japanese people import all kinds of systems, all kinds of *isms,* and while toying with these, Japanese eyes are perpetually blinking. Everything and anything is turned into small play-things when fingered by us Japanese. So you don't have to be terrified if this thing or *ism* is at first quite dreadful. You don't have to arouse from their slumber Yamaga Sokō, the forty-seven samurai, or the masterless samurai of Mito and confront them with Ibsen or Tolstoy."

It was in this way Fuseki proceeded with his speech.

Up to that moment he had said nothing new, yet Junichi felt his own basic thoughts, maintained until then, were suddenly shaken to their very foundations, for after these humorous remarks by Fuseki, the speaker suddenly became quite serious as he began referring to the two sides of Ibsen's individualism. First, Fuseki noted that throughout Ibsen's work a "red thread" of thought consistently appeared that enabled a man to live as an individual by breaking away from the so-called bonds of convention. It was similar to the feeling one would have after "experiencing many kinds of separation."

While listening to Fuseki, Junichi felt himself pushing down a stream with a pole in the same boat the speaker was in. Suddenly, though, Fuseki changed the subject, concluding with the remark, "This is one aspect of Ibsen; that is, it's the part of Ibsen depicted in *Peer Gynt*. It's Ibsen's worldly self." And then Fuseki added there was another Ibsen with a self that had been in his makeup from the very start. "If it were not for this second aspect of Ibsen's self," Fuseki continued, "he would be advocating nothing but self-indulgence. But Ibsen wasn't the self-indulgent type. He had another self that can be termed his social self, a social self always aspiring to improve the world. And that self was given full play in *Brand*. Why had Ibsen tried to discard and destroy the rotten bonds of convention? He did not want to yield the freedom he had gained and find himself mired in the mud of social convention. He broke through those powerful bonds with his own strong wings and tried to fly high and far."

Even though the speaker had not tried to sound the least bit solemn and had maintained his simple conversational tone, Junichi, on hearing these words from Fuseki, felt as if the prow of the boat he was steering had been forced to turn, forced to move against the current. And for some time thereafter Junichi was engrossed in his own thoughts.

Figuratively speaking, those things he had gathered for a long time, things he had remembered and stored in the box of his heart, had been, Junichi felt, overturned and thrown into disorder. It was too difficult now to return them to their former positions. No, he did not want to restore them. True, he did not want to restore them to their former places, yet somehow he wanted to put them in some kind of order. And yet he knew he couldn't.

His inability to do so was quite reasonable because such a rearrangement could not be made overnight. All at once Junichi felt Fuseki's remarks were beginning to sound like static, meaningless and distant.

While Junichi was listening to this noisy static, he suddenly realized the audience was being agitated too. Almost instinctively he strained his ears to catch what Fuseki was saying just at that moment.

"Zola's Claude searched for Art. Ibsen's Brand searched for an ideal. In order to obtain what they were looking for, they did not mind sacrificing even their wives and children. And even they themselves ceased to exist. Some have even said Ibsen was viewing the world cynically, even satirizing Brand. But the truth is that Ibsen was not being cynical but quite serious. He was seriously searching for a way to improve the world. All or nothing— this was the ideal which Brand, the protagonist, was seeking, but what Ibsen was searching for was limited to the idea that this ideal world would come from one's self, would come from one's own free will. In other words, one has to blaze one's own trail in order to walk along it. In order to obey the ethics of this self, one has to create one's own ethics. In order to believe in religion, one has to establish one's own religion. In a word, one has to seek autonomy. Even for Ibsen, the formulation of autonomy was probably an impossibility. At any rate, it was Ibsen himself doing the seeking. He was a modern. He was a man of the new age."

Fuseki ended his speech with these words. While the audience was wondering whether this was his conclusion or not, he sauntered from the table and resumed his seat on the cushion he had occupied before.

There was some scattered applause, but it soon died down because so few joined in. The majority of listeners were lost in thought the moment the speech ended. The room became exceedingly quiet.

The secretary declared the meeting at an end.

The maidservants began carrying away the empty bowls of barbecued eel that had been served on rice. A hum of voices could be heard from various corners, yet even those voices were apparently deep in thought. Fuseki's speech had left the audience spellbound.

When the secretary saw Fuseki out, members of the audience gradually began leaving.

8

While Junichi was standing by the stairs, Seto hurried over to him. "Are you going home now?" he said.

"Yes."

"Well, if you'll excuse me, I've got somewhere I have to go."

They parted at the gate, Seto heading for Kanda. The man who had been talking with him at the club quickly ran after him.

Just as Junichi began walking toward Ogawa-chō, he noticed someone in shoes taking long strides following him. When Junichi turned back to look, he found it was the medical student Ōmura who had previously handed him his name card. Before Junichi realized it, Ōmura was walking along to the right of him.

"Which way are you heading back?" said Ōmura.

"I live in Yanaka."

"Is Seto a good friend of yours?"

"Not really. We were just classmates in middle school back home."

Junichi had replied as if apologizing for something. Ōmura with his healthy complexion and strong build seemed to be trying to adjust his pace so as to walk evenly beside him. For a while the two walked wordlessly along Ogawa-chō toward Suda-chō.

Already shop lights on both sides of the street were on. The wind rose slightly, stirring up particles of dust and rattling shingles and doorplates. As Junichi and Ōmura walked along the pavement in front of Tenkadō, Ōmura asked, "Are you catching a streetcar?"

"I feel like walking a little."

"You're quite energetic. Well, I'll stop being lazy and try to walk too. But it'll really be out of your way if you go toward Hongō."

"Not at all. That route won't make that great a difference."

Again they stopped talking a while. Since Ōmura tried controlling his pace, Junichi tried walking with long strides. While Ōmura tried to shorten his pace in order to balance it with Junichi's, Junichi felt the more he tried to extend his pace, the more irregular it became. And it was not only his pace that made him feel unsettled. Somehow everything about Ōmura was well balanced, while everything about Junichi himself seemed restless, wavering.

Junichi kept trying to analyze the nature of his own restlessness, but found it extremely difficult to pin it down. Even as his mind reverted to his encounter with Ōishi the other day, Junichi couldn't help feeling Ōishi had overshadowed this self Junichi had found so trivial. But that did not mean he thought Ōishi had something extra special about him. For while Junichi had thought he himself had been destroying long-established conventions and theories, the moment he had met Ōishi, he realized Ōishi had been much more thorough in destroying them. Junichi felt that if he improved his mind, he too could take on that very same stance Ōishi had. But while listening to Fuseki's speech, he realized Fuseki did have something special about him even though it was something that could be discerned only faintly. Junichi wanted to know what that special something in Fuseki was. Junichi knew his own uneasy wavering had been caused by that something.

Suddenly Junichi asked Ōmura, "What kind of person is this type referred to as a 'new man'?"

For a moment Ōmura stared at Junichi. A bit of a smile flared out around Ōmura's eyes and lips.

"You're asking because Mr. Fuseki referred a while ago to Ibsen as a new man, aren't you? Mr. Fuseki's quite an unusual person. He hates the expression 'new man,' so instead he deliberately uses the phrase 'man of the new age.' Once when I said the 'new man,' he poked fun at me by saying 'new man' in Chinese means 'bride.' "

Irritated because the talk was getting off the subject, Junichi rephrased his question.

"In Chinese the words 'old man' and 'new man' seem to refer only to women. If that's the case, let me use the words 'man of the new age' the way Fuseki does. I wonder if 'man of the new age' means someone who is not enslaved by ethical and religious ideals. Or does it mean someone possessed by something else?"

Again Ōmura flashed that same smile.

"The real point is which one is genuinely 'a man of the new age,' the passive new man or the active new man?"

"Well, maybe that's the point. But does a truly active new man exist?" said Junichi.

Again Ōmura came out with his brief smile.

"Well, I don't know if he does or doesn't, though I agree that there ought to be that kind of person around somewhere. If he's destructive, he's also a builder. Just as the man who demolishes stones ends by heaping them into a foundation. Have you read any philosophy?"

"Only some books on it. Not the philosophy itself," said Junichi, responding honestly without the slightest hesitation.

"I didn't think you had."

Shōhei Bridge in the evening was quite congested. It formed a narrow link to Uchi-Kanda. Crowds of people, their silhouettes seen in bursts of dust occasionally raised by the cold wind, busily passed along the narrow bridge. It was so dusty Junichi was unable to continue talking for a while. And while hurrying along with the crowd, he could see against the sky the Jintan advertising pillar flickering off and on, its lights sometimes red, sometimes green.

"In the same way philosophical theories are perpetually being constructed and refuted," said Junichi after thinking a moment about Ōmura's response, "a new man will also construct something positive, so won't he be bound once again by that something?"

"Of course he will. Since the rope that binds him is new and touches a different part of his body, he won't feel these fetters for a while. At least that's what I think."

"If that's the case, why doesn't he remain passive instead and live comfortably in his skepticism?"

"Is living in skepticism comfortable?"

For a while Junichi didn't know how to respond. "I contradicted myself by talking about living comfortably. I should have said he'll live in eternal skepticism."

"You sound as if that were some kind of curse."

"No, skepticism isn't the right word either. I mean he can live in the eternal pursuit of desire. That is, in eternal aspiration."

"Well, it might be like that."

Ōmura's response probably sounded cold. But since there was a warmth in his tone and facial expression, Junichi did not feel troubled. Walking behind a back wall of the sacred hall of a shrine, Junichi, after giving the matter some thought, began again: "As I told you at the club before, I've read almost all the works of Maeterlinck. I also began reading Verhaeren simply because I heard he was Maeterlinck's friend at school. I came across his *La Multiple Splendeur* just before I left my hometown, and I read the book on the train. I found it presented quite a coherent view of life. It was quite unique, quite devout. I had the strange sensation that Verhaeren was quite different from what we Japanese think of as the new man. Or what you would call an active man of the new age. When I read works of the new men in Japan who write only about passive subjects, I do admire the way they undo the ropes that bind them, but I can't find anything in them which really attracts me, really overwhelms me. As for Verhaeren's poems, they too contain a unique view of life. And even though his view doesn't agree with mine, I'm drawn to a pious quality I find unique. I heard Rodin was Verhaeren's friend, and I found this same religious quality in Rodin's sculptures. When I look at these men in this way, it seems to me that what Europeans call the 'new men' are quite different from Japan's 'new men' in that those in Europe have something in them full of life, really active and humane. The same is true of the Ibsen that Mr. Fuseki talked about. As Fuseki said about the Japanese new men, they seem to be men of small caliber."

"Of course they're small. Actually what we call the 'new man' is the name given to a kind of clique," Ōmura said calmly.

Both he and Junichi continued walking along Hongō, each lost in his own thoughts, Ōmura thinking that men from the rural areas were not to be looked down on, for this self-taught young man was obviously superior in insight and ability to some of the students in the literature department at the university.

Passing Daigakumae, Ōmura suddenly said as they were approaching Morikawa-chō, not too wide a street, "You'd better be careful when you're with Seto."

"Yes, I know. He's quite a bohemian."

"Well, if you know that, I guess you'll be all right."

Promising to visit Ōmura soon at his boardinghouse on Nishikata-chō, Junichi turned at the corner of the First Higher School.

9

Ibsen's *John Gabriel Borkman* was performed on November 27 at the Yūrakuza Theater.

Since Junichi felt this was an important event from the viewpoint of contemporary thought, he became a member of the Free Theater immediately after the play's announcement as if he had been waiting impatiently for just this moment. Earlier, when he was still at home, one of Shakespeare's plays had been performed. When it came to performances of Shakespeare or Goethe, no matter how good the acting, and there could be no doubt about the quality of the plays, they would have had difficulty in making a profound impression on today's Japanese youth. Not only would these plays not affect young men, but the majority of our youth could not possibly appreciate such classical works which, to use a term applied to *haiku* poetry, have eternal fame and not merely transient popularity. To put this in a more extreme fashion, if a new Shakespeare-like play were to be published now, young Japanese would probably not even call it a drama but would dub it theater. They might say its poetry was too wordy. And they would probably say the same about Goethe's works. What would they say if *Faust* had just been published as a new work? They might not hesitate to say that the first part of the play, and of course the second as well, were not symbolistic but allegorical. And the reason for this reaction might have been that the tongues of these young men, accustomed to the strong stimulus of realism in the modern world, would find it difficult to appreciate the deep calm tastes of a century or more ago. How had classical Shakespeare been performed in Japan up to now? According to today's newspapers and magazines, Venice had become the town of Yashiki-machi in Surugadai, and the actor playing

Othello appeared on stage in the braided uniform of a Japanese army general wearing the Third Order of Merit for his role in the Sino-Japanese War. Just to imagine such a setting and costume would certainly have caused today's youth to feel they had been insulted.

The night of the twenty-seventh, Junichi took a streetcar to Sukiyabashi and went into the Yūrakuza. He was led to his seat in the fourth row on the main floor. All the spectators were already seated, the theatrical producer's speech was over, and the first act was about to begin.

Though this kind of Western-style evening theater was considered the thing to do for those who had come to Tokyo for the first time, it held no real surprise for Junichi, since he had already become well acquainted with theaters through various books and illustrations.

The spectators sitting around him were all women. To his left were two young women, probably students still attending school, their hair in a low pompadour. One wore a light blue *hakama* skirt, the other a violet one. To his right was a married woman wearing a Western-style coat with a thick fox furpiece. The seat to the right of this woman was not occupied.

When Junichi had sat down, both young women, who had been huddled together talking, and the woman seated to his right turned at once to look at him. The girl in the light blue *hakama* had a round reddish face; the one in the violet *hakama* was square-faced with a fair complexion. This squarish face reminded him of something: one of those dolls with a fearful mouth that Westerners use for cracking nuts. Her face, in spite of being gentle and feminine, reminded him of that kind of doll. And that face also reminded him somehow of the politician Shimada Saburō, who had once delivered a speech in Junichi's town. Neither woman was beautiful. Quite different from them was the exceedingly attractive woman with the fox furpiece. Her nose was just the right height, and something excessively coquettish was in her large dark eyes. Junichi had once heard a story about a man who had introduced his wife to a friend and said to him just after the introduction, "Don't worry. She gives everyone that kind of look." Somehow Junichi felt this beautiful lady's look was like that. It seemed to him that her jet-black hair was so thick and long she did not know how to manage it. The two younger women frequently looked around the theater and kept talking in low voices as if they had some important topic to discuss. The lady, though, had continued her bold look at Junichi.

"I say, the curtain's opened!" said the young woman in the light blue *hakama*, poking her friend in the violet *hakama*. "Oh dear, I was so absorbed in talking I didn't notice!"

The theater darkened. Since the audience consisted only of members of the Free Theater, the murmuring voices heard here and there died down at once. On the stage was the egoistic Mrs. Borkman, who was speaking such rational lines as would please any Japanese audience interested in drama. She was waiting for her son, but instead of him there came the altruistic Ella, Mrs. Borkman's younger sister who in the days of their youth had been her rival in love. Ella was speaking about something in sentimental slovenly tones. An excessively long exchange began between the two women. While listening, the audience found that Mrs. Borkman, who had sounded quite rational and gave the appearance of being strong, was turning into a weak woman and gradually losing sympathy, while the weakness of the younger sister, who seemed to be perpetually whining and looking more and more fragile, was actually made of much sterner stuff underneath and was gaining the sympathy of the spectators. The audience was beginning to realize the play was turning in a slightly different direction from what had been anticipated. While somewhat tired by the long dialogue, the audience was listening with suspense, expecting something to happen. Unaccustomed to this rambling exchange of dialogue in a play, the members of the audience received a new stimulus when they realized that the heavy footsteps upstairs were those of the bankrupt bank president. Then Mrs. Wilton, the son's sweetheart, appeared, and then the son did too, so that gradually the audience was even more stimulated. After all the characters withdrew from the stage except for Mrs. Borkman, she threw herself in agony on the floor, and the curtain descended.

The seats in the audience suddenly became visible in the lights.

"I had thought Madame Borkman's tossing around on the floor would be funny, but, quite the contrary, it wasn't in the least," said the woman in violet.

"No, it wasn't. Well, the play's unusual, quite interesting," replied the other in light blue.

The minute the curtain came down, the woman to Junichi's right stood, but she soon returned without her coat and furpiece probably because the theater had become much warmer. Though she wore a kimono of silk crepe patterned with figures of quail, a *haori* coat, and a gorgeous *obi* sash of gold brocade, Junichi had noticed only that the dark *haori* was quite elegant. And then he noticed that on almost every finger of the hands she had crossed on her lap was a glittering ring.

The woman's eyes were again concentrating on Junichi's face. "You've probably read today's program notes, haven't you? Where does the next act take place?" she said in a calm, clear voice. Junichi felt something firm and resilient in her tone, yet he was much more strongly impressed by the gleam in her eyes. Lurking in those eyes was, he sensed, a brazen cheeky smile as if the words she had uttered were completely different from this expression in her eyes. At the same time he had this thought, Junichi felt the eyes of the two younger women to his left had simultaneously turned toward him.

"I haven't read the program notes, but I've read the play in a French translation. In the next act we'll see the second floor where we heard the sounds of footsteps earlier."

"So, you're a scholar of French?" said the lady, a broad smile on her face as if remembering something.

Just then the curtain rose, and Junichi didn't have time to conjecture what had made her ask that question, a question to which, though, he thought it unnecessary to respond. On the stage, that "wolf in his cage" Borkman had secretly unlocked the tender feelings of a young girl who often came to play the piano for him. He had also found in this disappointed girl a seed of agony already beginning to sprout and forcing him to comfort her depressed and disconsolate heart. On hearing the lonely voice of Frida, the young girl, a voice like a twittering bird's, the spectators felt as if they had entered an exhibition of dolls fashioned from chrysanthemum flowers in Asakusa Park or were standing in front of a cage of linnets.

Junichi heard the woman in the blue *hakama* whisper, "Oh, how adorable she is!"

After the birdlike Frida leaves, her old father-bird, an unsuccessful poet, comes on stage, and he too leaves. Then Ella, who had been deprived by her coldhearted sister of the man she had long ago loved to the very marrow of her being, a woman whose body was being corroded by an incurable disease, enters the cage of her aged lover, a candle in her hand. And then Gunhild, Borkman's wife, a large shawl coiled over her head as if it were some triumphant symbol showing she was the one who had become his wife, suddenly appears after eavesdropping behind a door, and again she disappears like a fearful apparition. Encouraging the staggering wolf, whose claws and fangs have been weakened by the great power of love, Ella is about to lead him to the cavern of this phantom down below when the curtain falls.

With the lights on again, the spectators' seats were visible. A chorus of murmuring voices rose like a wind whistling through a forest. Once more Junichi felt the lady's eyes were on him.

"What happens from now on?"

"The next act takes place downstairs again. Almost everything will soon be settled."

After being spoken to by this lady, Junichi had the feeling the two younger women to his left had made him the object of their hidden observation. While he would be looking at them, the two kept looking away from him, but the moment he looked to the front or a little to the right, he felt them shooting glances straight at the nape of his neck. It felt uncomfortable to be looked at while pretending not to be aware of it. Junichi suddenly thought of his old middle school science teacher Yamamura in Y Prefecture. His old teacher had some strange superstitious beliefs on spiritualism. According to him, each human being has a special kind of atmosphere around his body which enables him to be aware of things without using his five senses, so he is able to tell which friend, for example, is following behind without having to turn back to see who it is. Junichi couldn't help feeling uncomfortable, even without using his five senses, when he was aware of being looked at from behind.

The curtain rose. Any man facing imminent death is not satisfied with temporary comfort. Ella, the elderly virgin, led the caged beast to his elderly wife's chamber downstairs. Erhart, the spoils from the chase all three were contending for, had been summoned by Mrs. Borkman, and he appears on stage. He refuses to obey his mother. He refuses to obey his father as well. Nor does he obey his aunt, who is trying to bind him with the rope of family affection. His piercing shout as he said, "I want to live my own life!" was applauded by the spectators, most of whom were students. He was going to ride in a sledge with silver bells which would set out in the snow and head toward southern climes with Mrs. Wilton, who looked like a flower trying to absorb as much sunlight as possible before withering.

The intermission came. Since the program had indicated that the time would be slightly longer than usual, most left their seats. A little before Junichi stood up, the lady on his left got to her feet. Pushed by persons in front and behind even while sometimes touching the lady and sometimes breaking away from her, Junichi made his way toward the lobby. Every so often a whiff of perfume assailed him. The lady turned back, a smile revealed in her eyes. Though Junichi could not make out why she smiled, he politely smiled back.

Junichi came into the lobby. Since the crowd was thinning out, he felt he should refrain from following the woman so closely, and he deliberately slowed his pace. But before there was not too much distance between them, the woman turned back to him and said, "Since you're interested in French, why not come visit my house? We have lots of books. You probably read only the latest ones, but I'm certain you will find some good books even among our old ones. Please feel free to visit my home."

While walking, the lady spoke in an easy, casual manner, as if she had known him for a long time. Junichi took out his name card and, handing it to her, said frankly, "I've come from the country, and I've rented a house in Yanaka. I've brought almost no books with me, so it would really be of help. If you have any literary works, I'd really like to read them, even if they're a little old."

"I see. We do have literary works. We even have complete collections. What's more, we have lots of books on history too. My late husband was a law scholar, and I donated all his law books to his university library."

It was at this moment Junichi learned the lady was a widow. He guessed she was now in control of her home or she would not have invited him, a stranger she had met for the first time, to come and examine her books. After briefly glancing at his name card on which only his name was printed in small characters, she brought out from between the folds of her *obi* sash a purse of embossed satin and put his name card in it. She gave him her own name card, saying, "Where are you from?"

"From Y Prefecture."

"Good heavens! That's the same prefecture my husband was from. Though you said you've just come to Tokyo, you haven't the slightest provincial accent, have you?"

"That's not so. I often come out with it."

On her name card was printed the name Sakai Reiko. When Junichi saw her name, he said at once, "So, you're the wife of Professor Sakai Kō, aren't you?" Junichi made a polite bow.

"Did you know my husband?"

"No, I know of him by name only."

Professor Sakai had been a famous scholar born in Y Prefecture. His translation of Montesquieu's *Esprit des Lois* into classical Chinese had earned him a good reputation, though his book had not met with a broad reception. But his translation of the *Code Napoléon,* considered the model of its type, not only earned him wide admiration, but the book had increased in reputation even after his death and even now continued to earn handsome royalties for his family. When Junichi was in middle school, he had heard that the professor had remained a bachelor until after forty years of age, had married a beautiful woman young enough to be his daughter, and had died from a spinal disease less than a year later.

Junichi found out that what he had heard was not rumor. In addition to being a professor at a college of law, he had been asked for decades to offer professional guidance to various government officials and had also lent his expertise to quite a number of fields. So after he died, he had a considerable fortune. His widow had managed that fortune by herself. She severed her ties with the people of Y Prefecture, including the family of the former feudal lord. She found that her life left her without any expectations, left her without real direction. Though she had no child, she did not want to adopt one. She did not even seem to have anyone she was on friendly terms with. She had lived in a Western-style villa in Negishi which had been completed a little before her husband's death, but she did not seem to be living in quiet contemplative grief over her husband's soul. She had been living a much more ostentatious life than when her husband had been alive, and that way of life had been a kind of private mystery. When Junichi had heard in his hometown these various rumors about her, there had been etched into his recollections the image of Mrs. Sakai as the heroine of an interesting novel.

When he had looked at her after replying that he had heard the name of Professor Sakai, he again witnessed that meaningless or covertly meaningful smile drifting across her face. At that moment the two of them were standing at the foot of the western staircase.

"Shall we go upstairs?" Mrs. Sakai asked.

"Yes."

Just as they started up, someone called out from the upstairs lobby, "Koizumi, is that you?" Junichi, who was on the fourth or fifth step from the top, looked up to discover it was Ōmura who had called out.

"Oh, Ōmura!"

When Junichi had responded in this way, Mrs. Sakai made an almost imperceptible bow, quickly finished climbing the stairs, and went off by herself to the left.

Junichi and Ōmura stood at the top of the landing, just below a sign on a pillar with the word "Buffet" on it, an arrow pointing upward to the left. Looking as if he had missed Ōmura, Junichi said, "I didn't expect to see you here. What a coincidence!"

"What's that? A coincidence? The play's only on for two days, and all of us have to see it. So the possibility of meeting one another is fifty-fifty. But most members of DIDASKALIA will come both days, so the possibility of meeting is one hundred percent."

"I wonder if Seto's here."

"I believe I saw him."

"This is such an elegant theater that it probably has something like a foyer or promenade."

"No, it hasn't. First of all, the corridor we're in corresponds to a foyer. There's a large room over there, but it serves as a dining hall. The Japanese prefer eating and drinking to walking and talking, and that's why so much space is taken up for dining."

Passing were the two young women seated to Junichi's left, their hands held as they continued their incessant talking. Many other people passed, as well, and every so often Ōmura indicated to Junichi who the persons were.

While continuing to talk with Ōmura, Junichi walked as far as the entrance to the dining room, and for a while they stood near a shop that sold souvenirs. The two observed those who went in and out of the dining room. Suddenly the warning bell rang.

Junichi left Ōmura and went downstairs. As he made his way to his seat and was being pushed along the narrow aisle between the rows of seats, he again caught the odor of perfume. Looking back, he noticed Mrs. Sakai's enigmatic eyes.

The curtains rose on a scene of a door to a house in the snow. The clerk, that ill-fated yet optimistic poet whose daughter had been taken away by Mrs. Wilton, had been knocked flat by the sledge with its ringing silver bells. Even though he had injured his leg, he had offered a blessing to his daughter's future and returned to console his wife, who was crying under a lamp in their lonely house. The setting was changed to a scene at the top of a hill. As the old hero, the ambitious industrialist, closed his eyes while sitting on a bench covered with snow, behind those eyes the vision of the great factory he had always envisioned, his former gentle love and now his widow who had been so hostile to the life of her rival in love shook hands over the dead body, and the curtain fell.

Thinking the exits would be crowded, Junichi stood waiting in the aisle for a while and looked toward the stage. The curtain, which had fallen, rose again, and in the midst of the final setting the actors and actresses posed for group pictures.

"Good-bye. Come any time you wish to see the books."

The moment Junichi looked back, the figure of Mrs. Sakai was disappearing in the crowd at the exit. He did not have a chance to respond. While following her with his eyes, he thought to himself: "I usually feel ill-at-ease when I talk to women, so why was it I didn't feel that way when I talked with her? Besides, she has such mysterious eyes. I wonder what's behind that glance of hers."

He looked around as he left, but he did not see Ōmura or Seto. To his left the two young women were repeatedly calling out for a rickshaw.

10

An entry from Junichi's diary . . .

November 30. Weather fine. It's strange to write down something about the weather as if I methodically write in my diary every day. No matter how hard I try, however, I find I cannot keep up my diary on a daily basis. When I visited Ōmura the other day and mentioned this difficulty, he said, "Since human beings are fettered to so many things in their lives, why is it they fetter themselves even to their own wills?" I think he's right. We don't have to worry that much about keeping a diary to prove we are alive. But the problem is how to prove we're living without fettering ourselves to keeping a diary. The real problem is to discover what the purpose is in liberating ourselves from diaries or anything else.

To make. To create. To create just like God created everything. This was my initial intention. But that has proved to be impossible. Each time I hear some critic say, "What can you expect to write idling away your time on the second floor of a lodging house?" I want to retort, "Are you saying that if a person cruises around the world, he can write a masterpiece?" Yet at the same time I make my rebuttal, another thought germinates, and I feel ashamed of myself for not even knowing enough about the second floor of my lodging. At that moment I feel like a midget in a dunce's cap who is grimacing and laughing at Tithonus as he pulverizes boulders and hurls their fragments toward heaven.

What should I do then?

To live. To lead my life.

Answering is easy. But what the answer means is not at all that easy.

I really do wonder if the Japanese actually know what it means to live. After they enter primary school, they try with all their might to finish, to hurry up and finish. They think there is a life ahead of them. Once they leave school and get a job, they try to perform and complete that job. And again they think there's a life out there ahead of them. But there isn't.

The present is a single line dividing past and future. If you can't find your life on this line, you can't find your life anywhere.

So what on earth am I doing now?

Already it's past midnight. Today is no longer today. Yet I feel so strangely clearheaded that I don't think I can sleep no matter how hard I try.

This today which is no longer today is now part of my own past history. That "today" ought to be called part of the history of existence, part of the history of my life. In order to write down this experience as a memorable incident in my idle life, I opened a new page in my diary with only the date printed on it.

But I don't know what it is that I'm writing about now. Though I thought I had a great many things to write out, I can find almost nothing to put down. I almost feel I should leave this page blank except for its worthless date.

The morning had been as ordinary as any other morning. From back home I had received a letter from my dear grandmother, who always writes me every two or three days. "Be careful about your food," she had written, "and don't get hurt by being hit by a streetcar, a carriage, or an automobile." She seemed to think food and vehicles were the only dangers I had to take precaution against.

Then Seto dropped by, saying he had come because it was Sunday. He spoke to me as if we were intimate friends. He behaved as if we shared some enormous secret and conspired together in concealing it. He always suggested two or three plans for killing time, and then he would let me choose one. Among them was always one which could be called *une direction dominante*. And like the needle of a compass, one of these plans would point to that secret we supposedly shared. I would endeavor as much as possible to choose a plan different from the one he expected me to choose. This time, however, just to make a test of it, I rejected all his suggestions and said, "Today I'm going to read at home." The result was just what I expected. Seto hesitated for some time before finally asking me to lend him some money.

It wasn't the least bit difficult to satisfy his request. But I didn't want to repeat those experiences I had had as early as my middle school student days. The most innocent borrowers would begin by saying, "I'm terribly sorry I haven't yet returned what I borrowed from you the other day." The most common trick would be to return the debt first and say, "I'll be obligated to you for a long time," and then to ask for even more money than what had been returned. But the cleverest one of all would say, "If you'd lend me this much more, I could round the figure off on what I owe." It would have been fine with me to arrange another loan, but I couldn't understand how anyone could be audacious enough to add to his debts by asking for more money just to round off the numbers. As I said, I didn't want to go through this kind of unpleasant experience again. So I decided to flatly refuse Seto's request. Yet I wasn't experienced enough in refusing requests. To make ends meet, even I have to budget the money I am sent from home, so I don't have much money to spare. But if I juggle my expenses, it's not impossible to lend Seto something. Actually I had enough money on me to meet his request. Ought I to tell him I had no money? But I didn't want to lie. On the other hand, if I told him a lie, he would easily know it. All that would be quite unpleasant.

I remembered something that had happened just before I left my hometown. It also had to do with someone who had hesitated to repay me, so I finally said to him, "It's all right if you don't return what you owe me, but I'll never again lend you anything." Afterwards that friend of mine severed all relations between us. Actually it was all due to my naive forthrightness. Simply because one does not want to lie, one ought not to make the other person lose face. It's probably better in such instances to make up a lie.

Summoning my courage, I said to Seto, "I've had some bad experiences lending money. I don't want any monetary difficulties between us. So please don't ask me for any money." Seto kept looking at me in total surprise, but after bringing up two or three irrelevant topics, he left in a hurry. He's much more experienced in the ways of the world than I am, so perhaps this incident won't make him break off our relationship. Yet he'll probably change his attitude toward me. He will no longer say, "You're a remarkable person." On the other hand, perhaps he'll have a slightly higher opinion of me.

At any rate, I hadn't opened my diary with the intention of writing about such trivial matters. A person who makes a visit without any definite purpose deliberately proceeds in a roundabout way. Am I not myself setting down these superfluous things against my will because I don't clearly know what I ought to write?

This afternoon I visited Mrs. Sakai. From the moment I had met her at the Yūrakuza until I visited her today, I had actually been in a kind of dilemma. I had asked my rational self whether or not I should visit her. I had reasoned that as she had informed me she had put together a collection of books in French, it would be in my own interest to see them. Yet I wondered if it would be wise to go to the villa of a woman on whom doubts and rumors had frequently been cast. In my mind the pros and cons about the visit were contending with one another until my own will in the matter began to interfere. I wanted to visit her. It could not be denied I wanted to go see those books. Yet when analyzing myself mercilessly, I had to admit that was not the only reason for visiting her.

Actually I wanted to discover the secret lurking behind her eyes.

After returning from the Yūrakuza, I had again and again recalled those eyes. Sometimes I was startled to find myself unconsciously recalling them. In a sense, those eyes had been pursuing me. It's probably more accurate to say those eyes had been trying to lure me. Though I said my will had interfered with the rational battle I was waging, that remark can be called similar to putting the cart before the horse. That battle between the rational pros and cons was probably nothing more than my helpless resistance against the magnetic force of those eyes.

It was today that my will finally triumphed over that resistance. I set out for her home in Negishi.

I easily found her residence. An oak tree whose top branches had been trimmed flat towered over a black wooden fence, but the house looked gloomy from the outside as if it contained some hidden mystery.

The grilled gates attached to stone posts were closed, but a small side door was open. Beyond the gate was a path with a low bamboo fence on each side, and at the far end of the path was a closed Western-style door. I pressed the doorbell, and a pretty parlormaid, perhaps fourteen or fifteen years old, came out. She took my name card and disappeared inside. Before long she came again and showed me in, saying, "This way please."

I was led to a Western-style room on the second floor. The first thing that caught my eye was a beautiful Gobelin tapestry, probably designed from a portrait by Watteau or someone like him. It depicted a grove in a garden before which a young woman was standing while a young man was kissing her hand. The green of the grass and leaves, and the red, purple, and hazy yellow of the costumes of the man and woman, were now dazzling, seen in the setting sun which streamed in the windows of a mansion, and produced a feeling of contentment.

The maid brought in some tea. "Madame will be here soon," she said and went out. After taking a sip of tea, I went over to some shelves filled with books.

Most of the books were those I expected to find. There were handsomely bound editions of the complete works of Corneille, Racine, and Molière. In addition, there were a number of books by Voltaire and Hugo.

Just as I was looking at some of the titles on those leather-bound books, Mrs. Sakai entered.

Again I saw those enigmatic eyes. Once more I could detect in her eyes some contradictory expression which no one could describe with simple, everyday words. The minute I saw those eyes, I knew I had come not because I was attracted to Corneille or Racine but because I had been lured by those eyes.

I can't remember what kind of conversation I carried on with Mrs. Sakai. This loss of memory can't be due to any great damage to my intellect. Yet, strange as it may sound, my memory isn't the least bit blank. Though it's odd that I've forgotten what we talked about, I do remember some of the words. To put this more accurately, I've forgotten the words, but I remember their sounds. In short, it's the reverberations of the words themselves, not the actual words, that still linger in my ears.

Another memory I can evoke now is Mrs. Sakai's behavior. That is, the movements of her body. I can recall how she stood, how she sat, how the tapering slender fingers of her hands were locked immovably or almost symbolically on her lap, and yet how those same hands expertly received the tea the maid brought her and how they quickly handed the tea to me.

The sounds of those words and the movements of Mrs. Sakai still clearly remain one after another in my memory, though I can't recall the order in which they occurred.

Here I ought to mention one more strange thing. Though I can remember Mrs. Sakai's movements, I have only the vaguest memory of those moments when she remained stationary, static. I can recall her beautiful face only by remembering its expression, not its actual features. The same can be said of her eyes. When I was living in my hometown, an old man once asked me about a bull's horns and ears—which were above and which were below. Since I felt I knew at least that much about bulls, I replied immediately. "Very few gentlemen in polite society," the old man said, "can easily know that." It seems that it is difficult for anyone to remember the actual forms and shapes of things. A woman's face is only one such form that is not remembered in detail.

If so, how much do I remember about Mrs. Sakai's kimono? Hopelessly little. In fact, I can only picture it by recalling what she was saying at the moment. While I was staring at the striped patterns on her *haori* coat without even realizing I was, she had said to me, "Odd, isn't it? For an old woman like me to be wearing such gaudy clothing. Nowadays I'm wearing the formal clothes I wore long ago, wearing them as my everyday clothing."

When I heard these words, I felt from the first that what she was saying made good sense to me. I hadn't thought her outfit too gaudy. I had simply felt that the beautiful colors of her kimono were in harmony with her figure, though I had felt there was something extraordinary about the colors.

But I'm still taking a roundabout way with this brush with which I'm writing my diary entry. I'm really quite a coward.

Why had I decided to open this diary and write in it, a diary I had neglected for such a long time? Isn't it because I want to set down a certain experience of mine? Why is it that even though it took courage to go through that experience, I don't have the courage to write it down? Or am I trying to say that the experience didn't happen because of some daredevil courage in me, but rather because I had recklessly plunged into that experience out of obligation to someone? If it happened out of sheer recklessness, then ought I not to feel ashamed of myself?

When I ran out the iron gates of that house in Negishi, my blood was seething with excitement. Furthermore, I was exhilarated beyond words. I felt a kind of power in me. What I was at that moment was quite different from what I usually am. If I compare myself at that moment with what I usually am, I feel as if my ordinary self has stored in its veins blood as cold as that of a fish.

But that was how I felt in my body. My thoughts were in total chaos. At first I took long swinging strides. My Satsuma *geta* resounded loudly against the cool night earth. But gradually my pace slackened, and by the time I turned west at the top of Uguisuzaka Slope and passed a mausoleum surrounded by rows of stone lanterns, I felt my blood, which had ignited my flesh, had drained away somewhere. My face seemed to have turned pale, and I felt my skin was crawling with gooseflesh. At the same time my thoughts were gradually restored to order. A serene pleasure was surging up inside me. It was a condition similar to that of a person who had gone through the paroxysm of some acute attack and then felt relief after the attack had passed. I had been carrying a book by Racine. I felt just then as if the duty of going to her house and returning that book would not be a pleasant one. I felt as if her eyes had already lost their magnetic power to lure me.

Suddenly there arose in me the memory of a strange scene. It had to do with Mrs. Sakai's posture. Just as I was about to leave after borrowing that book by Racine, she told her maid to bring in some warmed wine because it was a cold day. While Mrs. Sakai was gazing at me as I drank the wine, she suddenly leaned back against the sofa on which she had been leaning forward up to that time, and she stretched out before her both her feet in their white *tabi*. What had drifted into my memory had been this meaningless posture she had assumed at that moment.

And at the same moment I recalled the scene, I tried to think back to the conversations between us from the moment of my arrival to my departure. I was surprised that we had not exchanged a single word of affection. I couldn't help suspecting that every novel and play was complete fabrication, a tissue of lies. And I suddenly remembered the name of Aude. It was just that Aude's eyes were dead, hollow, drifting from person to person just as the sea drifts, whereas Mrs. Sakai's eyes were quite different, enigmatic, alive. Her eyes conveyed a number of meanings. But her posture as well communicated something to me. And the way it had communicated was very rare. I thought her similar to Aude in that she could in an instant alternate absolutely proper behavior with a frivolous type of behavior. While carefully thinking about these things as I walked along, I turned the corner between the Art School and the library only to be startled by a policeman who thrust his square lantern in front of my face.

I've already mentioned that in making my entry in my diary for today I've been taking a roundabout way in reaching my destination, but thus far I've merely been wandering about the peripheries to avoid my real destination. Until today I've been "a man of no experience," but today I've become "a man of experience." It's only a little more than two hours since that momentary turbulent wave died down, yet my heart has become as serene as a philosopher's. I had never foreseen that an intimacy with a woman could be like this.

And not only had I not foreseen this. I hadn't foreseen that my becoming a man of experience would be due to this kind of chance occurrence. Though I hadn't thought I had to fall in love before I became a man of experience, little did I expect that the mind which wants to preserve itself could so easily be overturned without falling in love. For Mrs. Sakai could never be the kind of woman who could be the object of my love.

It was long ago that I began to feel that inner urge, that instinctive stimulus. Once I had felt so apprehensive and ill-at-ease that I tried to divert myself by reading a book. My eyes were aimlessly following the printed words, but my mind was unable to grasp their meaning. All of a sudden I wanted to rush outside without any purpose, and I walked hurriedly along this road and that. On the way I realized I was looking for something—I realized, like the young man in Gautier's *Mademoiselle de Maupin,* that I was searching for a woman. I didn't censure myself, but I ridiculed myself. At that time I had some strange feelings. I had wanted to encounter *une aventure.* If it involved a woman, so much the better. And yet I wasn't sure whether or not I could commit myself to that encounter. I would wait either for a moment of prudent choice or yield to the judgment of my will.

One should prize one's body. No one wants to yield that body up too easily. If by chance I met a woman and she yielded herself to me, I might decline to accept her, but without insulting her, I might calm and comfort her if possible before departing from her. It would probably be interesting to do so. And if I could, it would not be impossible perhaps to establish a platonic relationship with her. No, that wouldn't do. That would be impossible. Judging from novels in the West, a woman in that situation could not help feeling insulted. Or even if a platonic relationship were possible for a while, it would be quite different from pure love. Such a chaste relationship would simply be the deferring of a stain, a blemish. In the final analysis, no one can predict what lies ahead. At any rate, such speculations can come only after encountering *une aventure.* Well, such were the thoughts that had occurred to me at that time, half consciously, half unconsciously. At that time, when I realized all these feelings and when at the same time I seemed to have clearly undeceived myself, I was equally ashamed. What a coward I am! Why don't I seek a real life? Why don't I look for a passionate love? I am ashamed of myself for being so spineless!

But I did have, at any rate, my inner urge. I don't deny that I had external temptations. From my youngest days I had been loved by people. I had been labeled a "good boy" as if it were another name for me. When I was playing with friends, elderly people, especially elderly women, would have contempt for my friends and show only praise for me. Even without being aware of it, I began to fancy myself as a good boy. I began to cultivate the feeling that I was proud of my features. Vanity was something I also cultivated in myself. Then not only was I conscious of my good looks, but gradually I came to make use of them. When I used my eyes in a certain way, even obstinate elderly people easily caved in. At first I used that look almost unconsciously only when I felt I was being resisted. But gradually I came to realize that mine was a look that played up to people. After I was aware of what I was doing, I told myself that heroic men would not use the dirty tactics of a eunuch, but even today, when I have grown from a good boy to a good-looking young man, I can't completely rid myself of this kind of coquetry. This blandishing look is attached to my body more like a visible deformity than an invisible bad habit. It seems to me that because my sober consciousness has tried to destroy this look of mine, it has, on the contrary, become even more *raffiné,* and wearing a mask of innocence and hiding behind it, that look has been wielding its powers all the more wildly. Moreover, since external temptations, especially those from the opposite sex, seem to be in collusion with my narcissism and my blandishing look, it is actually quite difficult for me to resist these temptations.

I feel today's incident is nothing but a seedling sprouting from these cultivated fields I've been referring to.

I have no regrets over what happened today. The reason is that even if the act of maintaining a man's virginity, which seems quite rare and uncommon in present-day society, should be highly esteemed, that purity seems to have no other meaning than to satisfy the egoism of esteeming one's own body. I too have this same kind of egoism. At the moment of that incident, I was actually illuminated by the light of reason, but a cloud of nervous excitement, which aroused my flesh too intensely for me to control, suddenly overpowered that light. When that momentary light disappeared, I shouted to myself, shouted to my very core, "What do I care! She's a widow!" I remembered that Hiraga Gennai once said somewhere, "When another man's wife makes overtures to you, you ought to remember you end up being tattooed on your neck for the crime of adultery. But to make a pass at a widow. . . ." That was how I felt at that moment.

At any rate, I admit I suffered a certain loss of egoism. But I am also aware that I don't want to incur this kind of loss again. And yet I have not the slightest taste of bitterness that can be called repentence.

I don't feel any bitterness, nor do I feel any sweetness. Both the powerful feelings generated at that moment and the feelings of exultation completely vanished in an instant. Now that I have returned to this room and have been sitting at this desk, I have no positive feelings. I don't feel any real physiological change has occurred in me. I do think I feel lonelier than I usually do. But that loneliness does not come from the feeling of being attracted to Mrs. Sakai in Negishi. I feel neither love nor yearning for her.

Is what I experienced life at all? I think not. This is decidedly not a real, full life.

Is it possible that I can't lead a full life? Am I nothing but a floating weed sprouting in a bog of decadence, a weed which can only have a pale illusory flower even if it blooms?

I have nothing more to write. Shall I take a short sleep before dawn breaks? I do wish I could sleep. Except that this sleeplessness may be a memorable token of that earlier excitement. Or perhaps the reason I cannot sleep even after the embers of that excitement have died out is due to my having written too long in my diary.

II

The day after Junichi had gone to Negishi, the weather was as good as it had been a few days ago.

Usually, even when he had stayed up till all hours of the night reading books, he would feel refreshed on waking the following morning, but as he sat this morning in front of a sliding door in the sun, he had a headache that made him feel sluggish, the sun blinding him. He thought if he washed his face, he would feel better, and he hurried out to the veranda.

Everything looked pale, steeped in the morning air charged with minute particles of vapor. Chōjirō had said he would spread fallen pine needles around the washbasin because he had some free time to do it, and Junichi noticed patches of frost on the thick straw rope circling the carpet of pine needles.

Suddenly Junichi slipped into some garden clogs and went out to the gate, and squatting there, he watched the traffic along the street. Two workmen in the short coat laborers wear walked by, fragments of their conversation heard, their breath white in the morning cold.

While squatting on his heels for some time, Junichi realized his headache had disappeared. He returned to the veranda, and while picking at his teeth with a toothpick, the memories of the previous day vaguely came back to him. He felt as if he had to think over the incident, slowly and carefully this time. Behind the sliding doors he suddenly heard someone sweeping his room. The old woman was picking up his *futon* bedding, opening the door to the east, and beginning to dust.

Junichi hurriedly washed his face and returned to his room, finding on entering that it was already cleaned. His eyes were immediately drawn to the diary left open on his desk. What troubled him was not the actual incident that had occurred yesterday but what he had written in the diary. One memory evoked another, and an uneasy feeling crept over him. He felt uneasy because his psychological analysis of what he had experienced yesterday was not thorough enough, and his overall judgment seemed wrong. Even the same phenomenon assumes a completely different appearance if it is examined at night or analyzed during the daytime.

The incident of last night could not be dealt with as merely an event of a single night. What course would it take from now on? It was certainly true that there was no love on his side. But the question was whether or not Mrs. Sakai had the power to attract him any longer, and he could not answer that with any certainty. Last night he had thought everything between them was over, but he wondered if his feeling was similar to what a sick person would feel after he had completely recovered from an attack of ague. Was there not a possibility that he would again want to see the enigmatic eyes of Mrs. Sakai? Unlike the psychological state he had been in late last night, he felt that those captivating eyes were again beginning to work on him even a little more powerfully.

Moreover, he could not make any speculation without the woman being present. It was not merely a question of what he himself thought about her. He had to consider what she herself felt. Ever since he had first met her at the Yūrakuza Theater, she had been advancing directly toward her objective while he himself had been on the defensive. The real question was probably concerned with what measures she was going to take rather than what direction he would take from here on in. He thought it presumptuous of him to argue about loving or not loving, for it might be the woman herself who had no love for him. If that was the case, was not the real issue how long she would continue this relationship that he ought to feel quite ashamed of? He had no doubt that the affair was obviously quite temporary, but temporary was a relative concept.

While he was indulging in these thoughts, the old landlady brought in his breakfast. Junichi picked up his chopsticks. Serving the meal, the old woman said, "Last night you were up late studying, weren't you?"

"Yes. I went to a friend to borrow a book. Without intending to, we had a long talk, and I got home late. And then I did some work." Junichi offered this lame excuse even as it suddenly occurred to him it was the first time he had told a lie since moving into this house. He felt disgusted with himself.

When he finished his meal, the old woman added some charcoal to the brazier and left.

Junichi took out the Racine he had borrowed last evening. Though he flipped through two or three pages, he didn't feel like reading. He justified himself by reasoning that a classical book of this sort ought to be read when he was in a calmer state of mind. Remembering the Huysmans novel he had discovered a few days ago at the Sansaisha Bookstore in Kanda and purchased, he started reading it.

He came across a dialogue between the hero, who is a novelist, and his guest, a doctor. The discussion concerned the merits and demerits of naturalism as a movement that had passed. What naturalism had achieved was to give once again flesh and blood to art and literature which had gradually become so far removed from the real world that both were almost totally divorced from it. But there was some truth in the remarks of the guest who had thoroughly rejected the naturalistic writer who ended up expressing commonplace and indecent thoughts in complex and verbose expressions.

In the section designating the achievements of naturalism, the names of Balzac, Flaubert, the Goncourts, and finally Zola were given. All these writers belonged to the highest ranks of naturalism.

When Junichi looked back to the miniature naturalist movement in Japan, he could not appreciate it that much, even when he tried to view it in the most favorable light. After he had come to Tokyo and had approached one of its prophets, Junichi's ardent longing for naturalism had cooled considerably.

When the discussion ended, the guest returned home. The hero was left to his own thoughts. In this section Huysmans had written something like the following: "Realistic content, detailed description of each and every part, and rich and sensitive and careful language—all these characteristics realism must preserve. But, in addition, realism must take into consideration spiritual values. Miracles must not be explained away as a sensual disease. Life has two aspects, the spiritual and the physical, and these are integrated. No, not so much that as inextricably bound together. If at all possible, I want my novels to have these two aspects. I want novelists to write about their reactions, their conflicts, and their reconciliations between these two aspects. In a word, while treading along that road which Zola dug out so deeply, I want writers to trace another road in the air. The latter is a back road, a road that runs from behind. In other words, it is a road on which to erect a naturalism of the spirit. If we can create this road, it can provide another aspect of naturalism to be proud of. It can provide another type of perfection for naturalism, another type of power for it. This type of splendid naturalism has not yet been possible, for there are two schools of naturalism in conflict with each other, one the liberal school which tries to make naturalism palatable to refined society, and the other which blindly imitates to no avail a spiritual art in a badly affected telegraphic language which can never conceal its poverty of thought."

When Junichi had read this far, he found his own thoughts moving away from the book. Though his eyes were fixed on the printed words, his mind was on something else. He felt that his experience of the previous night had only been physical and that his spirit was now walking along that skyward road. This was the start of his moving away from what had been written in the Huysmans book.

How long was Mrs. Sakai going to continue a relationship divorced from spirit? Like Aude, whom Junichi had suddenly recalled the previous night, was she going to pursue him the rest of his life? Or having advanced in a straight line to reach her objective, would Mrs. Sakai at the moment of achieving her goal regard it as only the end of the beginning of her real pursuit? The only thread binding him to her was the Racine he had borrowed and returned home with. When he brought it back, would she cut that thread? Or would she change that one thread into two threads or even three? Would she write to him? Would she visit him?

With these thoughts in mind, Junichi felt he could hardly wait to read her letters. He felt he could hardly wait to see her. That girl Oyuki had often visited his room. Yet no matter how friendly they had become, he could not open up to her, and after she left, he would heave a sigh of relief. As for Mrs. Sakai, from the moment he had seen her, he felt he could tell her all. And should she come into this room, she would probably behave in a natural and spontaneous way. She would probably never be troubled over what to talk about. And she might even behave as if words were unnecessary to understand what she wanted.

At this point in his thoughts, Junichi realized he had let his imagination run wild. He felt ashamed of his cowardice.

Was he not a real man, a respectable one? Due to inexperience he had remained on the defensive up to now, but he could not expect to remain defensive forever. No matter what she thought about him, it was up to him to decide how to respond to her. If he decided not to be at her beck and call any longer, that would settle the matter. He could return the book he had borrowed, return it by parcel post. He could leave her letters unopened. If she visited him, he could flatly refuse to see her.

Having come this far in his thoughts, Junichi wondered if he could really do any of these things. He wavered. He felt a kind of pleasure in leaving these attitudes undecided. As if taking advantage of that void in which he wavered, various memories came to him. He recalled her graceful body when she stood or sat, her suggestive facial expressions, her voice he yearned to hear. He would never be able to obliterate his feelings of longing for those precious qualities in her. Once more he wondered what he would do if he saw her behaving in this room. How vividly her behavior came to him as if now in his own room she were tossing aside her long overcoat and throwing on it her muff.

Junichi suddenly came out of his reveries, mocking himself, deriding himself. Again he began the Huysmans. If one might call his hero Durtal a traveler exhausted by his journey as a literary artist, Junichi might himself be called a person who had not yet started on his travels. Durtal, disenchanted with the actual world, had thought he would rather cast his lot with Catholicism. Though he had thought of trying to several times, he had not dared "leap into the void," and he had turned back from what he came to regard as a dead end. When he wondered why he had rejected the world, his reasons seemed quite inept. Numerous miracles never cease to exist in the actual world. Money, among other things, is a great mystery. Those who want to do something in the world are, however, penniless. And those who have money are unable to achieve anything. If the rich gain even more money, corruption increases. Should the poor obtain money, they proceed down the ladder of depravity. When money accumulates and is turned into capital, enterprises which ruin an individual are completely transformed into enterprises that destroy humanity. Millions of people perish through hunger because of capital, yet the world adores it on bended knees. If money is not the devil's work, it will be called a mystery. That is, it will be called a miracle. If one can believe in this miracle, it can be said that one can thoroughly believe in the dogma of the Trinity.

Junichi frowned. Though he sympathized slightly with the author's pessimism, even seeing that Catholicism was Huysmans' only retreat, he felt how strong were the roots of convention.

Around 11:30, Ōmura stopped by. He suggested they go on an outing because the professor who was supposed to give an hour lecture the last period Monday morning and also a clinical lecture in the afternoon was absent due to an accident. Junichi immediately accepted the proposal.

"I don't know anything about the suburbs. Since the weather's so good, I'll go wherever you wish."

"It's just these last few days that it's been this nice out. An onlooker, they say, sees better than a player—anyway, they say the weather's best just before the onset of winter."

"Really? Well, which direction should we go?"

"Let's see. I myself haven't decided where to go yet. At least let's catch a train at Ueno station."

"It'll soon be noon."

"We'll grab something to eat at Ueno and then set out."

While Junichi was putting on his formal *hakama* skirt, Ōmura picked up the book lying on Junichi's desk.

"You're doing some serious reading, aren't you?"

"I suppose. I've only just read the first few pages. Somehow what he's written is awfully pessimistic."

"That's it exactly. That's the point, isn't it? The hero's Catholicism ends up in a blind alley, and he turns back halfway to become a spiritual naturalist."

"Yes. That's as far as I've read. What in the world happens after that?"

With these words Junichi finished putting on his *hakama*. He picked up his cloth cap. Ōmura stood up, went over to the doorway, sat down, and began tying his lace-up boots.

"Wait a while for my answer because I want to talk about the book as we walk."

Junichi easily slipped into his *geta* and, glancing through the back door of the gardener's house, told his landlady that lunch was not necessary. He started out with Ōmura, but as they walked together side by side, Junichi couldn't help feeling he was being overwhelmed by this strongly built large man.

"Let's walk leisurely." Ōmura, as if he had sensed Junichi's feeling, glanced at him.

Ōmura's voice sounded as if he were conceding to Junichi or patronizing him, but Junichi didn't feel the least bit troubled.

"What happens in the novel we were talking about a while back?"

"It's disgusting. Quite serious though. The heroine, who comes to meet her lover, is a real *sataniste*. But Durtal is overwhelmed, and once more he backs away. He concludes that in French society, both ethics and religion have disappeared, and only diabolism remains. Haven't you read any of his other novels yet?"

"No. I've just now had a chance to read one. That's not one of the books I ordered and paid for. Since Seto told me there were lots of French books at Sansaisha, I went there and bought the book on impulse."

"Seto can't read French, can he?"

"Not at all. Since his school recommended he buy a French text for conversation or something, he told me he went to Sansaisha and discovered quite a few French novels there. He told me to go look at them."

"I thought as much. Well, read the entire book. There are some quite violent things written in it. It's not the typical book young men read."

With his eyes full of glee, Ōmura looked directly at Junichi. Junichi walked on without responding.

They came to Tennōjimae. Though the weather remained fine, there was little traffic. They came across some girls in a horse-drawn carriage, probably on their way to a visit to a cemetery. On a straw mat in front of a tradesman's house and shop were some children basking in the sun while playing.

Junichi and Ōmura passed the entrance to Ueno Zoo, cut across the precinct of the first *torii* gate to the Tōshōgū Shrine, and went into the Seiyōken Restaurant through a back door.

As they passed the front counter and went into the dining room, they found there were no customers yet, so the two or three waiters were talking together before the fireplace in the room. With a surprised look, they dispersed. One of the waiters followed Junichi and Ōmura to the table near the veranda. The meal was ordered.

When asked about drinks, Ōmura ordered beer, Junichi citron. Ōmura said, "Citron makes me feel too cold."

"Well, it's not that I can't drink *sake*. It's just that I don't like it that much to order it on my own."

"If that's the case, will you drink some if I offer it to you?" To Junichi, Ōmura's words sounded strangely sharp and critical.

"I guess so. I guess I can't help being passive."

"No one can put up a front that he's active and aggressive in everything."

The waiter brought their soup. While they were eating, they engaged in small talk when out of the blue Junichi said, "What do you think of the question of male chastity?"

"Well, as a medical student, physiologically speaking, it seems to me men have a more difficult time than women in maintaining it. But it's not at all impossible to maintain, nor is it harmful to. If you ask my opinion, I'm all in favor of guarding it."

Junichi felt himself blushing slightly. "I would want to, too, but it seems to me chastity's significance is only a form of egoism. What do you think?"

"Why do you say that?"

"To put it briefly, it's probably no more than a kind of self-love."

Ōmura seemed lost in thought for a while. Then he said, "There's some truth in your words. I questioned you because I tried to see the significance of chastity in terms of our daily impulses and the preservation of the species. From these points of view, guarding one's chastity means controlling our impulses, and by doing that we become more altruistic than egoistic. That point of view may seem too offensively philosophical, but it seems natural for me to think so."

As he put down his fork, Junichi's eyes gleamed. "Of course, you're right. It's my hope you'll go on being philosophical. All the time I was back home, I thought over and over again it was ridiculous to be a slave to convention, and I've come to negate everything and anything around me. Possibly I was influenced by novels and the like. But lately I've had the urge to really scrutinize my ideas. The other day, you remember, I talked with you about the 'new man.' And it was just our talk that made me feel the urge to again scrutinize my thoughts. We talked about the new man being active, but you really didn't clarify for me what active means."

The waiter came to remove Ōmura's plate of fried food, and he glanced at Junichi as if asking if he could remove his. "Go right ahead," said Junichi, putting his fork on the plate to let the waiter take it away, all the while continuing their discussion. "Since our talk I've frequently tried thinking things out by myself. And so, all my thoughts seemed to be sheer egoism. Rather my own petty egoism. Or perhaps it's better to think of it as an almost thorough self-righteousness. It occurred to me I shouldn't go on in this way. I thought that without sacrificing something, I would gain nothing in return. And yet of all the things I've done up to now, not one thing involves either sacrificing something or sacrificing myself. Everything I've done, even after thinking I should make a sacrifice, whether this or that, has been completely egocentric. And so when I thought about chastity, I did so not from the idea of using it in our daily lives or the continuity of the species but from the idea of the preservation of the self, the preservation of one's egoism."

The smile that suddenly appeared on Ōmura's face did not seem contemptuous. "And that's why you tried to gain someone's love in order to make a sacrifice, didn't you?"

"No, it isn't. It's not that. It's not that I don't expect to love someone. But since I don't feel love is the be-all and end-all in life, to achieve love is not, I believe, one of the real achievements of the aggressive new man." Junichi deliberately came out with a slight smile. "In other words, I counted out my moral attributes the way a poor man examines the little property he has, and I came out with the question of my chastity."

"I understand. As far as a man's actions are concerned, especially good actions, some are motivated by egoism, some by altruism, and some by both. So if the new man wants to be aggressive, whether it be to establish ethics or religion, he won't be able to achieve his goal through egoism."

"You mean—don't you?—that eventually we're all tied to something like convention. When I asked you that same question the other day, you said that a rope touches different parts of a man's body. I still don't understand what you meant by that."

"You've remembered terrible things! Well, what I meant is this. It's in the nature of convention to bind things instinctively and unconsciously. As for the new man, since he too is bound, he wants to be bound consciously. If we compare the bonds of convention to a rope which eventually binds a run-away thief, a new man is like some robber baron ready with a laugh of derision to be bound. Somehow the rope that binds is an expression we all have to use."

Ōmura came out with such an unrestrained laugh after these words that Junichi couldn't help laughing too.

After a while Junichi said, "If that's the case, the kind of ethics created by one's self is altruistic and social, isn't it?"

"Of course it is. Ethics made by an individual become public ethics, and we call that a leap, a resurrection. And so if an active new man emerges, social problems will be solved from within society."

For some time they sat there silently. Placed before them were their orders of grilled chicken and lettuce salad. These they ate, and for their coffee they went out to the veranda.

They paid the bill, and with the winter sun on the university cap of one and the cloth cap of the other, the two of them, breathing an air unusually dry for Tokyo, left the Seiyōken.

12

Junichi and Ōmura went across Ueno Hill, came down a short slope at the back of the Tokiwakadan Restaurant, and entered Ueno station. With the weather so good, numbers of people had come to Tokyo from the outlying districts, and now groups of people wearing straw sandals and carrying bundles wrapped in *furoshiki* cloth stood tightly packed in front of the ticket counter.

"Where shall we go?" Ōmura asked.

"I haven't been to Ōji yet," said Junichi.

"That's too close. Let's go to Ōmiya." With these words Ōmura walked past the second-class waiting room and bought two first-class tickets.

They had about twenty minutes before departure. While Ōmura went to buy some cigarettes in a corner by the third-class benches, Junichi went into the waiting room for first-class ticketholders.

An unusual scene attracted him.

A woman was standing by a table in the middle of the room. Though she was probably well over fifty years of age, to Junichi she looked as if she were only forty or so. She was dressed in quiet and simple clothing, but Junichi sensed a kind of refinement about her. She had no conspicuous ornaments in her swept-back hairdo, but she had on a gray furpiece and carried a muff made of the same material. She was surrounded by five or six men and women. Junichi was startled by the woman's bearing and manner.

To begin with, he could not help thinking she was like a queen inspecting her circle. She informed an old woman, perhaps her maid, about what to do during her absence. To a man of about thirty in a business suit, apparently the man accompanying her, she gave various instructions. And individually, to each of the studentlike girls who seemed to have come to see her off, she offered words of caution. Her commanding words rang out sharply through her light-reddish lips. Like words in a well-polished sentence, not a single word she said was wasted. Without blurring the ends of her sentences, she spoke clearly. Once, when Junichi had been back home and had been taken to Kyūshū to see a full-scale review, he had seen a division commander order a soldier to sound a bugle to muster the officers. Not once until now had Junichi again heard anyone speak in that commanding way.

Junichi couldn't help comparing this unknown woman to Mrs. Sakai. Both were conspicuous, and both seemed to be resorting to some kind of artifice, and yet their artificiality seemed almost natural. Compared to them, other women looked like amateurs on stage. In the same way that Japanese art has in it a kind of mannerism, so have Japanese manners and customs the same kind of mannerism, a mannerism that is far inferior to the natural ways of European women depicted in novels and paintings. And among these Japanese women with their use of artifice, Junichi thought Mrs. Sakai was representative of those who were feminine and clever, while this other woman he was now looking at was representative of those who could be categorized as brave and wise.

Only at that moment did Junichi notice Ōmura peeping through the glass doors to the waiting room to look for him. Immediately Junichi went out of the room and walked together with Ōmura here and there along the stone-paved floor near the benches for third-class passengers. Junichi said, "I just saw a woman in the first-class waiting room who looked different from ordinary women. Didn't you notice her?"

"How could I not help noticing! She's the famous Takabatake Eiko, you idiot!"

"Really?" said Junichi, inwardly feeling she had to be. She had been the head of a girls' school in Tokyo, a person whose public image had been both praised and censured. Various rumors had circulated as to why she had resigned from the school. Back home, Junichi's teacher, Mr. Tamura, had told him that Eiko was a fine speaker and that when she had a certain aim in giving groups of students a lecture, her speech reminded one of Napoleon's oratorical powers in bolstering the morale of his troops. Junichi had heard that even as she was being violently attacked in the scandalmongering tabloids, her farewell speech had moved the entire student body to tears. Furthermore, the emotion had not been that of the moment. When the student representatives of each class proposed giving her a farewell gift, virtually no students had objected. Junichi could think of her only as someone heroic, and he imagined she was able to control her emotions at will.

"I heard how brave she was," Junichi said, "but I never thought that a mere glance at her would reveal she was that remarkable."

"Yes, she's the exemplary woman in her deportment and manner."

"Not only that, but she's probably a great woman."

"Definitely great. Do you remember the Austrian scholar who committed suicide when he was young? That was Otto Weininger. Of all the books written after Nietzsche, his has had the greatest impact on me. His argument goes something like this: In the same way that each man has some feminine elements in him, so do all women have some masculine traits in them. All human beings have M + W elements in them. And so he apparently said a great woman had a greater proportion of M elements."

"If that's the case, Eiko must have a good many M's," said Junichi, even as he thought in a rather disturbing way that there were many W elements in himself.

For some time the group of passengers carrying loads wrapped in cloth *furoshiki* were crowding round the ticket gate with its black signboard. As soon as the barrier was opened, they pushed their way out to the station platform. Usually Junichi would wait at such moments until the crowd thinned out, but since Ōmura moved along without shoving anyone and yet without giving way either, as if he regarded the crowd as so much air, Junichi hurriedly followed along behind him through the barrier.

When they entered the first-class coach, no one else was there. But soon that man in the business suit Junichi had seen in the waiting room rushed in followed by a redcap carrying a leather bag. The redcap put the bag in the middle of the long seat to the left and laid a rough checker-striped camel-colored blanket by the bag. Then the man in the suit left. Since Ōmura had sat down on a seat just across from this man's, Junichi sat down beside his friend.

An old woman, probably a Tokyoite, came in, followed by a young woman. Even though Junichi was a man of little experience, he could easily tell that this young woman with her elaborate hairdo and coral ornaments in it was a geisha. They sat down with their small leather bags between them, but soon they took off their *geta* and then sat quite properly, Japanese-style. Their immaculately white *tabi* could be seen symmetrically from the back edge of their seats.

The woman who looked like a geisha kept peering nonchalantly in Junichi's direction.

Feeling slightly embarrassed, Junichi looked at Ōmura as if asking for help. Ōmura feigned indifference as he regarded the people hurrying in all directions along the platform.

When almost all the passengers had boarded, Miss Takabatake came into their car. The business-suited man was perhaps in third class, and he had run off after greeting her. Four or five of the studentlike girls were standing in a row outside her train window. Eiko said something to the old maid through the open window.

The starting whistle sounded.

"Have a good trip!"

"*Sayonara!*"

These words and others like so many warbling sounds came from the mouths of these amiable girls. Standing erect by the window, Eiko nodded to them. The oldest of these students had a very lively expression on her lean face, her handkerchief steadily waving its farewell until the train moved farther and farther away.

Eiko quietly sat down on the laid-out blanket, put her hands into her muff, and sat up straight.

No one in the car said anything for a while. When the train passed Nippori station, it was the geisha and her companion who broke the silence. When the geisha said, "Is it expected I'll come?" the elderly woman said, "No reason for them not to." The two spoke in unexpectedly modest voices. And yet every word they said could be heard in the quiet car. Still, it was difficult to make out to whom they were referring.

Since Ōmura remained silent, Junichi kept quiet in order not to disturb him. Miss Takabatake continued to sit there quite rigidly.

All Junichi could see out the window was the same type of rice field along the way. A flock of sparrows rose from the stubbled rice paddies. On a billboard with an ugly face printed on it a crow had perched, and as the crow's beak opened wide when it cried out, the bird flew off.

Fine particles of dust danced in the rays of sun coming in through a coach window on the left.

The woman who looked like a geisha and her elderly companion also fell silent. Junichi remained silent even though he felt bored, wondering why Ōmura was so uncommunicative.

As the train was about to pass Ōji station, Junichi, who had continued to stare out the window, said, "This is Ōji, isn't it?" All Ōmura said was "This train doesn't stop here," and again he lapsed into silence.

At Akabane a railway employee came in, touched the pot of green tea set on a table to see if it remained hot, and went out. Passengers boarded and got off at Akabane, Warabi, and Urawa stations. But the number of passengers in the quiet first-class car where Junichi and his friend were sitting did not change. All this time Miss Takabatake had continued her upright posture.

Shortly after three o'clock they reached Ōmiya station. With half their tickets torn off by the station employee as they left, Ōmura said, "Well, that's a relief."

"What do you mean?"

"I know this sounds ridiculous, but I don't like being observed by certain kinds of people."

"Does Miss Takabatake belong in that category?"

Ōmura laughed. "I guess you could say so."

"Whatever kind of people do you mean?"

"Well, it's hard to explain. In short, I guess I can say I don't like being observed by people who might misunderstand me." Ōmura noticed Junichi's eyes widen. "Well, that's too abstract, isn't it? People in our so-called education circles, they're of that kind."

"Oh, I get it. You mean, I suppose, they're hypocrites."

Again Ōmura laughed. "Well, that's being too harsh on them. Even I don't think that badly of educators. They do, though, make it a habit to mold people into patterns, and so they try to make everyone fit these patterns."

While talking in this way, the two men entered a park gate. Through the two gateposts a thicket of miscellaneous trees with yellowing leaves could be seen mixed in among the evergreen trees, each post bearing a wooden marker which was blackened with age and which indicated in large letters that this was Ōmiya Park.

On the broad path littered with fallen leaves, not a soul could be seen.

Junichi thought he easily understood why Ōmura wanted to walk in this spot. Suddenly from somewhere the sounds of a *shamisen* were heard.

"What does that Weininger you mentioned a while ago think about women?" Junichi asked.

"About women? Well, his idea's quite unique. He casts women into two types only, the prostitute type and the maternal type. To put it more simply, woman as prostitute and woman as mother. It can be inferred from this theory that wives out to buy actors that the *Tōkei* newspaper and the *Anonymous News* attack, if the items carried in these stories are true, are all prostitutes, no matter how high their social status or how wealthy their fathers and husbands. It's probably not a surprise that the prostitute type has been flourishing in Japan, which has provided the dictionaries of the world with the word 'geisha.' In France, where the inhabitants have decided they want no more than two children so that the population will gradually decline, it is nothing less than a victory for the prostitute type. All things considered, this type of woman has a tendency to be antisocial. Fortunately, though, we have the other kind of woman, and this type will never become extinct. The maternal woman is desirous of children, and not only does she show affection to her children, but from the time of her girlhood, she loves dogs, cats, and birds. When these maternal women marry, they are motherlike in their affections even toward their husbands. It is this type of woman whose outstanding contribution is the perpetuity of the human race. Consequently, it's natural for a nation to train women under the principles of being good wives and wise mothers. In the same way that a horse trainer does not have to train a horse to run even though he breeds it, there is no need to give the prostitute type any special education."

"Then what does Weininger think of the recent tendency of women to become independent and attempt to take on various kinds of work?"

"We ought to think of them as M > W type, and in raising that type we should not prevent their entering all the schools boys can enter."

"I do understand. But what about love then? If a man has a maternal type as his object, he won't be able to satisfy himself, I should think. And if his object is the prostitute type, isn't that a kind of moral degradation?"

"Quite right. And that's why Weininger's theory is extremely brutal to men like you who hope to win someone's love in the future. Women are not open to your kind of love. The prostitute type has only carnal desire. The maternal type desires only to breed. The object of love is nothing but an illusion created by men. Weininger was so very serious about his theory that it probably was the root cause of his suicide."

Though Junichi said, "Of course, it must have been," he was stunned into silence for a while. He suddenly pictured Mrs. Sakai as the representative prostitute type. He had an unbearable sensation of having been enfolded like some innocent bait in her avaricious octopus arms.

"It's ideas like that," Junichi said, "that make me pessimistic."

"And they do. If we follow in Weininger's footsteps, we can't help being drawn into pessimism. And yet the idea of love contains in it an intoxication with life. It contains a sense of *ivresse*. Something like opium or hashish! True, opium's prohibited outwardly even in China, but I doubt if a human being can ever abandon such a drink. Even if he's punished by Apollo, Dionysius will never become extinct. The problem is how we're punished. It might be better to put it in terms of how we're bound or how we're imprisoned."

They came near the sanctuary of Hikawa Shrine. As a voice called out to them from a teahouse on their left, they avoided the invitation almost instinctively and turned toward the back of the shrine.

Ahead of them on a small path strewn with fallen leaves, they saw a tiny cottage surrounded by a cluster of trees. From inside they could hear a *shamisen*. Mixed in with the music was the loud laughter of four or five people and a woman's singing voice.

The woman was singing a vulgar song to the accompaniment of a poorly tuned *shamisen* that was hard on the ears. Since the sun was beginning to wane by then, the sliding doors were luckily closed so that they were spared seeing the faces of this unrestrained group of men and women. The two of them steered themselves away from this house.

They came to the edge of a marsh on the east side of the shrine. A wayside teahouse, already closed, was circled by a shelter of reed screens.

"This is a nice spot," Junichi said, almost without thinking.

"It's not bad," said Ōmura, his simple response tinged with a kind of pride. They sat down on a bench.

As Ōmura lit a cigarette, Junichi looked out over the marsh. In front of him about seven or eight feet away was a crow perched on a stake rising above the dead reeds. The bird turned in Junichi's direction, its round black eyes on him as it slightly moved its shiny purple wings to steady itself, for it did not fly off.

"Haven't you written anything yet?" Ōmura suddenly asked.

"No. I haven't taken flight or sung yet," said Junichi, still looking at the crow.

"They say a man of letters makes quite a coup. But this compares art to gambling, to tossing down a pair of dice. Apparently one can become a popular writer or a best-selling novelist by mere chance. But apart from the problem of being censured these days, when one can express one's thought freely, there's no fear that a worthy work will go unnoticed by the perceptive. So you neither have to hurry nor hesitate. Once you're determined, you can start writing at any time."

"Do you really think so?"

"I'm quite optimistic when it comes to that kind of problem. No matter how extensively a clique makes use of newspapers and journals, there are always some leading members who become independent eventually so that the clique becomes as empty as a cast-off shell and is doomed to self-destruction. That's why you don't have to ask to belong to a clique, and if you are passed over and spoken badly of, there's no need to feel depresssed about it. There isn't the slightest need for you to join some narrow group!"

"But don't you want an older advisor to talk things over with?"

"That would be nice, but only those with important connections can meet such a person, and we can't force ourselves to look for connections. It's almost totally impossible to establish a useful relationship."

While they talked, the *shamisen* and the singing voice were no longer heard. Junichi looked at his watch.

"It's already way past five."

"No wonder I feel a little chilly," said Ōmura, standing up.

The crow cried out and flew off toward the woods.

Watching it go off in that direction, they suddenly realized gray thin clouds had covered the sky.

For a while they walked along the leaf-strewn path up to their waiting train.

13

Junichi's diary again remained with many blank pages. Before he realized it, half of December had passed. With an unusual run of good weather, he had yet to experience the cold weather in Tokyo he had heard about when he had been in his hometown.

Even the chrysanthemums in his landlord Uechō's garden had been cut, and the long-blooming camellia flowers had fallen. The only colors Junichi could see were from those trees mixed with evergreens, trees with red berries here and there that looked like holly.

It had occurred to Junichi that Nakazawa's daughter Oyuki had not been to see him for quite a while, but he had not asked about her until the old landlady mentioned her to him one day. Oyuki had a younger sister who had caught diphtheria and had gone into the university hospital. The diphtheria had been cured by a serum, but then she contracted a kidney disease and could not leave the hospital easily. Oyuki visited her sister every day on the way from her lessons so that she reached home quite late. On her free days, she would go to the hospital early in the morning after buying toys and the like for her sister, and she would remain with the sick girl all day. "I've never seen such a good-natured child as Oyuki," the landlady said, praising her.

A few days ago Junichi had visited Ōishi Roka after quite a long interval. Roka had changed his lodgings to Tomizakaue in Koishikawa. Junichi was ashamed that he had not completed a piece of writing and even more so in not having started to work on anything, and he was worried about how to answer if he were suddenly asked what he had been doing. And yet Ōishi did not ask him a single question about that. On the contrary, Junichi couldn't help feeling that Ōishi would probably take it for granted that his visitor was doing nothing. Just as Junichi entered, Ōishi seemed to be writing something at his desk on which there were scattered pages of a manuscript.

Junichi said, "I can come again if I'm interrupting you."

"Don't worry about it. I'm just writing mechanically, so I can stop at any point and pick up on it again whenever," said Ōishi, his face serious. "It's a piece of no importance." And quite unlike his usual taciturn response, he offered comments on his present circumstances. Ōishi spoke about these things in an extremely calm tone of voice as if he had no interest in the report, as if, in fact, the events had happened to a third party. Immediately Junichi realized that Ōishi's story had a close connection to the piece he was writing. And while talking, Ōishi seemed to be arranging the threads of the progress of the affair. Apparently he did not care to whom he was telling the story.

The *Tōkei* newspaper for which he wrote was originally started as a small paper written to carry simple news items in easy sentences so that even lower-class readers could read it, but it had gradually raised its quality. Its style had changed several times along with its reporters. But it had never been so seriously oriented toward the literary arts as it had been in recent years. This trend had occurred only after it had become the one organ for what came to be called naturalism. But after the death of the president of the paper, it passed to his son as an inheritance. The growth of the paper had not been due to the deceased president's conscious efforts. Its popularity had been a mere matter of chance as reporters with new ideas joined the paper, as young readers, for example students, happened to increase, and as news items for some reason or other began to find favor with those numbers of youthful readers. All these factors interacted with one another to help the newspaper

establish itself as the voice of naturalism. The former president had let this
trend take its own course. And then the newspaper passed into the hands of
its new owner. With a grip of steel like that of some youthful politician, he
began a conscious assertion of his own intentions. According to the newspaper employees, Baron Honda, the new president, his short corpulent body
encased in the latest Parisian frockcoat, would flash an impudent smile at
those sharply critical eyes surrounding him. One night, he let loose his social
savoir-faire by trapping some celebrities in the dining room of Peers Hall, a
savoir-faire which he had acquired in the *corps diplomatique* of a certain
great nation in Europe. These celebrities agreed to contribute from various
aspects of society news items to the *Tōkei*. And who were these celebrities?
The majority were from all the departments of liberal arts of Tokyo Imperial
University. From this point on the newspaper would be more academic.
Social events would be seen from a bird's-eye view under the rubric of time-
lessness, of eternal truth, and such high aspirations would adorn the *Tōkei*'s
reputation. Instead of reporting, say, an item that one might put in the
same class as sweet potatoes roasting on a smoldering charcoal brazier, the
same phenomenon would be reported as if one had viewed an elegant snow
scene through greenhouse windows behind which tropical flowers were in
bloom. The coverage would be superb. It might be good to have such a
newspaper. But among the newspaper staff, the only one who had not
drained his cup of champagne over the Peers Hall declaration was Ōishi
Roka, who now seemed a useless third wheel to a cart. And yet Roka, his face
calm, kept saying, "Behold, our newspaper will be the peers' gazette."

Junichi felt he ought not to continue to disturb Roka while he was writing, so he offered some words of farewell and left the lodging house at Tomizakaue. On his way home he was absorbed in various thoughts. He felt the
Tōkei newspaper had formed what Ōmura would call its own small clique
and provided its own biased criticism, and even though he himself was an
outsider, he couldn't admire that. But at least it had its own point of view. It
had its own distinctive characteristics. Yet Junichi found himself conjec-
turing on this entire situation. Since the newspaper had not installed Roka
as its president, it had to be that Roka's thoughts had naturally become
dominant among the entire staff in shaping the paper's distinctive characteristics. But what would happen with the change of presidents if the new
owner found that Roka's values were poisoning society? It was inevitable
from the president's point of view that the majority of readers were immature. Yet what was really surprising was the new president's attempt to rem-
edy the evil by making the newspaper more academic. That approach was
merely reactionary. Or perhaps it was more accurate to call it suppressive.

Why not permit freedom of thought and then try to carry out reforms? From Roka's point of view, he ought to complain. And that complaint ought to show itself in red hot anger, and if not that, in irony blistering as green rust. And what kinds of bitter or ironic articles would Roka write? Nothing of that sort. As usual, his sentences, which would be like the light from radium which never refracts against anything, would say, "Oh dear, my brain's empty," as if none of the problems had anything to do with himself. Literary circles nowadays, Junichi felt, were so infirm that they were unable to confront power except by complaining. And if so, one could not expect them to arouse any antipathy.

With these thoughts swarming in him, Junichi walked through Sasugaya Street to his house.

14

Only a few days remained in December. Junichi recalled there had been about forty rainless days since mid-November. He was so bored with taking walks it was more natural for him to remain mostly at home and read. Yet after spending two or three days in this way, he would get headaches, feel sick, lose his appetite. At such times he would suddenly have the urge to go out just about the time the shops on Sansaki-chō were about to close, and, his Satsuma clogs clattering heavily, he would wander along Ueno Hill, deserted at that hour.

One such night after wandering around the Sacred Hall Shrine in Ueno Park, he passed along a road lined with many stone lanterns and reached the summit of Uguisuzaka Slope. At that moment the train for Aomori passed just below. On the outskirts of the dead metropolis the electric lights of the Yoshiwara shimmered phantomlike in a sea of fog. As he stood there momentarily lost in this vision, he heard the park bell toll the eleven o'clock hour. A policeman, having climbed the slope from the direction of Negishi, lit up Junichi's face in the glare of a square lantern. The policeman stood briefly staring at Junichi before walking off toward the Mausoleum.

Junichi scanned in his line of vision the dark-roofed Negishi dwellings. Most of Negishi could not be seen, obstructed as it was by shrubs on both sides of the slope and the woods behind the Mausoleum.

He suddenly wondered about the direction to Mrs. Sakai's house. All at once he felt warm blood stirring in him like waves, brimming over into his cold ears and nose and the extremities of his hands and feet.

Almost twenty days had elapsed since he had visited her. Whether sitting at home or walking outdoors, he had wild fancies that occasionally made him recall her face. Compared to those generally ambiguous longings for women which had attacked him up to now, this capricious desire to see Mrs. Sakai assailed him much more frequently, the intensity much greater, so that he felt an anguish he had never experienced before. Though it was a night in which the fog gathering round him seemed to creep in under his collar and sleeves, Junichi's body was burning with passion. A terrible blind carnal impulse clouded the light of reason and made him indulge in feelings in which he wished he could run right then to her house, run and ring the bell at her gate. In the same way he was thinking of her as he stood on this hill, so must Mrs. Sakai in a dim light and under her *courte-pointe* coverlet have been thinking of him.

All at once Junichi felt his skin crawling with gooseflesh. And suddenly he felt ashamed of these momentary vagrant fancies.

What a fool he was! How thoroughly stupid! He had met her only once at a theater, and only once had he visited her. Beyond a doubt he was no more than one out of her many playthings. As long as he continued to keep his distance, she would not even send him a postcard. For these twenty days or so he had told himself that he would not wait for her letter, that he had no desire to wait, and yet even against his will he had been waiting for that very letter. It had all been a ridiculous waste of time. With his *geta* he kicked at some pebbles under his feet. The pebbles flew through the bushes and fell over a cliff. Brandishing his cane, Junichi started for home.

The day after he had walked along Ueno Hill at night was the twenty-second of December. The clear morning sky had turned to cloud in the afternoon. Putting aside the magazine he was reading, Junichi stared blankly at the closed paper-covered sliding doors. All at once it occurred to him he hadn't glimpsed a single line of the Racine he had intended to read one of these days, and that thought inadvertently recalled Mrs. Sakai's face, a face he had tried to block out of his mind. He remembered what she had said to him: "Do come any time you wish to exchange the Racine for something else. I'll tell my maid, so if you should come when I'm not home, just go right up and exchange it for another." Junichi had not yet availed himself of this privilege. Though he had cautioned himself that he ought not to look forward to receiving even a postcard from her, he found himself waiting for a reply, and this thought frustrated him. He was the one who ought to make the first response. Was not her refraining to write clear proof she was modest, the antithesis of *frivole*? Or by deliberately detaching herself from him, was that not, on the contrary, her trick in order to capture him the more securely? And if that was so, he had the feeling her device was about to take effect at any moment. Already he had sufficient experience with her to know she was not a woman who was the least bit hesitant. He had no doubts she had taken measures not to allow him even to moisten his lips with a drop of water unless the water container was tipped in his direction and he was dying of thirst. Absorbed in these thoughts, Junichi let his imagination run wild.

At that moment he heard quiet footsteps on the garden steppingstones.

"Anyone home?" The voice was that of a woman.

Junichi was startled. He was sitting quite properly at his desk, so it was all right with him if someone opened the sliding doors, but he felt so embarrassed by his wild thoughts that all he could do was sit up straight in utter confusion.

"Who is it?" he said, opening the sliding door himself. Oyuki was standing there, a broad smile on her face. Today her long strands of dark hair were fully pleated into three pigtails bound together with her usual cream-colored ribbon. Junichi could not tell if the kimono of coarse silk cloth with yellow stripes was the same she had worn the other day. The only difference he noticed was her *haori* coat of purple striped crepe.

"Please sit down on the veranda. If it's cold out there, do come in. I heard your younger sister was ill. Is she all right now?" Thus far when it came to talking to Oyuki, he had felt it painful to force himself to speak to her, but at this moment he sensed a waning of this feeling. The difficulty had not yet disappeared completely, but he was certain some of it had abated.

"Oh, you know about that? You probably heard it from the old landlady, didn't you? Since a disease of the kidneys can't be cured quickly, she came out of the hospital only yesterday. I haven't seen the old lady and her son's wife Yasu for more than ten days, so I wondered if you had moved." As she said these words, she sat down quickly on the veranda. Since she hadn't come for the past several days, she seemed somewhat hesitant, her manners better than usual.

"Why did you think I moved?"

"I don't know," she said pointlessly. But a moment later she added carelessly, "I just thought so."

The setting sun appeared through a rift in the clouds, and a cypress tree beyond the lattice fence cast its shadow on the veranda, but as the clouds moved, the shadow disappeared.

"If I sit here, you'll catch cold," Oyuki said, putting her slender fingers on the veranda as she started to stand.

"Come in and close the sliding door."

"May I?" she said, and without waiting for Junichi's reply, she kicked off her Chiyoda sandals and came in.

The sliding doors shut this well-matched couple into the small room, severing them from the outside world. Not that this was the first time they had been alone together. Up to now such a situation had frequently occurred, and each time Junichi was overjoyed.

"Oh, you've some pictures? Let me have a look."

Sitting next to Junichi, Oyuki kept flipping through the foreign magazine on his desk.

She sat on a cushion Junichi hastily set down for her, the bottom of her *haori* coat forming a gentle jet of drapery, her ample brownish braids trailing behind.

Junichi's restless eyes roamed back and forth across the light pink of her cheeks, her chin, and the nape below her ears, skin that would leave a slight impression of resistance even from the gentle touch of his fingers, his eyes roaming even to each of the deep ridges in the knuckles of her fingers as she turned the pages of the magazine.

Landscapes, no matter how beautifully printed, did not absorb Oyuki's attention. Nor did other pictures attract her unless they contained persons. Pointing to a small figure in a landscape painting, she asked, among other questions, "What's he doing?" and Junichi had to explain that and other illustrations.

Their kimono sleeves touched. Mixed into the sensation from some sort of cosmetic she used, he caught the odor of a healthy woman. All of a sudden Oyuki said, "My! How pretty!" and she moved her body in an exaggerated way. His hip came in contact with hers, and he felt the blunt, resilient resistance of her body.

The moment he experienced that sensation, Junichi, almost by reflex, stood up and went over to the brazier, which had been pushed into a far corner of the room. "Oh, the fire's dying," he said, picking up a pair of tongs. "I'll rebuild it."

"I'm not that cold," Oyuki said, her voice quite calm. She didn't seem to realize why Junichi had changed his seat.

"Can there really be hats this large?" she said. Poking at the fire, Junichi looked up to glance at her. What Oyuki had referred to was an advertisement at the back of the magazine.

"They say that hat is quite popular now. Even in this neighborhood I've seen women wearing those large hats."

Oyuki finished looking at the magazine. With her hands against her cheeks, she glanced directly at Junichi as she said, "I thought I had many things to talk to you about if I was able to see you today, but somehow I've forgotten everything."

"You probably wanted to tell me about the hospital, didn't you?"

"Yes. That was one of the things." And she started to explain. The doctor had told her sister she would have to remain in the hospital a week or two, but the moment she was hospitalized, all she thought about was going home. Each new day she desired to return, but each day her hopes were frustrated. Oyuki spoke as if she couldn't help but feel sorry for her sister. Junichi found himself listening to many other things as well. The way the sister cried when Oyuki was about to leave, for example, or how the patient would cry so that Oyuki had to remain until her sister fell asleep. How the nurse to whom her sister had become so attached, the one Oyuki had wondered so much about, turned out to be the best of all, a fact Oyuki discovered after she herself had long become familiar with her. How a fat doctor always happened to come along doing his rounds and quietly pinched Oyuki's cheek.

While listening to her, Junichi found himself staring at her face. To put this figuratively, he found that in the same way a light breeze ruffles the surface of water in a basin one foot in diameter, so were there little waves of expression continually seen on Oyuki's lovely face. He could not remember how many times she had visited him up to now, but each time she had looked at him more than he had looked at her. Today for the first time, though, he could closely observe her face.

Junichi realized something that he might have stated in the following way: Oyuki was aware she was being observed by him. It was quite natural for her to be conscious of that, but as far as he himself was concerned, the moment he realized what he was doing, he felt as if he had made a great discovery. And the reason he thought it great was that he felt her allowing him to look at her was the same as letting him do what he wanted. It would not be correct to say she had resigned herself to being looked at. No, it would be more accurate to say she was waiting for him to act; rather, she was urging him. But if he took one step forward, would she allow that step? Or would she move one step back? Or would she be on the defensive and attempt to hold out? He didn't know what she would do. What's more, she herself probably didn't know. At any rate, she had a passionate desire for knowlege, and that strong desire made her assume an attitude of waiting or urging.

At the same time Junichi had these thoughts, he felt he had to protect Oyuki, this person who was so easy to break, a person so vulnerable, so fragile. Had he not been the one present in this room, Oyuki, he felt, would be exposed to real danger. At that moment the uneasy impulsive feeling that had been set adrift in him ever since Oyuki came into his room vanished as if it had been erased.

Oddly enough, these cooled-down feelings he had suddenly experienced while he was smoothly raking the ashes in the brazier were communicated to Oyuki in the same way that actions in dramas can take their own free course without hesitation. Gentle and obedient, she seemed to hate to leave, but soon she knew she must.

"I'll come again," she said as if apologizing for having done something wrong, and she stood up.

"Yes, please do," Junichi said, his voice more gentle than usual as if compensating for a debt he owed her. He gazed after her as she walked away, her pigtails swaying heavily.

That evening he hastily prepared to go out of his Hatsune-chō house. He didn't understand why he kept looking at himself in the mirror for a long time before he left. Yet when he finally did, he brought the Racine collection with him.

15

An entry from Junichi's diary . . .

I don't want to add pages of disgrace to my diary. But I can't distort the facts.

When I left my room with that volume of Racine in hand, my thoughts went something like this: I often take a book with me when I go out for a walk. Today too I will go out and bring the Racine along.

The only difference between this book and others is that it provides me with a possibility of visiting Mrs. Sakai. I felt, though, that it was up to me whether or not I'd go there.

But this kind of reasoning is akin to deceiving oneself.

Actually, an uneasy feeling accompanied by a kind of sexual yearning had gradually been growing stronger during the last several days. I had made an all-out effort to repulse that feeling. But even when I repulsed it, it returned. It kept attacking me like those endless skirmishes between contending enemies.

Ōmura said that suppressing sexual desire is not harmful to one's health. It may not be harmful, but no longer can I bear this annoying desire. Once I even thought this kind of troublesome existence might destroy one's dignity as a human being.

Ōmura also said that the person who inherits nervous tendencies is unable to control them and that if one is forced to suppress them, he will become ill. Remembering his words, I suspected I might have some such hereditary trait in my own nervous system. Yet I feel that's unlikely. Both my parents were healthy until they died together in an epidemic.

It was Oyuki's visiting me after a lapse of several days that destroyed some of my self-control.

When I was sitting beside her, I saw flickering above my head the trap nature was hurling toward me.

Oyuki must have seen that trap too. But I had been the one trying to flee from it.

It had been my own insight that had helped me escape that trap, and so I had felt a kind of contempt for her.

At that moment I admired the power of my own self-control, but I hadn't thought that at the same time part of my self-control was being destroyed. Even as I was avoiding the rope the enemy would have bound me with, a rope that would have been difficult to cut once it had bound me, I was thrown off guard by a fragile rope that would have been easy to undo even if I had been bound with it.

The innocent and lovely Oyuki had not taken it upon herself to notice this erosion and this carelessness.

If Oyuki had not visited me, I probably would not have left my room carrying the Racine with me.

With the Racine in my hand as I walked aimlessly along Ueno Hill, my feelings of uneasiness intensified, and I became aware that my pulse had suddenly accelerated. It was exactly as if the impact of indulging in too much *sake* was beginning to take effect.

When I came to the entrance to Ueno Park and looked down at what seemed like the excessively noisy thoroughfare of Hirokōji, I felt dizzy as if I had a fever, and my body seemed too heavy for my legs to carry its weight.

I turned back with no real purpose in mind, and I stopped when I came to the top of a flight of stone steps leading to the Benten Shrine. I found an empty bench there, and I sat down and began flipping through the Racine, but it was getting too dark to read. Still thumbing aimlessly through the book, I read only its titles in big letters, for example *Phèdre* and such, more wrapped up in my own blank thoughts than anything else.

When I suddenly recovered from these vagaries, I realized a street light by the side of the stone steps had come on. The light, strangely large, was casting out its unpleasant yellowish glare. I couldn't believe the light's glass cover could be that yellow, and I thought I'd take a closer look at it the next time I ventured this way.

The human mind is really quite bizarre. Looking at that light, I decided to go to Negishi. I felt a close relationship between the glow from that light and my decision to go. When a person wavers about doing something, it seems he ascribes the motive for his action to something close at hand.

After I started for Negishi, I took rapid strides. My pace took on more and more speed. Even after the hedge and gate came into view, images I remembered vividly, I did not slacken my pace because I wanted to show some regard for Mrs. Sakai's feelings. Though I wondered how she would welcome me, I didn't feel she would do anything to embarrass me.

There was a small light above the nameplate on her gate, and by pushing a small side door, one could easily enter. When I walked through that door and pushed the doorbell at the entrance, my heart leaped in spite of myself. That emotion did not emerge from any consideration for Mrs. Sakai's feelings, but from the situation itself.

I didn't know if there would be any other servants besides the parlormaid I had met before, but since it was already dark out, I was afraid an unfamiliar face would greet me. But soon after I had rung the bell, the parlormaid I knew appeared. I remembered Mrs. Sakai had called her Shizue. Perhaps this was the name given to her parlormaids from generation to generation. And perhaps it had been decided no servant other than the parlormaid would welcome guests at that door.

A moment after the bell rang, a lattice window near the porch lit up. Seeing me, the maid said, "Oh dear, I'll go tell Madame," and she hurried off. Mrs. Sakai had told me to come in unannounced and just go up to the library, but I couldn't do that. The maid returned so quickly I wondered if she had even gone away. "There's no fire in the stove in the Western-style room, so please come this way." She offered me a pair of house sandals with red thongs.

We turned two or three times along the corridor. Except for a light at each corner we turned, all the rooms were pitch dark, deathly quiet.

The slight footsteps of Shizue and my heavy steps reverberated along the corridor. The elapsed time was quite short, but I felt as if I were in a dreamlike fairy tale.

At the end of the corridor was a cedar door painted with the design of a peony and a peacock, the door bordered with a lacquered frame. I took off my house slippers and went into the room. It had two sets of sliding paper screens, one at the entrance, another set further into the room. A light was seen through the inner screens. I recalled a room built like this one in my house back home where an important chief magistrate had once spent the night a long time ago. I don't know what the technical name is for a room in this style. For the time being I thought of it as a colonnade in the *shoin* style. Professor Sakai, I felt, seemed to have tastes that reminded me of those of a *daimyō*.

Shizue stooped over as she slipped open one of the sliding screen panels. Only one dim light was on in this room. My eyes were attracted to a large clothesrack on which no clothing had been hung. Shizue went over to the inner sliding screen, and kneeling this time, she said, "He is here," and then after a slight pause she slid open the screen.

At long last I met Mrs. Sakai. I had hoped not to realize this third meeting with her. I had tried to push it away into the future, but I had finally brought the meeting about. And under my own free will.

"Do come in," said Mrs. Sakai. "It's really been quite a while since I last saw you." Pushing aside a light pink quilt with large patterns covering the *kotatsu* footwarmer, she was stirring the fire in the round paulownia brazier. From the center of the room she selected a purple crepe cushion for me to sit on, one of those cushions young women seem to prefer when sitting. Laid face down beside the *kotatsu* footwarmer was Kosugi Tengai's novel *Chōja Boshi*.

I sensed an unexpected seriousness in her behavior, an unexpected calm. The only point I recognized was the flicker of a slight smile radiating in her usually enigmatic eyes. I couldn't guess what her attitude toward me would be, but I felt at once that her behavior was quite different from what I had expected. There arose deep within me a kind of dissatisfaction, a germ of something desiring to rebel. It was at this moment that I first began to see Mrs. Sakai as my "enemy."

Not a single hair of her hairdo, swept back into a chignon, was out of place, as if she had been expecting someone. This time, as I write, I clearly remember her clothing. Her *haori* coat was made of a yellowish green crepe material I had never seen before. Her padded kimono was probably what we call *omeshi-chirimen,* that is, silk crepe. It had a delicate pattern of black latticework against a light brown background. Her *obi* sash was in a coarse arabesque pattern the color of subdued silver. Her sash bustle, pale pink in color, was conspicuously charming and gave off an impression of youth, of juvenescence.

With some slight qualms of conscience, I returned to her the volume of Racine I really hadn't read after all. Without even looking at it or taking it in hand, she said, "When you leave, select any other book you wish."

A paulownia brazier of the same type I had noticed earlier was brought in. Tea was served. Cakes were offered. Shizue quietly brought these in and quietly stood up and left. The room was so quiet that when there was a lull in the conversation, even one's breathing was audible. Beyond the double-closed sliding doors the wind could not be heard, and only the whistles of passing trains communicated to me I was living in the everyday workaday world.

Mrs. Sakai paid no attention to the brazier I had pushed over to her. With her left hand on the light pink patterned quilt over the *kotatsu* footwarmer, her transparent fingers surprisingly slender as they tapered at their tips, she nervously kept opening and closing those fingers. She gazed at me, her eyes wide, and she kept asking me such meaningless questions as "Don't you smoke?" or "How have you been these days?" I tried to make my responses equally meaningless. While offering these vague replies, I couldn't help comparing her face with Oyuki's.

And how great was the difference. As for Oyuki's, which is plump and not as smooth as Mrs. Sakai's and is a face whose blood is rushing through its capillaries, there is always room for a sudden change in Oyuki's facial expression. Even in trivial conversation, Oyuki responds word by word with a corresponding change in facial expression in the same way a sensible accompaniment goes along with a naive piece of music.

Compared with Oyuki's face, Mrs. Sakai's, which is pale and regular like a face in Greek sculpture, is almost like a mask. It is masklike. My eyes, persistently searching for a delicate shade of expression on her face, always stop at her dark brown eyes. Only behind those eyes is there something. And because of that something, her face takes on an oppressiveness similar to overloaded electricity which threatens to cause a thunderstorm at any moment in a summer sky. I'd like to say that those eyes are those of a predatory bird, of a beast of prey, though of course her eyes are not that savage. If a nymph existed in a tropical sea, it would have eyes like hers. If not for Mrs. Sakai's eyes, her face might perhaps be called a *mine de mort,* that is, the face of a beautiful dead woman.

What makes this feeling increasingly strong in me is the lack of coherence between her facial expression and her talk. Her mouth utters one thing, her eyes another. And it is this discrepancy which makes her enigmatic eyes even more mysterious and reminds one of the face of a sphinx.

I once heard a certain theologian say "dogma" was a word, while another theologian objected that "dogma" was not only a word but a *forced* word. My interpretation of her enigmatic eyes is also a *forced* interpretation.

Will a time come when I will publish this diary in its present form, or will I do a revised version? I still don't know how I feel about this question. Suppose someday someone reads my diary. I'd like to tell that reader, "Dear Reader, I must make a certain mysterious confession to you. And that confession begins right now."

Mrs. Sakai's enigmatic eyes are contagious. My eyes must respond to the words conveyed by those enigmatic eyes. In this room in her house in Negishi, behind the woods of Ueno steeped in the quiet and darkness of the night, an electric light is casting its soft rays, and a brazier fire covered with white ashes is sending forth its gentle warmth like the warmth of flesh through thin cloth. And I am talking with her in the same way that travelers share a seat on a train or a table at a hotel dining room. We talked on topics anyone might discuss openly in public. These were topics I never anticipated after what I had experienced on my first visit to her home.

At the same time I am receiving these impressions, her eyes indicate different things from the words uttered through her lips as if those eyes were saying, "Between you and me, such trivial matters don't concern us." Her eyes have *une persuasion puissante et chaleureuse*. And my eyes are mercilessly and irresistibly enticed by the words in her eyes and play along with their meaning.

We were sitting about two or three feet away from each other, and the two braziers were between us, one over which Mrs. Sakai was holding her hands and the other which she ignored.

Each of us was attracted by the eyes of the other, our spirits embracing. A column of flame enveloped us.

I felt the time too slow in passing. It was an agonizing time. And then at a certain moment during this long interval, I realized this acute agony in the faint form of pangs of conscience had subconsciously and persistently been in me ever since I had come to know her. This thought flickered across my mind like lightning as I was enveloped in infernal flames and smoke.

And all this time I was in agony, I had come to regard Mrs. Sakai as my enemy. And as the time continued to extend itself, this feeling became all the more intense. If my will had been strong, I would have flung myself out the room at that very moment and gone back home. And then I would have regretted not having slapped that smooth white face of hers.

Suddenly without any conspicuous motive . . . (One page after this entry is torn off.)

At that instant I saw the smile in her eyes transformed into a triumphant joyous cry. And then again we continued our meaningless and distant talk which had momentarily been interrupted. More and more certain was my feeling that Mrs. Sakai was my enemy.

"On the twenty-seventh, I'll be leaving for the Fukuzumi in Hakone," she said. "I'll be there alone, so if you have time, please join me."

"Well, I've some work I've been thinking of doing, so I'm not sure if I can. Oh, I'm afraid it's already quite late."

"Well, if you do have time, do come."

Mrs. Sakai pushed a button at the end of a cord wound with red silk thread lying beside her, and the sound of a bell could be heard in the distance. For a while I recognized the clear sound of footsteps along the corridor, and then Shizue's voice called out from the adjoining room and asked her mistress what she wanted. I believe she had been trained not to enter a room unless she had been called in.

Shizue led me to the Western-style room with its many bookshelves. I had thought a good deal about the volume I had carelessly borrowed, but it had never occurred to me to borrow another. With no time to think about it, I had stood up to borrow a book in exchange for the one I had used as a pretext for my visit. The sensation of helplessness, that of a defeated man, seemed to stab my chest.

When I was standing in that Western-style room with Shizue, who turned on the lights for me, I felt a much stronger tension and excitement than I had felt when I was with Oyuki, probably because the sea of my own sensations was still roiling. But unlike a chambermaid in a French novel or drama, this girl stopped by the entrance to the room and gently and modestly waited, the fingers of both her hands crossed on her red-dappled sash bustle as she remained standing there, serious, without any fear, and without even smiling.

I grabbed another book by Racine, not even bothering to examine it, put the book I had formerly borrowed in the other's place, and went out the room with Shizue.

Though I had returned the Racine that had so tormented me, I now had another book. And that book would again cause me a great deal of anguish.

I looked into Mrs. Sakai's room to say goodbye. She stood up to see me off. Shizue, who rearranged Mrs. Sakai's house slippers for her mistress to easily step into, followed us at a distance so that she could not see us turn the corridor corner.

"If you have time, please come to Hakone," Mrs. Sakai repeated at the front door, her voice quiet and gentle.

"Yes," I said, casting a final glance at her.

Not a single hair in her hairdo was in disorder. She was standing there with her kimono neckband in perfect harmony. Her little figure again suddenly prompted in me feelings of antipathy to her. Thinking this enemy of mine would definitely try to entice me to go to Hakone, I started out after putting on my hat, which I was carrying in my right hand.

Though the sky was clear, I walked along a Negishi lane with low-hanging dense fog clouding the area. I thought about Mrs. Sakai's personality. And suddenly there arose in me a clear and strong image of Aude, the character created by Lemonnier, that eminent writer in the Belgian literary world. When I had read his book, I felt he had exaggerated several aspects of women, but having come to know of the existence of a woman like Mrs. Sakai, I was convinced a woman like Aude was not mere fiction.

Here these pages of my shame and disgrace come to an end.

I have written my diary entry as if I were writing a clumsy novel.

16

It was the twenty-fifth of December. Seto, a big smile on his face while con-jecturing as usual that Junichi was probably not angry with him, had dropped in at Junichi's rented house at Yanaka the day before to invite him to an end-of-the-year party for persons from their prefecture, the party to be held on the night of the twenty-fifth at the Kamesei Restaurant.

At first Junichi thought he ought to decline because he didn't want to be associated with others from his own prefecture, even though he had paid a courtesy call at the mansion of his former feudal lord in Takanawa, merely leaving his name card at the time. But Seto had kept on insisting. Seto's rea-soning was that since various people from various social classes and profes-sions would be attending, Junichi, who was trying to write a novel, would thus be able to gather a number of interesting observations. Because Junichi had nothing particular to do that night, he gave in to Seto's demand.

Just as Seto had entered Junichi's room, Yasu, the wife of Uechō, the gar-dener, came in carrying a lacquer box filled with rice, red beans, and cooked vegetables she had prepared in honor of her husband's birthday. Junichi thought this a stroke of good luck, for he had nothing to serve, and he asked Yasu to bring in an extra cup and plate for Seto. She also brought in some tea for them. Looking rather impertinently at Yasu in her short padded coat with its black satin collar, her hair neatly combed, Seto said, "If I could find a nice landlady like you who takes such good care of her tenants, I'd rent a house too."

"I'm merely someone up from the country, so I'm no help," Yasu said modestly. "It's my mother who likes to keep busy and take good care of Mr. Koizumi."

"What do you mean you can't be of help?" Seto said. "From those navy blue *tabi* socks you're wearing, I can see you're a real worker."

"In the rural area I'm from," Yasu explained, "all the women wear blue *tabi*."

Seto said it was strange to hear her say she was a countrified person, for it was impossible for someone as chic as a landlady to be a country bumpkin. Finally Yasu disclosed she was from Chōshi. As they continued talking, Seto said that once when he was on a sketching trip, he had stayed in Yasu's hometown. The two of them said a number of things about Chōshi, and after Yasu left, Seto noted with a sly look on his face, "Even if we go to Yanagibashi tomorrow, I won't be able to find any good models. Right here at your own place there's a fine model." When Junichi asked him what he meant, Seto said that he could probably find a geisha that would be a good model for studying the effect of white face powder or rouge, but it was impossible to find among geisha a natural unaffected woman like the landlady's daugher Yasu. Junichi and Seto began discussing whether or not any truly beautiful geisha existed. They concluded that even though they could not say there were no beautiful geisha, they had to admit these beauties were so artificial that even if there were some geisha good enough to serve as a rough sketch for the geisha-type woman, it was impossible to find among them one with feminine naturalness. Having called his attention to the fact that "feminine naturalness" could be found in Yasu, Junichi could not help but agree. Having exhausted the topic, Seto left.

"Generally speaking," Junichi thought when he was suddenly by himself, "I'm deficient in *esprit non préoccupé*. Until I made the discovery through Seto's frivolous eyes, I regarded Yasu merely as the wife of my landlord. She was merely somebody's wife. Though I sympathized with her for her strong sense of duty, her willingness to do anything by sacrificing herself, and other general traits like faithfulness and diligence, I hardly noticed anything about her physical appearance. After Seto put me on the alert, I tried to call to mind her features, and I found that from a physical point of view there was something beautiful about Yasu, who had formerly worked as a maid in the rural district where she was born and was now a gardener's wife. Her complexion, though, is bad. And even when she is neatly dressed, she's not concerned about her hairdo. And yet in those eyes and that mouth on her round face there's something coquettish, something similar to what I once saw in a print of the *Mona Lisa*. Of course the expressions on Yasu's face are quite different from those so artificial on the face of a geisha. Now that I think of it, nothing's easier to create than abstract arguments. Though Seto had himself formulated such an abstract argument, there seem to be few paintings in the Meiji era which depict simply and representatively the facial expressions and manners of the ordinary Meiji woman and the Meiji geisha. The Meiji period has yet to produce a single Constantin Guys. How I wish I could be a person with eyes, only with eyes that are not bound by convention." Junichi suddenly had the deep conviction that if he continued the usual path he was following, he would never have the qualifications to stand as an artist in the world.

Around five in the afternoon Seto came to call for him.

"Why is it Yasu's not waiting on you today?" Seto said, flashing his nasty smile.

"She rarely comes here."

Even as Junichi gave this accurate yet dull reply, he felt uneasy because if Oyuki had been there when Seto came, there was no knowing how much Seto would have teased him. At this moment Junichi was reminded of an episode at the time of Yasu's marriage, an episode involving Oyuki that Yasu had told him about. When Yasu had left her job to go to her new home as a bride, Oyuki's mother, Mrs. Nakazawa, had bought her a chest of drawers. Mrs. Nakazawa had helped Yasu put on her wedding makeup. As a result, she actually looked like a totally different person. For a while Oyuki was observing Yasu, who had been such a good friend, and as Yasu carefully bowed and kneeled to the mats to say goodbye, Oyuki began to cry so bitterly that everyone was surprised, uncertain what to do about it. Even now, the Nakazawa family talked about this incident with Yasu and called her "Yasu, our bride."

Junichi, who had long been prepared to leave and had merely been waiting for Seto, finally left with him. They passed through a grove of trees in the winter cold of Ueno Park and caught a streetcar at Hirokōji.

After they got off at Suda-chō to transfer to another streetcar for Kudan-Ryōgoku, Seto walked over to an old man who looked like a confirmed tippler. The man was sitting on a bench, an ill-fitting overcoat on and a derby hat, which was seldom worn in these days. Seto bowed and asked, "You going to the gathering? I'm on the way there too."

Soon Seto introduced Junichi to the old man. Born in Y Prefecture, the man, Professor Takayama, was a scholar of Chinese literature. At the art school Seto attended, many scholars had been invited to give special lectures ever since the school was under the direction of Okakura Tenshin, and their lectures had been published in book form. When Professor Takayama had given his lecture, Seto had become acquainted with him simply because they were from the same prefecture.

Professor Takayama was employed by the imperial household. Though a scholar of Chinese literature, he was also well versed in Buddhist literature. He did his calligraphy in the *tenshō* or seal-script style of the Den Wanbai school. Owing to his knowledge of Chinese literature, he was often asked to select inscriptions to be dedicated to the people from Y Prefecture. Junichi had heard about this professor.

Since the streetcar became fairly empty, Junichi and Seto sat together.

"Even though he's a scholar of Chinese literature," Seto said in a low voice to Junichi, "he's quite the joker. He knows a lot about red light districts too."

Looking at Takayama, whose face was as wide as that of Ebisu-saburō, the God of Wealth, and imagining him flirting with women, Junichi could hardly help from bursting into a laugh, but he controlled himself and kept a straight face.

They got off the streetcar at Hashidemae in Ryōgoku, turned left to cross Yanagibashi Bridge, and following Professor Takayama entered the Kamesei Restaurant.

As the professor slowly entered, a maid knelt and asked, "Do you wish to see Mr. Sone?"

"Yes," said Takayama. The maid led the way upstairs, and since Seto followed, Junichi did too. Seto explained that Sone was the chief editor and head clerk of the Hakubunsha Publishing Company and was secretary for the year-end party that day. Junichi had also seen Sone's name in magazines.

At the top of the stairs was a waiting room, and already a number of persons had gathered.

Though it was still bright outdoors, the lights had been turned on in the room. Through a glass partition in one of the sliding doors, the Sumida River could be seen. From Junichi's angle of vision he noticed a streetcar passing over Ryōgoku Bridge. On entering the room, he had looked for an unoccupied cushion and had sat down on one. He kept staring at the other side of the river where lights began flickering on one after another in the milky gray atmosphere of evening.

The most animated group in the room had gathered round a *go* board set in the center of the room. Usually two experts in *go* were known to take on horrendous looks, but here the two contenders, one an old man, the other young, were both quite easygoing. Since Junichi played neither *shōgi* nor *go,* he felt that people he saw playing *go* did it merely to kill time. Not that he was so narrow-minded a utilitarian as to feel one had to use one's time for something useful. Unlike *shōgi* or dominoes, games which do not take much time to win, *go* does require time. Junichi had a naive and shallow cynical idea that as long as the game was played as a kind of social pastime, there would be no possibility for dangerous thoughts to be passed among the spectators. And although he thought it understandable that people liked playing it, it was beyond his comprehension why so many people had gathered to watch these players.

Next to this group was a small one in the center of which was Professor Takayama, whom Junichi had met for the first time on the streetcar a while ago. Holding his hands over a brazier, he was talking in a loud voice about something. Junichi, who was bored with nothing to do, listened to the professor's words. The subject had to do with badgers.

"Well, you know, the Sacred Hall Shrine in my younger days was quite different, much more elegant than the dormitories of Tokyo University now. And badgers would often appear in the Sacred Hall. We were assigned to rooms partitioned off along the shrine corridors. And then every night after midnight small steps could be heard along these corridors. These were not human footsteps. That thing would walk along and peek into the rooms one after another. When one of us was awake, it would go past our room. And if we were asleep, it would lick the small tray of oil at the base of the paper-covered lampstand. And so it would clean the dish for us. All we had to do was put the lantern in the corridor and the badger would lick the dish clean. That was fine with us, but there was a rumor that a badger was entering the shrine sanctuary, so we made a fake badger. In the summer heat when we couldn't sleep, we tied up a bunch of cedar leaves with kite string, and then we waited for someone to come by while we sat outside on a fence. The fellow that passed along the fence was in for trouble. His head and cheeks would be tickled here and there by the cedar leaves. Then he would call out, "Look! It's a badger!" and the bumpkin would run away. If he carried swords, large or small, he would pass by posturing as if to draw them at any moment and would stare up at the sky. Oh, we did some terribly devilish things. But if you think we students in those days did nothing but these childish pranks, you're wrong. Often we climbed over the fences and stayed out all night, returning over those same fences before day broke. It's quite wrong to think students will behave morally if we force them to read the Analects of Confucius."

The story about the badger had taken a surprising turn. Junichi listened in astonishment.

Seto came over to ask if Junichi had paid his party fee. Junichi was suddenly aware he hadn't, and he asked Seto to take him to the secretary.

Sone was a diminutive man who was apparently quite shrewd. "The student fee's one yen," he said.

After a moment's thought, Junichi asked, "How much is it for non-students?"

With an expression on his face that seemed to say, "It's none of your business," Sone replied with studious politeness, "Five yen."

"I see," Junichi said and pulled out a five-yen bill. Seto, who was standing behind him, said, teasing him, "You're putting on airs." With a serious look on his face, Sone asked Junichi his name and entered it in his notebook.

Meanwhile, more and more people came. Most of the names in Sone's notebook were marked with a circle.

When a certain minister of state finally arrived, it was the signal for the sliding partitions sealing off the adjoining room to be opened.

Junichi had no idea how many mats were in it, but the room was extremely large. Cushions had been laid out in a huge square, a twelve-foot space left empty on the side of the room facing the corridor, several braziers having been placed at various intervals. The room was so huge the cushions and braziers before the alcove looked quite small.

When Sone was about to lead the minister of state to his seat of honor in front of the alcove, the minister urged a man about thirty years old in the same type of frockcoat the minister was wearing to come with him, and together they got up from their seats. While the minister had a decoration in the buttonhole of his coat, the other man did not. Later Junichi heard the man was a steward in the household of the Marquis Takanawa and had attended the party as a representative for the marquis.

Since no nametags were placed by the cushions, people began to compromise the seating order. While laughing, they pushed one another, jostling this one and that, and there were even some men of modest disposition who were forced to sit on the seats of honor. All was confusion.

At long last each guest had his cushion to sit on. Some of those taking inferior seats were Tokyo University students, their uniform collars bearing the insignia of their departments. Some wore the uniforms of other schools, and some, like Junichi and Seto, wore their Kokura *hakama* skirts. Altogether there were about six or seven students present.

At parties and the like, Junichi usually felt at ease. Just as he was about to take one of the inferior seats at the very rear, he was told it was the secretary's seat, so Junichi was forced to sit next to Sone.

As Junichi looked around, he seemed to feel there were comparatively few people from the upper classes. "Tonight," he said to Sone, "it seems only a small number of the people from our prefecture who are now in Tokyo are present. Who in the world are the people responsible for this meeting?"

"You're right," said Sone, "there are only a few. At first we decided to have the party only for younger government officials, but each time we talked about who would come, various names were thrown in. Even a new actor's here tonight."

As Junichi and Sone engaged in this kind of talk, the maids began bringing in the meals. Since the party was being held at the Kamesei in Yanagibashi, Junichi had taken it for granted they would be served by geisha. Furthermore, according to Seto when he had visited Junichi the day before, he had said it was the usual practice at such parties to have geisha serve, so Junichi wondered why only the restaurant maids were bringing in the trays.

Sake was served. The secretary made the opening speech of greeting and announced at one point that the *sake* had been contributed by the marquis' family. He added that among the many elder dignitaries from Y Prefecture, he especially wanted to thank the minister of state for attending a party being given to encourage young people.

The minister of state, his face large and red, was sipping *sake*. Looking from a distance at the body of this robust man, Junichi felt that in order to cope with the turmoils of the world, it was quite apparent that one had to have that kind of strong physique. Every so often the minister spoke with those near him. And each time he did, he would smile. That was probably his method for dealing with people. But when he stopped talking, deep wrinkles appeared on his forehead. It was as if carved into that brow, contrary to his wish, was a kind of runic writing due to innumerable difficult occasions in the past.

Just about the time the sliced raw fish had been devoured and the soup was almost finished, one person after another came up to the minister in front of the alcove to offer him *sake*. At various places in the room acquaintances gathered in groups. This person and that began introducing each to the other. Here and there the conversation grew animated. Suddenly someone shouted out, "How come we don't have any geisha present?" Someone laughed. Another shouted out in agreement. And still another said, "Be quiet!"

At that moment Junichi realized several people near him had surrounded the secretary and were having a lively argument with him. As he listened, Junichi discovered they were debating about whether or not they should call in some geisha.

After listening for a while, Junichi was surprised to learn the quarrel had turned to the question of whether or not geisha were necessary at a banquet. The argument seemed to focus on the students present as if they were *tertium comparationis,* irrelevant. It was really not a question of whether geisha were essential at banquets. But because students were present, at least the anti-geisha faction had arrived at the conclusion that geisha ought not to appear. And then the question was raised as to who indeed had brought up the issue.

Secretary Sone, who had been listening quietly and seriously to the ironic arguments raised so enthusiastically by both factions, was forced into disclosing the following details: while he was planning the year-end party, he had met Shioda one day, a person on the staff of a board of education. Shioda had said that geisha should not be invited because students would be attending. So Sone decided to consult two or three seniors, and since they had not raised any objections, he had decided their party would be without geisha.

One of the listeners said, "They're such hypocrites! If they'd been asked *their* opinions, how could they very well say they wanted geisha? The hypocrisy of those who raised the issue obliged your seniors to be hypocrites!"

"That can perhaps be said from your own penetrating insights," said another man, "but it troubles me to think we should consider what is virtuous as hypocritical."

"Virtuous, you say! If you really detest geisha, that may be a virtue. Or even if you don't hate them, if you are seriously trying to overcome the temptations of these likable geisha, that too may be a virtue. Yet inviting geisha to a party students do not attend but not inviting geisha when students do attend, well, neither can be a virtue."

"But that's how the world operates. So I think we have to regard both attitudes as virtuous."

"Your opinion's reprehensible! If that's true, then the world becomes completely hypocritical!"

This comment only fanned the fury of the dispute. Junichi listened, thoroughly enjoying the debate. And the argument became even more heated. But the debate, though very energetic, was as transitory as a firecracker. And the reason was that in this group of bickering men there was not a single person who really hated geisha or thought them useless. For each of these men wondered to what extent he should confess or not, while they talked, what his own feelings really were about geisha. And so there was no doubt they were being hypocritical themselves. But what about the man who had branded the others hypocrites? He had not rejected hypocrisy because he himself believed in absolute goodness. He was probably expressing his irresponsible, unruly opinion only for the sake of argument. Junichi felt the man's idea was based on a shallow and consequently worthless cynicism.

At any rate, the disputants decided to send for Mr. Shioda. After glancing around the room a while, Sone found him sitting in front of the minister and bowing to him. Sone went over to Shioda.

Junichi knew Shioda by name since he had often appeared in newspapers and magazines. Wondering what kind of person Shioda was, Junichi was waiting for Sone to bring him over. And when the man appeared, he was quite different from what Junichi had imagined. Shioda had preached that as long as there were no new ethics to rely on, we ought to rely on the old ethics so that returning to traditional morality was a kind of awakening; consequently, Junichi had thought Shioda would look like a narrow-minded moralist, somewhat like a misanthrope swimming against the tide of the world. Shioda, dragged along by Sone, seemed to look as much like a clerk as Sone did. Sone was short, Shioda tall. Sone's face was slender, tapering to a pointed chin, but Shioda's face was full-cheeked, round, his thick side whiskers shaved, traces of blue seen from his shave.

Yet both looked like shrewd operators, and in their eyes Junichi sensed a quite accommodating ironic gleam. In Shioda's eyes, which were continually busily shifting, was a kind of expression as if to declare, "I had to say what I did because I know the ways of the world. You keep batting the problem around. But the truth of the matter is that things don't work the way we preach them. And you know that too."

"As for geisha," Shioda said, "it wasn't that I had flatly rejected them. I merely said it would be proper not to call in geisha to a party at which students were present." From the very start he sounded as if he were ready to make concessions.

"Then if you can deny your feelings of 'impropriety' a little while, it'll all be settled," the man who detested hypocrisy said bluntly.

Soon they reached an agreement. When Shioda asked how they would pay the geisha fees, their argument was almost brought to a deadlock, but Sone said they didn't have to worry because they had already collected more than they needed for the party and the marquis' family had made a further donation. Sone left his seat to arrange things.

Seto, seated four or five cushions away, hurried over to Junichi. "Students like me," he whispered, "have been quite insulted. You've been listening to their argument, haven't you?"

As Junichi merely sat there in silence while smiling, Seto added, "I know you're not a student."

"Stop teasing me. Because I didn't know anyone at the party, I didn't want any special favors. I expected to hear our hometown dialect, but everyone's become a Tokyoite."

"Not everyone. Go listen to those speaking around the state minister. You'll find lots of our hometown accents."

"Well, at least I'll be able to see Yanagibashi geisha close up."

"Still, since we're calling them in without advance notice, I doubt if there will be any decent ones. There'll only be geisha no customers want."

"Is that the way it works?"

While they were speaking in this way, Sone stood in the middle of the room and said in a loud voice, "Everyone, his excellency the state minister has left because he had another party to attend. He gave his regards to all of us. Take your time, everyone, and enjoy yourselves. At any minute some pretty girls will be coming."

There was scattered applause. Junichi saw that the center seat in front of the alcove was empty.

At almost the same moment Junichi saw five or six geisha enter the room.

17

Already those at the party, abandoning all the courtesies, started sitting wherever they wished. Small circles formed here and there discussing this and that, empty cushions seen at various intervals. For a while geisha kept serving *sake,* but after whispering to one another, they all stood at once and picked up their *shamisen* instruments. Then, near the entrance, in a line parallel to the alcove, they sat side by side and started strumming and singing, two of the geisha dancing in front of the musicians. Almost all the noisy murmurs stopped, and the groups suddenly became serious in order to observe the dancing.

Seto, who had been sitting in front of Junichi and smoking a cigarette, said as if offering an explanation to a student, "That's *nagauta,* and they call the song 'Oimatsu.' " A moment later he added, "Take a look! That geisha dancing to our right's pretty—isn't she?—for an unsolicited geisha."

"I can't tell if their dancing is good or bad," Junichi said. "But I think professional dancers are better, prettier. Why couldn't we have professional dancers today?"

"That's what I think. Maybe none were available," said Seto, suddenly standing and going off somewhere.

Noticing that the cushion seats to his right and left were empty, Junichi felt uncomfortable at that moment. It occurred to him he might as well go over to Professor Takayama, whom he had met on the train and with whom he had come to the hall. When Junichi looked toward the staggered shelves to the left of the alcove where he thought he might find him, he discovered the old man engaged as usual in a heated discussion.

"It really jolted me when I was at Qinhuai," Takayama was saying. "Really surprised me. The water was terribly dirty. Compared to it, Lake Xihu is really worthy of the name lake. There were some places in China where the scenery was good. As for other lakes, Lake Dontinghu, perhaps because I visited it in winter, was a mess. All I saw were some shallows. It didn't look the least bit like a lake."

He was apparently talking about the trip he had once made to China. Noticing Junichi's eyes focusing on him, Takayama said, "Oh, excuse me. Here's a *sake* cup for you," and he offered it to Junichi. The moment Junichi took the cup, a white hand by his side emerged from within its kimono sleeve that showed the kimono's red undergarment. That hand served him some *sake.* It belonged to the woman Seto had praised for her beauty when she had been dancing a while back.

Junichi offered some *sake* to Professor Takayama on returning the cup to him. After listening without interest as Takayama continued to talk about

Chinese drama and tea served with watermelon seeds, Junichi returned to his seat. The seats to his right and left remained unoccupied, and he glanced around, a blank look on his face.

In the same row beyond Seto's empty cushion seat he had left a while ago, a man about forty years old, a gold watch chain hanging from the buttonhole of his suit, was talking intently to a somewhat aged geisha who had played the *shamisen*. Her hair was arranged in the small butterfly style, the middle-aged woman's *obi* sash black satin. Though the man seemed to feel he was entertaining the geisha, she herself was not showing the least bit of interest in him. He seemed to think he was teasing her, but she was thoroughly bantering him. Was it that she was treating him like a child? Not at all. When an adult deals with an innocent child, the adult will show some kind of sympathy to the youngster. Not only was this geisha contemptuously treating her guest with malicious intentions, she was actually making no effort to conceal or suppress her malice. Without realizing she was taking advantage of his ignorance, the man was laughing innocently, amused by her light jokes, which were really full of bitter irony toward him.

As Junichi listened to them a while, he felt quite uncomfortable. The forty-year-old person making a fool of himself was not worthy of any sympathy. Furthermore, Junichi could be quite indifferent to him. Yet he couldn't help feeling disdain for the geisha.

Geisha are cruel animals. This was the first impression Junichi had reached about them.

Suddenly Atropos broke off the conversation and stood up.

At that moment a beautiful geisha with a Shimada hairdo, as if she had been waiting for the older geisha to stand, replaced her and sat down, a *sake* container in her hand.

"This has just been warmed, sir," she said to the man with the gold chain as she abruptly held out the container to him.

Letting her pour the *sake,* he looked inquisitively at her face. "What's your name?" he asked.

"Ochara," she replied without so much as forcing a smile. That is to say, unlike that of the older geisha, Ochara's expression had nothing contemptuous in it. Her face was governed by a calm that was utterly pure. Her face was the quintessence of calm.

Junichi looked at her from the side. She was quite young. She had probably been only a fledgling geisha until recently when at last she had become fully experienced. A natural pink appeared on the cheeks and nose of her slender face, and on that face overflowed a trace of something slightly reddish. As Junichi glanced at her from the side, her bright eyes gave off a greenish reflection. Junichi noticed that not only were her kimono colors subdued, but the undergarment was different in its light and dark tints. He found her purplish-gray silk crepe kimono rare in its colors, and he noticed her unusual *maruobi* sash with its elaborate brocade pattern. The bustle of the *obi,* the waistband under it, as well as the scarlet color that divided the center of the *obi* into two parallel lines and the scarlet undergarment that seemed like a triangle with its turned-up hem, all stimulated Junichi.

As he devoured the fish before him, he glanced in the geisha's direction every so often, and occasionally she too furtively glanced at him as she smoked her *kiseru* pipe. When the chignon of her Shimada hairdo suddenly drooped forward, he could see the white nape of her neck, a triangular patch with its peak pointing downward under her kimono collarband. Perhaps, Junichi thought quite suddenly, this girl wanted to come sit by him. A while ago when she had come over to Professor Takayama, she had sat by Junichi's side without his being aware of her. And the reason she was perhaps sitting in front of the man with the gold watch chain was that his seat was near Junichi's. Yet a moment later he derided himself. No matter how truthful Seto's words to him were and even though the geisha who had come this night were geisha called on the spur of the moment, there couldn't be a geisha who would chase after a mere student in a Kokura *hakama* skirt. As he considered himself foolish for having such thoughts, he changed his mind and began digging into the steamed egg dish which had just been served.

At that moment a foppish man in a skirtless kimono under a black silk *haori* coat with five family crests on it came over to the man with the gold watch chain to accept a *sake* offering from him. He was a sophisticated-looking man in his twenties. Each time he spoke there appeared on his cheeks, which seemed to have some makeup on, three deep vertical wrinkles. The voice in which he spoke was indescribably unnatural and squeaky. It was a falsetto voice, *une voix de fausset.*

With his left hand on the *tatami* mat, he accepted the *sake* cup the man with the gold chain offered him. Ochara served him more *sake,* and he thanked her, his voice quite feminine. A handful of his hair shimmering with scented pomade tumbled down over his narrow forehead. "The other day," said the man with the gold watch chain, "my children went to the Yūrakuza to see you, and when they came home they talked quite a lot about you. They said your performance was really enjoyable."

"Oh, no, I'm still a beginner with almost no chance of being successful. But when you have time, please come see our play."

Junichi suddenly recalled that Sone had said a new actor would be present at the party. Junichi couldn't help feeling a kind of pity for this actor in

terms of his future. Actors, Junichi thought, had to portray different kinds
of characters. They had to speak their lines as naturally as possible. And so
when this man was portraying himself, he would lapse into speech as unnatural as his sounded now. What would happen if he had to portray a young
actor like himself? It couldn't possibly be a serious drama. It would be a
farce. It would be some improvised buffoonery. First of all, what in the
world had happened to his voice? Surely he wasn't born with a voice like
that. He must have deliberately worked at having a good voice, and this was
the voice he had ended up with, one that became second nature to him. It
was similar to a child's being told to behave himself so that he comes out
with an ugly frown. Again Junichi felt the pathos of the actor's situation. At
the same time he was having these thoughts, Junichi had not neglected to
observe what kind of attitude Ochara would have toward the actor.

Whenever Junichi had a chance to come in contact with various elements
of society, his illusions were mercilessly destroyed. Especially after he came to
Tokyo, each time he saw someone, no matter what that person's status, even
someone who was barely keeping his head above water and swimming in
that society, Junichi never expected that person to have any artistic taste. So
from the very first he had never anticipated that geisha would be able to
appreciate and understand real art.

Nevertheless, he wondered how Ochara would regard this effeminate-
looking man. Would she look on him with indifference or sympathy?

What Junichi discovered completely surprised him. As she served the man
sake, Ochara glanced at him for only a moment and then looked away. From
whatever angle of vision Junichi observed her, she remained completely neu-
tral.

The actor sat so close to her their kimono sleeves touched. He put his *sake*
cup before him, his left hand against the *tatami* mats as he talked.

"As for the comic interludes between *nō* plays, I think it's sufficiently satisfying just to get the audience to understand the plot. Otherwise, it's too
difficult to perform. It's too trying for me to memorize long speeches word
by word. The plays of the great masters are too difficult to memorize. The
role of an actor impersonating the female, did you say? Well, it's not that
difficult once you get the knack of it. It won't be long before actresses will
be appearing on the stage, and yet some people maintain that there are still
some roles that would be better played by men than by women. It's come to
my attention that even in the West, in the past, of course, all the female
parts were played by males."

The gold watch chain was listening to them, its face like that of an admirable patron. Ochara, seemingly bored, was tying and untying the stitched

cord of the *kiseru* pipe case on her lap. As Junichi was observing her small fingers toying with the cord, he found at the same time she was stealing glances at him.

While they exchanged glances for a while, Junichi felt more and more tense. He was assaulted by tension and uneasiness, as if he had been given a problem he had to solve. Had he been able to talk to her, he thought, this unpleasant rope binding him would be undone. But it was almost impossible to talk to her because she was sitting in front of someone else. No, that wasn't so. Even if she had been sitting in front of him, Junichi doubted he could talk to her with ease. If she wanted to look at him that much, she ought to come over and sit before him. Yet even if she came over, he wondered whether or not he could offer her his *sake* cup to drink from the way other guests did so easily. He felt he could not bring himself to offer the cup to her naturally. He'd bungle the whole thing because it was out of character for him to force himself to do it. Of course, it would be simplicity itself for her to offer him *sake* the way she did to everyone else. Why then hadn't she come over to him? And why hadn't she offered him any? She had no obstacles to overcome, had she, so why hadn't she come up to him?

As his thoughts proceeded this far, Junichi became aware of his usual antagonism toward women. He felt the wench was silently, wordlessly, trifling with him, playing fast and loose with him. At the same time, of course, he felt these impressions were so wide of the mark that he was more or less making unfair accusations against women. And yet even that realization was insufficient to extinguish the antagonism he felt.

Fortunately he did not feel her temptation was that strong, and because there had been no direct collision between them, he retained within himself the freedom to retreat from this pretty adversary.

He decided on a path of retreat toward Seto, Seto having returned to his seat near the gold watch chain. Junichi discovered him laying waste to the fish before him. The distance between Ochara's seat and Seto's was not great, but at least from this position Junichi would not have to face her.

With a feeling somewhat akin to the petty triumph of a man who had surmounted the lure of temptation, Junichi left his seat. But the moment he stood up, so did Ochara, who went off somewhere. With his eyes evoking a greeting, Seto called out to Junichi, "How do you like the party?"

"It's not very interesting," Junichi said, his voice subdued.

"My thought exactly. That's how these parties are. Oh, take a look. Seems like they're going to dance again. They're really doing us a great service."

Junichi looked back to find the older geisha with the *shamisen* at the spot the geisha had been before. In front of her were Ochara and another geisha making some fairly extensive preparations for the dance. Each was rolling up the bottom of her kimono and undergarment and firmly tucking these into the *obi* sash. From just below Ochara's knees Junichi could see her scarlet undergarment with its silk pattern; hers and the other geisha's light red undergarment were similar in design.

As the older geisha sat plucking her *shamisen*, the two girls performed their animated dance.

"What are they dancing?" asked Junichi.

"It's the old tale of Momotarō. They're singing about the old man and his wife doing something or other."

Junichi admired Seto's having various kinds of information at his disposal, especially since that was probably expected at parties where one drank, parties Seto would be the first to head for.

A maid brought in a platter of *sushi*. Seto instantly grabbed a piece topped with raw tuna, took a bite, and over his tray surveyed the room. He was looking for some soy sauce for the *sushi*. Since he had finished his dish of thin slices of raw fish, the maid had already removed it along with his small plate of soy. All he had on his tray were some oysters in shells with a vinegar sauce for this dish. He dipped the remainder of his piece of *sushi* into the vinegar and popped the tidbit into his mouth.

"What about you? Don't you eat *sushi?*"

"That steamed egg mixture we had a while ago filled me up. And this *sake* isn't very good."

"The *sake* they serve depends on the class of customers."

"Oh, is that so?" Junichi said, looking around toward the alcove since he had nothing to do. "What's that? That big tiger?"

"It's by Ganku. Had it been entered in an art exhibition sponsored by the Ministry of Education, it would have been rejected."

"Tell me. Do you think it would be all right if I left?"

"Who would care if you did?"

A moment later Junichi wordlessly got to his feet.

"You going home now?" asked Seto.

"Well, that depends," Junichi said. He passed through the middle of the room, headed out to the corridor, and went down the stairs. He wanted to leave inconspicuously if he could.

Just as he reached the bottom of the staircase, two of the men he had seen at the party came out of the men's room. Since he was embarrassed to be seen leaving alone so early, he went into the lavatory.

As he left the room after washing up, he saw Ochara leaning against a pillar in the corridor. Somehow her presence startled him.

"Are you leaving already?" she said, gazing at him. She was the type who could suggest laughter merely by her look. Her eyes gave off their greenish reflection. Bending her supple body forward, she moved a step toward him. As her slightly reddish face drew nearer, Junichi found himself dazzled by it.

"Next time, come by yourself." She took her name card from its small case and handed the card to him.

He took it, unable to say even a word. And that was because he was too befuddled to think.

Before he was able to recover from his surprise, Ochara turned around and rushed with quick steps through the corridor to the stairs.

Without looking at the name card in his hand, Junichi put it into his kimono sleeve, came in a daze to the foot of the staircase, and glanced around.

The only persons he saw were four or five men squatting on their heels around a brazier under a shelf on which hats and overcoats were piled. Junichi looked uneasily up the stairway along which, fortunately, no one was descending. He took this opportunity to move toward the shelf.

One of the men got up from this place by the brazier to ask, "Your number, sir?"

Junichi handed him his wooden marker, received his hat and coat, and left through the cold entranceway.

18

On his way home from the Kamesei, he stood at the foot of Ryōgoku Bridge and waited for his streetcar, finally boarding one that came along the riverbank at Hama-chō. Probably because it was near the year's end, the car was crowded. He had seen the red plate hanging on the car that indicated no seats, but with a few passengers getting off at the stop, he could just about manage to squeeze through.

While he stood at the end of the car holding onto the brass bar above a rear window, the conductor told him to move further in. He tried to step up onto the elevated platform to make his way toward the interior, but a young man in a short coat stood at the entrance, his arms folded and refusing to budge. Junichi stepped back and remained at the entrance as before. The conductor did not force him to move further in.

It was not long before the streetcar made a sudden turn. It was at that moment Junichi realized he was headed for Asakusa. The various emotions he had experienced at the party had so filled his head with confusion that he had paid no attention to the direction.

He took out his return ticket and got a transfer to Ueno Hirokōji. According to the conductor's instructions, he changed cars at Umayabashi-dōri.

The streetcar from Honjo was not too crowded, so he was able to hold onto a strap. Observing those along the street from the waist down, Junichi was reminded of Ochara as she sat with the nape of her neck so elegantly poised, her long undergarment revealed slightly from her hips as she stood. Finally, as he recalled the incident before the men's room, his imagination remained rooted to that moment. Her words to him and her movements were so vividly revived in him that at that instant he no longer had any interest in the pedestrians outside the car.

At that moment there occurred to him the question of Ochara's motive for her words and actions. Though he was aroused by the circulation of his young blood, his thoughts were so much cooler that even he wondered about himself. He found some justice in Seto's having once said to him, "You reason just like an old man." Junichi wondered if Ochara had acted as she had out of carnal desire or greed or possibly both, the causes often cited in newspaper columns on the psychology of women. And yet he was modest enough to reflect that if her words and actions were based on momentary desires, she would have chosen someone other than him, a mere student. He could feel at the back of his mind that his vanity was making him think this way. And so he sensed he would never fall in love. Though he thought he might happen to fall in love one of these days, just as he might fall into debt, he would never truly fall in love. And it seemed to him it was this kind of reasoning that made him think in such a detached and calm way.

When he got off the streetcar at Hirokōji, it was somewhat windy out, the leaves of bamboo rustling in the storefront decorations of the brightly lit shops celebrating the coming New Year. He raised his overcoat collar, his head buried in it, and began walking, his Satsuma clogs loudly resounding.

As he started to long for the brazier in his small room facing east in Yanaka, he was hailed by a rickshaw, so Junichi finally took the ride. Because he was still slightly intoxicated, he found the fairly strong wind against his face all the more pleasant.

Going through a familiar street leading to the zoo beside the large gate of Tōshōgū Shrine, he wondered as he passed under the semidarkness of a cluster of cryptomeria trees what in the world he was now achieving. He was afraid that with his perpetual inactivity, he would end up like that old man who had told him the story of the badger at the sacred shrine, but the idea struck him as so ridiculous he dismissed it at once.

When the rickshaw turned at Tennōji Temple, he found the shops in the

Sansaki Kitamachi area still open. This rural district, separated from the city by the park in between, was bustling with people out shopping for the year-end celebration.

He sent off the rickshaw at his house gate and entered his room. He took out a match from his kimono sleeve and lit the lamp. He saw how the old woman had offered him her services, the bed not only neatly laid out, but the kettle on the brazier already steaming. He removed the kettle only to discover the Sakura charcoal burning red in the brazier. He stirred the fire, adding a good many pieces of charcoal.

On his tidied-up desk was Maeterlinck's *L'oiseau Bleu,* which he had left half-read. He discovered a single postcard on the book. The minute he picked up the card his heart throbbed, intuitively feeling it had to be from the woman who was leaving for Hakone the next day. But it was from Ōmura: "I'd like to call on you tomorrow," it read. "If you've nothing planned, please wait for me, though I've no special business with you." Thinking this short note typical of Ōmura, Junichi smiled to himself as he put the card into the wire filing basket under his desk, the basket he had suddenly come across and bought at Jinbō-chō station.

He pulled out a small box he had placed in a corner of the alcove. Removing his wallet, watch, and several other items from his kimono sleeves, he tossed these into the box. Among the items was a small name card. It was the name card he had put into his sleeve without even glancing at it. He picked up the card, a lithographic one, the name Ochara from the Sakaeya on it in a clumsy hand. Not only did he think the name clumsily printed, but he found himself musing the name was odd even for a woman whose profession it was to be the plaything of men. As he looked carefully at the letters on the card, he couldn't help feeling this way. Even as he held the card in his hand, he could not clearly call to mind Ochara's facial expression, not even her voice. Besides this or that thing she did, he could recall only such trivialities as the color of her kimono or the way she dressed. But to Junichi the name card was not so meaningless as to be torn up or tossed into a wastebasket. It was certainly not so unimportant as to be thrown aside at once. If this was so, he asked himself if he wanted to go alone to see her, but he found the question not that urgent. And yet he couldn't bear to throw the card away. What significance, he wondered, did this name card have for him? He had no clear idea. Or was it not merely the token of a woman he had felt some slight kindling of love for? And again he could not clearly understand.

Junichi put the card between two pages of *L'oiseau Bleu.* And then without so much as changing out of his kimono, he crawled into bed.

19

Junichi had slept soundly, and when he awoke the next morning, he felt good about himself, felt healthy. And yet it seemed as if some phlegm had lodged in his throat. He wondered as he cleared his throat two or three times if he had caught cold. But the phlegm had apparently been caused by the *sake* he had drunk the previous night, for after gargling and washing his face, he felt relieved, refreshed. As he sat at his desk, his hands held over the brazier whose charcoal had been kindled by the landlady even before he was aware of it, he suddenly remembered something and whispered to himself, "Ah, it's today, isn't it?" His remembrance was similar to walking in the morning when he was a student and asking what day of the week it was only to find himself recalling at the very moment his school schedule for the day.

What Junichi had recalled was that it was the day Mrs. Sakai was to leave for Hakone. He had not yet decided whether to go, though he had been tempted to. What had made him recall the day of her departure more than anything else was that she had somehow suggested he should come too. There had always generally been something suggestive in all her words and actions. She was apt to use that technique half-unconsciously or, even more than that, to abuse it in order to control the will of another. Had she become a mesmerist, she would probably have been quite successful at it.

After remembering this day of her Hakone departure, Junichi let his imagination run so far afield he evoked a strange memory. It concerned a dream he had had near dawn the previous night. Just as he was about to enter that dream, he had awakened with a start, but soon had fallen asleep again. It appeared to him he had not slept long after he had that dream. And this was why he thought the dream had occurred near daybreak.

At any rate, in his dream he had gone on a trip with Ōmura, and they were resting at a teahouse somewhere. The teahouse was different from the deserted one at Ōmiya they had once rested at with its circled shelter of reed screens. The two had had their tea and had eaten some foul-tasting sweet buns, something of the sort. Junichi had no idea what the season was, but everything he saw lacked those colors that make for warm tones. The afternoon was somewhat cloudy. As he was talking and laughing with Ōmura, a woman suddenly cried outside the teashops, "A tidal wave's coming!" Junichi was the first to stand and head out to the road.

The road was a straight and long coastal lane between wide fields. A ditch was on each side of the road, and along the ditches was a row of lanky alders. Junichi glanced in the direction to which the woman had said, "Over there!

Look!" All he saw was a grayish line under a gray sky. He could not tell if any water was in that direction. And yet he was seized by some violent fear. And then speaking to Ōmura, who had just come out, Junichi asked, "Which way is nearer the mountains?" Ōmura remained silent. No matter which direction Junichi looked in, he could find no mountains to speak of. Except that, in a direction opposite the one from which the water was coming, he could see a low hill. Junichi broke into a run in hopes of reaching that hill. And as he ran, he let his feet take him across wide extended fields.

From time to time he looked back to find Ōmura still standing motionless on the road. The woman could not be seen. In dreams numbers of persons freely appear and disappear. Even though the woman had disappeared, Junichi did not wonder about her, did not even question the why of it.

All at once the scene changed. Changes of place in dreams are also made freely. The moment Junichi felt the water approaching his ankles, he clambered up a big nearby tree. He did not know what kind of tree it was except for the fact that it was big, its green leaves thick, luxuriant. He climbed and climbed until his hands touched a tree limb that spread out like a fan. The moment he had leaped onto that branch, he found several people had taken refuge on it even before he had. And there, crouching among the green leaves reflecting a white light, was a woman, her long hair disheveled; disheveled too were her long sleeves and her kimono skirt.

Wherever he looked the land was inundated with yellow muddy water except for this one tree that stood prominently like a small solitary island. And just like Adam and Eve newly born in a ruined world, Junichi and the woman boldly moved closer to one another, the body of each supported by one hand on the bough.

Junichi moved so close to her he could almost touch her. The face of this unknown woman suddenly changed into Ochara's, but he thought it not the least bit odd. And then during an interval when they were exchanging quite familiar expressions and fragments of words, the woman suddenly turned into Mrs. Sakai. While he was tormented with his endeavors to support his body in that precarious position even as he tried to shorten the distance between himself and the other, that face was transformed into Oyuki's before he realized what was taking place.

It was at this moment that Junichi was jolted and returned to a state of half-wakefulness. He recalled reading somewhere that in dreams men can perform the most beastlike actions with nonchalance, that this ability was due to some atavism in returning to ancient times when morality had not yet been created in the conventional world. Junichi had thought it a quite radi-

cal inference. Whether or not it was correct, he had not fallen into such atavism. Possibly he had not because he had awakened from his dream and had
somehow regained some portion of consciousness.

Half-awake, Junichi felt the flames of passion in him. Again he pulled to
his neck the quilt he had kicked down to his feet, and as if burying his chin
under the quilt, he was instantly asleep, vaguely conscious that his unfinished dream was lingering as if reluctant to leave. But soon he seemed to
enter a short but deep sleep. Those images in Junichi's long dream repeated
themselves within a short space of time with that unimpeded speed typical
of human thought. And as he repeatedly kept up his dream, he could so
clearly sense its outlines and colors it was as if he had grasped the dream with
his very hands. He wished he could write his novel that clearly. With this
thought he tried to repeat his dream, but its outlines blurred, its colors
faded. Only unnatural or irrational things, like a small stone one trips over
along a street, seemed to be prominent, to be so distinct and vivid.

20

Around ten in the morning, Ōmura Sōnosuke, with a healthy complexion, a
look of exhilarating freshness on his face, came into Junichi's room on Hatsune-chō. The sliding door facing the street had a pale yellowish light from
gray clouds, the sun's rays so faint that the colors could hardly be made out.

"Well, you've waited for me. I mailed you my card, but I was afraid you
might have to go somewhere. When I got up this morning, it was cloudy
out, but for Tokyo the day's not that unpleasant. I wonder if we can't head
off somewhere."

Junichi felt as if Ōmura had brought a kind of vigor and energy into the
gloomy room. Looking at Ōmura as he sat tailor-style on the other side of
the brazier, Junichi, attracted by Ōmura's bright way of talking, replied,
"Why, you've come exactly at the right moment! I've no place in particular
to go to."

Ōmura told him he had come to say good-bye before taking off on a trip
through some of the nearby prefectures during the holiday celebrations until
January 10. This show of friendship moved Junichi.

After they began talking about a few topics, Ōmura noticed *L'oiseau Bleu*
lying on Junichi's desk.

"You're reading something now?" he said, about to go over to the book.
Junichi was startled. He felt uneasy because Ōmura might notice Ochara's
name card inserted inside. So Junichi, outmaneuvering him, picked up the

book as he said, "It's *L'oiseau Bleu.*" He flipped through the opening pages and turned to page eighteen.

"It says here, *'A peine Tyltyl a-t-il tourné le diamant, qu'un changement soudain et prodigieux s'opère en toutes choses.'* This part is so beautifully written we don't even realize it's merely an ordinary stage direction. When I was a middle school student in my hometown, I was often taken by a friend to the home of a learned priest. One day, just as we visited him, he was giving a lecture on the Vimalakirti Sutra. The way Vimalakirti's shabby quarters change into a sublime world is quite similar to what's depicted in this play. I've read much further into the book, but I can't sympathize too much with the plot in general. A woodcutter and his family exist only on bread and water, and even at Christmas the poor man can't afford to buy candles to light up the fir tree even though the bluebird of happiness lives in a cage in the woodcutter's hut. And still Tyltyl and Mytyl, the brother and sister, wander in search of the bluebird to such places as Remembrance Land, the Palace of Night, and Future Land. And when they look in on Future Land to see what the children of the future are doing, they see some children devising elaborate machines. Some are being devised to allow men to fly without wings. Some children are trying to invent a medicine that will cure every kind of disease. Others are attempting to create a machine by which to overcome death. It's a world, you see, saturated with physical and material things.

"I wonder if we humans can become happy in these ways? I can't help feeling the play's full of contradictions. The nineteenth century was the era of natural science, and it brought about our materialistic civilization. But we couldn't be satisfied with that kind of world, so we turned our eyes from the outer world to the inner. What does it matter if children of the future bring us various kinds of machines or apples big as watermelons? Oh, now I remember. One of those kids was picking his nose. It reminded me of Ōson, perhaps thinking of putting out an addendum to his *Great Discoveries.* I wondered what that child was scheming while picking his nose. Apparently he was trying to devise a way of warming the world once the sun died out. Don't you feel all these machines and devices are no more than substitutes to make up for our losses once our present happiness vanishes? True, there were some children trying to devise ways of getting rid of inequalities. It's not that I'm saying there are no future ways by which to penetrate our inner lives for the better. It's just that all these devices are so jumbled I can't find any chain to bind them into some kind of systematic order. What's contradictory remains contradictory. What do you think?"

Junichi had waxed eloquent in spite of his intentions. For from start to finish he had been worried about Ochara's name card. He had fervently been hoping Ōmura would not reach out to ask for the book.

"That's it exactly," said Ōmura, not even putting out his hand to touch the book. "The weakness in the play is exactly that the contradictions remain contradictions. But philosophers, for the most part, tend to make observations on those ultimate problems human beings must face. They glance at life from the outside. That's true for Nietzsche and even for Weininger, whom we talked about the other day. The inner life, to use your words, is neglected. Their philosophy is deficient in that comprehensive view which knows the symbolic significance behind ordinary daily life. Except for Simmel, I feel the only person who observes from this perspective is probably Maeterlinck. I think he wanted to write in such a way that all kinds of work which the children in Future Land share—which you said was arranged in a disorderly way—would fuse into one symbolic theme in *L'oiseau Bleu,* but he failed to bring it off."

While Junichi was listening to Ōmura, the fear that the name card might be discovered gradually abated, and at the same time he found the questions Ōmura had raised about *L'oiseau Bleu* quite intriguing.

"As a matter of fact," Junichi said, "I can't help being attracted only by the commonplace, even banal, aspects of our ordinary daily life. I really believe these commonplace elements are probably of no real value. And this attitude of mine may have something to do with egoism, which we talked about the other day."

"I think it has a lot to do with it."

"You do? Then I'd like you to tell me frankly what you think about that." Junichi, his eyes large and cool and bright, looked up at Ōmura.

Ōmura stubbed out his cigarette into the brazier ashes and began a further explanation. "Well, if you wish, I'll speak frankly—I'll tell you exactly what I think," he said, laughing a little and revealing his white teeth. "Generally speaking, the happiness in *L'oiseau Bleu* boils down to this: finding spiritual peace and enlightenment in oneself and exerting a strong influence on others. Nowadays, there are those who try to explain happiness by means of Chinese morality. If possible, everything can be resolved at once by behaving oneself, supporting one's family, governing one's country, and pacifying the world. If you add a further transcendental aspect, the results are no more than something similar to the thoughts of Lao-tzu and Chuang-tzu or Chu-tzu and Yang-ming introduced into Japan after the coming of Buddhism. If we look at the Western world, Greek ethics were transcendentalized after Plato, and Christianity developed his thought to a considerable degree. This philosophy, based on a transcendental world, became supremely awe-inspiring, and this world itself became meaningless, empty. As a result, the bluebird, caged in the woodcutter's hut, went unheeded and had to be searched for elsewhere.

"It's my belief that Buddhism's renunciation of the world and Christianity's renunciation are the same. And I feel that the future development of man's ideas can only occur in the West. You see, there's never been a Renaissance in the Orient. The Renaissance made it possible for men to find the bluebird in their own homes. Bold voyagers appeared and created the real maps of the world. Astronomy came to be truly understood. The sciences developed. The arts bloomed. Machines became more and more significant, and everything in the world turned into what the Buddhists call the material world. Production and capital absorbed all our energies so that the other world became neglected, meaningless. And then that eccentric Schopenhauer suddenly awoke and attempted to peer into that other world. Wishing for that other world, he reflected on this world we were in. He envisioned all creation as fundamentally a product of blind will. This is his pessimism, a pessimism which can't accept life affirmatively. And then Nietzsche appeared and handed down a totally opposite thesis. He said that one cannot escape suffering in this life, but that it's cowardly to avoid it by running away. He proclaimed there was a way of comprehending life's significance while fully being immersed in its suffering. That is, he turned the problem of What into How. You have to find, at any cost, the significance of life as it is.

"Even if one talks about returning to nature the way Rousseau did, memories persisting from ancient times to the present are undeniably real, and no one can obliterate them. In Japan, some people have said the Chinese thought advocated by the school of Ogyū Sorai and the ideas expounded by Keichū and Kamo no Mabuchi and their disciples were a kind of Renaissance, but their ideas were merely reactionary, not a rebirth of human thought. Of course, it's not good either to drive one's soul to the country of beautiful dreams where past memories reside and to yearn for the blue flowers of the romantics. Even Tolstoy, great as he is, is pessimistic. In the long run, you have to confront your own daily life directly and immediately. This direct confrontation of life is Dionysian. And if while doing so and while immersing yourself in that daily life, you can also defend spiritual freedom without letting your resolve budge even an inch, that's Apollonian. Somehow, if life is comprehended in this way, you can't help becoming individualistic. That attitude is definitely individualistic, but there's a dividing line between what we call egoism and altruism. Nietzsche's egoism represents its dark side, that is, the will to power. Its basic idea is to become great by defeating others. If men fight each other in the search for power, that leads to anarchism. And if this is individualism, it goes without saying that individualism is bad. But altruistic individualism doesn't work that way. Even as you stoutly defend the cast of your ego without budging an inch from that principle, you try to find significance in every aspect of life. You remain loyal to your master as a citizen, so it's not like being the so-called servant of the master as in ancient times in which one's public and private life were all muddled together. You are loyal to your parents, but as a son you aren't your parents' slave, whereas in the old days you could be sold by them or killed. Faithfulness to your master or parents is no more than those real values of life your ego finds significant. Everything in our daily lives is of significant value in our lives. And if this is so, can we so easily cast away ego? Can we sacrifice the ego? Actually, that's possible. Just as the greatest affirmation of love can result in the suicide of lovers, the greatest affirmation of loyalty to one's master can result in death in battle. If every aspect of life is significant, a person can significantly kill himself. In this instance, individualism turns into savage valor. And that is different from a death based on negating life from the principle of pessimism. Well, what's your reaction to this type of argument?" Ōmura said, again laughing and revealing his white teeth.

"I suppose you're right," said Junichi, who had been listening intently. "I'm not sure, though, until I can give it more thought. And yet it seems to me these fragments of modern ideas have in them something in common with each other if only we can tie them to one another. The other day I read about a theory of a person holding a doctor's degree. According to this idea, we Japanese can't sacrifice ourselves to the principle of individualism since individualism is a Western idea. So in the Orient individualism is transformed into family-ism, which in turn becomes nationalism. The writer goes on to say, therefore, that one can forsake the self for the benefit of one's master or father. Since his theory equates individualism with egoism, it's completely different from your concept of altruistic individualism, isn't it? Furthermore, since his theory says that individualism develops into family-ism and then into nationalism and that it's un-Western, don't you think it rather odd in Japan, funny even?"

"Well, of course, it's ridiculous. That type of theorist not only equates individualism with egoism or self-centeredness, but also with anarchy. His idea that ancient humans probably crawled out of their caves to live separately like chemical atoms completely ignores the history of mankind. If his theory's right, we have to say man's life originated in anarchy. But that kind of life never existed in any period in the history of the world. Anarchic life is merely the imaginative product of present-day anarchists. The theory that human beings who originally led an artificially isolated life created societies and then countries probably originated in Rousseau's theory of the *Contrat Sociale*. I doubt if there's anyone who still believes that. The further we look back into the history of mankind, the more strongly do we find men bound by ties of communal life. Gradually men broke those ties, gained more freedom, and became individualistic. Since we're both studying literature, an analysis of the history of literature tells us this is so, doesn't it? Plays in which fate plays a role and plays in which the environment triumphs become plays of character, so that means plays became vehicles for individualism. To attempt to suppress individualism at this time in history is like pushing into bed and holding down by force a child that's awake and ready to rise. It's impossible, don't you think?"

Although Ōmura was disclosing confidences in this animated discussion, his voice contained no trace of agitation. He continued talking in his usual calm voice. Junichi simply listened, chiming in occasionally with "That's so right" or "Exactly."

"I've got a funny story to tell," said Ōmura as he continued his talk. "After the Russo-Japanese War, some Western scholars, feeling that the Japanese did not value life, offered a kind of analysis for that tendency. Since the concept of family or nation has not yet developed in Japan, the Japanese, they said, do not sacrifice themselves for these concepts. Due to their blind hatred of foreigners and due to the fact that they don't prize life, they die a cheap death in war. Look at any of these books and you'll find that almost all of them make that observation. On the other hand, our Japanese scholars say Westerners become anarchists one after another because they have been individualistic since ancient times and know nothing of family or nation. While much misunderstanding is mutually exchanged between East and West, Germany and the United States have gradually been expanding their exchange of university professors. They've almost finished building an international university in Belgium." Ōmura suddenly said, "We're having a strange discussion, aren't we?" and just as suddenly he became silent.

Junichi too was lost in his own silent thoughts. Yet at the same time, because he felt the distance between Ōmura and himself had been transformed into respect for one another, he was so happy he smiled in spite of himself.

"What are you smiling about?" Ōmura asked.

"It's just that I'm happy we're having a stimulating discussion today."

"Me too. It's the privilege of young men like us to say whatever we feel like saying without weighing each word on a scale."

"Why do men become hypocrites once they get older?"

"I guess they do. It may be too unfair to use the word hypocrites, but there's no doubt we become much less flexible. Just as there's no life eternal, there's no eternal youth."

Junichi thought a moment before saying, "But isn't there some way to keep us from getting less flexible?"

"It's not just our flexibility we lose. It gets to be a problem of preserving the elasticity in our bodies. There's a Russian called Metschnikoff at the Pasteur Institute in Paris. He's trying to work out a method to prevent the body from becoming more calcified as it gets older. If you want to cope with the problem of eternal youth now, well, there's no other way except to follow Metschnikoff's method."

"Do you really think so? Is there still one man left with such a belief in eternal youth? I don't think I'm trying not to die, but I'd like to escape that calcification!"

"Actually, that's what Metschnikoff himself says. He says you can't escape death, but at least he'd like to preserve his elasticity until he dies."

Realizing they had been probing into the far-off future, they both smiled at the same moment as if it had been prearranged. To them age and death seemed to be infinitely remote phenomena. They had never experienced having in their hands some scale by which to calculate the lifetime of a man.

Suddenly they heard a clumping sound outside the sliding doors to Junichi's room. The old housekeeper had been considerate enough to prepare their lunch and was now carrying it in to them.

21

Sipping tea after lunch, the two young men were silently enjoying their camaraderie. They realized they didn't have to talk of anything they didn't want to, for to speak of things because they are forced to socially is the loosest of all ropes that bind the minds of acquaintances. To remain calmly silent as long as one wishes without being bound by that rope is impossible for those beyond a certain age. Both Ōmura and Junichi were still young enough to ignore that danger.

Junichi drew the scuttle to him and added some charcoal to the brazier as Ōmura stood to go out to the lavatory. After he left, Junichi suddenly looked at *L'oiseau Bleu*. It had been bound loosely in its blue cover by the publisher, Charpentier et Fasquelle. Hurriedly he thumbed through the rough uneven pages he had cut apart with a paper knife. He pulled out the small name card he was searching for. It narrowly escaped being torn, but because of its pliant paper, the card crumpled when he tried to put it into his sleeve. Junichi felt as satisfied as a criminal feels when he has succeeded in suppressing evidence.

Returning from the restroom, Ōmura said, "I guess I'll have to be on my way," and he warmed his hands over the brazier, half-sitting before it.

"Do you have to make some preparations for your trip?"

"Nothing like that."

"Well, why not stay longer then?"

"You seem like someone who can't stand being alone," said Ōmura, and he sat with his legs crossed tailor-style and lit another cigarette. "Men who don't feel lonely are insensitive, or, if not, they've dulled their senses in order to get through life—you know, with *sake,* gambling, women, or hashish."

They looked at each other and laughed.

"To dull the mind to satisfy one's physical appetites is the same as killing oneself spiritually," said Junichi. "But there are times when my nerves are strangely stimulated or strangely suppressed, and I don't know what to do with my body." And he asked, "What do you think I should do at those times?"

Ōmura's theory was that the healthiest way was to practice something like Swedish gymnastics. "But you ought to prepare a target in the same way one needs a hypothetical enemy at military exercises, or you're apt to get bored. When you prepare a target, the effort becomes a sport. And when it becomes that, the competitive spirit appears directly or indirectly. Victory or defeat emerges. In the long run, never getting tired or bored means having the incentive that allows you to win at any cost. But, on the whole, artists have little of this competitive spirit, though the degree of competition may vary from person to person. Even when they're doing their artwork, even as they are actually competing as a matter of form, they forget about the competitive spirit while they are engaged in the work itself. There's a short story by Paul Heyse in which a rival breaks into his opponent's house during the night and smashes a statue, but this destructive act is based on his hatred of the other's personality and, furthermore, comes from a grudge about some love affair that's mixed into the action. In short, the story seems to say that artists worthy of being called artists will probably find it difficult to become sports enthusiasts."

As if reminded of something, Junichi said, "I don't mean to pose as an artist, but I can't get enthusiastic about competitive sports."

"Well, soon it'll be the season for competing in the One Hundred Poems game, so I guess that's bad for you, right?"

"No, it's true I can't enjoy the game, but they always ask me to read the poems, and that's good enough for me," said Junichi smiling.

"I see what you mean. Among those hundred poems there are several that begin with the same word, and unless you learn the poems by heart, you won't be able to pick up the two or three cards the moment the first five characters are read. In that case, you can't be called a skilled player and then it's not worth playing. The child's card game 'i-ro-ha' is the same kind of thing. To state this in an extreme way, you put the cards in your mind, say, beginning with A or B, in sets of two or three, so that if you hear A read aloud, all you have to do is pick all the cards beginning with A. If this game of poem cards has any value at all, it's limited to the time before you memorized the hundred poems and you had to search and probe mechanically to see how many of the poems began with the same word. Rather than being burdened with this kind of memorizing, I prefer memorizing something more intelligent."

"Generally, the participants are merely reading the cards and picking them up without paying attention to the poem's meaning or even to its pure rhythm or sound. I don't like being made a fool of by people with such humdrum minds."

"If that's true, then you still have something of the competitive spirit!"

"Perhaps because I'm still young."

"I wonder if you really are."

They looked at each other and again laughed.

Each time Ōmura saw Junichi laugh, he thought how charming Junichi's eyes were. Just at this moment the question of homosexuality occurred to him. In the mind of man, Ōmura thought, there exists a dark bottomless region. He had usually enjoyed associating with men older than himself, but after he had met this young man, he had suddenly begun alienating himself from others and had come only to Junichi's place. And though Ōmura usually hated lecture-like conversations more than anything and had found it annoying to listen to discussions of this kind, he could not come to dislike being talkative before the young Junichi. Ōmura didn't consider himself a homosexual, yet he couldn't help feeling that even in the minds of the most normal of humans, seeds of homosexuality lay buried.

Suddenly Ōmura stood up. "Well, I've really got to be off. What are you doing now?"

"Nothing, really. At any rate, I'll go part of the way with you."

It was not yet two in the afternoon.

Junichi along with Ōmura in his university uniform left the house on Hatsune-chō and turned on to Dangozaka.

At the entrance to each residence were the usual New Year decorations, a
combination of bamboo stems and pine tree branches and the sacred straw
rope with white paper streamers, the *shimenawa,* stretching horizontally
under each roof. Between a flourishing liquor store and an equally prosperous vegetable shop was a quiet paperhanger's shop whose sliding doors were
papered with a serene beauty, the result, after all, of his trade. No matter
where one looked, added embellishments were in evidence in preparation
for the New Year, and even those working in the shops were bustling about
with unusual energy.

On the north side of the street was a shop dealing in antiques, its frontage
quite narrow. Possibly because of the many temples in Yanaka, there were
such odds and ends in the shop as a wooden Buddhist gong whose red lacquer was peeling in various places and a wooden statue whose Chinese chalk
was scaling, these items placed between some old coins and an incomplete
set of cups and saucers. From the ceiling hung implements used at Buddhist
altars, such as gongs swung by a rope and an ancient Chinese musical instrument. There were also hanging potted ferns.

Each time Junichi passed this shop, he would look at it. It goes without
saying that his interest in stopping was different from that of an old man
who enters a curio shop to make a lucky find. Junichi's peering inside came
from curiosity. He recalled one of the storehouses constructed of mud and
mortar back home which were loaded with odds and ends of all kinds of
tools. Inside were strange utensils whose use was unknown, and there were
chipped and damaged pieces of scrap metal and wood so disfigured that the
uses of these items were incomprehensible to him. When Junichi had been
a small child, he often spent entire days rummaging aimlessly through
junk of this type. He remembered those occasions when his mother, now
dead, had at times gone out to look for him at the dinner hour, her eyes
wide in astonishment when she found him inside the storeroom. Junichi's interest in this antique shop contained a trace of his former feelings
for that old storehouse. It was a sort of investigation. From a rusty iron
kettle to a restored dish, he could imagine the history of these various arti-
facts.

Passing in front of the store and looking in, Junichi felt this shop was the
only one that had not undergone any kind of influence from its environment.

Seeing Junichi glancing into the shop, Ōmura said, "You seem to have
diverse interests."

"No, not really. Since there are so many unusual things lined up here, I've merely gotten into the habit of looking at them."

"Well, there are people whose minds are cluttered with odds and ends like that shop!"

With words this trivial, the two men went down the street in front of Zenshōan.

At that moment a female student coming up the street greeted Ōmura. Slightly tilting to the side her downcast face with its disheveled forelock, she shot a rapid glance at the two men as if examining their features, attitudes, and characters.

Ōmura took off his square university cap to return her greeting.

Junichi thought her an ordinary female student. Except for the purple bundle she carried, which probably contained books, all that attracted his attention were her blouse, tied with ribbons at the neck and wrists, and her violet *hakama* skirt. Actually she looked no different from a typical woman student. Her skirt was made from Ōshima fabric, her *haori* coat having a slightly larger splashed pattern than was ordinarily seen. Though she wore an *obi* sash of silk crepe with its red and yellowish-green design against a purple ground, Junichi couldn't see it because the sash was hidden behind her *hakama* skirt. The white neckband of her undergarment seen above her blouse was somewhat grimy, but Junichi obviously could not see the inner side of the girl's collar.

Yet what made a strong impression on him was her face, its strong lines seen through thin amber skin, and he found too that her sharp-looking eyes attracted him.

Even before Junichi began to wonder what her connection was to Ōmura, his friend blurted out, as if muttering to himself, "I never expected to see her!" And when the two men looked back at almost the same time, she had already gone about ten steps past them.

The two men went down one slope and up another before Ōmura volunteered his story.

He had met her the first time at a social gathering the previous year sponsored by a journal, *The World of Female Students*. As he found himself bored by the young pianist playing a piece for the *koto* entitled *Rokudan*, he noticed a girl student who had come in late, embarrassed at not being able to find a seat. Giving his seat to her, Ōmura stood by her, and then he was attracted to the name Saigusa written on the turned-up corner of the same cloth wrapper she had carried her books in. In those days, Ōmura had been asked by the chief editor of this journal to select some *tanka* poems for it. He had often chosen strikingly bold and passionate ones. And the writer of these poems had been Saigusa Shigeko. Since Saigusa was not a common surname, Ōmura suddenly felt like asking, "Are you Miss Shigeko?" And at almost the same moment she said, "Are you not Mr. Ōmura?" Later they had engaged in a lively discussion. While they were on various subjects, Ōmura happened to ask her if she was studying any foreign languages. "German," she said. This was Ōmura's first contact with a woman who was studying that language.

The day after the gathering, Shigeko's postcard arrived. And a few days later she suddenly called on him at his lodging house. She had come to ask him about some passages in Sudermann's *Zwielicht.*

Her questions were not in the least irrelevant, and Ōmura was not ill-natured enough to question her understanding of other passages she did not ask about.

On her next visit she had brought Tovorte's short story collection *Nicht Doch.* Ōmura told Junichi how embarrassed he was when the girl asked him, "How should I translate *'nicht doch'?*" Ōmura explained to Junichi the special meaning of this German expression. It was somewhat similar to *point du tout* or *nenni-dà* in French, even though the words did not exactly correspond. After one read the first story in Tovorte's collection, a story written quite simply, even quite shallowly, its language probably used to gain the cheap applause of mediocre readers, it was impossible not to understand the meaning of *nicht doch* from the story's contents even though the phrase's precise meaning was difficult to catch. If Shigeko had understood what Ōmura meant, she ought to have been able to offer some concrete examples to illustrate the meaning of the words. In fact, even if she knew how to read just a bit of German, she ought to have known those words. And if she knew that much, was she actually that innocent in asking questions about her reading, innocent without any ulterior motive? If she was that innocent, the novelist-critic Aeba Kōson might have said of her, "She's overly fond of being a modern student in her purple kimono with its splendid pattern of arrows." Ōmura wondered how she could have composed those revealing *tanka* poems. Had it been possible for a present-day sixteen-year-old girl to write them? Or else . . . Yet he was afraid to continue to think about it, to make further conjectures.

After that Shigeko no longer visited him. "We approached each other out of curiosity," Ōmura said, "but neither of us was able to obtain what we wanted." So without obligation or hard feelings they had parted. Of course, she of her own free will had been the one to approach him and to distance herself from him, but due to his own curiosity about her, he accepted his own responsibility in the matter by currying favor with her and encouraging her. After these remarks Ōmura laughed.

With these words the two stopped talking. They were walking before the gate of Seson'in Temple. Though it was cold, a group of children was playing tag in the vacant lot in front of the temple gate without showing any signs of feeling the cold.

"What kind of personality did she have?" Junichi suddenly asked.

"Well, from her poems I thought she behaved according to her feelings, but when I met her, I found she was quite a little politician."

"Strange, don't you think? What kind of family did she come from?"

"I didn't ask her and she never mentioned it, but later I heard from someone that her mother lived in Kyōbashi and was a masseuse who used the Yoshida method."

"That's a little odd, isn't it?"

"Well, I thought it strange when I first heard she was. Now that you call it odd, I believe I thought so too. I'm trying to recall the girl's behavior now that I think of it from that angle. Though she was only sixteen, she had acquired a certain kind of past even by that time. According to the man who told me about her background, Shigeko had entered the Japan Medical School with the intention of becoming a doctor. Apparently in a class with only male students, she had opted to study German. It wasn't known after that how many times she changed schools. Girls' schools offered only English and French in foreign language study, and for this reason she had tried to enter several private schools for boys after she quit the medical school. Every day she went to the lodgings of a teacher who taught German at a government-run school. At times she was seen walking with this teacher. The man who gave me this information also told me she was an odd woman. At any rate, she seems to be a woman who is quite problematic."

Junichi and Ōmura turned onto Sakana-machi. When they passed a mason's workshop in the area, Ōmura suggested they drop in at his boardinghouse, but even though he said he did not have to prepare for his trip, he indicated he definitely had two or three letters to write, so Junichi politely declined and parted at a corner where a funeral home was located.

For a while Junichi watched Ōmura walk with long strides along a narrow alley, his words *"Au revoir!"* lingering behind. Junichi moved toward Oiwake, the street gradually enveloped in the gathering dusk. He passed a laborer from a company that lights gas lamps, a footstool in the man's hand as he ran along the street.

22

A frown on his face, Junichi was sitting alone in his room at the Kashiwaya, a hot spring inn in Hakone Yumoto.

Since it was the thirty-first of December, those working at the inn were bustling about doing their various duties and preparations for the New Year, but since few guests were at the inn, almost no noise reached Junichi's room. All he could hear, in fact, were the turbulent sounds from the Hayakawa River. His bag had been left open in front of the alcove where a small scroll was hanging with a Chinese poem by Count Itō. Open beside it were two or three loosely bound octavo Western books in addition to a large European magazine which had also been left open. The journal was printed in two columns and had illustrations. Just as Junichi was leaving Tokyo, he had received *L'Illustration Théâtrale* and had tossed it into his bag.

He had left Tokyo the previous night and had arrived in Hakone on the thirty-first. He had gone at once to take a comfortable bath. He felt dissatisfied with himself for venturing to make the trip. And that dissatisfaction had unconsciously appeared all over his face.

≈

Ōmura had himself gone on a trip to several of the nearby prefectures. Junichi had no other friends. It would be natural and not at all surprising to say Junichi was quite lonely in Tokyo at year's end. Thus far in his life he had never suffered from loneliness should he have no one to talk to for two or three days if only he had some books to read.

Loneliness. Was it really loneliness that had driven Junichi to make this trip to Hakone, or could it have been solitude? Neither actually. No, unfortunately it had been neither loneliness nor solitude. To use Nietzsche's words, it had not been *einsam* Junichi had feared, for he had hoped to be *zweisam*.

Had he been able to say the journey was for love, he could have justified his coming to Hakone. But he was not in love with Mrs. Sakai. If he had been forced to indicate what it was that had influenced him, he would have had to admit it was, after all, nothing but animal impulse. And if such was the case, that left no room for him to offer any defense or embellishment.

On the morning of the thirtieth when he had decided to leave Tokyo, the melancholy he felt he ascribed to the cloudy weather. Even as he read his books, he had no interest in them. In the afternoon when the skies cleared, the sun's rays poured down against his sliding doors, so he had thought he would feel better, but the opposite occurred. A lump of uneasiness lurking deep in his mind rose to the very center of his consciousness, and that uneasiness grew rapidly. He began to hear cries of resistance against his own rational will. He had no doubts that he had been urged to leave Tokyo by the cry "To Hakone! To Hakone!"

In the evening he had begun making preparations to leave. Gathering this and that, he thought of putting his things in a leather suitcase he had brought with him from his hometown, but since he felt the bag too large and inconvenient, he had put everything in a cotton *furoshiki* wrapper. Then he took out a rug of camel hair he had bought just before coming to Tokyo. Telling the old landlady he preferred spending the New Year holidays at Hakone because it was too much trouble to pay the traditional New Year calls, he asked her to get him a rickshaw. Actually he was not obligated to pay his respects for the New Year at any home in Tokyo.

The decision was so abrupt the landlady's eyes were wide in astonishment even as she sent him away in the rickshaw. Junichi hurried off to Shinbashi station. As he passed through the Ginza, thronged even at night because of the year's end, he happened to notice his *furoshiki* wrapper did not look appropriate for such a trip, so after he stopped off at the Tomoeya, a luggage shop, and bought a small leather satchel, he stuffed the entire bundle into it.

At Shinbashi station when he checked the train schedules, he found the 7:50 train had already left. The next train, an express, was due out at nine and was expected to reach Kōzu at 10:53. The train would not arrive at Hakone at a convenient hour. "Never mind," he thought. He would take his chances. He finally decided on the nine o'clock train. He left with a porter his leather bag and the rug he had taken to warm his knees, and in addition he asked the man to buy him a ticket. Junichi went upstairs to the second floor to eat at the Tsuboya Restaurant. The Tsuboya had not yet been superseded by the Tōyōken.

Passing the buffet section, he entered the first of the dining rooms. Since the dinner hour was over, the room was empty. The old-fashioned fireplace built into the plastered wall was covered with dirty ash from the lumps of coke, but the electric lights gave a brilliant glow to the room. Junichi hung his cap and inverness on a wall hook and sat in an area partitioned off from the buffet section. He ordered two dishes and merely for the sake of form some beer, which he took in small sips every now and then.

Junichi's feelings, which had been in a state of irritation until he left his home at Hatsune-chō, finally calmed the minute he realized he would be able to get to Hakone and would at last take the night train. These feelings calmed as if the flowing tide were about to ebb. He couldn't help indulging, though, in various thoughts. Whenever he had been a witness to the vulgarity of Seto's personality, he had felt a wide disparity in everything between his own personality and Seto's. This was especially true in terms of sexual behavior, since this kind of activity ought to be pardoned if it were merely a question of accepting or rejecting an encounter should the chance of the moment allow it. "It's base to have it so arranged beforehand that it becomes just a filthy act," he thought. Seto was the type who left his lodgings with the intention of going to a house of ill-fame. As for himself, he had never felt he would venture out like that. And yet he was deliberately on his way to Hakone. "And so I'm gradually becoming more and more degraded and probably getting to be the same type Seto is." Thoughts like these seemed to Junichi to seriously damage his self-esteem. So he tried to defend himself even though he realized he was exaggerating the point. That is, even though he was headed for Hakone, it did not necessarily follow he was going to continue his relationship with Mrs. Sakai. Once he arrived, he could still decide what to do. The freedom of his course of action was still in reserve.

While Junichi was engaged in these thoughts, a waiter brought him his order of ham and eggs. Just as Junichi started to eat, a lady entered the room. She was so thin and ugly he thought she looked like a poorly paid family tutor. Her figure was as straight and stiff as a pole, her long lean neck seen under her tight, swept-back hairdo. She settled her umbrella against a chair of the corner table just diagonal to where Junichi was sitting. He could plainly see her narrow back. She ordered coffee and a *crème,* and the minute the *crème* came, she devoured it and ordered another. And then she ordered another. She devoured four plates of *crème* in that short interval. She looked as if she wanted to eat *crème* to her heart's content at least once in her lifetime. Junichi found this desire so peculiar that he somehow lost his own appetite. He felt as if one of the *lemures,* those frightening specters the Romans had created, had separated from its group and come into the room. Possibly his awareness of the ghosts of hunger in Buddhism had helped him form the image. At any rate, Junichi, though he did not believe in superstitions, somehow felt the appearance of this woman was an omen that his trip would end in misfortune.

As the train gradually approached its nine o'clock departure, more diners began to trickle into the room. Among these was a large group consisting of an old man and some children. What Junichi saw finally caused his melancholy mood to vanish. A student fifteen or sixteen years of age stirred the fire in the fireplace, calling out to the younger boys and girls, "All of you come over here." Some of the other diners began ordering food. Others complained that the food they had ordered had not yet arrived.

Amidst this clamor the departure time arrived, and then first one and then another person began leaving.

The ominous woman who had eaten those *crèmes* stood bolt upright as well and left with her umbrella against her body. The porter came up to Junichi with a ticket and urged him to leave.

The train platform was quite congested, but Junichi's second-class carriage was not that crowded, and even the passengers who had come in later without the help of the porter were easily able to find their seats. A man who had led in his wife and taken a seat across the aisle from Junichi said to her, "The first-class car is more crowded."

After the train pulled away, Junichi opened his leather bag, searched inside his *furoshiki,* and took out a book, Henry Bernstein's *Le Voleur,* blue-covered, the same size as *L'oiseau Bleu.* Though he heard the book was not a masterpiece, he had ordered it to gain information about its dramatic quality, or rather its theatrics, which had appealed to the masses. He had not yet read the book.

He cut open the first few pages with an ivory paper knife. He realized at once while reading the first act's dialogue, after turning over the pages of the captions and list of characters, that the play had been created in a sensible, light, and easy-to-fathom manner so that the dialogue existed merely to carry through the plot. He was not bored, but neither was his interest aroused.

After reading two or three pages, he found his eyes tiring. Not only was the light in the car bad, but the book, printed in small type on yellowish paper in fascicle form, was jostled up and down by the train's vibrations so that reading became unbearable. He suddenly remembered Ōmura's comment that motion pictures were quite bad for the eyes. And to make matters worse, Junichi was irritated by the man in the seat next to him, a merchant apparently, who kept glancing rudely at the book. Junichi, with the book on his lap after closing it, kept a finger between the pages where he had stopped. He turned his eyes for a while toward the window across the aisle.

The train increased its speed only after it had stopped a while at Shinagawa. Every so often lights somewhere in the darkness sped backward like shooting stars. Suddenly somewhat larger lights drew near the window as the train roared past a small station.

All at once, without any inducement, images of his hometown came to him. His grandmother's letters had reached him as regularly as the periodicals he had ordered. The contents of those letters were always the same. "Time" in his hometown passed as methodically and uneventfully as ever. His responses to her had sometimes been prompt, sometimes late. And the letters he wrote were sometimes long, sometimes short. But generally his responses were apt to be made later and to be shorter. He had every intention of writing a kind and considerate letter, but always as he confronted his writing paper, he was embarrassed to find he had nothing to say. Except for some vague intangible instinct, no inner life connected him to his grandmother. He thought this lack of connection was due to the letter writing itself, for he felt that if he returned home and met her in person, there would probably be a good deal to talk about. Twice had his grandmother written him in rapid succession that he should come home during the New Year holidays. And with this thought in mind he regretted he was going to get off the train at Kōzu. He suddenly felt slight pangs of conscience.

The merchantlike man beside him began reading a newspaper, and as if stimulated by this action, Junichi opened his book again. Apparently increased expenses for paying Paquin, the dressmaker, had induced the heroine, Marie Louise, to desire more money, a desire she secretly inserted in her dialogue with her husband, who, both overtly and covertly, kept referring to his sexual needs. Junichi thought the only merit the writer deserved was in the clever way he had intertwined intrigue and sexual desire so that the plot advanced without boring the spectators. Junichi could imagine eyes turned toward the stage, eyes without the least bit of boredom in them. Yet those who read these lines would not be moved at all. In other words, it seemed to Junichi that the playwright had merely developed the unadulterated theatrical aspect any play can have.

Whenever Junichi felt an itchy sensation in his eyes, he closed his book and looked outside. This time he found the train had slightly changed direction, for it seemed as if the wind were blowing the smoke to the side, the sparks beyond the window flying backwards like the tail of a comet in darkness. When his eyes felt better, he resumed his reading. His desire to read on was the same as his wanting to keep up with a detective story. The moment Marie Louise's crime of stealing money was about to be disclosed by the detective Fernand, the young man who had fallen in love with her assumed responsibility for the crime. Instantly clouds of anguish hung over the innocent youth and his parents, robbed of their money. With total indifference to their situation, the lighthearted Marie Louise entered her husband's bedroom and immediately began cajoling him. Denying him in an easy manner while urging him on, both openly and subtly, she forced her husband to help her with her bedtime preparations. Word by word, the conversation

between them, half-innocuous, half-blunt, stripped away like a bamboo
sheath the woman's mask. In the final analysis, Junichi couldn't help feeling
this scene could never be performed in a Tokyo theater. The woman's purse
was suddenly brought into the conversation.

"Will you be carrying my photograph in your purse your entire life?"

"Yes, I'll carry it with me all my days."

"Let me have a look at it."

"Don't lay a hand on it. Oh, no!"

"Why?"

"Never, oh, no!"

"The more you say don't, the more I want to see it."

"Well, if you give it back at once."

"And if I don't, then what?"

"I'll never speak to you for the rest of my life!"

"That I rather doubt."

"I'm superstitious. That is, if anyone looks into my purse."

"It's strange. It's really strange. The way you're so determined to keep it
from me makes me suspicious."

"Please don't open it!"

"I will. I have to look at the photograph of your paramour."

At the end of this dialogue the purse was opened, and an enormous sum
of money was discovered. Sultry words of love turned into cold words of suspicion. Forgetting about the pain in his eyes, Junichi finished reading
straight through to the scene where Marie Louise confesses because she feels
sorry for the lad who is about to be transported to Brazil. So strong was
Junichi's impression of having been made a fool, he flung the book into his
leather bag.

Soon the train arrived at Kōzu. Since he was unfamiliar with the town, he
felt he ought to find an inn before it got too late. He would leave for
Hakone the following morning. Carrying his bag and rug, Junichi sauntered
out the station. Beyond some towering pine trees lay the sea, the night
quiet.

The inns were still open, and in the shadows of the inside lights he could
see the maids going about their chores. Junichi entered the nearest inn and
asked for a room. A tidy maid diligent as a bee stopped her busy steps, and
standing at the entrance, she glanced him over from head to foot, only to
say, "I'm sorry, but there are no vacancies," and she turned away toward the
interior.

He tried the next inn. He was refused in the same way. It was the same at
the third and fourth inns. Certainly Junichi in his inverness while carrying a

leather satchel and rug was not very respectable, but surely his appearance was not so repulsive that anyone might feel uneasy about putting him up at an inn. He vaguely remembered hearing somewhere, though he wasn't sure when or where, that a person who travels alone won't be given a room at an inn. Yet he couldn't believe that could apply in this kind of flourishing town. Indeed, in Tokyo there had been no problem in allowing him to stop over.

He thought the refusals quite strange, but there was no one he could ask about the problem. He felt as if he had been transformed into a fairy-tale monster.

Finally he went to a police box and asked a policeman to help him find a place. The man, who was about forty years old, seemed phlegmatic, apparently half-asleep and taciturn, for after hearing Junichi's complaint, he did not say the treatment was natural or unfair. Having been warming himself close to a brazier with scorch marks around its edges, he indolently left his chair and, taking a square hand lantern, said, "If that's the case, come this way," and he walked off ahead of Junichi.

The place to which the policeman led Junichi was different from those newly built inns Junichi had tried to stop at thus far, for it was at the gate of a house whose walls and pillars were black with soot. The policeman made the owner open the locked door, and he began negotiating. Apparently whatever he said seemed to result in an immediate agreement. A man with closely cropped hair appeared from inside, a cotton kimono under a wadded cotton robe, and invited Junichi in. The policeman returned, the square hand lantern lighting his way.

Junichi went up some narrow black steps to the second floor. A handrail circled the landing. The room, which had no veranda, was actually a hall with fifteen or sixteen *tatami* mats. Except for the closed storm shutters, it had no furnishings. Inside a paper-covered lampstand was a tray with a kerosene flame; the man carried it in as he led Junichi into the room while setting the lampstand down on the worn-out *tatami* mats. He fell to his knees before greeting Junichi.

"Are you going to retire right away? Can I get you anything?"

Junichi, so dazed by the realization he had finally been able to find shelter under a roof, had no time to gather his thoughts. At the same time he was delighted that he would be able to stay, he realized in a flash that he ought to order something to reimburse the man.

"If you have a small side dish with some *sake,* please bring it. I've already eaten dinner."

"We have some boiled fish."

"That's fine."

The man with cropped hair opened a closet beside an alcove set up in this room for the sake of form only. The single structure in the second-floor room was this recessed alcove. From the closet the man pulled out a *futon,* some nightclothes, and a stuffed pillow. He laid out the bed before going downstairs.

Still standing, Junichi looked at the bed a while. Since the inn offered no cushion to sit on, as if that were a kind of luxury, Junichi flung his cap to the mats and still stood there without attempting to sit down. The *futon* quilt was so dirty its stripes could not even be seen. The white cotton cloth over the pillow was dirty gray from grime.

Junichi sat down nervously on his *futon* mattress. He took out his watch to find it was nearly midnight. A displeasure he could not define seemed about to curb the resilience of his youthful energies. It was not a displeasure that came from having to stay at this dirty inn. Since he had always been fortunate in his circumstances, he had always been careful not to become a vacillating, effeminate man. At times he had even thought of trying to live a Spartan life. But unless those difficulties could be confronted under his own free will, he found it annoying to face them. If he were forced into difficulties merely by the actions of those around him, he had no desire to act. After being refused entrance at the first inn, he had felt as if he were falling step by step into some disagreeable world, drawn into it under the power of a malicious witch. That he had found completely offensive.

The man with the closely cropped hair came up carrying a brazier. Round and ceramic, it was dark blue, strangely shiny in its glaze. Behind him was a fourteen or fifteen-year-old girl, her kimono sleeves tucked up with a sash as she brought in the *sake* and fish Junichi had ordered. On the tray she carried was a *sake* container, a *sake* cup, and a dish of foul-smelling blue fish cut into slices. She placed the tray with its several items by the bed, and after glancing with apparent curiosity at Junichi's frowning face, she silently went downstairs. Taking an account book from his kimono sleeve and holding the brush from a portable writing kit in his hand, the man said, "Your name?" Junichi gave it and the address of his Tokyo lodgings, but since the man did not know how to write the first character in "Junichi," Junichi had to write it for him.

Junichi wondered how he would be able to sleep. He was not yet that tired, but fatigue and discomfort had left his head throbbing. By no means did he feel like lying down on the bed. He took off his *hakama* skirt and wrapped it around the stuffed pillow. He then folded the camel-colored rug in two and inserted it into the collar of his night kimono. In this way he could get by without his face or hands touching the filthy thing.

He set his leather bag by the head of his bed. Then he grabbed the *sake* container and drank down a cup of the warmed liquid. Still wearing his inverness and his *tabi* socks, he carefully took his night kimono by the collar so that the rug would not be disarranged, and he lay down. For a while his face felt flushed, his heart beating wildly, but before he realized it, he had fallen into a deep sleep.

He did not know how long he had slept. He did remember hearing some sounds between sleep and waking. And then he thought he had heard voices. Moreover, these were the voices of a man and woman. At the same moment he had thought of those voices, he had awakened. "Your name," said the man's voice. And then the woman had responded. Her voice was that of someone young saying something like being from Aichi Prefecture, from some village in such and such a county, and sister of someone whose name he couldn't catch. The man went downstairs.

Junichi felt strange at the thought of sharing this second-floor room with a woman he did not know. Embarrassed even as he pitied the woman, Junichi lay quietly without turning his eyes toward her. A while later the woman said, "Excuse me . . ."

Certainly she had uttered those words to him. Junichi imagined she had come into the room while he was asleep. He felt she must have seen everything from the moment he awoke to his deliberately trying not to look at her. Since he did not know how to respond to her "Excuse me," he remained silent.

But the woman said, "I'm on my way to Tokyo. What time does the first train leave?"

"Oh, I see," said Junichi, obstinate in his refusal to look in her direction. "I don't know either, but I've got a travel guide in my bag. Shall I get up and look at it?"

She couldn't help coming out with a short laugh. "Don't bother," she said. "It'll be all right. In any event, I've already asked the office to wake me."

With these words she became silent. Junichi maintained his obstinacy in not looking at her. It seemed she was unable to fall asleep. He could hear her turning restlessly several times. He very much wanted to see what kind of woman she was, but it was all the more awkward to look at her now that so much time had elapsed, and he didn't. Before long he again fell asleep.

When he woke the next morning, the woman was no longer there. Since he couldn't bring himself to use the lavatory of the inn, he hurried away after paying his bill. The man with the cropped hair was about to follow him out to carry his bag, but Junichi declined his help. He wanted to break off his connection with this inn as quickly as possible.

He entrusted his getting from Kōzu to Asahi Bridge to Yumoto, a distance of some seven miles, to a horse-drawn tramcar, and as his face, still unwashed, was exposed to a morning wind that seemed to be dragging with it shreds of mist as the horse-drawn car plodded on through a pine forest and then to Odawara station, he couldn't help repeatedly recalling the images of that nightmarish stay at the inn in Kōzu, how he had slept in the same room with an unknown woman, how they had exchanged words, how he had not seen her after all. Probably she was a homely woman heading for the capital to work as a maid. That was not what concerned him though. His path had crossed hers without even knowing what kind of woman she was. Somehow it seemed their parting without any recognition of one another was absolutely intriguing.

After leaving the car, Junichi deliberately avoided the Fukuzumi inn where Mrs. Sakai was staying, and he put up at an inn called the Kashiwaya. He was worried about the rejection he had experienced in Kōzu and did not want to be turned down again. True, he had not been welcomed, but he had at least been able to stay in a small room. He tried to justify his action in coming to Hakone under the dubious pretext of still having the liberty to do as he wished. Yet no matter what sophistry he resorted to, he could not convince himself that the scope of his liberty would be enlarged in inverse proportion to the distance between him and Mrs. Sakai. He felt somewhat better after taking a bath. He took up a few of the books and magazines from his leather bag, but he couldn't regain sufficient composure to devote himself seriously to reading.

23

To go to the Fukuzumi or not to go? That was the hypothetical question Junichi found himself toying with. Yet he was deeply aware the issue had been settled long ago. It had been answered in the affirmative. If there still remained some question about this situation, it could only have been the question of time.

And yet there were things that were going to shorten that time period. A considerable number of minute but memorable incidents about Mrs. Sakai's action as well as her ambiguous words had unexpectedly remained anchored in Junichi's mind. A gesture, a word unspoken—that's what these were. Despite time's passage, these would not fade. They could not just disappear. Just as a rough stone is polished into a jewel and stands out in its surroundings, strong and powerful in its glow, so too were these incidents purified in his memory. Even when he was reading, memories intervened between the page and his eye to cast a veil that could not be rent or thrown aside, a veil that marred the meaning of the book he thought he had understood until then.

Had there been waters of Lethe to allow him to forget these memories, Junichi would have gulped these waters down. And still he tried to defend himself by arguing that even if he privately prized these memories, not discarding them, regarding them as a kind of elegiac element in the domain of his emotions, there was no harm in doing so. All of which was to say that because these were memories of anguish, he should have wanted to get rid of them, but because their anguish was equally sweet, he found it difficult to give them up.

Junichi couldn't help hearing a voice that kept deriding him in the following way: "You've deliberately come all the way from Tokyo to Hakone, haven't you? So why are you afraid of going from the Kashiwaya to the Fukuzumi?" To Junichi's ears, that voice was merciless in its insistence.

Telling an unnecessary lie to the maid at the inn, "I didn't sleep well last night," he had her put out his bed after lunch. He lay down and slept for about two hours.

When he awoke, he found another maid adding charcoal to the brazier. She was beautiful, her skin pale and fair. She was completely different from the maid who had served him lunch and laid out the bed for his nap. Even her kimono was different in that it was made of silk.

"If you wish to read a newspaper, I can bring it to you."

Raising her face, which she had kept lowered, she glanced briefly at him, her words sounding somewhat shy.

"Yes, bring one in."

Though he didn't particularly want to read, he had responded perfunctorily to her question.

With her face still looking down, she stood in a coquettish way and went out.

As he got up and sat by the brazier, a maid, different from the one who had just left, came in with two or three newspapers. This maid was poorly dressed, spoke in a loud voice, laughed without reserve for no reason at all, had a sturdy and heavily built physique; in short, she was a quite ordinary maid. Junichi imagined there were "special maids" other than ordinary ones like the one in his room, "special maids" who performed special services, but he didn't feel like probing into that issue.

He picked up one of the newspapers and glanced briefly at its literary column, but without trying to read it carefully, he set it down. To Junichi, who did not belong to what Ōmura had called a "clique," any critical article written from a one-sided, biased viewpoint had no value.

Thinking he'd take a short walk before dinner, he sauntered aimlessly out the inn. He walked along the bank of the Hayakawa, whose waters dashed violently against rocks. On Katagawa-chō, he came across a woodwork shop, flanked by several inns. The shop turned out various products made of wood and sold some of the handicrafts for which Yumoto was famous. Urged by the shopkeeper's wife to buy some souvenirs, Junichi selected two or three small items, among them a toothpick container and a tobacco box.

Just then Junichi noticed a man and a woman passing the shop, talking together and laughing, no doubt guests at one of the hot spring inns. He thought he had heard the woman's laughter before. While the shopkeeper's wife was counting out his change, Junichi, who had picked up a toy top and was examining it, happened to look up, directing his gaze toward the woman's voice only to accidentally exchange glances with none other than Mrs. Sakai.

Over her dark blue padded kimono of silk crepe in a splashed pattern was a pale green crepe *haori* coat with three family crests. Her hair was done up in a butterfly coiffure bound by a ribbon ornamented with pearls, a comb made from black tortoise shell and pearl oyster shell in her hair. Yet it was her elegant and coquettish figure that attracted his attention.

Mrs. Sakai's cheerful laughter suddenly stopped, and a discreet amiable smile came into her eyes. She seemed not the least concerned about the passage of time since she had parted from him at Negishi or about the distance between Tokyo and this hot spring area. In a quite casual tone she said, "Ah, so you've come."

Junichi had intended to say "Yes," but his voice had so lost its control, the words coming out so low, that he himself could hardly hear it.

Mrs. Sakai remained standing there as she looked back at her companion, a man in his forties, robust with square shoulders. His thick stiff hair cropped by clippers was streaked, gray among the black, but his face glowed with a healthy color.

"This is Mr. Koizumi, a student of literature," Mrs. Sakai said, and then she turned to Junichi. "This is Mr. Okamura, the painter," she said. "He's also staying at the Fukuzumi. Why haven't you come to our inn? I told you to come there, didn't I?"

"I carelessly forgot the name of your inn. I'm at the Kashiwaya."

"My, but you're forgetful! Why don't you come see me tonight?" she said. With these parting words, she began walking away. Drawing himself to his full height as he continued to stand there, the artist, like a giant looking down at a dwarf, said as if echoing her, "Yes, please come tonight," and he followed along after Mrs. Sakai.

Junichi kept gazing at the two of them a while. All this time the shop-keeper's wife, her knees on the wooden porch, the change on a small tray, had been kept waiting. Suddenly noticing her, Junichi hurriedly took the small silver coins mixed in among some large copper ones and put them into his coin purse made of alligator skin. Junichi left the shop.

The trees on the other side of the river, as if resembling the legs of a group of people dressed for Carnival, were, before he realized it, completely envel-oped in the evening fog, and here and there along a row of railroad tracks the hydroelectric lights began coming on.

Junichi was walking in a daze toward his inn. His head was permeated by a loneliness he had forgotten but of which he was suddenly reminded, and his mind was filled with something unpleasant that was beyond analysis. He consciously tried to explain this discomfort that did not seem to come from jealousy, but he found its justification difficult. And the reason for this was that he believed he would not have felt this discomfort if Mrs. Sakai had been alone when he met her by accident at that woodwork shop in Yumoto. His thoughts went something like this: "Somehow the existence of that big fellow Okamura really disturbs me. I've heard a painter with that name's quite prominent, a master in fact, a painter in the *shijō* style. I don't know anything about his personality. And I certainly don't want to. It's just that when I saw the two of them walking side by side, I felt they looked, some-how, like man and wife, and that certainly hurt my feelings. I didn't feel that way because of some prejudice against them, not at all. Had they been seen by the indifferent eyes of a stranger, they would definitely have been seen in the same way as husband and wife. In short, had the shopkeeper's wife talked to them, she would certainly have addressed them as Mr. and Mrs. I'm not the least bit envious of Okamura. Nor do I want to change places with him. But that guy's really a nuisance! I really despise him, and I can't help feeling a deep, really deep, dissatisfaction with Mrs. Sakai. I feel like calling her ungrateful, a woman who's broken her promise. Yet what obligation, if any, does she have to me? What promise did she ever make to me? I can't find a single word with which to answer these questions. From every angle these feelings of mine are almost indistinguishable from those of a jealous person. And these feelings are accompanied by feelings of loneliness as well, and it's a nasty loneliness I feel, a very nasty loneliness.

"The loneliness I felt for Ōmura after I parted from him in Tokyo is nothing compared to the loneliness I'm feeling now. Once, when I was a primary school student, I had a feeling somewhat similar to this. That was when I saw in the distance some of my friends in a group whispering something to one another. I was about fourteen at the time. At the school just then was a tall, thin girl named Okatsu. She detested me, and she often put me in awkward situations. Okatsu was always at the center of that group of whispering children, taller than they because of the way her hair was arranged in the butterfly coiffure. From time to time she would be looking back at me. It always seemed they were keeping some quite important secret from me. And yet when I'd ask one of the children in the group what they'd been talking about, I'd discover it didn't have the least bit of significance and made no difference whether I heard it or not. And each time I would admire Okatsu's ability in so skillfully gathering those children together and producing that illusion of their plotting together. It's true the loneliness I'm feeling now suddenly made me recall that childhood incident, but now that I think about it, the feeling I had at that time didn't come just from loneliness. It was probably Okatsu who first planted in me the seeds of jealousy."

While walking as these thoughts came to him, Junichi almost passed the gate of the Kashiwaya. Fortunately he was hailed by a voice from within the gate, and he went in. He passed the noisy office where a few men were either sitting or standing, and he got to his room, pushing open the sliding doors. A maid hurried past him from behind and switched on the lights.

After dinner Junichi picked up the newspapers he hadn't yet finished during the day and began thumbing through them. As he suddenly looked at the photograph of a woman in a column entitled "Colored Threads" printed in six-point type, he found the caption under the photograph: "Ochara of the Sakaeya." The print was so thickly smeared that the face was half-hidden, but it was certainly the geisha at Yanagibashi who had given Junichi her name card.

The news item ran as follows: "It has been the talk of the town that Ochara of the Sakaeya (aged sixteen) has been wild in her pursuit of men ever since she has been an apprentice geisha. When it comes to *kabuki* actors, she has been partial to Uzaemon—she is out to acquire handsome faces, so much so she does not know when to quit. The saving feature about her passion for these handsome faces, however, say those who know her, is that she remains disinterested. Yet her colleague Otatsu, a geisha who works in the same house, is apt to attack Ochara's behavior severely as if to castigate her. Ochara may not have followed the customs of Yanagibashi geisha handed down from the Edo period, but she has been severely berated by Otatsu for her recent passionate pursuit of a young craftsman dressed in a short livery coat, his name Matsu. Alas, it is too bad that Ochara has been quite depressed ever since this rebuke."

The end of the article found Junichi smiling in spite of himself. That Ochara followed her sexual desires and was indifferent to making money gave Junichi almost the same feelings of consolation as when he heard good words or saw good deeds performed. And the comment that Ochara was attracted to handsome faces quite satisfied Junichi's ego. The mind of the young is full of resilience. No matter what discomfort oppresses a youth's ego, as soon as the oppression relaxes ever so slightly, he unconsciously tries to regain his former resilience as if he had been waiting for the opportunity. On reading the article about Ochara, Junichi found his feelings had recovered somewhat.

At that moment a maid came in with a message sent from the Fukuzumi. Mrs. Sakai wanted him, the maid said, to visit her if he had time. Junichi did not hesitate in replying that he would come right away. It seemed impossible for him not to accept the invitation. For even though he had half a mind to sulk and refuse, to reveal such a cowardly defeatist attitude was bound to make him regret it later. At any rate, the news item in "Colored Threads" about Ochara seemed to soothe his feelings toward Mrs. Sakai and without a moment's hesitation helped him send off a positive response.

Junichi went to the Fukuzumi at once.

Led in by a maid, he passed the main floor of a three-storied building called the Bansuirō. As he came near the drawing room of a one-storied cottage at the rear of a garden, he could see bright electric lights spilling through the paper-covered sliding doors and could hear laughing voices inside. That laughter was like the whinnying sound of a bass singer. The moment Junichi thought that sound had to come from Okamura, an antipathy toward the man arose instinctively, and Junichi felt as if he wanted to turn back.

Mrs. Sakai at Hakone: that was the image he had often imagined. The detached cottage of this hot spring inn was surrounded by a thick grove of thousand-year-old trees. Certainly her living room at Negishi was free from the commonplace noise of the city, but this cottage was altogether removed from the frontiers of humanity. Junichi felt he was about to see in this tranquility a beauty like Ondine. But before he did, he first had to hear the laughter of a faun.

The maid who came out to meet him in the corridor was Shizue, whom he had seen in Negishi.

"Madame has been waiting for you. Please come this way."

Now Junichi was handed over to Shizue by the maid who had led him to the cottage. He felt as if there were a borderline, an outpost, between the inn and this cottage. What, he wondered, was there that had to be protected, sheltered? Even this sacred spot was no more than a place in which a man named Okamura was meeting Mrs. Sakai face-to-face, was it not? What Junichi had felt at Negishi to be delightful was here immediately transformed into something disgusting. Quite obviously things were different depending on where they occurred.

In the adjoining room, Shizue got to her knees to announce, "Mr. Koizumi has arrived," and she gently opened the sliding door separating the rooms.

It was Okamura who called out, "Well, please come in. Madame is waiting for you." Okamura, the main guest, was certainly well behaved. A small brazier was placed by each person. Tea and cakes were served. But the portable footwarmer beside Mrs. Sakai again made Junichi feel uncomfortable.

After ordering Shizue to replace the old tea with a fresh brew, Mrs. Sakai gazed at Junichi. "How long have you been here?"

"I've just come. I met you just after I arrived."

"I suppose there are some beautiful girls at the Kashiwaya," Okamura butted in.

"I don't know. I can't tell since I've only just arrived."

"I find that quite upsetting. The first thing I do in arriving at an inn is to be on the lookout for them."

From his voice and words, Okamura seemed to indicate the *sake* consumed at dinner was beginning to take effect.

"If people in society were like Mr. Okamura, the world would be a terrible place," said Mrs. Sakai, looking at Junichi as if to shelter him.

Okamura found it more and more difficult to remain silent. "No, Madame. That's not true. Men of literature are much wiser about the ways of the world than painters are . . ." And he started on some small talk about young men of letters he knew by name. It was nothing but mere hearsay— how the bohemians of the literary world who were just starting to become popular were evaluated in the eyes of the female restaurant proprietors and geisha with whom Okamura had become friends. Next he went on to give opinions on such novels as *Futon* and *Baien*. Thinking Okamura surprisingly well versed in literature, Junichi, after asking some questions, discovered Okamura hadn't read either of these books.

Junichi found it quite unpleasant in the room. But gentle in disposition, he couldn't bring himself to show annoyance in his look, and he tried to play along with Okamura as much as possible. And yet, in the meantime, Junichi indulged in these thoughts: "Most of the criticism by the public against the new literary arts will probably be launched and spread by people like Okamura. And they'll freely express their opinions without even having read the works. If that's the case, it's not the literary work itself the public rejects; they just blindly follow offensive criticism made by one clique against another. It's true that prohibition of the sale of literature is proclaimed and executed by public officials, but the government's attempt to interfere with the literary arts on the grounds they are naturalistic or individualistic is the direct result of these offensive criticisms. It might well be said that men of literature are endangering their own literary foundations by digging tunnels under the works their peers have constructed. Of course, *Futon* and *Baien* involved biographical problems. But those biographical details at the core of *Baien* were themselves seen as actions revealing only the superficial surface of reality. Since problems of realism in *Futon* and other novels were raised by literary men themselves, wasn't it that these problems of realism were originally exposed by the so-called stories in the journal *Rokugō Bungaku?*"

Shizue came in with fresh tea. She poured some into the teacups of the hostess and guests. After she withdrew, Mrs. Sakai said, "Mr. Koizumi, you're so quiet and submissive that Mr. Okamura keeps chattering away as much as he wants. You too ought to say nasty things about painters."

"Maybe I ought to refrain," said Junichi with a smile. But gradually his displeasure kept reasserting itself since he felt that ever since he had entered the room, she was apt to keep patronizing him. Wasn't she treating him formally, as if he were a stranger? And that meant she was treating Okamura in the opposite way, that is, with unreserved intimacy. To put this more strongly, to Junichi, Mrs. Sakai and Okamura seemed to be behaving like a married couple.

Okamura asked Junichi if he had come to Hakone with the intention of doing some writing. Junichi admitted he had no plan of that sort. Then Mrs. Sakai said, "Mr. Koizumi is so young there's no need for him to rush into publication." Again Junichi thought she was patronizing him. He suddenly felt somewhat defiant. "Mr. Okamura," he asked in return, "are you painting something now?" To which Mrs. Sakai said, "During the summer Mr. Okamura almost finished painting a sliding door and a screen in the Ban-suirō." Again the response revealed to Junichi her intimacy with Okamura, and at the same time he had the suspicion that she might have spent the summer with Okamura at the Fukuzumi.

Junichi wanted to confirm this suspicion, but since he was afraid that pos-ing such a question would be equivalent to forcing someone to say what she did not want to say, he refrained; he changed the subject.

"Summers are probably better in Hakone, aren't they?"

"They certainly are," said Okamura with a kind of innocence, only to be seemingly lost in thought for a while. Then as if suddenly reminded of something, he added, a smile on his big face with its square jaw, "No, the summer's not that good. At about that time the mists are hanging all over the place, and bugs head for the electric lights. All that's quite annoying. Pests such as beetles, you know. The kids in Tokyo call them *kana-bun-bun*. They catch them and play with them. Those pests never stop coming!"

"They're really quite awful," said Mrs. Sakai, interrupting. "If the sliding doors are closed, those bugs fly against the paper, bump against it, and then fall down. The men servants come noisily along the corridors bringing a bucket full of water, toss the bugs in, and carry them off."

As Junichi listened, he wondered if Mrs. Sakai and Okamura had wit-nessed this kind of event together or whether it was only a coincidence that they both knew what happens during the Hakone summer. Again Junichi was somewhat suspicious of them.

Okamura became even more enthusiastic about his own voice. "Those *kana-bun-bun* bugs were a real nuisance. But I've been thinking about get-ting revenge on them. I'm going to cut off their wings, and with a glue called *banjaku nori*, I'll paste a bug to a cart made out of cardboard and force the damn thing to pull the cart. It'll keep on living, continuing to pull that cart. I'm thinking of abandoning painting and standing at street cor-ners selling children these carts pulled by *kana-bun-bun!*" And he broke into a laugh with the same neighing sound Junichi had heard earlier.

"I wonder what kind of glue *banjaku nori* is," asked Mrs. Sakai.

"*Banjaku nori?* Oh, they sell it all over town."

"I'd really love to see you selling *kana-bun-bun* carts on a street corner in Tokyo, say Ueno Hirokōji."

"Well, I know they'll sell like mad. You do know they have a children's fair and other exhibits at Mitsukoshi's department store where they display all kinds of toys, but they've never shown a living toy."

"I'm sure many people will immediately imitate it. The way they did Russian bread after the Russo-Japanese War," said Mrs. Sakai.

"I'll monopolize the field!"

"Can one monopolize a living thing?" said Mrs. Sakai.

"Well, I haven't thought it out that far," Okamura said, again laughing. Then he added, "At any rate, those bugs are real pests. Though swarms of them fly into bonfires, as many as are killed come right back!"

"Oh, that bonfire was truly beautiful, wasn't it?"

Junichi was startled. Her expression uttered in the past tense, "Oh, that bonfire was truly beautiful!" was irrefutable proof that the two of them had seen the bonfire together. Judging from the situation, Junichi had found it perfectly clear they had both spent the summer together, but he refrained from asking about it. He had been paying close attention to their dialogue, desiring by whatever ways or means he could find to know exactly what their relationship was.

Junichi's discomfort suddenly intensified. The suspicion occurred to him that his presence was nothing more than a superfluous third wheel on a cart. Finally he felt as if he had to run from this place of discomfort.

"It's already late, and I have to go along now," said Junichi, trying not to show any rage in his voice. Pretending he had an appointment, he looked at his watch as he got up from his cushion. Actually he did not know where the hands of his watch pointed, nor were his eyes even conscious of them.

24

Having rapidly gone out the Fukuzumi's exit, Junichi slackened his pace once he was outside. He walked around the outer fence of the Bansuirō and paused in front of the room where Mrs. Sakai ought to have been. Since the building's stone wall had been built on elevated ground, it looked like a structure with a mezzanine. The shutters had not yet been closed, so the lights from the room came through the paper-covered sliding doors. For a while Junichi kept looking at these sliding doors, but no human figures were reflected on them, probably because the electric lights were closer to the sliding doors than the spot where the insiders were sitting.

When he had left the room, he had not had sufficient time to think things over, but now that he did have time to think, he wondered if Okamura himself ought not to have left with him. Had Okamura felt there was no need to worry about Junichi because he was no more than a youth? Whether or not Okamura was contemptuous of him, was Okamura so involved with Mrs. Sakai that there was absolutely no need for him to leave, so that he could remain there without reserve? These thoughts weighed on Junichi's mind as he continued to stare at those sliding doors through which the light was spilling. He was waiting, wondering if Okamura's shadow would fall on those sliding doors as he stood to leave. Suddenly, though, Junichi was angry for worrying about such matters, for waiting for that to happen. Mrs. Sakai was not his sweetheart or anything, was she? What was wrong with Okamura's staying in her room as long as he wished? Why should Junichi worry about it? How feckless, how cowardly, he had been! He could not help being indignant with himself.

For a while he continued to stand there. Though he had no need to feel ashamed of himself to anyone, he came to feel guilty, his conscience bothering him, and he began to saunter along. The sounds from the Hayakawa River, louder at night, seemed to merge with his tangled feelings, and a loneliness, stronger than he had felt during the day, assailed him as if to throw him off balance.

Junichi went back to the Kashiwaya. The *shamisen* he heard after he passed the entrance was still audible from the room above his. A maid entered to greet him. "You must be troubled by all the noise," she said. After Junichi asked her who the guests were, she said they stopped off from Nagoya every so often. The maid who had come into his room was of course an "ordinary" maid. It was probably a "special" maid who was entertaining the upstairs guests.

The second-floor crowd was having an increasingly lively time. They had probably come with the intention of having a wild interlude on New Year's Eve. The *shamisen* went on incessantly. A woman kept laughing. Another one, middle-aged, was chanting something like "The god of drunkards is an honest god. Turn your head toward the *sake*. To whom shall I give my *sake* cup? To this one? To that?" The chant was repeated over and over again. Each time it was, someone was supposed to receive a cup filled with *sake*.

Junichi crept into his bed, which had already been laid out. He remained perfectly still. He felt the pulsation of his arteries against his pillow as if they were urging him to do something. He turned over in bed to avoid hearing their sound. And still those arteries kept up their pulsation. His heart was probably beating quite rapidly. What was worse, the chant became louder and louder, as if the god of drunkards was going to persist in tormenting him.

Junichi wanted to forget everything, wanted to sleep, but he couldn't, not at all. His excessively overwrought nerves responded, strangely enough, to even the most trivial stimulus. And he was conscious, like a person observing himself from the outside, of urging his nerves to say, "It's no use making this boy's head think now. It's best to let him sleep somehow or other." His consciousness proposed that he simply decide what to do and thus allow himself to calm down, so that he might go to sleep. It was all right if that something was not elaborately worked out. It might even be better if the plan of that something were so rough it would not put too heavy a demand on him. Or, rather, the rougher the plan, the more appropriate it would be.

How would it be, to cite an example, to leave Hakone? That was a good idea. That would be a decisive step; moreover, leaving would not torture his mind at present, which needed a plan that would lead to repose, to calm. Such a step would at once cut off several electric wires transmitting various kinds of displeasure.

Leaving Hakone was a really good idea. Nothing could be better than that. If he did leave, he could demonstrate something to Mrs. Sakai. He could, he felt, show her that he would not stand being made a fool of. No, not that. He didn't have to worry about that. He could not have cared less about what Mrs. Sakai thought. In any case, he would leave Hakone. And then he could use this opportunity to break off his connection to Negishi. He would send back by parcel post the Racine he had borrowed from her. He wanted to hurry back to Yanaka as quickly as possible and mail back that book. Once he did that he would feel relieved.

The moment he hit upon this idea, his mind cleared more rapidly than he expected, as if alum had been thrown into muddy waters. In fact, various complicated and unanalyzable things, one after another, were all lumped together, removed as it were from the muddy waters of his mind. This was the stage of relief his mind reached that night. Probably because the relief bordered on the world of sound sleep, Junichi, with the quilt over his head, was able to fall asleep even though the god of drunkenness was still rampant.

The next morning, contrary to his intentions, he woke early, disturbed by voices near dawn. Wide awake, he had gone to the lavatory. In the corridor he saw some guests preparing for an early departure. Two men, who looked as if they were about forty years old, were wearing Western business suits. While hurrying one of the clerks to carry their luggage to the entrance, they were apparently talking about something urgent, heads turning to the side while buried in their overcoat collars. They seemed quite serious, quite straitlaced. Junichi almost felt like asking them why they had held that ridiculous wild party last night.

On his way back from the lavatory, he suddenly thought of taking a bath, and he glanced into the public bathing area. Someone was inside. Due to the thick steam from the bath, he couldn't make out the person clearly, but it seemed to be a woman. Surprised by a sign from someone, she suddenly stood up as if hurrying to finish. Junichi secretly escaped from the place, feeling as if he had committed a crime, and he returned to his room.

He found after coming into his room that no fire had yet been brought to his brazier. Except for the guests who had left early, almost all the others were still sound asleep. Junichi again went to bed, and without trying to get back to sleep, he simply lay there.

He was so wide awake he couldn't possibly sleep any longer. And so what he had thought about the previous night after he had gotten into bed gradually returned in detail as if each thought were being pulled like a thread into his mind.

Often he had had the experience that those thoughts which had come to him when he was exhausted at night turned out to be of little use the following morning, but the decision he had made last night still maintained its merit even now when reviewed with a clear mind. And not only did he find it retained its validity: the more he looked at it with his clear vision, the more he couldn't help feeling something bold, something heroic, was in it. As he retraced those thoughts now, he first felt his head had not functioned properly the previous night, so he conjectured that now, on the contrary, he could quickly make a decision without being restricted by various considerations he had insufficiently examined from various angles.

He pledged to himself that he would definitely carry out his decision today. Seeing that nothing in his mind or body would interfere with his resolution, he felt as if he had won a final victory. And yet this victory came from the fact that when one emotion gained dominance, another was quietly suppressed. Years after, when he faced similar temptations any number of times and repeated the same kind of struggle, he gradually came to realize quite poignantly that biological incidents would come and go like the ebb and flow of the tides. He found it interesting to think of that biological flow by recalling the primitive metaphor of the Confucian scholar Ōta Kinjō: "Like wind and rain in the heavens."

Well, now that he had decided to carry out his resolution today, his mind was regaining its composure. At the same time he found that various "guests" from worlds of the past, present, and future were visiting him at this hot spring inn as he lay in bed with the quilt over him. It had been only about two months since he had come up to Tokyo from his hometown, but what he had thought back home about what he'd be able to do in Tokyo had all disappeared like bubbles. He had done nothing positive in all that time.

It was a vain hope to rely on others to do what he himself could not do. And yet in contrast to that, from those persons he unexpectedly had come in contact with, he had received various kinds of stimulation; he had been able to "store" something in his mind in the same way a bee sucks honey from no matter what flowers it alights on. Unlike the period spent in his hometown, he had been so busy leaping from flower to flower he had made no attempt to write a novel, not even a poor one. Yet might it not be true, on the contrary, that this refusal to write had become a kind of medicine for him, had resulted in something beneficial to him? If he tried to write now, he would probably be able to produce something. Back home he had a friend who liked to play *go*. Once at a party his friend had told him that having refrained from playing *go,* his game had actually improved. Hearing his words, a schoolteacher, Mr. Yamamura, had said this happened because the player had been practicing *go* subconsciously. And so if Junichi himself tried to write now, he could probably produce something quite good. The moment Junichi had this thought, he felt like renting a room at this inn and beginning to write something after this long dry spell. But no, that wouldn't do. Not in the least. If he did that, he would not be able to carry out the plan he had gone through so much trouble to decide. Damn! Mrs. Sakai and Okamura be hanged! If he might use Ōmura's favorite expression, *"Der Teufel hole sie!"* Nothing mattered that much now. He would return to Tokyo as soon as possible and write.

Junichi pushed aside his *futon* quilt, got up, and sat cross-legged on his *futon* mattress. He had forgotten there was no fire in the brazier, so lost in thought had he been. The moment he had perceived he would at long last start to write, all the things around him at present together with all he had experienced in the past lost their value. He no longer cared about that beautiful lump of flesh lying in a cottage in the Fukuzumi only a short distance away. His face was flushed, his eyes large and shining. Up to now he had often been stirred by the sensation that he was about to write something, but he had never been so satisfied as he was at this moment as if like a cloud so overloaded with electricity it was about to bring on evening showers at any second.

What he wanted to write was something different from what was now popular. The subject he wanted to set down was a legend his grandmother had once told him when he was in his hometown. He had attempted to write about this legend several times. He had thought about setting it down in several modes, once in verse, once in prose, once even wanting to imitate Flaubert's narrative style in which the French author had written his *Trois Contes.* Once he had even thought of creating it as a play, using a short

script of Maeterlinck's as a source. Shortly before he had left Tokyo, he had
made his latest attempt, some twenty or thirty pages he had started, the
manuscript at the bottom of the leather bag he had left at Yanaka. At the
time of that writing he had been unconsciously influenced by the so-called
naturalistic novels of the period. But the archaism he had originally aimed
for in terms of its meaning and its diction got in the way as he developed his
story. So this time he would try to devise a way of writing in contemporary
language while carefully observing the people of his day without damaging
the flavor of the old legend.

Junichi had been lost in these thoughts without any awareness of the noise
that for some time had been coming from the kitchen of the inn when suddenly the light hanging from the middle of the ceiling of his room went out.
At the same moment, probably because it was already light outside, several
rays of bright sunshine were filtering through the paper-covered transom
above the lintel of the sliding door.

A maid came in carrying a pan filled with lit charcoal. "Dear me!" she
said. For some strange reason Junichi found it was a pretty one who had
come in this time.

"I had no idea you were up already," she said as she began to build a fire
in the brazier.

Though he felt she probably did not have much time to sleep, she had
combed her hair neatly and had put on fresh makeup. She was taking quite
a bit of time to build the fire. Possibly because she was a woman of few
words, she remained silent.

"Aren't you sleepy?" said Junichi, feeling obliged to say something
to her.

Even by the time she had answered in the negative, Junichi felt he had
said something awkward, something sentimental, and he was sorry he had
spoken.

"Weren't you disturbed by the noise?" she said, asking a question in
return.

"Not at all. I slept quite well," he said, trying to be as casual as possible.

Beyond the sliding doors he could hear the rattling sounds of the shutters
being opened. The maid, after building the fire, began wiping the edges of
the brazier. She stopped a moment as she said, "Shall I bring you some zōni
soup?"

"Oh, I see. Today's the first day of the New Year. Fine. I'll wash up first."

As he used his toothbrush after washing his face, he was thinking about
that pretty maid. He sensed something gentle about her, and he found he
liked her. He wondered if he ought to give her a special tip when he left.

No, he wouldn't. If he did, she might think he had some ulterior motive. He remained absorbed in these thoughts.

On the way back he met one of the "ordinary" maids at the entrance to his room. She had probably finished putting away his *futon* bed.

It was another "ordinary" maid that served him the *zōni*. He told her he was going to Kōzu to catch the 9:08 morning express, and he asked her to bring in his bill. In her surprise, which seemed to him exaggerated, she said, "Dear me! In that case, you're not taking care of your health!"

"But some people have returned earlier than me, haven't they?"

"They're quite different from you."

"In what way are they different?"

"They came here to have a wild time."

"I see. And I can't have a wild time, is that it?"

When she stood to get him another bowl of soup, she made doubly certain he intended to leave. Then seeing him nod that he did, she muttered as if talking to herself, "Well, Okinu will be very surprised."

He called out to stop her: "Who's Okinu?"

"Well, she's the one who came this morning to bring in your fire for the brazier. When you arrived yesterday, she said something about you right away. She said you had brought a lot of books, so she felt you surely must have come to study during the holidays."

With these words the maid went out to the corridor, a serving tray in her hands.

Junichi thought the name Okinu definitely suited the temperament of the maid, something he had imagined about her, and he experienced a kind of satisfaction. But although he felt gratitude to her for looking after him when she was so busy, he regretted having thought of her way of life in scornful and inconsiderate terms.

Another serving of the *zōni* was brought in. Junichi felt it would be too difficult for him to learn more about Okinu from this maid who was serving him, and he refrained from asking. It was too painful for him to have her think there might be some special meaning behind his inquiry.

As he began putting his scattered belongings into his leather bag, he once more started examining his feelings, calmer now than they had been last night and even when he had awakened in the morning. He had no thought of overturning his decision to return to Tokyo. Nor was there any necessity to do so. Nor had his resolution to go back to Tokyo and write faded. But merged with the purity of his single-minded resolve was a slight suspicion that had crept in, a whispering voice saying to him, "Often you began writing on the spur of the moment only to find yourself suffering a discouraging setback, haven't you?" Fortunately this whispering voice was not sufficiently powerful to paralyze his will. On the contrary, that whispering voice stimulated his desire to write, and he felt that it increased the power of resistance within him.

Contrary to his expectations, the feelings he had for Mrs. Sakai had undergone considerable change during the short period of his stay. Mixed into his continual sensations about her the previous night was the feeling that he would do something spiteful to her, that he would make her realize something, but now when he reflected on these points in the bright daylight, he found he had been quite wrong. How petty and mean he had been to think in that way. It was like the small-minded ideas of a slave. The way he was feeling now, he had a good deal to do to improve himself. Not only that, but why should Mrs. Sakai feel any remorse or pain if he left? Once the poet Albert Samain, who had died eight years ago, had written a poem about the love of a female doll called Xanthis. Among her lovers was a duke who was platonically devoted to her, and there was also a young musician who was as passionate as any artist. And yet that female doll needed a copper doll to satisfy her, a copper doll as strong as a *sumo* wrestler. Mr. Okamura was probably Mrs. Sakai's copper doll. And what was Junichi himself? He had not offered Mrs. Sakai as much passion as that young musician had offered that doll. What merits, what redeeming features, did he himself have? After he left Hakone, she would think no more about his departure than she would a lost coin purse filled with small change. And so he had no right to complain about her. And even if he had that right, what on earth could he complain about? It could not be a complaint in which he would feel sadness in losing her. It was no more than a wound suffered by his self-esteem. Once Ōmura had told him about a woman who had, without obligation or regret, separated from her lover. His own situation was different, but it would be well for him to separate from Mrs. Sakai, separate without obligation or regret. And still, no matter what his reasons for leaving, his loneliness was real, quite real. He couldn't help feeling as if he were surrounded by a void, by an emptiness. And that too was all right. It might be possible that out of his loneliness a novel might be created.

A man from the office brought in Junichi's bill. Seto had once told him that hot spring inns do not treat students as full-fledged guests, but this inn had not said anything rude or insulting to Junichi. Junichi gave him a generous tip, one that would raise the esteem of the world of students. And then, simply because he wanted to be generous to Okinu, he gave all the maids more money than he normally would have.

The maid who brought Junichi a receipt for his payment of the inn charges and his tips told him the rickshaw had arrived. He locked his leather bag and stood up. The innkeeper's wife came to offer thanks. What she said to him as she bowed with her hands touching the floor just outside the threshold of the room sounded quite respectful.

Junichi left the room, a maid following and carrying his bag. At a wide area along the corridor the maids gathered, whispering something to one another, and then all of them took leave of him. Okinu, seemingly dejected, was standing behind the group, and she bowed to him after everyone else had finished bowing. Junichi climbed into the rickshaw, and it pulled away. The New Year sky was clear, but over Mt. Yusaka the haze lingered. It was not that cold outside.

Before he crossed Asahi Bridge, he looked back at the room in the Fuku-zumi where Mrs. Sakai was staying. All its sliding doors were closed, not a sound heard from within.

1910–1911

Selected References in Youth

Aichi Prefecture: prefecture in the middle of the Japanese main island (Honshu).

Akabane: city in Saitama Prefecture, near Tokyo.

Andersen, Hans Christian (1805–1875): Ōgai's translation of Andersen's only novel, known in English as *The Improvisatore,* which he published in 1902 as *Sokkyō Shijin.* It was widely read and appreciated.

Aomori: northernmost city on the Japanese main island (Honshu).

Art School: institution located in Ueno Park, Taitō-ku, Tokyo; now the Tokyo University of Arts.

Asahi cigarette: a popular brand, cheaper than the Shikishima brand mentioned elsewhere in the novel.

Atropos: one of the Three Fates in Greek mythology.

Aude: character in a novel by Antoine-Louis-Camille Lemonnier. The specific work in which the character appears has not been identified.

Aurelius Augustinus (354–430): Saint Augustine, the dominant personality of the Western church of his time, considered the supreme thinker of Christian antiquity; author of *Confessions.*

Baien: (Soot and Smoke): a 1909 novel by Morita Sōhei (1881–1949), a disciple of Natsume Sōseki. The novel is based on the author's love affair with Hiratsuka Raichō (1886–1971), feminist, critic, and suffragette.

banjaku nori: glue made from rye or wheat flour.

Benten Shrine: shrine located in the middle of Shinobazu pond in Ueno Park, Tokyo. Benten was originally an Indian goddess of rivers, but in Japan she represents one of the Seven Deities of Good Fortune (the only goddess among them). She is the goddess of music, knowledge, and wealth.

Bernstein, Henry (1876–1953): prolific French playwright well known and respected early in the century for the violence of his dramas and the technical skill of his stagecraft.

Bertand, Father: character in *Youth* modeled after François Bertrand, a missionary and Ōgai's teacher of French when he lived in Kokura.

Chōja Boshi (Star Among Millionaires): a two-volume novel by the naturalist novelist Kosugi Tengai (1868–1952). Volume 1 was published in 1909, Volume 2 in 1910.

Chiyoda sandals: popular style in the latter half of the Meiji period (1868–1912). Similar sandals are still worn by women and girls on special festive occasions.

Chōshi: city in the northeastern part of Chiba Prefecture in central Honshu.

Chuang-tzu: Chinese philosopher in the latter half of the fourth century B.C. and the most prominent of the early interpreters of Taoism.

Den Wanbai (1796–1828): celebrated Chinese calligrapher who had a number of disciples in Japan. In Japanese, the artist is referred to as Tō Kampaku.

Der Teufel hole sie: German idiom meaning "May the devil take her!"

didaskalia: classical Greek term for notes given by the playwright to the actors or the playwright's explanations given at the beginning of the play.

Dontinghu: largest lake in the northern part of Hunan Province in China.

Ebisu Saburō: one of the Seven Deities of Good Fortune. Ebisu (for short) is a god of fishing, farming, and commerce; his face, all smiles, is large and round; he is the third son of the deities Izanagi and Izanami. Usually represented as holding a fishing rod in his right hand, he carries a sea bream, traditional symbol of good luck.

einsam: German for "lonely," "solitary," "lonesome," "alone."

Emperor's Birthday: the Emperor Meiji's birthday was November 3.

Emperor's Portrait: before and during World War II, children had to go to school on the Emperor's Birthday and pay homage to his portrait (placed on the podium of an auditorium), listen to the principal read the imperial rescript, sing the national anthem, and thank the emperor for his benevolence. Students also prayed for the emperor's longevity.

family crest: a formal *haori* coat for men has five family crests: two in front, one on each sleeve, and one on the back of the coat. For women, the coat has three family crests instead of five.

Figaro: French newspaper first published in 1825; since 1866, a daily newspaper, often satirical.

First Higher School: institution now part of Tokyo University.

forty-seven loyal retainers: the revenge of the forty-seven *rōnin* (masterless samurai) is one of the most celebrated examples of loyalty and warrior ethics in Japanese history, and the incident has been the subject of innumerable plays and stories. Early on the morning of December 14, 1702, a band of former retainers of Asano Naganori (1665–1701), the recently deceased lord of Akō, attacked the heavily guarded home of Kira

Yoshinaka, retainer of the Tokugawa shōgun, and assassinated him, thereby avenging the crime they believed had been done to their lord.

Fukuzumi: an inn located at Hakone Yumoto, a hot spring resort in Hakone, Kanagawa Prefecture. The inn still exists today.

Fuseki: character in *Youth* representing the famous novelist Natsume Sōseki (1867–1916).

Futon (Bedding): the 1907 novel by Tayama Katai (1871–1930), a famous naturalist writer. The narrative frankly discusses the love and jealousy between a middle-aged writer and his female disciple. The work is considered to be the first "I-novel" in Japan, that is, an autobiographical work of fiction with its author as hero.

Ganku (1756–1838): Edo period painter famous for his depictions of tigers.

Great Discoveries (Dai Hakken): short account by Mori Ōgai, written in 1909, chronicling the accomplishments of those who have contributed to humanity's knowledge of the world, ranging from explorers to writers, philosophers, and intellectuals.

Guys, Constantin (1802?–1892): French ink and watercolor artist who did sketches of Paris life and customs under Napoleon III. He also worked as a cartoonist and comic illustrator of the demimonde of the Second Empire.

Gyōsei School: at the time of *Youth,* a private school now called Gyōsei Gakuin. The school was established in 1898.

Hakone Yumoto: the eastern part of the Hakone region, which has the oldest hot spring in the area.

Hatsune-chō: street in Tokyo on which Junichi, the protagonist of *Youth,* lives.

Hayakawa River: river originating from Lake Ashino at Hakone and flowing into Sagami Bay, Kanagawa Prefecture.

Heyse, Paul (1830–1914): anti-naturalist German novelist whose works won him the Nobel Prize in 1910.

Hikawa Shrine: located in Takabatake in the city of Ōmiya in Saitama Prefecture, the shrine is dedicated to Susanoo no Mikoto—younger brother of the sun goddess of the Shintō religion, Amaterasu Ōmikami—and to two other deities as well.

Hiraga Gennai (1728–1780): doctor of herbal medicine, scientist, and writer famous for his experiment with *"erekiteru"* (electricity). He killed his disciple in an apparent fit of madness and died in prison. He also wrote some ballad dramas *(jōruri)*.

Hirokōji: wide avenue in Ueno, Tokyo, near Ueno station.

Huysmans, Joris-Karl H. (1848–1907): French novelist, first a naturalist writer, then an aesthete and mystic. His novel referred to in *Youth* is *Là Bas,* published in 1891.

i-ro-ha karuta: children's card game using two packs of cards; the pack with writing contains a proverb or ethical axiom; the other pack contains pictures illustrating the proverb or axiom. The child searches among the cards spread out on *tatami* mats for the proper picture.

Itō, Count Hirobumi (1841–1909): Japan's first prime minister and speaker of the House of Peers. He became prime minister four times (1885, 1892, 1898, 1900) and was the architect of Japan's first constitution.

Japan Medical School: institution, now called the Japan Medical College, located in Tokyo.

Jintan: oral deodorant pills sold in a small container without a prescription as a kind of over-the-counter drug. Jintan advertising signs used to show the figure of a naval officer with red and green lights flickering on and off.

Kameshirō: famous restaurant located near Yanagibashi Bridge in Tokyo.

Kamo no Mabuchi (1697–1769): scholar of Japanese literature and language and a poet of the mid-Edo period, famous for his philological studies of ancient *Man'yōshū* poetry.

Keichū (1640–1701): scholar of Japanese literature and language and also a poet of the early Edo period; well versed in Chinese literature and the Buddhist sutras.

kiseru: Japanese-style pipe with a bamboo stem (usually a foot long) and a metal head and mouthpiece.

Kita Ward: district in Tokyo famous for its Nanashi waterfall.

Kokura *hakama:* Kokura is a city on the southern island of Kyushu, famous for its special style of textile fabric; a *hakama* is a formal skirt worn over the kimono.

Kōson: Aeba Kōson (1855–1922), a novelist and theater critic well educated in Edo literature.

Kudan–Ryōgoku: railroad line betwen Kudan and Ryōgoku in Tokyo.

Kurama rock: often used as a garden rock (mostly buried underground) produced in Kyoto.

Kyōbashi: section of Tokyo near the Ginza in Chūō Ward.

Kyūkin (1871–1945): Susukida Kyūkin, a well-known Japanese symbolist poet.

Lao-tzu: Chinese philosopher who flourished about 300 B.C., known for his teaching of Taoism.

Lemonnier, Antoine-Louis-Camille (1845–1913): Belgian novelist and short story writer, also known for his art criticism.

maruobi: the most expensive kind of *obi* sash, distinguished from other sashes by a design decorating the entire length of the *obi,* both in front and in back; it is slightly wider than the usual *obi.*

Mausoleum: edifice located in Ueno Park in Tokyo.

M badge: insignia worn on a student's uniform collar; the M is short for "medical" or "medicine."

Mito: now the capital of Ibaraki Prefecture in central Honshu, the main island of Japan. After the battle of Sekigahara in 1600, Mito became the city inhabited by Tokugawa Yorifusa, the eleventh of Tokugawa Ieyasu's sons. Throughout the Edo period (1600–1867), the Mito domain remained highly influential and became the center for a school of learning (the Mito School) which was emperor-oriented, deriving from Shintōism and Confucianism. In *Youth*, Fuseki in his speech refers to those Mito masterless samurai who helped overthrow the Tokugawa feudal military government.

Miyajima: famous tourist spot in Hiroshima, in western Honshu, the main island of Japan. The deer mentioned in *Youth* are at the Itsukushima Shrine in Miyajima.

Miyake Setsurei (1860–1945): pen name of Miyake Yūjirō, a philosopher and critic; a man of few words, his way of stuttering was reportedly impressive to his audiences.

Momotarō (Peach Boy): famous character in an old Japanese folktale. An old man and wife once lived in a certain village. The old man would often go to the mountains to cut firewood; the old woman would go to the river to wash their clothing. One day the old woman saw a large peach floating down the river. She brought it home, cut it in half, and found a beautiful male child inside. They named the child Momotarō. The child grew into a strong youth who one day decided to conquer some demons who were harassing the villagers. With a dog, monkey, and pheasant as his retainers, he went to Onigashima (Island of Demons) where a fierce battle ensued and the demons were defeated. Momotarō and his crew returned to the village with treasures given by the demons as tokens of their subjugation. Momotarō lived happily ever after with the old man and woman.

Mōri Ōson: character in *Youth* represented as Ōgai himself.

nagauta: traditional Japanese type of song sung to the accompaniment of the *shamisen*. Sometimes dances were performed as well.

Natsume Sōseki (1867–1916): famous Japanese novelist. Sōseki gave a lecture entitled "The Attitude of a Writer" (Sōsakuka no taido) at the Tokyo Youth Hall in February 1909, but the text of this lecture bears no relation to that presented in *Youth*.

nenni-dà: French for the emphatic negative *not*, translated as "no," "but no," "don't," "certainly not."

Nicht Doch (Certainly Not): title of a collection of stories by Hans Tovorte (1864–1946), a German novelist.

November 27, 1909: evening of the first performance of the Free Theater (Jiyū Gekijō) at the Yūrakuza in Tokyo, when Ōgai's translation of Ibsen's *John Gabriel Borkman* was performed.

Ogyū Sorai (1666–1728): famous Tokugawa-period Confucian scholar whose wide interests ranged from language and linguistics to literature and military affairs.

Oimatsu: literally "old pine tree," which symbolizes longevity. Both the music and lyrics of this song were composed by Kineya Rokusaburō VI in 1802.

Ōishi Roka: character in *Youth* modeled on the novelist and critic Masamune Hakuchō (1879–1962).

Okakura Tenshin (1862–1913): critic, art historian, and author of *The Book of Tea,* Tenshin was head of the Tokyo Art School from 1890 to 1898; later he served as Oriental curator at the Bostom Museum.

Ōmiya: city in Saitama Prefecture, near Tokyo.

Ōmura Sōnosuke: character in *Youth* modeled after Kinoshita Mokutarō (1885–1945), a well-known poet and playwright who was also, like Ōgai, a doctor of medicine.

One Hundred Poems: traditional Japanese card game played during the New Year holidays. The game is played with two decks of cards. One deck has one hundred cards, each with a thirty-one-syllable poem composed by one of the hundred famous poets of classical Japanese literature. The other pack consists of the same number of cards which have only the last fourteen syllables of these poems. The cards in the latter pack are spread out at random on *tatami* mats. One person reads aloud a poem from the cards in the first deck; the contestants, seated on the floor around the scattered cards, try to pick the matching card as quickly as possible. Skilled players can find it as soon as the reciter utters the first few syllables of a "reading card." The game is won by the player who gathers the most cards.

Ōshima: type of hand-spun silk made on Ōshima Island off the coast of Kagoshima Prefecture in Kyushu, the southernmost area of Japan.

Ōta Kinjō (1765–1825): Japanese Confucian scholar of the mid-Edo period.

Peers Hall: two-storied Western-style brick building built in 1883 and formerly called the Rokumeikan (Deer Cry Pavilion). It was destroyed by fire in 1941. Built to help in the westernization of Japan, its architect was the Englishman Josiah Conder. Celebrities and dignitaries, both Japanese and Western, held balls and banquets in this building almost every day and night in early Meiji times until 1896, when it became known as Kazoku Kaikan (Peers Hall).

Phèdre: celebrated tragedy by the French dramatist Jean Racine, first performed in 1677.

Qinhuai: formerly a pleasure district in Nanking, China.

Rokudan: music for the *koto* composed by Yatsuhashi Kengyō (1614–1685).
Rokugaku Bungaku: a journal cited in *Youth;* the translators are unable to iden-
    tify it.
Russo-Japanese War: conflict (1904–1905) in which Japan defeated Russia.

Sakaeya: name of the geisha establishment in *Youth* that employed the geisha
    Ochara.
Sakana-machi: street in Hongō, Bunkyō Ward, Tokyo.
Samain, Albert (1858–1900): French poet and writer. Ōgai translated one of his
    stories and published it in 1911.
Sansaisha: bookstore once located in Kanda Ward, now Chiyoda Ward, Tokyo.
Sansaki-chō: street in Taitō Ward, Tokyo.
Satsuma: old name for the southernmost part of Kyushu, the southern island of
    Japan. The area was once governed by the feudal lord Shimazu. Famous
    for its textile named *Satsuma-ori.*
Segantini, Giovanni (1858–1899): Italian landscape painter who settled in the Enga-
    dine region of the Swiss Alps.
Seiyōken Restaurant: famous Western-style restaurant in Ueno, Tokyo.
sen: unit of old Japanese currency; one hundred of these coins equaled one yen.
sensei: Japanese term of respect used for a teacher at any rank or level or for a mem-
    ber of the Diet.
Seson'in Temple: temple at Komagome in Bunkyō Ward, Tokyo.
shijō style: school of painting in the Japanese style, originated by Matsumura
    Goshun (1752–1811).
Shikishima cigarette: more expensive than the Asahi brand at the time of *Youth.*
Shimada Saburō (1852–1923): Japanese statesman; speaker of the House of Repre-
    sentatives in 1915.
Shimada hairdo: formerly the coiffure of an unmarried woman; today, geisha or
    brides may use a variation of the style.
shimenawa: Japanese New Year decoration consisting of a thick twisted straw rope
    with strips of white paper hanging from it. It is strung across the top of a
    gate or at the entrance to a house. The rope is fastened together with
    oranges, a piece of seaweed or lobster, and green ferns. The orange rep-
    resents continuity of good health in the family, the seaweed good for-
    tune, the lobster long life, and the green ferns humility and purity. A
    house with *shimenawa* is believed to be so pure that devils cannot enter.
shoin-style or *shoin-zukuri:* Japanese-style residential architecture, developed in the
    middle of the sixteenth century, used in homes of the military, in guest
    halls, in temples, and in the quarters of Zen abbots during the Toku-
    gawa period (1600–1867).
Simmel, Georg (1858–1918): teacher, sociologist, and neo-Kantian philosopher

famous for his sociological methodology. He helped establish sociology as a basic social science in Germany.

Stage Society: the Free Theater (Jiyū Gekijō) was founded after Ishikawa Sadanji, a *kabuki* actor, had observed at firsthand the management of the British Stage Society. At each performance, a member of the Japanese Free Theater paid 2.5 yen and was allowed to take a member of his family with him. On the night of the first performance at the Free Theater, when Ōgai's translation of Ibsen's *John Gabriel Borkman* was performed, Ōgai's mother Mineko, his son Oto, and his daughter Mari attended. On the second night, Ōgai and his wife Shigeko went together.

Sudermann, Hermann (1857–1928): German playwright and novelist; a leading writer among the naturalists. His play *Heimat* (Homeland), produced in 1893, brought him international fame. The heroine of the play, Magde, fights for a woman's right to independence; the influence of Ibsen's *Hedda Gabler* is evident.

Takabatake Eiko: character in *Youth* modeled after Shimoda Utako (1855–1936), a poet and educator. Director of the Peers School for Girls (Gakushūin Joshibu); president of the Patriotic Women's Society.

Takanawa: district in Minato Ward, Tokyo.

talar: German for "robe" or "long jacket"; a clergyman's vestment.

telegraphic style: reference to the German naturalist poet Arno Horz (1863–1929), who wrote free verse in what he termed the "telegraphic style."

tenshō style: one of the four basic styles of calligraphy, used nowadays in Japan for seals, epitaphs, and other inscriptions.

Tōkei: Tokyo newspaper for which Ōishi Roka wrote in *Youth. The Tōkei* may refer to *The Yomiura,* a "small" newspaper first published in 1874 and now one of the largest in Japan. Newspapers in the Meiji period were classified as either "small" or "large." The small papers did not carry editorial or political items; space was devoted mainly to social events and various kinds of entertainment. These small papers used simple sentences; the Chinese characters were accompanied with *furigana* (pronunciation syllabaries to the right of the character) so that the uneducated could read more easily.

Tokiwakadan Restaurant: establishment once located in Ueno Park, Tokyo.

Tōshōgū Shrine: shrine sacred to the memory of Tokugawa Ieyasu (1542–1616), the first shōgun; located in Ueno Park, Tokyo. A larger and more famous Tōshōgū Shrine is located in Nikkō, in the northwestern part of Tochigi Prefecture.

Trois Contes: three tales written by the renowned French author Gustave Flaubert (1821–1880), first published in 1877.

Turner, Joseph (1775–1851): famous British landscape painter.

Uechō: short for Uekiya-Chōjirō, the gardener in *Youth*. *Uekiya* in Japanese means "gardener," and Chōjirō is the man's first name.
University Hospital: reference to the hospital attached to Tokyo University.
Urawa: capital of Saitama Prefecture.
Uzaemon: doubtless a reference to the *kabuki* actor Ichikawa Hazaemon XV (1874–1945).

Verhaeren, Émile (1855–1945): Belgian poet who wrote in French. His *La Multiple Splendeur* was composed in 1906. He also wrote plays in verse.
Vimalakirti Sutra: Buddhist text, read in Japan in a Chinese translation, long considered important for literature and the arts.

Warabi: city in southeastern Saitama Prefecture; in Edo, one of the postal stations along the Nakasendō highway.
Weininger, Otto (1880–1903): Austrian philosopher whose *Geschlecht und Charakter* (Sex and Character) was published in 1903. He committed suicide at the age of twenty-three.
World of Female Students: probably a reference to *Jogaku Sekai*, a magazine first published in 1901 by Hakubunkan in Tokyo.

Xihu, Lake: lake in Hangzou, Zhejan Province, China.

Yamaga Sokō (1622–1685): Confucian scholar, strategist, and historian.
Yōmeigaku: philosophical school, based on the teachings of Wang Yang-ming of the Ming dynasty (1368–1644), which centers on the means by which one awakens to the ultimate universal principle; the emphasis is on the unity of thought and action.
Yoshida Method: school of acupuncture that was founded in the 1560s by Yoshida Ikyū, a Shintō priest.
Yoshiwara: elegant prostitution quarter in Tokyo that thrived during the Tokugawa period.
Y Prefecture: Yamaguchi Prefecture, at the western tip of Honshu, the main island of Japan.
Yūrakuza: first Western-style theater built in Japan, constructed in 1909.

Zenshōan: Zen house built by Yamaoka Tesshū (1836–1888), a vassal of the Tokugawa shogun and a skillful swordsman and calligrapher. The house has a splendid belfry.
zōni: soup with pounded rice *(mochi)*, chicken, and vegetables; served especially during the New Year holidays.
zweisam: German for "two alone," "two people by themselves."
Zwielicht: reference to *Im Zwielicht* (At Twilight), a novel written by Hermann Sudermann (1857–1928) published in 1866.

GLOSSARY

bon: the Festival of the Dead, held each year in the seventh month of the traditional calendar.

daimyō: the lord of a manor, or a feudal lord, usually the ruler of the area in which he resided.

furoshiki: a large cloth in which objects can be wrapped and carried.

fusuma: sliding panel doors in a traditional Japanese room, usually covered with paper.

futon: bedding designed to be placed on traditional *tatami* matting.

geta: wooden clogs.

go: a game similar to checkers.

habutae: a standard variety of glossy silk.

haiku: a traditional seventeen-syllable verse.

hakama: a kind of divided skirt, worn by men on important formal occasions.

haori: the traditional coat or cloak worn by men and women.

hibachi: a charcoal brazier.

kabuki: the most spectacular of the traditional forms of Japanese theater, using male performers and elaborate costuming and scenic effects.

kakemono: a hanging picture scroll.

kotatsu: a footwarmer with a coverlet placed over it.

koto: a stringed instrument sometimes compared in sound to a Western harp. It usually has thirteen strings.

kyōgen: a comic play performed as an interlude to the serious *nō* drama.

netsuke: a small ornamental carving, sometimes of ivory, used to suspend a medicine bag or tobacco pouch from the waist.

nō: the medieval poetic drama.

obi: a traditional sash.

sakaki: a variety of tree sacred to the Shintō religion.

sake: rice wine.

-san; -sama: a suffix added to a title or proper name indicating respect to the person addressed.

shamisen: a three-stringed musical instrument often used to accompany singing.

Shimada: a popular hairstyle, named for a *kabuki* actor. Formerly the coiffure of an unmarried woman; today geisha or brides may use a variation of the style.

shōgi: a Japanese version of chess.

shōji: paper sliding doors.

sushi: a popular food consisting of rice cakes topped with raw fish or sea-weed.

tabi: traditional bifurcated socks.

Takashimada: a variant on the Shimada style, with a topknot tied high on the head.

tanka: classical thirty-one-syllable poems.

tatami: rice straw matting, in units measuring roughly six by three feet and two inches thick, used on the floor of traditional Japanese houses.

tokonoma: the alcove in a traditional Japanese room where pictures, flowers, or other artistic objects are placed.

torii: the ceremonial gateway to a Shintō shrine.

yatsude: a tree with eight-fingered leaves.

yōkan: sweetened bean jelly.

yukata: a thin cotton garment, usually worn in the summer.

zabuton: cushion for sitting on the floor.

zōni: rice cakes boiled with vegetables and chicken; served especially during the New Year's holidays.

CONTRIBUTORS

RICHARD BOWRING, professor of modern Japanese studies at the University of Cambridge, is the author of *Mori Ōgai and the Modernization of Japanese Culture.* He has also written on Murasaki Shikibu, author of *The Tale of Genji,* has published a complete translation of her diaries, and is coeditor of *The Cambridge Encyclopedia of Japan.*

KAREN BRAZELL, professor of Japanese literature and theater at Cornell University, is highly regarded for her research and publications in the field of Japanese literature, and in particular for her work on the *nō* theater. Her most recent book is *Traditional Japanese Theater: An Anthology of Plays,* forthcoming from Stanford University Press.

JOHN W. DOWER, the Luce Professor of International Cooperation and Global Stability at the Massachusetts Institute of Technology, is a leading specialist on modern Japanese history. His recent publications include the prize-winning *War Without Mercy: Race and Power in the Pacific War.*

SANFORD GOLDSTEIN, professor emeritus at Purdue University, has cotranslated Japanese stories, novels, and *tanka* collections. SHOICHI ONO, professor of English at Joetsu University of Education, has been a cotranslator with Sanford Goldstein for almost a decade. Their English versions of Japanese short stories have appeared in *Western Humanities Review, Arizona Quarterly,* and *Mānoa.*

HELEN M. HOPPER, formerly associate professor of historical studies at the State University of New York–Empire State, is currently adjunct professor of history at the University of Pittsburgh. She is the author of "Mori Ōgai's Response to the Suppression of Intellectual Freedom 1909–1912," *Monumenta Nipponica* 29 (4), and is currently doing research on the role of women in the Taishō and early Shōwa period.

IVAN MORRIS (1925–1976) taught for many years at Columbia University. His publications include translations of such diverse classical writers as Sei Shōnagon and Ihara Saikaku, and his books *The World of the Shining Prince* and *The Nobility of Failure* remain classic studies of Japanese literature and culture.

J. THOMAS RIMER has written widely on various aspects of Japanese literature and culture. He is the editor, with David Dilworth, of a collection of translations, *The Historical Fiction of Mori Ōgai,* and has also written a short biography of Ōgai for the Twayne Series. He is a professor of Japanese literature at the University of Pittsburgh.

GREGG M. SINCLAIR was president of the University of Hawaii from 1942 to 1955. His translations of modern Japanese literature, published in 1919 and 1926, including several undertaken with Kazo Suita, were among the first to bring the work of several important authors to English-speaking readers.

TORAO TAKETOMO was a well-known Japanese scholar and poet active in the first half of this century under the pen name Taketomo Sōfū. In addition to his own poetry, he was widely appreciated for his translations of Dante and the classical Greek poets, among others. As a young man, he studied at Columbia University in New York.

JAMES M. VARDAMAN, JR. teaches at Surugadai University near Tokyo, and has served as coeditor for a collection of essays entitled *The World of Natsume Sōseki.* He has published translations with Kodansha International and at present is working on the English version of a novel by the contemporary writer Nakagami Kenji.